## DESTINY: *Child of the Sky*

"Haydon culminates her powerful fantasy saga with adventure, treachery, mystery, and romance . . . an exciting read that will pique new readers and delight fans of Haydon's first two books. Her superbly rendered characters incite us to share their triumphs and sorrows, even as her lyrical prose casts its wondrous invitation to visit her world."

—*Romantic Times* Gold Medal Review

"Though inspired by music theory, Norse and Celtic folklore, and by such authors as Tolkien, C.S. Lewis, Patricia A. McKillip, Anne McCaffrey, and Palmer Brown (*Cheerful*), the author uses a fluid writing style to build a world uniquely and compellingly her own." —*Publishers Weekly*

"Much to the delight of readers bored to tears by doorstopper clones, Elizabeth Haydon's tale is unique, thrilling, and utterly romantic from start to finish."

—Amazon.com, Best of 2001

## PROPHECY: *Child of Earth*

"*Prophecy* proves that Elizabeth Haydon is a superstar and not a one hit wonder. Haydon's world is so real the audience will feel that we too have been transported in time and space to a wondrous vision." —*Midwest Book Review*

"One great book (*Rhapsody*) might be a fluke. But its sequel, *Prophecy,* keeps right on developing great characters in a believable fantasy world without sacrificing the momentum of a terrific story. Fans of epic fantasy will find Haydon a worthy successor to Tolkien, ranking with Robin Hobb and Guy Gavriel Kay." —Amazon.com, Best of 2000

"As strong and compelling as its predecessor, the action is exhilarating; and sometimes broad, sometimes wry humor leavens the story's horror. As in high fantasy at it best, the sense of foreboding is palpable, the world building is convincing and consistent, the evildoers are truly wicked, and the battles are ferocious." —*Booklist*

# RHAPSODY: CHILD OF BLOOD

**Best Fiction of 1999, Borders.com**
(Top 10 Fiction Titles of 1999)
**Best Book/Editor's Pick: Amazon.com**
(Top 10 SF/Fantasy titles of 1999)
**The Readers' Choice List: SF Site**
(Top 10 SF/Fantasy titles of 1999)
**A Best Book of the Year in SF/Fantasy:**
BarnesandNoble.com

★ "Distinguished by superior wit and intelligence, this fantasy debut opens what looks to be an outstanding saga."
—*Publishers Weekly* (starred review)

"A stunningly told tale by a new fantasy author who is sure to go far." —Anne McCaffrey

"An epic saga worthy of Eddings, Goodkind and Jordan."
—*Romantic Times* (4¹⁄₂ stars out of 5)

"*Rhapsody* is movingly-written, epic fantasy. I read this book with a growing sense of pleasure, impressed not only with the author's deft plotting but also with her use of language. Haydon is a *writer*." —Morgan Llywelyn

"Filled with detail and a complex, multi-faceted plotline, it's an epic beginning to what is being billed as a major fantasy series, and readers will quickly pick up on the echoes of J.R.R. Tolkien's Middle Earth and David Eddings Belgariad series, as well as Celtic and Norse mythology, and even a dash of Mozart's Magic Flute." —*Toronto National Post & Mail*

"This author will surely go far. I am amazed at the growing number of strong new voices in fantasy, hitherto mostly male. Elizabeth Haydon is sure to change that."
—Piers Anthony

# Tor Books by Elizabeth Haydon

*Rhapsody: Child of Blood*
*Prophecy: Child of Earth*
*Destiny: Child of the Sky*
*Requiem for the Sun*
*Elegy for a Lost Star*

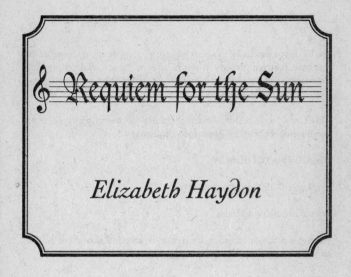

# Requiem for the Sun

## Elizabeth Haydon

**TOR®**
fantasy

A TOM DOHERTY ASSOCIATES BOOK
NEW YORK

This is a work of fiction. All the characters and events portrayed in this novel are either fictitious or are used fictitiously.

REQUIEM FOR THE SUN

Copyright © 2002 by Elizabeth Haydon

www.elizabethhaydon.com

All rights reserved, including the right to reproduce this book, or portions thereof, in any form.

Edited by James Minz
Maps by Ed Gazsi

A Tor Book
Published by Tom Doherty Associates, LLC
175 Fifth Avenue
New York, NY 10010

www.tor.com

Tor® is a registered trademark of Tom Doherty Associates, LLC.

ISBN: 0-812-56541-X

First edition: September 2002
First mass market edition: May 2003

Printed in the United States of America

0  9  8  7  6  5  4  3  2  1

Because he saw *Rhapsody* in curlers and a mudpack
and didn't slam the manuscript shut
Because he is willing to take risks
that others would not
Because he refuses to accept less than my best
Because it matters as much to him as it does to me
this book is dedicated
with gratitude and affection
to
James Minz
Visionary
Editor
Friend

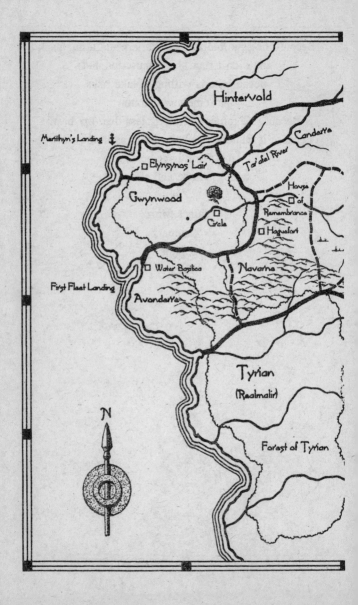

Ylorc
(Canrif)

Yarim

Roland

Batha
Carbair

Kravensfield
Plain

Fire Basilica

Wind Basilica

The Moot

The Cauldron

Bethany

Sepulvarta

Ether Basilica

Jakar P

The Teeth
(Manteids)

Night Mountain
Earth Basilica

Dasart

Sorbold

# ACKNOWLEDGMENTS

Many thanks to the Musée des beaux-arts de Montréal; the Sinclair gallery and The Cloisters/Metropolitan Museum of Art, New York, New York; the Getty Museum, Los Angeles, California; Corning Glassworks, Corning, New York; the Hicks Collection and the Lindtfelder Collection, Louisville, Kentucky; and the Henry Mercer Museum, Doylestown, Pennsylvania, for their assistance in the research of medieval glassmaking techniques.

My sincere gratitude also to James Meeker, United States Navy, for his generous assistance with nautical fact checking and skillful technical support.

Additional thanks to Shane McKiness, for the loan of his name.

Love and appreciation to my friends and family, without whom it wouldn't happen.

And to all the great folks at Tor, as always.

# Ode

WE are the music-makers,
And we are the dreamers of dreams,
Wandering by lone sea-breakers,
And sitting by desolate streams;
World-losers and world-forsakers,
On whom the pale moon gleams:
Yet we are the movers and shakers
Of the world forever, it seems.

With wonderful deathless ditties
We build up the world's great cities,
And out of a fabulous story
We fashion an empire's glory:
One man with a dream, at pleasure,
Shall go forth and conquer a crown;
And three with a new song's measure
Can trample an empire down.

We, in the ages lying
In the buried past of the earth,
Built Nineveh with our sighing,
And Babel itself with our mirth;
And o'erthrew them with prophesying
To the old of the new world's worth;
For each age is a dream that is dying,
Or one that is coming to birth.

—Arthur O'Shaughnessy

Seven Gifts of the Creator,
Seven colors of light
Seven seas in the wide world,
Seven days in a sennight,
Seven months of fallow
Seven continents trod, weave
Seven ages of history
In the eye of God.

## SONG *OF THE* SKY LOOM

Oh, our Mother the Earth;
Oh, our Father the Sky,
Your children are we,
With tired backs.
We bring you the gifts you love.

Then weave for us a garment of brightness. . . .
May the warp be the white light of morning,
May the weft be the red light of evening,
May the fringes be the fallen rain,
May the border be the standing rainbow.

Thus weave for us a garment of brightness
That we may walk fittingly where birds sing;
That we may walk fittingly where the grass is green.

Oh, Our Mother Earth;

Oh, Our Father Sky.

*—Traditional, Tewa*

## THE WEAVER'S LAMENT

Time, it is a tapestry
Threads that weave it number three
These be known, from first to last,
Future, Present, and the Past
Present, Future, weft-thread be
Fleeting in inconstancy
Yet the colors they do add
Serve to make the heart be glad
Past, the warp-thread that it be
Sets the path of history
Every moment 'neath the sun
Every battle, lost or won
Finds its place within the lee
Of Time's enduring memory
Fate, the weaver of the bands
Hold these threads within Her hands
Plaits a rope that in its use
Can be a lifeline, net—or noose.

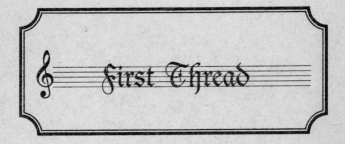

First Thread

The Warp

*One man with a dream, at pleasure,*
*Shall go forth and conquer a crown;*
*And three with a new song's measure*
*Can trample an empire down.*

## ARGAUT, CONTINENT OF NORTHLAND

The light of the harbor torches fluttered on the waves and reflected back at the night sky, a dim imitation of the waxing moon that hung stubbornly above the end of the quay, ducking in and out of the clouds racing past on the wind.

Long into the dark hours, scores of even darker figures had sworn, sweated, and spat, reaching endlessly into the bowels of the ships that lined the jetty, dragging forth their treasures in the forms of barrels and chests and loose bales of goods bound for market in Ganth, then throwing them roughly into wagons or carrying them, corded muscles straining with exertion, into the dray sleds amid muttered cursing. The dray horses, sensing the onset of a night rain, danced in their hitchings, fearing the coming thunder.

Finally, when the docks were silent, the torches had burned down to the stalk joints, and no light remained but that of the obstinate moon, Quinn emerged from the belly of the *Corona* and made his way down the gangplank, glancing behind him several times until he reached the pier.

The longshoremen had joined the ship's crew in warmer, louder haunts, and were now undoubtedly drinking themselves into belligerent fits or pleasant stupors. The stench in their quarters the next morning would be a fine one, to be sure. But the smell of intestinal gas and sour vomit tomorrow would be welcome compared with what Quinn faced now at the end of the dark quay.

Quinn's eyesight had always been acute. He had sailor's eyes that scanned the endless horizon for a fleck of variation in the swimming expanse of monotonous gray-blue; he could tell a gull from a tern from the crow's nest in the glare of the sun at distances that befuddled his shipmates. Still, he always doubted the accuracy of his vision in the last few moments of this familiar walk, for the person he was meeting always seemed to change before his eyes as he approached.

Quinn was never quite certain, but it seemed as if the man *thickened,* and grew more solid, his long, thin fingers subtly gaining flesh, the shoulders broadening slightly beneath the well-made cloak. Once Quinn thought he had caught a glimmer of blood at the edge of the seneschal's eyes, but a closer look proved him to be mistaken. They were clear blue, cloudless as a summer sky, without a trace of red. The warmth of those eyes was almost enough to dispel the chill that never failed to creep though Quinn like a slithering vine whenever they met.

"Welcome back, Quinn." The heat in the seneschal's voice matched that of his eyes.

"Thank ye, m'lord."

"I trust your voyage was successful."

"Yessir."

The seneschal still did not favor him with a glance, but instead stared into the lapping waves cresting under the pier. "And was it she?"

Quinn swallowed, his throat suddenly dry. "I'd say sure as certain, m'lord."

The seneschal turned finally, and looked down at Quinn with a contemplative expression. Quinn caught it then, that smell, the faint, foul reek of human flesh in fire. He knew the odor well.

"How do you know this, Quinn? I don't want to sail across the world for nothing; I'm sure you'd agree."

"She wears the locket, m'lord, a shabby piece amongst all 'er jewels."

The seneschal studied Quinn's face for a moment, then nodded distantly. "Well, then. I suppose it's time I paid her a visit."

Quinn nodded dumbly in return, almost unaware of the raindrops that had begun to spatter the dockside planks.

"Thank you, Quinn. That will be all." As if in enthusiastic agreement, the rippling glow of heat lightning undulated across the docks, punctuated a moment later by the rumble of distant thunder. The sailor bowed hurriedly and turned, scurrying back to the *Corona* and his tiny, dark hole below-decks.

By the time he reached the gangplank and looked back, the figure had become part of the windy rain and the darkness again.

## HAGUEFORT, NAVARNE

On the other side of the world it was raining harshly. Night was coming, bringing with it the relentless downpour that had been dogging Berthe's mood from the moment the storm had begun at dawn, though early on it had taken the form of a mild but insistent shower. Every hour or so a wayfarer had pounded on the scullery door, begging shelter and tracking rainwater and mud from the road over her newly washed floor.

By nightfall she was livid, berating the last of the men with language so acid that the chamberlain himself had rebuked her, reminding her of the recentness of her hire and the strict standards of courtesy the Lady Cymrian expected to be in place at Haguefort, the keep of rosy brown stone in which the royal couple lived while the beautiful palace her husband was building for her nearby was being completed.

But the lady was away and had been for weeks, her absence evident in the ever-souring mood of her husband. Lord Gwydion was passing the remaining fortnight before her return in all-night meetings with his weary councilors, who privately expressed the hope that the next two weeks would come and go rapidly, given his ugly state of mind. Berthe had never met her, never even seen her, but unlike the rest of the palace staff, she did not pray for the lady's speedy return, the lord's bad mood notwithstanding. From what Berthe had been able to discern in her ten days' tenure at Haguefort, the Lady Cymrian was an odd duck given to some fairly strange ideas.

Now the vast kitchen was dark, the polished stones of the floor finally scrubbed clean, the firecoals burning down to flickering ash. Upstairs in the meeting rooms on the other side of the main wing lights still burned, and voices were occasionally raised in barely audible laughter or argument. Berthe leaned against the hearth wall and sighed.

As if in blatant mockery, the door knocker sounded.

"Be off wi' ya," the scullery woman scowled through the latch. Silence reigned for a moment; then the knocker sounded again, louder this time.

"Go away!" Berthe roared back before her better sense took hold; she glanced around furtively, fearing the return of the chamberlain. When she had ascertained that no one important, or likely to report her to someone important, had overheard her, she lifted the bolt, cleared her throat, and opened the door a crack.

Before her was nothing but the gloom of the dreary night.

Seeing no one at the threshold, Berthe started to close the door, a growl of annoyance emanating from the wrinkled folds at her throat.

A flash of lightning blazed, and in its momentary light a figure could be seen lowering the hood of a cloak, the outline of which she could barely make out, and had caught no sight of the moment before. A crackle of electricity hummed over her skin as she peered out into the murkiness of the night. Berthe had to look closely through the sheeting rain to see even this shade of a person; had she not squinted into the darkness at the same moment as the flash, it was unlikely she would have noticed anything at all. She interposed herself in front of the figure that was preparing to step into her clean and buttoned-down kitchen.

"There's an inn down the road a piece," she growled into the rain. "Everyone's to bed. The buttery's closed down tight. I don't mean to keep the staff up all night."

"Please let me in; it's very cold out here in the rain." The voice was that of a young woman, soft and a little desperate, heavy with the weary tone of a tired traveler.

Berthe's annoyance was apparent in her answer, though she struggled to maintain the civility she had heard the lady was insistent upon, even to peasants. "What do you want? It's the middle of the night. Be off wi' you, now."

"I want to see the Lord Cymrian." The reply came as if from the darkness itself.

"Days of Pleas are next month," Berthe answered, beginning to close the door. "Come back then; the lord and lady hear requests beginning at sunrise on the first day of the new moon."

"Wait," called the voice as the opening narrowed. "Please; if you'll just tell the lord I'm here, I think he will want to see me."

Berthe spat in a puddle of dirty water forming near the scullery step. She had dealt with such women before. Her former employer, Lord Dronsdale, had a veritable flock of them, assigned to different nights of the week; they gathered outside the stable, waiting for the Lady Dronsdale to retire, then began preening beneath the back window, each hoping to be selected by the lord, who signaled his interest from the balcony. It had been her job to shoo away the girls not chosen on a given night, and an onerous task it was. She had hoped not to have to repeat it here at Haguefort.

"Well, now, aren't we the cheeky wench?" she snapped, her recent training forgotten. "It's past midnight, my girl, and you're here unannounced, on a day not in keeping with the law. Who are you that the lord would want to see you at this hour?"

The voice was steady. "His wife."

Later Berthe realized that the clicking she heard following the words was the sound of her jaw dropping open; it remained thus for much too long. She closed her mouth abruptly and pulled the heavy door open wide, causing the metal hinges to scream in protest.

"M'lady, forgive me—I had no idea 'twas you." *Who would expect the Lady Cymrian, dressed in peasant garb, unguarded, at the buttery door in the middle of the night?* she wondered, clutching her icy stomach.

The darkness shifted, and the cloaked figure hurried inside. Once she was silhouetted against the firelight, Berthe could see that the Lady Cymrian was no taller than she, and slight of frame. Her jaw trembled as the young woman untied the hood of her cloak amid a cloud of mist that rose from the folds of it, then pulled the garment from her shoulders.

First to emerge from the shadows of the plain blue-gray fabric was as fair a face as Berthe had ever seen, crowned with golden hair the color of sunlight pulled back in a simple black ribbon. The expression on that face was clearly one of displeasure, but the lady said nothing until she had carefully hung her cloak, still surrounded with an aura of mist, on a peg over the fire grate, followed by a quiver of arrows and a white longbow. Then she turned to Berthe.

When the lady's eyes, deep and green as emeralds in the shadows of the firelight, took in the scullery maid's face, however, the look of annoyance faded into a serious aspect devoid of anger. She brushed the rainwater from her brown linen trousers and turned back to the fire on the hearth, which leapt as if in welcome, warming her hands.

"My name is Rhapsody," she said simply, looking at the scullery maid from the corner of her eye. "I don't believe we've met."

Berthe opened her mouth, but no sound came out. She swallowed and tried again.

"Berthe, m'lady; I'm new here in the kitchen. And I apologize most humbly—I had no idea 'twas you at the door."

The Lady Cymrian turned again, and folded her arms. "You didn't need to know it was me, Berthe; any traveler who has come to this door is to be let in and welcomed." She saw terror come over the old woman's wrinkled face, and her hand went unconsciously to the tangled gold locket around her neck. She smoothed the chain and cleared her throat.

"I am sorry that this was not explained to you upon your hire," she said hurriedly, casting a glance in the direction of the buttery's inner door. "And also for disturbing you so late in the evening. Welcome to Haguefort. I hope you will like working here."

"Yes, mum," Berthe muttered nervously. "I'll go tell the chamberlain to alert the lord you're here."

The Lady Cymrian smiled, the firelight dancing off her locket. "No need of that," she said pleasantly. "He already knows."

The buttery door banged open with a force that made Berthe jump. She leapt even farther away as the maelstrom that was the Lord Cymrian rushed past her in a flurry of billowing garments and speed born of long musculature, his odd red-gold hair catching the light of the roaring fire and glinting ominously. Her hand went nervously to her throat, watching the man who was said to have the blood of dragons in his veins sweep down upon the small lady, gathering her into his arms. Berthe would hardly have been surprised to see him tear her limb from limb, or consume her, on the spot.

A moment later the buttery door opened rapidly again. Berthe leaned against the wall for support as the chamberlain, Gerald Owen, and a number of the lord's royal visitors crowded in the opening, some of them with weapons drawn.

Owen's wrinkled face relaxed upon seeing the lady in the arms of the lord.

"Ah, m'lady, welcome home," he said, pulling out a handkerchief and mopping his brow in the heat of exertion and the blazing hearth fire. "We weren't expecting you for another fortnight."

The Lady Cymrian tried to extricate herself from the lord's embrace, managing to merely to raise her head above his shoulder.

"Thank you, Gerald," she replied, the words partially muffled by the fabric of her husband's shirt. She nodded in the general direction of the nobles crowding the buttery doorway. "Gentlemen."

"M'lady," returned an awkward chorus of voices.

The lady whispered something into the lord's ear that made him chuckle, then patted him and slid out of his arms. Lord Gwydion turned to his councilors.

"Thank you, gentlemen. Good night."

"No, no, please don't abbreviate your meeting because of me," the lady objected. "Actually I'd like to sit in; I have a few matters of state I need to discuss with some of these good nobles." She looked back up at the lord, who stood a head taller than she. "Are Melisande and Gwydion Navarne to bed?"

Lord Gwydion shook his head as the chamberlain crossed to the fireplace and took her cloak down from its peg, still radiating its aura of mist. "Melly is, of course, but Gwydion is keeping council with us. Has made many good suggestions, in fact."

The lady's smile grew brighter and she opened her arms as her husband's namesake, the tall, thin lad who would one day be the Duke of Navarne, made his way through the convocation at the doorway and came into her embrace. As they conferred quietly, the lord turned back to his councilors.

"Give us a few moments, please," he said. "We'll resume our conversations—*briefly*—at half the hour." The nobles withdrew, closing the buttery door behind them.

Berthe eyed the chamberlain, gesturing nervously toward the back door to her chambers; Gerald Owen nodded pointedly. The scullery woman bowed clumsily and made a hasty retreat to her room, wondering if the Lady Dronsdale would consider taking her back.

℣he Lord Cymrian watched as Gerald Owen walked slowly over to his wife, who was unbelting her scabbard without breaking her conversation with their ward. Owen had been the chamberlain of Haguefort for many years, serving both Gwydion Navarne's father, Stephen, and Stephen's own father before him. Even in his later years, his staunch loyalty and service to Stephen's children, and their guardians, was unfailing. He carefully took Rhapsody's sword and cloak, and left the buttery without causing so much as a pause in her conversation.

"Twenty center shots in the same round?" she was saying to Gwydion Navarne. "Excellent! I've brought you more of those long Lirin arrows you liked from Tyrian; they've fletched them in your colors."

Gwydion's normally somber face was shining. "Thank you."

The Lord Cymrian tapped his wife on the shoulder, gesturing toward the door through which Gerald Owen had left.

"I made a loan of my cloak of mist to you so that you might travel unseen by highwaymen and thieves," he scowled with mock severity. "Not so that you could return without my notice."

"Trust me, my return will garner your notice later," she said teasingly. "But I really must speak to Ihrman Karsrick before he returns to Yarim; did I see him among the councilors in the doorway?"

"Yes."

"Good." She slipped her hand inside the crook of her husband's arm. "Now, let's go attend to affairs of state—so that we can retire to our chambers and discuss the—er—state of affairs."

𝒜s she walked arm-in-arm with both Gwydions through the towering hallways of Haguefort, past ancient statuary and carefully preserved tapestries from the First Cymrian Age, Rhapsody found herself suddenly battling a wave of conflicting emotions, some warm, some bitterly painful, all deeply held, none changed in any way by the passage of time.

The loss she and Ashe, as her husband was known to his intimates, still felt at the death three years ago of Lord Stephen, Gwydion Navarne's father and Ashe's dearest friend, was still acute. It was impossible to traverse the corridors of Haguefort, the keep that Stephen had lovingly restored and filled with priceless artifacts, or tend to his historic exhibits in the Cymrian museum on the castle's grounds without being overwhelmed with the memory of the young duke and the great joy he had held for life. Each time she left Haguefort, she returned to find his son resembling him more.

The thought caught in her heart; Rhapsody blinked. Gwydion Navarne was staring down at her from the first step of the grand staircase, offering her his hand on their way up to the keep's library, where Ashe had been meeting with his councilors, looking for all the world like his father. Beside her Ashe squeezed her hand; he understood. Rhapsody squeezed back, then took their young ward's hand, allowing him to lead her up the stairs.

Colored light splashed the steps from the stained glass in the chandeliers above them, illuminated by scores of tallow candles. Rhapsody thought of how carefully Stephen had chosen that beautiful glass, and everything else in the keep and the museum. The musing made the next breath she drew heavier than the one before.

They had chosen to stay in Haguefort after Stephen's death, keeping it exactly as it had been, for the sake of Gwydion and his young sister, Melisande. Stephen, himself widowed when the children were very young, had endeavored to make certain that life went on for them after their mother died. In their love for him, Rhapsody and Ashe had tried to do the same. Nonetheless, the time was coming when Gwydion Navarne would be of age to assume his father's title. Now, watching him ascend the grand staircase, Rhapsody couldn't help but acknowledge that that day was coming sooner than she wished.

As she stepped in a pool of blue light, a chill whispered over Rhapsody's hair and the skin on the back of her neck. She stopped quickly and turned; in the flickering light of the chandeliers she thought she saw the tiniest of movements. But when she looked more closely, nothing was there but dancing shadows.

Ashe's hand closed gently on her elbow.

"Aria? Are you all right?"

An old dread, stale from the crypt of memory in which it had been long locked, rose like bile; the acid burned the back of her throat. Then, with a flicker of candlelight, it was gone.

Numbly Rhapsody put her hand to her throat; the burning fear had subsided completely. She smoothed the gold locket at the hollow of her neck and the collar of her cambric shirt, then shook her head, as if shaking off a bad dream. Sometimes visions of the past or the future came to her, unbidden, and had since childhood, but there was no more to the fleeting chill; it had vanished.

The Lady Cymrian looked up at her husband and smiled to soothe the worry she saw in the lines of his face and his eyes, cerulean blue scored with vertical pupils, a subtle vestige of the dragon blood that ran in his veins.

"Yes," she said simply. "Come; let us not keep your councilors waiting."

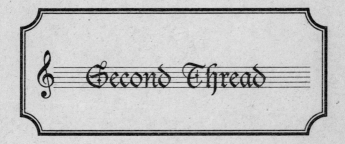

# Second Thread

## The Weft

## TILE FOUNDRY, YARIM PAAR,
## PROVINCE OF YARIM

Just as rivers flowed inevitably to the sea, in Yarim Paar all knowledge, public and hidden, all secrets, made their way, sooner or later, to the ear of Esten.

And Slith knew it.

Whether the secret was uncovered in the bright, unyielding sun of Yarim Paar that baked the red-brown clay of the crumbling northern city to steaming in summer, or in the dark, cool alleyways of the Market of Thieves, the opulently decadent bazaar in which trade, both exotic and sinister, flourished at all hours of the night and day, Esten would eventually hear of it.

It was as unavoidable as death.

And since death could come from standing in the way of such information, it was usually better to be the bearer of the secret to Esten than the one who might be perceived as trying to hide it from her.

Though not always.

Slith glanced up nervously. The journeyman who was overseeing his work and that of the other apprentices was stretching out in the shadows of the large, open kilns, seeking relief from the blasting heat, paying the boys no mind. Bonnard was a corpulent man, a skilled ceramicist whose touch with tile nippers and mosaic tesserae was unrivaled, but he was not much of an overseer. Slith exhaled, and cautiously reached into the greenware jar on the lower shelf again.

What he had found was still there where he had seen it yesterday, wedged at an angle in the unfired clay at the bottom of the urn.

Another backward glance reassured him that Bonnard's attention was otherwise engaged. With a smooth movement, in the attempt to avoid the notice of the other lads stoking the dung fires and stirring the slip, Slith plucked the clay container from the shelf and tucked it quickly under his arm, then made his way out the back door of the tile foundry to the privies beyond.

Slith had long been accustomed to the stench of waste that slapped him each time he drew the rotten burlap curtain open; he ducked inside and pulled it closed carefully. Then, with moist hands that trembled slightly, he reached gingerly into the open mouth of the vessel again. With a firm tug he pulled out its contents and held it up to the light of the rising moon that leaked in through the gaps in the privy curtain.

A blue-black gleam stung his eyes in the dark.

With great care Slith turned the circular disk, thin as a butterfly's wing, to the side, catching the moonlight that ran in ripples off its pristinely balanced rim. The outer edge was razor sharp—Slith had shaved several layers of skin from the back of his hand the previous day when he reached, entirely by accident, into the greenware jar while moving the older urns waiting to be fired from the dusty storage room to the kiln area.

He would probably have limited his curiosity to the curse he had muttered under his breath and assumed that the odd metal disk was an unfamiliar scraping tool of some sort, except for the dark, tacky shadow that marred its surface. Slith's hand shook as he turned the disk over.

It was still there.

The shadow of blood, long dried.

A memory flooded Slith's mind. Three years before, he and the other first-year apprentices had been jostled awake in the dead of night by bells ringing frantically deep within the foundry. He and his fellow novices in the art of tile-making had crept out to see what the emergency was, only to be shoved roughly aside by the journeymen hurrying to respond to the alarm. What they all had found when they came into the kiln areas had kept him awake every night for months afterward.

The huge vats of boiling slip had been upended from their fires, spilling a sea of hot, molten earth in lumpy waves throughout the vast foundry. Three of the apprentices who had been working the late shift tending the slip and kiln fires had vanished, though one was later located, under a hill of cooling slip, drowned in the wet clay. The bodies of the other two, Omet, a bald-pated fifth-year apprentice whom Slith had liked, and Vincane, a brutish boy with a penchant for cruel pranks, were never found. A dozen or so journeymen were also missing.

But, worst by far, the alcove that led down to the tunnel where the slave boys were clandestinely digging had filled with boiling slip and somehow been fired, baking it to an impenetrable ceramic wall.

The night of the calamity was only the second time in his life that Slith had laid eyes on Esten, the foundry's owner and Mistress of the Raven's Guild, the trade association of ceramicists, tilemakers, glassblowers, and other artisans that was the cover for the most brutal and nefarious ring of thieves in the Market.

The first time had been the day he had been apprenticed to her in the tile foundry. Even though her face was darkly beautiful, her physical form slight, and her smile glittering, there was such menace, such inherent *threat* in her aspect, in the way she moved through the air, that Slith, then nine years of age, had begun quaking uncontrollably when he was brought into her presence. Esten had looked him up and down like a hog she was considering purchasing, then nodded and waved a dismissive hand. He was bound over, the papers signed, his life no longer his own, if it ever really had been. From that moment on, there had been no real abatement to the fear that was born in him that night.

But it was able to grow.

The night of the accident he had seen Esten for the second time. The cool, detached demeanor he had observed on the day he was bound over in her service was gone, replaced by an anger so complete that it seemed to call thunder from the sky above. Slith tried to put the image out of his mind of Esten stalking purposefully around the mounds of cooling slip, breaking suddenly into sharp, lunging movements, kicking the dim firecoals, slamming the open doors of the cold kilns shut, pulling over shelves of bisque pots and racks of fired tiles in explosions of black rage. The remaining journeymen winced at her cobra-like eruptions of fury, but grew even more agitated as that fury cooled to a seething, contemplative concentration.

Finally, after staring at the disaster for more than an hour, still as death, Esten turned around and leveled a chilling gaze at the assembled men and boys.

"This was not an accident," she said softly, with a deliberateness that froze Slith's spine. The faces of the journeymen, lit only by the dying embers of the slip fires, went paler at her words.

It was unnecessary for her to add the thought that followed.

Yet three years later, as far as Slith knew, there had been no clues found, no answers to the riddle of that night.

Life in the tile foundry was even more restricted now than it had been before. Prior to the accident, everyone was on alert because of the highly sensitive nature of the operations taking place in the tunnels below the foundry. Now the pressure came from the unresolved question of who had been suicidal enough to dare to disrupt Esten's secretive digging, would be reckless enough to destroy something so important to her. Whether the answer would eventually point to a clever and powerful adversary, or an extremely lucky fool, mattered little.

Because, inevitably, like rivers to the sea, all secrets made their way, sooner or later, to the ear of Esten.

And Slith had just found one.

## THE CAULDRON, YLORC

The fire on the mammoth hearth in the council chamber behind the throne room crackled and blazed with smoldering anger, neatly matching the mood of the Firbolg king.

Achmed the Snake, the Glowering Eye, the Earth Swallower, the Merciless, and owner of a host of other fear-invoking titles bestowed upon him in both honor and fear by his Bolg subjects, leaned forward in his heavy wooden chair and tossed a handful of broken shards of glass into the fire's maw, muttering ugly Bolgish curses under his breath. The long fingers of his thin hands interlaced in a viselike lock, coming to rest against the lower half of his face, veiled, as always, in black cloth, as his mismatched eyes, one light, one dark, stared in savage silence into the fire.

Omet ran a hand absently over his beard and leaned back against the wall, but said nothing. He had always been given to judicious observation, rather than helpful interjection, and had learned almost from the moment he came to live in Ylorc three years ago that when the king had finished aligning the innumerable thoughts, images, plans, counterplans, and impressions that his vibrationally sensitive physiology was routinely bombarded with, he would speak.

Any disturbance to the sorting process was generally not appreciated.

Unlike his fellow artisans, many of them Bolg, Omet was comfortable with silence. After many long minutes of watching them shift uncomfortably from foot to foot, or sweat nervously in the presence of the Bolg king, he stretched, then leaned forward and picked up the last remaining shard from among the glass splinters on the floor, ran it in between his forefinger and thumb, then held it up to the firelight himself.

*The king is right,* he thought. *Too thick.*

When the king finally lowered his folded hands from where they rested against his upper lip to beneath his chin, Omet stood up noticeably. He had become quite good at recognizing the subtle signs that signaled changes in the Bolg monarch's mood, and he tried to pass them along discreetly to his fellows. He cleared his throat slightly.

"Too much feldspar," Omet said.

The Bolg king blinked but didn't say anything.

Shaene, a big, brawny ceramicist from Canderre, leaned forward, picking fretfully at his leather apron.

"Gold smalti?" he asked apprehensively.

The Bolg king's head did not move, but the mismatched eyes shifted to Omet. Omet shook his head.

Shaene snorted impatiently. "Vitreous glass then. What do you say, Sandy?"

Omet exhaled deeply. "Not strong enough."

"Peh!" Shaene growled, tossing his acid-stained leather glove down on the enormous table. The muscles of King Achmed's back tensed.

The room went suddenly still.

Rhur, a Firbolg mason, the only other man in the room besides Omet whose brow was still dry, met his glance. "What then?" he said, his voice marred by the harsh whistle that characterized the language of his people.

Omet's dark eyes went from Shaene to Rhur, then finally to the Firbolg king.

"We can no longer experiment like this," he said simply. "We need a stained-glass artisan. A sealed master."

King Achmed kept his back to the ceramicist long enough for Omet to count ten beats of his own heart. Then, without a word, he rose from his chair and left the room, making not even a whisper of sound, or disturbing a current of air in his passing.

When Omet guessed that the Firbolg king was well out of earshot, he turned to Shaene.

"Master Shaene, my family was originally from Canderre, so our mothers may have been friends in childhood," he said evenly, using the tone in which a lad of not-yet-eighteen summers could address an older man without requiring confrontation. "In honor of that possible friendship, perhaps you could refrain from striking the flint of the king's patience with the steel of your foolhardiness when I am the one standing closest to him."

\*    \*    \*

$\mathcal{A}$s he traversed the dark hallways hollowed into the mountain, soon to be brightened by torchlight, Achmed suddenly felt the need for air.

Following the main causeway of the Cauldron, his seat of power within the mountains, past clusters of Bolg soldiers and workers who nodded deferentially as he passed, he stopped long enough to step into one of the viewing stands that looked out over the cavernous capital city of Canrif, now in its fourth year of renovation.

A warm updraft carrying a cacophony of noise and vibration from the rebuilding that was taking place below slapped against his hands and forehead, and swept over his eyes, the only places on his body not shielded by veiling. His skin-web, the network of sensitive veins and exposed nerve endings bequeathed to him by his mother's Dhracian blood, could feel the disturbance anyway, even swathed as it was in cloth, muted. It was an irritation, a constant stream of stimulation that the Bolg king had learned to live with a lifetime before.

When he had first come to this place, four years ago, the vast cavern below his feet and towering above his head was the sepulcher of a dead city, silently rotting in the stale air long trapped within the mountain. Within its broken hallways, along its desolate streets roved clans of Firbolg, demihumans who had overrun Canrif at the end of the Cymrian War and now walked its crumbling tunnels, oblivious of the glory that had once been.

A thousand years before it had been a masterpiece of architecture and a paean to ingenuity, carved into the belly of the Teeth by the design and sheer will of Gwylliam the Visionary, the only other man ever to claim the title of king within this forbidding range of jagged mountains.

It was well on its way to becoming that masterpiece again.

Four years of focused attention from thousands of Firbolg workers, as well as the costly and limited guidance of expert artisans from outside Ylorc, as the Bolg called this land, had reclaimed almost half of the city, restoring it to the model

of art and efficiency it once had been. The ancient culture
that had built the place, naming it Canrif, might not have
understood the priorities the Bolg king had employed in the
restoration; though Gwylliam would have agreed with Achmed's emphasis on reinforcing the defenses and infrastructure, he might have found the king's penchant for adding
tusks and other Firbolg features to ancient Cymrian statues
more than a bit perplexing.

The tumult below him dimmed slightly; Achmed looked
down to see a section of the massive city below the viewing
stand motionless in the midst of all the movement. The
workers who were hauling loads of stone, tiling roofs, laying
bricks, and a thousand other tasks in the reconstruction of
Canrif stood stock-still, staring up at him from below. The
paralysis was spreading in waves as more and more of the
Bolg saw him up in the reviewing stand, halting in their
tracks.

Quickly he withdrew from the stand and hurried down
the corridor, feeling the waves of motion resume a moment
later, dissipating in long ripples of vibration.

A cleaner wind caught his nostrils as he neared the opening of the tunnel. As he stepped out onto the rocky ledge,
the cool air of the open world whisked around him, tugging
at the edges of his veils and robes, carrying with it different
vibrational patterns, scents of campfires burning, sounds of
distant troop movement in the canyon beyond.

Achmed walked to the end of the ledge and stared down.
A thousand feet below in the dry river canyon the watch
was changing, the troops doubling with the coming of night.
Torchfires flickered in thin streams of light, twisting on the
canyon floor like fiery serpents as the lines of soldiers ran
their evening drills. He could hear snippets of the cadence
being called when the wind favored it.

Satisfied, he turned his gaze skyward. The firmament
holding the heavens in place had blackened patchily, with
blue clouds smudging the panorama of stars that winked in
the night wind.

He stared beyond the darkened rim where the canyon turned southeast; then he took down the veil and closed his eyes, letting the wind rush freely over his face and neck, bristling against the veins of his skin-web. He opened his mouth, and let the breeze fill it.

In his mind he sought a heartbeat, a distant rhythm on the wind. It was his blood-gift to be able to match his own to those ancient rhythms born in the same land as he had been born, the lost Island of Serendair, silent beneath the waves of the sea a thousand years again by half. A gift now shared only with a few thousand other living souls, all ancient beyond years, caught at whatever age they had been when they left the Island, frozen forever in time.

He quickly caught the heartbeat he was seeking, felt his pulse slow slightly and beat in the great, voluminous tympani of his oldest friend. Achmed exhaled; the nightly ritual brought him something akin to relief.

*Grunthor lives,* he thought, satisfied as always. *Good.*

He turned and sought another rhythm on the wind, a lighter, quicker one, more difficult to find, yet still unconsciously familiar. He knew it as well as his own; he was bound to its owner, bound by history, by friendship, by prophecy, by oath.

By Time.

He caught this one quickly as well, far away, past the Teeth and the seemingly endless Krevensfield Plain that lay beyond, over the rolling hills of Roland, almost to the sea. It was there, flickering in the distance, like a comforting song, the ticking of a clock, the ripples in a stream.

Achmed exhaled again. *Good night, Rhapsody,* he thought.

He sensed Omet's presence even before his polite cough sounded, and waited until the tile artisan had come up to his side, continuing to stare down into the canyon.

Omet stared down into it as well.

"Quiet night," he observed.

Achmed nodded. "Are the last deliveries in yet?"

"Yes." Omet handed the king a leather pouch, then shook his head as the wind caught his hair, blowing it into his eyes. It had finally gained the length to do so again, after he had shaved it off while apprenticed to the tile ovens of Yarim, and their dark mistress. The thought made him shudder involuntarily. He stood quietly as the Bolg king leafed through the messages from the aviary. Achmed's system of messenger birds was as reliable as the rising and setting of the sun.

"Nothing from Canderre yet," the king said, turning the small slips of vellum over one by one, holding on to one in particular.

Omet nodded. "Francis Pratt, their ambassador, has been in ill health, I hear."

"From Shaene?"

Omet chuckled. "Yes."

"Then Pratt's probably in a brothel bedding half of Canderre. Shaene is more consistently wrong than any form of life I have ever encountered." He kicked a pebble into the canyon, knowing he would never hear its impact. "Pratt's probably had trouble finding an artisan in the western provinces."

"Probably." The word came out lightly, but the night wind caught it and held on to it, adding weight, leaving it hanging in the air above the ledge.

The Bolg king turned the remaining piece of paper over in his hand. "If Pratt can't find us one in Canderre who can be trusted, perhaps there is one in Sorbold. Or we can send across the sea for one from Manosse."

Omet let his breath out as lightly as he could. "We could take our chances in Yarim. The best are there."

Finally the Bolg king turned, leveling his mismatched gaze at Omet, and smiled slightly.

"Well, it's interesting you should mention Yarim," he said, "because there is a message here from Rhapsody. She wants Grunthor, you, and me to meet her there two fortnights from today." He chuckled at the look of shock on the young man's face.

"I'll be happy to stay behind and look after the works while you and the Sergeant are gone," he said hastily when he recovered the use of his tongue.

"I thought you might see it that way," Achmed said. "So if you'd rather, you can stay here with Rhur and the Bolg artisans, and that idiot Shaene, listening to him call you Sandy."

Omet sighed. "I can endure that, I suppose. Better than the alternative."

Achmed nodded. "If you say so. Me, I would take any chance I could to spare myself from Shaene." He pulled the veiling back over his lower face, made one more check of the mountain walls, the canyon, and the Blasted Heath beyond, then turned and strode back down the causeway into the depths of the Cauldron again.

On his way to his bedchamber, he stopped in the smithy, where Gwylliam's ancient forges, refitted now with his own accoutrements, blazed through the night, turning out steel for weapons and tools, armor and architecture. Three thousand Bolg toiled through each shift in the blinding light and heat, adding to the strength of the mountain with every pull of the bellows, every clang of the hammer.

The Bolg Master of the Forge nodded to him, as he did every night at this time while Grunthor was away. The Firbolg king completed the Sergeant-Major's tasks quickly, checking to make certain the cull pile was not being pilfered, the smiths were not using excessive amounts of iron ore in the mix as they had a few seasons back, and that the balance of the *svarda,* the circular, triple-bladed throwing knives that the Bolg exported to Roland, was being attended to.

Finally, assured that the smithy was functioning properly, he bade the forgemaster good night and headed for his chambers, stopping to finger the newly minted supply of disks for his cwellan, the primary weapon he used. It was of his own design, similar to an asymmetrical crossbow, curved to employ greater recoil on the spring. Instead of firing bolts, however, it made use of thin metal disks as the ammunition, razor-sharp, three at a time, staggered, each disk forcing the previous one deeper into the wound made by the first.

He held one up for a moment to the blazing light of the forge fires burning below, smelting steel into fiery near-liquid to be beaten into an endless number of shapes. The fireshadows danced across the cwellan disk, sending waves of rippling light over the blue-black rysin-steel surface.

Suddenly weary, the Firbolg king hastened to bed.

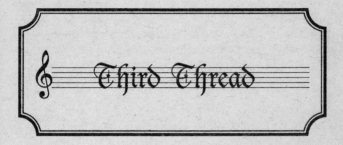

Third Thread

The Lee

# JIERNA TAL, THE PLACE OF WEIGHT, SORBOLD

The realm of Sorbold was a place of relentless sun. Mountainous and arid, it stretched like the fingers of a grasping hand southward from the rim of the Manteids, the mountain range known more commonly as the Teeth, arthritic phalanges of spiny hills reaching across the barren desert and into the rocky steppes of the Lower Continent, to the ghostly inland seacoast, where the skeletons of ships lost centuries before still littered the black sand, shrouded in mist coming off the warm sea.

In winter the icy winds swept across the land, scattering crystals of snow, howling through the bleak dunes, shifting the desolate landscape like a child playing in a box of dirt. At night those winds carried sprays of golden sand aloft into the sky, where they drifted for a moment among the stars, mirroring the silent streaks of blazing light above, shooting stars that fell into the edges of endless blackness encompassing the vast, echoing desert.

In spite of the harsh reality of the land, the occasional sense that the Creator had forsaken the place and its people, Sorbold was a realm of deep magic.

The harsh climate did not engender a hospitable nature in the people of this rocky land. Sorbolds were known for the shortness of their attention, of their tempers, of their alliances. The only thing that seemed to be long in the national personality was memory. Sorbold held its history tightly; every battle loss, every betrayal, every perceived injustice counted and recounted silently but consistently as the years turned into centuries and eventually millennia. Ages and dynasties came and went with the shifting sands of the desert, but the memories remained, hidden, brooding, deep within the vaults of Time.

For three-quarters of a century Sorbold had been under the rule of Her Serenity, Leitha, the Dowager Empress, a humorless woman whose cold attitude stood in marked contrast to the climate of the realm she held locked in her tiny but iron grip. The empress was short of stature but long of will. When she was coronated she was almost a perfect globe in shape; as the years of her reign passed she desiccated slowly, like a drying apple, as if the heat of Sorbold were sucking the water, fat, and muscle tissue bit by bit from her body, leaving her withered, hard, and leathery well into old age. The process made her stronger, like steel that was tempered in fire, or leather cured in smoke. For all that the bordering nations of the continent had quietly distrusted her father, the Fourth Emperor of the Dark Earth, they openly feared his daughter, who seemed bound and determined to live forever, and was doing a fair job of accomplishing that goal.

The bravest of her subjects and adversaries on occasion referred to the empress (well out of her earshot, of course) as the Gray Assassin, after a poisonous spider commonly found in dark, cool hiding places in the mountainous clime. Like the arachnid, the empress was rumored to have mated only once. Her consort, a pasty-faced noble from the Hintervold, was found the morning after their wedding, his rigid body carefully dressed and lying on top of the neatly folded sheets in the royal bedchamber, a hideous grimace sealed forever into his features by the richtus of death, while the empress was out for her morning ride.

The momentary union produced the empress's only progeny, the Crown Prince Vyshla. The Crown Prince favored his father; his skin was sallow and pale, even in a clime that produced swarthy complexions in everyone else who lived there; his hands and body were soft as a woman's, some soldiers of the Columns were known to have joked once, though in doing so they learned quickly that the mountains, and even the desert sand, had ears. Their eyeless remains, dried and mummified by the harsh winds and waterless air, swung for more than a year from a parapet outside the palace of Jierna Tal before the prince was finally prevailed upon to have them removed so that they did not clash with the street decorations celebrating the rites of spring.

It was not the prince, however, who was responsible for the grisly ornaments, but his mother.

The Crown Prince had remained unmarried all his life. At first it had been rumored by those outside his realm that the reason was his deeply held standards, set too high for any mortal woman to reach. As the years passed, however, other reasons were proffered when the topic came up over tankards of ale around inn hearth fires or in sewing circles.

Perhaps it was the prince's own noxious personality that kept him from winning a bride; he was said to be fussy and high-strung, easily offended and given to spates of impotent smoldering. In addition, other types of impotence were widely rumored. But, for all that Vyshla was, without question, annoying and childlike, he certainly was not the first ruler of a powerful nation to be devoid of a pleasant personality. That lack of personal charisma had never been a barrier to a royal marriage before; on the contrary, it had been more or less proven that the most attractive appendage in a royal man was the scepter he held in his hand by divine right, not anything more centrally attached to his body.

As time went on, the gossip shifted. Crown Prince Vyshla's lack of betrothal, marriage, and progeny, it was now believed, had been engineered entirely by the Dowager Empress. Jealous and avaricious, the woman who had ruled Sorbold for more than seventy-five years had broken the aggressions of her enemies, held armies at bay, and elevated a dry, resourceless land into a realm of tremendous power and influence by the mere force of her will and vision. Quite simply, the stories said, she was not willing to entertain the possibility that an heir was necessary, because she was never planning to leave the throne. One of the more exaggerated tales claimed that she had wind-dried the unfortunate soldiers who joked at her son's expense as an experiment to see how better to preserve herself post mortem, so that she might continue to rule without interruption after her death.

For all the iron-clad avarice of the self-serving dowager, and the finicky, spoiled behavior of the pampered prince, however, there had been one moment in recent history that showed that the Empress of the Dark Earth and her son were levelheaded monarchs, reasonable in their policies of international relations, acting in the best interests of Sorbold.

They had more or less willingly agreed to, and ultimately signed, treaties of trade and nonaggression with the new Cymrian Alliance.

Initially the elderly queen and her son worried when the benison of Sorbold, the foremost clergyman in their land and the dowager's personal confessor, had returned from Sepulvarta, the independent city-state that was the capital seat of the religion of the realm, with news of the alliance between the central human nation of Roland to their north, the forested Lirin realm to their west, and Ylorc, the savage kingdom of Firbolg monsters across the mountainous barricade to the east.

The new queen of the Lirin, a half-human woman named Rhapsody whom Vyshla had halfheartedly sued for the hand of, and Gwydion of Manosse, the Heir Presumptive of the Cymrian line that had ruled Roland, Ylorc, and Sorbold itself for a time a thousand years before, had been selected by a council of the surviving Cymrians and their descendants to reign over a loose alliance of the realms of the central continent, while each kingdom retained its sovereignty. The empress was able to see the value in being perceived from the outset as a friendly independent nation, rather than have the alliance of men, Lirin, and Bolg test their mettle as a possible conquest later on.

The Dowager Empress had a remarkable gift for looking forward. Her visionary glance saw down the road into a future where cooperation from the outset would yield protection in later days.

As with most visionaries, what her eyes couldn't see was the shadow that loomed behind her.

*        *        *

𝒯he three-quarter moon rose heavily over the streets of Jierna'sid, the capital seat of Sorbold, glowing sparingly on the sand that blasted the formal gardens and well-kept roadways, a constant reminder of the endless desert that flanked the city on two sides. The wind seemed to laugh in time at the moon, teasingly blowing wisps of clouds in front of the pale sky-lantern, shrieking fitfully over the sleeping city. *Try to tame me,* the wind seemed to taunt. *I dare you.*

That moon, in answer, doused the central object of the city with a particular shine.

Towering above the palace of Jierna Tal, the Place of Weight, stood the holiest artifact in the land. It was a gigantic set of ancient scales, the wooden column and beam planed smooth by artisans of the old Cymrian empire a thousand or more years before, the ancient metal pans even older, trays of gleaming gold carried across the ocean on ships fleeing the destruction of the place they had been smithed, burnished by the relentless sand and wind.

The last time those mammoth scales had been used to weigh a decision of heavy import had been three years prior, when the Patriarch in Sepulvarta died. The Patriarch had decreed in his final moments that, rather than naming his own successor, he wished to allow the Scales to select one. The benisons of the religion, those clergyman directly beneath the Patriarch in power and influence, had gathered in Jierna Tal for the Weighing, a long-revered rite in which the ancient Scales passed judgment on a candidate's worthiness. Historically the Scales had at one time made determinations on many different kinds of offices, as well as the innocence or guilt of accused criminals, and whether treaties were balanced and fair, but in recent memory their wisdom was only consulted on matters of state or great import. The selection and investiture of a new Patriarch was deemed a worthy cause for consulting the Scales.

The Ring of Wisdom of the Patriarchy had been placed, amid solemn ceremony, into the tray that aligned with the west wind, *Leuk,* the wind of justice, to serve as the weight.

One by one, each of the benisons had stepped onto the eastern tray.

One by one the Scales had tilted crazily and the eastern tray upended, finding the candidate unworthy, and depositing him unceremoniously onto his hindquarters at the base of the enormous scaffold amid roars of amusement from the immense crowd that had gathered to watch the selection. The youngest of the four benisons, Ian Steward, had bravely volunteered to go first. He landed with a resounding splat, his body splayed out in such an unflattering manner that the eldest benison, Colin Abernathy, had decided to forgo the process and pass up a chance at the Patriarchy altogether.

Finally, when each of the existing benisons had been deemed unworthy of the Ring and the Patriarchy by the Scales, another man had stepped forward. He was tall and broad of shoulder, despite being advanced in years, his white-blond beard and hair curling in streaks of gray. He had stepped onto the scale tray as if it were something he had done many times before, and stood, as if listening to a voice in the clouds, as the enormous arm and chains of the Scales raised him on high, over the heads of the now-silent crowd, then balanced the trays.

As the stunned crowd recovered from its shock and roared assent, the man quietly spoke but one word, his name.

*Constantin.*

The noise from the crowd dimmed for a moment. The name was renowned in Sorbold, shared with a famous gladiator in the western city-state of Jakar, a cool and bloodthirsty arena killer who had disappeared from the gladiatorial complex some months before. The thought that this elderly holy man, soon to be anointed and invested with the powers to become the most potent healer in the land, had the same name as the gladiator was such a great irony as to invoke a sea of rippling laughter across the city square that rattled the bell towers of Jierna Tal.

Later that day, long after the decision of the Scales had been officially inscribed in the holy tomes of Sepulvarta, many hours after the crowds in the square had dispersed, the new Patriarch could still be seen, standing at the foot of the Scales, staring up at the holy instrumentality, a look of reverent amazement etched into the lines of his face.

In the light of the waxing moon a man again stood, a different man, gazing at the Scales, a look of similar awe molding his heavy facial features into an aspect of reverence. His swarthy hands were at his sides, awash in the silver illumination, fingering something smooth as he watched the magnificent instrumentality of justice gleam in the intermittent brightness.

The last watch of the night had changed while he stood in the shadows of the palace of Jierna Tal. The soldiers of the Second Steppe Column, sweating beneath their helmets of cured leather banded in steel and wrapped in linen, passed by within a few strides of him as if he were not there. Now the street was silent, the lights in the palace dimming, then winking out into blackness.

He exhaled, then took a deep breath of the hot summer air, dry, rich with portent, letting it fill his lungs.

Then he slowly mounted the steps leading to the titanic Scales.

The inconstant moonlight gleamed off the golden trays, large enough to hold a two-ox cart and more. He stared contemplatively at the center of the pan, at the fine lines long ingrained in the metal, the surface marred by time and weather, shining with their own radiance. This had been the birthplace of many new beginnings.

His left hand opened.

In it was a weight shaped like a throne.

The carving on the weight was in and of itself worthy of appreciation; the tiny throne was rendered, curve for curve, angle for angle, engraving for engraving, in the likeness of the throne of Sorbold, down to the image of the sword and sun that decorated the ancient seat of power now occupied by the Dowager Empress.

But more of notice was the material that comprised the weight. It was cool to the touch, even in the heat of the desert night, its rockflesh striated in colors of green and purple, brown and vermilion.

It hummed with life.

Carefully the man set the throne weight into the western .tray. He then walked deliberately around the massive machine and stood in front of the eastern tray. He opened his right hand.

The fleeting moonlight had vanished; at first, darkness cloaked the item in his hand. After a moment, as though curious, it returned, shining on the irregular oval, violet in color, though when the light touched the surface it seemed to shimmer radiantly like the flames of a thousand tiny candles. In its smooth-weathered surface a rune was carved in the tongue of an island long settled beneath the rolling waves of the sea.

It was a scale of a different kind.

With consummate care he placed it in the empty tray, marveling at the waves of violet light that rolled to its edges like ripples of a pebble thrown in smooth water.

The man's dagger, worn a moment before at his side, glinted in the dark.

He rolled up the sleeve of his *belaque* and drew a quick, thin line, black in the darkness, across the back of his wrist, then bent down and held his bleeding hand above the tray.

Seven drops of blood dripped onto the scale, each one meticulously counted.

Then the man stood up, ignoring the oozing of the blood into the sleeve of his garment, watching the Scales intently.

Slowly the enormous plates shifted, skittering across the stones of the square slightly.

Then the plate bearing the bloody scale was raised aloft, the light of the moon flashing off the golden tray as it moved.

The Scales balanced.

The piece of Living Stone carved in the shape of the

throne of Sorbold ignited and burned to ash in a puff of crackling smoke.

The man at the foot of the Scales stood stock-still for a moment, then threw back his head and raised his arms in triumph to the moon overhead.

He did not cast a shadow.

𝔍n the opulent darkness of his bedchamber, the Crown Prince was thrashing about in the clutches of disturbing dreams.

He began to sweat, struggling to breathe.

### YLORC/SORBOLD BORDER AT KRIIS DAR

𝔖ergeant-Major Grunthor had been somber all night.

The entire ride home to the Cauldron he did not speak a word, did not allow his eyes to move from the ground in front of him. He just spurred his horse to as consistent a canter as he could maintain, rushing to get back to the Firbolg seat of power.

He had actually been quite cheerful earlier when riding the enfilade line, shouting playful obscenities in the Bolgish tongue at the guards on the Sorbold side of the border, grinning widely and waving to the stern-faced sentries, trying to crack their resolve while appearing as nonthreatening as seven and a half feet of green-skinned, tusked musculature can appear. It was his favorite way to end a border check.

"Hie! Sweet'eart! My 'orse 'ere wants a word with you! She thinks ya might be the jackass who fathered the mule she popped t'other night!" The light from the border fires illuminated his broad face, causing his impeccably kept teeth and tusks to mirror the waxing moon overhead.

The Sorbolds, strictly trained not to respond unless attacked, continued to stare due east into the lands of Ylorc, steadfastly holding their watch.

The giant Sergeant-Major tugged at the reins, guiding the heavy war horse to retrace its steps, then stood in the stirrups, balancing perfectly against the skill of his mount.

"Speakin' o' fathers, did ya know Oi coulda been *your* dad, but the dog beat me up the stairs?"

Not so much as one Sorbold eyelash fluttered. The Bolg line of guard under his command snickered intermittently.

A wicked gleam appeared in the Sergeant's eye as a new taunt occurred to him. He reined Rockslide, his war mare, to a stop and began to dismount, still shouting taunts at the border guards.

"Why are you all so sore-balled, anyway? What, 'ave you been knobbing the sagebrush or—"

As his foot touched the earth Grunthor stopped.

His skin, generally the color of old bruises, went pale enough to be noticed by his men, even in the dim light of the fires.

He bent quickly and placed his hands on the ground, struggling to maintain consciousness over the din in his ears; the internal noise rocked him, made him weak, threatening to bowl him over in pain and despair.

The earth beneath his hands and knees was wailing in terror.

> For each age is a dream that is dying,
> Or one that is coming to birth.

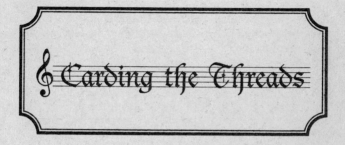

Carding the Threads

# Red

## Blood Saver, Blood Letter

### Lisele-ut

# 1

## HAGUEFORT

𝒯he members of Lord Gwydion's advisory council had reconvened in Haguefort's richly appointed library and were grouped in pairs and triads in various parts of the voluminous room, examining papers or talking quietly among themselves. To a one they rose from their seats and fell into a pleasant, welcoming silence as the lord and lady entered.

First to greet the returning lady was Tristan Steward, the Prince of Bethany, the most powerful of the provinces of Roland. He had been hovering near the doorway by himself, away from the other councilors, and stepped quickly into Rhapsody's path, bowing politely over the ring on her left hand.

"Welcome home, m'lady," he said in a thick voice, oiled with the fine brandy of Haguefort's cellars. The light from the library's lanterns pooled in his auburn curls, making them gleam darkly in red-gold hues similar to those in Ashe's hair, though not with the same odd, metallic sheen that the Lord Cymrian's dragon heritage bequeathed him.

Rhapsody kissed the prince on cheek as he stood erect again. "Hello, Tristan," she said pleasantly, extricating her hand from his grasp. "I trust Lady Madeleine and young Malcolm are well?"

Tristan Steward's eyes, green-blue in the tradition of the Cymrian royal line, blinked as they looked down at her.

"Yes, quite well, thank you, m'lady," he said solemnly after a moment. "Madeleine will be honored to know you asked after her."

"Young master Malcolm must be getting ready to take his first steps," Rhapsody said as she continued into the library, her hand resting on Ashe's forearm.

"Any day now. How kind of m'lady to remember."

"I remember every child at whose naming ceremony I have sung. Good evening, Martin," Rhapsody greeted Ivenstrand, the Duke of Avonderre, who smiled and bowed deferentially; she nodded to each of the other councilors and slipped hurriedly into an empty seat at the long table of polished wood where Ashe and his advisors had been meeting. The dukes of Roland and the ambassadors from Manosse and Gaematria, the Isle of the Sea Mages, all member nations of the Cymrian Alliance, took their seats as well, following the lead of the Lord Cymrian.

"I can see you've been keeping these good councilors far too long and far too late into the night in my absence," Rhapsody said to her husband as she gingerly moved aside a half-eaten turkey leg that lay on a plate amid crumpled sheets of parchment and empty cordial glasses on the table before her, eyeing the refuse that was clumped in piles around the rest of the table and other parts of the library.

Ashe rolled his eyes and sighed dramatically. "Revisions to the Orlandan tariff structure," he said with mock angst.

"Ah. Well, that explains it." She turned to young Gwydion Navarne, seated to her left. "Where were you in your discussions when I interrupted, Gwydion?"

"The impasse seems to have occurred in the discussion of the exemption that the province of Yarim has requested on foodstuffs, owing to the drought conditions of the last two growing seasons," the young man said.

"Indeed," Ashe agreed. "Canderre, Avonderre, and Bethany oppose the waiver of such tariffs, while Bethe Corbair agrees."

"Bethe Corbair shares a border with Yarim, and does not have the cost of transportation of goods that Avonderre has," protested Martin Ivenstrand, whose coastal province was the most distant from Yarim.

"Nor do I remember Yarim agreeing to reduce tariffs on their opals or their salt in the past when restrictions on sea trade threatened *our* revenues," said Cedric Canderre, the older man who was the duke of the province that bore his name, known for its production of luxury goods, fine wines, and rich delicacies. "I am unclear as to why this drought is any different than the obstacles Canderre or the other provinces of Roland have faced."

"Because this drought is *beggaring* my province, you imbecile," growled Ihrman Karsrick, the Duke of Yarim. "Those so-called obstacles did not make even a nail's worth of a dent in your fat treasury, and you know it. Yarim, on the other hand, is facing mass starvation."

Rhapsody leaned back in her chair and looked to Tristan Steward. "And what is Bethany's position, Tristan?"

"We are certainly sympathetic to Yarim's plight," said the prince smoothly. "As such, we are more than willing to extend them generous extensions on their tariff payments."

Amusement sparkled in Rhapsody's green eyes, but her face and voice remained passive. "How kind of you."

The mild look on Tristan Steward's face hardened a little. "More than that, m'lady, Bethany is concerned that this matter was brought up for discussion at the level of the Cymrian Alliance at all," he said, a terse note entering his otherwise warm voice. "Hithertofore each province of Roland has always had the right to set its own tariff rates, as it deemed fit, without interference from any—er, higher authority." His eyes met Ashe's. "At the Council that named you Cymrian lord and lady, we had been assured that the sovereignty of the realms within the Alliance would be respected."

"Yes, that assurance was given, and it has not changed," said Rhapsody quickly, noting the darkening of her husband's expression. She turned again to the young man who would soon take a place at this table as the Duke of Navarne. "What is your opinion of this, Gwydion?"

Gwydion Navarne shifted in his chair, then sat forward.

"I believe that, while the sovereignty of provincial tariff rights is important to observe, there are some things that transcend tariff," he said simply, his young voice husky with change, "emergency foodstuffs being one of those things. Why should those of us blessed with more fertile lands and

plentiful food profit excessively from the suffering of a fellow Orlandan province, rather than going to its aid in a time
of need?"

The Lord Cymrian smiled slightly. "Your father would
have proffered the same solution," he said to Gwydion Navarne, while keeping his eyes locked with Tristan's. "You
are a compassionate man, as he was."

"Well, I am sorry to intrude at what is clearly a sensitive
stage of the talks, but if you will allow me, I believe I may
be able to proffer an alternative solution to the tariff quan-
dary," Rhapsody said, squeezing Ashe's hand.

"By all means, do tell, m'lady," said Quentin Baldasarre,
the Duke of Bethe Corbair.

"Yarim needs water." Rhapsody folded her hands.

The councilors looked to one another blankly, then stared
in turn at the table, amid the occasional clearing of throats.
Ihrman Karsrick's brow furrowed, barely containing his
annoyance.

"Does m'lady have a way of beseeching the clouds for
rain, skysinger that she is? Or are you merely stating the
obvious for amusement at my expense?"

"I would never taunt you on so grave a matter for amusement, m'lord, that would be cruel," Rhapsody said hastily,
pushing down on Ashe's arm to guide him back into his
seat as he began to rise. "But Yarim has a great source of
water in its midst, a source which you do not currently make
use of, and which would doubtless spare you from some of
the effects of the drought."

Karsrick's expression resolved from anger into confusion.
"M'lady does understand that the Erim Rus has run dry, and
that even when it was still flowing in spring, it was contam-
inated with the Blood Fever?"

"Yes."

"And that the Shanouin well-diggers are finding surface
veins of water less and less often?"

"Yes," Rhapsody said again. "I was referring to Entudenin."

Silence fell over the dark library, the lanternlight dimming as the oil reserves began to run dry, the firelight on the hearth burning strong and steady, casting bright shadows on the faces of the bewildered councilors.

Entudenin in its time had been a towering geyser, a miracle of shining water spraying forth from a multicolored obelisk of mineral deposits sprouting from the red clay of Yarim, in cycles roughly akin to the phases of the moon. For twenty days out of every moon cycle it showered the dry earth with sweet water, water that made the dusty realm bloom like a flower in the desert. In its time it had gifted the province with liquid life, allowing the capital city of Yarim Paar to be built, a jewel in a vast wasteland at the northern foothills of the Teeth, and had nourished the outlying mining camps and farming settlements as well.

But its time had come to an end several centuries before, when one day, without explanation or warning, the marvelous artery of life-giving water dried to a shriveled shell, never to give forth water again. Centuries had passed; the obelisk withered in the heat, dissipating into a shrunken formation of monocolored rock, unnoticed every day by hundreds of oblivious passersby in the town square of Yarim Paar.

"Entudenin has been dead for centuries, m'lady," said Ihrman Karsrick as pleasantly as he was able.

"Perhaps. Or perhaps it is merely sleeping." Rhapsody leaned forward, the fireshadows gleaming in her eyes, which sparkled with interest.

"And does m'lady have a song of some sort with which to awaken Entudenin from its sleep of three hundred years?" Karsrick was struggling to maintain his patience.

"Perhaps. It's the song of the drill." Rhapsody folded her hands. "And I am not the singer to make use of this song, but within the Cymrian Alliance there are such singers."

"Please elaborate," Ashe said, noting the looks of bewilderment on the faces of the councilors.

Rhapsody sat back in her chair. "Entudenin was the embodiment of a miracle; fresh water in the middle of the dry clay of Yarim, heralded as a gift from the All-God, and the gods that the indigenous population worshipped before the Cymrians came. As such, when Entudenin went silent, it was assumed to be some kind of divine punishment. What if, in fact, it is not?"

The silence that answered her was broken only by the crackle of the hearthfire.

"Please go on," Tristan Steward said.

"It is possible the water that flowed from Entudenin in its lifetime came from the sea," Rhapsody said. "That would explain its lunar cycle—the phases of the moon have similar effects on ocean currents and tides. I have just recently been to the lava cliffs along the southern coastline of the lands of the sea Lirin, similar to the ones that line the coasts near Avonderre. There are thousands of crannies and caves in those cliffs, some of which are quite shallow, others of which go on for miles.

"It made me wonder about the source of the water for Entudenin. It is possible that an inlet there or even more northward fed water through an underground riverbed or tunnel of some sort all the way to Yarim. The complexities of the strata that make up the earth are immeasurable." Rhapsody inhaled deeply, having traveled through such strata long ago. "It is possible that the right combination of underground hills and valleys, riverbeds, inlets, and filtering sand led to this sweet-water geyser a thousand miles from the sea, swelling and ebbing with the cycle of the moon and the tides. If all this is possible, it is also possible that this pathway became clogged, closed somehow. If it could be opened again, the water might return."

"M'lady, how would anyone know?" Quentin Baldasarre asked incredulously. "If, as you suggest, a blockage occurred somewhere along a thousand miles of subterranean tunnel, how could one ever find it?"

Rhapsody sat forward. "One would ask those who know the subterranean maps of the Earth, who walk such corridors in daily life, and have the tools to mine them."

Realization began to spread through the features of the councilors, leaving unpleasant expressions on the faces of the dukes of Roland.

"Please tell me that you are referring to the Nain," Martin Ivenstrand said.

"I am referring to the *Bolg,* of course," Rhapsody replied testily. "And I do not appreciate your tone or your implication. The Nain want as little contact with the Cymrian Alliance as is necessary to maintain good standing. The Bolg are full participants in its trade and support." She turned to Ihrman Karsrick, whose face had gone an unhealthy shade of purple. "You seem suddenly unwell, Ihrman. I would think that this opportunity would bring you great joy and anticipation, not indigestion." She glanced at the turkey leg again. "Though I am not surprised if you are suffering from that, too."

The Duke of Yarim coughed dryly. "Surely m'lady does not believe me so daft as to want to enter into dealings of some sort with the Bolg?"

The expression on the Lady Cymrian's face resolved into one of sharp observation.

"Why ever not, Ihrman? There has been a trade agreement between Roland and Ylorc for four years now. You sell them salt, you buy their weapons, they are members of the Cymrian Alliance—why would you not seek their expertise in solving your greatest problem?"

"Because I have no desire to be beholden to the Firbolg king, that's why," snapped Karsrick. "We share a common border. I do not wish to have him feel he can cross that border and take remuneration from Yarim at any time he wishes."

"I would never think that you would put yourself in such a position," Rhapsody replied. "His doing so would not be tolerated. My suggestion is that you contract for the services of his artisans, just as you do with those of Roland, Sorbold, and even from as far away as Manosse. Do you have some objection to making use of the talents of Firbolg artisans?"

"I do not wish to invite hordes of Bolg—*artisans* into Yarim, no, I don't, m'lady," Karsrick retorted. "The possible repercussions hold great horror for me."

"Surely that is not an unreasonable stance," interjected Tristan Steward. "King Achmed does not look happily on Orlandan workers coming into *his* realm. The handful of them that have been invited to work on the rebuilding of Canrif have been subjected to unbelievably intense scrutiny, and even then only one or two have been hired. Why should we issue invitations to his people when he has not been particularly welcoming to ours?"

"Perhaps the reason for King Achmed's lack of hospitality may be that the last time your people came into his lands they were carrying torches and clubs, Tristan," Ashe commented. He had been sitting back in his chair, hands folded in front of his chin, watching Rhapsody press her argument. "It will take some time for the Bolg to get over the annual Spring Cleaning ritual that was practiced, at their grievous expense, for so many centuries."

"If I recall, you took part in one of those raids yourself when you were a young man training with the army, Gwydion," said Tristan Steward darkly. "We rode in the same regiment."

"Regardless, you are missing the point," Rhapsody said. "The Bolg may be able to help restore water to Yarim, sparing it from the drought that now threatens your people. If there is any possible chance that they can, do you not have an obligation to seek their assistance?"

"Do I not have an obligation to the safety of those people as well, m'lady?" asked Karsrick, a note of desperation in his voice.

"Yes, you do," Rhapsody replied, "and so do I. Therefore, I offer to take full responsibility for the comportment of whatever Bolg craftsmen, miners, or artisans come to Yarim to examine Entudenin, and for whatever work they do. I am well aware that this is, at least historically, a holy relic, and that you are greatly concerned with preserving it."

"Yes."

"So again, let it be on my head. I will take full blame for anything that should occur in this undertaking."

The Duke of Yarim threw his hands up mutely, then sat back in his chair with a dull thud. The other members of the council looked at each other in bewilderment. Finally Karsrick sighed in resignation.

"Very well, m'lady."

Rhapsody smiled brightly as she rose from the table. "Good! Thank you. We will meet King Achmed and his contingent four weeks hence in Yarim Paar at the foot of Entudenin." She looked around at the blank faces staring back at her. "Well, good councilors, if you do not have anything else pressing that needs to be attended to this evening, I think I shall commandeer my husband and leave you all to get some rest."

Ashe was on his feet in an instant. "Yes, indeed, thank you for your patience. I shall see to it that you are all able to sleep in late tomorrow; we will not be convening until the day after. *At least.* Good night, Gwydion." He pushed the chair back under the table, bowed to his councilors, and his namesake hastily accompanied Rhapsody out of the library. On the way across the room he leaned down to her ear and spoke softly.

"Well, darling, welcome home. It's good to see that causing strife among the members of the council is still a family trait."

As they passed the large open hearth the flames of the fire roared in greeting, then settled into a quiet burn again. Rhapsody stopped and looked quickly over her shoulder.

She stared into the fireshadows dancing on the colorful threads of the intricately woven carpet, then looked up to the balcony doors on the other side of the library, where raindrops dashed intermittently against the glass.

"Did—did someone just come into the room?" she asked Ashe softly.

The Lord Cymrian stopped beside her. His dragonesque eyes narrowed slightly as he concentrated, reaching out with his dragon sense to the corners of the vast library. His awareness expanded between two beats of his heart. Every fiber of carpet, every candleflame, each page in each book, the breath of each member of the council, each drop of rain outside the keep was suddenly known to him in detail.

He detected nothing different. But now his blood ran colder.

"No," he said finally. "Did you feel something disturbing?"

Rhapsody exhaled, then shook her head. "Nothing tangible." She slipped her hand into her husband's palm. "Perhaps I am just eager to quit this place and be alone with you."

Ashe smiled and kissed her hand.

"As always, m'lady, I defer to your wisdom."

In a remarkable show of restraint, he waited until the doors of the library had closed securely behind them before sweeping Rhapsody off her feet and carrying her, in a few bounding steps, to their tower chambers.

Inside the library, the damask curtains that lined the glass door to the balcony overlooking the Cymrian museum in the courtyard below fluttered gently, unnoticed by the councilors, who had immediately returned to their arguments, oblivious of the howling storm outside the library windows.

A heartbeat later, they hung motionless, still as death, once more.

## Orange

# Fire Starter, Fire Quencher

Frith-re

# 2

## ARGAUT, NORTHLAND

The night rain fell in black sheets, twisting into showers of dark needles on the wind before it spattered the muddy cobblestones of the streets leading to the Hall of Virtue, the towering stone edifice that housed the Judiciary of Argaut.

The seneschal paused for a moment at the top of the marble steps of the hall, listening as if to distant voices in the turbulent wind.

The streets of the city were silent, muted no doubt by the frigid wind and insistent rain. Even the wharfside taverns and brothels had doused their lamps, closing their shutters tight against the gale that blew in off the waterfront.

The seneschal stared out over the harbor, to the far end of the cove where the lighttowers burned, even in the downpour, serving as guide to the ships at sea, their hulls battered by the pounding storm. *We well may lose one tonight,* the seneschal thought, pondering the signals from the tower; the light was flashing in broken beams, gleaming with increasing brightness as more oil was added to the flame. He inhaled deeply. When death hovered in the sea winds, it was invigorating to the lungs.

He closed his eyes for a moment and turned his face up to the black sky above him, letting the icy wind buffet his eyelids, allowing the rain to sting his skin. Then he opened his eyes once more, shook the water from his face and cloak, and climbed the last few steps into the Hall of Virtue.

The great iron doors of the hall had been bolted against the night and the storm. The seneschal shifted the small burlap sack he carried to his lesser hand, grasped the knocker, and pounded; the sound thudded like a bell tolling a death knell, echoing for a moment, then was swallowed by the howl of the wind.

With a metallic scream the enormous door was pulled open, flooding the opening with dim light. The guard stepped quickly aside; the seneschal patted the man's shoulder as he passed from the fury of the storm to the warmth of the echoing quiet in the palace's vast foyer.

"Good evening, Your Honor," the guard said as he closed the heavy iron door behind the seneschal.

"Has my lord sent for me?"

"No, sir. All is quiet."

The exchange was the same as it was each night, the soldier thought as the seneschal handed him his dripping cloak and tricornered judge's hat. The lord never sent for the seneschal; he never sent for anyone, in fact. The Baron of Argaut was a hermit, living in an isolated tower, and tended to in gravest secret by only a trusted handful of advisors, chief among them the seneschal. The soldier had been standing guard duty in the Hall of Virtue for more than four years, and had never seen the baron even once.

"Good. A pleasant evening to you, then," said the seneschal. The guard nodded, and returned to his post by the door. He listened to the fading click of the seneschal's boots as he crossed the polished marble foyer and made his way down the long hallway into the judiciary chambers. When the last echo had died away, the soldier allowed himself the luxury of breathing once more.

The candleflames in the wall sconces that lined the long hallway to the Chamber of Justice flickered as the seneschal walked past, causing the light that pooled intermittently on the dusky slate floor to dance frenetically, then settle back into a gently pulsing glow again.

At the end of the long central corridor he opened the door to the dark courtroom and stepped inside, his eyes adjusting quickly in the absence of light, then quietly closed the door behind him.

The seneschal's eyes burned at the edges as he gazed lovingly about the place where so many judgments were handed down, where so many men and women stood accused, then condemned. The prisoner's docket, the barrister's podium, stood silent now in the dark, the echoes of the wailing that had occurred here today, and every day before today, vibrating invisibly in the air, leaving behind a delicious hum of agony.

The seneschal strode quickly across the floor of the shadowy chamber, past the empty witness gallery, pausing for a moment at the clerk's desk, a two-compartmented, cagelike table with wooden slats above it. Draped over the slats was a long piece of parchment curled at the ends, stretched out to allow the ink to dry. Many names were neatly inscribed on the document, tomorrow's court agenda, a list of condemned souls who did not know that their fate had been decided long before they had even been accused. The seneschal fingered the parchment with an air of bemused melancholy. *No time for this. Ah, well.*

His mind wandered to the street wench he had killed earlier this night beneath the pier, her body doubtless being battered now against the pylons by the raging surf of the storm. His thoughts then shifted to the sailor who would burn for the crime tomorrow, at this moment sleeping off his evening's rum, oblivious in his drunkenness, the blood of a woman he had never seen drenching his clothes, clotting in dark, sticky pools. It was bound to be an exciting trial, and an even more exciting bonfire, especially if the rum vapors were still fresh on the bewildered man's breath.

Such a shame that he would not be here to appreciate it.

The seneschal exhaled sharply, refocusing, silencing the building din of dark voices calling in the depth of his ears.

A slight movement in the burlap sack he carried brought him back to the task at hand.

Framing the bench where he sat daily in judgment was a red curtain, heavy damask that smelled of mildew and earth hanging behind his chair. The seneschal climbed the steps to the bench, then drew the curtain aside, revealing the stone wall behind it. He ran a finger over an all-but-unseen crack, felt for the handhold, then turned the doorway aside and stepped into the darkness of the tunnel behind the wall, closing it carefully behind him.

Down the familiar passageway he descended, his feet finding their way automatically in the blackness. A left turn, then three more to the right; his eyes closed to slits.

His body flooded with warmth when the greenish glow in the distance became visible. His steps quickened as he called into the darkness.

"Faron?"

From the floor of the catacomb steam began to rise, thin tendrils of twisting vapor hovering over the glowing pool.

The seneschal smiled, feeling the heat rise inside his own body.

"Come forth, my child," he whispered.

The gleaming mist thickened, writhing in waves that reached outward, above, into the blackness that surrounded it.

The seneschal peered into the vapor.

Finally, from within the glowing pool bubbles of air crested the surface of the incandescent water. The meniscus roiled, then broke open, causing the ghostly mist to swirl and vanish.

From the center of the pool a head emerged, human in shape though not appearance. Wide, fishlike eyes occluded with milky cataracts blinked as they came into sight from below the surface, followed by a flat, bridgeless nose; then the creature's mouth, or near lack thereof, appeared, lips fused in the front, open over the molars, black horizontal slits through which small streams of water gushed. Its skin, golden, sallow, appeared almost a part of the pool from which it had been summoned.

The gleaming water surged as the creature, with great effort, pulled itself up on forearms that curled and bent under the weight of its torso, its limbs misshapen and mutable, as though they were formed not of bone but only of cartilage. The silky garment that draped its body bulged slightly in spots to cover both nascent male and female bodily traits, set in a slight, buckling skeletal frame, grotesquely twisted and soft.

A fond look came into the eyes of the seneschal, eyes that burned red at the edges in excitement. The demon spirit that clung to his physical form, recognizing the presence of its own, crowed in excitement, scratching at his ribs.

"Good evening, little one," he said softly. "I've brought your supper."

The creature's cloudy eyes burned red at the edges in response. With a forward movement of its twisted arms it drew nearer, its lower body hovering in the shining green water of the pool.

The seneschal drew forth the blade he wore at his side and opened the cloth sack. Reaching inside, he pulled out two marinus eels, blind, oily creatures, black of flesh and thick of heft, that bit wildly at his forearm, lashing about as they dangled over the pool. He tore the heads off and tossed them into the darkness, chuckling as the creature's eyes widened hungrily.

Then, with exquisite care, he sliced the still-twitching bodies into thin slivers and tenderly fed them to the creature through the side openings in its mouth, eliciting grisly popping and slurping sounds as the soft teeth ground the flesh to bits.

When the creature had consumed the eels it backed away from the pool's edge and began to sink slowly into the green water again.

The seneschal's hand shot out and caught its head gently under the chin; the layers of loose, wrinkled skin reverberated, sending ripples through the glowing pool.

"No, Faron, tarry."

He stared down at this child of his creation, the end result of one of his favorite and most brutal conquests, an Ancient Seren woman who fell quite literally into his hands a thousand years before. The atrocities he had committed upon her still made his blood burn hot with pleasure; impregnating

her had been well worth the diminution of power that he
had suffered as a result. The innate magic she and all those
of her race possessed—the element of ether left over from
Creation when the Earth had been nothing more than a flaming piece of a star streaking across the void of the universe—burned in Faron's blood, just as the fire from which
his own demonic side had come did. There was a perverse
beauty in their misshapen offspring, this denatured entity,
its features at the same time old and young, all but boneless
in its deformity, yet still his child, and his alone.

The creature's enormous eyes fixed on his face unblink-
ingly.

"I have need of your gift," the seneschal said.

Faron stared at him a moment longer, then nodded.

The seneschal released the mute creature's face, caressing
it gently as he did. Then from an inner pocket of his robe
he brought forth a square of folded velvet and opened it
carefully, almost reverently.

Beneath the folds of cloth lay a lock of hair, brittle and
dry like straw, hair that once was golden as wheat in a
summer field, now yellow-white with years, tied with a
black velvet ribbon that had decayed almost into threads of
dust. He offered it to the creature floating in the pool of soft
green light and watery mist.

"Can you see her?" he whispered.

The creature stared at him a moment longer, as if gauging
his weakness; the seneschal could feel it searching his face,
wondering what had come over him. He contemplated the
same thing himself; his hands were shaking with anticipation, his voice carried a husky note of excited dread that he
could not remember it having before.

Probably because he had not considered the possibility in
more than half again a thousand years that she might still
be alive.

Until this night.

The creature apparently found whatever it was looking
for in his face; it took the lock of ancient hair, then nodded

again and slipped beneath the surface of the pool, reappearing a moment later.

In one of its grotesquely gnarled hands it carried a thin blue oval with tattered edges that gleamed iridescently in the reflected light of the pool water. Each side of the object's surface bore an etching; it was the image of an eye, obscured by clouds on one side, clear of them on the other, the engraving worn almost to invisibility by time.

The seneschal smiled broadly. There was something so pleasing about seeing the scale in the hands of his child that he could barely contain his delight. Faron's mother had been the last in a long line of Ancient Seren seers to possess some of the scales, and her power to read them had passed through her blood into Faron's. Imagining the horror she must be suffering in the Afterlife made the demon that clung to his soul shout with joy.

He watched reverently as Faron plunged the ancient scale beneath the surface of the gleaming green pool. Clouds of steam from the heat of the fire that burned naturally in Faron's blood began to rise, white vapor that filled the air like ghosts hovering above, longing for a view.

*Earth, present in the scale itself,* the seneschal mused, staring through the billowing mist. *Fire and ether, ever-present in Faron's blood, water from the pool.* The cycle of the elements was complete but for one. Given the distance over which he wished Faron to see, great power would be needed.

Slowly he took hold of the hilt protruding from the scabbard at his side, and with great care drew Tysterisk. A rush of wind whipped through the catacomb, stirring clouds of mold spores from the floor as the blade came forth from its sheath, invisible except for a shower of sparks of flame as if from a brushfire in a high breeze.

A deep tug resonated through both his human flesh and his demonic spirit, the bond of connection to the elemental sword of air within him blazing as it always did when the weapon was drawn. Holding Tysterisk in his hands was the most powerful pleasure of the flesh he had ever experienced, an orgiastic sensation that dwarfed all others his body had felt. He held it over the glowing green pool, sending waves crashing over Faron where a moment before there had only been gentle ripples.

The elemental circle was complete.

Beneath the surface of the green water the scale glowed.

The clouds in Faron's occluded eyes cleared; their bright blue irises shone like stars in the reflected brilliance of the pool. The seneschal noted the change, the demon within him crowing with excitement.

"Can you see her?" he asked the ancient malformed child again, struggling to keep his voice steady.

The gnarled creature stared into the windy water, blinking in the dark, then shook its head, the hanging folds of skin beneath its chin quivering.

Impatiently the seneschal fumbled in the bag that had contained the eels and withdrew a soft tallow candle, formed from caustic lye and human fat rendered from sickly old people and children, the useless booty of privateered ships that had been picked clean of more valuable captives and treasure. He tapped the wick with his finger, calling forth the black fire from within his demonic soul, his very essence, and sparked the flame. When the taper began to glow he held it up over the pool, casting more illumination over the submerged scale.

"Can you see her?" he demanded again; the fire burned in his voice, dark with threat.

Faron squinted, studying the scrying scale. A moment later the monstrous face turned up to meet the wild blue eyes of its father, and nodded.

Blazing excitement, replaced a moment later with impatience, roared through the seneschal.

"What do you see? Tell me more."

The mute creature stared at him helplessly.

"What is she doing? Is she alone?"

The creature shook its head.

The fiery excitement soured to blinding fury.

"*No?* She is not alone? Who is with her? *Who?*"

The creature shrugged.

The wild storm in the seneschal's eyes broke, like the wind-whipped waves in the gale.

He plunged both his hands up to the last joints of the fingers into the misshapen creature's soft skull, twisting them as its fishlike mouth dropped open at the sides in agony, a silent scream bursting in waves of gushing air exiting its quivering lips.

As Faron's body went rigid with shock, the seneschal closed his eyes and concentrated. Intently he focused his concentration inward, untying the metaphysical bonds by which his immortal demonic nature clung to his corporeal form, seeking the vibrations in Faron's blood that matched those of his own. He found them easily.

Like threads of spun steel, the tiny tethers of power stretched between his body and his soul. Meticulously he unhooked them one by one and retied each one to the misshapen mass of human flesh writhing in his hands, whose blood burned with his own.

As the fire of his essence slipped into Faron's body, his own corporeal form cooled, withered and sank into itself, shriveling like a mummified skeleton. It clung to Faron, its ossified fingers still protruding from the child's head.

Faron's twisted form, now the vessel, the host of the immortal soul of the demon, straightened and grew substantial, the cartilage hardening into bone. The demon peered out through Faron's clear blue eyes.

He stared into the blue waves of light reflecting in the scale just below the surface of the glowing green water.

At first he saw nothing but a distant shadow. Then, a movement, and his bearing sharpened.

In the rippling waves of the pool he could make out the watery image of a face, both alien and innately familiar to him. It was a face he had studied at great length a lifetime ago, stared at in portraits, gazed at intently when in close proximity. He knew every line, every angle, though in the clouds of steam it was not exactly as he remembered it.

Perhaps it was the expression that was confusing him. The face he had known was a guarded one, one that rarely smiled, and when it did, that expression was wry. The emerald eyes within the face had burned with contempt, coolly disguised beneath an aspect of disinterest, especially when fixed on him.

Now, though, in whatever blue light through which it passed half a world away, this familiar, unknown face was wreathed in an expression he did not recognize.

There was laughter in her eyes, caught in this moment of time, and something more, an expression he could not place, but did not like, whatever it was. Her face was shining in the reflected glow of candleflame, but more—it was generating its own light.

She was talking to someone.

More than one person, it seemed, from the way her head moved, someone whose face was at an equal height to her own to the left, and another who was taller to the right. When she looked in the latter direction, her eyes took on an element of excitement that burned like elemental fire, pure and hot from the heart of the Earth. There was something so inviting, so compelling, about this face that involuntarily he reached into the glowing water and touched the back of her neck, where the golden hair he had dreamed about for more than a thousand years hung in a silken fall. He drew Faron's gnarled finger through the ripples in an awkward caress.

Half a world away, she froze. A look of revulsion, or perhaps fear, washed the smile from her face, leaving it blank, pale. She glanced over her shoulder, then put her hand to her throat, as if shielding it from a bitter wind, or the maw of a wolf.

His touch had made her recoil.

Again.

*Whore,* he whispered in his mind. *Miserable, rutting whore.*

His anger exploded, causing Faron's body to jerk and quiver with the physical manifestations of rage. With a furious sweep of his squamous hand he slapped the surface of the water, sending the scale spinning out of the pool and into the dank darkness of the catacomb.

He breathed shallowly, trying to regain his focus.

When reason returned, he closed his sky-blue eyes, concentrating on the metaphysical threads that bound him to Faron's human form, loosing and retying them once more.

As the demonic essence rushed back into the seneschal's body, the withered mummy swelled with life again, the angry light returning to his dried-out eye sockets. Faron's body, by contrast, grew supple and twisted again until it collapsed under its own weight.

The seneschal breathed shallowly as he pulled his remaining fingers from the soft skull of his child, stanching the blood that dripped from the holes. Tenderly he gathered Faron, who wept silently, deformed mouth gasping at the edges, into his arms and caressed the wisps of hair, the quivering folds of skin, gently kissing the creature's head.

"I am sorry, Faron," he whispered softly. "Forgive me."

When the creature's soundless moans resolved into light panting, the seneschal cupped its face in his hand and turned it so that he was staring into its eyes, now cloudy again, though still the same blue as his own.

"I have wondrous news for you, Faron," he said, stroking its flaccid cheeks with his fingers. "I am going on a long voyage, far across the sea—" He pressed his forefinger to the creature's fused lips as panic came into its eyes.

"And I am taking you with me."

𝕿he dark staircase that led to the Baron of Argaut's tower was built, except for the last few steps, of polished gray marble veined in black and white. The stairs, like the passageway itself, were narrow; the noise of footsteps ascending or descending was reduced to soft, ominous clicks instead of the echoing cadence that walking through the other corridors in the Hall of Virtue produced.

At the top of the staircase the last few steps were hewn from blood coral, a stinging calcified sea plant—a living creature when in the sea, it was said—that formed poisonous reefs thousands of miles long near the Fiery Rim, many ocean leagues away. It blended with the marble of the steps, forming a deadly barrier to anyone not immune to the bite of fire, the sting of venom.

The seneschal climbed the last stair and stopped before the black walnut door bound in steel. He knocked deferentially, then opened the door slowly.

A rush of dank wind and consuming darkness greeted him.

He stepped quickly into the chamber and closed the door behind him.

"Good evening, m'lord," he said.

At first no sound replied except the skittering movements of mice and the flutter of bat wings in the eaves above.

Then, deep within his brain, he heard the voice, words burning his mind like dark fire.

*Good evening.*

The seneschal cleared his throat, casting his eyes around the black tower room, the darkness impenetrable. "All is progressing well in Argaut. We had another successful day in the Judiciary."

*Very good.*

He cleared his throat again. "I will be leaving tonight on an extended voyage. Is there anything m'lord requires before I go?"

The silence swelled around him in the dark. When the voice spoke again, it burned with menace, stinging his ears and the inside of his brain.

*An explanation, to begin with.*

The seneschal inhaled deeply. "I've had some news today that someone who owes me a very great debt, an oath struck on the Island of Serendair before the Great Cataclysm, survived the awakening of the Sleeping Child and is alive." He let his breath out with the words. "I need to collect on that debt."

*Why?* the burning voice demanded. *Send a lackey.*

Wisely the seneschal swallowed the retort that rose, unbidden, to his lips. It was not prudent to enflame the baron.

"That is not possible, m'lord," he said in a measured, respectful tone. "This is something to which I must attend personally. I assure you, however, the prize with which I will return will be more than worth my absence."

*In your estimation, perhaps. But mayhap not in mine.* The anger in the voice seared the inside of the seneschal's head. *If you leave, who will procure the slaves? Maintain the terror? Who will sit in the judiciary? Attend to the burnings? Who will fulfill the law?*

The seneschal's eyes burned red at the edges in response as he struggled against his own wild ire.

"The infrastructure is well in place, m'lord. All of that will be done, and more." Impulsively he dropped to one knee and bowed his head. When he spoke, his voice carried an excitement that the expansive darkness of the room could barely contain. "But to please m'lord, before I go I will attend to your will. I will accomplish a rash of burnings sufficient to light the sky to a crimson glow that will linger for days! I will move up the dockets, deploy the fleet, set in motion whatever m'lord desires. But I must leave with the tide ere morning; I have a contract to enforce." He raised his eyes to the darkness again. "An oath to make someone uphold."

The silence echoed around him. The seneschal stared into the endless darkness, waiting.

Finally, after what seemed like an eternity, the voice spoke. It was filled with reluctance, a disappointment that was palpable.

*Very well. But be certain to return as soon as you have claimed whatever is owed to you.*

The seneschal rose quickly and bowed from the waist.

"I will, m'lord. Thank you."

The dark voice spoke softly, the tone in its words fading into the blackness again.

*You may go now.*

The seneschal bowed once more. He backed away in the darkness, feeling for the handle of the door. Once he found it, he opened it, stepped through quickly, and closed the door behind him, taking his leave.

Of a completely empty room.

# Yellow

## Light Bringer, Light Queller

### Merte-mi

# 3

## THIEVES' MARKET, YARIM PAAR

It never failed to amaze Slith how much power could reside in a single word, a word that was merely someone's name.

Particularly Esten's name.

Now as he followed Bonnard's quivering form, the rolls of flesh vibrating with each step along the cobbled alleys of the Market of Thieves through which they were traveling, he pondered whether invoking that name had been wise or not.

Bonnard's sneer, upon finding him shirking his duties in the privy, had melted quickly into an expression that straddled the border between consternation and fear when he had uttered his need to be taken to the guildmistress. Slith cast his eyes down at the dusty red cobblestones and smiled to himself, remembering their exchange.

*What—what would the likes of you need to see Esten about?*

*Certain you wish to know, Bonnard? That will make you the only other one besides me.*

The journeyman had considered the question for the span of ten heartbeats, then scowled, shook his great jowled head quickly, and motioned for Slith to follow him.

Now, as they traveled deeper into the Market of Thieves, Slith wondered whether invoking that name had been the most foolish thing he had ever done.

As a young child he had once ventured as far as the Outer Market, the bazaar of merchants and goodsellers from all over the known world, and undoubtedly parts of the unknown world as well. He had found it to be a place of open-air shops and street booths, of exotic animals prowling the areas near shopkeepers' wares, of brightly colored silks and bags of pungent spice, the scent of incense and perfume mixed with the slick, heavy odor of the peat fires over which meat was roasting. His mother had brought him along with her in a vain search for a tonic to heal his ailing father; after seeing her pay every coin she had for a bottle of glittering liquid that had proved completely ineffective, Slith understood on an innate level at the age of six how the market had gotten its name.

Never, however, had he been this deep in, this close to the poisonous danger of the Inner Market. He could feel the threat in the air around him; it was somehow heavier here in these back streets, these dark alleys, where the color and pageantry gave way to hidden alcoves and shadowy porticos. The mudbrick buildings, dried to the color of blood, as all of Yarim was, the kiosks of straw and sheets of oilcloth dotting the streets, teemed with secrets.

Gone were the merchants loudly hawking their wares, the chanters and the singers and the screaming carnival barkers. The Inner Market was a place of thick silence, furtive glances, where hidden eyes followed every move.

Slith kept his eyes downcast, as instructed, watching the heels of Bonnard's hobnail boots. He could feel the gaze of what seemed like a thousand of those hidden eyes on him, but knew that attempting to meet that gaze could be fatal.

Finally Bonnard stopped. Slith looked up.

Before him loomed a tall, wide, one-story mudbrick building, dark from the coal dust that had been mixed with the red Yarimese clay when it was fired. Like most of the buildings in Yarim it was in a state of advanced decay, the coal dust clay flaking off the building's edifice ominously, signaling a deeper rot. The inconsistent patches made the building look like it was bleeding.

On the door was a crest, the sign of a raven clutching a gilt coin. Slith suppressed a shudder; he had seen the guild-mark before, on the day of his indenture, when his mother brought him to the counting house of the Raven's Guild to be inspected by Esten. The Raven's Guild in the city center of Yarim Paar was a grand building, housing the largest trade association in the province, a confederation of tile artisans, ceramicists, and glassblowers, as well as smiths of all sorts. The guild also provided an intraprovince messenger service. It was the worst-kept secret in Yarim that they were a formidable coterie of professional thieves, thugs, and highwaymen who ruled the dark hours of Yarim.

And Esten was their undisputed leader.

Cold beads of sweat trickled down his neck as Bonnard opened the door and motioned him impatiently inside. He followed the journeyman's gesture to an alcove to the left of the door, and watched nervously as Bonnard disappeared into the darkness before him.

Slith blinked rapidly, trying to force his eyes to adjust quickly in the absence of light. The room seemed to have no visible boundaries; the space before him melted into the farthest reaches of his vision. A battered table, rough-hewn from ragged wood, stood a few yards from the door to his right; at least that was what it appeared to be by shape. Around it were mismatched chairs of various heights and styles. He thought he could see a cold fireplace behind the table. The harsh odor of coal and rancid fat hung thickly in the stagnant air.

"You wanted to speak to me?"

Slith reared back in shock, a numbing cold sweeping through him.

Almost as close to him as the air he was breathing was a face, its pale contours blending into the darkness. It appeared disembodied, dark eyes staring directly into his own.

Slith swallowed, then nodded wordlessly, his mouth too dry to form sounds.

The black eyes twinkled as if in amusement.

"Then speak."

Slith opened his mouth, but no sound came out. The eyes in the darkness narrowed slightly as a look of annoyance entered them. He cleared his throat and forced the words out.

"I found something. I thought you should see it."

The face inclined at a slight angle.

"Very well. Show me."

Slith fumbled inside his shirt pocket and pulled forth the roll of rags in which he had wrapped the blue-black disk. Before he could reach out to hand it over the roll of cloth disappeared from his grasp.

The dark eyes cast their gaze downward; then the face turned and vanished.

In the distance a glow of light pulsed, then brightened into a ring, as one by one a circle of lanterns was unhooded.

As the room was illuminated Slith saw that it was much smaller than he had imagined when the darkness still reigned unchallenged. In the far corners several grizzled men were watching him as they brought the room to light with the lanterns.

Esten stood before him, turning the blue-black disk carefully over in her long, delicate hands, her face, unlike those of most Yarimese women, unveiled. In the half-light he could see that she was no taller than he, with long raven hair and garments the color of a starless night that had blended perfectly into the darkness a moment before. Her tresses were bound back in a braid that was knotted at the nape of her neck, further accentuating the sharp angles of her face. Slith imagined she must be of mixed blood, her face possessing some but not all of the characteristics of Yarimese faces. He pondered where she might be from for a moment, but the thought disappeared as she leveled her dark gaze into his own.

"You are one of Bonnard's apprentices?"

Slith's father had imparted few words of wisdom that he remembered, but one oft-repeated phrase stood out in his mind: *Look every man in the eye, friend or foe. Your friends deserve the respect, your enemies warrant it even more.* He returned her stare as respectfully yet directly as he could.

"Yes."

Esten nodded. "Your name?"

"Slith."

"What year are you?"

"Fourth."

She nodded again. "So you are, what—eleven? Twelve?"

"Thirteen."

A look of interest came into her eye. "Hmm. I took you on rather old, then, didn't I?"

Slith swallowed, determined to hold his ground, and shrugged.

Esten's expression of amusement widened. "I like this one, Dranth. He has steel in his viscera. Make sure he is getting enough to eat." The blue-black blade appeared between her long, thin fingers. "Where did you get this?"

"I found it in a greenware jar on the back storage rack in the firing room."

"Do you know what it is?"

"No," said Slith. He watched as Esten's gaze returned to the disk. "Do you?"

Shock washed over her face at his impertinence, as if he had attacked her. Within a breath she had recovered in time to gesture to the men behind her, staying their hands, and leveled her shining gaze at him again.

"No, Slith, I don't know what it is," she said evenly, holding the disk up to the streaks of light pulsing from within the hooded lanterns. "But you may sleep in deepest peace tonight, assured in the certainty that I will find out."

"At first I thought it was a seam scraper of some sort," Slith said, watching the firelight ripple over the surface of the disk in her hands. "But it occurred to me that it has probably been in that jar a long time."

When Slith looked at her again, her eyes were glittering with cruel excitement, looking past him.

"You may be right," she said softly. "Maybe for as long as three years." She turned to one of the men in the corner. "Yabrith—give Slith here a reward of ten gold crowns for his sharp eyes, and a good meal; tell Bonnard he will be ready to return to the foundry after he has supped." She looked at Slith once more. "Your attention has served both of us well. It would be a good habit to cultivate. Tell no one what has transpired."

Slith nodded, then followed the sullen man who gestured to him.

Dranth, the guild scion, watched as the boy had left, then turned to the guildmistress.

"Do you wish him removed?"

Esten shook her head as she turned the disk over in her hands again. "Not until we discover what this is. It would be a shame to toss away four years of good training if it merely *is* a seam scraper."

Dranth's eyelids twitched nervously in the lanternlight. "And if it is more? If it is indeed something we missed, something left behind from—that night?"

Esten held the disk up to the light, ripples of blue reflecting against the dark irises of her eyes.

"Bonnard knows where the boy sleeps. And you know where Bonnard sleeps."

She finally broke her gaze away and nodded to the remaining men, who slipped out the back and disappeared into the darkest part of the Inner Market.

$\mathcal{A}$ll but one of the lanterns had been extinguished and night held sway within the walls of the guildhall when the men returned with Mother Julia.

Esten smiled wryly as she watched the wizened crone enter the antechamber of the hall. She was a withered old prune, hunched and shrouded in myriad colorful shawls, the second most powerful woman in the Market, accustomed to receiving those who wanted information from her in her own lair, on her own terms. Being summoned in the middle of the night and hauled into the depths of the Inner Market undoubtedly did little to improve her normally crotchety and imperious disposition but, like everyone else in the realm of thieves, she could not refuse Esten, or show any sign of annoyance.

A false smile, minus more than a few teeth, spread across the wrinkled face.

"Good evening, Guildmistress. May Fortune bless you."

"You as well, Mother."

"What may I do to be of help to you, then?"

Esten studied the weathered face, its aged features a deceptive setting for the bright, quick eyes that stared back at her. Mother Julia was by trade a soothsayer, a fortune-teller who procured an extremely comfortable living from the fools who sought her advice. Although her ability to predict the future was no better than anyone else's, she was a source of generally reliable information about the past and, even more so, the present, largely owing to her extensive network of spies, which was centered in Yarim but also crossed provincial and even national borders, the majority of them members of her own family. She had seventeen living children at last count, Esten knew, having been the agent by which that tally had been diminished by one, and more grandchildren, cousins, and relations by marriage than the stars in the night sky.

She was anxious, Esten knew as well. The wrinkled face was placid, but the dark eyes within it burned with nervous light. Usually Mother Julia played the information gambit better than anyone in the Market, but she had led too early, had tried in her second breath to entangle Esten into indebtedness. *She's losing her touch,* the guildmistress thought, tucking the observation away as she did all information. She turned away and walked toward the fire, denying Mother Julia a clear look at her face.

"Nothing at all, Mother."

The crone coughed, a consumptive sound of rattling phlegm and fear. "Oh?"

Esten smiled inwardly, then set her face into a serious mask and turned to face the old woman.

"I have been singularly disappointed in your lack of response to the one question about which I did seek your help."

An arthritic claw went to the soothsayer's throat. "I—I have—have been scrying diligently, Guildmistress, peering through the—the red sands of Time to try and discover—" Her words choked off and she sank into silence when Esten raised her hand.

"Spare me your prestidigitation and claptrap; I am not one of the imbeciles who seek it from you. You have had more than three years to bring me an answer to a simple question, Mother—who destroyed my tunnel, stole my slaves, killed my journeymen? Who snatched the sleeping water of Entudenin out of my hands, leaving Yarim to wither in thirst and depriving me of the wealth and power it would have brought? This should be an easy thing to find at least one clue to, and yet, yet you have brought me nothing, nothing at all."

"I swear to you, Guildmistress, I have searched diligently, night into day following night, but there is no trace!" the crone stammered, her voice quavering. "No one in all of Yarim knows anything. Outside the Market, not one soul even knew of the tunnel. The destruction must have been the work of evil gods—how else except through the hand of a demon could all that slip be fired into hardened clay, when all your ovens together could not have done it?"

A blur of movement, and Esten's eyes were locked on the crone's from a breath away, a gleaming blade at her throat, pressed so lightly and yet so close that tiny droplets of blood were spattering the air with each of the old woman's nervous tremors.

"You old fool," Esten growled in a low voice. "Gods? Is that the best that you have for me after all this time?" She lashed out violently, contemptuously, and shoved Mother Julia into the table behind her, causing the old woman to stagger and crumple against the table board with a moan of pain. "There are no gods, Mother Julia, no demons. Certainly a charlatan of your caliber, who finagles idiots out of their precious coin in return for bursts of colored smoke and disembodied voices, must be aware of that, or you'd already be burning in the Vault of the Underworld."

"No, no," the woman moaned, struggling to stand but only managing to clutch the table before falling to the dirt floor. "I give homage to the All-God, the Creator who made me." She made a countersign on her heart and ears, her arms trembling.

Esten exhaled, then strode to where the woman was cowering on the floor, seized her arm, and pushed her into the chair.

"The gods do not make us, Mother Julia; we make the gods. If you understood this, you would be a much more powerful and respected woman, instead of just a pathetic impostor who swindles the naïve and vies with Manwyn for the idiot trade."

At the sound of the Oracle of the Future's name, the old woman made her countersign again, her eyes wide in terror. "Don't invoke her," she whispered. "Please, Guildmistress."

Esten snorted contemptuously. "Too late to fear that now. Manwyn only sees the Future. She knew what you were going to hear a moment ago before I said it; she can no longer remember it now." She crouched before the frightened soothsayer, moving slowly, deliberately, like a spider stalking a victim. "All she knows is what lies ahead for you." She cocked her head to the side, dark eyes gleaming. "Do you think she is afraid on your behalf?"

"Please—"

"Please? You are asking me for favors now?" Esten leaned closer, her limbs moving in a deadly dance. "Did you think your time was infinite, my patience endless? You are an even bigger fool than those pathetic vermin who seek you out for answers to their insignificant questions." She stopped within a hairsbreadth of the trembling crone, and the glint in her eyes grew harder, like greenware firing in the kiln into bisque.

"I employ you because your network, your leprotic clan, has so many eyes," she said steadily, her voice low and deadly. "Those hundreds of eyes must all be blind, then, to have been unable to find even one clue in three years, wouldn't you say, Mother?" A terrifying smile spread slowly over her delicate face. "Perhaps they no longer need the use of those eyes." She turned to the guild scion. "Dranth, issue an order to the Raven's Guild: from here forth, any member of this simpleton's family that they come across is to have its eyes put out immediately, including her wretched grandchildren who prowl the street, spreading filth and breathing the air reserved for others who have some actual worth."

"Mercy," the old woman whispered, her arthritic hands clasped in front of her. "Please, Guildmistress, I implore you—"

Esten settled back on her haunches and regarded Mother Julia, whose face was gray and covered in beads of sweat.

"Mercy? Well, I suppose I can consider your entreaty, can offer you one last chance to redeem your sorry family. But if I do, and you fail me again, all the world will regard your clan as monsters, because that which is useless on their heads—eyes, ears, and tongue—will be removed from them and cast into the alleys to feed my dogs. Do you understand me, Mother?"

The crone could only bring herself to nod feebly.

"Good."

From within her garments Esten pulled forth the bundle of rags Slith had given her. With great care she moved the layers aside and revealed the blue-black steel of the whisper-thin disk; it gleamed in the inconstant light of the lantern.

"Do you know what this is?"

Mother Julia shook her head.

Esten exhaled. "Study it well, Mother Julia—use your eyes for what may be the last time. Within one cycle of the moon I want the word spread within your clan alone as far as your miserable influence extends; I want to know what this is. And more importantly, I want to know to whom it belongs. Bring me that information, and I will keep you within my protection. Fail me, and—"

"I will not fail," the crone said softly. "Thank you, Guildmistress."

Esten patted the woman's wrinkled cheek gently. "Good. I know you will not, Mother." She reached into the folds of cloth that formed the trousers of her garments and pulled forth a gold coin minted with the head of the Lord Cymrian on one side, the crest of the Alliance on the other. "Take this gold crown for your newborn grandson—what was he named?"

"Ignacio."

"Ignacio—what a lovely name. Give this to Ignacio's mother for him, please, and extend my warmest wishes to her upon his birth."

The old woman nodded shakily as two of Esten's men took her arms and raised her to her feet.

"See to it Mother Julia gets home safely, please," Esten instructed as they led her to the door. "I would not want anything untoward to befall this dear lady."

She waited until the door had closed soundly, then sat down before the lantern, watching the watery patterns of light ripple across the smooth surface of the disk and off the razor edges, like bright waves rushing headlong over a shining cliff to a dark sea.

*Soon,* she thought. *I will find you soon.*

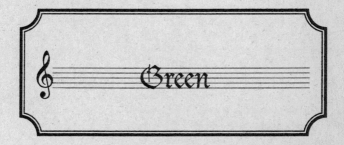

# Green

## Grass Hider, Glade Scryer

### Kurh-fa

# 4

## THE CAULDRON, YLORC

℞ven if he did not have the kingly sense that allowed him to perceive the movements and changes within his mountains, Achmed would still have known that Grunthor had returned to the Cauldron.

Centuries before, in the old life, Achmed had traversed a fjord near the Fiery Rim, a desolate inlet of churning sea currents between towering black basalt cliffs. In the thick woods atop those cliffs, teeming with wildlife but uninhabited by humans, dwelt Firewyrms—giant, chameleon-skinned beasts akin to dragons, which legends claimed were formed from living lava with teeth of brimstone. Dormant much of the time, the serpents, when hunting, prowled through the undergrowth below the forest canopy in relative silence, and yet it was always obvious to him when they were approaching, because the fauna would disappear utterly; the incessant birdsong that rattled over his ultrasensitive skin would suddenly cease, as if the forest was holding its breath, hoping the predators would pass.

It was much the same in Ylorc whenever Grunthor returned.

Achmed had never been able to divine exactly what it was about the Sergeant-Major's training that enabled him to strike such abject fear into the hearts of the Firbolg soldiers in his command, but whatever it was, it had needed to be applied only once.

From the moment he was sighted, still three or more leagues away, the corridors and mountain passes of Ylorc scrambled to attention, clearing away any tomfoolery in favor of regulation dress and behavior. The Firbolg could sense his approach from great distances, like the birds and creatures of the fjord hiding from the Firewyrms, and, like them, took great pains not to draw his notice.

Despite their obvious fear of their commander, a fear he cultivated continually, the Firbolg army was devoted to Grunthor in a way that Bolg had never been. It was a source of amusement to Achmed how in little more than four years' time the primitive nomads they had discovered when he, Grunthor, and Rhapsody had first come to this place had learned to hold watch as well as any soldier in Roland, Sorbold, or Tyrian, and were better trained in tactics and weapons use. Such skills were only partially imparted by training. Most of them came from pure loyalty.

Grunthor's impending arrival this day, however, seemed to be generating more than its usual consternation. Rather than snapping to attention, as the Firbolg soldiers generally did when word came down that the Sergeant was within range, the Bolg were scattering before the scouts that heralded his arrival.

This did not bode well as to whatever Grunthor had found on his border check.

A few moments later Achmed's foreboding was borne out. Over the rim of the steppes that led up to the foothills of the Manteids, as the Teeth were officially called by cartographers, rode a party of eight horses, one enormous, heavy war horse in the lead. Achmed's extraordinary vision could make out the Sergeant-Major, the many hilts of his weapons collection jutting from behind his back, urgently spurring Rockslide, cresting the battlements and riding through the gates in the recently erected walls of baked brick and bitumen.

The Bolg king jogged over to the quartermaster, who was standing ready to take the Sergeant's mount, and waited.

The ground beneath his feet rumbled ominously with the party's approach, the dust of the steps and rocky terrain rising like smoke from bursts of fire around them. There was a look in Grunthor's eyes that Achmed could see even from a great distance and didn't like; those amber eyes had seen more than their share of death and devastation, had faced foes of human and demonic nature, and always maintained a steady gaze. What he saw now was confusion, something Grunthor rarely exhibited.

"What's happened?" he shouted into the mountain wind as the Sergeant brought his mare to a halt and tossed the reins to the quartermaster.

The giant Bolg stared down at the king, then shook his head. "Oi was about to ask you the same question, sir," he said as he dismounted. "Oi 'alf expected to find the place in flames." He dismounted with an earthshaking thud.

Achmed watched until the quartermaster led the war-mare away. "What has you so worried?"

Grunthor bent down and laid his hand reverently on the ground. The earth, the entity to which he was tied on an elemental level, no longer wailed in fear, but was quiet.

"Somethin' was wrong at the pass, somethin' terrible," he muttered, running his thick fingers through the dust and pebbles on the ground.

The Bolg king watched silently as the Sergeant stood and turned around several times, then shrugged.

" 'Twas like there was a rip, a gouge of some sort," he said, more to himself than aloud. "Can't explain it past that. Like the Earth was bleeding to death."

"Is it still there?"

The giant shook his head. "Naw. Everything's quiet now."

Achmed nodded. "Any guesses as to what it was?"

Grunthor inhaled and let his breath out slowly, feeling the heartbeat of the Earth pounding in his own blood. His union with the element had come to him during the trek he, Achmed, and Rhapsody had once made, refugees from their doomed homeland, crawling through the depths of the world along the roots of Sagia, the World Tree. In the course of that seemingly endless journey across time, he had absorbed its ancient rhythms, breathed in the secrets that lay dormant in its depths, had come to know it intimately, innately, though he could never give voice to what he had learned.

*Grunthor, strong and reliable as the Earth itself,* Rhapsody had Named him in the moments after walking through the purifying fire at the Earth's heart. The name had come to embody his bond to the element. Being above ground now made him feel somehow bereft, away from the comforting warmth of the Earth.

So the wound the Earth had sustained, whatever had caused it to scream in fear, had reverberated in his soul, leaving him frightened, a feeling he had rarely experienced in his life.

He shook his head again. "Naw."

Achmed glanced through the gate over the battlements to the steppes below. Dawn was coming, wrapping the world in cold light; the wind whipped across the desolate plain, making the grass bow low in supplication, unbroken waves of vegetation that covered the bulwark of hidden battlements, ditches, and tunnels that formed the Firbolg first line of defense. There was something ominous in its passage.

When he looked back his eyes met Grunthor's, and an unspoken thought was passed between them.

Together they hurried into the Cauldron.

Achmed carefully checked the corridor outside his bedchamber before locking and bolting its door. He nodded to Grunthor, who carefully removed the intricate traps and opened the many locks on the heavy chest at the foot of the Bolg king's bed, finally lifting the top to reveal a dark portal. He climbed inside, followed a moment later by Achmed, closing the lid of the chest behind him.

They traveled the dim corridor in silence, the rough-hewn walls of basalt swallowing all sound of their passage. The air of the upworld, clear with the relative freshness of morning, quickly flattened and became stolid, dank, as they traveled deeper into the mountain.

The farther in they went, the harder it became to breathe. The heavy odor of destruction, smoke-stained air that hung heavy with grit, still remained, three years later; the fire that had raged deep in the belly of the mountain had long since burned out, leaving behind acrid soot and bitter dust that stung the eyes and the lungs.

Neither Bolg spoke as they traversed the tunnel Grunthor had built to the Loritorium. There were ghosts in these passages; specters of people and dreams, both of which had died horribly. They concentrated instead on avoiding the traps Grunthor had set, which would seal the tunnel in the event it was broached by anyone other than the two of them or Rhapsody, who came once a year to tend to the Child.

Deep within the mountain, at the bottom of the tunnel, a hill of rubble rose, ominous, in the dark, a moraine of stones and broken basalt that served as a bulwark, a last barrier before the Loritorium. Achmed paused for a moment and hung back, waiting for Grunthor to open a passage in the mound of stony wreckage.

While he was waiting, he looked up at the ceiling above him, stretching into the darkness of the Loritorium's dome. Seeing this place never ceased to cause him to reflect sadly on the overwhelming loss of it all, the ruin of what had once been a masterpiece, a deeply hidden city of scholarship, once a shining example of the genius of Gwylliam, the Cymrian king who had fashioned Canrif and the lands around it many centuries before. Now it was but a metaphor to the destruction that comes when vision gives way to ambition, and ambition to the avaricious hunger for power.

*Bugger it,* he thought, anger burning in the back of his throat. *I can only rebuild so much of what that idiot destroyed.*

Even as the thought formed, it dissipated. There was no end to what he could, and would, build and rebuild in these mountains, because ultimately it was not the outcome of the construction that was his purpose, but the process. The renovation of Canrif, and the additional projects he was fomenting, were all undertaken with one motive in mind: the building up of the Bolg, his unknown father's race, from scattered tribes of primitive, demi-human, nomadic cave dwellers into a real society—a warlike, austere society to be certain, but nonetheless a culture with value, a contribution to be added to history.

And he had an immortal lifetime to spend on that undertaking. How else was he to spend forever?

*But not this place,* he thought. *Never this place. This remains as it is, undisturbed.*

He took stock of the hidden measures he had set in place to insure the sacrosanctity of the place in the event something happened to either of them, musing idly for a moment about the devices attuned to their heartbeats, their own innate vibrations, set to seal the tunnel in the presence of any intruder. *If Grunthor were to die, I would have to bring in a score of work crews to open and clear the tunnel and then kill them afterward,* he thought. *Such an unfortunate loss of manpower.*

An orange-red glimmer caught his eye; he turned to see the wall of shale and dust gleam like molten lava around Grunthor's hands, which were outstretched, forming an entryway in the mound, leaving a tunnel with walls as slick as glass. Achmed blinked away his musings and followed the giant Bolg through the opening.

On the other side of the mound was what remained of the Loritorium, silent now. A haze of old smoke snaked heavily through the space beneath the overarching dome, disturbed perhaps by the vibrations of their movements and the introduction of the air from the world above.

In the center of what remained of the courtyard the altar of Living Stone appeared undisturbed; the Sleeping Child, formed of the same elemental earth, lying supine upon it.

Achmed and Grunthor approached the altar quietly, careful not to disturb the Earthchild. The chamber in which she had once rested before its destruction had borne a warning inscribed in towering letters:

LET THAT WHICH SLEEPS WITHIN THE EARTH REST UNDISTURBED;
ITS AWAKENING HERALDS ETERNAL NIGHT

The two Bolg had long paid heed to that warning, having seen the threat to which it referred, a far more deadly Sleeping Child, with their own eyes during their travels through the center of the Earth.

The child still rested as she had when they had first found her, her eyes closed in eternal slumber. Like the altar on which she slept, her skin was a polished gray surface, translucent, beneath which veins of colored strands of clay in hues of purple and green, dark red, brown and vermilion could be seen. Her body, tall as that of an adult human, seemed at odds with the sweet young face atop it, a face with features that were at the same time coarse and smooth, roughly hewn but smoothly glossed; she was like a living statue of a human child sculpted by a being that had never really seen one in close proximity, without any sense of perspective.

The hair of the child was long and coarse, green as spring grass, matching the lashes of her eyelids. Those eyelids twitched intermittently but remained closed, as did her heavy lips.

Mutually the Bolg sighed, unspoken relief evident in the relaxation of their stances. They drew closer to the altar.

"Does she look—smaller to you, sir?" Grunthor asked after a long moment.

Achmed squinted, examining the outline of her form on the altar. There was no shadow, no visible indication that her body had lost any of its size; still, there was something different, a frailer air to her that he couldn't place, and didn't like.

Finally he shrugged. Grunthor crossed his arms, staring down at the Earthchild intently. Finally he shrugged also.

"Oi think she's lost some of 'er, but it must be a very small amount," he said, his heavy forehead wrinkling in worry. He tucked the eiderdown blanket beneath which she slept around her tightly, then gently caressed her hand.

"Don't ya worry, darlin'," he said softly. "We got yer back."

"She doesn't seem ill, or hurt?"

"Naw."

Achmed exhaled. Grunthor's description of the wound he had felt in the Earth had unnerved him, had made him fear that the Earthchild might have been compromised or injured, or worse. It was an unending worry anyway; she was, to his knowledge, the last living Child of Earth, a being formed long ago from the pure element and sparked into life by an unknown dragon.

The rib of her body was a Living Stone key that could open the Vault of the Underworld, where in the Before-Time the demons of elemental fire, the F'dor, had been imprisoned. It was the blood oath of the Dhracians, his mother's race, to guard that vault, to keep the F'dor locked away for all time, to hunt down and destroy any that might have escaped. Likewise, it was the endless quest of upworld F'dor to find a way to free their brethren from the Vault, unleashing the chaos and destruction of the world that they, children of fire, craved incessantly. The Earthchild, therefore, was the fuse, the catalyst that could light a sequence of events that could not be undone. The fate of the Earth was dependent on her safety, and he, as a result, was sworn to an eternity of guardianship to see that she remained unharmed, hidden here, away, in the dark vault that once was to have been a shining city of scholarship and lore.

It was a small enough price to pay, though not an easy one.

"Sleep in peace," he said quietly to the Earthchild, then nodded toward the passageway.

As they passed through the tunnel Grunthor had made in the moraine, Achmed looked up one last time at the firmament of the dome that towered into the blackness above the Loritorium and, finding that it appeared sound, glanced back at the altar of Living Stone.

The Earthchild slumbered on, oblivious, it seemed, of the world around her, and of whatever might have threatened it.

The Firbolg king watched her for a moment, then turned and walked back through the tunnel ahead of Grunthor, who closed the hole in the moraine behind them, his black robes whispering around him.

"What do ya think did that, then, caused the Earth to scream that way?" the Bolg Sergeant asked, glancing one last time over his shoulder before turning to follow the king up the corridor.

"I have no idea," Achmed replied, his voice echoing strangely off the irregular walls of the ascending tunnel. "And there's little more we can do, other than prepare, because sooner or later whatever it is will no doubt find me. Let's make our way from one ruined landmark to another." Grunthor nodded and caught up with him, traversing the rest of the corridor to the upworld in companionable silence.

They were on the other side of the moraine, halfway home, and so were unable to see the single muddy tear slip down the Earthchild's face in the darkness of her sepulcher.

Grunthor stepped gingerly over the scattered shards of colored glass and looked up into the thin, towering dome hollowed into the mountain peak Gurgus, the Bolgish word for *talon*. The levels of scaffolding that ringed the interior of the structure were silent now, the artisans gone, leaving only the king and himself.

And an increasingly large pile of broken glass.

"Not going particularly well, Oi take it?" he said humorously, kicking aside the debris. He reached down and picked up a crumpled piece of parchment lying beneath the detritus that bore the markings of an architectural plan.

"Don't open it," Achmed advised sourly. "It's full of spit. I encouraged everyone to take a turn at it after a particularly trying day early last week. You might want to stay away from any other wads, too; as the week wore on, the bodily fluids we applied to the plans reflected our progress, or lack thereof. You can imagine where we ended up."

Grunthor grinned, his neatly polished tusks gleaming in

the half-light, and tossed the wad of parchment back into
the pile.

"Why ya driving yourself mad with this, sir?" he asked,
his tone at once light and serious. "If you really feel the
need to be irritated to the point o' going insane, why don't
we just send for the Duchess? She generally 'as that same
effect on you, and she costs less than rebuilding the dome
of a mountain, at least if you pay by the hour."

Achmed chuckled. "Now, now, let's not reference our
beloved Lady Cymrian's sordid past. We'll be seeing her
soon enough. I heard from her last night by avian messenger; she wants us to meet her four weeks hence in Yarim."

"Oh, goody," the giant replied, staring up into the tower
again. "What now?"

"She wants our assistance—your assistance, actually—in
bringing Entudenin, that dead geyser obelisk, back to life."

Grunthor nodded, arranging the piles of colored glass
with the toe of his boot.

"Oi told 'er a long time ago 'twas probably a blockage
o' some sort in the strata. She got 'em to agree to let us
drill?"

"Apparently."

"And you're willing to drop everything and leave at 'er
request?"

Achmed shrugged, then went back to the pile of colored
rubble.

The giant raised an eyebrow, but said nothing, returning
his attention to the tower.

When Gwylliam founded Canrif he seemed to have a penchant for hollowing out mountain peaks. The Teeth were
full of them, jagged summits that stretched into the clouds,
multicolored, threatening, dark with beauty and secrets.
They must have posed a challenge to the arrogant Cymrian
king, because he spent a good deal of his time reinforcing
them while chipping away at the mountain strata inside
them, filling them with needless rooms and grand domes.

Grunthor, tied to the earth as he was, found the practice repulsive to the point of feeling violated.

When he, Achmed, and Rhapsody had come to Ylorc, they had found and restored a ruined guard-tower post in the western peak of Grivven, attached to a fortress and barracks that housed more than two thousand Bolg soldiers, and a towering observatory above the Great Hall, from which thirty miles of the Krevensfield Plain could be seen in all directions save east.

He, as a military man, understood the need for these renovations. He could even grudgingly abide the rebuilding of the inner mountain cities and the restoration of the art and statuary, things he had little use for. But none of the reconstruction projects had taken on the import, or produced the aggravation, that the Bolg king's current undertaking had, and for the life of him, he had no idea why.

The Sergeant squinted as he looked up into the pinnacle of the broken tower, trying to discern what it was about this Cymrian artifact, this particular hollowed-out mountain peak, that so captivated Achmed's attention. Each time he returned from maneuvers the king's mood was blacker; now it had taken on approximately the same hue as pitch.

There were endless opportunities for renovation in the Bolglands. The place had once been almost a country, a multiracial settlement nestled in the protective arms of the mountains, inside the earth and in the open-air realm beyond the canyon, housing the greatest minds of the times, undisturbed for three hundred years, allowing great advances in every aspect of science and art to germinate and grow, unfettered. Even the seven hundred years of war that followed had not destroyed those engineering feats and architectural marvels completely. Besides, Grunthor reasoned, Achmed had all the time in the world to build them back up again.

All the time in the world.

"What is it about this thing that has ya so bollixed up?" he asked finally, gesturing at the tower. "Oi think it might be a good idea to 'ead off ta Yarim just ta get you away from this place. It's enslaved your mind. Ya look downright awful."

"I'm Dhracian. I always look downright awful."

"More awful than usual, sir."

"You can tell that even behind the veils?"

"Yup. Yer eyes're all yella and red. Thought for a moment ya might 'ave gone F'dor on me while Oi was away."

"Now that would be interesting; a Dhracian F'dor. I wonder what would happen if a demon tried to possess me. My guess is that I would explode or dissolve, so diametrically opposed are the two races, which might be worth it; at least I would take one of them with me. But no, I'm not possessed; we have merely been meeting with failure at each turn here. The domed ceiling is defying me, and I hate being defied by glass." Achmed sighed and crouched down, running his gloved hands through the colored sand and shards. "Omet says we need to find a glass artisan of a much higher level of expertise, a sealed master."

"Well, 'e would know."

"Yes, and he has even acknowledged that the place to find one is Yarim."

Grunthor whistled. " 'E must really be growing desperate."

"Or he knows that I am." The two friends exchanged a smile; Omet's terror of Yarim and his sensitivity even to the mention of the place had made for many entertaining moments over the last three years. It was a source of great amusement among the Bolg to see the calm young man who lived casually among them and was rarely at a loss for a wry comeback become instantly flummoxed at any reference to the province, going white and trembling violently. The guildmistress he had served there, whose name he had only mentioned once, must have been formidable; Omet had whispered to him, back when he was still a bald teenager they had rescued from the ceramics works, that evil in a purer form did not exist.

But of course, Omet had seen nothing of the world. Achmed knew that no matter how terrifying the guildmistress was, evil had a whole array of purer forms it could assume.

He had met a number of them personally.

"So Oi suppose that means we're going," Grunthor said.

"Yes, unless you can't spare the time away."

"Naw," the giant said, stepping over the debris and going to stand directly under the tower. "Hagraith and the others can 'andle it while Oi'm gone for a bit. An' it'll be wonderful ta see the Duchess again; been too long."

"Indeed," Achmed agreed.

"Is that really why you're going, sir?" Grunthor said, avoiding the king's gaze. "It's been fair on to impossible to break you away from this secret glass-tower project."

Achmed exhaled shallowly, then went to the draftsman's table and drew forth a sheaf of vellum pages, weathered with age, from a box beneath it.

"These are the plans I could find for this place," he said, his voice soft, as if speaking more to himself than to the Sergeant. "They are incomplete, unintelligible in places, written in code or ancient languages in others. I can follow the basic diagram, but there is so much missing that I can't find in Gwylliam's library or the vault underneath it. I know that the dome is supposed to be formed from colored glass— it says thus in Gwylliam's notes, and there were seven glass test blocks buried in the vault, one of each color, to use as a gauge—but which colors are arrayed where is not clearly spelled out. There is one manuscript—this one"—he separated out a ragged page—"that seems to make reference to the tower, but I can't decode it. Perhaps Rhapsody can. Besides reading Serenne, as a Namer she is knowledgeable about the science of the vibrational scale. Some of the notations in the manuscript look like musical script of a sort."

"Ah," Grunthor nodded. "Oi knew there 'ad to be a connection between this and Yarim for you to be willin' ta go, even more than the chance to see 'Er Ladyship again." He sighed as Achmed held the ratty diagrams close to his eyes. "Perhaps could you finally break down and tell me what is so all-fired important about rebuildin' this tower, sir?"

Achmed blinked. "What?"

"You're obsessed, if ya forgive me for sayin' so. An' Oi can't fathom why." The Sergeant crossed his arms. "Ain't never seen ya like this except when you're huntin'. The troops are fully trained, the borders secure; the Alliance seems ta be goin' well, from what an 'umble soldier like me can tell. We got plenty o' battlements, outposts, lookouts. So why does this one 'ave you in its grip?"

The Bolg king's olive complexion darkened as he contemplated the question. Grunthor waited patiently until he was able to sort out his thoughts enough to give voice to them.

"When Gwylliam and Anwyn battled during the Cymrian War, it took her five hundred years to make it from the western coast to the Teeth," he said finally. "Their sons had been divided against their wills, pressed into service by each parent, so as a result, Anwyn couldn't even approach the Teeth to assault them for most of the war. Anborn held back his mother's armies for his father with tremendous success. All across the continent there was zero-sum warfare; Llauron would take a town or a province for Anwyn, Anborn would take it back for Gwylliam. As long as the brothers were the generals, it was hardly a real conflict; you can tell they were not prosecuting the war too enthusiastically by the length of time over which nothing of any note was accomplished. That is not surprising, given that neither of them really wanted to be participating in it the first place."

Grunthor nodded, having studied the battle records.

"But when Anwyn finally did return to the Teeth, what was her first objective?"

The giant exhaled. "Gurgus," he said.

"Right. This peak, this tower was the first thing she attacked—*why?*" The Firbolg king began to pace, leaving little or no trail through the colored dust on the floor. "She didn't bother to secure her perimeter, to advance her borders. She ignored Grivven and Xaith and the westernmost outposts, left her army well behind the line of engagement, and instead sent a stealth brigade, three cohorts of her best troops, into the depths of the Teeth, knowing none of them would ever return, *specifically* to destroy this tower. But why? It had no weapons, no battlements, nothing but a ceiling of rainbow-colored stained glass and some sort of metal support piping and a wheel. What could possibly have been so important about this tower that Anwyn would compromise her position, sacrifice her best-trained soldiers, to destroy it before engaging Gwylliam?"

"Dunno," Grunthor said, shaking his head. " 'Twas a long time past, that war; damned thing ended four 'undred years ago. You met 'er at the Cymrian Council; she was off 'er flippin' track. Maybe she was just crazy then, too. 'Avin' seen 'er in action, Oi'd say there was probably a *stupid* reason, like she 'ated the colors of the roof windows or ol' Gwylliam 'ad once said 'e liked it. These people were fools. Now they're both dead, an' we're all better off for it."

He stood straighter, casting an enormous dark shadow across the room. "But you, sir, you're no fool, and neither am Oi. So why don't you tell me the real reason you're bent on rebuilding something, when ya don't even know what it is?"

Achmed's mismatched eyes studied his longtime friend for a moment, then looked away.

"I've seen an instrumentality like it before," he said. His voice was distant, a world away. "Same cylindrical tower; same piping. Same colored glass ceiling. Same wheel."

Grunthor waited in silence until it became too heavy to bear. "Where?" he said finally.

"In the old world. Someone in Serendair had one."

" 'Oo?"

The Bolg king let his breath out slowly, as if trying to hang on to the word for as long as possible.

"Glyngaris," he said at last.

It was a name that he had only uttered once before in Grunthor's hearing, and never in the new world.

The Sergeant stood still for a long moment, then shook his head, as if shaking off sleep, and nodded.

"If that's all, sir, Oi'm going to go and see about settin' up to leave in a few weeks."

Achmed said nothing, standing still as death, as the Sergeant left the room.

# Cloud Chaser, Cloud Caller

Brige-sol

# 5

𝕿he rush of wind and sun that blew the tower window open awakened Ashe, filling his eyes and causing him to turn for a moment away from the warmth beside him, shielding his forehead from the brightness of morning invading his chambers and his sleep. He muttered vulgar, muted curses that he didn't particularly mean in a variety of tongues, some common, some obscure, then rolled back over and stared down at Rhapsody, sleeping deeply, undisturbed in the filtered light.

His good mood returned upon beholding her again. The lacy curtains at the window, fluttering on the wind of dawn, cast moving patterns on her delicate face, striping her cheekbones and brow with fleeting shadows that darted a moment later over her hair, which spread in silken waves over the pillow and white bedlinens like a golden sea.

Within his dichotomous soul, he could feel the swell of divided emotion, the love the man felt for her vying for dominance with the satisfaction in her safe return that was appreciated by the dragon side of him. It was an interesting disparity; his draconic, covetous nature counted her as treasure, struggling with jealousy and bereft despair when she was gone from his sphere of awareness, juxtaposed with the simple, uncomplicated adoration his human side accorded her as the other half of his soul.

Either way, he was wholly glad she was finally home.

He reined in his breathing and moved away slightly so as not to awaken her, settling back against the pillows to study her face while she slept.

With her eyes closed in unconsciousness, she appeared younger, slighter than she did when awake, almost childlike. The heat of the element of pure fire that she had absorbed long ago during her trek through the Earth from her island homeland to this place on the other side of the world burned latent in her cheeks, much dimmer than it did in her eyes, where it could be seen most clearly when she was awake. That elemental magic living within her had a powerful effect on the people who beheld her; it caused some to stare at her as if hypnotized, others to cower in fear as they would in the presence of a roaring inferno. It was an aspect that was misperceived by the masses as an intimidating beauty, because they were unfamiliar with the power behind it.

He, unlike them, was not bespelled by that beauty, but recognized it for what it was, because his dragon nature could sense the power within her, could almost see it. Indeed, because he was tied as powerfully to the element of water as she was to that of fire, he understood on the deepest possible level the gift and curse of such an elemental bond. As a result there was a perfect balance between them, an opposition and a commonality that had made him fall inescapably into enchantment with her even before he had ever seen her; just being within a few miles of her had been enough for the dragon to sense her magic and succumb inexorably to it.

The man, on the other hand, living himself with immense natural powers but imperfect in his humanity, could see beyond that magic, that beauty, to the imperfect woman beneath it. What his human heart felt for her was the love any man had for the woman who completed him, whom he in turn completed, flaws and strengths endured and appreciated, arguments and petty annoyances fought over and forgiven in the course of weaving the tapestry that was a shared life. Being of the lineage from which he came, with its vast powers and terrible history, it was this ordinary love, this common, perfectly imperfect union that he treasured above all else, the sense of normalcy and reality she brought to him.

And she was home.

From the moment he had laid her carefully on their marital bed the night before, as she extinguished the bedside lamp with a simple gesture toward it, there had been no words between them; no words were ever necessary. The fireshadows on the hearth across the room had leapt and danced in time with their lovemaking, the flames roaring with abandon, diminishing down to glowing coals as their passion was sated, dissolving into the contented sleep of lovers blissfully reunited.

And now she slept still, pale, undisturbed by the morning wind rippling through her hair, as he watched her, content with his world.

Finally, when the sun had risen fully above the rim of the horizon and the window ledge, flooding the bedchamber with light, she stirred, then opened her deep green eyes and smiled at him.

"You're awake?"

"Yes."

"You're awake."

"Apparently."

"You're never awake before me."

"Now, that's an insulting overgeneralization."

Rhapsody rolled over and stretched, then slid her small, callused hand into his. "Very well, I don't believe I've ever seen you awake before me until this morning. You are usually deep in the sleep of a hibernating dragon and almost impossible to rouse with anything short of the overpowering stench of that nasty coffee you like so much."

Ashe drew her into his arms and rested his nose against hers. "I dispute that utterly. It is remarkable how easily I am roused when you are here, m'lady. If you are complaining, I insist on the opportunity to prove my point."

"You'll get no complaint from me," Rhapsody said. "On the contrary, I am impressed at your prowess, as always, even more so after last night. You must have been practicing in my absence. I hope you were alone." She laughed as Ashe's face colored, then kissed him warmly.

"Well, I am happy to hear that you were not disappointed

after traveling all that way to come home." He pulled her against his chest and lay back on the pillows with a contented sigh, reveling in the contrast of the warmth beneath the down coverlet and the cool sting of the wind above it. "Did you manage to attend to all your affairs of state in Tyrian?"

"Yes."

"Good; glad to hear it, because I don't intend to let them have you back any time in the foreseeable future. And as you know, dragons can foresee quite a way into said future, so I hope Rial obtained your signature on whatever he needed for the next several years."

Rhapsody chuckled, then sat up and regarded Ashe with a thoughtful expression. "I did indeed make certain that all of Tyrian's business requiring my attention received it duly, because I now hope to undertake a project that would have me here in Navarne for an extended period of time. After the excursion to Yarim to rejuvenate Entudenin, that is."

Ashe sat up as well. "Oh, really? I'm intrigued. What project might that be?"

"The care and education of a child."

"You adopted another honorary grandchild? How many does this make now? Are you over one hundred yet?"

Rhapsody shook her head, her green eyes kindling to a darker emerald shade. "No, only thirty-seven. And that is not what I meant."

"Oh?" Ashe felt a slight chill hum through his skin at the tone in her voice. "What did you mean, then, Aria?"

The coals on the fireplace, a moment before nothing but cooling gray ash, gleamed red again, matching the blush in her cheeks.

"I think it's time we had one of our own," she said, her voice steady, though Ashe could feel a slight tremor in her hand.

He stared at her, trying to force the words that she had spoken to pass from his ears into his mind, until he saw her wince in pain; quickly he released her fingers, which he had unconsciously clutched to the point of unwelcome tension.

Slowly he sat up more fully, swung his legs over the edge of the bed, and leaned forward, bringing his chin to rest on his folded hands. He could tell by the change in her heart rate, her shallow, rapid intake of breath, and a dozen other physiological signs his dragon sense was aware of that his reaction was distressing her, but he was too upset by her words to do anything to relieve her anxiety. Instead he concentrated inward, trying to beat back the jumble of words from the past that were echoing in his mind.

In a sudden swirl of muscle and bedsheets Ashe rose and went to the wardrobe, trying not to see the look of astonishment and hurt on his wife's face. He pulled on a shirt and trousers, then turned finally, not meeting her eyes.

"I must return to my meetings with the councilors," he said flatly. "I am sorry to have wakened you; I should have let you rest longer after your long journey."

"Ashe—"

He strode rapidly across the room and took hold of the door handle. "Go back to sleep, Aria," he said gently. "I will have them bring you a tray in an hour or so."

"You told them you would not be meeting today."

"That was inconsiderate of me. They have been held captive here for weeks; they doubtless want to finish and return to their provinces."

Rhapsody tossed back the coverlet and rose from the bed, pulling on her dressing gown.

"Don't be a coward," she said evenly but without rancor. "Tell me what has you so frightened."

The vertical pupils of Ashe's eyes expanded, as if drawing in the light and her words. He met her gaze for a moment, then opened the bedchamber door.

"Rest," he said simply.

He closed the door quickly and silently behind him.

She found him later that afternoon at the top of one of the carillon towers that flanked the main gate of Haguefort.

Rhapsody knew her husband was aware of her presence, would have felt her coming from a great distance away, so she assumed he was willing to be found. She waited in the doorway at the top of the tower stairs, following his gaze over the rolling hills of Navarne, where the sun was painting the highgrass in swaths of yellow light and deep, cool green. Finally, when she saw his shoulders rise and fall as he exhaled deeply, she spoke, breaking the silence that heretofore had been interrupted only by the occasional whistling breeze.

"Is it Manwyn's ranting? Is that why you are afraid?"

Ashe said nothing, but continued to stare over the foothills toward the Krevensfield Plain. Rhapsody stepped through the doorway and stood beside him, resting her hands on the smooth stone crenellations of the parapet, newly rebuilt after being destroyed in rank fire and burning pitch three years before. She waited in silence, breathing in the sweet summer air, following his gaze over the hills.

Finally, when he spoke, his eyes were still fixed on the seemingly endless sea of green meadow beyond the walls of the keep.

"Stephen and I used to roam these fields endlessly in childhood," he said quietly. "Sometimes it is as if I can see him there still, chasing imaginary warriors, flying kites, lying on his back staring at the clouds and reading the future in them." He shook his head, as if shaking off a chill, then turned and regarded her seriously. "Did you know his mother, like mine, died when he was young?"

"No."

Ashe nodded, then looked back over the Plain. "Consumption. It withered her away from the inside. His father was never the same afterward—took his spirit with her when she left. Stephen barely remembered her. Just like Melisande doesn't remember Lydia."

Rhapsody sighed. "I am not going to die, Sam," she said, using the name she had once given him long before, in their own youth when they had met on the other side of Time. "Manwyn told you that as well. She said so directly, in fact—*'Gwydion ap Llauron, thy mother died in giving birth to thee, but thy children's mother shall not die giving birth to them.'*"

Ashe shook his head slightly in the vain attempt to silence the words in his mind, recounted in excruciating detail by the dragon in his blood. It had been more than three years since he stood in the dark temple of the Oracle of Yarim, Manwyn, the mad Seer of the Future, who by a curse of birth was also his great-aunt, and shuddered at the odd inflection in her voice as she pronounced a prediction she had not been asked for.

*I see an unnatural child born of an unnatural act. Rhapsody, you should beware of childbirth: the mother shall die, but the child shall live.*

Rhapsody's hand came to rest gently on his bare shoulder but he shrugged it off, trying to break the grip of other words in his mind, spoken in his father's voice.

*I assume you are aware of what happened to your own mother upon giving birth to the child of a partial dragon? I have spared you the details up until now—shall I give them to you? Do you crave to know what it is like to watch a woman, not to mention one that you happen to love, die in agony trying to bring forth your child, hmmm? Let me describe it for you. Since the dragonling instinctually needs to break the eggshell, clawing through, to emerge, the infant—*

*Stop.*

*Your child will be even more of a dragon than you were, so the chances of the mother's survival are not good. If your own mother could not give birth to you and live, what will happen, do you think, to your mate?*

Without looking at his wife he shook his head again, concentrating on the waving green sea of highgrass below him.

"I have seen too much death to risk it, Aria; I have known too many divinations that have been misheard, misunderstood. With the very last words of advice my father gave me he warned me that I should not trust prophecies, that their meaning is not always as it seems."

"If you are discounting prophecies, then why does the first one worry you at all?" Rhapsody said, taking his hand. "It seems to me that you are giving credence to those that would prevent us from living our lives as we see fit, in order to avoid peril, but shun those that nullify those dire warnings. Either accept both, or neither, but do not choose to fear one and refuse comfort in the other."

Ashe's skin darkened in the light of the afternoon sun. "There are so many children in your life, Rhapsody, in *our* lives. Anywhere you go, from this very keep you live in to the mountains of Ylorc, from the Lirin forest to the Hintervold, you have 'grandchildren' to love and look after. I don't think it is wise to tempt Fate by risking your life giving birth to the child of wyrmkin, an infant with dragon's blood in its veins. There are enough motherless children to tend to without bringing another into the world." His voice carried a bitter sting.

Rhapsody took him by the arms and turned him around, slipping into his embrace.

"I refuse to make my choices based on the maniacal rantings of your aunt," she said humorously, "which is why I never use the hideous brocade table linens she sent us as a wedding gift." Her tone grew more serious, and she caressed his cheek tenderly. "I want to make the life with you that we planned, Sam; I want to mix my blood with yours, to carry your children within me, to raise a family of your line and mine that is entirely our own. I thought this is what you wanted as well."

Ashe did not break his gaze away from the windy plain. *More than you can know,* he thought.

"If there is good reason not to have children, I will yield the idea in a heartbeat, but in the face of two conflicting prophecies, I see no need to live in terror of something that she has told you will *not* happen. Besides, the prophecy you fear has already been fulfilled; it was not directed at me, but at the mother of the last child fathered by the F'dor we destroyed." Her eyes darkened at the memory. "I witnessed the birth, and the death. The mother died. The child lived. It's over. The prophecy was fulfilled."

"You don't know that for certain, Rhapsody."

She threw up her hands in exasperation and turned away from him. "What do we ever know for certain, Ashe? Moment to moment, life is unsure—you can't live in fear of it." Another thought occurred and she turned back. "Manwyn cannot lie, can she?"

"Not directly, but she can obfuscate and evade, and she knows the distant future as well as the immediate, so she can give an answer to a question that qualifies as truthful, but may not be pertinent for a thousand years. She is not to be trusted."

"But if she answers directly, yes or no, that cannot be false, can it?"

Ashe shook his head. "Supposedly not."

"Well, then, since I am headed to Yarim in the next few days, and Manwyn's temple is in Yarim, I will have ample opportunity to ask her directly, yes or no, if giving birth to your children will cause my death or permanent infirmity. Perhaps she can lay this ambiguity to rest then and there."

Ashe's face went pale, then red. "A moment ago I was grateful beyond measure that you had returned home," he said stonily. "Now I wish you had remained in Tyrian, where at least you would be safe from your own foolhardiness. Rhapsody, didn't you learn the last time we addressed Manwyn in her temple that it was an experience not to be repeated?"

"Apparently not," she snapped, pulling away and turning back to the tower doorway. "Apparently I've also been wrong in assuming you shared my desire to have a child; if you did, you would not be deterred by so flimsy an excuse."

She started down the stairs, only to be caught by the arm and turned around.

Ashe stared down at her for a long moment. Rhapsody's anger, white-hot a split second before, cooled at the sight of the pain in his dragonesque eyes, the depth of the agony she knew he had suffered, and the love that ran even deeper. Inwardly she cursed herself for the pain she was causing him now, the fear her selfishness had rekindled. She opened her mouth to recant but was stopped when he rested his forefinger on her lips.

"We will go together," he said, cupping her face gently. "We will put the question before her, and I will try and live with her answer. It's the only way to reclaim control of our lives."

"Are you certain you want to do that?" she said, arching an eyebrow. "If memory serves, *you* were the one she attacked last time we were there. She didn't give me any difficulty."

"Well, she and I are family, after all," Ashe replied, a hint of humor returning to his eyes. "If you can't fight with family, with whom can you fight? Look at my grandparents. Their marital spat led to a war that took down an entire empire."

"Hmmm. Perhaps we should reconsider adding to our family after all," Rhapsody said. She looked off across the whipping highgrass and smiled as a brightly colored kite in the shape of a copper dragon caught the wind, streaking suddenly higher on a strong updraft. She waved to the tiny figure in the distance, and Melisande waved back.

Ashe exhaled. "No, you're right," he said at last. "If it is at all possible, I would dearly love to see the children of the House of Navarne and those of the lines of Gwyllium and Manosse playing in these fields once more."

"Well, in a sense that decision is entirely up to you." Rhapsody spoke the words gently, knowing that to do so heavily would sting; as a descendant of a Firstborn race, Ashe had to make a conscious decision to procreate. "But once you decide in favor of it, whenever that may be, I promise to make that decision worth your while."

Ashe laughed and kissed her hand, then went back to watching Stephen's daughter draw pictures in the sky with her dragon kite, lost in memory.

## TEMPLE OF THE ORACLE, YARIM PAAR

𝒯he darkness of the inner sanctum of Manwyn's temple was broken intermittently by fires burning in decaying receptacles and the tiny flames of countless candles, thick with the stench of burning fat barely masked by pungent incense.

Mother Julia stared across the jagged well in the floor to the dais suspended above it, trying to hold the Seer's gaze and failing; the eyes of the mad prophetess were perfect mirrors of quicksilver, devoid of any iris, pupil or sclera. They reflected the myriad flames, making Mother Julia's head spin crazily.

"How—how long will I live?" she whispered, dotting her gray forehead with the colorful fringe of her shawl.

The Seer laughed, a maniacal, piercing sound, then rolled suddenly onto her back, pointing the ancient sextant in her hand at the black dome of the temple above. She began to swing the dais wildly over the jagged pit beneath her, singing in mad, toneless words.

Finally she righted herself and leaned over the edge of the platform, fixing her reflective gaze on the trembling crone.

"Until your heart stops beating," she proclaimed smugly. She waved a dismissive hand at Mother Julia, her rosy golden skin, scored with tiny lines of scales, gleaming in the half-light.

"Wait," the old woman protested as the doors to the inner sanctum opened. "That is no answer! I made a generous offering, and you have told me nothing!"

A blank look of confusion crossed the Seer's face. Mother Julia turned away from the guards gesturing at her, realizing that she had phrased her objection incorrectly; Manwyn could not comprehend the Past, only the Future and enough of the Present to allow her a stepping-stone in Time. With a trembling hand she reached into the folds of her garments and extracted her last gold crown. She held it up; the light caught the surface and reflected in the prophetess's eyes.

"You are not telling me anything. You will cheat me for Eternity if you do not provide me more of an answer. I will be forever a bad debt of yours."

Manwyn cocked her head to one side, her tangled mane of flame-colored hair billowing in the updraft from the dark well; its metallic silver streaks caught the reflection of the candlelight for a moment and flashed, causing Mother Julia to wince in pain. Her lips pursed as she considered, then nodded briskly like a child.

"Very well. One more question. Consider carefully; I shall answer no more for you in this lifetime."

The old woman shuddered, racking her brain to combine her questions into one which would suffice while the ancient Seer spun the wheel on the sextant beneath her fingers, humming tunelessly. Finally Mother Julia took a deep, ragged breath and squared her shoulders.

"Who shall tell me what the disk of blue-black steel is?" she stammered.

The prophetess looked into the sextant, then up at the crone again. When she spoke, her voice was plain and clear of madness or singsong.

"Your son Thait will tell you what you have been commanded to discover," she said simply. "Five weeks and two days hence this night."

From the depths of her belly the old woman sighed, relief glistening in her eyes and on her brow. She bowed to Manwyn, tossed the coin into the well, muttered her thanks, and hurried out through the heavily carved cedar door past the guards, eager to quit the temple as quickly as possible.

As the cedar door closed behind the woman, Manwyn looked up as if startled. She nodded to herself, then called softly into the darkness in the distance.

"He will whisper it to you through his tears as he sits beside your grave, arranging the stones."

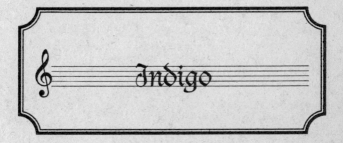

# Indigo

## Night Stayer, Night Summoner

### Luasa-ela

# 6

## PORT OF ARGAUT, NORTHLAND

The scent of fire in the wind was always an exciting thing, the seneschal thought, inhaling deeply. Pungent ash mixed with the tang of salt sea air was like a perfume to him, especially in the aftermath of morning, when the white smoke of the infernos gave way to the stolid gray miasma that hung like dirty wool in the wind above the smoldering coals, the dingy causatum of so much glorious flame the night before. It was an odor he had loved all his life, but in the last thousand years or so it had taken on a special appeal, particularly when laced with the olfactory undertones of human flesh, which added a pleasant causticity to it.

The previous night he had stood in the darkness of the reviewing stands, watching the burning pyres be lighted like signal flames along a giant battle wall. It had been an unprecedented inferno; the chorus of wailing, rising and falling on the summer wind, had been especially melodic, a symphony of pain that enflamed his soul with excitement.

The thrill had still not worn off, even in the bitter light of dawn observed now from the rolling deck of the *Basquela* on which he stood. The bonfires had burned down to seething ash, cooling, waiting for the farmers of the Inner Crescent to come and haul the detritus away, sowing it into their fields to enrich them.

The seneschal ruminated on that for a moment, the beneficial balance he had achieved since coming to power. The shipping lanes had never been so profitable; Argaut's fleet was one of the most commanding and respected in maritime trade throughout the civilized world, plying the seas in extended cycles, braving some of the most dangerous coastlines in the process—the rocky archipelago of the Fiery Rim; the shark-infested waters of Iridu and the Great

Overward, where the predatory fish could reach a hundred feet in length; the burning swells that still foamed over the watery grave of the sunken Island of Serendair in the south seas, its former mountaintops of Briala, Balatron, and Querel now making for treacherous pocketed reefs of boiling volcanic blasts.

The real danger in those places was not the natural phenomena that existed there, but the pirates who used them as hunting grounds. Privateers from deadly, centuries-old familial lines, their ships, swift and silent, plied the shoals and crosscurrents as if immune to the perils of the sea, mastering the wind with merciless efficiency. The remains of the vessels they plundered were never found, the able-bodied among the crew and passengers sold as slaves in a variety of ports around the world, most especially in the diamond fields of lower Heraat in the Great Overward, and the gladiatorial arenas of Sorbold. The old, the sick, and the weak were used as chum for the sharks.

The Brigands of the Sea Wind, as the pirates like to call themselves, were the scourge of the shipping lanes, the terror of the seas, and made the passage of travelers and the plying of trade hazardous at best. Even the nations that supplied military forces to escort their merchant vessels watched in hope that turned frequently to dismay for their return. Owning a strong, reliable fleet of swift ships that could run the privateers' blockades, outsail them, and escape with their crew and contents intact was one of the greatest assets any merchant guild or nation could have. Argaut's merchant fleet and navy were without peer in the world.

Because the Baron of Argaut, who owned the fleet, also owned the pirates.

It made for a perfect cycle, a very profitable way to suppress competition. The seneschal was extremely proud of the beautiful simplicity and interconnectivity of it all. The Brigands occasionally attacked ships in the waters near Northland, but by and large stayed far enough away from port to avoid suspicion. The slave trade fostered friendship in places like Druverille, the frozen wasteland to the north of Manosse, and Sorbold, a key nation in the western continent on the southern border of the Wyrmlands. The northern continental coastline of the Wyrmlands had been held in protection for thousands of years by the dragon Elynsynos, who allowed no ship to broach the misty shores. The slave traders of Sorbold were Argaut's favorite trading partners, paying a high premium for captives who could serve in their famed gladiatorial arenas.

And so the cycle had continued, year after year, century after century. The shipping lanes filled Argaut's coffers with the bounty of respectable trade by the merchant fleet and the booty of privateering by the Brigands. The slave trade provided an easy dumping ground for any victims of piracy who would have survived to tell the tale; the less valuable captives were accused, along with the occasional local upstart, of being the pirates themselves and were burned in great bonfires that lighted the night sky, sating the righteous indignation of the population while convincing them of the efficiency of their government. The remains of the unfortunates were sown into the fields to produce a bountiful harvest, or rendered as fat for tallow candles, both of which in turn provided more products for the shipping trade.

And, above all else, they satisfied the bloodlust of the seneschal and the baron, both of whom craved the thrill of the fire.

*Indeed; I have no wish to abandon this.*

The seneschal whirled, caught off guard by the baron's voice.

"M'lord—"

*Disembark. We are not leaving.*

The pleasant musings vanished, leaving the sensation of acid burning in the seneschal's eyes.

"Forgive me, m'lord, but we are." Involuntarily he winced at the stabbing pain in his head.

The voice, when it whispered again, was low and soft; the seneschal could barely make out the words over the waves of nauseating thrum in his head and the crying of the gulls.

*In sixteen centuries you have only dared defy me once; remember what you wrought.*

"Twice," the seneschal corrected. He clutched his brow in agony, shaking his head like a boar shaking off the hunting dogs beset upon its neck. He glanced woozily in the direction of the dark hold where Faron waited, frightened, in his transplanted pool of gleaming green water. He had been secreted aboard in the middle of the night, carried in soft blankets, while the fires were burning down and the sea winds tugged at the moorings. The terror in the child's eyes haunted at him again, and feelings of protective rage rose inside his breast. "And what I wrought is a lifeline for you; remember that."

The threat in the reply was unmistakable.

*You remember it as well.*

"Yer Honor? Sea-shakes got hold o' ya already? We haven't even cast off yet."

The seneschal struck violently at the air behind him, knocking the man flat with a gesture.

"Leave me in peace."

The sailor, long accustomed to the strong arm of command, rose quickly from the deck and slipped away. When the sailor had gone, the seneschal focused his attention again on the voice in his mind, the demon that shared his soul.

"I will not be questioned by you in this," he said in a low voice, fighting the grip behind his eyes.

*You are taking us away from our place of power, where our dominion rests, unchallenged. Why?*

The seneschal stood a little straighter.

"A debt is owed me, a debt I had written off a lifetime ago and a world away."

*So if you decried this debt a lifetime ago, why pursue it now?*

The seneschal ran his fingers angrily through his hair, as if seeking to gouge the nagging voice from his scalp.

"Primarily," he spat, "because I *choose* to. And I do not wish to answer to you about it."

The dark fire of F'dor spirit that clung to his essence burned blacker within him, making him nauseous.

*I can see we have a misunderstanding of roles here.*

"Yes," the seneschal agreed, "though I am certain we have differing opinions on who is transgressing on the terms under which we have agreed to associate with one another."

The voice of the demon was silent for a moment, leaving only the sound of the wind and the sea, the cry of the gulls, and the distant noise of the port growing busy as morning came. When it spoke there was a crackling sound in its tone, like a fire, the flames calm but seething underneath in the coals.

*I have allowed you far more autonomy, far more independence, than most with our arrangement would have.*

The seneschal exhaled sharply.

"Perhaps that is because I took you on voluntarily, if you recall," he said. "You have benefited greatly from my strength, from retaining my independence. If you wanted a passive host whose life essence you could suck out, use as a parasitic moss uses a tree, surely there were thousands of sickly, pathetic rabble after the Seren War ended that you could have taken on; a flower-seller, perhaps; a fishwife, an infant? You chose me because I offered you a host healthy of body and mind, a soldier, a leader of men, with power of my own that you could share, but it was never part of the bargain that you would possess that power outright. If you had wanted a servile lackey, you should have chosen a host within your ability to subdue, with strength less than your own, one you could conquer, could make your own unwillingly, could hollow out and feed off of until you moved on to someone better. You would never have been able to take me on then, never would have conquered me against my will." He paused, feeling the ebb and flow of the demon's spirit coursing through his veins. "You cannot do it now."

The sea wind gusted again, snapping the mains'l violently, then settling into a calm breeze again. The seneschal felt the heat within him dim as the demon considered his words.

*You have not done poorly in this bargain yourself,* the voice said when finally it spoke again. *You wanted life unending. You have had it.*

"Yes," the seneschal acknowledged, "yes, I have. And so have you. I might point out that when I came to you your host was dying, alone, unable to drag the sorry remains of his crumbling body out of the water that was filling the dungeon in which you were held captive. I saved your sorry life, have brought untold glory to you, the power of elemental wind to mix with your fire—"

*In return for immortality.*

"Yes. A fair trade. And all in all, it has been a beneficial, in fact, inspired pairing." The seneschal clutched the railing, prepared for another onslaught of demonic rage. "Except on those occasions when you forget that I have the final decision as to where we go, what we undertake. You, sadly, have no choice but to come along. Unless you wish to leave now."

The demon chuckled; it was a harsh, rasping sound that scratched against the seneschal's ears. *You always were foolhardy. Think which of us will have the worse of the bargain if I should decide to do that.*

"My wager is on you," the seneschal said as the sun crested the horizon, splashing the ocean with golden light. "After sixteen centuries of unquestioned dominion, feeding your hunger for fire and ruin, I think it would be amusing to see how you fare as a cabin boy or a whore strolling the docks. Look around you; is there anyone in particular that you crave to move on to? Perhaps there is a tavern wench you might like to have as your host? Then perhaps you too can know the feeling of being fornicated over and over again, as I do when you try to assert yourself."

The voice of the demon cackled.

*It might be interesting to take you up on that. Were we to part company in the next beat of your heart, I would not die; I would be weaker, 'tis true, but when one is immortal, a setback in merely a delay, not an ending. It would almost be worth the loss of stature and power to take up residence in another, any other, just to watch your body shrivel to dust and blow away in the wind before my eyes.* The fire returned, soaking into the internal edges of the seneschal's consciousness. *You do know that is what would happen, do you not? Without my essence you would not only be a dead man, but one who owes Time a dear debt he has no means to repay.*

"Go then," the seneschal snarled. "Cast yourself out. Better still, allow me to do it for you."

*Your rashness will be your undoing, if not now, then later,* the demon said solemnly.

Again the voice fell silent, and the seneschal gripped the deck railing. The demon was the embodiment of chaos, of destructive impetuosity. He prepared himself for battle, or being tossed into the sea, or into oblivion.

*You are in pursuit of a woman, once again.*

The seneschal clenched his teeth, seeking to bar the F'dor spirit from the inner reaches of his mind, but it was like trying to hold back the sea; the hot fingers in his brain probed mercilessly, unyieldingly, violating what little space was left to him. He could feel it searching the hidden realms within his head, finally coming upon the thoughts he had sheltered from it, grasping them, digging them out like a root from the dirt.

*Have you learned nothing?* the demon chided angrily. *Do you not recall what happened the last time you let your lust get the better of us?*

"Yes," the seneschal said bitterly. "I recall it well, and would change nothing about it, given the chance. It gave both you and me a night of unmitigated joy in the glorious suffering of an Ancient Seren, and the boon of a bloodline in the child that was born of that night."

*A useless freak. A monster.*

"Nonesuch!" The seneschal's voice, low and guttural to avoid calling attention to himself, ground against his throat as if against shards of glass. "Faron is a beautiful creation, unique, with powers only beginning to be realized. And should either of us ever be in need of a vessel in which to seek refuge, Faron is perfect."

*Thank you, no. I have higher expectations of a host than that. I have no desire to share my life's essence with what is essentially a human* fish, *blind in daylight, boneless, timid—*

Violently the seneschal raked his nails down the sides of his head, gashing stripes of blood across his cheeks.

"Enough of this! If you wish to move to another host, do so now, or submit to my will! I will brook no more of this nonsense!" In his rage the seneschal closed his eyes, concentrating on the spiritual tethers that bound the demon to him, hooks in the core of his essence that he had untied the night before, to allow their combined spirits to inhabit Faron. All thought of self-preservation vanished; he quickly found one metaphysical tie and in his mind seized upon it, preparing to cast off from the demon as the ship soon would from the dock.

*Stop.* The scathing voice quavered.

Silence returned to his mind. The clouds that had blanketed the sun as it rose thinned and broke open, causing the morning light to shimmer in dusty streams across the water. The seneschal held his breath, waiting for the demon's reply, longing for the cool darkness belowdecks where Faron waited. He wondered whether the monster he had carried voluntarily, its metaphysical talons embedded in his soul, would make good on its threats. There was nothing he could do but wait.

Finally, when the voice spoke again, it was subdued.

*Tell me of this woman, and why this is so important to you.*

The seneschal inhaled, allowing the salty air to fill his

lungs to their depths. He allowed his mind to wander back over ancient fields of summer grass, the Wide Meadows of the Island of Serendair, now nothing more than seagrass in the sand beneath the boiling waves of the sea. He concentrated on the memories he had made there.

"Her name is Rhapsody," he whispered, struggling to keep the word light on the air, reverent, like a psalm, a holy laud, though he knew it was far past impossible for his profane mouth to ever utter such a prayer. "I knew her in Serendair, before the cataclysm. She is beautiful; eyes green as the emerald forest, hair of gold like ripened sheaves of wheat. But that is not why."

*Then why?*

The seneschal tried to form thoughts, words around the memory. "She is spirited, alive; passionate." The thought of the disdain he had routinely seen in her eyes many centuries before rose up like bile in his throat, stung his pride all over again now as it had then. "Stubborn, surly, defiant, argumentative. Foolish." *And she loved me,* he thought, allowing himself a fraction of a second to bask in the rumination, then driving it from his mind before the demon could seize upon it.

The knowledge that she had sworn her fealty to him had salved many a difficult moment, had kept him warm through a thousand dark nights in the time before the demon, when he was a mortal man in the vanguard of a coming war. He could still summon up the memory of the oath she swore to him before he had left her for the last time, a memory he had consigned to the dark vault of loss long before, too painful to think about without going mad.

*I swear by the Star that my heart will love no other man until this world comes to an end.*

The fact that he had forced her into the pledge, had made her promise it, knowing that she was unable to lie, as he held the life of a young girl in his hands before her eyes, had dissipated in his recollection long ago. She had given her word, and Lirin had rules about such things inbred in their blood.

If she had said she loved him, it must have been the truth.

The loss he felt when the word had come to him as he was embroiled in the early battles of the Seren War that she had vanished, when he was within a hairsbreadth of reclaiming her, had almost killed him. She had been stolen by the Brother, the Dhracian assassin known as the most proficient killer the Island had ever seen, even more proficient than he himself had been. There was no trace of her to be found, and so he had assumed that the Brother had killed her and tossed her body into the sea, as the Dhracian's disinterest in temptations of the flesh was renowned. He had wept, for the first time in his memory, tears that rained like acid and had driven him into even greater fits of destruction, sacking villages and torching the Wide Meadows in the vain hope that the wildfires he ignited would help purge his soul of the despair he felt at her loss.

And now he had come to find that she was alive, had survived the destruction of the Island just as he had, had undoubtedly sailed away before the cataclysm with the other Cymrian refugees who had made their way across the world to the Wyrmlands and had taken shelter there. She, like he, had cheated Time, had robbed Death of a conquest, had obtained the same immortality that the other Cymrians and their descendants had obtained.

And she had married. Word had come via the shipping lanes of a royal marriage in Roland, but he had paid it no mind, until the name *Rhapsody* had come to his ears again, after sixteen centuries of silence.

It was then that the jealousy had begun to brew. He took to walking the docks at night, passing by dock wenches and drunken sailors that otherwise would have been easy prey, wondering if the Rhapsody he had known and this new queen that he had heard tell of could possibly be one and the same. When the curiosity turned to obsession he had summoned Quinn, one of the sailors who was his unwitting thrall, and sent him on a mission to discover if by the smallest stroke of Fate it might be the woman who had pledged herself to him. Until last night, it had seemed almost impossible to believe that it might be true.

And then Quinn returned, confirming his greatest hope, and his greatest dread.

She was alive.

After all these centuries, the death of the Island in volcanic fire, a journey that had taken the lives of many of the refugees, and the war that followed, she was still alive, half a world away. Still wearing the locket she had worn when he knew her. She was alive.

And married.

And happy.

His thoughts blackened as the rage returned.

She had lied to him.

She had broken her oath.

She needed to be taught the consequences of such actions.

"Why?" he said aloud, his voice beginning to shake in the effort to suppress his fury. "Because she is the single best knob I have ever experienced; a bedwench of limitless charms. A talented slut, a rutting whore who broke an oath to me. I seek to reclaim what I lost when that happened."

The voice of the demon was weak, like the graying ash of a long-burning fire that had expended much of its fuel.

*Not again. Let us not do this again. Remember the consequences: remember how weak we were left the last time you gave in to the desire to knob a woman. Each child you father breaks open my essence, our essence, leaving us diminished. Sate your lust in blood and fire, not between a woman's legs. What you leave behind there—*

"I will leave no seed behind this time," the seneschal retorted, gripping the railing as the light from the rising sun flattened over the sea. "When Faron was conceived I was still human, my blood only slightly tainted by your essence, because you were still so weak from the transfer of hosts. Now I am F'dor, having carried you for sixteen hundred years. There is very little, if any, human blood left in me. And F'dor, like all other Firstborn races, choose whether or not to break open their souls in the act of procreation. Believe me, I have no intention of doing that again; I want nothing between Rhapsody's legs but me. I plan to spend a goodly amount of time there, making up for all the time she owes me. So rest easy; your power is safe."

There was another long silence while the demon considered, peppered now by the increasing noise from the docks, the cacophony of activity as the harbor swelled with life and traffic. Finally the voice within his mind spoke; it was soft, as though tired, resigned, but still bore a resolute tone.

*Very well. Let us be off, but with the intent on returning as soon as you have retrieved that which is owed to you. I wish to get back to the terror, the burnings, the mad beauty of the destruction we have wrought here.*

The seneschal absently fingered the hilt of Tysterisk as he thought back for one last moment to the image of Rhapsody's face as she swore her pledge to him; she had called him by a name he had long forgotten until now.

*There; is that enough for you now, Michael?*

*Michael,* he had been called in that other life. He had all but lost the memory of it.

Michael, the Wind of Death.

"Believe me," he said again, "where we are bound, there will be more than ample opportunity for terror, for burnings. I promise you, the mad beauty of the destruction we have wrought here will pale beside what is to come when we make landfall on her shores."

# The New Beginning

## Grei-ti

# 7

𝕿he master of the range flashed the signs from one hundred fifty yards—twelve centers, two inner ring, nine outer ring, one perfect alignment.

Gwydion Navarne sighed, then signaled for the targets to be moved back. While the rangekeepers dragged the hay-butts about in the distance he gave his longbow a shake, then gently ran his fingers up the grip. He had spent more than a year in its making, had carefully blended wood, horn, and sinew, cured it lovingly. It was a weapon of which he was greatly proud, even if it was still not a masterpiece; it, like he, was in training, learning, stretching to its potential.

This afternoon he was not proving worthy of it.

He was so focused on trying to sort out the problem with his angle of flight that he did not hear the approach of the hoofbeats until Anborn was already upon him.

"You disappoint me, lad."

The snort of the black stallion shook Gwydion from his concentration, and he looked up into the face of the Lord Marshal, the ancient general of the Cymrian army, who was staring down at him from his high-backed saddle, watching him as intently as a bird of prey watches a mouse. Gwydion shook the bow again.

"My apologies, Lord Marshal. I'm working on my free-flights, albeit dismally this afternoon." He nodded to Anborn's man-at-arms, an older First Generation Cymrian with gray hair and a deeply lined face, weathered from the sun, who always traveled on horseback with a pair of crossbows drawn. "Well met, Shrike." The soldier nodded in return, dismounting.

The general snorted in the same timbre as his war horse,

then reached behind him and unstrapped his crutches from their saddle bindings.

"I'm not disappointed in your accuracy, boy, but in your choice of projectiles. I see you have a fondness for those flimsy Lirin sticks." Anborn sighed dramatically. "I should have had a long talk with you before your adopted grandmother moved in here and destroyed your sense of arrow flight with her Lirin preferences."

Gwydion laughed, then took the reins as the Lord Marshal dismounted slowly, Shrike standing ready, as always, to support him should he lose his balance. In the three years since Anborn's crippling, Gwydion had never seen it happen.

"Actually Rhapsody has little preference for arrows, and not too much interest in archery anymore," he said. "She brings me back the long whitewoods whenever she goes to Tyrian if she can."

Anborn steadied himself on the two specially made canes and stared at Gwydion in mock disgust. "So you came to this tendency on your own? Appalling."

"I am still studying the crossbow as well, Lord Marshal."

"Well, then at least you shouldn't be taken out and fed to the weasels yet."

Gwydion Navarne laughed. "Perhaps someday you can enlighten me as to why your family is so fascinated with the feeding of incompetents to weasels," he said, glancing at the squire who was approaching with the general's chair. "If I recall correctly, your brother, Edwyn Griffyth, declared the same fate should befall Tristan Steward at the Cymrian Council."

"Being devoured by weasels is far too good a fate for Tristan Steward," Anborn said contemptuously. "In addition, it would be cruel to the weasels." He observed the gesture of the rangekeeper. "They are ready for you, lad."

"So what have you been occupying yourself with, Lord Marshal?" Gwydion Navarne asked as he nocked his arrow.

"Rhapsody said you had gone south to the Skeleton Coast of Sorbold."

"Indeed." The Lord Marshal allowed Shrike to assist him into the wheeled chair, then laid the crutches across his now-useless legs.

Gwydion Navarne watched the general thoughtfully as he settled himself. He had met the legendary soldier as a child of seven at his mother's funeral, and had been terrified by the experience. He was too young to have yet heard of the general's cantankerous reputation, so Anborn's very appearance was intimidating to him; the broad, menacing musculature of back and shoulders, gleaming azure eyes set within a face dark with terrible memories, black hair streaked with white flowing angrily to his shoulders—everything about the general was sufficient to make him want to hide behind his father, who had understood his fear innately and did not require him to come out and shake hands until the general was ready to leave.

And now, since the council held in the wake of the great battle three years ago, he had come to know and admire the man, to love him much the way his godfather, Gwydion of Manosse, did—respectfully and from a safe distance.

There was something in the general's eyes that Gwydion Navarne didn't grasp. He recognized, in the incomplete wisdom of youth, that there were thoughts, emotions, and insights in the head of someone who had lived for as many centuries as Anborn had, seen as many horrors as Anborn had, and contemplated life in ways that Anborn had that he himself could not comprehend now, if ever.

Gwydion Navarne drew back and let fly; the arrow's arc was slighted a hint to the lee; it struck the hay target at one hundred sixty yards and glanced off.

"Drat!"

The Lord Marshal stared at him as if thunderstruck.

"Drat?" he said disdainfully. "*Drat?* Dear All-God, what has my useless nephew been teaching you? Is that the best oath you can muster, lad? After you finish here we will go directly into Navarne City and find a suitable tavern, where we will tend immediately to your proper education in the essential things—drinking, wenching, and swearing properly."

"Oh, I do know how to swear fairly well, Lord Marshal," Gwydion Navarne said pleasantly. "I just didn't want to offend your ears, knowing you to be the frail and discreet gentleman that you are."

Anborn chuckled as Gwydion Navarne drew back again. "Well, I would certainly hope so. My nephew, your namesake, has been schooled by the best—that would be *me*—in the finest curses ever wrought of the dragon tongue, which is the preeminent language in which to swear. You don't have the physiology for that, alas—without the serpentine aperture of the throat you could never manage the double glottal stop—but certainly you should have acquired an impressively vulgar vocabulary after living with him for a few years. And your 'grandmother'—well, a Namer of her power should have access to some utterly splendid oaths."

"Oh, she does." Gwydion Navarne let fly, piercing the inner edge of the outer ring, then kicked the ground in annoyance. "*Hrekin!*"

"Ah, a Bolgish profanity, if an uninspired one. Not bad." The general's face twisted in amusement. "Can't imagine who you caught that one from."

"Well, when you and I served with Sergeant-Major Grunthor as honor guard at Rhapsody's coronation in Tyrian, he taught me many useful things, such as nit removal from private skin folds and how to clear the nasal passages of blockage while rendering an assailant momentarily sightless at the same time."

"Ah." Anborn cleared his throat as Shrike looked askance at the young duke-to-be. "Well, one can never have too many weapons in one's arsenal, though that one was unknown to me until just now."

Gwydion Navarne unstrung the weapon, allowing the bowstring to relax. "So are you going to share with me where you have been? Or am I committing a social misstep inquiring?"

"Both." The ancient warrior looked him up and down, but with a different expression in his eyes than before; there was a sharper intensity in his glance that was tempered with another, deeper emotion, one that the boy did not see this time as he turned back to his bow. "I was looking for a Kinsman on the Skeleton Coast."

Gwydion Navarne did not look up as he strung the bow again. "Oh?" He gave the bowstring a perfunctory pluck and, satisfied with the draw, glanced up finally. The serious expressions on both men's faces made him blink. "Was this a kinsmen on your father Gwylliam's line, or from your mother Anwyn's family?"

Anborn exhaled deeply and looked out over the meadow, his eyes unfocused, as if seeing into another time.

"Neither. I don't mean a kinsman who is merely a blood relation. I am speaking rather of an ancient society of men, a fraternity forged in the old world, from another time; brothers. Warriors. Dedicated soldiers who mastered the craft of fighting over a lifetime's devotion to it, at the expense of self. Kinsmen were sworn to the wind and Seren, the star which shone over the Island of Serendair, resting now below the waves on the other side of the world. And to each other. Always to each other."

Gwydion Navarne brought his hands to rest atop the bow respectfully, waiting to hear the rest of what the Lord Marshal, usually a man of few words, was saying.

He felt Shrike's eyes on him, but he didn't turn to meet the glance of Anborn's man-at-arms. The intensity he felt in their stare told him that what the general was sharing was something he was imparting carefully, with great import. He resolved to be worthy of the telling.

Anborn looked out over the rolling hills to the high wall that surrounded the fields beyond Haguefort; atop the rampart guardsmen walked, patrolling the battlement, their shadows long and spindly in the afternoon sun.

"To some extent, all soldiers are brothers of a kind, relying on one another for their very lives. This kind of life forges bonds that can't be formed any other way, not by birth, nor by the mere desire to do so—it is a commitment of the soul that transcends any other; the willingness to die to save a comrade, the participation in a cause greater than oneself.

"After a lifetime of such soldiering, two kinds of men remain—those that are grateful to have survived the experience, and those that are grateful that the experience survives.

"The first kind gathers his belongings and whatever pieces are left of himself at the end of his service and goes home to farm and family, knowing that no matter what befalls him thereafter in life, he was part of something that will never leave him, tying him to others he may never see again, but who remain a part of him until death takes him."

He cleared his throat and looked back at Gwydion Navarne, studying him for a moment. "The latter kind never goes home, because to him, home is the wind. The wind is never in the same place for more than a moment, but is always there, around him, wherever he is; it is both ephemeral and stalwart; he learns to be the same way. And the more like the wind one becomes, the more one loses a sense of self. Of course, any soldier who serves, any man-at-arms who puts his life at risk daily for not only his comrades and his leader but for those he never sees, has little sense of self anyway.

"Kinsmen were the elite of men who lived this way. They were accepted into the brotherhood for two things: incredible skill forged over a lifetime of soldiering, or a selfless act of service to others, protecting an innocent at threat of one's own life."

He took the bow from the young man's hand and turned it over, making adjustments to the grip and examining the string. "Your nocking point is too high," he said. He made a motion with his hand toward Shrike, who wordlessly plucked a white longflight from Gwydion Navarne's standing quiver and handed it to him. The general flexed the wood of the shaft, then raised his eyebrows.

"Good spine," he said with grudging admiration. He nocked the arrow, then handed the bow back to the young man.

Gwydion nodded silently.

"When one has achieved the right to become a Kinsman, it is the wind itself that selects him," Anborn continued, watching him closely. "Air, like fire, earth, water, and ether, is a primordial element, one of the five that make up the world, but it is often overlooked. Its strength is always underestimated, rarely seen, but formidable. In its purest form, air has *life*, and it knows its own: Kinsmen, who were also called Brothers of the Wind. Serendair was a highly magical place; the wind blew freely there, and strong. Alas, the birthplace of the element, Northland, is on the other side of the world from here, so wind is not as strong in this land as it was there.

"When a man becomes a Kinsman, whether he has earned the title through a lifetime of service or a moment of selfless sacrifice, he hears the wind in his ear, whispering to his heart, telling him its secrets. He can use those secrets to hide within it, to travel by means of it, to call for help on it. The Kinsman call is the most compelling summoning a man can ever hear; it ensnares the soul, reaches deeply into the heart, demanding to be answered. It is used only in the direst of circumstance, when the Kinsman uttering it feels he is on the threshold of death, when his death will have impact beyond itself. And any Kinsman hearing it would never think of ignoring such a summons; to do so would leave him haunted unto insanity for the rest of his days."

"And you heard the Kinsman call from the Skeleton Coast." Gwydion Navarne tried to keep his voice low and respectful, but the excitement in it boiled over, breaking the solemn mood in the meadow.

Shrike stared sharply at him, but Anborn merely nodded.

"Did you find him? This Kinsman, was he there?"

Anborn exhaled, remembering the sound of the waves crashing against the black sand, the steaming mist from the sea swirling around the wreckage of ships from the old world, broken fourteen centuries in the timeless sand. The wind had fought for dominance with the sound of the sea, had faltered and drowned in its roar.

"No," he said.

Gwydion Navarne lapsed into silence again. He turned away from the Cymrian soldiers and drew back, then loosed his arrow at the popinjay suspended from a pole at one hundred and fifty yards. The straw bird snapped back at the force of the impact, then swung wildly, eliciting subtle sounds of approval from the two men.

Feeling somewhat vindicated, the young duke-to-be turned back to them.

"Perhaps he was answered by another Kinsman," he suggested.

"Doubtful," Anborn growled. "Kinsmen were rare in the old land; in this world they are all but imaginary. I have met but two in the last seven hundred years. One was Oelendra, the Lirin Champion, who led the First Fleet of refugees from the Island itself, and passed from this life after the royal wedding. The other—" His words broke off and he smiled slightly to himself.

"Who, Lord Marshal?" Gwydion Navarne could not contain his curiosity. "Who was the other?"

The two soldiers exchanged a glance, and Anborn's smile broadened.

"Perhaps you should ask your 'grandmother' the answer to that question," he said.

"Rhapsody?" Gwydion Navarne's brows drew together above an incredulous expression. "Rhapsody is a *Kinsman*?"

"Perhaps I neglected to mention that Kinsmen come in all shapes and sizes, lad," he said, echoing the words she had once used on him in the same incredulous state. "They come in all walks of life—some of them even are Singers, Namers."

"Women can be Kinsmen?"

"Both the Kinsmen I have just mentioned were women. You think only men are willing to sacrifice for a greater cause?"

"I'd like to have one sacrifice a few hours, a few scrapes on her knees, and a sour taste tomorrow morning for the greater cause of my satisfaction," muttered Shrike. "Are you finished here, Anborn?"

Gwydion Navarne ran a hand through his mahogany-colored hair. "This has been a curious day," he murmured. He looked up at Anborn's man-at-arms. "Are you a Kinsman, Shrike?"

The elderly Cymrian snorted. "When you are one yourself, then you may ask me that," he snapped. "Not until."

"Sorry," Gwydion said, but already Anborn was nodding in the direction of the black stallion. Shrike, obviously relieved to be quitting the conversation, wheeled the chair quickly over to the horse and took Anborn's canes, strapping them quickly to the saddle again.

"You really should reconsider the longbow, lad," Anborn said as Shrike prepared him to mount. "A crossbow or stonebow penetrates better and is more flexible in war."

"Yes, but we are at peace, and have been since the lord and lady ascended the throne," Gwydion replied, looking at the ground as the man-at-arms lifted the ancient general with his shoulder from the wheeled chair and boosted him like a child into the saddle. "I don't expect to see war anytime soon, Lord Marshal. For now as an archer I only need to be proficient enough to penetrate a haybutt."

The general paused in his ascent and stared down at him. "Only a fool thinks so, lad," he said shortly. "Peacetime is good for but one thing: practicing skills to be ready for the next war. Your father knew this; you can tell by that wall he built. Woe unto your province if you don't know it as well."

When the Lord Marshal had been hoisted back onto his mount, he gestured for Gwydion Navarne to bring him the longbow. The youth complied, fascinated, as the Cymrian general closed his eyes, drew the bow easily back to an anchor point well behind his ear, a draw length Gwydion had never seen on the bow before, and fired.

The arrow whistled past him; the wind on which it sailed tousled the young man's hair, blowing it into his eyes, but not before he saw the arrow slam into the direct center of the hay target, vibrating rigidly in waves he could feel in his teeth from one hundred sixty yards away.

Anborn opened his eyes.

"Did you hear it?" he demanded.

"The wind? Yes. It whistled like a teakettle."

The general tossed him the bow impatiently.

"That was the *arrow*," he said curtly. "Did you hear the *wind*?"

Gwydion Navarne considered, then shook his head.

"No."

Anborn exhaled sharply. "Pity," he said as he lifted the reins and Shrike mounted his own horse. "Perhaps you are not meant to, then."

"Why did you tell me this?" Gwydion Navarne called as they turned to leave.

Anborn came alongside the young duke and leaned down as far as his fused vertebrae would allow him, steadying himself against his high-backed saddle.

"Because soon there will be no more Kinsmen," he said quietly. "The brotherhood all but perished when the Island was swallowed by the sea. MacQuieth, probably the greatest of all Kinsmen, died soon after that; he led the Second Fleet to safety in Manosse, then waded into the sea, standing vigil for the death of the Island. When the cataclysm came, he walked into waves and drowned. What few remained in this place—Oelendra, Talumnan—all have passed from this life now. One day the legendary Kinsmen will be nothing more than that; a legend. I thought you might want to hear the lore while there was still someone qualified to tell you, lad." He took up the reins. "I am sorry if I was mistaken. And if I *was* mistaken, then you, too, are sorry."

"I am honored that you chose to tell me, Lord Marshal," Gwydion said hastily as Anborn nodded to Shrike, preparing to depart. "But what about Rhapsody? She is a First Generation Cymrian, and therefore should be unaffected by the passage of time. As long as she lives, won't there always be Kinsmen?"

Anborn sighed. "Apparently you don't understand the meaning of the word," he said, a touch of melancholy in his voice. "One cannot be a Kinsman alone."

He clicked to his stallion, and cantered off over the glossy fields of highgrass bending in supplication before the late-afternoon sun.

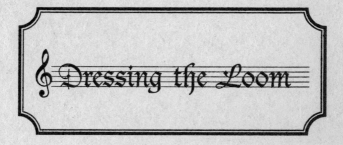

# 8

## HAGUEFORT, NAVARNE

Rhapsody raised her hand to her face to shield her eyes from the glare of the sun. The wind was gusting hot, even now, at dawn, the portent of a scorching day ahead.

The green fields of Navarne were silent beneath the sun, the dawn wind rippling the highgrass in waves beyond the trans-Orlandan thoroughfare, the ancient roadway that spanned the length of Roland from Avonderre to the Manteids. The quiet hills looked in all their vast motion like a green-golden sea, ebbing and flowing with the gusts of the wind. They put her in mind of earlier days, other meadows, another world now long gone, and in the midst of the excitement brought on by the upcoming journey a pang of melancholy struck, resonating for a moment in her soul.

Peace reigned across the Cymrian Alliance, and had for three years now; it was both a fragile and a resilient accord, with the occasional flare of tempers and disputes, but by and large harmonious. She could see it in the faces of the people of the continent, from the Lirin of the western forest to the delegates from Bethe Corbair, the last Orlandan province before the Bolglands, a relaxation of a long-held guard. Even Ashe seemed to be relishing the end of hostilities that had gripped the land for decades. This formerly hunted man, who had spent twenty years hiding and alone, now walked the world openly, happily, his face to the sun. That a wyrmkin's dragon blood, notorious for its paranoia, was allowing him the optimism he was experiencing must surely be a sign that all was right with the world.

But there was something in the wind.

She could not really put her finger on what she felt; it was transitory, ephemeral as the wandering breeze itself. But a change was coming; she could feel it. And it made her skin prickle in cold, even beneath the growing heat of the summer sun.

The noise of preparation dimmed; she looked away for a moment from the soldiers making ready the horses, wagons, and supplies that would accompany them on their trek to Yarim and turned from the ocean of billowing grass westward toward the real sea, one hundred leagues away.

*Is that where it's coming from?* she wondered, trying in vain to find the thread in the wind, the change in the air, whatever alteration in scent or heat or density that was causing her melancholy. Attuned as she was to the vibration in the world around her, in the tone of the music that life made, as a Lirin Singer, a Namer, she could seek such changes.

But she found nothing.

There had been no dreams, no nightmares that foretold of anything looming, warnings like the ones that had once nightly plagued her sleep. When she was wrapped in Ashe's arms, the bad dreams stayed at bay; a dragon guarding one's dreams was the most peaceful means to a night's rest. But even more, when she was away from him, in Tyrian or journeying back again, there had been no visions, no premonitions, no omen to give credence to this sudden change in the wind.

Perhaps she was only imagining it.

Yet as she stood, peering futilely into the distance, she felt another chill, a different one, this time at her back. The tiny hairs at the nape of her neck bristled and beads of sweat appeared, cooling a moment later in the morning breeze. Rhapsody turned quickly, staring over the battlements of Haguefort eastward, toward the ever-reaching expanse of the Krevensfield Plain, but the sensation was gone. Nothing met her eyes but endless swimming fields of highgrass.

She put her palm to her temple, seeking to dispel the throbbing that had arisen from deep within her brain; as she did, to the south she felt yet another quiver, like a tremor in the ground. She bent quickly and touched the earth beneath her feet, but found nothing out of the ordinary.

And then, as quickly as it had come, it too was gone.

"Aria?"

Rhapsody looked up to see Ashe, on the roadway below, watching her along with the guards, the soldiers, and Gerald Owen. She mustered a smile and shook her head, a gesture that sent everyone back to his appointed task except Ashe, who handed the chest he was carrying to one of the escort troops, then headed up the grade to her side.

"Is something wrong?" he asked as she stood and brushed the dirt from her hands.

"I'm not certain," she replied, shielding her eyes again and looking around. Whatever had disrupted her thoughts, had given her pause, was gone now, if it had even been anything to begin with.

"I don't think so," she said finally.

"We can still send an avian message to Achmed if you wish to stay home," Ashe said, running a finger through a loose strand of her hair. "He won't be leaving Ylorc for another day or more; Yarim is so much shorter a trek for him."

Rhapsody took his hand and pulled him back toward the wagons. "Not at all. I am very much looking forward to this journey," she said as they walked to the caravan. She stopped as a carriage marked with the royal standard plodded into the line, drawn by a team of bays. "What is that?"

Ashe bowed deeply. "M'lady's coach."

"Surely you jest."

The Lord Cymrian blinked. "No. Why?"

"You want me to ride in a carriage?"

"Why not?"

"Coaches are for—for, well—"

A wry look of amusement came into Ashe's blue eyes. "For what, my dear?"

"For—well, for nobility and the like."

"You are nobility, Rhapsody. You're royalty now, as much as it pains you."

She cuffed him playfully. "You're right, it does, but that's not the problem. Coaches are for the pampered, or the old, or the ill. I don't wish to be any of those things, not yet at least."

"Are we never to overcome your distaste for royal amenities? It might afford us a private place to sleep."

"I'm sure the regiment will appreciate that. No."

Ashe gave a mock sigh of annoyance. "Very well," he said, and gestured to the quartermaster. "We don't need the coach, Phillip. Thank you."

"It would just slow us down anyway," Rhapsody said, going to her roan mare and patting her affectionately. "And Twilla would be jealous."

"Let it be noted that I attempted, indulgent husband that I am, to spare your hindquarters from the saddle, and you rebuffed my efforts," Ashe said, attempting an injured air.

"Well, my hindquarters thank you, and please do not comment further on that statement," Rhapsody said, patting the roan again. "Are we almost ready?"

"Yes."

"Then perhaps we should find Melisande and Gwydion Navarne. And I wanted to be certain to bid farewell to Anborn."

Ashe nodded in the direction of the crest of a hill. "He's over there," he said. "I'll gather the children if you want to go say goodbye."

Rhapsody kissed him appreciatively. "Thank you."

She waited until he had ascended the steps of Haguefort before heading toward the hill he had indicated. She stopped halfway up, listening to the moan of the wind again, but there was nothing in it out of the ordinary that she could discern. Finally she sighed and hurried up the hill face to the summit.

At the top of the hill Anborn sat, alone in his wheeled chair. His back was to her, but as she approached he spoke.

"It's coming from the west, I believe," he said.

Rhapsody stopped where she stood: "What is it?" she asked apprehensively.

The ancient soldier didn't move. "I don't know," he said.

Rhapsody slowly came forward until she was beside him. Even standing upright she was only slightly taller than the Lord Marshal was when seated. She waited, not wanting to disrupt whatever he was listening for. Together they stared out over the endless meadow to the horizon, brightening now with the full ascent of the sun. Finally the general spoke.

"I thought I heard the call," he said.

"You had said. On the Skeleton Coast."

Anborn turned his azure gaze on her. "No; again, last night."

The chill returned, prickling her flesh, but this time Rhapsody knew that the source was the general's words. "Where?"

Anborn looked away again. "If I knew, I would be there." He rolled his shoulders, the massive muscles rippling beneath his shirt, then straightened his useless legs with his hands.

"I heard nothing, though I sense a change in the air," Rhapsody said, brushing the hair from her eyes as the breeze blew through again. "I have never heard the call of the Kinsmen on the wind, Anborn; I've only been the one to cry for help, and you answered. I thought that if a Kinsman called, and there was one within the hearing of that call, he would come; that the elements themselves would aid in bringing him."

The general nodded. "That was my understanding as well."

"So then how could this be?"

Anborn shrugged. "I have lived more than a thousand years, Rhapsody. If I live a thousand more, I will still not know the answer to every question you would have."

Rhapsody smiled slightly. "Indeed that is true," she said, putting her arm across his shoulder. "And even if you knew, I doubt you'd share the information. You cannot even deign to tell the buttery cooks what you want for supper."

"Your new one is wretched, by the way. I've had better swill and hardtack in the belly of a cargo ship."

The light words dissipated on the wind, leaving an image ringing in Rhapsody's mind.

"Could the call have come from the sea?" she asked. She felt Anborn's muscles tense slightly beneath her arm. "Llauron used to say that the wind over the sea sometimes caught sounds and spun them, like raveling wool, keeping them flying about forever, battered by the vibrations of the endless waves. Is it possible you are hearing a call that came from someone on the sea, maybe yesterday, maybe a hundred years ago?"

Anborn scowled. "If we are to debate all of what is possible, you will not arrive in Yarim in time to meet the Bolg king," he said gruffly, though the affection was unmistakable in his voice.

"Perhaps that is why you are hearing it and I am not," Rhapsody said. "Perhaps it came from a time before I was even here, before I became a Kinsman." Her face colored slightly in the morning sun. "It is still so hard for me to believe that I am one; I haven't the lifetime of soldiering service that most have."

Anborn shook his head. "Many lies are put on the wind, but the wind itself never lies. You called and I heard you, so whatever you did to obtain the status must have been worthy. Hard as it sometimes is to imagine it." He pinched her hip playfully.

"What do we do, then?" she asked, slapping his hand and trying to keep the desperation she felt at bay.

Anborn shrugged again. "Nothing."

*"Nothing?"*

"Nothing." The lines in the general's face crinkled as he squinted into the sun, then turned his gaze to the fields again. "You cannot save the entirety of the world, Rhapsody; no one can. If it is to be, if there is a Kinsman in distress, and he is able to be saved, the wind will see to it that he will be. I stand ready—well, all right, I *sit* ready."

He chuckled and patted her face gently, allowing his hand to linger on her cheek for a moment. "And I know you do as well. So we will wait and see what is to pass. In the meantime, go and live your life. Go to that dry red brick of a city and flood it; drown it, for all I care. It's a place of dry rot, and deserves to blow away in the wind, as far as I'm concerned, but if this is what you seek to do, by all means go do it. You cannot wait on destiny; it comes to you, usually when you are least ready for it."

Rhapsody took the hand that rested on her face and kissed it, then bent and kissed the general's cheek.

"Thank you, Anborn. Are you staying in Haguefort for a while?"

"A short while, long enough to undo the miserable lessons my useless nephew has been giving the young duke. That boy doesn't even know how to spit properly; it's a crime."

Rhapsody laughed. "Oh good. Well, I'm sure he will be a whole new man when we return."

"Count on it. I may not be here to welcome you home, alas. You know how much I dislike staying in one place for too long."

She nodded. "Yes. I will miss you, as always."

The general waved a hand at her. "Go. The caravan was almost ready when I came out here an hour or more ago. They are doubtless waiting for you. Travel well."

He waited until she had disappeared over the rim of the hill before he spoke.

"And, as always, I will miss you, too."

## THE CAULDRON

Achmed marveled at how quietly the Bolg had assembled.

The caravan to Yarim had been stocked and made ready during the night, so as not to disrupt the morning muster or early maneuvers; the work had been accomplished in virtual silence, impressive because the wagons with the drill bits and gears were seven yards long, with four axles each, weighty, cumbersome equipment that clanked and groaned under the best of circumstances. It was a tribute to Grunthor's training and the natural grace of the Firbolg body, made flexible and stealthy by necessity.

Despite the efficiency of their actions, the king could see that the Bolg who had been selected to travel to Yarim were nervous.

The scars from the centuries-old tradition of Spring Cleaning still remained, four years after he had taken the throne, a hideous annual ritual in which the Orlandan army, drunk on power and better armed and trained, came to the foothills of the Teeth and laid waste to a Bolg village, thinking that their bloodthirsty actions were keeping the demi-human population in check and preventing the cannibalistic hordes from attacking the border provinces of Bethe Corbair and Yarim.

In their haste to destroy and hurry home, the soldiers of Roland had seemed to miss the fact that the site of their devastation was the same every year. The Bolg manipulated the situation masterfully; a ramshackle village was hastily constructed and populated with the castoffs of the semi-nomadic society—the old, the infirm, the sickly. The solution, to his mind, was pragmatic and clever; it kept the herd stronger, while appeasing the bloodlust of Roland, and prevented them from coming deeper into the Teeth where the Bolg really lived. The deception had been the convincing factor to Achmed that this populace, the race of his unknown father's people, was worth his effort to protect.

From horseback he could see them now in the light of dawn, gathering their foodstuffs and weapons, hitching the dray horses to the wagons—oxen might have been better, but would never have survived in the Teeth. Bolg didn't care for the taste of horseflesh, and could be threatened into treating the animals as transportation, not food, unlike the four unfortunate teams of experimental oxen he had purchased from Bethe Corbair a few years back. He still occasionally saw Bolg pass him in the tunnels, their crude headpieces sporting the bovine's horns, usually just one from the center of the forehead or sprouting from their heads atop a helmet. He had once even seen one adorning a lesser commander's codpiece, and muttered a silent apology to the late ox.

So for all that the human inhabitants of Yarim would no doubt tremble at the sight of a cohort of the Firbolg army approaching from the east, they could hardly be as unsettled by it as the Bolg were at the thought of entering into the heart of the former enemy's territory in a small, sparsely guarded group. They had more justifiable reason to worry, in his opinion.

The ground rumbled to his right, and Grunthor appeared atop Rockslide.

"Oi think we are ready to depart, sir," the giant said.

Achmed nodded and turned to Rhur, who wore an apprehensive expression, noticeable in the gray light. Since the aspect usually seen on Bolgish faces was taciturn, it was especially unsettling.

"As ordered, look to Omet for guidance in matters of Gurgus, and to Hagraith in administrative ones," he said. "If there is something about which you are uncertain, await my return." The Bolg artisan nodded.

Achmed took up the reins, signaled to the quartermaster, then urged the horse forward until he was at the head of the supply column. He cleared his throat.

"Ready?"

The dark faces and hirsute heads nodded silently.

"Very well, then. We'll be in and out quickly, so as not to have to endure these people any longer than absolutely necessary. Fall out."

With a grinding scream of wood, the noise of the animals, and a flash of the summer sun on the blue-black steel of the drill bit, covered a moment later in canvas, the Bolg engineers set forth for the red clay of Yarim.

## AT SEA, AT THE CROSSING
## OF THE PRIME MERIDIAN

𝒯he seneschal could hear the sailors calling to each other from the riggings of the *Basquela,* even over the bellow of the sea wind.

"Point o' No Return, Cap'n!"

"Point o' No Return! All hands hoay!"

The shout was picked up by a dozen voices, then a score, then two score, passed all around the decks like the warning of wildfire or flood.

Fergus, the seneschal's reeve, stood up from the sea chest on which he sat and motioned to the armsmen the seneschal had brought from Argaut to gather abaft the mainmast. A man of few words, Fergus communicated largely in a lexicon of terrifying growls, grunts, and snorts, but in the building gale he resorted to sweeping arm gestures and a black glower.

The seneschal grabbed for a nearby stay and clutched the mouse, the metal ball on the stay's collar. The Prime Meridian, the invisible line that sundered the sea and was said to have been the exact place where Time began, was the fabled Point of No Return, where a ship might pass silently and without incident, or be caught and scuttled by an errant crosscurrent; worse, the wind had been known to suddenly die down, becalming the ship on the open sea. It was the place that sailors dreaded, but were forced to brave on any circumnavigation. The metal under his hands was slippery and cold in the salt spray and stiff wind.

"Ease the ship," the pilot shouted to the helmsman. "We're gonna close-haul 'er."

Clomyn and Caius, the seneschal's trusted crossbowmen, staggered to their feet, looking for a place to grab hold and ride out the crossing of the meridian. Twins whose hearts beat in unison, and whose skill with their weapons was unmatched in all of Argaut, the brothers had been green since leaving port, and now lumbered, pale, as their stomachs rushed into their mouths.

"Bear a-hand, mates!" the captain called, steadying himself. " 'Tis a heavy sea today; look alive. Warp her, or we're gonna be all in the wind."

The ship's crew, long accustomed to braving the Point, scrambled aloft or manned their posts, preparing for a violent ride. The heave of the sea was strong, slapping high waves over the sides, drenching the armsmen in the seneschal's regiment.

The seneschal, himself unsettled by the pitching of the vessel, clung to the stay, gasping for breath as he caught the spray from a cresting wave full in the mouth. He shouted for Fergus, and the reeve made his way across the slippery deck.

"Secure me," he ordered his reeve, who nodded and braced himself, then grabbed hold of the seneschal's arm.

"Luff! To the lee, man!" called the pilot to the helmsman again.

The seneschal felt the black fire within his soul rage with anger at the helplessness he now felt. The ship was pitching violently, the sailors scrambling, when only a few moments before they had been following a fair wind, making good time. That his journey, and thereby his goal, was in jeopardy, infuriated both man and demon.

"Right the helm!" the captain shouted.

"Hold sound," the seneschal said to Fergus, who nodded his understanding.

Fighting off the gale, he grasped the hilt at his hip and drew Tysterisk.

A shower of infinitesimal sparks of fire gusted forth from the scabbard, visible only in the blink of an eye.

The seneschal held the sword hilt aloft, slicing through the gale with a vicious sweep.

To any eye other than one as close as Fergus's, it would have appeared that the seneschal was merely in possession of a handle of black steel. But Fergus, being close enough to touch the man, caught for a split second a glimpse of the blade, its edges faint black outlines that held within their boundaries a swirling of tiny currents, invisible except for the droplets of water from the spray that were caught and spun within them.

And in that split second, the reeve could see the tiny, formless faces of spirits, eyeless wraiths with dark mouths open in howling agony, that spun within the invisible blade; for that moment he could see the weapon's heft, its power, crackling in the air around it.

That power radiated instantly through the seneschal, causing his body to stiffen, to surge with a strength that Fergus could feel in his grasp. The skin beneath the seneschal's robes grew warm, then blistering, too hot to touch. With a guttural sound of pain, Fergus relinquished the lord's arm.

There was little need to secure him now anyway.

Lightning crackled in the wind that swept the deck and sails.

Like the sword blade, the seneschal's lean body seemed to take on a greater heft, a sinewy muscularity, as the power from the weapon surged through him. He threw back his head and laughed, then shouted into the wind.

"Bow to me!"

The twins, prone on the deck, stared up from the pools of vomit through their sodden hair, watching the transformation.

Watching their master instruct the wind itself.

"I am your lord!" the seneschal bellowed into the gusts that tugged at the mains'l. The sound of his voice was deep, cutting through the scream of the gale like the blade of the sword through snow. "Bow to me; I command it."

In answer the thundering wind crackled with static, whipping in a cyclone-like spiral skyward.

Then, in a twinkling, the wind died down; the waves, absent its tormenting buffets, calmed. The sails, aback, their surfaces pressed aft against the mast by the force of the wind a moment before, slackened and fell, then filled again as a fairer breeze blew through, catching them.

The crew stood stock still, their eyes riveted on the seneschal.

The seneschal closed his eyes, a wide, triumphant smile on his lips. He raised his face to the sun, visible now that the clouds had been blown away. He stood for a moment, reveling in the glory of his mastery of the gale; then, as if coming to clarity, opened his eyes again quickly and leveled a displeased glance at the crew. The breeze around the hilt in his hand sparked angrily, tiny sparks of flame like windswept embers of a campfire taking to the air.

"Get on with it, then," he said in a low, deadly voice.

The captain turned quickly to the pilot.

"Thus!" he called, the order to maintain the course. The crew, dumbstruck the moment before, scrambled to attention, returning quickly to their posts.

Fergus dried his stinging palms, blistered from the heat of touching the seneschal, on his breeches, then crossed the deck to where the crossbowmen still lay, sundered by nausea.

"Rise up," he said in his gruff voice. "Get back belowdecks 'til you're needed."

The mate paused as he passed the captain on the way back to the quarterdeck, leaning close to his commanding officer so as not to be overheard, not realizing that the wind heard everything.

"What have we taken on, sir?" he asked nervously.

The captain did not flinch.

"I couldn't say," he answered, watching the seneschal return to his quarters below decks. "But surely our voyage is blessed. How can we ask for more than to have the wind itself with us?"

# 9

## ON THE SKELETON COAST, SORBOLD

𝔚ith the morning came the wind.

The man stood with the rising sun behind him, his face to the west, watching the rolling mist billow in waves half a heartbeat behind the surf as it broke over the black sand of the beach.

All around him the towering wrecks of ships dozed, their ancient timbers jutting from the sand like the cracked bones of giant mythical beasts, wrapped in dense blankets of fog.

*The sea looks calm this morning,* he thought, watching the gentle ebb and flow of the waves, foaming as they ran up the dark, sparkling sand of the beach, then retreating shyly. He knew it was all a pretense. The riptide a few feet from shore was deceptive and merciless, the rocky bottom jagged as broken glass from the volcanic shards of sand. Here on the lee of the Skeleton Coast, peace was only a pretty mask for a deeper, deadly threat.

The thought amused him.

On the windward side of the coast, the waves made no attempt at concealing their rage. They rolled in high white breakers, pounding the shore with an unforgiving fury, crashing against the rocks, blasting their spray violently into the air, churning madly until they were sucked back into the maw of the sea again, only to return insistently a moment later, over and over and over endlessly.

There was something much more appealing to him about that undisguised sea rage, that unapologetic hostility, unfettered by the need to hide, to appear passive. It was a rage he felt himself, an anger that lurked deep inside, needing to be disguised, tempered, cloaked in a gentle face, an amiable aspect, for the sake of cooperation. Like the leeward sea.

For now.

A beam of gold broke through the ever-present haze, illuminating the vapor in the cloudy air, making his dusky skin shine coppery, the color of the earth in sunlight. Sorbold skin, burnished by the desert wind, the unrelenting sun. There was a beauty to his people that did not exist in the other strains of the human race of the continent, a superior mettle that withstood the relentless sun, the pounding blasts of desert wind, the harsh clime, the brutal nature of the culture, and came out the other side stronger, honed, like a clay pot tempered in fire.

Soon to be put to the test.

A creaking whistle interrupted his musings, a groaning that could be heard from time to time along the Skeleton Coast. It was only the wind bending around the ruined masts of the ancient ships, whipping over the remains of the hulls, blasting the wood clean. The dead ships had been built from a strange wood, from a kind of tree not seen on this side of the world, wood that had not rotted even with the passage of fourteen hundred years. The wind seemed to caress the ruins lovingly, wrapping them in the steam of morning, moaning its plaintive song.

The man looked up, his thoughts refocused on the task at hand. He had been scouring the beach in the gray light of predawn, as he had been the day he first found treasure here, as he had done endless times since, to no avail. There were only a few moments left before full sun, when the misty beach would turn white and cloudy, the haze impenetrable, blocking any chance for a glimmer of magic to be seen. Quickly he cast his gaze around one more time, his eyes scanning the foaming waves, the black sand.

He saw nothing out of the ordinary, just as he had every time he had looked save that first time.

The man let out a deep sigh, resignation in his breath. The failure was not unexpected; after all, how many times in one lifetime can one be handed the keys of Time?

He dug dispiritedly beneath the prow of the skeletal ship he had been searching through, trying to catch sight of any scrap that the sea had not claimed, any glint, any tiny sparkle like the one he had seen that day, but to no avail.

The red-orange arc that had cracked the horizon at daybreak swelled to a complete sphere, filling the heavy, vaporous air with opacity. Full sun.

He sighed deeply, remembering the moment of his discovery fondly.

He had been a much younger man then, a man with unrealistic dreams of youth and the itching desire to see them to fruition being lessened a little each year as those dreams dissipated. He had all but settled into the resentful acceptance that his life would turn out to be no more than ordinary when an impetuous dawn stroll along the black sand beach had yielded a fortuitous glimmer.

He had almost missed it; he caught it out of the corner of his eye, like a distant movement, and it had set his heart to heavy, painful thudding; legend said that gray lions, living ghosts of hunter-predators, prowled the Skeleton Coast, blending into the mist to invisibility until they were upon their unfortunate prey. He had seen enough human bones scattered amid the bones of ships to believe the tales. The purple glimmer on the periphery of his vision had terrified him, caused him to stop, frozen, where he stood, praying to the All-God to allow him to blend into the mist, to escape the jaws of the ghost lions.

When nothing sprang out of the fog at him after a few minutes he had cautiously made his way to the dark bones of the ship, the outlines of its crushed timbers turning from shadows to gray, then black, until he was there, inside what had been the hull. He had dug carefully in the sand, brushing the grains on the wet surface gently away, oblivious of the blood that was seeping from his fingers, his skin sliced into thin ribbons by the volcanic shards.

About a knuckle's depth down, hidden in the lee of a broken timber, he found it.

At first he had thought it was a shell of some kind, or perhaps a piece of mother-of-pearl; it was violet in color, irregular in hue, flat as a whisper, with a ragged edge running the perimeter of an asymmetrical oval. It had taken him several moments to work up the courage to touch it, in fear that it might be a kind of poisonous coral or other sea plant he had never encountered before. When finally he did, he found it smooth as glass, but scored with fine lines, as if inlaid with countless tiny, perfect tiles.

However long it had been wedged in the sand had given the sea the opportunity to grind it down, blast the surface with uncounted gusts of wind and grit, and yet, still etched into its surface was a rune of some kind, a type of writing he had never seen. Gingerly, and with the greatest of care, he picked the odd thing up and held it up before his eyes.

At that moment the sun broke through the mist again. The ray of light touched the glass like surface and caught each tiny line; the object flashed with a glamour that almost blinded him. Ray upon ray of multicolored light rippled in a heartbeat over the pale violet surface, running in glistening rivers off the thin, tattered edge, dazzling his eyes.

And then, when the light moved on, it darkened again to the flat violet hue once more.

He did not feel the pain in his bloody fingers, or the sand in his eyes, or the growing heat of the sun as it climbed into the sky. All he felt was the magic radiating in his hands, the beating of his own heart keeping time with the ticking of some great unseen universal clock, a melodic hum in his mind telling him, without words, that his life would never again threaten to be ordinary.

He had feverishly sought its origins from that moment forward, had indentured himself as a ship's cook on voyages to Manosse and the Hintervold, taken a position as an acolyte in Terreanfor, the great cathedral of Lord God, King of the Earth, Sorbold's basilica of Living Stone, had served scholars and clerics and Filidic foresters, all to no avail. None among them had in their libraries, their memories, or their recounted lore a story of such a thing, and of course he could not ask anyone directly what it was, let alone show it to him.

He grew more and more frustrated as the years went by, searching for any clue, any explanation, but could not even find a sample of the writing that formed the rune on the object's surface.

Until the day, quite by accident, he had happened upon the Cymrian museum, a little repository of dusty relics, rarely open and even more rarely visited, in the small keep known as Haguefort in the Orlandan province of Navarne.

The keeper of the museum was a pleasant young man named Lord Stephen Navarne, the duke of the province and an unabashed aficionado of Cymrian lore and history. He had inherited the responsibilities of the position of Cymrian Historian from his own father, who, like the other historians before him, had kept artifacts and records of that era locked away in secret, ashamed to be of the lineage of the people who had come to this continent as refugees from a disaster, and ended up consuming it, first in colonization, then in war. Those who were descended of that line rarely spoke of it, and almost never acknowledged its shameful history, its atrocities and destructive arrogance.

Stephen Navarne had been different, however. Knowing the advances that had been made before the Great War, the building of roads and cities, harbors and lighthouses, castles and cathedrals, he had chosen instead to be proud of that heritage, albeit subtly. He had lovingly built a small, unassuming depository of the historical treasures of that era with an eye toward preserving them, displaying them with a pleasant combination of pride, humility, and scholarship. He was always more than willing to give of his time to those seeking to know more about the time period and the race, the diverse, fragmented population that had escaped the volcanic fire of the Sleeping Child that had consumed their homeland, only to turn around and revisit that destruction on the lands of their hosts, then disappear into history.

It was there, in that tiny museum, amid the carefully

tended displays, that the man who now stood beneath the
Sorbold sun, wrapped in the mist of the Skeleton Coast, had
discovered, in the tattered, water-soaked pages of a fragment
of a book rescued from the same skeletal ships, several of
the answers he sought.

The book, from the looks of its remains, had once been
a thick tome, bound in leather and calligraphed in a careful
hand, the annoyingly meticulous hand of a scholar. It existed
now only in pieces, crumbling bits of pages and smeared
ink, carefully preserved under glass. A few sections were
intact, but by and large what remained was unreadable, or
torn beyond recognition, or paste.

But one thing that had survived was the title, embossed
on the tattered leather cover.

*The Book of All Human Knowledge,* it read.

He had missed a good deal of the explanation that the
Duke of Navarne had proffered about the book, struggling
to contain the exhilaration that was ringing in his ears, making him sweat in nervous euphoria, all the while attempting
to come across as calm and mildly disinterested. It was the
first of many subsequent performances in which he was able
to utterly deceive the person talking to him, appearing in
one face, while hiding a very different other one.

What little he had heard he had mostly forgotten now; it
was some sort of incessant babble about an old-world Nain
explorer named Ven Polypheme, who had compiled all the
great lore and teachings he had discovered in the course of
his travels around the world. It had also been necessary for
him to inquire of several other meaningless entries in the
book in order to avoid allowing Lord Stephen to suspect
which item he was interested in, and so a good deal of the
historical background had blended together.

But a few salient facts had penetrated and remained
lodged in his brain.

The item he had was a fortune-telling talisman of some
sort, a card in what the Nain explorer had described merely
as the Deck. The Deck had belonged to an Ancient Seren

seer named Sharra, and so on occasion Ven Polypheme referred to it as Sharra's Deck. The seer, according to the explorer, was able to draw upon some elemental power with which to manipulate the cards to bring about significant events, though what that power was, or what those manipulations led to, had been lost to Time and the sea.

The symbols on some of the other cards in the deck had been crudely sketched in the book; indeed, if he had not recognized the throne symbol on one of the more intact pages he might have missed the connection altogether. But miraculously that drawing was intact in the exhibit, the inscription below it clear enough to be recognized.

He had struggled to remain blasé as he gestured absently to the runes below the sketch of the throne, runes he had committed to memory, even though he could not read them.

"What language is this?" he had asked the young duke casually.

"Ancient Serenne," Stephen had replied, his blue-green eyes snapping with excitement. "It's really more a magical code or musical notation than a language. Here; I have a small volume that is a folio of sorts on Ancient Serenne, if you would like to see it."

He had searched feverishly through the slim book, writing the words and symbols with trembling hands, until a single phrase stared back at him, the translation of the runes he had struggled for so many years to decode.

*The New Beginning,* it said.

The only other information of note that he had discovered in the scant remains of *The Book of All Human Knowledge* regarding the Deck was that Ven Polypheme believed the cards were formed from dragon scales, though he acknowledged he had never seen their like in any of the many dragons he had apparently been privileged to meet in the course of his travels.

And since dragons were the race formed of elemental earth, he had a suspicion he knew what might help power the scale.

The time was almost right to test his theory.

He had already put the steps in motion; the Scales of Yarim had weighed in his favor. From the moment he had placed the totem of Living Stone on one plate and the violet scale of the New Beginning on the other and they had balanced, he had felt it, a blood-deep power coursing through his veins, an entitlement that transcended any other.

As the sun rose in the firmament, and the thick mist of the Skeleton Coast swallowed him into invisibility once more, the man knew that the time was at hand to see if he could wield it.

# 10

## ON THE ROAD OUTSIDE YARIM PAAR

The sweet morning air rang with the sound of a glorious bass, slightly flat, echoing off the Teeth beyond.

> My lover snores like a bear in its den,
> She smells like a moose in 'eat,
> She's covered in mud like a pig in a pen
> Six toes on each of 'er feet.
>
> Oh, 'ow Oi 'ates to leave 'er side
> When Oi 'ears the call to duty,
> Oi 'ad to look far and 'ad to search wide
> For a thing o' such endless beauty.

A score or so of raspy Bolgish voices picked up the chorus to the cadence:

> Aye-eh, Aye-ah, a wondrous sight to see,
> Aye-eh, Aye-ah, my girl in Ter-I-lee.

Achmed was only half-listening to Grunthor and his troops extolling the praises of the Sergeant's favorite bedwench in song; he was watching instead for the approach of the Yarimese guards. He suspected that Ihrman Karsrick, paranoid old goat that the duke was, would do whatever he could to contain the presence of the Bolg in his province, escorting them grudgingly into the work zone, perhaps under cover of darkness, to avoid exposing his subjects to the cannibals, as Bolg were frequently referred to by humans.

He didn't need to wait long to be proven correct.

Just as the Bolg chorus had arrived at the place in the tune where Grunthor's wench's nose ring was being compared favorably to that of a local prize-winning bull, a thin line of horsemen appeared in the distance.

The melody choked off, swallowed with precision.

"Ah, 'ere comes the welcoming committee," the Sergeant said, smirking. "Was wonderin' when the royal treatment was gonna begin." He turned to the two dozen Firbolg workers and signaled the caravan to slow to half speed. "Ya all remember ta use yer napkins and fingerbowls like Oi taught ya. Now set to."

The Bolg guard that was riding escort, numbering a dozen more, nonchalantly aimed their crossbows, targeting the forelegs of the Yarimese guards' mounts as the Sergeant and the Bolg king rode slowly out to meet the soldiers of Yarim.

A single rider, a dusky-skinned man with light eyes, separated from the contingent in turn and urged his mount forward gently.

"Well met, sire," the officer from Yarim said when he was within earshot, addressing the Bolg in the Orlandan vernacular. "Welcome to Yarim; I am Tariz, and am to be your escort and aide while you are here in the province."

Achmed did not favor the man with a glance. "Lead."

The soldier reined his horse around, and rode back toward the Yarimese contingent, his shoulders twitching as if he expected a crossbow quarrel to be planted between them at any moment.

*       *       *

ℑn all seasons save for summer, Yarim Paar was a cold, dry place, a flat wasteland nestled between the fertile fields of Canderre to the west and the towering peaks of the Teeth to the east. It was an older city than most others on the continent, and the most ancient of all the provincial capitals, having preceded the Cymrian era in its building by more than a thousand years. Exactly how long it had been standing was lost to Time and the wind that blew the red clay around in spiraling clouds across the wide, arid plain.

In summer, the current season, the dry red clay clotted the air, making it difficult to breathe in the heat. The parched ground had baked at the surface and cracked, sending forth spirals of red clay dust with the tramping of the horses' hooves, stinging the eyes along with the glare of the sun.

Achmed had seen the bright white cloth of the construction tents that had been erected around Entudenin long before any of the rest of the decaying buildings in the center of the capital could be discerned. In the massive expanse of what had once been the jewel of the cold desert, the gleaming fabric of the site glowed against the backdrop of blood-red clay. He inclined his head toward it, and Grunthor nodded.

Tariz noticed their exchange. Nervously he shifted the reins into his right hand and pointed with his left.

"That is the site, sire," he said awkwardly.

"Then why are we riding away from it?" Achmed asked, already knowing the answer. The sensation was similar to being a cat playing with a bird it had caught. His head hurt with the game, and it annoyed him.

"Er—we, ah, well, I have specific orders from the Duke of Yarim to first take you and your contingent to the barracks complex that has been set up for you outside the city to the northeast. You will be most comfortable there; we have arranged for housing for the men and animals, as well as for the machinery."

"The men *too*?" asked Grunthor in mock amazement. "Oh, goody! Ya mean we don't have ta sleep in the rocks amongst the snakes? You truly are a gentleman, sir."

"The duke intends to see to your every need while you are his guests," stammered the aide.

"I presume that includes our need for constant guard," Achmed said.

"Yes, yes indeed." Tariz looked relieved.

The Bolg king reined his mount to a halt and gestured for the aide to stop alongside him. He leaned nearer, locking eyes with the man.

"Let me make one thing undeniably clear from the outset, Tariz," he said quietly. "Whatever your orders, my men and I are not your prisoners. For practicality's sake I will tolerate your presence, your needless vigilance, your standing guard over us while we work, for as long as it suits me. But bear in mind always that it is the ignorant fools in your own province you are watching for and holding arms against, whose curiosity is injurious in some way in the mind of your duke, not the Bolg artisans he has hired. If for one moment I feel a shift in that understanding, if any of my workers are harassed or made to feel like anything less than the hired experts that they are, come to save your province from dying of thirst, we will be gone before you draw a second breath, leaving you to wither and desiccate in the sun. Do you understand my words?"

The Yarimese soldier nodded, his eyes bright in the sandy wind.

"Good. Then let us move out more quickly; the men deserve a rest from this sun before we begin work at nightfall."

From the gleaming marble balcony of her guest room in the Judiciary, the palace of Yarim's duke, Rhapsody watched the procession of wagons and horses as it turned to the east. The gown of green Yarimese silk in which she was clothed, the duke's welcome gift, gleamed in the sun passing over it as she turned to follow the caravan.

"Where are they going?" she demanded, shielding her eyes from the bright glare radiating off the balcony railing, inset with precious opals and lapis lazuli, the gloriously colored products of Yarim's famed mining camps.

Ihrman Karsrick cleared his throat. "I have arranged for them to be quartered in the Bissal Crescent, a few miles outside of the city," he said blandly. "They should be easy to protect there."

"That's nothing but a dust bowl," said Ashe, crossing his arms. "Have you recently built a garrison there, Irhman?"

"No, m'lord, not a permanent one, but a full camp has been erected, with a ring of guards around it."

Rhapsody turned to the duke. "Let me understand this. You have invited King Achmed to your province for the purpose of benefiting from his expertise, in a matter that could remedy the possible starvation of your people and save your treasury from being emptied, and you are expecting him to quarter outside the city, sleeping on a cot in a tent in the middle of a barren wasteland, under continuous guard, much in the same manner as you once housed the murderers from the Market of Thieves?"

"Not at all, m'lady," replied Karsrick, his teeth set in annoyance. "The murderers from the Market of Thieves were given bedrolls, not cots. Where did you expect me to house the Bolg?"

The Lady Cymrian turned and strode angrily to the door. "I expected you to house them as you would any other guests in your province, Ihrman, and I am embarrassed on your behalf, as well as my own, that you didn't expect to do this as well. As for the Bolg king, who is a visiting head of state, and a fellow member of the Cymrian Alliance, I expected you would put him up in your very own bedchamber, if need be, and sleep yourself on the scullery floor with your fat arse to the fire before you would disgrace both of us like this."

When the duke turned, purple with fury, to her husband, the Lord Cymrian merely shrugged.

"Namers must tell the truth as they know it, Ihrman," he said, following Rhapsody to the door. "Speaking anything other than the truth dilutes their power. So perhaps it would have been more politic of me to address you myself, rather than leaving it to Rhapsody, and tell you what a graceless, mannerless idiot you are." He caught her arm before she went through the doorway.

"You are right, of course, Aria," he said quietly. "But practically speaking, do you not think the Bolg would be uncomfortable here in the Judiciary? Wouldn't they, in fact, have chosen the same sort of accommodation that Ihrman has provided had they been asked?"

"Undoubtedly," his wife replied, kissing him on the cheek. "But they *weren't* asked. Sometimes the etiquette is more in the question than in the answer. I will return before supper."

Ashe caressed her face gently, then returned to the balcony, watching in silence, listening with Karsrick as the palace guards repeated her orders to bring forth her mount and open the gate.

"Make certain she is accompanied and guarded on her way to the Bissal Crescent," the Lord Cymrian directed Karsrick, who nodded angrily and left the room, leaving him to stand alone on the balcony, observing his wife ride off to meet the other two of the Three, the men who had brought her across Time, through the belly of the Earth, unknowingly returning her to his life and his world again.

He swallowed, willing himself to be grateful.

$\mathfrak{W}$ell, would ya look at that."

Grunthor laughed aloud at the sight approaching the camp. From the west a rolling cloud of dust rose, in front of which a Lirin roan could be seen, in full canter transitioning to a gallop. Atop the roan was a woman in a green silk gown, her lower legs bare, the skirts streaming behind her in the wind, similarly to the way the blond tresses of her hair were flying, her scabbard slapping at her side. Behind her, a small retinue of guards struggled to keep pace.

"Looks like she's bent on losing them, eh, sir? Think she might be 'appy to see us?"

Behind his veils Achmed smiled as well. He knew it was only a matter of moments before she would descend upon them, because he had been tracking her heartbeat for most of the morning. It was racing in time with the galloping mare.

"Yes, I believe she is," he said.

As she crested the rise where they were encamped, the roan slowed, then came to a graceful halt in a swirl of red dust. Rhapsody vaulted from the animal's back, and ran toward them, bare of foot, grinning.

She threw herself first into the waiting arms of the giant, allowing him to lift her from the ground and swing her about in his embrace like a child.

"Grunthor! I am *so* glad to see you! Thank you for coming!"

"My pleasure, miss," the Sergeant grinned in return. "Been far too long."

"I agree," she said as he put her down gently on the ground. She turned to the Bolg king and embraced him. "Hello, Achmed."

"Hello yourself," Achmed replied. "That was quite a spectacle, the Cymrian Lady riding astride with her skirts flying up in the wind. If you decide to give up the royal life and go back to your previous profession, that might be a good way to attract business."

"Thank you, I'm glad to see you as well," she said, ignoring his comment and taking his arm, then Grunthor's. "I'm here to escort you to the Judiciary in Yarim Paar."

"Why?" Grunthor asked.

"Well, it's bound to be more comfortable than billeting in the middle of the desert."

"Naw, that's all right, miss. The troops are more comfortable 'ere actually; fewer 'umans gawkin' at 'em. They can get some rest and a good meal and be ready ta work tonight. An' Oi'd just as soon stay with 'em, if ya don't mind."

"Well, what about you, Achmed? Do you wish to remain here as well?"

"Did your husband accompany you to Yarim?"

"Yes."

"Then I'll pass on the invitation," the Bolg king said. Rhapsody's face fell, so he quickly added, "It's better that I remain with my 'men,' as you are so fond of calling them." He stopped at the top of a sandy rise, watching the deployment of the Yarimese guard around the perimeter of the camp. "But as long as you're here, I need you to look at something."

Rhapsody glanced around the Bissal Crescent. Far away at the horizon to the east she could see the shadow of the Teeth, their multicolored peaks faded by distance into a muted gray, ringed with a haze of clouds; it was raining there, filling the watersheds, no doubt, with the life-giving rain that was denied by Nature to the vast expanse of the province of Yarim.

To the north and west of the Crescent, great red rocky formations were strewn about the desert floor, some reaching heights of over one hundred yards. Their curves and hollows spoke of a time when they might have been supple clay, now fired in the kiln of the wind and sun into the hard, dry skeletons that baked in the heat along with the rest of Yarim.

There was something unnerving about this place to her, this open land ringed with dead red rocks and Yarimese guards; it was as if there were eyes somewhere, watching her, watching them, but hidden from sight in a place that had no natural cover.

She shook her head to clear it. "Very well. Show me." She waved to the Yarimese guards, dismissing them. The guards looked at one another helplessly, then assumed parade rest.

Achmed reconnoitered for a moment, then took her elbow

and led her to a sheltered place in the lee of a rocky formation, ten or so feet in height, where a small tent had been
erected. He led her inside, then pulled off one of his outer
veils that served as a cloak and tossed it on the ground at
her feet.

"Sit."

Rhapsody obeyed, heedless of the clay dust that crept into
the drapes of the silken gown.

The Bolg king shrugged off the pack he wore across his
back, removing from it a thin locked box fashioned of steel.
Beeswax sealed the edges; Achmed ran his finger around
them, melting the wax, then produced a tiny wire, with
which he sprung the lock. With the greatest of care, he removed the contents of the box, wrapped in several layers of
protective oilcloth. The cloth contained a few pages of brittle parchment, an ancient manuscript that Rhapsody sur-
mised must have come from Gwylliam's library in Canrif.

He handed the drawings to her with the greatest of care;
she took them with similar gentleness. The schematics were
detailed in the painstaking detail she had seen in other ex-
amples of Gwylliam's work, meticulously rendered in a fine
architect's hand, for that had been the training of the ancient
Cymrian king before he had led his people away from the
doomed Island of Serendair.

The schematic was of a tower of sorts, supported by
beams or pipes of some kind, its fan-shaped ceiling set in
panes of colored glass, ordered as the colors of the rainbow.
The key that indicated each of the colors was in Old Cymrian, the common tongue of the Island that she, Grunthor,
and Achmed had each spoken when they lived there, now
considered a dead language by the people of this land, who
spoke Orlandan, the language of the provinces of Roland,
or the vernacular of their individual homelands. A separate
drawing detailed a wheel of some sort, also set with panels
of glass, or something like it, though clear, not colored.

She pointed to a series of notations near the bottom of
the page. "Gurgus," she read. "Wasn't that the mountain

peak in the Central Corridor of the Teeth that had been smashed to bits by Anwyn's forces early in the siege of Canrif?"

"Yes."

"Hmmm." Rhapsody turned the sheaf of papers slightly to better catch the diffuse light shining through the fabric of the tents. "This is interesting, but why are you showing it to me? You can certainly read this yourself."

"This part I can, yes," Achmed agreed. He ran a perennially gloved finger along the edge of the top page. "It is the page below it that I cannot, and am hoping you can."

"What is this apparatus? Do you know?" Before the Bolg king could speak, Rhapsody quickly handed him back the parchment and put a finger to her lips. "Tarry a moment, Achmed."

She rose from the dirt floor of the tent, pulled the flap aside, and stepped out into the blinding light of noon again. The wind whipped warm across her face, slapping her hair into her eyes; she turned in to it, allowing it to blow the strands clear. Then she drew her sword.

Daystar Clarion, the elemental sword of fire and starlight forged millennia before, came forth from its sheath with a whispering ring, a note that sounded quietly, a muted call of a battle horn. Drawing it in peace, as she had, caused it only to ring softly, vibrating gently in the sandy wind, but when it was drawn in battle, the call of the sword could be heard across continents, could shake the foundations of mountains.

Rhapsody held the sword aloft in the hot breeze, focusing on the metaphysical tie that bound her to the weapon. She could feel it resonating within her, humming in the same note, pulsing in time with her heartbeat and the breath of the elemental fire within her. Quickly she drew a circle in the air around the tent, a thin ring of light that remained even after the sword had passed from it, hovering on the wind. It was a circle of protection, a musical tone that would divert the currents of air around it and keep what was said within it from escaping onto the wind.

The silver circle undulated on the air, expanding and contracting with the changes in the breeze, but continued to hover, steadfast, flexible but unbreakable. Satisfied, Rhapsody returned to the tent.

"I have an uneasy feeling lately that someone is watching me. I don't know if it has to do with the work here in Yarim, but I think it's best we take extra precautions. What we say now cannot be overheard," she said as she sat back down beside her friend.

He was staring at the pages, his mind clearly far away from the windy plain of Yarim. She noted the absence of focus in his eyes, and thought to herself how much his other nature, the Dhracian bloodline, was showing at this moment. Rather than the heavy, rough-edged angularity of the Bolg features that were apparent when he was around Grunthor and his Firbolg subjects, she could see instead the thin, fine veins that scored the surface of his skin, the long, sinewy musculature and dark eyes of the race of his mother. He was very far away, she knew, lost in thoughts, most likely from the other side of Time, so she waited in silence until he was ready to speak again.

When his eyes finally cleared, he fixed them on Rhapsody for a moment, then turned back to the manuscript.

"I have seen something like this once before," he said, his voice as sandy as the Yarim wind. "It was long ago, in another lifetime, long before we met in the streets of Easton in the old world." He fell silent again.

Rhapsody pulled the green silken folds of her dusty skirt around her knees and waited.

"Someone I once served as guardian for—a rare and magical being—had an apparatus that looked very much like this. I only saw it once, but it would be impossible to forget such a thing. Like this, it was built into a tower in a clifftop monastery, though not in a mountain peak; Gwylliam had delusions of grandeur that made him feel he could mold the very Earth itself. In the language of its owner, the apparatus was called the Lightcatcher."

"What did the apparatus do?"

Achmed shook his head, his eyes heavy with memory. "I am not certain. I do remember, however, that when the gravely injured were past the point of being healed by the monks or the priests there, they were taken to the Lightcatcher. Many of them returned, whole. When knowledge was being sought, the priests often asked—" He caught himself, his olive skin turning darker for a moment. "The one who possessed the machine was frequently asked questions that required the ability to see into the future, or across great distances, or into hidden places, and those questions were answered. There were other things as well—things that defy explanation that the Lightcatcher brought about. It was an instrumentality of great power. How it worked, and what its exact capabilities were, I am not certain. I have tried to follow Gwylliam's directions in the reconstruction of the one he built, but I cannot get the colored glass in the ceiling to the right thickness and porosity."

"You are rebuilding this?" Rhapsody asked. "Why?"

The Bolg king studied the drawings before him. "If the scant records of the Cymrian War that were preserved in the library of Canrif are to be believed, part of the reason that Anwyn was not able to assail Gwylliam's stronghold for more than five hundred years was this instrumentality, and whatever powers it had. When she finally broached the mountains, the destruction of the instrumentality was her first objective. Such a powerful tool would aid in making the mountains secure."

Hot as the day was, a sudden chill swept over Rhapsody. "Do you not believe the mountains to be secure, Achmed?" she asked, concern darkening her green eyes. "Is there a threat that is unknown to the Alliance?"

The Firbolg king shrugged. "There are always threats, Rhapsody. There is no such thing as a lasting peace, only long pauses between episodes of war."

"Are you certain you and Anborn aren't related?" Rhapsody asked jokingly.

"If I were to be related to someone in your husband's odious family, I suppose he is the one I could endure with the least bad taste in my mouth. I respect his ability to not give a roasted rat's damn what anyone thinks of him. But as for your question, remember that I guard a mountain, and a Child who is the key to the Underworld for the F'dor. Even if we are at peace, I can never be overly prepared. The risk is far too great. And since you were named as the Earthchild's *amelystik,* you should be willing to do whatever it takes to tend to her as well, to assure her safety. Helping me in this regard will do that."

Rhapsody sighed, then carefully separated the top pages of the sheaf from the older, more delicate page at the bottom of the pile, handing them to Achmed as she studied the last one. It was thin and cracked with age, the paper crumbling at its edges. The markings on it were in a script she recognized immediately, being the language in which Lirin Singers trained to become Namers: Serenne, the tongue of the Ancient Seren race, the progenitors of her homeland.

"There is a poem, or frontispiece of a sort here," she said, studying the whisper-thin strokes of ink. "Serenne is based on musical script, and so it is somewhat hard to equate to spoken language."

"Your best effort should suffice," Achmed said impatiently.

"The poem is a sort of roundelay, a verse of a song, but the main lines read something like this:

*Seven Gifts of the Creator,*
*Seven colors of light*
*Seven seas in the wide world,*
*Seven days in a sennight,*
*Seven months of fallow*
*Seven continents trod, weave*

*Seven ages of history*
*In the eye of God.*

She turned the parchment slightly toward the light. "It's graphed like a musical scale, which, by the way, is another seven—seven distinct notes in an octave, the eighth note being the same as the first. It looks as if this is just a part of the poem; the rest is missing."

"Does it make any sense to you?" Achmed asked.

Rhapsody exhaled. "Not really, except that it is a list of significant sevens." Her brow furrowed. "One of them seems out of place—the Seven Gifts of the Creator. I had always heard the elements referred to as the Five Gifts, fire, water, earth, air, and ether, so I am not certain what that means."

"Can you read anything else?"

"There is a list of names beside the words for the different colors in the rainbow—shall I read them to you?"

"Yes."

She tucked a lock of hair behind her ear and bent closer to the parchment page.

"They are marked with the musical symbols for sharp and flat, almost like the signs for positive and negative, all but the last one.

> *Lisele-ut,* or red, Blood Saver, Blood Letter
> *Frith-re,* orange, Fire Starter, Fire Quencher
> *Merte-mi,* yellow, Light Bringer, Light Queller
> *Kurh-fa,* green, Grass Hider, Glade Scryer
> *Brige-sol,* blue, Cloud Chaser, Cloud Caller
> *Luasa-ela,* indigo, Night Stayer, Night Summoner
> *Grei-ti,* violet, The New Beginning.

When she looked up again, Rhapsody's face was pale.

"What have you found, Achmed?" she said nervously. "This is old magic, sacred and secret ancient lore; it worries me to see it out in the open like this. Only the most revered of Namers in the old world were allowed access to this sort of lore. These words are the basis of all vibrational code, which gives power to Singers' music, spell-weavers, healers, and others from the old land that could manipulate power through the vibrations of the living world."

Achmed said nothing. He made use of vibrational lore himself, in his elemental tie to blood, the tie that allowed him to track and distinguish heartbeats. It was a power that had made him an unerring assassin on the other side of Time.

"What are you going to do with this once you have reconstructed this instrumentality, Achmed?" Rhapsody asked, handing him back the parchment sheets with great care.

The Firbolg king smiled from behind his veils.

"The same thing you have asked me to do here in Yarim—make the lives of your subjects more secure."

"Why don't I believe that's the end of it?" Rhapsody said, rising from the ground and brushing the dry red clay from her gown.

"Because, your choice in husbands notwithstanding, you are not a fool. Now, come. I'm sure there is some stew or gruel left from dinner that you can have, so that you can properly thank Ihrman Karsrick for his hospitality when you return this evening."

## AT OPEN SEA

The seneschal's reeve spotted the continent even before the lookout in the crow's nest had opportunity to do so.

"Land, m'lord," Fergus called, lifting his voice to be heard over the gusting sea breeze.

The seneschal nodded, staring over the starboard bow to the dim gray at the horizon's edge.

"How much longer?" he asked the captain, his voice dry and crackling in the wet air.

"We have to skirt the coast, m'lord; there's a dangerous reef between that barriers the Lirin lands between Sorbold

and Avonderre. Five days to a week 'til Port Fallon, I would
hazard."

The seneschal nodded, struggling to keep the impatient
voice in his head at bay. He listened to the scream of the
wind, the snapping of the sails as they filled and slackened,
then filled again, bringing him, moment by moment, closer,
ever closer. He closed his eyes and let the sun beat down
on them from a cloudless sky.

*Soon.*

# 11

## TOWN SQUARE, YARIM PAAR

𝔒hrman Karsrick's efforts notwithstanding, when Achmed, Grunthor, and the Firbolg miners arrived in Yarim
Paar that evening, the square was teeming with townspeople.

A fourth contingent of soldiers from the Yarimese army
had been sent in to bolster the efforts of the three previously
assigned divisions; they ringed the town square around the
ancient obelisk and pushed the noisy horde back to the first
ring of streets, away from the dry central fountainbed in
which Entudenin stood. But word that the Bolg were coming
had spread like wildfire throughout the capital, so as the
afternoon waned to evening, more and more of the populace
of Yarim Paar continued to crowd the dusty roadways, hoping for a glance. By the time Tariz and the other escort
troops reached the city center, Yarim Paar was in a state of
barely controlled chaos, a carnival-like atmosphere of waving firebrands, shouting and curious merriment bordering on
pandemonium.

"Oh, lookee! A splendid buffet of fresh meat!" Grunthor
said, loud enough for the escort to hear him, pointing to the
clamoring throng. "Oi likes it when my dinner is 'appy,
makes the taste sweeter. That Karsrick sure knows 'ow ta

make a Bolg feel welcome and well fed. What an 'ost, eh, sir?"

Tariz, who rode at the fore, wheeled and stared at the giant Sergeant, then at the Bolg king.

"He's speaking in jest, I take it, Your Majesty?"

"Probably," Achmed replied. "Grunthor doesn't tend to like dry meat, and Yarim has been without water for so long that you all seem a bit on the stringy side."

"Too true," the Sergeant agreed with a comic sigh. "Give me a nice, fresh Lirin! Now, that's a juicy treat, moist an' tasty. But ya never know. Ain't too many Lirin around 'ere. Local cuisine might be just fine."

The escort troops looked at one another, then halted and dismounted quickly.

"Send an advance guard up the Marketway to the town square, meet up with the second division and bring back enough troops to open a corridor," Tariz ordered his soldiers. "Push the peasants back; try not to bloody the fools too badly."

Achmed's eyes narrowed in annoyance. His personal reasons for coming to Yarim, Rhapsody's assumptions of his altruism aside, had been to seek her assistance with translating the manuscripts and to find a stained-glass artisan who was a sealed master. In a city known for its tile manufacture, he reasoned, it was not impossible that one might be for hire. He had been assured by Omet that there were many masters from the old school, now scratching out their livings in more humble labors, longing for a return to the days when Yarim had supplied the ceramics, tile, and glass for the great cathedrals and buildings of state, back before the Cymrian War had put an end to all such things. With the swirling chaos filling the streets, however, it would be nearly impossible to find the opportunity to locate such an artisan.

He looked back over his shoulder at his own troops. The Bolg were standing at attention in their simple garb, which seemed grotesquely primitive by comparison with the red tunics, articulated leather armor, and horned helmets of the

Yarimese army. Every Firbolg face was set in a mask of stoicism, their eyes directly ahead, disregarding the uproar before them, but he could tell that they were unnerved by the wriggling mass of humanity crowding the streets, shouting and laughing and fighting for the chance to catch a glimpse of them.

①utside the enormous tents that surrounded Entudenin, Rhapsody was growing anxious.

"It's a spectacle gone mad," she said nervously to Ashe. "I am not certain they will be safe in the crowd, even with the guards. Right now the townspeople are just curious, but what if the atmosphere turns violent? If either group becomes more afraid than curious, there's no telling what could occur. If the citizens swarm them, the Bolg may panic, and they will be crushed."

Ashe nodded in agreement, then turned and pulled the tent flap open and went inside. He came back a moment later, a length of rope in his hand.

"Ihrman," he said to the duke, whose eyes were glazing in alarm, his skin mottled with sweat, "there is quite a bit of rope in this tent. Lash the lengths together—probably at least four street lengths here—and give it to the soldiers to demark a corridor through the city; open it right through the crowd, wide enough so the Bolg can pass comfortably. Position the soldiers inside the rope, and make the closest townspeople help them hold it. Beg the Firbolg king's pardon and indulgence; tell him we will have this problem cleared up in a few moments."

The duke signaled to his captain of the guard, who carried the Lord Cymrian's orders to the rest of the troops. Ashe turned to Rhapsody.

"Step back inside the tent, Aria. There will be a good deal of shifting and pushing for a moment, but it will settle into a controllable chaos shortly." He pulled the tent flap aside.

"What are you doing?"

"It's impossible to quell the curiosity that has been sparked by trying to hide the Bolg; they have become an irresistible attraction, thanks to Ihrman's bungling. But we can use it to our advantage." He turned to the captain of the guard unit that was forming a barrier between the dais on which they stood and the crowds. "Captain, summon your best hornsman."

A chain of shouted orders rippled over the building din, swallowed as it moved through the air. Within a few moments a trumpeter had appeared.

"M'lord."

"Hornsman, make ready," Ashe addressed the soldier. "Play a volley of welcome for a head of state."

As the hornsman prepared himself, Ashe turned to the Duke of Yarim again.

"Once the Bolg have come into the work tent, have the original contingent of soldiers continue to ring it, but keep adding as many as you can, gradually. If you gently insert a few troops here and there, the circle will expand slowly but resolutely, without necessitating any confrontation with overeager onlookers. Keep expanding the ring until the crowd is two street corners away from the work site. Then announce the times of the changing of each shift."

Karsrick's mouth dropped open. "Is that wise, m'lord? The townspeople will know when the Bolg are arriving and leaving, and will gather at those hours in these same unwieldy numbers."

"Yes," Ashe agreed, "and they will go back about their business during all the other hours. At first many of them will stay, hoping to catch a glimpse, but, being dissuaded that this will come to pass, they will settle for watching the changing of the guard. After a short time, even this will cease to be interesting to all but a few." He clapped Karsrick on the shoulder encouragingly. "Buck up, Ihrman; this is temporary, though Rhapsody was right when she told you if you had just treated them like guests, instead of like monsters that needed to be guarded, and guarded against, this would not be a problem. Had you done that, you would never have incited this level of curiosity in the first place."

"Yes, m'lord," Karsrick muttered.

"All right, hornsman, set to," Ashe instructed. "Play a lively tune that will make the Bolg feel welcome."

Peering through the tent flap, Rhapsody chuckled.

"I suggest a rousing instrumental of 'Leave No Limb Unbroken,'" she said. "Last I knew, that was their favorite march."

Once the roped corridor was opened in the sea of onlookers, and the townspeople themselves enlisted in holding the barrier lines, the Bolg were able to hurry quickly into the work site without incident.

When the flaps of the enormous tents had closed behind them, muting the noise of the rabble, and the soldiers established in a ring around it again, Achmed turned to the Lord and Lady Cymrian and the duke.

"Perhaps I misunderstood the invitation," he said angrily. "I was under the impression you were hiring us to work on your dried-out shell of a geyser, in the hope that bringing our skills to bear on it might rescue your withering province from dying of thirst. Had I known you were recruiting for your menagerie, or a traveling circus, I would have remained in Ylorc and left you to shrivel in the heat. There are far more interesting freaks among your own subjects, Karsrick; you certainly don't need our help to fill your sideshow."

"My deepest apologies, Your Majesty," the duke said, bowing from the waist and struggling to appear sufficiently contrite. "We could not have foreseen the interest that the townspeople of Yarim Paar would have in the arrival of their—neighbors from the southeast. Please forgive the rudeness of our welcome; it was not intended. Tell me what I can do to make it up to you."

The Firbolg king's expression shifted slightly in the flickering shadows from the torches outside the tent, the light changing in his mismatched eyes. He lingered for a long, uncomfortable moment in silence before the duke; then finally, when he spoke, his voice was calm.

"You can find me a stained-glass artisan, a sealed master, who is willing to be hired at an extremely generous rate to work on a project in Ylorc." He turned away from the duke as he took a few steps toward the Bolg assemblage, then looked back over his shoulder. "No ninnies. I've had enough of those today."

The Duke of Yarim exhaled, looking doubtful. "I will put the word out to the guilds, sire, though I can't guarantee an artisan will come forward."

Achmed walked over to Grunthor. "How do you want to proceed?" he asked the Sergeant.

The giant Bolg considered for a moment. "Clear the tent o' all unnecessaries, and let me examine the dry wellspring."

Achmed walked back to the royal couple and the duke. "Get everyone out of here," he said curtly, "except for yourselves."

Ashe nodded, overriding the protest that was bubbling on the duke's lips. He turned to the Yarimese soldiers gathered under the tent.

"Out, gentlemen. Thank you."

As the Bolg Sergeant came forward and stood before the obelisk, it was as if the rest of the people standing beneath the strung canvas in the town square faded into the gray darkness of oblivion, leaving only himself and Entudenin, alone together in the universe.

Even in its state of decay and petrification, the geyser was, like himself, a child of the Earth, one born of fire, the other of water, both unique creations that had known the magic of the Mother's touch.

As he walked around it in wonder, the first thing he felt was an overwhelming sense of loss. How beautiful it must have been in its living time, a towering pillar twice as tall as he was, arched at the top in an angle that jutted westward in the direction of the setting sun, beckoning to the wide ocean a thousand miles away. He could almost see how it was formed, and must have once looked, layer upon layer of multicolored rings and stripes in rich hues of vermilion and rose, deep russet, sulfurous yellow and aquamarine, mineral deposits that grew ever taller with the passage of time, until their height surpassed anything on the flat dry prairie of clay for as far as the eye could see.

Now the obelisk stood, lifeless but unbowed, shriveled and covered in a baked red clay, like the rest of Yarim.

Grunthor stepped over the broken stones of the fountain-bed at its base and approached it slowly, almost reverently, wondering what could have happened to cause such a vibrant, growing source of life-giving water in the middle of the cold desert to suddenly cease, then fade this way. He put out a hand to touch its shrunken flesh.

Beneath the tips of his fingers, the desiccated clay felt surprisingly warm and supple. Grunthor blinked; his eyes told him that the geyser was dead, its once-moist clay now hard and inflexible, but a deeper part of him, the place where he and the Earth were indissolubly bonded, was taking over his sight, his senses.

From deep within the ground he could hear the voice of the Earth, the slow, melodious song that had first crept into his unconsciousness, permeating ever fiber of his being, when he, Achmed, and Rhapsody were crawling in the depths of the world, pulling themselves along the spidery roots of Sagia, the World Tree, fleeing from their hunters to this new, strange land. The song wound around his heart, whispered invisibly in his ear, and it told him the tale of Entudenin.

The song recounted the birth of the region known as Yarim in the language of men, a place forgotten by the trade winds, in the shadow of the mountain, at the base of the glacier, on the continental divide, where the ground was barren but the earth held riches, deep and hidden. Ore of copper and manganese, iron and rysin, the blue metal so beloved of the Bolg in the making of steel, healing mineral springs, opals and precious salt all were concealed beneath the thick red clay, but with no regular prevailing sea winds, no cool gusts from the mountains, the ground hardened stubbornly, refusing to give up its bounty easily.

Grunthor stood, rapt, transfixed, the tale forming images he could see inside his mind, as the song grew more melodious, more fluid. The tale changed to the story of the Erim Rus, the Blood River, a muddy red watercourse stained by the slough of the manganese-red mountains. The Erim Rus had eventually met up with a tributary of the mighty Tar'afel, and their marriage had formed a beautiful oasis at the riverhead. From that marriage Entudenin had been born.

The Tar'afel, like any great river that bisected a continent, had a network of underground tributaries that scored its riverbed and the floodplain that surrounded it, some reaching for many miles from the actual banks of the river. One of these veins was particularly fortunate in its placement; it connected, in the vast, spidery network of subterranean springs that form a watershed, to a strong line fed directly from the sea, through a volcanic cave in the northern coastline of the icy Hintervold. That cave was pocketed in the rockwall at the exact place where the Northern Sea met the open ocean, producing an immensely strong crosscurrent that backwashed for a thousand miles.

This backwash was the lifeline of Entudenin.

Along the way east the seawater traveled through the glacial fields of the Hintervold, where it was sweetened by icy drainage and deprived of some of its salt; it passed beneath the verdant fields of Canderre, through the peat bogs and rich loam that gave that province its bounty, until it finally reached the sandy, mineral-laden red clay of Yarim, where it decided to stop—that decision forced by the deep, heavy layers of all but impenetrable clay and bedrock that had been left over from the formation of the mountains to the east. Filtered by ice, sand, and time, and ramming up against the underground barrier, the water, now sweet, had nowhere to go but up.

And up it went.

At its birth, Entudenin had been little more than a puddle, emerging with a gurgle, then spreading out with a great muddy burp. Had there been any human eye around to witness its arrival, it might have gone unnoticed entirely, but the region would not be inhabited for several thousand years. It was not a monumental beginning, but it was an important one; the seal of the earth over the water had been broken.

From then on it was merely a matter of the passing of time and the tides of the ocean, dictated by the phases of the moon. When the sea current was at rest, Entudenin rested as well, its water source withering to a trickle that pooled beneath the fields of Canderre, never traveling into the region of red clay at all. But when the tide turned, and the moon was at the height of its strength, the seawater poured in violently, racing along its course until it erupted in a joyful shout from the evolving geyser, spraying glistening drops into the air to mingle with the sunlight. As this continued over the millennia, the minerals that remained around its mouth began to grow thick and harden, forced upward by pressure, until the obelisk that had been Entudenin in its glory had risen, tall beneath the countless stars of the endless desert sky, reaching toward the moon.

That obelisk, formed of sea and earth, well traveled from many places, containing precious minerals and ores, salt, ice, and time, took on a life of sorts, a child of pure Earth, a wonder of the world; sweet water in the middle of a vast, dry land. The glistening mica that scored its walls, glittering back at the stars, was a silent sign of the magic that it held.

And so it had remained for thousands of years more. Eventually this life-giving wellspring was discovered by man and put to use, almost worshipped, tended by priestesses of the Shanouin tribe, an extended family of humans who had a Mythlin ancestor. Mythlin were one of the five ancient races, formed at the beginning of time, from the element of Water; thus the Shanouin had talents for divining it even beneath the desert sand. They were talented well-diggers, and it was assumed that they would be the appropriate guardians of Entudenin.

The Shanouin managed the cycle of the Fountain Rock, as Entudenin became known in the language of Yarim. They kept those who longed to harvest the water away for a full day after its cyclical Awakening, when, with a deep rumble and a glad shout, the backwash roared forth with enough force to break a man's back. The Shanouin maintained control as the water was gathered during the Sennight, or Week, of Plenty, that followed the Awakening, where the flow was abundant; then through the Sennight of Rest, when the copious spray settled into a smooth, bubbling stream. As the current turned fallow in the sea, the water of Entudenin would subside into a quiet trickle, known as the Sennight of Loss. During that week, only those with grave illness in their households or the elderly and frail were allowed to collect from the wellspring. Finally, as the moon went new, Entudenin slipped into the Sennight of Slumber, when it slept, waiting for the moon to shine again and turn the tide.

And so it went on, year after year, to century and millennium, until the day of the Shifting.

Grunthor's head snapped back at the change in the voice of the Earth. The song it had been weaving was a lilting roundelay that had come to lull him into a sense of peace; now, with a sudden jolt, the melody changed, screamed into a searing crescendo, then stopped altogether. Beneath the images in his mind, the voice of the Earth whispered sadly.

Miles to the west of Entudenin, at the border of Canderre, was one of the great opal fields of Yarim, Zbekaglou, whose name in the language of the indigenous people of the continent meant Rainbow's End, or "where the skycolors touch the earth." Zbekaglou had been scoured for centuries for its treasures, the earth rent in great delves and mined of its soft, colorful gems, then left empty, open. Where the earth had been mined, the ground was instable, even below the water table. A strong vibration, a normal occurrence in the heartbeat of the earth, had shaken loose a landfall of the disturbed clay beneath the ground, plugging the watercourse completely.

Since this happened in the middle of the Week of Slumber, the water merely never returned. Entudenin went dry, overnight, never to shout with the joy of the Awakening again.

While Rhapsody had told Grunthor the lore of the humans of Yarim, and how the people had reacted with horror, then blame, then finally resignation to the loss, allowing their jewel of a city to wither in the heat, but going on with life, the Earth told him in quiet tones the end of the tale of what had happened to Entudenin.

It was a slow, painful death.

Like the great Trees of the Earth, or vast canyons carved over time by rivers, or the pounding sea itself, or any of the other places where elemental earthen magic is embodied, Entudenin had a soul of sorts. In its time it had been a vibrant entity, a natural formation with almost human moods, roaring with joy at the Awakening, laughing happily as the water flowed copiously, filling the vessels, the fountains, the canals of Yarim Paar. Sinking into sober reflection at the Sennight of Loss, contemplating the mortality of the world. Silent in its slumber, to awaken again, beginning the wondrous cycle all over, never tiring of it.

The beautiful obelisk, deprived of the gift of water, at first experienced a sense of what in human terms might have been bewilderment. It could hear the prayers of the humans that had tended it, feel their vibrations, even though it could not comprehend them, but their desperation translated, transcending the differences in consciousness, and that desperation became its own. As time passed, and the water did not return, the Fountain Rock yearned for salvation, prayed in supplication in its own way to its Mother, but the Earth could not undo what man had caused.

Finally, in sorrow, the obelisk succumbed to the inevitable. It continued to stand beneath the sun, feeling the moisture leach out of it more and more as each day, year, and century passed, baking from the outside, withering. It lost some of its height, a good deal of its girth, and all of its myriad colors, passing from the beauty of a child to the ugliness of a crone over time. As each drop evaporated beneath Yarim's blistering heat, Entudenin mourned.

But it refused to crumble.

Stalwartly, what tiny remains of soul had been embodied in the Fountain Rock held fast, standing tall beneath the stars, the mica that remained in its surface still gleaming in their light on occasion.

Grunthor's head swam, then snapped back again at the abrupt end of the Earth's song.

When the voice went mute, his stomach turned; he felt the connection to the warmth that had been coursing through his veins, winding its way through the chambers of his massive heart, shatter suddenly. It was an internal blow so strong that it buckled his knees. He fell to the ground, his hands on the earth, searching unconsciously to reestablish the connection, but the Earth had gone silent.

A moment later he felt hands on both his shoulders; he waved them away, fighting the nausea that had rushed into his mouth, swallowing to choke it down again. He sat back with effort and waited for his head to clear.

When finally it did, his amber eyes blurry as the vision righted itself to the world around him, away from the pictures that accompanied the Earth's song, he looked up to see Rhapsody and Achmed standing over him, Ashe at Rhapsody's side. The Bolg in the tent were whispering among themselves with fear at the sight of their felled Sergeant-Major.

Again he waved away Achmed's hand, and rose, unsteady for a moment, inhaling deeply through his great nostrils. After a moment he turned to the king and nodded once. An intricate view of the inner pathways of the obelisk and its feeder lines was etched in his brain.

"Right. 'Ere's the plan: we take off that angled arm—it's withered to the point o' being solid anyway, and it's too fragile to withstand the bit."

"Take off the arm?" Ihrman Karsrick interjected nervously. "You can't do that—it's a holy relic."

"It's a holy relic that doesn't function," said Achmed, his back to Karsrick while he continued to watch Grunthor, who had lapsed into silence at the higher-ranking official's interruption. "Do you want to maintain a dead decoration, or do you want water?"

The duke thought for a moment, then put his hand on the Bolg king's shoulder. "Can you guarantee that the water will flow if I allow you to remove the Obelisk's arm?" he asked hesitantly.

"No, but I can guarantee that blood will if I remove yours," the Bolg king replied, staring at Karsrick's hand.

"Achmed," Rhapsody chided. "Some courtesy, please."

The Bolg king exhaled as the duke quickly withdrew his hand. "I can guarantee very little in life, Karsrick. The return of the water is not something I can warrant. But I can guarantee that if you do nothing, the water will not return. If he says the arm must be removed, then it must be. Now kindly be silent and allow us to hear the rest of his directions."

The duke cleared his throat and nodded at Grunthor.

"We'll drill out the obelisk itself, and the first thirty yards below it," the Sergeant said, wiping the sweat from his wide forehead, his skin having returned to its normal hue, the color of old bruises. "That'll get 'er ready to withstand the return of the water, if it comes. Right now she'd shatter." He glanced up at the dry red geyser. "The pathway beyond that is clear; the real blockage is farther away, almost to the border of Canderre. That's somethin' Oi can 'andle myself, sir; no point in draggin' the men there. Once they finish 'ere, you can take 'em back to Ylorc and Oi'll ride out to the border, clear the blockage, an' then come on 'ome."

"Will you need any of the equipment?" Achmed asked.

The giant grinned broadly, then fumbled in his pack for

a moment. He produced a small hand spade, battered and worn, and held it up for Rhapsody to see as well. It was Digga, the retrenching tool he had used to dig the three of them free from the Earth after their journey through its belly four years before. Rhapsody laughed.

"This is all Oi'll need, sir," he said.

"All right," Achmed agreed. He turned to the assembled Bolg craftsmen. "Unpack the rest of the equipment and we'll set to work."

Outside the tents the ring of Yarimese guards was slowly, subtly growing larger. The ever-expanding ring had pushed the crowd gently but resolutely back to two street corners away from the town square, where the flickering torches that lighted the tent from the outside did not reveal the movements of the shadows within.

At the edge of the rope, Esten waited, struggling with the throng of townspeople to get closer, to catch a glimpse of what was happening. She was preparing to leave, having seen nothing, when Dranth touched her elbow and shook his head, indicating that thus far none of her spies had managed to broach the work site either. Esten inhaled deeply, then pushed her way through the crowd to the empty streets beyond.

"I have no patience in this matter," she said to the guild scion. "Karsrick is benefiting from all the work I undertook before the disaster; if the Bolg restore Entudenin, he will have the water that should have belonged to me. Why has no one gotten inside? The guards have always been easy to bribe or threaten."

"The Yarimese guards, yes, mistress," Dranth replied darkly. "But the Bolg are standing guard as well; their king brought his own security detail with him, and they are steadfast and thus far unapproachable."

The guildmistress's black eyes glistened angrily.

"I want to know what is going on in that tent," she said

in a low, deadly voice. "And I need to have someone get
inside, to prevent the theft of my water. Before night falls
tomorrow, it will be done, or blood will spill like the water
from Entudenin."

# 12

Within three days, Ashe's prediction had come to pass.
The Bolg followed a regular schedule of workshifts, labor-
ing silently in the heat beneath the tents that surrounded the
work site, and the villagers of Yarim Paar settled for watching them enter and leave the tents and the city as their ro-
tations changed, from the boundary two street lengths away.

The throngs that had gathered during the first days began
to grow sparse, and while there was still considerable interest in the primitive men whom the Lady Cymrian had said
were Entudenin's hope for resurrection, the majority of the
town returned to its work and its daily routine, occasionally
happening by the square at the appointed hours to see the
Bolg hurry out of the tents to their waiting escorts. No in-
teraction was allowed, and since the Bolg never initiated
any, or showed any interest in meeting or touching any of
the citizens of Yarim Paar, it became unconsciously clear to
the townspeople that the Firbolg were being protected from
them, and not the other way around, which changed the
mood from resentful and fearful curiosity to that of embarrassed interest.

The linen tents, bleached white as snow at the onset of
the project, rapidly took on a brownish-red cast from the
clay dust spattered into the air by the drilling. Great beams
of wood were brought in on the Bolg's supply wagons,
lashed together in articulated sections that were driven into
the ground by massive apparatuses of tampers and gears,
sophisticated machines designed centuries before by Gwylliam and used to hollow out the passageways of Canrif. The
townspeople of Yarim Paar, accustomed only to the well-

digging practices of the Shanouin, marveled at the sights and sounds of the tools that the Bolg were making use of, though most of the smaller equipment was kept from their sight, like the craftsmen themselves.

The disembodied arm of Entudenin was removed first, and, in a quiet ceremony, brought into the Judiciary's main rotunda beneath the palace's famous minarets. There it was put on display, because Yarim had no elemental temple, its people worshipping under the auspices of the Blesser of Canderre-Yarim, Ian Steward, who held services in the Basilica of Fire in Bethany a hundred leagues away. The first day it was available to be viewed by the public, more than four thousand people came to reverently observe it, ten times the number that had paid their respects when the body of Ihrman Karsrick's father had been lying in state in the same rotunda many years before.

Ashe watched the crowds filing into the rotunda from the balcony of their tower guest chambers west of the central palace, chuckling at the look on Rhapsody's face.

"What is it now, my love?" he asked teasingly. "You seem amazed."

"I *am* amazed," Rhapsody said, staring over the railing at the snaking line that stretched down the streets, almost to the central Marketway. "That bloody thing stood in the center of their town for hundreds of years, ignored and unnoticed. Virtually every merchant, every tradesman who had business in the center of the city, walked by it every day, and no one paid it a bit of attention except a few pilgrims and a little boy I once saw stop there to relieve himself. And now it is a holy relic of vast interest to the same people who were oblivious to it three days ago. It *is* amazing."

Ashe put his arms around her. "Indeed. Well, do you suppose I might be able to draw your interest away from this amazing sight for a while?"

"By all means," she said, smiling. "What do you have in mind?"

"I thought we might go out into the city in disguise—you

could put on a ghodin and I can wear a hooded veil like the Shanouin well-diggers or some other pilgrim."

His wife laughed in delight. "Back to the days of hiding your face, are we? Well, I did wear a ghodin the last time I was here with Achmed, so that I would not be recognized. There are not too many yellow heads in Yarim; I would have been a curiosity, and since we were here to snatch the slave boys from the tile foundry, that would not have been a good thing. I can wear one again; all that flowing white linen keeps the heat out. So where would we go? It might be a good time to shop the market; all the townspeople are in the Judiciary, bowing to a dead rock formation. The crowds shouldn't be too pressing."

"Not quite what I had in mind."

"Oh?"

"I thought we might make a visit to Manwyn's temple."

The laughter in Rhapsody's eyes resolved to a clear, sober expression.

"Are you certain you want to do that, Sam?" she asked gently.

"Yes," he answered, taking her hand and leading her back into the tower chambers. "Let us obtain the answers to our questions, knowing we may only get some insane babble, and then we can make an afternoon of it. We can take noon-meal in a tavern or over one of those open-street firepits, and then find something quaint in the market to bring home for Gwydion and Melly."

Rhapsody made a deep reverence before her husband. "Lead on, m'lord."

𝔐anwyn's temple stood at the western edge of the city, the centerpiece of a section that had been a thriving water garden in the time when Entudenin still brought forth her liquid gifts, now all but deserted. Deep, dry depressions that had once been immense pools lined the decaying streets, along which broken statuary of sea nymphs poured empty vessels into dusty fountains.

The temple itself was, like Yarim Paar itself, large, majestically built, but decaying from neglect. Formed of marble which must have been magnificent in its time, the Temple of the Oracle was composed of a central building with two annex wings sprawling at the end of the main thoroughfare, crumbling in places. Cracked marble steps led up to a wide, inlaid patio, where eight huge columns stood on the unevenly paved surface, marred by expanding patches of lichen.

The central building was a large rotunda topped with a circular dome in which two large cracks could be seen. A tall, thin minaret crowned this central building, shining like a beacon in the sun.

Rhapsody stopped at the base of the grand staircase.

"Are you *certain* you want to do this?" she asked Ashe again. "It was very strange the last time the two of you saw each other here; I don't want to repeat that, if possible."

"You do not enjoy being in the center of a battle of dragon will in a moth-eaten temple?" Ashe replied, looking into her green eyes, the only part of her visible beneath the ghodin. "Teetering on the brink of her yawning well as the ground shakes, dodging falling pieces of the firmament of the dome?"

"That would be accurate, yes."

"I will do my best to behave," he promised. "Come, Aria."

Rhapsody's green eyes glittered nervously. "Do you remember the wording we planned?"

Ashe caressed her hand reassuringly. "Yes. Come."

They climbed the great stair and passed through the large open portal that served as the entrance. The inside of the temple was dark, lit only by dim torches and candles, keeping the entranceway in a perennial state of half-light.

The interior of the temple, unlike its edifice, was well maintained. In the center of the vast room a large fountain blasted a thin stream of water twenty feet into the air, where it splashed down into a pool lined with shimmering lapis lazuli. The floor was polished marble, the walls adorned with intricately decorated tile, the sconces shining brass.

To either side of this room were small antechambers where Manwyn's guards stood, wearing the horned helmets traditional in Yarim and armed with long, thin swords. A large door of intricately carved cedar stood across from them, behind the fountain and its pool, also guarded.

Rhapsody stopped again suddenly and grasped Ashe by the arm.

"Oh! Wait! Remember the last time we came here for a prophecy, Manwyn was very angry because you were hiding your face. Perhaps it is best to remove the ghodin and the veils now; I don't want to provoke her again."

"Very well; we will as soon as we are inside."

Ashe pried her fingers loose from his forearm, took her hand again, and led her around the fountain, stopping before the guards of the great door.

"Ten gold crowns to see the Oracle, for the Seer's sustenance," the man said rotely.

Ashe reached into his coin purse and drew forth the amount the guard had demanded.

"If this is really being used for the maintenance of the Oracle, I expect that she will have a new gown since the last time we saw her," he said, dropping the coins into the offering box. "She looked thin and in a fair bit of disarray, though I see that *you* are well turned out and of a healthy girth, soldier. But I'm certain that you would never usurp any of the alms given to the Oracle for yourselves, now, would you?"

The guard spat on the floor and opened the beautiful cedar door, motioning them angrily inside.

"You are doing an *excellent* job of behaving already," Rhapsody said dryly as they entered the Inner Sanctum.

"I'm a dragon. It's my job to annoy people."

"I see that."

"Well, if we are to reveal our faces in the attempt not to disturb Manwyn, we had best do it now." Ashe pulled the veil from his face, then gently took down the head veil of her ghodin. He blinked; Rhapsody's face was almost as pale as the white robe she was wearing, ghostly in the glow of the candleflames around them.

"Aria? Are you all right?"

She nodded wordlessly.

Ashe took her hand; it was cold and trembling slightly.

"Rhapsody, if you don't want to do this, we can leave now, without a second thought."

She shook her head, though her grip tightened slightly.

"It's just all coming back to me now," she said nervously. "I had forgotten how intimidating a place this is. Manwyn frightens me."

"Then let's go back to the bazaar." Ashe turned and curled his knuckles to rap on the cedar door, but Rhapsody stopped him.

"No. We have to hear what she has to say, have to ask her about her last prophecy, or else something that should be a wonderful, exciting event in our lives will only bring worry and fear," she said. "I am sorry I am being such a coward. Let's go in."

Ashe squeezed her hand, and together they went deeper into the Inner Sanctum.

The room beyond the cedar door was immense, illuminated by a series of small windows in the dome of the rotunda and countless candles. In the center of the room was a dais which was suspended precariously above a large, open well, sideless, flush with the floor.

Manwyn sat, as she always did when in her temple, in the center of the suspended dais. She was tall and thin with rosy gold skin and fiery red hair streaked with silver. Her face bore the lines of middle age. In her left hand she held an ornate sextant, and she was dressed, as Ashe had expected, in a ragged gown of green silk, once a magnificent garment, now frayed and worn with age.

The Seer of the Future had eyes that were perfect mirrors, with no pupil, iris, or sclera to delineate them. The first time

Rhapsody had beheld her, it had almost felt as if she were drowning in those eyes, deep, reflective pools of quicksilver that gazed only beyond the present, into the realm of what had not yet come to be.

She had learned, over time, how dangerous it was to the conscious mind to meet the gaze of a dragon or its kin. So she lowered her eyes respectfully and waited for the Seer to address them.

At first Manwyn ignored them altogether. Her long fingers were engaged in spinning the wheel of the sextant, which she did while humming a tuneless melody to herself. The lord and lady stood silent while she played, glancing occasionally at each other but saying nothing.

Suddenly, as if she had caught the scent of fire in the wind, Manwyn lurched upright, sniffing the air. Her liquid silver eyes darted wildly around the circular room, finally settling on them. She rose up slightly on her knees and pointed to the great dark hole that yawned raggedly in the floor.

"Gaze into the well," she commanded in the same harsh voice Rhapsody had heard the last time she had been here, a raspy croak that scratched at the edges of Rhapsody's skull.

Against her will she began to tremble again; Manwyn had attended the first Cymrian Council and their wedding, and had not been intimidating or frightening at all, merely detached and confused. But here within her temple, she was terrifying, smiling with a confidence that bordered on cruel amusement.

"May the All-God give thee good day, my great-nephew and his lady-wife," the prophetess said, bowing deeply and saluting them with the traditional address of the Island of Serendair. "And indeed, He shall; it shall be a very interesting day for you."

"Thank you, Aunt," Ashe replied, returning her bow. "I hope that's not the extent of our prophecy. I paid generously at the door."

The Seer chuckled. "You will always be my favorite great-nephew, Gwydion of Manosse. And your lovely bride; she is quite a hat in your feather. Hat and feather, hat and feather!" She giggled, grinning broadly.

Rhapsody bowed in greeting, glancing askance at Ashe, who shrugged.

"Speak, then, your question," Manwyn commanded, her solemn expression returning.

The Lord and Lady Cymrian exchanged a glance, remembering what they had planned to say.

"I seek a clarification of two conflicting prophecies you gave to us a few years ago," Ashe said.

Confusion passed like a cloud over the Seer's face. "Prophecies?"

"Yes," Rhapsody said quickly. "To me you said, 'I see an unnatural child born of an unnatural act. Rhapsody, you should beware of childbirth: the mother shall die, but the child shall live.'"

"And yet to me, her husband, you declared, 'Gwydion ap Llauron, thy mother died in giving birth to thee, but thy children's mother shall not die giving birth to them,'" Ashe added. "We seek to know what you meant, Aunt."

The confusion on Manwyn's face deepened to bewilderment. She ran a hand over her head through the tangle of matted snarls that was her hair, pulling at it nervously as a child, then shook her head briskly.

"You ask of the Past," she said petulantly. "I will never be able to see the Past. I know nothing of what you speak."

Rhapsody's throat constricted. "Of course she wouldn't," she whispered to Ashe. "How stupid of me to phrase the question like that."

The nervous confusion cleared in an instant from the Seer's reflective eyes; her back straightened, and she turned in Rhapsody's direction slowly, like a predator stalking its prey. She slid down onto her belly, causing the suspended dais to swing crazily over the well, and fixed her silver gaze on the Lady Cymrian.

"One should beware the Past, lady," she said in a grim voice, though she was smiling. "The Past can be a relentless hunter, a stalwart protector, a vengeful adversary. It seeks to have you; it seeks to aid you." She moved forward even more, her upper body suspended over the well, and whispered, "It seeks to destroy you." She sat back, pleased with the sight of Rhapsody's pale face, and twirled her fingers through her knotted hair. "Just as the Future continually seeks to destroy me."

"Answer this," Ashe commanded, disturbed by the look in the Seer's eyes that was bringing fear into Rhapsody's. "If Rhapsody and I conceive a child, will she or the baby come to any harm of it? I seek a direct answer, Manwyn. I tire of the game."

The Seer stared at him for a moment, as if stunned, then calmly pointed the sextant at the firmament of the cracked domed ceiling above her and peered into it. Rhapsody huddled closer to Ashe as a dark wind rose from the well in the floor; the thousands of candleflames dimmed suddenly, blackening the room. Above their heads, the dome had faded into a night sky, dotted with stars between which ephemeral clouds passed, unhurried. A cold breeze rippled across their backs, snapping the fabric of the ghodin like a sail on the high sea.

Finally, after what seemed an eternity, Manwyn lowered the instrument from her eye and turned her gaze back to Ashe, her face sober. She held the golden sextant aloft, the navigator's tool that guided his great-grandfather, her father, Merithyn the Explorer, across the sea to the shores of the dragon Elynsynos. Ashe understood the gesture; she was reminding him that she was born of that union, as was he, even if consciously she could not see the Past in which it happened, a commonality of dragon blood and ancient lore that was both their bane and blessing.

"You will always fear your own blood, Gwydion," she said calmly, her voice absent of any wildness. "You need not. Your wife will not die in bearing your children."

Ashe pointed at her accusingly. "Rhapsody," he said sternly. "Say that *Rhapsody* will not die."

"Rhapsody will not die in bearing your children."

"Nor become injured or infirm by it? Don't hedge your answer, Aunt."

Manwyn shrugged. "The pregnancy will not be easy, but it will not kill or harm her. No."

Ashe inhaled, gauging the new clarity with which she spoke. "Swear it to me, Manwyn, as your great-nephew, and as your lord. I want your oath; swear to me, descendant of our common ancestors, Lord Cymrian, duly invested, to whom you swore allegiance, that you are *utterly certain* that my blood will not cause this woman who stands before you harm in the bearing of our children."

"It will not," the Seer said patiently. "I swear it."

Ashe exhaled, watching her carefully. "Thank you, Aunt."

"You are most welcome, m'lord," the Seer said, bowing respectfully.

"Anything else you wish to impart us of the Future before we go?" Ashe asked as Rhapsody began to pull the hood of the ghodin over her head again.

Manwyn considered his question, her curled fist tucked beneath her chin, a finger resting on her cheek.

"The Pot and Kettle will be serving an excellent spiced lamb at the noonmeal," she said pleasantly. "And today the fletcher will have some wonderful arrows, sparred in feathers dropped from an albatross in Kesel Tai; they will bring your ward luck in his bowmanship."

"Thank you." Ashe pulled up his own veil. "God give thee a good afternoon, and a peaceful night." He took Rhapsody's hand and started to lead her away.

"Gaze into the well before you go," Manwyn said, her voice soft.

The two exchanged a glance, then Ashe nodded and released his wife's hand, turning to approach the well.

"Not you, m'lord," Manwyn chided. "The lady."

"Do you wish to, Aria?" Ashe asked, running his thumb

over her knuckles. "We can leave right away if you wish."

"That might offend her; I don't wish to do that," Rhapsody said quickly. She turned and walked carefully across the dark floor, taking care to stay as far from the cracks in the jagged opening as possible.

When she reached the well, she peered hesitantly over the edge into the endless darkness below, where once she had seen the poor Lirin mother who had fulfilled Manwyn's childbirth prophecy. A soft howl, the whine of the wind, ululated and echoed deep within the black pit in a discordant wail, but nothing more. She stared, trying to see whatever it was the Oracle was trying to show her, but all she could make out was blackness.

"I see nothing," she said finally.

The prophetess smiled widely, her silver eyes gleaming with wicked light once again. "No? Pity. I suppose there are no more divinations coming to you today." She slid down on her stomach again, her chin resting on her hands, and cocked her head to one side.

"Such it is with all those unlike yourself, who are not prescient," she said, a tinge of haughtiness entering her voice, "who are not Singers, who are not blessed with dreams of the Future—in short, the rest of the world, lady. Who walk the earth, go about their lives, never having any warning of what is coming for them." She began to giggle again; the mirth increased rapidly, until she was shrieking with laughter.

"Rhapsody—come now." Ashe's voice had the tone of a king, a quiet command that sliced through the madness and beckoned unwaveringly. Rhapsody shook her head to clear it, then turned away from the well and hurried back to him, taking his hand and walking rapidly toward the cedar door.

Behind them Manwyn began to call loudly.

Long ago a promise made,
Long ago a name conveyed,

Long ago a voice was stayed—
Three debts to be paid.

Against her will Rhapsody stopped and turned around. The Seer was not looking in their direction, but was dancing on the suspended dais, clutching the wires that tethered it to the domed ceiling, swinging crazily over the pit.

Manwyn began muttering madly. "Betrayed! Aid! Delayed! Your eyes—the color of jade!" Then her gaze locked on to Rhapsody's, and a broad smile wreathed her face.

"Afraid?" she asked solicitously.

Rhapsody straightened her shoulders angrily, annoyed with the game.

"No," she shouted back across the dark room. "No, Manwyn, I'm not afraid, not of the Past, nor of the Future, nor of your senseless babble. I will live happily in the Present, thank you very much, a place you should consider visiting sometime. But thank you for the lunch recommendation. If it produces a satisfying belch I shall dedicate it to you. But since it will be in the Past, you won't know it." She turned and stormed out through the cedar door, Ashe close behind her, struggling to keep his laughter in check.

"Well, Aria," he said, wiping back a tear, "you are doing an *excellent* job of behaving as well. Come; that lamb sounded tempting, and I would pay an immense sum to watch you belch."

Plaiting

# 13

## INSIDE GURGUS, YLORC

Almost ready, Rhur?"

The Bolg artisan nodded his agreement, followed a moment later by Shaene.

"Ready, Sandy," the Canderian artisan said.

Omet took a deep breath, then grasped the newly assembled wheel, forged from steel and inlaid with clear glass wedges. The others took hold as well and lifted, groaning under the strain.

Carefully they guided the wheel over to the wall where metal piping was attached in a semicircular track beneath the open dome of the tower above them. The beveled edges of the wheel, after a few moments of maneuvering, aligned with the metal track; once they had it in place, the wheel hung, suspended at an angle, above the floor of the tower. The artisans carefully stepped back to survey their work.

"All right, Sandy, it's up. Now what does it do?" Shaene asked, panting and wiping the sweat from his forehead.

Omet shrugged, ignoring innately Shaene's joking reference to the sands of Yarim from which he had come, feeling winded himself. "Don't know. I think it is some kind of healing device. Once the stained glass in the ceiling is in place, the plans seem to indicate that the wheel works with the colored light shining through the ceiling. Purely speculative on my part, however; I can't read the language of the plans. If you want to know more you'll have to ask the king when he returns. But at least we know we followed the plans correctly."

"And no easy feat it was, either, since much of 'em's missing," Shaene hastened to add.

"Too true. All right, let's take it down, wrap it in the oilcloth, and lock it in the storage room before something happens to it," Omet said, brushing his hands on his breeches. "This is the only part of the project that has worked so far; we shouldn't risk compromising that."

"Right," Shaene agreed. He grasped the top of the wheel a moment before Omet and Rhur were in position to do so. His sweaty palm slid off the cool metal, jostling it and setting it, inadvertently, into motion.

With a scream of metal the wheel spun quickly across the track, following it around the mountaintop tower for several yards while the artisans, shouting and cursing, ran after it. As it rolled it caught the sunlight shining above the mountaintop, and cast bright, quick patches on the floor of the tower that sparkled in elaborate patterns for an instant, then vanished.

Once they had regained control of the wheel, the three artisans stared at the floor in silent unison.

"What was *that*?" Shaene asked when he recovered his voice.

Omet shook his head. "I don't know."

"It must do *something*," Shaene insisted. "Seems like an awful lot of trouble to go through for a moment of pretty amusement."

"Well, it does do something," Omet said, taking hold of it again. "It goes into storage. Come on, now, help me take it off the track." He looked up to the open tower ceiling, where sunlight glinted off the metal framework on which the stained glass was expected to go, then looked back at Rhur and Shaene.

"And whatever you do, don't tell anyone about it."

## THE WORK SITE, YARIM PAAR

Grunthor raised a hand for the drilling to stop, wiping the sweat from his massive brow as the relentless thundering of the gears and the pounding of the bit slowed to a dull cadence, then ceased.

He watched the men for a moment, all dripping with similar perspiration, their normally dusky skin pale and sallow in the heat. Accustomed to the cool depths of the Earth, already two Firbolg artisans and a soldier had succumbed and were being tended inside the Judiciary.

"This is ridic'lus," the Sergeant muttered. "We've run out o' today's water already; is Karsrick gonna bring the additional rations 'e promised or not?"

"We have put out a call to the Shanouin, sire," the duke's aide-de-camp said to Achmed, who was pacing back and forth the length of the hot tent. "They are commanded to deliver three more barrels each morning. Will you similarly instruct your soldiers to allow them through the guard line? They have been turned away twice already."

"That may be because my soldiers do not speak Orlandan," Achmed said, stepping around the growing piles of red dust and gaping holes in the ground. He pulled the tent flap aside. "Come."

A few moments later a parlay took place at the exterior ring where the Yarimese soldiers were holding the guard line. The soldiers, who had been told to deny access to anyone other than the commanding officers, the duke, lord, lady, and the Bolg themselves, were instructed to make certain that the water bearers, and the water bearers alone, were brought into the work site, under careful guard, and allowed to deliver their barrels.

After the outer ring had been given instructions, Achmed moved with the aide-de-camp to the inner ring, manned by Firbolg soldiers, and addressed them in Bolgish.

"An hour before each shift changes, water carriers will be allowed through the first guard line. Be sure to check their barrels without fail, pry open every one of them and run a clean sword through the water, make certain there is nothing or no one hiding in them. Then escort the water carriers back to the first guard line. If anyone attempts to slip away from you, or enter the tent, subdue him. Try not to crack his head open against the stones in the street, but if you should happen to do so by accident, at least the blood will blend in with the bricks." The Bolg soldiers nodded in assent as the harsh, noisy cranking of the drill started up again.

"And if anyone broaches the guard line, kill him and eat him, in whatever order you prefer," Achmed said loudly in Orlandan, for the benefit of the Yarimese.

When the bells of the tower tolled noon, six anxious-looking women in pale blue ghodins, priestesses in the Shanouin tribe, approached the work site under guard, bearing between them three great water casks. The Bolg soldiers ringing the tent grudgingly moved aside and allowed them to come through the second guard line, up to the exterior of the tents. They quickly set their burdens down outside the tents and hurried back through the Firbolg line, into the custody of their human guards.

As the tent flap opened, one of the women glanced over her shoulder fleetingly, only to meet the mismatched eyes of the Bolg king, staring at her from within the tent, clothed in black and standing in front of a great pumping machine that groaned and screeched like the damned. In the split second of sight she thought she was gazing straight into the Underworld itself.

The Shanouin woman wheeled around and hurried to keep in step with her sister priestesses.

𝕴nside the cool marble walls of the Judiciary's library, Ihrman Karsrick and his captain of the guard watched the work site, seeing nothing but the occasional exit of a figure from the enormous tents. For three days the Bolg had labored in consecutive shifts, entering and leaving the tent at their appointed hour with the same precision as the changing of the guard at a royal palace, completely undisturbed by any onlookers.

A knock on the library door startled him; it was his chamberlain.

"Yes?"

The man came in and closed the double doors behind him.

"The Hierarch of craftsman's guilds has sent a message, m'lord."

"What is it?" Karsrick dreaded the answer, expecting it at the same time.

" 'With respect and regret, there is none in our ranks suited, available, qualified, or willing to accept the Bolg king's generous offer. Our apologies and best wishes.' "

"There's a surprise," Karsrick muttered. "Now what am I to do?"

"There is another avenue, another source, m'lord," the captain of the guard proffered nervously.

"What source? Where?" the duke demanded.

"The Raven's Guild in the Market of Thieves."

"Are you out of your *mind?*" Karsrick shouted. "You want me to consort with thieves and assassins, and send one of them into the realm of Ylorc?"

The captain shrugged. "There is no love lost between you and the Firbolg king. Sending an artisan who might be an assassin as well—"

Karsrick's hand sliced through the air in a gesture of silence.

"I do not condone the assassination of heads of state, however much I distrust them, thank you. Do you have any idea what the Lady Cymrian would do, not to mention the Lord, if I were to engage in such chicanery, especially if it led to the death of her friends, the Bolg king, or his sergeant? She would melt my flesh from the inside with hideous musical torture, or some such thing. No."

"M'lord, the Raven's Guild is not entirely composed of assassins and thieves. On the contrary, they operate, as you know, some of the most prestigious and well-respected foundries, metal and glassworks in Roland. If there is an artisan left in Yarim to be had, one that might be willing to perform their craft in such odious circumstances—"

"No!" Karsrick stated again, more firmly this time. "I will not do that. I would prefer to make my apologies to the king and hope against hope for his understanding, than even *think* about opening that door, do you hear me? Is that clearly understood?"

"Yes, m'lord. It was only a suggestion."

"A very bad suggestion." Karsrick leaned heavily on the ornate metal molding that surrounded the library window, suddenly weary. "Do not allow this conversation to leave the room, Captain. The last thing I need is for word to get back to Esten about this." He turned to look at the captain of the guard, who nodded, and met his glance.

It was a glance that acknowledged that Esten undoubtedly already knew.

## JIERNA'SID, SORBOLD

*How easy it is to be overlooked in broad daylight,* the man observed, standing in an alleyway shadow. He was watching the beggars of the city taking refuge from the heat of another blistering summer's noon, supplicating for water or coin from passersby in the central streets of the capital city. The townspeople, oblivious of them, walked on without a break in their conversations, or even a glance of notice.

As if they were invisible.

He looked up at the high towers of Jierna Tal beyond the massive Scales, rising proudly to the sky above, thankfully free of any desiccating bodies or other grisly ornamentation. One had to admit that it was a beautiful palace, a place of visionary architecture that elevated the city beyond the dull little collection of animal markets, street booths, linen weavers, and dingy buildings in which the populace found shelter. One could even describe it as magnificent.

*One day,* he mused, *all of Sorbold will be described thus.* One day soon.

His gaze fell on the Scales, their golden plates gleaming brightly in the light overhead; he closed his eyes, remembering with relish the feel of their approval, the rush of air as he was lifted up, held aloft in their approbation.

*A few more days,* he thought, fingering the violet scale in his pocket, relishing its warmth, its humming vibration. *I await the moon.*

He stepped off the portico step and over the beggar lying before it, then strolled into the light of the marketplace without a flicker of notice.

The crowd passed around him as if he were not there.

## OUTSIDE THE PORT OF AVONDERRE

The seneschal held the candle aloft in the fallowing darkness, taking pains not to allow the wax to drip onto the child or his makeshift pool of gleaming green water deep in the ship's hold.

The ship lurched suddenly as it hit a cross-swell; the current from the Northern Sea made approaching the harbor of this province of the Wyrmlands difficult, occasionally treacherous. The hold shuddered; Faron squealed tonelessly as the water around him stormed in tiny breakers.

"There, Faron, there, there," the seneschal crooned comfortingly, trying to quell his impatience and that of the demon. "Don't be frightened; read the scales and tell me if we can put into port here. Is anything lying in wait for us? Or do we have clear passage to the harbor?"

The creature struggled to maintain its balance, its soft bones and flaccid muscles no match for the pitching of the ship. With trembling, gnarled hands, Faron held a jade-green scale up to the flickering candlelight. The large, liquid eyes blinked rapidly in the intermittent dark and light. Finally the creature shook its head.

"No?" the seneschal demanded angrily. "No? Why in the name of Void not? Do you see any danger to us, any resistance, hidden in the waves? Is someone coming?"

The child stared at him in terror, then nodded vigorously.

"Are you certain?"

Faron groaned and nodded again, then disappeared beneath the meniscus of the green water.

The seneschal doused the light and groped his way to the ladder. He climbed up on deck and, spying the captain, shouted into the wind.

"Change course! Veer now; sail further north, along the coast, until we reach the reef of Gwynwood." He brushed the wind out of his light blue eyes, squinting in the heat of the sun's glare.

The captain stared at him as if he were mad.

"Your Honor, there's nowhere to weigh anchor there! Avonderre is a sheltered harbor, with a guardian light to spare us from the shoals. We can't wind the ship now." He raised a hand to his brow and stared east toward shore. "That aside, we're about to be boarded."

The seneschal stumbled to the rail and followed the captain's stare.

A small cutter in the harbormaster's fleet was giving chase, flying the flag of approach.

As acid splashed the back of his throat, the seneschal cursed silently in the profane words known only to F'dor and unutterable in the language of men. He had feared this happening; the *Basquela* did not have valid docking papers in Avonderre, or any other Orlandan port, nor did it have clearance to dock in the other ports of the Cymrian Alliance. The potential of challenge by the authorities in the port had been weighed at the time of departure against the need for speed; Quinn had warned him of this when he hired the *Basquela,* rather than waiting for the *Corona.*

And now it seemed they were about to be confronted by the harbormaster's crew, just outside Avonderian waters.

"Drop anchor," the captain ordered the crew.

The seneschal turned to Caius, who was, as always, cleaning and refitting his crossbow.

"Pass word to Quinn, quietly, and tell him and the others to make ready," he said to the crossbowman, while his brother and the seneschal's reeve listened nearby. "I sense an unfortunate maritime accident may be about to occur."

## RAVEN'S GUILD, MARKET OF THIEVES, YARIM PAAR

𝒯he leaping flames of the enormous hearth all but obscured Dranth's approach.

The guild scion was used to entering into the guildmistress's presence with no fear; as her most trusted officer, he had come to believe that she valued his candor, even when it angered her, although she had been so irrational since the devastation three years ago, and even more so of late, that he didn't take anything for granted where she was concerned.

Especially now, when she was as angry as she was; none of her spies had yet been able to broach the Firbolg guard line. The drilling was continuing, contrary to her wishes. Even the uproar that had erupted when a half-eaten body of a child had been tossed into the desert near the Bolg camp had failed to stop the excavation; a few hours of rioting had been quickly quenched, and the Bolg exonerated, causing the human sheep of Yarim Paar to return to their gawking outside the drilling tents, preventing her assassins from bringing the work to a halt.

It was frustrating her more than he had ever seen.

Being near Esten in a state of frustration was similar to playing carelessly with the volatile acids used in the foundry. It was not a matter of whether one would be burned, merely of when and how badly.

He cleared his throat softly.

Esten didn't seem to hear him. She was staring into the roaring fire, her chin resting on her curled fist, deep in thought. Her long black hair, freshly washed and still damp, hung to her knees, gleaming in the dancing light. It was a dark and lovely image; Dranth could almost see the woman there in the fireshadows for a moment. Then reason returned, and he remembered where he was.

And who she was.

And what she was.

He would never forget his first sight of her, a ratty urchin, the child of a Yarimese craftsman and a dark Lirinpan mother, long gone. She was eviscerating a soldier four times her body mass in a back alley of the Inner Market, a tiny, crude blade jutting from the hollow of his throat, another moving like captured light in her hand. The look she had shot Dranth had been so deadly that he had merely stepped back and marveled as she coolly completed her grim task, her blade flashing with a speed born of a precocious talent, an inbred agility, and an utterly ruthless lack of fear. Dranth was no stranger to masters of the knife, but that day, in the dark backstreets, he knew without question that he was witnessing the most skilled artisan of murder he had ever seen.

She was eight years old.

He cursed himself; the momentarily human impression of sensuous womanhood, incorrect and dangerous as it was, left him feeling light-headed, weak, as if he had been walking carelessly along an abyss, thinking it merely an irrigation channel, not seeing it for what it really was in the darkness.

Dranth cleared his throat again, louder this time.

"Visitor, Guildmistress."

Esten turned finally and stared at him, her gaze as devouring as the desert sands that were said to have swallowed the legendary city of Kurimah Milani more than a thousand years before. Dranth gestured into the darkness, motioning the young woman to come forward.

Like a pale ghost she appeared, swathed from head to toe in her light blue ghodin, her face white in the fireshadows. She was trembling, and the tremors redounded through the fabric of her ceremonial garb, making her appear as a ship's sail on a windy sea. Darks curls peeked out at her forehead, the only part of her hair showing, framing her face.

Esten seized her own long locks and, in a lightning-quick motion, bound them into a knot at the nape of her neck, then stood slowly as the taller woman approached.

"Well, well, this is indeed an honor," she said, venom dripping from every syllable. "A Shanouin priestess has deigned to come and visit me. How interesting. What is your name, Holiness?"

The tall woman squared her shoulders and folded her arms beneath her flowing garment. "Tabithe, Guildmistress." Her voice was soft, respectful.

"What do you want?"

The priestess coughed, then nodded an apology for the disturbance. "I have come to beg for the life of my mother-in-law," she said.

"Ah. And whom would that be?" Esten folded her arms, mirroring the priestess's stance.

The Shanouin woman coughed again, this time from deeper within, a rattling sound that hinted of red-lung, a common illness among the well-digging tribe.

"Mother Julia," she said finally.

Esten began to walk in a slow circle to the woman's left, nodding exaggeratedly. The priestess remained rigid, her eyes toward the firelight, while the guildmistress completed her stroll. Finally Esten stopped directly in front of her. She leaned forward, her face wreathed in a sinister smile.

"Too late," she said.

The woman blanched but otherwise her expression did not change.

"Truly, Guildmistress? Are you jesting?"

"Truly, Holiness. I never jest."

The woman was silent for a moment, then inhaled deeply. "Then may I barter for the body?"

Esten snorted. "I doubt you would want it in the state that it is in, Tabithe; my hair is still damp from washing the blood out of it. I suggest you return to your husband—which of the wretched charlatan's litter would he be?"

"Thait, Guildmistress."

"Ah. Well, I suggest you return to Thait and tell him that his impostor of a mother is resting in peace—pieces, actually—and that I did him a favor excising such a blight from your family."

The pale young woman struggled to remain focused. "I

have information I believe to be valuable, Guildmistress," she said, her voice betraying her slightly.

"Really? That's interesting. Your mother-in-law did not. Hence her current state."

The priestess nodded. "I did not have a chance to tell her, or anyone else, this information," she said haltingly. "I have only come upon it this afternoon; I had gone to Mother Julia's house to tell her, but—"

"What is this information?" The guildmistress's tone became suddenly intense.

Tabithe blinked several times, her face otherwise a mask. She inhaled, her lips set in a thin line, then spoke. "For my mother-in-law's body, Guildmistress?"

Before she could exhale, there was a dagger at her throat, a blade that had sprung forth from the leather sheath at Esten's wrist. The edge pressed across her gullet to the point of stopping her breath, just before breaking the skin. Esten's prowess with a blade was renowned, and it was said that, no matter the size or speed of the opponent, once Esten decided to employ said blade, it would sever the jugular before the next beat of the victim's heart.

"For the continued soundness of your own, Holiness. Speak."

The woman winced. "I delivered water to the work tent of the Bolg today."

The blade disappeared, and the priestess exhaled, drawing another ragged breath before the bright black eyes were next to her own.

"What did you see?"

"Very little—the flap was only open for an instant."

The voice dripped ice. "And why do you think this would purchase the pieces of your mother-in-law?"

"I—I saw the Firbolg king," the Shanouin stammered. "He was swathed in black garments, his eyes of different colors, the skin of his face mottled with veins. It was an unholy sight."

The black eyes narrowed. "And you think this would interest me? I know the Bolg king is there, and that he is hideous. Both are common knowledge. You are trying my patience."

"Behind him the Bolg were operating an enormous drill; there were a half-score or so of them turning the handle of a machine. It had great metal circles lined with teeth that interwove like weaver's threads."

"Gears." Esten took a step back. "I am listening."

"I could see the bit," Tabithe said. "At first I did not realize what it was; I had never seen one of such length and breadth before. It was curved, like a twisted tallow candle, driven into the ground by the machine, not a tamper as we use."

"Is that all?" Esten began to stalk the dark shadows, disappearing in and out of the light.

"It was made of steel, I believe, Guildmistress," the priestess said, summoning her courage. "Steel that glinted both black—and blue."

All the noise went out of the room as Esten stopped pacing. She turned slowly to the priestess.

"Say that again," she said quietly.

Tabithe hugged herself tighter beneath the pale blue ghodin. "The bit of the drill the Bolg are using is forged of blue-black steel, similar to the thin circle you described," she stammered. She stood in silence as Esten stared at the floor; what she was cogitating on, Tabithe had no idea, but she could see that the epiphany she was undergoing was enormous.

Finally the guildmistress looked up again; whatever deliberation had been going on in her mind a moment before was no longer reflected in her eyes.

"Thank you, Holiness," she said politely. "Your information is indeed valuable, and you shall be rewarded handsomely for it." She turned to the guild scion. "Dranth, reassemble Mother Julia and have her body wrapped in fine Sorboldian linen. Put the body in a wagon for Her Holiness, and deliver to the house of Thait." Her eyes returned to the priestess as she finished her directive. "Collect from him the lowest delivery fee."

"Yes, Guildmistress." The guild scion disappeared into the dark reaches of the guildhall, returning a moment later. "It is ordered."

"Good. Thank you for the information, Tabithe. I'm sure your husband will be grateful for your efforts, given what stock your family places in the burying of kinsmen and the like."

"Yes, Guildmistress," the priestess said.

"Nonsense, if you ask me," Esten added. "I know that the clan you married into is a superstitious lot, but even your own people have the same silly practices. I never cease to be amazed that a tribe such as the Shanouin, who dig in the earth, laying back the blankets of uncounted bones, can still have a belief in the Afterlife. Tomfoolery, all of it. But enjoy your little rituals, if they make it easier for you to face the inevitability of mortality."

The priestess bowed respectfully and followed the hands that beckoned to her from the darkness into the alleyway beyond.

When the door closed behind Tabithe, Esten turned back to the fire.

"Dranth, did you make certain that a wide wagon was hired for the delivery?"

"Yes, Guildmistress." He had anticipated the request.

"Good. Please instruct the driver to collect a double fee when he delivers the bodies. And extra for the linen—perhaps as a kind gesture you can wrap Tabithe in blue."

"It is being arranged as we speak."

The guildmistress kicked a burning ember that had spattered out of the hearth back into the fire grate with the toe of her boot. "Make certain that you tell the head journeyman at the tile foundry to adjust the schedule to replace the boy, Slith, and Bonnard. I don't want to fall behind on any orders."

"Bonnard as well? He knows nothing; it's a shame to lose so competent a ceramicist."

Esten turned and leveled her gaze at the guild scion. Her voice, when she spoke, was flat, her words carrying double meanings.

"What do *you* know, Dranth?"

Dranth swallowed, his eyes signaling his understanding.

"Did you see that she is pregnant?" he asked hesitantly.

"Tabithe? She is?"

"Yes. Hiding it under the folds of her ghodin."

"Ah." Her gaze returned to the fire as she pondered the information. After a moment she crossed her arms.

"Her information *was* useful."

"Yes, Guildmistress."

"Perhaps we should be lenient then."

"If you wish, Guildmistress."

"Very well, then. No extra delivery fee for the baby."

# 14

### AVONDERRE HARBOR, PORT FALLON, OUTSIDE THE SLUICEWAY

Port Fallon, at Avonderre, was the largest and busiest in all of Roland; with the exception of modest fishing villages and harbor towns, it was the only port, and the only combined shipping and naval center in the Cymrian Alliance.

Farther south along the coast were Tallono, the great sheltered harbor that had been built by the Gorllewinolo Lirin thousands of years before with the help of the dragon Elynsynos, and the two great western seaports of Minsyth and Evermere in the unclaimed region known commonly as the Nonaligned States. But none of those ports had the size or the open access of Port Fallon. Tallono was restricted only to Lirin vessels, while Minsyth and Evermere were dwarfed by the massive inner harbor of Ghant in Sorbold, which lay to the east above the Skeleton Coast. The combined size of all four was still not quite that of Port Fallon.

In the heyday of the Cymrian Empire, a lighttower one hundred feet in height was constructed at the mouth of the harborway, where the southerly currents of the Northern Sea cleared from the easterly ones of the open ocean. The light from the tower could be seen, it was said, on the clearest of nights by ships as far away as the outer archipelago to the east of Gaematria, the mystical island of the Sea Mages that straddled the Prime Meridian.

In one of the most ambitious engineering projects of the Cymrian era, an enormous sluiceway had been constructed, a floodgate of a sort being formed from the natural curve of the coastline, to keep the tides from damaging the ships in port. What nature had already provided to Avonderre's coastline was embellished, a new causeway built that turned the harbor into an enormous lagoon, eight miles wide from the outer villages, protected from the elements. In the most virulent of storms, the harshest of winter weather, or even in the wake of a tidal wave that crashed to the north on the coast of the Gwynwood reef, destroying not only the port but the villages nearby, the mighty, bustling harbor of Port Fallon remained unharmed, safe in her natural shelter.

The existence of the sluiceway made the all-but-impossible task of patrolling the harbor achievable; the harbormaster had outposts that flanked the entry channel into Port Fallon from which his large fleet of guidance, rescue, and interdiction craft could be launched. Thus the ships that made Port Fallon a destination were protected both by nature and by law from the misfortunes of the sea; the favorable geography improved upon by Gwylliam's engineers saved many a ship from sundering in a storm, while the vigilant patrols of the harbormaster and his sailors prevented the more brutal scourge: pirates.

To keep the trade flowing in and out of Port Fallon, the harbor patrol ships were on constant dispatch, routinely trolling for anything entering or leaving the harbor that seemed untoward. Their moorings were on the two causeways to the sides of the harbor's mouth, so their launchings were easy, and the sea at the sluice was glasslike. It was certainly impossible for them to inspect every ship, check every cargo, even interdict every act of privateering, but by and large they maintained order in the harbor, and that in turn made Avonderre one of the safest and most prosperous headwaters of the shipping lanes the world around.

Avonderre's wharf stretched along the north-south coastline for as far as the eye could see, peaking in the center at the pinnacle of the lighttower, then gradually diminishing down over the harbor proper, where along the colossal jetty a hundred merchant vessels could be off-loaded at once, in a meticulously choreographed dance of longshoremen, deckhands, barrels, crates, horses, and wagons drawing forth treasures from around the world with the precision of an anthill, only to be equally efficiently reloaded and sent on their way again.

It was this massive amount of seafaring traffic that had made the seneschal decide to risk sailing into Port Fallon in an unregistered vessel, without the papers of special waiver he had represented to the captain that he possessed. In the course of an average day, a thousand ships or more might pass through the waters of the sluiceway. How likely, then, that a modest little frigate like the *Basquela*, hovering at the harbor's outer edge, politely waiting its turn in the queue, would be assailed by the harbormaster?

Far too likely, it now appeared.

The seneschal cursed again at the sight of the masted cutter skimming quickly over the smooth waves toward them, signaling them with the harbormaster's inspection flag.

He glanced around quickly to ascertain that no other ships were within easy sight, then motioned to the reeve, who in turn nodded to Clomyn and Caius. The twin bowmen slid into position at the rail, casually balancing their ever-present crossbows on one arm.

The captain was signaling to the cutter his preparation to be boarded for inspection. A three-man scull was being launched, with two rowers and the harbormaster's agent climbing into it as the other three crew members on the cutter lowered it over the side. The seneschal could hear their voices on the wind, calling to one another.

"Handsomely, now, lads," the agent was shouting to the sailors. "Have been in the drink already once today."

"And you *still* need a bath, Terrence," one of the men on board shouted back to him. "You stink of bilgewater and Mistress Carmondy's perfume."

" 'Twas a rough night," the agent said agreeably.

Good-natured cursing and laughter was keeping the harbormaster's crew occupied for the moment. The seneschal turned away from the rail for a moment and stared at the captain, who was chuckling along with the first mate, waiting for the arrival of the boarding party. The captain turned, still smiling, to the seneschal.

"You should lay hands on those documents of waiver, Your Honor," he said, signaling his crew to lower the rope ladder, though the scull had barely touched the water and was just being cast off. "The harbormaster's agent will want to inspect them upon coming aboard."

"I have no such documents," the seneschal said calmly.

The smiles faded from the faces of the captain and the mate; they both turned in to the wind to stare at the seneschal, the expressions on their faces indicating they thought they had misheard him.

"Pardon, Your Honor?" the captain said.

"I said I have no documents of waiver," the seneschal repeated, louder this time so as to be heard over the snapping of the sails.

The captain left the rail and came to the seneschal. "I am quite certain you said that you had arranged for waiver before we sailed, sir," he said, his face growing flushed.

The seneschal shrugged. "Perhaps I did. If I did, I lied. I apologize most sincerely. I cannot possibly afford a trail of documents that would lead back to Argaut."

"What? Why?" The captain's face darkened from red to purple. "This may be nothing more than a fine for you, sir, but I could have my ship seized."

"I would not despair of that, Captain," the seneschal said, nodding to Clomyn and Caius.

"I took your word, sir, as a high official of Argaut, and I am shocked that—" The captain's next few words were lost in the sound of the crossbows unleashing their bolts.

The brothers had fired three shots each before the mate had recovered enough to gasp; the captain was at the rail in time to see the last of the three sailors on the cutter fall back with a quarrel in his throat. He looked down in horror at the scull to see the agent and one of the rowers, the agent supine, the rower prone, bolts in the throat and neck as well.

On the floor of the scull one sailor remained, a quarrel lodged in his lower spine, his legs useless, as he flailed helplessly in the bilge. Caius laughed aloud and cuffed Clomyn on the ear.

"Blunderer! Cheese-fingers! Look at that!"

His brother shouldered him angrily, aimed, and fired again. The sailor lurched and then lay still. Caius shook his head and clucked in mock disapproval.

"*Two* quarrels for one man? What a waste! A sin, I tell you. A *sin!*"

"I could keep my scale of bolts used to men killed one-to-one if I bury my bow's stock in your forehead, Caius," his brother growled.

"Hoist the scull, aboard," Fergus ordered the *Basquela*'s crew; the sailors stared at the bewildered captain and the horrified mate, then quickly jumped to the rail, drawing the long rowboat to the ropes.

"What is going on here?" the captain demanded, striding toward the seneschal. "Desist! What are you—"

The seneschal grabbed the man's throat and, with a

wrenching swing, slammed him into the mast. Fury burned in his eyes as he squeezed, pressing his bent knuckle in between the bones of the man's clavicle. The captain gasped and flailed helplessly, his eyes blinking in an attempt to remain conscious.

The seneschal pulled the captain back and battered his head against the mast again, and again, over and over, shaking the mast, pounding relentlessly until blood spattered the mains'l in stripes and flecks, bits of the man's brain caking the timber.

Finally, with a vicious tug, he dragged the captain's corpse to the outer rail, the side of the deck aligned with the open sea. He snatched the binnacle, the box containing the man's beloved compass and navigational maps, lashed it quickly with a length of rope and tied it around the dead man's neck, then tossed his body overboard. He stared as corpse hit the waves and sank. Then he turned back to the crew; he took a moment to straighten his triangular hat and brush the green-gray matter from his cloak.

"I *do* so hate being questioned," he said casually.

Fergus stared in dismay over the side.

"Why, if I might ask, did you toss the binnacle too, Your Honor? How are we to navigate now?"

The seneschal inhaled. "I wanted the captain to have clear directions to the Underworld," he said, his tone light. "And we don't need those petty tools. Faron will guide us with the scales."

The sailors looked to one another doubtfully. "Yes, sir," Fergus said.

"And now," the seneschal continued, striding up to the first mate and stopping before him, "now there is a question of you, sir. Do you wish to ascend to the captaincy?"

The man squared his shoulders and looked the seneschal directly in the eye.

"No," he said, quietly and firmly. "I know that you will kill me in the end, whether I aid you or not. So I choose not to."

The seneschal's muscles rippled with anger. "I will not kill you in the end; you are wrong in that," he said, his voice seething. He turned and walked away from the mate, then nodded to the twins.

The crossbows fired again within a breath of one another. The mate's body only lurched once as it tumbled over the side.

"I will kill you in the beginning," the seneschal said. He turned to the reeve. "Where is Quinn?"

"Here, sir," came the sailor's voice, shallow and thready. The seneschal motioned for him to come forward.

"It seems you have command now, Quinn. Prepare to weigh anchor, after securing the scull and once the cutter has moved on."

The sailor's blue eyes blinked rapidly in the unfiltered sunlight on the open water. "Moved on, sir?"

In reply the seneschal turned back to the cutter. He walked to the rail, studying the listing ship for a moment.

"Spill the sails," he called to Quinn, who quickly repeated the order. The crew leapt to grab the sheets and discharge the wind, gathering the flapping canvas as quickly as they could.

The seneschal closed his eyes and drew Tysterisk, reveling in the gust of air, the rush of power that came forth with it, the harnessed wind itself. He opened his eyes and looked to the sails of the cutter, which began to fill with wind.

The *Basquela* remained at anchor, riding the shallow waves, as the cutter began to bear away, into the wind, sailing briskly out of the harbor toward the sluice. From any distance it appeared as if the harbormaster's ship, satisfied, had departed from the *Basquela*, moving on to patrol the outer port.

The seneschal looked about the immense harbor, where many ships were passing, some moving into dock, others already moored, some dealing with their own inspections by other vessels of the harbormaster. The cry of the gulls, the glare of the sun, the slap of the wind as the cutter sailed away; ordinary business in Port Fallon.

"Bear away, against the wind," he ordered Quinn. "Take us out of the harbor, across the sluiceway and around the point." Quinn scrambled to obey.

When the *Basquela* was no longer in sight of the wharf, the seneschal tapped Clomyn on the shoulder.

"Here's your chance to make up for your miss earlier," he said, the gleaming blue of his eyes mirroring the sky.

Clomyn came to the rail. "Where, sir?"

"The mains'l, I think."

The crossbowman sighted his weapon, out of range for a normal archer by more than three times. "Ready, sir."

The seneschal touched the tip of the quarrel, and spoke the word *kryv*; ignite.

The tip of the bolt gleamed red for a moment, then blazed forth in a spark of dark fire. It hissed menacingly as it snapped to life.

The seneschal nodded, and Clomyn fired. The wind lay eerily still for a moment as the bolt soared over the ocean currents and out of sight.

Then, at the very edge of their vision, a tiny finger of smoke rose from the mains'l.

"Well done," the seneschal said to Clomyn. He raised the sword and reached down into himself, where the element of air, of wind, was bound to his dark soul.

The breezes that scudded along the sea between the *Basquela* and the cutter picked up, gaining strength, then bound together; a small waterspout appeared for a moment as they passed over the waves, gusting toward the empty ship. A heartbeat later, the crew of the *Basquela* saw the cutter's sails go full.

Within another heartbeat the cutter's mains'l exploded in flame. The fire leapt high up the mast, then raced from the forecastle to the stern, all in the twinkling of an eye. All on the deck of the *Basquela* stood and watched, rapt, as the red-orange fireball resolved itself in black ash, burning caustically, the ship a bright, skeletal outline in the smoke.

"Bear a-hand, Quinn," he said to the new captain, who was trembling slightly as the horns and bells began to sound in the distance. "Follow the coast. I want to drop anchor again in the morning. It is ungentlemanly to keep a lady waiting."

# 15

## YARIM PAAR

On the morning of the eighth day, the drilling stopped suddenly.

Ihrman Karsrick, who had finally become accustomed to the grinding rumble outside the windows of the Judiciary, leapt up from the breakfast he was sharing with the Lord Cymrian and hastened to the window. He looked out over the streets to the place where Entudenin stood, and the work had been progressing.

In the distance he could see that the internal ring of Bolg guards had broken in places; Firbolg soldiers and artisans alike were milling about, apparently packing up equipment, carrying it out of the tent to the large wagons that had brought it in eight days before. He could not see any sign of a restored fountain, no breach of water, no change in the tent, no pool on the ground.

"Gods, where are they going?" Karsrick said, crumpling his napkin in panic.

Ashe took another bite of his hot buttered scone and shrugged.

"They aren't finished—they can't be finished, it's only been eight days. I don't know whether to be thrilled or horrified," Karsrick muttered, his eyes darting around the room to the window, at the Lord Cymrian and back again.

Ashe swallowed and wiped his mouth on the linen napkin. "Perhaps they are. Achmed does not waste time."

"We must go to them, m'lord," Karsrick insisted, hurrying across the conservatory to the door. "Where's the Lady Cymrian?"

"I believe she is in the garden, singing her morning devotions."

Karsrick summoned the chamberlain, clanging the bells so frantically that Ashe rose from the table and folded his napkin, his breakfast half finished.

"Ihrman, why are you so distressed? You have been beside yourself since the Bolg arrived; I would think their departure would gladden your heart immensely."

Karsrick stared at him glassily. "There is no water, m'lord. They have dissembled Entudenin—disemboweled it, really—sliced away the relic's upper arm, disturbed the city for eight continuous days without stopping, robbing the entire square and all the streets surrounding the Marketway of any peace, any sleep whatsoever as they continued their hellish drilling into the dark hours of the night. They've destroyed the walkways and the fountainbed in and around the town square—*and there is no water.*"

Ashe sat back down to finish his meal. "All right, Ihrman, all right, calm yourself. Rhapsody will return in a moment, and then we can make our way to the square and ascertain precisely what is happening."

When the duke, lord, and lady arrived in the square, the Bolg had half finished packing up the equipment. Karsrick hurried to the Firbolg king and tapped him nervously on the arm.

"Where are you going, King Achmed? Surely you are not ready to leave yet."

The Bolg king turned around and regarded the duke as he would someone with cauliflower sprouting from his ears.

"Surely we are," he said as if addressing a five-year-old or a mental defective. "It's finished. We've done as much as we can. We hate this place, this place hates us; seems all in all like a good time to leave."

The duke gazed in dismay at the disarray of his town square beneath the tent and beyond it. Clay dust was everywhere, piled in great heaps like miniature red mountains. Deep crevices had been dug that were hastily filled in, lending the appearance of new graves, while the cobblestones of the street and the bricks of the walkways were strewn about in abandon.

And worst of all, Entudenin stood, naked and dismembered, looking as sad and shriveled as it did eight days before, shorter, with a great hollow hole in it.

"It's—it's not finished!" the duke cried, waving his hands wildly.

"As far as we're concerned, it is. We've done what we can do."

"But there's no water."

"No, there isn't."

"You've broken the Fountain Rock down, sliced its arm off, delved the streets, made a colossal mess, and there is still no water. Yet you are preparing to *leave?*"

Achmed crossed his arms and looked for a long moment at Rhapsody; he narrowed his eyes, inhaled, and addressed the duke in a barely civil voice.

"We, unlike you, have been following the phases of the moon, Karsrick," he said, stepping out of the way of three Bolg soldiers carrying a long, heavy wooden box. "If there is water still available to Entudenin, it would be in its sleeping phase right now; five days or so hence, if there is water to be had, it should come back. It may, it may not." He shrugged. "We've done what we can to make the Fountain Rock capable of withstanding the flow, should it return. We removed a great deal of debris and detritus from the feeder tunnel, and there is another place below the ground where the passageway is partially barred, near the Canderian border, which will be taken care of. I'd say we're finished here.

"Since we cannot predict for certain how the cycle of the flow corresponds to the moon's phases, I deemed it necessary to get the miners away from the subterranean chambers

now. The force of water at Awakening was said to be violent, damaging in fact. I don't want my men in harm's way
when it returns, if it returns. I will not lose any of my subjects on your behalf."

"What he says makes good sense, Ihrman," Rhapsody
said, staring at the dry red geyser. "There is really no point
in the Bolg remaining here, in the heat, now that the digging
is done. I'm certain King Achmed is looking forward to
returning home."

"Please, sire, reconsider and stay," Karsrick said, eyeing
the building crowds that had come to investigate the silence.
"I will host you and your artisans in the Judiciary—"

"Did you find me a stained-glass artisan?"

Karsrick stopped in midword, his mouth open, then closed
it quickly.

"I put out a call to every legitimate guild, sire, but alas,
no, I was unable to locate anyone qualified to do the level
of work you asked for who was also available to travel to
Canrif."

The Bolg king exhaled. "Ylorc. It's called Ylorc, Karsrick."

"My apologies; of course. Ylorc."

Achmed directed three soldiers carrying an enormous
metal gear to a specific wagon, turning his back on the duke.
"I wish I could say that your inadequacy surprises me," he
said sullenly, "but I was prepared for it. Grunthor—are we
close?"

"Yes, sir. Just 'ave to pack the bit, and a few o' the odds
and ends."

The duke trailed along behind the Bolg king as he continued to make preparations to leave.

"Please—just a few more days. Stay until the water returns."

"No." Achmed took hold of one end of a jointed timber,
and Ashe caught the other end, helping him carry it to the
waiting wagons.

"Why are you so insistent that they stay, Ihrman?" Rhapsody asked, coiling a great length of rope.

"I—in case—well, if there should be some residual need—"

Achmed gave the timber in the wagon a ragged shove, then turned to face the duke.

"He's afraid the water will not return, which is a very good possibility," he said to Rhapsody, staring at Karsrick in contempt. "And if that comes to pass, he wants the Bolg here to take the blame, and whatever ugly reaction the citizenry may visit upon whomever they blame. You're a coward, Karsrick; when a man starts being afraid of the reactions of his own subjects to the point where he is unwilling to acknowledge his own decisions and take responsibility for them, he ceases to have any credibility as a leader, in their eyes, and in the eyes of those who rule alongside him." He picked up a pair of wrenches waiting in a pile to be loaded and tossed them into the wagon.

"He's right, Ihrman," Ashe said. "Bid your thanks to the king and move out of his way."

"I do appreciate the irony of your invitation," Achmed said, signaling to the Bolg soldiers to pull forth the last wagon, the one that transported the bit. "You didn't want us to come; now you don't want us to leave. It's touching."

"Sire—" Karsrick protested.

"Have the bill of tender prepared immediately; I expect to be given the down payment within the next hour," Achmed said to the duke, cutting his protest off with a mere glance. "And make certain those powdered mineral ores I ordered—the manganese, iron, cobalt, and copper—are delivered here, ready to be packed."

Karsrick swallowed, and left the square, motioning to his aide-de-camp.

"Thank you for doing this," Rhapsody said over the building din of the crowd as a dozen Firbolg workers ducked into the tent. She took Achmed's hand as Ashe and Grunthor held the tent flaps aside. "I am sorry you were not able to find a stained-glass artisan, but I do appreciate your doing this for me."

Achmed and one of the soldiers pulled open the gates of the wagon. "Once again, you overestimate your importance to me," he said dryly. "Karsrick is paying me handsomely, satisfied with our work or not. And he is giving us a tariff waiver that extends beyond the ten-year proviso you negotiated with Roland four years ago. If his credit papers are not in Ylorc with the next mail caravan, I will stop all trade with him until they arrive." The first two Bolg soldiers emerged from the tent, the blue-black rysin-steel bit in their hands, followed by four more; Achmed motioned them over to where the wagon waited. He lifted his voice for effect. "Who knows? If they don't pay the balance, perhaps we'll invade and round up some of the townspeople to stock the larders of the Cauldron."

Rhapsody's expression hardened. "Why must you do that?" she asked in annoyance.

"Do what?"

"Say things you do not mean, just to be ugly. Be deliberately obstreperous, obnoxious. Make people unnecessarily wary of the Bolg."

The Bolg king watched as the enormous bit was loaded into the wagon, then wrapped in heavy canvas for the trip, more for the protection of the wagon than for that of the bit. Then he turned and smiled slightly at Rhapsody.

"Who is to say that I don't mean it?"

"I am. Stop it. I know you better after fourteen hundred years, all but four of them alone with you and Grunthor in the dark, facing death daily. I know when you are bluffing and when you mean what you say. You didn't just now."

The Bolg king's face grew serious. He took Rhapsody's arm and led her to a sheltered side of the tent, away from the tumult of the onlookers and the noise of the Bolg preparing to move the equipment out. He looked down into her face, studying her for a moment, then sighed and looked away.

"You once asked me whether I desired the Bolg to be viewed by the world as men, or as monsters. Do you remember?"

"Yes," Rhapsody replied. "I remember very well; you chose men, albeit monstrous men."

Achmed nodded in assent. "Indeed I did, and that is what we are: both man and monster. But remember, Rhapsody, for all that you struggle to make the humans accept the Bolg for the men that we are, it is the monster in us that may prove to be their more valuable ally in the end."

Rhapsody jumped at the sound on the other side of the tent of the wagon gate slamming suddenly shut.

"Why?"

"Don't you remember your childhood nightmares?"

"Yes." The corners of Rhapsody's mouth twitched as a smile began, then was abruptly halted. Achmed was not smiling in return. "Because monsters never sleep?"

Achmed merely nodded.

"In any event," she said, "whatever disappointments there have been in this undertaking—Entudenin is still dry, you did not find your artisan—perhaps there will be a better understanding now between humans and Firbolg. That alone was worth the price."

Achmed shook his head. "Perhaps, though I would not say the Firbolg opinion has improved much. And it will take months to wash off this cursed red dust."

The impulse to smile came again, and Rhapsody surrendered to it. "With good reason. But at least there has been some enlightenment on the side of the Yarimese; perhaps it will extend to other humans as well."

"Perhaps. But in my experience, enlightenment has a very short life span. It tends to shrink, not spread. Do you want to say goodbye to Grunthor before we go?"

"Of course. I thought perhaps he might stay for a few days after you and the Bolg leave, get a good rest and have a chance to replenish his stock."

"If he agrees, that's fine; then I only need one more thing from you."

Rhapsody moved deeper into the tent's shade. "Yes?"

"When I have the Lightcatcher assembled, when I believe it is time to test it, or if I need your help determining what it does, will you come?"

Rhapsody inhaled deeply. "You do understand that I am uncomfortable with what you are doing? That I think you should have a greater hesitancy to make use of power you don't fully understand?"

Achmed nodded shortly. "I do. And *you* do understand that I take nothing in life lightly; therefore, you should trust that I will never employ anything of this nature without absolutely needing to do so."

"I do," Rhapsody said quickly. She reached out and pulled the Bolg king into her arms and embraced him tightly. "And you understand that whenever you need me, I will come." She kissed him on the cheek, hugging him more tightly. "Travel well, and put a little time aside to be happy, Achmed. I know that is something that won't happen unless you specifically schedule it."

Achmed chuckled and returned the embrace.

The noise from the townspeople of Yarim had grown into cacophony by the time the Bolg departed. Another division of Yarimese guards had to be activated to keep the corridor through the streets open; the Bolg rode out from under the tents, without looking back, leaving the lord and lady, the duke, and the giant Sergeant-Major behind.

Moments after the Bolg disappeared from view, a murmur ran through the crowd that was rapidly picked up by more and more voices, until the streets were full of chanting.

"Take down the tent!"

"Where is the water?"

"Show us Entudenin!"

"Water! Give us water!"

Ihrman Karsrick began to shake. He turned to the lord and lady in terror and fury.

"This is exactly what I feared," he hissed. "They are going to tear us limb from limb."

"Don't be ridiculous, Ihrman," Ashe said in annoyance. "Address them; tell them that we hope the water will return within a cycle of the moon, and that they must be patient."

"I will not," the duke retorted. "I am not certain that it will, and I do not wish to be seen as an even greater fool than they already think me for bringing the Bolg to Yarim in the first place."

"Life is an uncertain entity, Ihrman," Rhapsody said. "They have lost nothing if the water does not return."

"You are more than welcome to inform them of that, m'lady."

Rhapsody sighed and turned to Ashe. "Perhaps I should." Her husband considered a moment, then nodded. She squeezed his hand, then climbed to the highest place that remained in the stone wall surrounding the fountainbed, in front of the work tent.

Ashe leaned over to Karsrick as she reached the top and steadied herself.

"Watch this, and learn how it's done by a master," he said.

Rhapsody closed her eyes and began to chant softly, using her skills as a Namer, weaving the words of her song in and out of the tones she heard and felt around her in the marketplace. Over and over again, the volume increasing incrementally, she spoke the true name of silence, until the cacophony of the town square subsided.

She opened her eyes and regarded the townspeople with a direct, calm expression.

"Fellow Orlandans, people of Yarim, the Firbolg king and his craftsmen have finished their work here. They have ended the drilling to coincide with the lunar phases, because in its living time Entudenin's cycle followed the moon as well. Whether the water returns to Entudenin, and to Yarim

Paar, is in the hands of the All-God now. If it does, the drought will be averted, and life will most likely be easier, and more bountiful. If it does not, you will be no worse off than you were before the Bolg came. We must await the ruling of the Creator, and the Earth. Until then, we must be patient."

The tone of her voice was melodic and clear, her face set in a straight, emotionless expression. Ashe smiled. She was using her Namer's ability of True-Speaking to address the boisterous rabble, and it was working well; the crowd appeared bespelled, settling down into tranquillity, lulled by the music and the innate beauty of the fire that burned within her.

The musicality of Rhapsody's voice changed; she was weaving a suggestion into her True-Speech.

"Return to your homes, or your labors. If the Fountain Rock awakens, you will not miss it. But your carts stand empty, your ovens cold, your houses unattended, while you wait here for something that may be a long time in coming."

The crowd stood for another moment, absorbing the magic in her words, then quietly began to disperse.

Rhapsody climbed down from the tiny stone wall and took Grunthor's arm.

"Return with us to the Judiciary," she said fondly, smiling up at her friend. "The duke will make certain that the very best his kitchen has to offer will be prepared for your supper—and I do *not* mean any of the scullery workers."

"Awwww." The giant caught sight of the duke's face out of the corner of his eye, and broke into a wide grin. "Why, that'd be lovely, Duchess. Maybe 'e'll even give me a lit'le tour o' the place."

At the front of the crowd, standing close to the rope corridor, a woman in the flowing, pale blue robes of a Shanouin priestess had been standing, watching every movement of the Bolg as they packed up their gear and made ready the wagons for leaving. While others around her had peeled

off and joined in good-natured merrymaking, she had remained at the front of the line, struggling to see owing to
her slight stature.

When the rysin-steel bit was brought forth and wrapped
for its journey, she moved closer, forcing her way between
two of the Yarimese guards for a better look. The guards,
ordered by law to protect the Shanouin, glared at her but
did not sweep her back into the crowd as they might have
someone who was not a water priestess.

When the Bolg finally departed, she, along with most of
the onlookers, followed them to the outskirts of the town,
watching until they were out of sight. But when the other
townspeople returned to the square to be addressed by the
duke, she had continued on, to the rocky outer reaches of
Yarim Paar, staring after the wagons and horses until they
were swallowed by the distant horizon.

She reached into the folds of her robe, and pulled forth
the cwellan disk; it caught the light of the sun overhead and
flashed like a beacon.

She held it up to her bright, black eyes for a moment
longer, then slipped it back into her slightly long robes.

Then she herself slipped back into the pleasant mayhem
that was erupting as the town let go of its breath with the
exit of the Bolg in the red streets of Yarim.

# 16

## THE PALACE AT JIERNA TAL, SORBOLD

*T*he evening lamps had been doused; the nightly cones
of pungent incense and balms of sweet sandalwood were
burning down to ash in their golden receptacles lining the
hallways outside the cavernous bedchamber of the Dowager
Empress as night crept in, silent, on a warm, moist breeze.
The heavy silk damask curtains at the open window crackled
slightly with its passing.

Within the opulent chamber Her Serenity, Leitha, Dowager Empress, daughter of Verlitz, the Fourth Emperor of the Dark Earth, was watching the night sky from the silken pillows of her mammoth bed as she was accustomed to do each evening. The full moon cast an illumination as bright as midday against a gray sky filled with visible clouds and scattered stars beyond the burning moonlight; it was a strange sight, magnificent in its clarity.

Outside the bedchamber, the palace servants moved quietly in the completion of their daily tasks: spiriting away the empress's gowns for cleansing and pressing; discarding the still-fresh flowers in dozens of porcelain vases which would, in the morning, be graced with another crop of blooms; removing the trays containing the remains of the empress's nightly bedtime repast—for a tiny, shrunken woman who weighed no more than a feather, the empress had an appetite that would shame a sailor or a gladiator—and sweeping the desert sand from the thick, densely woven carpets and tapestries that lined the high corridor walls. Several halls away, a string quartet played a sweet concerto, muted enough to spare the empress any disturbance while lulling her to sleep.

Despite the care the servants took in moving quietly, the empress could hear them. It was the curse of her dominion; the palace of Jierna Tal, with its high towers and thick ramparts, bulwarks and fortifications, had been so long under her rule, and the rule of generations of ancestors who handed the crown down to her, that it was part of her consciousness, just as everything that took place in the realm of Sorbold was. Indeed, she was even distantly aware of the changing of the watch, the entire column of soldiers whose sole duty was to guard her stronghold from the slightest disturbance. She sighed in annoyance and pulled the gleaming coverlet up around her wrinkled neck.

"Good evening, Your Serenity. I trust you are resting well."

The voice, crisp and distinct, came from the darkness itself.

The empress sat up starkly, or tried to. Instead of her normal ease of movement, she found herself unable to do anything but straighten her back. Her arms lay, useless, at her sides, her hands, spotted and gnarled with age, motionless on the smooth edge of the thick coverlet. She opened her mouth to speak, but her jaw was clenched, rigid, unable to open.

At tiny glimmer of violet radiance caught her eye near the window, swallowed a moment later by the darkness.

In the shadows a figure of a man appeared, silhouetted against the bright light of the full moon. The empress could not distinguish his face at first; it was the same heavy-featured, bearded, swarthy face that most of her subjects possessed, but the eyes within it shone with an incandescence she had never seen before. Internally, she felt a tumbling rush of cold, though her body did not tremble or quake, but merely lay as still as death.

The figure approached her bedstead, pausing for a moment to examine the heavily carved mahogany bedposts, then came forward and sat down on the feather mattress beside her. His body made no impression in the plumped coverlet; it was as if he had no mass, no weight, at all.

The man leaned forward and gently tucked the coverlet around the empress, taking great care in folding the silken sheets under her motionless arms. Then he sat back and cocked his head to one side, observing her with interest, as though she were an objet d'art or an interesting exhibit in a menagerie. When he finally spoke, his voice was soft, and warm as the desert wind.

"In case you are interested, the bells you will hear shortly will be summoning the royal healers to the bedside of your useless son, the late Crown Prince."

The eyes of the empress snapped open wide, the only movement still under her control.

The shadow man chuckled quietly.

"Yes, it's true, your fair-haired, pasty-skinned boy is gone. But do not despair; you will be following him imminently into the Vault of the Underworld, so there will be no need to pretend to mourn him. I know you despise him every bit as much as the rest of the population of Sorbold does."

The empress blinked rapidly, her breath shallow and rasping.

The figure moved, slightly, catching a ray of moonlight from the balcony window; backlit thus, the empress saw that he was filmy, the colors of his robe gleaming as the moonlight passed through them, through his skin, his hair, his face.

Now she recognized him.

Her heart pounded painfully, thudding loud in her chest and ears.

The filmy man noted her panic and genially patted her rigid hand.

"Calm yourself, Empress. This is to be a momentous experience for both of us. Your son—now, that was truly regrettable and unimpressive; I took his birthright from him, his scanty authority and lore, without a whisper of struggle; he was as disappointing in death as he was in life. But you, Leitha—if I may address you thus—you are a lioness, aren't you? Your squamous claw here has held back Time itself, when death should have come for your decades ago. By sheer will you have clung to the throne of Sorbold, and life, in a magnificent show of spirit. I look forward to its testing!"

The tiny, shrunken body of the empress began trembling vigorously, but now it was more from fury than from fear. The man saw the change in her eyes, and smiled broadly.

"Much better! Gird your soul, Empress; I am come for it."

The man relinquished the empress's hand and rose from the bed. From his pocket he took forth a gleaming purple oval, the scale he had found so long ago in the wreckage of the Cymrian ship. It glowed in the light of the moon, the runes shining with a light of their own.

He stared down for a long moment at his prey, then seized the silk coverlet at the bottom of the bed, wrenching it off the Dowager Empress's feet, clothed in white linen bed-shoes. He took one of them in his hand, stripping off the slipper and cupping it as the empress shuddered.

"Ah, the heel that you kept on the neck of the populace all these years—strangely small for such a crushing force," he mused, running his fingers gently over the thick yellow calluses, the ropy purple veins, the dry skin parched white with age. He held the scale up to the empress's eyes, his own shining as brightly as the runes.

"This, Empress, is a New Beginning, the passing away of a dynasty before your eyes. The Divine Right of Kings your ancestor claimed three centuries ago passes now, like the light from a dying torch, to a new, stronger firebrand, one with sufficient fuel to blaze before the nations."

The gleam in his eyes turned cruel.

With a savage twist he seized the empress's heel and squeezed with a grip of iron.

The old woman screamed silently, her mouth unable to open, her throat to issue forth any sound, locked in an agonizing rictus.

The shimmering ripples of light cascading from the scale in his hand pulsed for an instant, then glowed more brightly.

From within the empress's heel a thin wash of light emerged, diffuse as a dusty sunbeam. It hovered in the air, formless, for a moment, then arced with a sudden force into the scale.

The translucent man's head arched back, his shoulders convulsed as well, as an expression of joy crept over his filmy features.

After a moment he righted himself again and looked back down at the quivering old woman. He released her foot; it fell to the bed with a graceless thump, the heel desiccated and hollow, powdery skin hanging loosely over a skeletal bone.

His eyes twinkled as he ran his fingers up the dowager's leg, smirking as she groaned wordlessly. His hand came to rest on her knee, fingering the wrinkled skin which only a few hours before had been anointed with a balm of precious oils and ambergris.

"This knee, which never bent in supplication, even to the All-God—how much strength much reside there. Give it to me, for it is mine now."

With a sickening pop, the kneecap crumbled beneath his hand, sending forth a burst of light, denser this time, flooding into the scale and the hand of the man who held it. His body rocked again as a jolt of power shot through him, making his muscles contract, his heart pound, as blood raced through him, leaving him flushed, tumescent, more solid than a moment before; it was a sensation of bliss so deep that he barely needed to witness the agony that racked the dowager to make his pleasure complete.

He closed his eyes, allowing his head to swim in the new sea of power that was engulfing him; it was a sensation almost painful in its sweetness. In distant thoughts he could hear his weaknesses, his lowborn failings, melting in the rushing sound of Divine Right as it entered him, filled him, made him whole.

He was jolted back to consciousness by sickening blow of a small, hard foot to his genitals.

The glory vanished, replaced instantly by a rush of cold that shocked him to the neck, nauseating him. His vision blurred for a moment; when it returned he looked down to see the wizened old crone glaring at him, the rigid muscles of her face struggling to contain the triumphant smirk that shone clearly and without fetter in her eyes, fighting with the agony that gripped her, and emerging victorious.

A primal rage reared forth from the depth of him, to be suddenly quashed by a newer, higher-minded emotion, a sense of amused pity that tasted gloriously rich in the back of his mouth. Nobility, newly won. After his breath returned, the man smiled without more than a hint of a wince.

"Well struck, Your Serenity; I see I was correct when I predicted this would be a delightful struggle."

He grasped the empress's nightgown and jerked it up to her neck, laying her body bare. Without a hint of revulsion he fondled her sagging flesh, watching intently the look of horror and humiliation in her eyes, drinking it in, smiling broadly.

"These breasts never suckled, never gave life, nor joy, of any kind; there is no power to be harvested here, alas. You probably can't feel much of this anyway, can you, Empress? You have been dead below the neck your entire life."

Finally, when he was finished playing with her, his hand slid up her arm to her hand, the arthritic joints swollen and distended with age. He bent over her and raised the hand to his lips, brushing the palm with a kiss.

"This is the hand that has gripped the arm of the Sun Throne, has held the Scepter of the Sword in its grasp for far too long," he intoned. "The Scales have weighed in my favor now, Serenity. Time to loose your grip."

He turned her hand over and caressed the ring that adorned her middle finger, a large oval of shiny black hematite surrounded by a ring of blood-red-rubies from Sorbold's eastern mountain mines, the Ring of State her father wore, and his father, grandfather, and great-grandfather before him. Carefully he slid it over the distended knuckles and onto his own hand; he held it up to the light of the moon, causing the hematite to gleam brighter, the rubies to sparkle like dark fire.

He turned and held his hand up before her eyes, ignoring the blistering rage in them.

"Do you like the way it looks on my hand?" He admired the ring a moment longer, then sighed and removed it from his finger. "Alas, I shall have to wait until my investiture as emperor to keep it." He leaned over to return the ring to her finger and choked, then laughed aloud. The empress's rigid hand was frozen in an obscene gesture.

"Bravo, again, Serenity. This has proven quite enjoyable." He slid the ring back in place, roughly this time, then seized the elderly hand, dragging forth the power it held into the scale as before, leaving the flesh withered to the bone.

A look of solemnity settled over his swarthy features. He knelt down and leaned against the bed, his eyes locked with hers; the defiance in the empress's gaze dimmed in the face of what she saw in those eyes.

The man ran his finger delicately around the perimeter of her head, tracing a circular path through the wisps of thin white hair at her temples.

"This head bore upon its brow the Crown of Sorbold, the golden acknowledgment of sovereignty, of dominion," he said softly, his voice barely above a whisper. "Ingrained in this skull are many of its secrets, whispered to it from monarchs past, wisdom handed down through the ages, ruler to ruler, in one, unbroken line." The gleam in his eyes softened as tears came into the old woman's eyes, and his voice became even more gentle. "Those secrets, that wisdom, belongs to me now, Empress," he said, nodding slowly, as if to soothe her.

With great difficulty the dowager wrenched her head away.

The man rose, leaving his hand in place. The soft look in his eyes hardened as his fingers gripped the fragile skull at the temples.

He held up the scale once more.

The runes glowed, fiercely bright.

"Please give my best regards to Crown Prince Vyshla when you see him in the next few moments," the man said. "How lucky it is that you have lived all your life in Sorbold, Serenity. The climate here should be a good preparation for what is to come."

With a sudden contraction of muscle and will, his fingers clutched the top of the small skull and squeezed mercilessly.

A blisteringly bright line of light appeared in the flesh of the empress's head at the precise line where the crown was worn. It jumped, as with a life of its own, in a blazing arc, lighting the woman's contorted face, into the violet scale, exploding with brilliance and sending frenetic waves of colored light spilling in ever-replenishing waves off the scale's tattered edge.

The man's body convulsed violently, orgiastically, as a harsh guttural sound ripped forth from his throat. His body stiffened and became opaque, growing instantly warm with the sensation of power and authority visited upon him. He shuddered, trying to maintain his stance, and fell to one knee, overcome by the lore of dominion over the land, its treasures, and its people.

How long he knelt, regaining his breath and his balance, he was uncertain, but eventually when his legs could bear his weight again he struggled to a stand, and looked down into the royal bed.

The Dowager Empress of the Dark Earth was gray and cold, the color of clay. Her body no longer trembled, her chest giving only the slightest of indications of breath. All the pigment that had tinted her skin, her hair and eyes had faded from her, leaving her pale, colorless. Not even a hint of defiance remained in her glassy stare, but her skeletal hand still clutched the Ring of State in a death grip. The man exhaled slowly, amusement returning. They would have to pry it from the claw of her dead fingers. It seemed fitting.

He bent over the shell of the dying empress and softly kissed the cold, papery skin of her forehead.

"Thank you, Serenity," he whispered.

Then he stepped back into the moonlight. The illumination wrapped him in its glow, making him shine, translucent again, against the heavy damask silk of the royal bedchamber's draperies.

He waited thus, unseen, as the bells began to ring frantically down the hall, watching the understanding of their import pass through the reflective stare in the old woman's eyes.

In her last moments of fading consciousness, the empress could make out the whispered words on the other side of her heavy mahogany door, spoken in a voice clogged by tears.

"Should we waken her?"

A long moment of silence followed, finally broken by the final words the dowager heard.

"No, let her sleep. Morning will come soon enough; give her one last night of happiness before we tell her that her son is gone."

# 17

## THE GUEST CHAMBERS OF
## THE JUDICIARY, YARIM PAAR

Come away from the balcony, Aria."

Rhapsody looked over her shoulder and smiled. "I'm waiting for dusk, so that I can sing my sunset devotions," she said, turning back to the sight of the all-but-empty town square and the dry rock formation at its center.

The five days Achmed had believed would pass before the water would return had come and gone; Grunthor had remained three more until the moon began to wax full, then departed for the Canderian border, shaking his head.

"Don't know what's keepin' it," he had muttered as he mounted Rockslide. "Shoulda been 'ere by now."

"Be careful traveling alone through the areas near the mining camps to the west," Rhapsody had said, handing him a kerchief tied with a knot. "That's a fairly rough area."

"Oi'm tremblin'."

Rhapsody laughed. "Well, be careful anyway. Once you get in range of the border, things will be better. The people

of Canderre tend to be a friendly lot; many farms in the
eastern part of the province. It reminds me a good deal of
where I grew up."

Grunthor reached down and caressed her small cheek with
his enormous hand. "Look after yerself, Duchess, and don't
be a stranger. Come back for a turn in Ylorc; don't ya miss
Elysian?"

Rhapsody exhaled deeply at the pang that was summoned
by the reference to the beautiful underground cottage in the
center of a subterranean lake in the Bolglands where she
and Ashe had fallen in love. It was a haven for them both,
a place away from the world and its cares. "Yes, more than
I can say. But not as much as I miss the people in Ylorc. I
will try to come and visit, Grunthor. I just can't say when
it will be. There are a few things that require me to be close
to Haguefort for the time being."

"All rightee. Well, fare thee well, miss. Be'ave yourself."

"I promise nothing."

"An' kiss Miss Melly for me; give my regards to my
mate, the young Duke o' Navarne. Tell 'im next time we
meet Oi'll show 'im 'ow to pick 'is teeth with a fallen enemy's 'air. Works with yer own, o' course, but it's much
more fun when it's a foe."

"I shall tell him." Rhapsody clenched her jaw to stem the
sadness she felt at his leaving, the loss that ached intensely
whenever she was parted from him, or from Achmed, the
only two living people who really knew her in her other life.

"What's this, by the bye?" Grunthor had asked, lifting the
kerchief and taking the reins in hand.

"A memento of Yarim, just for you, since you were so
good and didn't consume any of its inhabitants. Even though
I know you really were tempted."

"Damn right," Grunthor had chuckled. "With all of 'em
standing around the square all day, it was pure torture. A
lot like workin' outside a bakeshop and never able ta go
inside for a taste."

Rhapsody, still at the balcony, smiled, remembering the

exchange, and hoping he had enjoyed the gingerbread men decorated with horned helmets like the ones the Yarimese guard wore, and the note—*Eat vicariously*. She was certain he had enjoyed the joke.

The door closed quietly behind her, and she felt Ashe's shadow fall on her from behind; he often came to listen to her evening vespers, the requiem that Liringlas sang for the sun as it sank below the edge of the world, welcoming it again in the morning with the dawn aubade, the love song to the morning sky. He always stood in respectful silence until she was finished; Ashe had Lirin blood in his mother's line, but not from the Liringlas strain. Nonetheless, all Lirin were called Children of the Sky, so it seemed fitting that he share the devotions she kept to the sun, moon, and stars, the other Children of the Sky.

She began the vespers, an ancient melody, in sweet major tones that turned quickly minor, a song of natural sadness and daily loss, resolving to a major key again, hopeful in its ending, a pledge of devotion that would last the long night and be there to greet the return of the sun in the morning. It was a song handed down in Lirin families from parent to child; in her case, her Lirin mother had imparted the melody to her, a twice-daily ritual that now brought her comfort in the memory.

Her human father had stood, much as Ashe did, in the shadows during these times, listening to the beauty of her mother's voice, and her own awkward attempts to imitate the sacred air. Her brothers, their Lirin heritage an afterthought to them, ignored the tradition, busying themselves instead with farmwork in the golden light of the morning sun, still at work in the red light of its setting.

A tear crept down her face, unbidden. It dried on her cheek in the warm wind.

Strong arms, comfortingly strong, encircled her.

"Lovely as always. Coming inside?"

"In a moment." Rhapsody pulled his arms tighter around her and laid her head back against his chest. She closed her eyes and felt the wind on her face, the heat of day beginning to wane with the cool of oncoming night.

Behind her eyelids she could remember the placement of the evening star; its memory still burned bright in the darkness, much like the ones she had just been recalling, though all the people bethought had long since passed into the realm of the Afterlife.

Ashe buried his face in her hair, exhaling deeply.

"Worried? Anything of concern to you on the wind?"

Her eyes still closed, Rhapsody listened carefully. The wind was muted, still; it gusted intermittently, dying down to the stagnant air of summer, only to pick up again in a moment. She concentrated, trying to discern the vibrations it carried.

Like the breeze in which she stood on the windy hilltop near Haguefort, the wind of Yarim carried a sense of arrival, of portent; something was coming. Yet unlike the sense she gained in Navarne, that something evil was brewing, it was a gentle omen, seeming to be a harbinger of something good.

A sense of hope, of good cheer, rippled over her skin, leaving it tingling.

She leaned back against Ashe, listening to the beating of his three-chambered dragon heart; it was a comforting sound, musical, slow, like the rhythm of waves in the sea. The vibration she felt in the air around her, the sense of peace and good fortune, blending with the heartbeat of her soulmate—it was intoxicating, making her face flush warm in the rosy luminance of the setting sun.

She struggled to come back to consciousness, back to calm, knowing that if she remained in Ashe's arms a moment longer she would succumb to a deep and blissful reverie, one from which it would be painful to rouse, and would remain on the balcony into the dark hours, reveling in the sounds of the night, the warm wind on her face, her husband's enduring embrace, his breath on her skin, the spicy scent of summer mixed with the intoxicating perfume from the Outer Market.

Rhapsody gently broke free from his hands and turned around to him, her face shining. Ashe blinked, then smiled.

"All right, I will assume that your answer is no, there is nothing worrying you on the wind."

"Nothing at all. Not on the wind, not anywhere else."

"Good." He took her hand and kissed it gently, then led her from the balcony into the inner chamber that had been lighted while they were outside with dozens of scented tapers.

All around the room were porcelain vases overflowing with fragrant summer lilies in fiery shades, dianthus and tuberoses, and sweet woodruff, known to the Lirin as ease-the-mind. On a table in the center of the room a silver platter of rich red berries coated in white and dark chocolate lay next to a bottle of Canderian brandy, two crystal snifters beside it, light dancing off their bowled surfaces. And in the middle of the table, a tiny fountain danced and splashed around a glass cylinder of flame, causing watery, fire-colored ripples of light to flicker on the chamber's walls.

It was Rhapsody's turn to blink. "What is all this? Do you think this means Ihrman has forgiven me for forcing the Bolg on him?"

"Probably not," Ashe said, walking to the table and uncorking the brandy. "This is from me."

"From you? Why? Are we arguing?"

Ashe chuckled. "I don't think so. Not yet, at least."

Rhapsody bent close to a vase of tuberoses and inhaled the sweet-spicy scent. "Then are we celebrating?"

"Yes."

She looked up at Ashe; the light of the candleflames was glistening in his cerulean-blue eyes, a half-smile on his face.

"What are we celebrating?"

Ashe poured the gem-colored liquid into the snifters, then swirled them both gently.

"Your birthday."

Rhapsody cocked her head and looked askance at him. "My birthday is not for another two months."

"Not the upcoming one, Aria. Next year's."

"Next year's birthday? Why?"

He ambled across the room and stopped in front of her, handing her a glass.

"Because the gift I plan to give you for your birthday next year will take time to craft; about thirteen months, I think. I need to be certain you will want it before it is started."

Rhapsody lifted the glass to her lips and took a sip. The liquid was warm, like fire, and it burned pleasantly in her mouth. She swallowed, inhaling over the fiery sensation in her throat. "Why don't you tell me what it is?"

Ashe took a sip himself, then stood, regarding her, one hand in his pocket. After a moment he pulled out a small leather drawstring bag and tossed it to her. She caught it, sending rolling waves through the brandy in her glass.

"Goodness; you'll make me spill," she chided, setting the glass down on the table and opening the pouch. She shook the contents out into her hand.

Five heavy gold pieces, older coinage than she had seen in Roland, slid out, clinking pleasantly as they came. Rhapsody turned the top one over slowly and examined it.

" 'Malcolm of Bethany,' " she read, squinting at the inscription, then looked up at Ashe, a puzzled expression on her face. "Was this Tristan's father?" Ashe took another sip of his brandy and nodded. "Thank you," Rhapsody said doubtfully.

"Do you remember ever seeing coins like this before?"

"I don't think so."

He sighed in disappointment. "Ah well. I had antiquities merchants scrambling all over Yarim to find them. What a waste."

"Where would I have seen them?" Rhapsody asked, her voice betraying a hint of impatience.

Ashe set his glass down and came over to her, taking her

shoulders and staring down into her questioning eyes.

"In a windy meadow, on the other side of Time," he said gently. "I offered you coins just like these, because I had nothing else to give you on the eve of your birthday."

Rhapsody turned away, clutching the coins tightly in her hand. She braced against the flood of emotions that swept over her, some stinging, others sweet, all treasured memories of their meeting in the old world, a story that no person other than they knew.

Sometimes, even now, she wondered if it had all been merely a dream that lingered until it had formed a memory.

Ashe took her by the shoulders and turned her around. He tucked his forefinger under her chin and lifted her gaze to meet his own, the vertical pupils in his eyes expanding and contracting in the flickering light of the candles.

"Through all the years, down all the roads I have traveled, after every nightmare, every dream, I have never forgotten how you looked in the moonlight that night, Emily," he said softly, using the name her family called her in the old world. "I still do not know what magic, what hand of Fate, plucked me from the road to town that I was walking and deposited me where I could find you, outside that foreharvest dance, but whoever it was, I owe them my soul. Because without you, I wouldn't have one."

"Do not be so quick to feel gratitude," Rhapsody said, her eyes on her fist, gripped tightly around the golden coins. "Whoever it was must have been the cruel person who also ripped you away from me the next day."

Ashe smiled broadly. "Exactly. And the pain nearly killed both of us—all but ruined our lives."

"And you're grateful for that?"

"Yes. All of it. The good and the bad, the pain and the ecstasy. Because it was our beginning, Aria. And in that beginning we knew, without question, what we wanted— each other, in any way we could have that. It was simple; there was no questioning it. You were willing to leave behind everything you had to come away with me; I was willing to give up the life I had known in the Future, knowing the war that was to come, in a heartbeat, to be with you. Risk was something we never even considered; that is what is so pure, so holy, about a new beginning. And nothing— not being dragged back to this time, not the cataclysm that took Serendair to the bottom of the sea, not having to travel for centuries through the belly of the earth, not separation, misunderstanding, pain, death, betrayal—nothing has thwarted the love that began that night." He reached out then and caressed her face, receiving a smile in return.

"And nothing will," she said.

"Each new beginning we've had in our lives has been a renaissance for us. There is a risk that is weighed, then discarded, when we forge ahead, trusting in what we are doing," Ashe continued. "Look at your undertaking with Entudenin. There was considerable risk there—the ire of the citizenry, the potential for conflict between the Bolg and the Yarimese, the possibility that you were destroying an ancient holy relic, which I know as a Singer and student of lore would be devastating to you—and yet you understood that the need for the water outweighed the risk. You forged ahead, staked your credibility with the dukes, the people, and with the Bolg, unable to promise any of them results or protection, but undertaking it anyway. As you said to me in Navarne, what in life is not worth risk? Even Achmed was willing to assume his part in that risk, for whatever his reasons were."

"What makes that so astounding is that, except for Grunthor and me, Achmed trusts no one," Rhapsody agreed. "Trust is the thing that allows you to risk, but the concept of risk is not in his personality. He hates acting without a plan, without the ability to control every aspect of the situation, even though he has so many skills that he can call upon in a crisis or an unexpected circumstance. He's consummately impatient."

Ashe's smile faded a notch.

"I don't know if you are right about that, Aria," he said.

"I think Achmed is more patient than we think. It all depends on what he is waiting for."

Rhapsody laid her hand on top of his that lingered on her face.

"What are you telling me, Sam?" she asked softly.

Ashe entwined his fingers with hers. "That if you agree, if you are willing to undertake with me a new beginning, I think we can set about ordering your birthday present tonight."

Rhapsody leaned closer so that her lips were just a breath away from his.

"And what do you plan to give me for my birthday?"

Ashe gazed into her eyes, the love in his own burning as brightly as the lanternlight, the candleflames.

"Someone to teach your morning aubade, your evening vespers to," he said.

All of the worry, the concern that had plagued both their minds over the years was gone, banished from the room as if by the hand of an unseen guardian, leaving nothing but the soft, inconstant light of the candleflames, the scent of tuberoses, the crackle of the lantern fire, the splash of the fountain, and each other.

And yet there was anticipation, a nervous, dizzying excitement that they had felt once before, so long ago, on the other side of Time.

The sense of portent, the good cheer that Rhapsody had felt on the balcony, blew in on the evening breeze and wrapped itself around the bedchamber; there was an utter lack of foreboding, a palpable good cheer that drove any doubt from the room.

Only once did Rhapsody speak.

"Why—?"

"Shhh, love," Ashe said, resting his finger on her lips, then replacing it with his own. "Don't ask why tonight; leave that for the morning."

She returned his kiss without hesitation of any kind.

The lanternlight within the fiery cylinder that shone on the falling water of the fountain mirrored their movements, a slow, gentle dance of melding, opposing elements, improbable in their attraction, beautiful in their union.

Those bonds of elemental power, tied inexorably to their souls, sang deep within each of them; the crackling passion of the fire that was she, the patient relentlessness of waves of the sea that was nascent in him, oscillating, undulating, building and cresting as it joined with her, warmed by the pure, gleaming fire within, forming a new element, one that burned with heat, ebbed with the tides of the sea, remaining stalwart, unending, as their love for one another.

The element of Time.

In a fleeting moment of conscious thought amid the blissful oblivion of lovemaking, Rhapsody felt a tone sound within her, a melodic note that was different from *ela,* her own Naming note, and *sol,* the musical pitch to which Ashe was attuned. This new tone resonated through her body and mind, then disappeared, leaving a mark she could sense, but only distantly.

It was the most beautiful sound she ever remembered hearing.

The water in the fountain on the table leapt with joy; the fire in the lantern burned brightly in time with it, until its fuel was spent. Then it resolved to a gentle glow, reflecting in the ripples in the basin, no longer leaping, but smooth as glass.

The moon crept over the horizon's edge, bathing the red clay of Yarim in white light, making the city shine as if in a dream, the silent brick buildings and empty market stands gleaming in its radiance.

The moonlight glided through the open balcony window and came to rest on the two lovers, wrapped in sleep and the arms of each other, spreading to lovers like them all across the city.

It tiptoed into the apertures beneath which children slept, blanketing them in its light, shining in their dreams.

It shone around the sad, lifeless relic that stood in the center of a disrupted fountainbed, illuminating it to dazzling as the tiny flakes of mica in its surface reflected the light.

From the depths of the now-cleared earthen passageway came a whisper, then a gurgle, and finally a sigh.

A particularly bright moonbeam caught the first mist around the Fountain Rock's summit; it sparkled in the haze of the glistening vapor, bathing it with an ethereal radiance of mist.

And as the dry, weary city slept in the cool wind of an otherwise warm summer night, life-giving water began to pour forth, once more, from Entudenin.

# 18

$\mathcal{M}$orning clanged in on the clamor of the bells from the Judiciary's tower ringing over a swell of shouting in the still-dark streets.

Groggily Ashe sat up, deep in the fog of dragon-sleep, his head humming unpleasantly at the ruckus. He muttered an inaudible curse, then rubbed his eyes with one hand as he propped himself up with the other, the blissful ease of the night before dissipating around him.

His dragon senses came to awareness first; the fire in the room had gone out, and the heat of day had not yet come to dispel the chill of dawn from the chamber. In the scope of his awareness he could feel the water coursing forth from Entudenin a few street corners away, hear the glad tidings being shouted and acclaimed by voice, the ringing of bells, the clashing of pots, and the banging of drums as Yarim Paar awoke to the miracle. The minutiae of it all was mammoth; each individual in the square—*four hundred twenty three, four hundred twenty four,* the dragon counted—each of the three hundred and seven, no, nine, noise makers, each of the one hundred and eleven sparks in the fireplace, each drop of newly flowing water—*seven hundred million, four hundred sixty seven thousand, three hundred thirty six, seven, eight*—counted obsessively by his dragon nature. The resulting din made his head hurt, made him struggle to subdue his innate awareness, shielding it from his conscious mind so he would not end up with a colossal headache.

Rhapsody slept fitfully beside him, pale and whispering to herself. After spending half the night in deep slumber she had become restless, edgily twitching from side to side in the bed, embroiled in dreams that he could not chase away. He had, as a result, not gotten a great deal of rest, and he was certain, based on the reverberations from her body and the alabaster hue of her face, that she had not, either.

He leaned over her and kissed her neck, his lips warm against her cold skin; it was moist, perspiring. He laid his hand on her side and shook her gently.

"Rhapsody? It's almost dawn. Are you going to sing your aubade?"

She moaned in response, drawing her knees up and curling into a ball.

Alarm rushed over him. Ashe sat up, shaking off the tremors of cold worry and gathered him wife into his arms. She was breathing shallowly, face beaded in sweat.

"Rhapsody?"

Weakly she pushed away from him and rolled onto her side, then dragged herself to the edge of the bed. She stumbled as she stood, then hurried to the privy closet, slamming the door behind her.

The alarm that had gripped him was replaced a moment later with realization as the sounds of retching issued forth from behind the bathroom door.

He rose quickly and dressed, waiting for her to return. After a few minutes had passed he walked to the privy and stood outside the door.

"Rhapsody? Are you all right?"

Her answer was weak. "Go away, please."

"Can I get you something?"

"No. Go away."

He ran a hand nervously through his red-gold hair. "Do you—"

"Ashe." Her voice came through the door more loudly this time, still ragged but a little stronger. "Go away for a while, or I will have to kill you when I come out of here."

"Oh. Well, since I don't want to die just yet, I suppose I will go out on the balcony for a bit," he said, his smile fighting with the furrows of worry in his brow. "If you need anything, just snap your fingers, and I will be there."

"Thank you. Go away."

"All right."

"Now."

"At your will, m'lady."

The Lord Cymrian turned away from the renewed sound of retching and went out onto the balcony. Dawn was breaking over the city, coming to light over the red buildings and making them gleam with morning fire. Ashe took a deep breath, inhaling infinitesimal drops of moisture that had coated the air in the night, leaving it heavy, sweet.

In the streets below a crowd was gathering, larger than the crowds that had pushed into the Marketway to stare at the Bolg. There was an almost palpable violence mixed with the joy as the townspeople at the edge of the central streets, those who had obviously heard the news from those closer to the city square, shoved themselves forward, carrying jars and clay vessels for harvesting the liquid bounty that had returned in the night.

Ashe noted, lacking any genuine interest, that the Shanouin priestesses had been summoned; a thin corridor in the pressing crowd had been opened to allow a dozen or so of the veiled women in their pale blue ghodins into the town square where the fountainbed had already begun to overflow, spilling precious water onto the dry bricks of the streets. One among them seemed different, awkward in the ritual countersigns they were making as they approached the Fountain Rock; he might have thought it noteworthy if he cared at all, which he did not.

He stared at the wellspring; Entudenin had darkened, like wet clay, to a deeper hue of brown. Tiny rivulets of green and blue, too insignificant to be visible to human eyes yet, but within range of his sight, striated the clay; by the end of the cycle, the color would be starting to return to the Fountain Rock. There was something deeply pleasing about the knowledge of that. He closed his eyes, concentrating on the miracle a few streets away.

The element of water that formed the core of his soul sang within him; the waters that were issuing forth from Entudenin shouted in return. Ashe stood for a moment, lost in the silent song, then went to the sword rack and drew Kirsdarke, the ancient elemental sword that he carried as its bearer. His hand gripped the hilt more tightly than usual; the sword was more alive today, gladdened by the presence of the living water pouring into the streets of Yarim Paar.

He returned to the window and held up the sword in the light. The liquid blade, which normally ran in blue rivers from tip to tang, disappearing just above the wave-shaped hilt, was frothing like breakers rolling to the shore of the sea; it sparkled in the light of dawn, rejoicing in kinship with the fountain. Ashe could feel its power, enormously vibrant and strong, even at rest, surge and increase, celebrating now with renewed excitement, as if it were welcoming a child in this place of dry desert.

In his kinship with the sword, he could understand its thrill.

Soon he would welcome a child of his own, one who shared the same blood, the same history.

And love for the same woman.

The privy closet door opened with a slow creak and Rhapsody emerged. Ashe sensed her return and quickly sheathed the sword, then ran into the room from the balcony and took her arm. She was pale as milk and her eyes seemed to be struggling to keep a focus.

"I am all right, Sam," she said, forestalling his query, "but I can't see very well. Can you please help me to the bed?"

"You can't see?" Ashe asked nervously, guiding her gently across the cold tiles of the floor. "I have never heard of that before."

She squeezed his hand as a spasm shot through her, stopping where she stood, trying to regain her balance, then nodded when she had done so. "How many times have you witnessed a woman of human and Lirin blood who was carrying a wyrmkin child?"

"Never," Ashe admitted, "but I didn't think you would be ill so quickly."

"Neither did I," Rhapsody said, pushing back against the pillows as Ashe delivered her to the bed. "My mother carried six of us without missing a single morning's chores. It's frustrating to be so weak. And cold. I feel so cold." Her eyes cleared for a moment, and she took Ashe's hand and smiled. "But I am very happy."

Ashe kissed her on the forehead. The skin was still clammy, beginning to burn with feverish heat. "Yes. As am I." He looked down into her green eyes, which were beginning to cloud over again. "Tell me what I can do for you," he said, trying to keep the desperation out of his voice, and the worry from taking command of his mind.

Rhapsody winced as her abdomen contracted again; she rolled to her side, trying to keep from groaning in pain.

"Take me home," she said, her face buried within the pillow. "I want to go back to Haguefort."

Rhapsody had just reemerged from the privy closet when Ashe returned to the room. She was sitting in one of the chairs near the fire a few feet away, dressed in her traveling clothes, and looking as if she felt better, though still ghostly pale. Ashe came to her side, took her by the shoulders, and bent down, kissing her cheek.

"It should a fairly simple task to slip, unnoticed, from Yarim," he said, running the back of his hand over her hair, still damp from the bath he had given her before he left to make arrangements for their journey. "Every man, woman, and child in Yarim Paar, it seems, is dancing in the spray from Entudenin, filling jars and being generally jubilant or disruptive. No one is paying attention except our own guard regiment."

"Good," Rhapsody said, clutching the arms of the chair as another spasm rocked her.

Ashe sighed in a mixture of frustration and sympathy. "I hope you will forgive me, but we will be traveling by coach," he said, a note of humor in his otherwise-worried voice. "At the risk of having to brave your ire for being made to feel pampered, old, or ill, I thought you should be as comfortable and as contained as possible."

"Thank you," she replied, exhaling deeply as the tremor passed. "You have been most kind. At the risk of making myself ill again, can you answer the question I was trying to pose to you last night?"

"Yes. What is it?"

"When you said that we could, er, order my birthday gift, you commented something about it taking thirteen months to craft," she said, her hands moving back to her stomach. "Why?"

Ashe winced. "Well, you are half Lirin, and the Lirin have a longer gestation than humans do," he said, watching as the realization began to come over her face and trying not to laugh at the comic horror in her expression. "A child of a full Lirin mother and a human father generally is carried for about thirteen months, as you know. And that's being optimistic. With dragon blood involved, it's impossible to know how long this will take."

"How long was your mother pregnant with you?" Rhapsody asked shakily.

"Two and a half years. Close to three."

The Lady Cymrian stood up sharply, her hand over her mouth.

"Excuse me," she said quickly, then lunged for the privy closet again.

Ashe waited for a moment, then went to the door and summoned the guard.

"Tell the quartermaster to hurry with that coach," he said.

$\mathcal{T}$he jolting ride through the rocky outskirts of Yarim Paar was sheer agony. Every rocky rut the coach contacted brought on another spasm, another bout of nausea, leaving Rhapsody sallow and trembling. By the time they reached the foothills above the city, she was unable to remain upright and lay, curled under a heavy blanket, on the coach's bench, jostled violently with each lurch of the carriage.

Ashe was growing frantic, though he fought to keep his panic from his wife's notice. He kept repeating the words of the Seer over and over again in his mind, struggling to draw comfort from them but finding none.

*Rhapsody will not die bearing your children. The pregnancy will not be easy, but it will not kill or harm her.*

*If you have lied to me, Aunt, I will come for your blood,* he thought bitterly, endeavoring to remember the primordial mandate that the Seers could not do so, but failing to be consoled by it. After all, his own grandmother, Manwyn's sister, had deceived him about Rhapsody's survival more than a hundred years before.

When they reached the summit of the promontory that overlooked Yarim Paar, Ashe glanced out the window, then rapped on the window that opened onto the driver's perch.

"Stop here, please."

"Yes, m'lord."

As the call to halt traveled fore and aft of the carriage in the caravan, Ashe knelt on the floor next to Rhapsody's seat and ran a hand gently over her hair and face. Her body was still cold and trembling, her eyes still fleetingly glassy. He lowered his lips to her ear, kissing it, then spoke softly.

"Aria? Can you hear me?"

She nodded distantly.

"I'm going to stop here and take you outside for a moment to get a breath of air." Rhapsody didn't respond.

Carefully he gathered her in his arms and kicked open the carriage door, carrying her out of the darkness of the coach, down the steps and out into the blinding summer sun.

The wind at the top of the bluff snapped his cloak of mist behind him, spattering droplets into the hot air, as it blew her hair in front of her face. Rhapsody's eyes remained closed, but her grip on his arm tightened slightly.

He carried her to the edge of the rocky promontory and came to a halt there.

"Aria—look if you can."

At first Rhapsody did not respond, but after a moment of the wind in her face she opened one eye, then the other, and gazed out at the city of Yarim Paar stretching out on the flat red plain below.

In the center of the distant city, a glorious mist of blue and white was emanating forth from the tiny gleaming obelisk that yesterday had been dead, shriveled in centuries of heat and loss. The light of the summer sun caught the water droplets and refracted them into a glorious spectrum of color, reaching from the ground into the air above, disappearing in a shaft of gold from the sunlit clouds.

The water that was flowing now from Entudenin had spilled over the fountainbed and was coursing through the streets, turning the dry red clay to dark mud. The sound of merry laughter, of celebratory music and clamor could be heard, muted but unmistakable, in the distance; it echoed off the rocky hills on which they stood, a joyful vibration in the normally silent desert.

Rhapsody lifted her head, then slowly slid down to a stand, bracing herself against her husband, and smiled. She inhaled deeply, but said nothing, staring at the rainbow in the desert.

Where the skycolors touch the earth.

Ashe drew her closer, steadying her.

"See, Aria? See what your faith has wrought here?"

Rhapsody leaned against him, resting her head against his shoulder, and watching the combined celebration of humans and earth in the Fountain Rock's life-giving spray. Reveling in the song of it.

"Our faith, and the Bolg's knowledge of the right way to proceed. And Achmed's refusal to be deterred by the bigotry of the Yarimese."

"Perhaps that is all that a miracle is—faith and the knowledge of what is right in combination with refusal to be deterred." His hand came to rest on her abdomen. A moment later hers came to rest atop his.

"I am sure you are right."

He led her back to the carriage, leaning on his arm but walking on her own. Once she was settled inside, he took a final glance at the ancient wonder on the windswept plain below, then called to the coachman.

"Take us back to Navarne—gently, now."

## THE CAULDRON, YLORC, IN THE FORGE

€asy, Shaene—the glass will shatter before it anneals; it's not sufficiently cooled."

"Bugger yourself, Sandy," Shaene growled, clutching the giant pincers with the leather rags, his thick arms trembling with the effort. He shifted the cylinder of just-melted frit, the earliest stage of glass, to the edge of the forge and brought it to rest above the slab where it would be flattened into a sheet.

Achmed struggled to contain his impatience.

"The color is wrong already," he said through gritted teeth. "The red is too light; it's almost pink."

"Give it a few hours of heat," Omet suggested, interposing himself between the king and the craftsmen who were standing near the kilns that had been built near the iron forges; the men and Bolg were uniformly dripping with sweat and exhaustion. "The color changes in the curing. It will darken."

Achmed turned away in frustration and aimed a savage

kick at an almost empty pot of powdered cobalt ore that sat at the brink of the open fire. A streak of blue light erupted in the flames as the mineral ignited, then extinguished a second later.

Shaene started at the sound, dropping the pincers and bouncing the glass cylinder off the rock slab. The resounding *crack* echoed through the cavernous chambers around the forge, followed by the dispirited sigh of the glassworkers.

"Enough of this!" Shaene shouted, heaving the metal pincers against a nearby stone wall where they fell onto a wooden scaffold, sending pots, tools, and smalti flying. His demeanor melted before their eyes, like the glass in the kiln. "I cannot bear this anymore, not for all the gold in Gwylliam's treasury! This project is cursed, cursed!"

"Calm yourself, Master Shaene," Omet said, glancing between the livid craftsman and the narrowing eyes of the Bolg king.

A gruff cough drew their attention. Achmed turned around to see a Firbolg guard standing off to the side of the forge overhang, signaling to him.

"Get back to work, Shaene, or I will tell your mother you are having tantrums again," he spat, then strode over to the soldier.

"What is it?"

"Messenger, Sorbold."

"A messenger from Sorbold? From the mail caravan?" The soldier shook his head; Achmed scratched his own, slapping the sweat away. "Very well. I will be right down."

The man was waiting in the Great Hall when the king arrived, dressed in the livery of the empress and the armor of the mountain columns, staring at the domed ceiling above the hall. He turned immediately upon hearing the king enter and bowed perfunctorily.

"Majesty."

"What do you want?"

The soldier eyed him with a mixture of nervousness and

contempt. The Sorbolds were not a naturally courteous people; rudeness was so much a part of the national character that special regiments, like the one to which this soldier belonged, were trained in the politics of etiquette, so that messages could be delivered across borders without international incidents being started. He stood at straighter attention and cleared his throat.

"The Blesser of Sorbold, the benison Nielash Mousa, greets King Achmed of Ylorc, extending to him the salutations of—"

"What do you *want*?" Achmed demanded impatiently. "I am busy."

The messenger, caught up short, swallowed the words he had painstakingly prepared, then met the king's eye.

"Her Serenity, the Dowager Empress, has passed from this life in her sleep," he said shortly.

"I am sorry to hear that," Achmed said curtly. "Her son must be thrilled."

"Doubtful," replied the Sorbold soldier, abandoning royal protocol in the attempt to deliver the message. "He is dead himself."

"What happened? Did they hire a new chef?"

The soldier paused long enough to recover from the insult. "Her Serenity had seen ninety-four summers, the Crown Prince sixty-two. It was the will of the All-God, nothing more."

The Firbolg king eyed him in silence for a moment, then put out his hand.

"Do you have an official decree?" he asked.

"Yes, Majesty, and a request for you to attend the state funerals from the benison."

Achmed broke the seal and opened the folded parchment, scanning it rapidly. It contained the same information that had been relayed to him orally, in more flowery language, with the addition of a single long sentence at the bottom of the decree.

As the Crown Prince left no legitimately recognized heir, a Colloquium is summoned by invitation to address the absence of a line of succession to the Throne of the Dark Earth, issued to the Lord and Lady Cymrian, sovereigns of the Alliance to which Sorbold is a sealed ally, as well as rulers of bordering nations, namely His Majesty, King Achmed of Ylorc, Her Majesty, Rhapsody, Queen of Tyrian, Lord Tristan Steward, Regent of Roland, and Viedekam, Administrator of the Non-aligned States as well as representatives of the Church, the Nobility, the Mercantile and the Army, to convene directly after the burial during the Period of Mourning, eleven days hence.

The Bolg king stared at the decree for a very long time, then looked up into the face of the messenger, almost as if he had had forgotten the man was there.

"You may go now," he said, nodding to his own guards. The Sorbold representative bowed and left.

Achmed waited until the footsteps of the soldier from the rocky, secretive nation that bordered his own had died away, then sat down on the marble throne in the Great Hall, his stomach churning in rare-felt anxiety. He stared at the words on the parchment, words whose import he was only beginning to absorb, and swore in the language of the Bolg.

"*Hrekin,*" he said.

# 19

## ON THE TRANS-ORLANDAN THOROUGHFARE, BETHANY

The royal coach, already traveling at half-speed, slowed appreciably. The small internal window slid open, and the driver's voice could be heard over the noise of the decelerating caravan.

"One of your regiments is approaching, m'lord."

Ashe, leaning back against the leather bench with Rhapsody propped up, asleep, in his arms, reached for the velvet curtain on the carriage's side.

"One of my regiments?"

"Yes, m'lord. It appears that Anborn is at the lead."

"Very well, slacken the reins and roll gently to a stop. Make it as gradual as you can."

"Yes, m'lord."

The sound of hoofbeats and shouted orders grew louder as the coach came to a halt, amid squeaking and the clattering of the horses and tack. Carefully Ashe slid his wife from his chest to the pillows, covered her carefully with the carriage blanket, and stepped quickly from the coach, endeavoring to keep the blinding sun from encroaching on the cool and comfortable darkness within.

As he came around the front of the carriage he could see the Lord Marshal in the fore atop his beautiful black stallion, leading the second regiment of Haguefort in a steady canter eastward to meet them on the thoroughfare; the General motioned to the soldiers behind him to slow to a walk, and spurred his horse onward in Ashe's direction.

"Well met, Uncle," Ashe said, shielding his eyes from the sun as Anborn approached. "Please keep the regiment back—Rhapsody is sleeping, and I do not wish her disturbed."

The General laid on the reins and drew his mount to a brisk halt; the animal danced fluidly in place, then stopped completely, perfectly trained to the needs of the horseman who had lost the use of his legs.

"Sleeping?" he demanded, his voice terse on the hot summer wind. "Midday? Is she ill?"

Ashe motioned to Anborn to follow him out of the hearing of the carriage guards; when they were about fifty paces away, he glanced at the two regiments setting to a watch, then returned his attention to Anborn.

"She is not feeling well," he said, looking up from the ground at his uncle. "She is with child."

Anborn stared down at him from the stallion's back, absorbing his words for a moment, allowing the horse to edge uncomfortably close to Ashe. Then, with a speed born of years of soldiering, he pulled the greave from his useless leg and heaved it at the Lord Cymrian, striking him square in the chest.

"Are you out of your misbegotten mind?" he hissed, fury evident in his tone. "What have you done, you idiot?"

Ashe inhaled deeply, struggling to remain calm, though his fists curled at his sides, and the dragon in his blood began to rise.

"If you need ask, Uncle, I am sorry for you," he said as pleasantly as he could.

The General drew himself up in the saddle, anger radiating from his azure eyes. "You unspeakable fool! Did you forget, perchance, what happened to your own mother?"

Ashe finally took a step back. "Why are you here, Anborn?" he asked, the multiple tones of the dragon creeping into his voice. "I trust you have a reason other than to assail me with questions that are none of your concern."

The General spat on the ground to his right side, as if trying to clear a bad taste from his mouth, then walked the horse in a tight circle to return to court distance, reached angrily into the folds of his jerkin and pulled forth an oil-cloth packet, which he tossed to the Lord Cymrian.

"The Empress of Sorbold is dead, finally," he said contemptuously. "As is her fat bump of a son."

Ashe stared at him for a moment, then pulled the missive from the oilcloth and broke the seal, his dragonesque eyes scanning the document.

"This is worrisome," he said as he read the missive. "There is more than just a lack of a direct heir; over the empress's long life, even those distantly related to the crown have died out. Sorbold is a headless body now; it will be chaos there."

"You have your father's talent for understatement," Anborn observed, staring down at him from the saddle. "Mark this moment in your mind, nephew; this is the day when the war that is to come began."

"You see war in every waking moment, Uncle," Ashe replied, the more human tone of annoyance in his voice now. "There is a council in place, an Alliance to which Sorbold is a friend, not only through Leitha, but those who came to the Moot and pledged their fealty. Let us not borrow trouble, shall we?"

"The second regiment is outfitted with the appropriate state mourning finery and all that other nonsense of protocol," the General said, ignoring his words. "They are here to escort you both to the funeral."

Ashe glanced over at the carriage. "We cannot possibly attend," he said, rolling the parchment into a scroll and sliding it back inside its oilcloth sheath. "Rhapsody is fragile, ill, and I will not jeopardize her with such a long journey over mountainous terrain."

"You cannot possibly *not* attend," the General snorted, glaring down from the saddle. "This will be the moment when Sorbold's destiny is decided, the genesis of a new dynasty, or a new form of government altogether. Those distant royals who may attempt to stake a claim to the throne will face a possibly bloody challenge from the nobility, who, as head of their own city-states, may seek to dissolve Sorbold as an empire altogether. Then there is the army, the mercantile, and the church, all of whom have interests they will want to advance. You are the bloody high lord of all this mess; you have no other choice but to go."

"He's right, Sam." Rhapsody's voice, weak but clear, caused both men to turn abruptly toward the carriage, where she crouched at the door, preparing to disembark. Her long hair, normally bound back in a simple black ribbon, hung loose down her back, but otherwise she seemed alert.

"Rhapsody—wait," Ashe said, running to her side. He slid an arm behind her to brace her, then helped her out of the carriage, into the warm air. "I'm sorry to have disturbed you."

"Well, draconic tones tend to rend the vibrations of otherwise bland air," she said, entwining her arm through his to stand on her own. "I assume that the other multiple-toned voice could only belong to Anborn, yes?"

The General nudged his mount closer slowly. "Indeed, lady. Can you not see me?"

Rhapsody shielded her eyes and looked up at him. "I can see your shadow, your outline," she said, smiling wanly. "But I would know your vibrational signature anywhere, Anborn, whether my eyes are working or not."

The General gave her a slight smile in return, which quickly faded, as he looked at Ashe with a mixture of accusation and disgust.

"Did I hear correctly that the empress is dead?" Rhapsody asked.

"The empress and the Crown Prince both," Ashe replied, looking off to the south in the direction of the Sorbold border; even at this distance the rocky peaks of the Teeth could be seen, swathed in the intermittent clouds that cloaked the mysterious realm. "Within hours of each other."

"How awful," Rhapsody murmured. "Did they get a new chef recently?"

"It's not clear. But they were both quite aged, and they died in their sleep."

"Leitha probably had nothing left to live for, after accomplishing the one thing she still had to do—outlive anyone who was a challenge to her sovereignty," Anborn said, shifting in the saddle.

"Stop it. What a terrible thing to say." Rhapsody's face went pale, and she clutched her abdomen suddenly.

"You must go to the funeral for me, Anborn, as my representative," Ashe said, taking her into his arms and guiding her back to the carriage. "As you can see, Rhapsody is in no condition to be left alone."

The General's expression blackened. "So as to not risk offending the lady's ears, or senses, I won't curse you properly as I should, and tell you what a ridiculous thought that is. You agreed to take on this accursed lordship, if you re-call. I, being the more intelligent and sensible of us, refused to even be considered for it. Now you see why." He looked at Rhapsody, whose face was blank with illness and con-cern. "But you are correct in that the Lady Cymrian is not able to be left alone. So I will take her back to Navarne, and you can go off to Sorbold and try and sort out the situation there."

"If you think I would leave—"

"He's right, Sam," Rhapsody said, her voice strained but somewhat stronger. "If we can't both be there, you must go."

"Very well," Ashe said, looking displeased, "I will go once you are safely ensconced in Haguefort."

"The timing will not suit," interjected the Lord Marshal. "You will only be on time for the funeral services if you head straight from here to Jierna Tal in Jierna'sid. The rites take place in the Night Mountain, at the basilica of Earth, Terreanfor. That's a good five days' ride or more, with fa-vorable weather. They want to bury the old hellkite and her useless blob of a son before they begin to rot and stink in the heat."

"Oh gods," Rhapsody moaned. She turned away rapidly and retched.

"You think I would leave *you* to tend to her?" Ashe de-manded incredulously as he handed her his handkerchief.

For the first time since he had arrived Anborn appeared taken aback.

"My apologies, lady," he said quickly. Rhapsody, her back turned, waved her acceptance. "Listen, nephew, I promise to be on my best behavior—I will comport myself in the manner which she deserves in an escort. And I will protect her with my life."

Ashe's face was doubtful as he ran his hand over her back. "Rhapsody? What do you think?"

His wife ran her hand through her thick gold hair, pulling it back off her face, and turned around again.

"I will be perfectly safe with Anborn," she said, breathing deeply. "I want to get back and check on Melisande and Gwydion Navarne. But I don't want to remain at Haguefort."

"Where do you wish to go, then, Aria?"

"To Elynsynos."

Uncle and nephew looked at each other in shock. Anborn was the first to recover his voice.

"You wish to go to the dragon's lair? Unsteady as you are?"

Rhapsody nodded. "Yes. She alone of anyone alive that I know has carried a child of a totally different racial line, has blended the blood of dragon and human in her own body. I will be safe with her, and well, in her cave of the Lost Sea. The waves will lull my nausea until Ashe returns from Sorbold. Elynsynos will take care of me." She smiled wanly. "Those aspects aside, I miss her terribly. It will be good to visit and catch her up on the gossip."

Ashe exhaled deeply. "I suppose there is nowhere I can think of where you will be safer during your confinement, Rhapsody," he said at last. He looked at his uncle. "And there is no one else to whom I would entrust getting you there. Very well, Anborn; if you will escort my wife to Haguefort, and then to the northern wilds to the lair of Elynsynos, I will be in your debt." Anborn nodded. "I will take one of the falconers with me. If there is need of me, if anything goes wrong—"

"I will only send out a falcon if there is a catastrophe. Now go. The regiment is waiting."

"Travel well, Sam," Rhapsody whispered as Ashe took her into his arms. "I wish to hear good news when I see you again. And study the basilica; I've heard it is one of the hidden wonders of the world. I want you to tell me every detail of it when you return."

"I hope you know that I am only going because you want it that way, Aria."

"I know. Your presence there, at this time of upheaval,

will benefit not only Sorbold, but the Alliance, and the rest of the world."

"If you wanted me to stay with you, the rest of the world could be damned," he whispered back.

## BRINNE SEACOAST, NORTH OF AVONDERRE, GWYNWOOD

The scales had augured that the tiny fishing village would be deserted at midday.

*As usual, Faron is right,* the seneschal thought as the rowing scull made its way across the waves toward shore.

Caius, the more seasick of the twins, had elected to sit in the stern, rather than pitch with each wave, and was gripping his stonebow tightly, his face gray. Clomyn, comfortably ensconced in the bow, called to the boatswain, guiding him through the rocky edge of the shoals that were the bane of the fishermen of this desolate northern coast.

Finally, when the sun was directly overhead, and the world swam in billowing heat rippling off the sand, the seneschal's scull and the three longboats of soldiers he had brought with him from Argaut made landfall.

He stood for a long moment, drinking in the gentle crashing of the waves, the black, pocked cliffs rising tall beyond the shoreline to meet the sky, the cry of the gulls above, the whipping of the wind that dashed along the coast, and the scent of promise that hung in the air, waiting for him to fulfill it.

*One more sennight, Rhapsody,* he thought. *The scales have predicted our meeting.*

Within his mind he could feel the familiar boiling sensation as the demon woke and began to come to awareness.

*We have made landfall,* the voice whispered, excitement evident in the crackling tone. *I'll want a fire.*

"Not yet," the seneschal demurred. "We do not want to draw attention to our presence yet."

*When shall the burnings commence? When will the destruction begin?*

"Soon," the seneschal murmured, trying to remain calm; his excitement only served to enflame the demon. "But not yet; we have work to do, horses to purchase, plans to lay. It is best that we remain undiscovered until we have captured what we are after. Once she is safely stowed on the ship, the fires will begin."

He struggled to turn a deaf ear to the demon's impatient, wordless mutterings that followed, and looked instead to the men who were off-loading, dragging the longboats out of the surf.

"Signal the others to prepare to come ashore. When the men and the supplies have all landed, secret the boats up the beach, where the sand ends, in one of those rocky enclaves," he ordered, signaling to Fergus. "Make haste; we have a trap to lay."

From inside a cave in the volcanic cliffs farther north, black eyes clouded with the film of age watched as the ship unloaded its crew, observing the back-and-forth of the longboats, until at last they were stowed away in the rocks at shoreline. The ship retreated to deeper waters on the south side of the cove, out of plain sight. The soldiers combed the area around the beach, then slowly set forth east to the forest.

Had any of them been watching in return, they might have seen an elderly man with skin the color of driftwood, who stared in their direction for a moment, then shook his head in the throes of dementia and returned to drawing meaningless patterns in the sand.

# 20

Achmed had long despised cards and other games of chance.

Part of the reason might have been that long ago, in the old world, that other life, his true name had been won in a game of cards from the Bolg of Serendair and given by the winner, under duress, to the demon that was his enemy.

Part of the reason might also have been that his Dhracian mother was selected for capture by the Bolg with a toss of the bones.

But whatever the reason, what he detested most about gamesplaying was the uncertainty of it.

The thrill of the gamble that others so often relished never came to him; he hated risk, and spent the better part of his existence minimizing it whenever possible. And while on those occasions in his life when he had succumbed to the need to gamble, to risk, in order to achieve what he wanted, he had more oftentimes been successful than not, he still endeavored to minimize that uncertainty, that surrender of control.

He ruminated on how much he loathed those ambiguous, helpless feelings as he stood on the reviewing stand, the lone representative of Ylorc amid a sea of other dignitaries and their retinues.

From his place in the crowd of heads of state he was learning a good deal about both the actual capacities of his fellow sovereigns, and the perceptions they hoped to convey, by studying the retinues they had brought with them to the state funeral of Sorbold.

The Sorbold army had turned out in force, doubtless to underscore to the visiting dignitaries the unwavering power they still had. Achmed counted twenty divisions in the

square that surrounded the palace of Jierna Tal alone, with
that many again lining the streets from the Place of Weight
where the mammoth Scales stood to the mountains on the
outskirts of Jierna'sid, where Terreanfor, the hidden Basilica
of the Earth, was concealed in a place of endless darkness.
It was an imposing display of manpower, well managed and
obviously well trained. Grunthor would have been impressed. Achmed settled for merely being concerned.

Many of the other heads of state, including Tristan Steward, the regent of Roland, Miraz, the Diviner of the Hintervold, Viedekam, one of the chieftains of the Nonaligned
States, and Beliac, the King of Golgarn, whose borders
backed up to his own on the far eastern side of the Teeth,
had brought enormous retinues with them as well. It was
this genital-waggling posturing that flooded Achmed with
the sensation of being at a game of cards; the silent bluffing,
the position-staking, the puffery that irritated him beyond
measure.

The Lirin realm, Tyrian, of which Rhapsody was titular
queen, had sent a modest delegation headed up by her vice-
roy, Rial, a calm man with a sensible head on his shoulders.
He had come with the Lirin ambassador to Sorbold and a
handful of guards, as had Ashe, whose solitary presence
caused Achmed to raise an eyebrow. Rhapsody's absence
was rather disturbing; he knew that very little would have
been able to keep her from attending such a landmark service as this funeral in Terreanfor, a place she had never been
privileged to see, student of ancient lore that she was.

Achmed stepped out of the crowd as much as he could,
though the dais was so full that he could barely separate
himself at all. He concentrated, trying to locate Rhapsody's
heartbeat; it was there somewhere in the distance, but jumbled, whether from the conflicting rhythms all around him,
or for another reason he could not fathom. He resolved to
make certain to catch up with Ashe when the opportunity
presented itself.

As he stepped forward, what little space there was around

him widened. The other nobles and heads of state had taken the implication, as he expected they would, of his solitude: he did not need guards, soldiers, or a retinue around him.

He was deadly enough all by himself.

Achmed glanced around the central square of the city, flooded to overflowing with onlookers. The Sorbolds were a stern-faced people, dour and stoic in their aspects, so different from the exuberant idiots in Yarim who had crowded the Bolg work site a few weeks prior, hooting and cheering as if they were at a carnival. He had no doubt that such an occasion of state would have been even more celebratory in Roland, where emotions ran high and increased proportionally with attendance.

Here, however, the all-but-silent crowd was much more intimidating. While it did not have the volatile nature of a gathering in Roland, which might go from excited merriment to angry destruction with very little warning, there was a threatening air to them, these silent desert dwellers who stood, staring down from city walls and parapets, ramparts, window ledges and rocky crags, watching the rites that marked the passage of their empire from an age of steel-fisted autocracy into one of uncertainty.

Achmed knew exactly how they felt.

He noted silently how grateful he was at times like these that he was no longer subject to the heartbeats of each person who shared the land with him, as he had been in Serendair. His blood gift, the maddening pulses of millions of strangers beating in his mind, vibrating against his skin, had been horrific to endure, even if it had made him a handsome living as an unerring assassin. Now that was gone, left behind beneath the waves of the sea in the Island's watery grave; all that remained were the few distant pulses of those who had once lived there, now ageless, who still remained in the new world.

Like Rhapsody.

And Grunthor.

His attention was drawn to the steps of Jierna Tal by the

clanging of the brass bells from the palace's towers. Harsh and dissonant, the ugly clamor rang out over the land, silencing whatever noise had been present among the swell of troops and onlookers.

The funeral rite was beginning.

From the front palace doors a procession emerged, a double line of priests and acolytes dressed in robes in the colors of Sorbold—vermilion and green, brown and purple, twisting slashes of color that interwove like threads. Achmed recognized the pattern; it was the same colors that could be seen beneath the Sleeping Child's stone-gray skin, and in the altar of Living Stone on which she lay. They carried before them tall poles topped with the symbols of the dynasty, the golden sun bisected by a sword.

Following the line of clergy was the benison of the region, the Blesser of Sorbold, Nielash Mousa. Achmed recognized him by the rounded miter he wore on his head, and the amulet of the earth that hung around his neck, but otherwise would not have; in the intervening three years since the investiture of the Patriarch, Constantin, Mousa had aged at least a decade. He still carried himself with dignity, even as his shoulders were hunching under whatever weight was burdening him.

Behind Mousa came a pair of catafalques, each borne by six soldiers in the livery of the royal house, the bodies atop wrapped in simple white linen embroidered in gold. From the size of them there was no doubt that the empress was in the lead, consigning the Crown Prince to wait his turn unendingly, in death as she had done in life. A single line of mourners draped in black brought up the rear, silent and stoic.

The clanging bells slowed to a long, repeated knell tolled by the two deepest of them. As the sound diminished, one last figure emerged from the palace. A tall man in golden vestments, emblazoned with an ornate silver star on the front and back, his eyes scanning the crowd all around and above him; Achmed noted from the calm expression on his face that he had walked into his share of enormous gatherings.

The Patriarch, Constantin.

Alone among the clergy, the Patriarch's head was bare. He, like all those of Cymrian blood who had lived an extraordinary length of time, was a study in contrasts, his white-blond hair and curling beard streaked with gray, his face lined, while his shoulders remained broad, unbowed. He raised his hand to the people, moving it slowly across the panorama, and as he did, they bowed in a great wave of respectful motion. His presence, more than the death and burial of the two monarchs, caused an aura of awe in the square; generally Patriarchs remained unseen by the populace, even the faithful who worshipped in their cathedrals.

The procession moved through the city square, the dissonant bells tolling a clashing knell the whole while. Achmed shifted his stance; the vibrations from the bell tower were making his teeth ache, and sending spasms rattling down his spine.

He felt the touch of a hand on his elbow; Ashe had made his way through the cluster of nobles and heads of state to stand beside him on the reviewing stand.

"Achmed; well met."

The Bolg king nodded perfunctorily. "Where is Rhapsody?"

"Navarne," the Lord Cymrian replied, leaning forward to catch a better sight of the procession as it mounted the steps to the platform in the Place of Weight. "Though she may have left to visit Elynsynos by now."

The last knell of the brass bells sounded, then died slowly away, taking the noise of the crowd with it.

With great, grim care, the bearers of the catafalques mounted the steps that led up to the Scales, following the benison. The remainder of the clergy stayed below, ringing the great stand on which the holy relic stood. One of the priests who had led the procession was handed a pair of parchment scrolls and a quill; he unfurled the first one, the older of the two.

At the top of the steps, the benison was met by two pairs of sturdy soldiers bearing an elaborately carved box the size of a coffin hanging from two poles; they followed him to one side of the Scales, standing rigidly, their eyes on the sun.

Achmed's eyes narrowed as the linen-wrapped body was lifted, under the direction of Nielash Mousa, and placed carefully into one of the great golden plates. He and Ashe watched closely as the benison himself reached into the ornate box and removed many small sacks of sand known as Fists, a measure of weight used commonly in Sorbold and among the merchants who did business there. He carefully placed each Fist onto to plate opposite the empress's body, watching the balance closely.

Finally, after an agonizing amount of time, the Blesser of Sorbold signaled to the priest who held the scroll. The cleric hurried forward to hear what the benison conveyed to him; he scratched it onto the scroll with the quill, then stood erect and turned to the Patriarch.

"Her Serenity, the Dowager Empress, at birth twenty-three Fists, one Fingerweight. Upon her coronation, five hundred fifty-one Fists, one Fingerweight. Upon her marriage, six hundred sixty-six Fists, six Fingerweights. Upon the birth of her son, the Crown Prince Vyshla, seven hundred seventy-five Fists, two Fingerweights. Upon the occasion of her fiftieth jubilee, five hundred fourteen Fists, eight Fingerweights. Upon the occasion of her seventy-fifth jubilee, three hundred sixty-six Fists, three Fingerweights."

The priest studied the scroll for a moment, looking puzzled, then announced in a voice that quavered slightly, "At the Weighing following death, one hundred two Fists, three Fingerweights."

A buzzing rumble passed through the crowd at the number. Ashe and Achmed exchanged a glance.

"That can't possibly be right," the Lord Cymrian murmured. "If that was correct, she—she would have not weighed much more than she did at birth; she'd have had the body mass of a three-year-old."

"The Scales are obviously wrong," Achmed said.

A stifled gasp rose from the ground below the reviewing stand; the Bolg king looked down to see the first few rows of Sorbold townspeople staring at him in a mix of muted horror and dismay. Ashe leaned forward slightly and spoke into his ear.

"Not a politic statement in these parts," he said softly. "The Scales have long been trusted to be the unerring determinant in all grave matters. As you can see by the litany of her life, each Sorbold citizen is weighed at significant moments of passage—though only the royal family is weighed on these Scales."

Achmed swallowed angrily but said nothing. He had seen the plates of the Scales a lifetime before, affixed to another balance, in Serendair, and so knew better than Ashe their history.

"Declare the death weight again," said the benison.

"One hundred two Fists, three Fingerweights."

The benison and the Patriarch exchanged a glance. Then Nielash Mousa turned and addressed the crowd.

"Throughout her life, Her Serenity lived and breathed for Sorbold; it is not unexpected that she breathed the last of her life essence into the very air," he said in his gravelly voice. "She gave everything she had to her people and her nation; there is nothing left of her earthly body, but the lightness of it shows clearly that her spirit is free, in the warmth of the Afterlife."

The crowd fell into skeptical silence.

The Blesser signaled to the soldiers, who removed the small linen-wrapped corpse from the plate and returned it to the catafalque on which it had rested, then replaced the pile of Fists in their coffer. The soldiers who had borne the pall of the prince came forth and lifted his body, obviously with greater strain than the ones who had carried the empress, and placed it on the Scale plate.

Again the Blesser of Sorbold began the ceremony of weighing, slowly balancing the Scales against the corpse with the bags of sand. The crowd began to grumble quietly as the minutes passed, but the benison continued the task meticulously, adding each small bag to the ever-growing pile with precision, followed by a check of the Scales' balance. Finally he conveyed the result to the head priest, who turned to the Patriarch, and the crowd once more.

"His Highness, the Crown Prince Vyshla, at birth, twenty-eight Fists, eight Fingerweights," he intoned. "Achieving the Age of Ripening at eleven summers; six hundred-ninety three Fists." He coughed; then, in the absence of any other significant dates for the prince, read the death weight.

"At the Weighing following death, one thousand, three hundred fifty-six Fists, three Fingerweights."

A subtle combination of sounds conveying both astonishment and amusement whispered over the crowd, which fell silent again.

Nielash Mousa cleared his throat. "In contrast to Her Serenity, who gave the entirety of her earthly essence in the service of her people, what a sadness it is that Crown Prince Vyshla was so well prepared to serve, and yet passed from this life, never having had the opportunity, before he had the chance to share his potential. His contribution to Sorbold surely would have been a weighty one."

The Blesser of Sorbold stood for a moment, then, in the absence of something else complimentary to say, signaled to the soldiers, who removed the body from the plate and placed it back on its catafalque.

The benison signaled to the priests in the lead of the procession, who again formed their double line, and the benison, the head cleric, and the catafalques began the long march to Terreanfor.

They passed through the swell of the crowd without breaking their gaze from the path before them. Even if they had, they would most likely never have noticed the man at the edge of the crowd of onlookers, watching the procession with an uncharacteristically pleasant expression on his face.

A face that was somehow much more opaque than it had been the last time he stood at the foot of the Scales, in the light of the full moon.

# 21

The noise of the crowd had long died away by the time the funeral procession and the invited dignitaries arrived at the basilica in Night Mountain.

Each of the guests had been required to leave their retinues at the mountain pass that guarded the entranceway into the Earth basilica; twenty regiments of Sorbold guards were present for the purpose of ensuring cooperation in this matter.

The Bolg king and the Lord Cymrian had, by virtue of proximity, been paired up in the procession, and so walked uneasily beside each other, following the line of priests in the multicolored vestments.

"Why did she not come?" Achmed asked as they descended into a ravine in the rocky crags, a winding open tunnel that left rock walls towering above on both sides.

Ashe smiled to himself, watching the floor of the pebble-strewn trail.

"She had more important things to attend to."

The priest in front of them turned around and glared angrily at them both but said nothing. The two sovereigns fell into an awkward silence.

At the opening of the cave that led into the basilica itself, the procession came to a halt.

The two golden symbols that had preceded the funeral parade were brought forward to a place in the ravine where the sky was clearly visible overheard, and placed flat on an enormous ceremonial slab, on which oil was then poured. The guests waited while fire was kindled by the sun, then transferred to four small lanterns that would serve to light their path down into the darkness of the Earth cathedral.

Achmed glanced around at the dark walls as the procession descended into the passageway leading to the basilica proper. The earth, dry and stony at the exterior from contact with the heat of the upworld, quickly grew cool and moist as they traveled deeper in. The distant, dim light at the head of the procession cast occasional shadows in which the walls of the passage could be seen, smooth and trim, unlike cave walls, and gloriously colored by nature in random swirls, difficult to appreciate in the dark.

As the funeral procession moved deeper within Night Mountain, the sound from the world above disappeared, replaced by the slow, melodic song of the Earth. The deep timbre of it was subtle, so rarefied that most of the dignitaries could not even hear it; Achmed could tell because, unlike them, his breathing and heartbeat began to keep time with its rhythm, his footsteps marking cadence in an effortless synchronicity. Among the others, only Ashe seemed to have picked up on the pulse.

Ahead in the distance, light flickered off the passageway walls. The line of clergy, pallbearers, and mourners slowed their steps as they approached the dancing shadows; the dignitaries, relegated to the rear, came to a virtual halt, waiting to pass into the actual basilica.

Finally the funeral procession moved through a high archway into a vast, circular antechamber.

The dimensions of the room were intermittently visible in the reflected light that flickered in one of the three semicircular alcoves that were hollowed into the walls at each of three quarters of the circle. That alcove, directly across from what appeared to be another archway, twice the size of and to the right of the one they came in, radiated heat and light from a leaping flame that burned with the intensity found only in the pure fire of the Earth's heart. The tiny flamewell of moving light cast bright fireshadows around the antechamber, and a short distance into the basilica beyond the tall archway.

Across from the hallway in which they stood was another alcove from within which a deep, gurgling splash could be heard. The evanescent light glimmered momentarily on the bubbling underground stream that formed a low fountain, rising up from the ground and then back upon itself, to rise again a moment later.

As the procession came into the antechamber, a gust of wind, stale and heavy with the scent of wet earth, whipped from the final alcove, passing over them, trapped within the circular walls of the anteroom.

*Paeans to three of the other elements,* Achmed noted, looking around for the traditional fourth, ether, but seeing no alcove devoted to it.

At the head of the procession, a gesture was made. The four small lanterns were extinguished.

It was time to enter the basilica itself.

Slowly the funeral procession turned to the right, and passed through the large archway. Nielash Mousa, as the benison of Terreanfor, led the way, followed by the priests, the Patriarch, the catafalques, the mourners, and the dignitaries, into the cathedral proper, a place that only rarely was seen by anyone other than the benison and the chief priest.

As they stepped through the opening into the mammoth basilica, the song of the Earth grew louder, more distinct; it took on the muted tones of the mines, the ringing of distant hammers, the hollow whistling of uncountable caves, the slow sound of roots growing deeper with time. Within Terreanfor the song had a voice, a deep, slow melody that sang like the quiet chanting of a choir of monks in a dark monastery.

The thought made Achmed shudder involuntarily.

The unpleasant memory vanished instantly, squelched by the overpowering solemnity that was present in the utter darkness.

Backlit by the weak light from the flamewell in the basilica's antechamber, he could see that the mammoth cathedral was filled with statuary, carved from the living earth itself. Beyond pillars that reached to a towering ceiling, the height of which was too tall to be seen, a great menagerie of animals stood, life-sized sculptures of elephants and lions, gazelles and tirabouri that seemed to move in the shadows, their eyes fixed in stony silence. A closer examination revealed that the pillars were shaped in the aspect of trees, in which Living Stone birds could just be seen at the edges of the light, gleaming in the deep, rich colors of the earth.

As he passed a gargantuan pachyderm, silently marveling at the lifelike wrinkles in its stone hide, Achmed thought back to the early days after he, Grunthor, and Rhapsody had emerged from the Earth's belly into this new and unfamiliar world, a place to which those who had left the Island after them had refugeed, then conquered, and finally decimated with their foolish war and petty grudges. They had found much of the last history of their dead homeland, and the stories of what came to pass afterward, in the Cymrian museum of Haguefort, lovingly tended by the historian Stephen Navarne, one of the very few of his lineage that Achmed actually liked.

Stephen had proudly shown the three of them etchings of the five great basilicas that had been built to honor the Elements. Patiently he had named them all, though in many cases his translations of the Old Cymrian were incorrect—Abbat Mythlinis, the cathedral shaped like a great wrecked ship and built into the sand at the edge of the sea north of Avonderre, known in the common language as Lord All-God, Master of the Sea; Vrackna, the circular basilica in Bethany, fashioned to look like the sun, surrounding another, larger well of flame from the Earth's core, called Lord All-God, Fire of the Universe; Ryles Cedelian, the wind cathedral, where eight hundred-seventy-six bells tolled in the bell tower, sanctifying the ground with their windy music, known as Lord All-God, Spirit of the Air, though Achmed knew its literal translation to be *Breath of Life*; and Lianta'ar, the largest basilica of all, which stood in the holy city-state of Sepulvarta, towered over by an ether-tipped spire beneath which the Patriarch held services—Lord All-God, Light of the World.

He thought back to what Stephen had said about Terreanfor as he enthusiastically displayed the renderings of the peaks of Night Mountain, the only representation of the cathedral in his collection, since Terreanfor itself was hidden away.

*This is the only non-Orlandan basilica, the church of Lord All-God, King of the Earth, or Terreanfor. The basilica is carved into the face of the Night Mountain, making it a place where no light touches, even in the middle of the day. There is a hint of the old pagan days in Sorboldian religion, even though they worship the All-God and are a See of our religion. They believe that parts of the earth, the ground itself, that is, are still alive from when the world was made, and the Night Mountain is one of these places of Living Stone. The turning of the Earth itself resanctifies the ground within the basilica. It is a deeply magical place.*

Walking now beneath the soaring stone trees, past the immense statues of creatures honed from the living rock, Achmed could agree with the late duke's assessment.

By the time the procession had traveled deep enough into Terreanfor to move beyond the garden of animals and into the inner sanctum, where the statues were now stone renderings of soldiers, Achmed noted another light ahead, though a cold one that did not burn like fire this time. Closer examination showed that some of the rocks that were housed within the Earth cathedral were glowing on their own with a kind of phosphorescence he had seen only in his travels through the Earth; *the element of ether, finally,* he thought.

When he and Ashe were passing beneath the upraised blades of two stone swordsmen flanking the central aisle, the procession stopped.

Up ahead he could barely make out the movements of the pallbearers, who were positioning the linen-wrapped bodies on the altars of Living Stone, from which most of the song of the Earth was emanating. The vibrations of the song, soothing but with an undertone of pain, lulled him as first the Patriarch, then the benison, began to drone the funeral rites in Old Cymrian, the common tongue of the Island of Serendair, now a dead language used only in religious ceremonies.

*Oh our mother the Earth, who waits for us beneath the everlasting sky, shelter us, sustain us, give us rest.*

How long the ceremony lasted Achmed had no idea; it seemed like moments later, and an eternity as well, when the procession began to move again.

The benison led the clergy, pallbearers, and mourners deeper into the profound darkness, past the altars of Living Stone that hummed with the same mellow, orotund vibration of the sonorous earth all around them.

Deep within his soul, Achmed felt a painful tug, a desire to remain within the dark walls that in the light would shine green and rose, purple and blue with pure, undiminished life. There was a power here, a deep, elemental essence that spoke to both of his bloodlines, his mother's Dhracian love of the deep earth, his unknown father's kinship as a cave dweller. It was all he could do to spur himself to keep pace with Ashe, whom he could barely see in the dark.

The line processed to a tall, straight stairway that stretched up into the darkness beyond the altars. As they mounted the stairs, the air became warmer, lighter; a gray haze began to fill the space before them.

"This must be the stairway to the sepulchers," Ashe murmured as the darkness began to diminish.

Achmed merely grunted, wishing the endless ritual would end, so that the colloquium they were to convene afterward to discuss Sorbold's future could get under way.

Finally they ascended to a landing, a wide open floor with a low, vaulted ceiling above it. Light, more present in this area, was provided by a host of the glowing rocks Achmed had seen earlier.

Two scaffolds lay in the center of the floor of this open room, attached to ropes and pulleys that hung from the ceiling above, in which dark rectangular holes could be seen.

The benison intoned his concluding rites, the ceremonies of burial similar to those performed in the Patrician church of Roland, but with elements of the ancient ways, the more pagan touches that Stephen had long ago commented on. When he had finally finished, he turned to the assemblage.

"My children, the right of committal to our mother the Earth is concluded. There is only now the interment, the ascension of the bodies into their individual sepulchers in the royal crypt above us. If you wish to leave now, the acolytes will escort you back to Jierna Tal, where a funeral banquet will take place, after which we will convene the colloquium. If you would like to ascend to the viewing area of the sepulchers by way of the Faithful's Stair," he added, pointing to a tiny doorway in the wall near the scaffolds, which were already being drawn up toward the ceiling on the ropes, "you are welcome to witness the final burial rites. Please note that the Faithful's Stair is quite winding and close; if you are in ill health or uncomfortable with tight spaces, I gently suggest you return to Jierna Tal at this point."

The dignitaries, most of them in the throes of claustrophobia, hurried after the departing acolytes and into the air of the upworld.

Except for the Lord Cymrian and the Firbolg king, who looked at each other questioningly, then together made a quick path for the archway that the benison had indicated, and darted up the steps.

The benison had not exaggerated the tightness of the turning stairway. Achmed's shoulder, and all of Ashe's right side, brushed the curving walls as they climbed in evershortening spirals. As they ascended, the air around them grew warmer, the ground was distinctly drier, less alive.

"This was ill considered," Achmed muttered after the thirteenth full turn around the staircase's axis. "I really have no need to see the sepulchers; I was merely curious as to what it was going to take to haul the Crown Prince up into his tomb."

"Perhaps they have a few dray horses and an elephant on the upper floor to help," Ashe suggested, curling his shoulder in to avoid the continuous abrasion he was suffering from the wall.

"If there is more than another full rotation, I'm turning back," the Bolg king declared, climbing with a deliberate gait. "For all I know this staircase could lead all the way to the top of one the peaks in—"

Ashe heard Achmed's voice choke off abruptly.

"What is it?" he asked as the Bolg king stopped.

Achmed never answered him. Instead, he took a few halting steps forward, staring all around him.

Stepping into the upper burial chapel of Terreanfor, which housed the individual mausoleums of the monarchs of Sorbold, was like stepping into a living rainbow.

The chapel was small in girth, but tall in height. Thin supports of stone that connected with the ceiling and were decorated with statues of men, most likely legendary figures from Sorbold history, judging by their heavy facial features. The statues demarked sections of the tomb, almost invisible in the rest of the walls.

Which were made entirely of exquisite stained glass.

The Bolg king took another step into a gleaming patch of rosy light adjacent to a glimmering blue that pulsed gently as a cloud passed overhead in the sky beyond the window walls.

His mismatched eyes scanned the panorama of glorious color around and above him, drinking in the beauty, the artisanship, of a thousand years' time and scores of generations of craftsmen's labor which had combined to produce a paradise doused by the afternoon sun, facing west.

"A lovely final view."

Ashe's voice was muted to his ear. Achmed shook off the words almost without effort, lost in the majesty of the rainbows which had solidified into place along the mausoleum's walls and in the domed ceiling.

His conscious mind, a distant second to the workings of his aesthetic senses, made note of two things.

First, he could see that each of the individual sepulchers of Sorbold's royals had its own window, flawlessly rendered, depicting a stylized representation of that monarch's life. Leitha was immortalized, a beautiful, rotund woman in rich garments, one hand scattering bread to the nation's poor, the other stalwartly bearing a sword. Clearly the windows had been commissioned and all but completed many years before; they were probably begun at the time of her birth. The sheer artistry of it and the others that commemorated the lives of her ancestors took his breath away.

Second, from within the burial chapel he could see outside the windows that would seal the tombs of the empress and her son several shaded outlines, moving back and forth in front of the windows, bending down, then contacting the other side of the glass, carefully applying the final touches, the death weights, the last historical record for posterity, immortalized in sand and ash heated with minerals until it formed shiny shards of magnificent color for history to remember when all who knew them in life had joined them in death.

Glass artisans.

# 22

As he scrambled up the side of the western mountain that contained the windows of the tomb, Achmed rethought his position on retinues. While it was true that coming alone to the funeral, and the fray that would undoubtedly erupt afterward, had already conveyed the message he had intended, he made note that the presence of one aide would have saved him from needing to attend to all his errands himself, and spared him from being late to the colloquium.

By the time he crested the mountaintop the sun was hanging low in the sky, turning the land around him the color of blood. He shielded his eyes, looking for the glassworkers who he had seen as shadows outside the windows while in the crypt.

Most of them were gone.

Those that remained were, for the most part, packing up their tools and their materials, packing brightly painted wagons, preparing to descend from the mountaintop before nightfall. Achmed noted that this cadre was composed of both men and women, dark of hair, eye, and countenance, all dressed in the garb of nomads, each wearing a multihued sash or belt as a sign of whatever clan they belonged to, though they did not all seem to share the same ethnic background. Most of them were slight, wiry, of a similar build to his own. The men were uniformly clean-shaven and shorn. Like the men, the women wore their hair short, so at first it was hard to distinguish them. They called to each other in a tongue unknown to him as they tied their equipment onto their pack animals and loaded the three wagons that were with them.

He broke into a loping run toward the place where the artisans were putting the last coats of glaze on the newly inscribed windows, and cleaning some of the other, older panes, only to be stopped by a quartet of Sorbold soldiers who were guarding the glassworkers.

"What are you doing up here?" a heavyset column leader demanded as the others readied their pikes. "Turn back."

Achmed came to an abrupt halt, his hands at his sides. His mismatched eyes locked with those of the commander; after a moment of stony silence, one guard whispered something to another behind the column leader's back. He thought he caught the words *Bolg king*; apparently he was correct, because the column leader stepped aside, glaring at him silently.

Rank had its benefits, as did renowned ugliness.

"I want to speak to the artisans," he said evenly, moving

closer to the soldiers in as nonthreatening a manner as he could muster.

The soldiers looked at each other, then back at the column leader.

"Most of them don't speak the common tongue," the column leader said; "Majesty," he added reticently after a heart-beat.

"Who are they?"

The soldier shook his head. "Itinerants. Traveling crafts-men from the southeast. They call themselves the Panjeri. The empress must have hired them; they have come at times over the years to attend to her glasswork. One of the women says they will be leaving soon." An unpleasant note crept into his voice at the word *women*.

"Which woman?" Achmed asked, looking past the sol-diers at the artisans and seeing four of them.

The column leader shrugged, then turned and watched them for a moment.

"They all look the same," he said finally. "I commend you to that one, Majesty." He pointed past a rocky rise to the scaffolding that braced against the circular cliff face which held the crypt windows.

Atop the scaffold a single artisan remained while the oth-ers packed. She was crouched in a squatting position, in-tently polishing a small area of the newly installed portion of the Crown Prince's glass memorial, oblivious of the set-ting sun and the occasional shouts of her comrades.

Achmed nodded curtly; his head was throbbing with an unpleasant hum mixed with the annoyance of knowing the colloquium was either waiting for him or, worse, carrying on in his absence. He climbed the remains of the embank-ment and quickly crossed the rest of the rocky ledge, coming to a halt beneath the scaffold. Several of the Panjeri stopped in their transport of materials to stare at him.

"Who is your leader?" he asked three men and a woman who were watching him sharply.

The men exchanged a glance, then returned to staring.

"Do any of you understand me?" Achmed said, trying to contain his frustration.

The silence answered him.

Finally he moved away from them, feeling their eyes locked on him, and approached the scaffold.

The woman atop it was still intent on her work. She was edging the window with a small, crude tool, buffing the glass as she checked the seam once more. One of the other craftsmen shouted up to her impatiently in a language Achmed did not recognize, and she acidly called something back to him. As she turned to answer, her eye caught the Bolg king for a split second, but she did not favor him with a longer glance before returning to her work.

Finally, as the rest of the Panjeri began to descend with the crates and animals, two men came over to the scaffold. One grabbed the supports impatiently and shook it.

The woman atop it swayed slightly at the motion, then caught herself with a lightening-quick act of balance. She seized a small brass pot from which she had been dipping and hurled it at the man's head, missing it deliberately by a hairsbreadth, but splattering him with glaze. Then she tossed her tools down to the other man and descended the scaffold, her dark eyes flashing at the one who had shaken it.

Achmed stood by, trying to catch her notice, as she exchanged a few pointed words with her fellow craftsman, then stooped to pick up the pot. The men seized the scaffold and broke it down, carrying the pieces quickly to the remaining wagon. The woman, having retrieved her pot, turned to follow them. Achmed interposed himself quickly between her and the wagon.

"Hello," he said awkwardly, grinding his teeth and wishing Rhapsody were here to make the approach for him; he hated conversation in general, hated initiating it even more, and hated initiating with people with whom he could not communicate past the point of being rational about it. "Do you speak the common tongue of the continent?"

The woman's eyes narrowed. "No, I do not, my apologies," she said curtly, then attempted to step past him.

Achmed jumped to the side to block her again. "Wait, please." He looked down at her, a sense of guarded excitement coming over him.

The woman was not much taller than Rhapsody, if that. Like Rhapsody, she clad herself in practical clothing, trousers and a stained cambric shirt. She was breathing heavily from the exertion, so her cheeks were ruddy; short, dark locks of hair framed her facial features, which, while hidden beneath a layer of grimy sand and streaked with dried sweat from her work atop the scaffold, were delicate, her dark eyes large and interestingly shaped. Those eyes held a gleam of contempt that he couldn't help but recognize; he had seen it in his own reflection.

She shared his attitude; she did not brook fools, or anyone who interposed himself in her way.

"Are you finished here?" he asked.

The woman tossed the pot to one of the men who was waiting near the wagon. "Have you been sent to pay us?"

"No," Achmed said quickly.

"Then move out of my way." She strode past him to the wagon, and prepared to climb aboard; Achmed caught her arm.

The flurry that resulted caught him by surprise even as cursed himself for not expecting it.

Without hesitation the woman slammed her hand into his shoulder and pushed him back, loosing his grip. As she spun, the remaining artisans, men and women, pulled an assortment of small knives and sharp tools. Achmed dropped her arm quickly and held up his hands.

"Apologies," he said, cursing himself inwardly. "I am not good at this. I want to hire you."

The woman leveled her gaze at him for a moment, then shook her head at her companions, who went back to loading the wagon.

"Hire us?" she asked disdainfully. "You cannot afford the price."

"I—I am King Achmed of Ylorc," Achmed stammered.

"How fortunate for you. You cannot afford the price. Now kindly move out of the way." The woman turned her back and walked away.

Achmed felt like he was drowning. All of his normal calm had fled, leaving him feeling desperate, anxious beyond reason.

"What is the price?"

The woman turned and regarded him sharply. She considered his question, inhaling slowly to calm her breath, then spoke.

"Each of us is a sealed master. Two hundred thousand gold suns."

Achmed swallowed heavily. "Done," he said.

"In gems. We cannot carry that much in coin."

"As you wish."

"Today."

The Bolg king coughed. "Today?"

The woman nodded, her eyes fixed on his face. "Today. Before the setting of the sun."

"I cannot possibly do that."

She nodded. "As I told you—you cannot meet the price." She returned to the wagon and prepared to climb aboard.

Achmed chased after her. "Wait, please. I can have a bill of tender stamped this evening."

The woman laughed. She stepped off of the wagon's rim and came to stand in front of him.

"You do not know of the Panjeri, do you?"

The Bolg king shook his head, swallowing to keep from misspeaking.

"You know nothing of the craft, of the trade, then. Nor anything of our language. The word means 'the dry leaves.' We are called that because we blow about in the wind, racing along from place to place, never staying anywhere for longer than a fallen leaf would stay in a windy desert. It pains us to remain still for too long. To ask a dozen Panjeri to come to wherever you would need us, would be as to ask a dozen leaves to remain on the ground in a high breeze."

"I don't need a dozen Panjeri," Achmed said quickly, struggling to keep his tone from becoming imperious. "I need but one—the best one, the most talented, highly trained one. The leaf least likely to skitter in the wind." He raised his eyebrows and cocked his head to view each of the other assembled workers, a wry smile coming over his face. "Which one would that be?"

The woman's eyes narrowed in response.

"That would be *me*," she said haughtily.

"And by what name are you called, as the greatest of the Panjeri?"

"Theophila."

"I see. Since I have no way to ask the other Panjeri," the Bolg king countered, continuing to size up the artisans, who stared blankly at him from the wagon, "and would find it difficult to communicate my needs to them, I'll just accept that you are the heaviest leaf."

The woman crossed her arms. "Well, even if they did not agree, how would you understand what they said?"

Achmed nodded, his lips pressed together in a mock show of agreement. "You do have a point there. Very well, Theophila, assuming you are in fact the best stained-glass artisan of the Panjeri, what would the price be to hire just you?"

She considered for a moment. "For how long?"

"However long the project takes. If you would not commit to finish what you begin, I would not have you anyway."

The woman scowled. "I never leave any aspect of my work unfinished, even as the others pack to leave," she snarled. "I believe you have witnessed this."

"Indeed. So again I ask you, what is your price?"

The woman regarded him again, leaning back against the clapboard of the wagon.

"A reason," she said.

"A reason?"

"Yes. A reason to divert my travels, to separate from my kinsmen, to remain in an unknown place for however long you wish me to remain—can you give me a compelling reason to do so?"

Achmed considered for a moment. "Yes," he said finally, "I can promise you that the glass you will make for me, the project on which you will work, will be unlike any you have ever done before, or will do again."

Theophila shrugged. "That is not compelling enough," she said blandly. "That can be said of most projects we undertake. While the challenge of the work is well and good, it does not feed my family; it does not buy my tools." She put her foot back on the wagon rim once more and started to hoist herself aboard.

The Bolg king smiled slightly. "Tools? Yes. I did notice your nippers are rusty, and your filial files and groziers are awkwardly balanced. If your price is not in gems, perhaps you can be paid in better tools."

The woman froze on the rim, then looked back at him, a cool look in her dark eyes. One of the men in the wagon gestured impatiently to her and another of the women began to speak, but she waved them both into silence.

"Perhaps you do know a little of the trade," she said. "But what do you know of balance, of tools?"

"Everything," Achmed said brashly, feeling as if he were betting on a hand of cards and hating the feeling. He reached down into his boot and pulled forth a half-weight *svarda,* balancing one of the three blades on his gloved fingertip, then straightened his arm to demonstrate the perfect equilibrium.

The Panjeri in the wagon stared, their eyes riveted on the circular blade poised in the air above the Bolg king's index finger. Only Theophila seemed unimpressed.

"We have no need of throwing knives," she said contemptuously, but Achmed noted a waver in her voice.

She was betting on the cards in her hand as well.

"My craftsmen can make anything that is a tool or a

weapon, and make it from a material that will last through your lifetime, and the lifetimes of your grandchildren. It will remain sharp and true, within a hairsbreadth of the width it was when planed in the forge."

"Oh? Better than diamond-edged steel?"

"Better. Yes."

She tossed her head, running her hand through her short tresses, spattering the sweat. "I don't believe you."

Achmed pulled forth a cwellan disk. "Examine it yourself. But take care—if you are fumble-fingered, you will be maimed. This has no handle; it is a weapon, not a tool." He chuckled to see the angry reaction in her eyes to the insult, though her face remained stoic.

Delicately she took the disk, and turned it over carefully in her hand, holding it up to the last rays of the low-hanging sun. After a moment she knelt and struck the disk against a rock, then scraped it along the surface with a flicking motion. She stood again and returned the disk to Achmed.

"We are leaving Sorbold soon after we are paid," she said, walking away as she spoke.

"How soon?" he asked as she vaulted into the wagon and sat down next to one of the other women. The man who shook the scaffold, driving the team, clicked to the horses, and the wagon began to roll.

She shouted back over the noise of the cart as it disappeared over the first rocky rise.

"As soon as the wind changes."

When the Bolg king was no longer in sight, one of the women spoke in their dying language.

"Theophila, what did that strange man want?"

The woman stared back over the sideboard of the wagon, up into the rocky face of the hill. In the distance she could see a long, thin shadow, backlit by the setting sun, skittering down the cliff face like a spider, stopping from time to time, then hurrying down again as the cart moved farther out of view.

"I'm not certain entirely," she said. "He says wants to hire me for my expertise in glass."

The Panjeri looked from one to another.

"And will you go with him?"

"Perhaps. We shall see. If he has returned before we leave on the morn, I may. I doubt he will. But I must consult with the leader."

"It would be your choice," said one of the men beside her.

She covered her eyes with her hand, endeavoring to catch sight of the moving shadow, and failing. She put her hand down again and stared out over the ruddy desert below.

"I know."

Achmed watched until the wagon had descended the mountain to the flatlands, following it down along the ridge. He watched it pull into a campsite amid three other wagons and a handful of tents where the other Panjeri had already laid a celebratory bonfire.

He made careful note of the position of the camp, then hurried down the cliff face and back to the castle of Jierna Tal as night fell thickly, coating the dome of the sky above Sorbold with inky blackness through which no stars could be seen.

# 23

Nielash Mousa was growing weary of Fists and Scales, sand and Weighings.

Once the burial rites in the deep temple of Terreanfor and the internal peak of the stained-glass crypt were concluded, he had hoped to move on to the more important and difficult business at hand, the sorting out of Sorbold's future. Insuring Leitha's place in eternity, complete with pomp and ceremony, and the laying of her scrawny bones to rest in the brilliant light of the stained-glass chapel might have been what the dowager had believed would be the first order of things, but Mousa knew that the dead could wait, while the living might not.

Already there were rumblings in the army.

The empress's control of the military had been legendary. In a harsh land composed largely of shifting desert sand and impenetrable mountains, the concept of landownership among any but the monarch was more ephemeral than it would have been in other parts of the world, where the terrain was more stable. In Roland, a man could stake out a piece of the Krevensfield Plain or a river valley, build on it, farm it, hand it down to his children, in short, imbue his soul, and the souls of his descendants, into the very soil. Leaders might come and go, taxes might be owed and grudgingly paid to the Crown, but the lore of the land belonged to the one whose blood had shaped it, and continued to steward it.

It was the same with the great Orlandan cities. Every palace, every basilica, represented the dreams, aspirations, and sweat of far more people than the duke who lived in it, the benison who performed rites there. It was the vision of the architect, the toil of the carpenter, the labor of the stonemason, magnified a thousand times over, and a hundred thousand times, every shop, guild, and business reflecting the concept of *ownership,* individual power in the shadow of a loose, overarching leader.

The instability of the terrain of Sorbold, where the places to build cities were few and far between, led to the opposite: the desert disdained the puny attempts of man to conquer it, to mold it; it had much in common with the sea in that regard. The mountains had a similar attitude. As a result, the only real power that the land itself supported was the primacy of whatever ruler held the favor of the Dark Earth, the pure element of Living Stone.

For five generations, that power had been indisputably locked in the iron grasp of the Sorbold royal family. Each generation had produced but one heir; Leitha had been the single offspring of her father's loins, as he had been to his father before him, and as Vyshla had been to her. This concentration made the family all the more obviously powerful.

And the army respected obvious power.

But now, in a cruel twist, the sole heir had predeceased the monarch, and had died without producing a direct heir himself. This left no one with clear Right of Kings. The field of candidates with far-flung ties to the royal family was a dubious one; already there had been noise that the commander of the Western Face might not be willing to be directed by anyone whose claim to Leitha's throne was barely more defensible than his own would be.

Those rumblings notwithstanding, they had come, every pretender to the Sun Throne with a drop of blood in his or her veins that could be puffed into a pedigree. It was not the desire for the emperor's mantle that drove them to sue for the throne—indeed, the responsibility that came with the crown was far more grievous a burden than could be balanced against the pleasures of its power—but in an attempt to retain their own royalty and privilege. Without a family member, no matter how far removed, on the throne, those who had been by birth accustomed to the luxurious trappings and easy life of distant royal relations could be divested of those titles, and the privilege that went with them.

Mousa had stood in the heat of the Place of Weight for the better part of the afternoon, as candidate upon candidate mounted the steps that led to the Scales to weigh himself and his presumed right to rule, balanced against the Ring of State in the other plate.

One by one they stepped nervously onto the empty golden plate, eyeing the small oval of hematite and rubies on the other.

One by one, the Scales weighed, then discharged them, some more violently than others, as if the great instrumentality was not only declining their suit, but actively vomiting them off balance.

What remained of the crowd from the funeral that morning had brought rough blankets and food, camping out in the square to watch the spectacle. Their persistence was rewarded; some of the candidates had been dumped so comically on their heads or hindquarters that the onlookers felt as if they had been treated to a performance by a circus of clowns.

Now there was only one left, a distant cousin several times removed. He came to the top of the last step hesitantly, his long, loose shirt stained down the back and under the arms with nervous sweat. Nielash Mousa forced a benevolent smile.

"Speak your name."

"Karis of Ylwendar."

The benison nodded, then turned to the assemblage and repeated the name.

"Is it your wish to address the Scales, in suit for the Sun Throne of the Dark Earth, for stewardship of Terreanfor, and all the realm of Sorbold, from its dark depths to the endless sun above it?"

"It is," the man replied anxiously, his eyes darting around the square.

"Very well, Karis of Ylwendar. Step into the eastern plate and cast your lot to Leuk, the wind of justice."

The man stood frozen.

The benison exhaled tensely. "Do you wish to sue for the throne or not?"

Karis looked over his shoulder, then looked back at Mousa, shaking like a leaf in the desert wind.

"I do."

"Then set about it, man," the benison said as pleasantly as he could, mustering what little protocol was left in him. He did not want to be remembered as the cleric who insulted the next emperor just as the Scales confirmed him, though from what he could guess, there was little chance of that.

Nervously, Karis stepped onto the plate.

Just as his second foot came to rest, the wind blasted through from the west in a great hot gust; it spun the plate crazily, then tilted it with an enormous recoil and swung it like a giant sling shot.

Karis of Ylwendar sailed over the heads of the delighted crowd and into a fishseller's cart, sending dried herring and salted mackerel flying in every direction. A chorus of cheers and hooting saluted him as he landed.

Mousa struggled to maintain a solemn mien. "Is there anyone else claiming royal birth who commands a Weighing?"

Silence answered him.

The Blesser of Sorbold cleared his throat and spoke, the heaviness in his heart mixing with the inevitability of the outcome.

"Very well. Having performed ritual Weighing for each person of royal blood who requested one, and found none suitable in the eyes of the Scales to assume the Sun throne, I declare the Dynasty of the Dark Earth to have ended. A colloquium will commence immediately to determine the interim leadership; any candidates who emerge in the course of that, or any other discussion, will be summoned to the Scales by the tolling of the bells of Jierna Tal. Until such a time as that occurs, I command the bells to be silent."

He signaled to his guard retinue and descended the steps, the weight that he carried on his shoulders suddenly much heavier.

$\mathcal{S}$ilence reigned in Jierna'sid.

It held sway in the Place of Weight, where the mammoth scales now stood, still for the moment, glowing as the shadows of evening grew longer. The townspeople had been shooed from the square, replaced by an expressionless wall of swarthy, heavy-faced soldiers, all garbed in the livery of the now-defunct Dynasty of the Dark Earth. There was a pervasive nervousness about them that had made the crowds uneasy anyway; the townspeople had quickly gathered their blankets and the remains of their picnics and had fled the square, the carnival atmosphere now replaced with an ominous stillness.

Night fell heavily as the preparations for the colloquium were finished. The town square in front of Jierna Tal, from the castle entrance to the outside edge of the Place of Weight, was lined with blazing lamps, tall torch stands holding cylinders of burning oil to light, and perhaps enlighten, the discussion.

Two wide rings of tables, the smaller inside the other, had been set at the base of the Scales, along with chairs for the assembled guests. The evening was still warm in the grip of summer's heat, but the breeze, while hot, was more refreshing than the dank, stale air of the palace, which still reeked of death and incense left over from the burial preparations.

Watching each other with trepidation across the inner circle were representatives from each of the major factions of Sorbold; Fhremus, the empress's trusted supreme commander of the empire's army; Ihvarr and Talquist, the Heirarchs of the eastern and western Mercantile, the tradesman's guilds and shipping compacts that between them controlled nearly all of Sorbold's trade and industry; and the twenty-seven counts who were the magistrates of the empire's twenty-seven city-states. This combination of military, economy, and nobility was combustible, which might have been why the benison had put them into the center, so that if tempers flared, the outer ring of foreign dignitaries could be relied upon to act as a buffer, or at least throw a cloak over whoever ignited and roll him in the sand.

The invited guests from outside of Sorbold were fewer and farther between, seated in the outer circle with the members of the clergy. Ashe was there as head of the Alliance, with whom Sorbold had peace and trade accords, as well as the various sovereigns or their representatives who had their own realms within the Alliance, Achmed for the Bolglands, Tristan Steward for Roland, and Rial for Tyrian. Additionally, those sovereigns of the realms that lay beyond the Inner

Continent—the Diviner of the Hintervold, Miraz of Winter; Beliac, the king of the far eastern region of Golgarn; and Viedekam, chieftain of Penzus, the largest of the southern Nonaligned States—were eyeing each other, and the leaders of the nations their lands surrounded, with a mix of stoicism and suspicion.

Ashe struggled to maintain a calm, cheerful mien, though internally he was roiling. The air in the Place of Weight was charged with unsaid words, fraught with hidden agendas. He could feel it at the fringes of his dragon awareness, but did not doubt that even if he had no wyrm blood, it would have been clear to him anyway.

Nielash Mousa was standing near the palace entranceway with Lasarys, the chief priest whom Ashe had seen marking the scrolls with the death weights of the empress and the Crown Prince. Lasarys was the sexton of Terreanfor, the cleric responsible for the maintenance and protection of the basilica of the Earth, as significant a position in the Patrician religion of Sepulvarta as the Tanist, or official successor, was to the Invoker of Gwynwood, the religion of the Filids, the office Ashe's father had once held. Lasarys, a quiet, bookish man who spent his days in the dark depths of the earth, lovingly tending to the secret cathedral, seemed unnerved to be out in the open air of the Place of Weight, in the midst of so much unspoken venom. Ashe felt a pang for him; he, too, wished that he could unturn the Earth, move Time back to a place where what was about to happen could be avoided.

He crossed the dark square through the archways of flickering light and stopped before the benison, bowing politely.

"Your Grace. How are you holding up?"

The Blesser of Sorbold smiled. "I will be happy when the night is over."

Ashe nodded. "Will the Patriarch be attending? I do not see a place for him."

Mousa shook his head. "He intends to bless the proceedings, but will be departing immediately thereafter. He must return to Sepulvarta in order to be back in time for the mid-summer consecration rites."

"Indeed."

The deep voice of the Patriarch sounded behind them; Lasarys jumped, bowing respectfully, then withdrew quickly to the circle of chairs. The silence in the square became suddenly more profound as the other participants in the colloquium noticed the holy man's presence.

"I was hoping to have a chance to ask how you were faring before the colloquium began," Ashe said to Constantin, making the appropriate countersign in acceptance of the blessing that the Patriarch bestowed on him. "How are you, Your Grace? My wife will want to know."

The tall man smiled, his blue eyes gleaming. "Please convey to Rhapsody that I am well, and that she is long absolved from any need to worry about me."

"Can you not delay for another day?" the Lord Cymrian asked, watching the shifting of chairs and glances in the center of the square. "Wisdom of any kind is sorely needed here now, either from the Ring, or from your experience. You would be a welcome addition to the discussion. I'm sure you have some opinions about what should happen next." He smiled; he knew from whence the Patriarch had come, though, other than Rhapsody, no living soul did besides the man himself.

The Patriarch chuckled and shook his head. "I have opinions on everything, my son, but part of the burden of wearing the Ring of Wisdom is knowing without doubt when to keep those opinions to myself. And in this matter, it is not the place of the Church to be a party to the decisions of how Sorbold will continue, but to support those decisions prayerfully and respectfully." He looked sharply at the assemblage in the inner ring, then leaned forward slightly so that none beside Ashe caught his words.

"However difficult that may ultimately prove to be."

He raised a hand to the assemblage; all those who were adherents of the Patrician faith of Sepulvarta bowed reverently. Only the Diviner, Achmed, Rial, and the King of Golgarn remained standing straight, in polite silence. The Patriarch then bowed slightly to Ashe, who, as Lord Cymrian, was titular head of both the church of Sepulvarta and the faith of the Filids, the nature priests of Gwynwood.

"Nielash Mousa will serve his nation well as the church's representative," he said softly. "And I do not wish in any way to overshadow his authority here."

"Understood."

"Good. Well, then, Lord Gwydion, please commend me to your lady wife. I must be on my way."

Ashe cleared his throat nervously. "If you would entreat the All-God on her behalf when you perform the midsummer ritual, I would be most grateful," he said quietly.

The sharp blue eyes of the Patriarch narrowed. "Is she ill?"

The Lord Cymrian shook his head. "With child."

Constantin considered for a moment, then patted Ashe's shoulder.

"I will offer prayers for her each day of her confinement until your child is born," he said seriously. "If she takes ill, send for me. I learned some things long ago that might aid her."

Ashe bowed deeply. "Thank you."

The Patriarch, his face still solemn, signaled to his retinue and took his leave of Jierna'sid.

It was only matter of moments after the Patriarch had departed before the ugly nature of what was to play out became evident.

Hours into the discussions, that ugliness had taken root and begun to grow.

It began with the contention put forth by the nobility, the counts who had been given right of stewardship of the city-states by the empress or her ancestors. Though unrelated to the familial line, the noble families had served for generations as titular heads of those states.

The death of the empress who had granted them their titles had given them opportunity to cement that stewardship into something more autonomous.

"The empire is no more," stated Tryfalian, Count of Keltar, the third-largest of the Sorbold city-states. "You heard the Blesser state it: the Dynasty of the Dark Earth has come to an end. Every man with so much as a drop of the dynastic line in his veins was been weighed, and to a one, all were found wanting. There is no emperor, no empress, to command Sorbold as a nation. The empire has ceased to exist. What remains now are only the twenty-seven states, each with its own governance. It is here in which order lies." His eyes glittered as he looked over the assemblage. "It is here that it should stay."

"What are you saying?" demanded Fhremus, commander of the imperial army. "Are you suggesting that Sorbold be broken into twenty-seven pieces?"

"Not twenty-seven. There are nine major city-states: Keltar, Jakar, Nicosi, Baltar, Remaldfaer, Kwasiid, Ghant, Telchoir, and of course Jierna. The others are too small to be considered able to stand on their own, to support an army—"

"You are proposing to dismantle the *army?*" Fhremus shouted over the dozen and a half voices that rose in objection from the counts of the smaller city-states Tryfalian had just invalidated.

"Not to dismantle, Fhremus, merely to reassign, reapportion."

"You're insane!" The commander's chair screeched sharply as he leapt to his feet, only to be drawn gently back down into it by a tap on the shoulder from the benison.

"Actually, it has worked quite well for us," inserted Viedekam, representative of the southern coastal region known as the Nonaligned States. "Penzus, like each of the other Nonaligned States, maintains its own army, its own naval fleet, its own tax and tariff structure, which differs substantially from some of the other states', particularly the landlocked ones. The autonomy has been extremely beneficial to each of the member states, allowing it to determine its own destiny."

"And, judging by the wealth and influence the Nonaligned States exert on the world, you will only continue to consider that independence beneficial, I'm sure," snorted Tristan Steward contemptuously, drawing glares from the counts, Viedekam, and Ashe. "It was precisely the example of the Nonaligned States that convinced Roland to band together under a single regency, so that we might not continue be a loose and messy conglomeration of conflicting laws and priorities. In the three years since the consolidation of the provinces of Roland, we have found great economy, efficiency, and, above all, *strength* in unity, while retaining the provincial autonomy. Sorbold has that now. Why would you compromise it?"

"Thank you, chieftain, m'lord," said Nielash Mousa blandly, lifting a hand to forestall the angry chorus of replies rising from the nobility. "Mayhap it would be best to ask if there is any faction within Sorbold that would like to respond to the proposal that Tryfalian had placed on the table."

"Allow me to do so," said Ihvarr, the eastern Hierarch, smoothly, but with evident anger bubbling beneath his calm manner. "Talquist and I can assure you that a nation with the size and scope of Sorbold would fall to chaos under such a plan."

"Why?" demanded Damir, the Count of Jakar. "As the westernmost province, I have had little to do with Jierna Tal for the last twenty years. I am all but autonomous already."

"Perhaps," acknowledged Talquist, Hierarch of the guilds and shipping compacts in the western region and, like Ihvarr, a heavyset man with broad shoulders and skin burnished in the sun. "And you have been a fair and well-respected ruler, Damir. But, for all that I have been the one supplying you with workers for your salt and sulfur mines, transporting your goods, and building your city, my trade agreement was with the empress. I worked for the Crown, not, with respect, for you. If I had to negotiate trade agreements, exchange tariffs, make security arrangements, and all other sort of terms with you, and each of the twelve counts to whom I supply these things, I would go mad."

"As would I," added Ihvarr.

"But think of the advantage your shipping lines would have under such an arrangement, Talquist," said Kaav, the Count of Baltar. "You could sit in consultation with the rulers of the coastal states and persuade them to deploy a larger percentage of their forces to defend the shipping lanes, and they would be a more sympathetic audience to your request than the empress, who had to protect an entire realm, with far more land than sea."

"Leaving my workers unprotected?" Ihvarr demanded. "I will brook none of that. Then who will you find to ply your copper, anthracite, and silver mines, Kaav? Who would transport your goods? For surely I will have no dealing with you if you cannot protect my assets with armed forces."

"And where do you propose to find these forces?" Fhremus asked bitterly. "Remember, the might of the Sorbold army comes from two factors—commonality of purpose and love of our native land. Not to mention loyalty to the empress, may her soul fly freely among the clouds. I gainsay this plan because it will divide us, state to state, column to column—and we are weaker divided."

"Nonesuch," said Tryfalian angrily. He glared at Fhremus, his eyes lighting on the foreign dignitaries assembled in the outer circle. "And I charge you, man, do not again utter such treasonous words in the presence of those who might wish to take advantage of them."

Beliac, King of Golgarn, snapped to attention from what had previously been a somewhat drowsy state. "I resent that," he bellowed, rising from his chair. "We are here in this damnable heat, listening to your endless prattle, because Golgarn is your ally, not your enemy. I came to pay my respects to my longtime friend the empress, and her son, and to offer my support to the new rulership. And for this you insult me."

"Apologies, Majesty," Nielash Mousa said quickly. "No insult was intended, I assure you; we are grateful for your presence, and for that of all of Sorbold's true friends."

He turned, his eyes containing a clear look of despair, to the inner circle.

"I have a suggestion," he said to the divided group of nobles, soldiers, and merchants. "The Scales can weigh ideas as well as men. When the first emperor was chosen at the end of the Cymrian War, a colloquium similar to this one met, with many of the same concerns, expressed by the same factions. A symbol for each of the factions was placed on the Scales against the Ring of State. The scales weighed in favor of the military, whose goal was to see a single, united Sorbold, so it was from there that the emperor was ultimately chosen. I suggest that, as it is almost midnight, this might further the discussion to a better conclusion."

Stony silence answered him. Then, after a moment, heads nodded grudgingly, and the various factions adjourned to select their symbols and plot their next moves.

$\mathcal{A}$chmed waited until the inner circle had dispersed, then rose from his seat, pushing his chair back into the table. Ashe, sitting beside him, with Tristan Steward to his left, ran a hand through his draconic red-gold hair, which gleamed with a metallic sheen in the torchlight, then put his forehead down on the table.

"Gods," he groaned.

"No, I have no doubt these are mere mortals," Achmed said. "Well, best of luck with it."

"You're leaving?" Ashe asked incredulously as the Bolg king gathered his belongings.

Achmed nodded. "I made an appointment with the master of the empress's stable, and a bill of tender for the benison to sign before he collapses under the weight of all the stupidity being flung about here. I don't want to keep the stablemaster waiting any longer than I already have."

Ashe sighed. "Well, then, perhaps we can talk when you when you return."

"I am not going to return. I have a cramp in my leg, a horse to buy, and a few hours of sleep to steal before I leave for Ylorc on the morrow."

The Lord Cymrian sat up straight, thunderstruck. "You're leaving? Before this is decided?"

Achmed took a breath. "It could be days, weeks, before a solution is reached here. I have some important things to attend to in Ylorc, and no time to wait around for these fools to sort out their petty differences."

"I have to admit that I am amazed," Ashe said, a tone of wonder mixing with the aggravation in his voice. "You, more than any single member of the Alliance save my paranoid uncle, are utterly distrustful of Sorbold—for good reason, given that it borders your lands. Don't you feel at least some need to stay and see what comes to pass here?"

"I don't think so. Whatever happens is going to be for ill," Achmed said gravely. "Any outcome from this will be something with which we must deal, and prepare ourselves to survive. Watching it come about, being there at the moment it hatches, would only be deliberately dip the open wounds on my hands in salt water. While it's pretty to think that something I might have to say would tip the scales, it won't."

"Well, there's a positive outlook," remarked Tristan Steward, rising from the table as well and smoothing out his trousers.

"Go get another glass of wine, Tristan," Ashe said sharply. "Your comments at this colloquium have been bothersome, to the point of being embarrassing."

Steward stared at the Lord Cymrian in shock that molded in a matter of seconds into fury, then glared at the Bolg king and departed.

"Stay, please," Ashe said to Achmed when Tristan was

out of earshot. "Your counsel may be of great benefit."

"No. I came to listen, not to speak," the Bolg king replied.

"But what are your thoughts? I want to hear them."

Achmed rolled his eyes. "I am not your advisor, Ashe. If pressed to weigh in, if you will excuse the expression, I would lean in favor of stability, at least for my purposes, because there are many trade agreements and peace accords in place currently that would need renegotiating. They were a bother to enact in the first place, so multiplying that nuisance many times over might insure that it does, in fact, not happen again.

"More than that, a united Sorbold is worrisome enough. Sorbold in tatters would be worse; one can only imagine what would rise from a broken land where the army considers itself a faction in the decision-making process of selecting a new leader. If you did not shudder when that commander stood up and objected as if he were a head of state, you are a fool."

"I did."

"Well, you must understand, then, that no good is coming out of this. This dynasty didn't end because everything was going well. These tables aren't here because everyone is feasting a new monarch. Either the army will slaughter them all, or the merchants will have their thumbs on the scales, or the governors will break the empire by just going home. Whatever accord appears to be passed, whatever pleasantries exchanged, whatever support the losers in the contest demonstrate for the winners, this will end badly. It's inevitable." He turned to go, looking back only for a moment.

"If you must know, part of what I'm doing is to prepare for some instability on the border, and, in truth, I'd appreciate the details when it is settled, but I must go. I don't have the stomach or the time to watch what comes to pass just so that I am able to say I was there and could do nothing to stop it.

"Now I must find the benison. Good night."

# 24

$\mathscr{A}$chmed was awake long before dawn broke.

He crept from the sleeping palace, stopping long enough to stare up at the towering minarets, the dry, imposing edifice, where the bells had thankfully abstained from ringing since the evening before. His head still vibrated from the cacophony of the funeral.

Quickly he made his way down to the livery. The gardens were glistening in the light of the setting moon, the sparse dew on the shrubs and flowers shining like spidery lace.

The stablemaster was there, as he had requested, overseeing the morning's mucking and watering. The horse he had asked for was tacked and saddled, quartered beside his own. Achmed handed him the bill of tender, allowing his eyes to wander over the mount. The stablemaster has chosen generously; the mount was the one he would have selected himself. Achmed inhaled, pleased that, for once, his Firbolg blood had not been an excuse to be mistreated.

He withdrew from his pocket a platinum sun and gave it to the man for good measure, then led both horses away from the warm, heavy air of the stable into the cooler wind of dawn. It was the first time he remembered ever paying more than was asked; it was an interesting feeling.

He was not certain he liked it. But he felt no despair at it, either.

Quickly he vaulted onto his mount and, leading the horse he had just purchased, trotted off into the gray haze of pre-dawn to the cliff face that overlooked the camp of the Panjeri. The advent of sunrise was causing the sky behind him to lighten in anticipation of the dawn.

As he crested the last rise, Achmed reared to a halt.

The camp was gone.

As were the nomads.

His heart began to pound as his eyes scanned the vast

expanse of the steppes to the west, searching the gray mist of the world below for signs of the Panjeri caravan, but it were nowhere to be seen.

A sense of panic, or something like it, began to settle on him, burning in his thin skin. He had finally found the artisans for whom he had searched for months, one in particular who seemed precisely what he needed, a sealed master who was diligent and uncompromising in her work, who would brook no nonsense from Shaene, and could stare a Bolg in the face without flinching.

Who could help turn the Lightcatcher from a schematic into an instrumentality.

And she was gone.

*By the gods, no, I will not let this slip through my hands again,* he thought angrily.

He spurred the horse to canter, doubling back to the base of the hill that led up to the summit where the glass windows were embedded into the peak of Night Mountain.

As before, a quartet of guards was stationed near the crypt.

"Where are the Panjeri?" Achmed shouted to them as the two horses danced in place. The four soldiers blinked, the words rousing them from a state of half-sleep in the drowsy coolness of dawn.

The soldiers shook their heads. One of them shouted back.

"The mail caravan came through in the night. They might have gone with it for part of the way; nomads often do. It heads west through the Rymshin Pass and then north to Sepulvarta. You might try there."

Achmed raised a hand in acknowledgment and spurred the horses again.

𝕿wo days later, an hour's ride through the Rymshin Pass brought him in sight of the western Krevensfield Plain. The sun had crested the horizon, bathing the world below the foothills in a haze of steam, the green waves of highgrass, burned at the tips, waving in the wind as it swept through.

In the distance the guarded mail caravan, seven wagons escorted by two score and ten guards, was slowly winding its way, unhurried, north along the feeder road to the trans-Orlandan thoroughfare. They were headed to Sepulvarta, halfway through their four-week transcontinental cycle. Achmed was intimately acquainted with the schedule and workings of the mail caravan, because it was he who had established it.

Following closely behind the caravan were four crude wagons, gaily painted, each drawn by two teams of horses, with single riders traveling along at intervals alongside.

He had found the Panjeri.

Achmed considered for a moment the logistics of his approach to the caravan. The Krevensfield Plain was flat enough, unguarded enough, that even a single rider coming rapidly down from the foothills and across the steppes might be mistaken as a marauder, though surely the most foolish marauder even spawned. Having no desire to be brought down by an arrow from one of Tristan Steward's caravan guards, he looked around quickly for something to signal his peaceable intentions.

A banner depicting the Sun and Sword of the now-dead empress was flying dispiritedly at the entrance to the pass, its companion flag missing from its pole. Achmed rode to the entranceway and seized the banner, affixing it to his own riding staff. He looked up for a moment, contemplating the dynasty he had heard declared dead the day before, and its symbols of the endless power of the sun, the enduring might of the sword.

*Even these pass away,* he thought. *Perhaps better in life to take on symbols of less grandiose stature, so that in death one might not look as ridiculous.*

He checked the reins on the horse he had purchased in Sorbold, then spurred his own, guiding it down the rocky pathway into the open arms of the Krevensfield Plain.

\* \* \*

$\mathcal{A}$ shout went up simultaneously from the Orlandan guards in the rear of the mail caravan and the Panjeri riding alongside their wagons.

"Hie! South! A rider!"

The caravan continued to roll, picking up a half-gait of speed, as the southern flank of guards peeled off and formed a vanguard waiting to intercept the rider. The Panjeri caravan continued on as well.

Within the second wagon, an older woman grabbed the arm of the younger woman called Theophila, and shook it to get her attention.

"Theophila! Hie to the south! Isn't that the King of the Bolg in pursuit?" she said in the strange pidgin dialect of the nomadic tribe.

"It is! I recognize his veils," said another. "Look! He's come for you, Theophila!"

The younger woman shaded her eyes with her hand, staring south to the foothills. A smile, something the Panjeri had almost never seen on her face, crept across the corners of her mouth, but she said nothing. The women began teasing her as the wagon slowed, and two of the caravan guards rode out to meet the approaching rider, who was flying the standard of the dead empress and leading a second horse.

"It's not your skills as a glass-*shairae* that he covets, girl!"

"No, it's your arse! You do have a lovely arse, Theophila."

"Yes, but she's been waggling it in Krentice's face through this last project. Won't he be jealous?"

"Of the Bolg king? Hardly."

"Why not? He has the same sack in his pants that every man does—"

"Yes! A coin purse!"

"Stop that, you peahens," the older woman scolded. "Mind your manners."

The object of their teasing put her hand into the pocket

of her trousers, and fingered the coins she had taken from the eyes of the empress and the Crown Prince after the clergy and other mourners had left and sealed the tomb high up in the desolate mountaintop. She ran her thumb over the rough metal surfaces, still feeling regret and the sting in her abdomen of misjudging the width of the hole she had opened in the stained-glass window. It was this entranceway she had been sealing when the Bolg king had first seen her.

"Let them twitter," she said. "I pay them no mind, anyway."

She watched with interest as the caravan guards exchanged a few words with the rider, then tugged on the reins, peeling their mounts back to the caravan line. The Bolg king, swathed in veils as she had seen him on the rise of the mount of windows, tossed his Sorbold standard on the ground and eased his horse forward, leading a second one, an expensive, beautiful gelded bay. He came to a halt before the wagon in which she was seated and shielded his strange eyes, staring directly into her own as she rose to a stand.

"Have you considered my offer?"

She squinted in the sun. "To work for tools?"

"Yes. Any hand tools you can design, they will be made for you."

She thought for a moment. "And the two hundred thousand gold suns?"

Achmed blinked, his voice skipping slightly as he answered. "That was for the entire retinue of Panjeri."

"No, it was for hiring what Panjeri you needed. It was you who said you needed but one." She put her hands on her hips. "Are you reneging on your offer?"

"No," the Bolg king said quickly. He smiled as an afterthought occurred. "It is a fair price to purchase the unlimited time of a sealed Panjeri master."

It was now Theophila's turn to experience a skipping of voice. "Wait," she said, "Unlimited time? I did not agree to that."

"Indeed you did. I told you I would not have you unless you were committed to finish the project, and you rather stoutly informed me that you never leave any aspect of your work unfinished. For all you know, my project is to line every crag in the Teeth with intricate windows depicting the geography of the entire world, from each mountain's roots to it summit. Are you reneging on your acceptance of my offer?"

Theophila squared her chin defiantly.

"No," she snarled.

Achmed smiled slightly. "Good. Then bid your clan goodbye, assure them you will be well treated and well paid, and come with me."

The woman turned to the Panjeri, who were staring at her in confusion, spoke a few quick words, listening to the reply of an older man in the same wagon as she, the one that Achmed had determined to be the leader of the nomads based on his actions the day before. She turned back to the Bolg king.

"The leader wants your assurances that you will treat me with kindness." Her voice held a hint of irony, perhaps at the knowledge of how much kindness she herself tended to show.

Achmed sat up straighter in the saddle, then dismounted and walked to the wagon, where he stood beneath Theophila, looking up at her.

"I treat no one with kindness," he said quietly. "You may question both my dearest friends and direst enemies, and they shall both tell you the same thing. But you will be safe, well fed, well protected, and well outfitted. Beyond that, I promise nothing."

The woman stood silent, considering his words. Behind her the Panjeri began whispering to one another in their strange tongue. Achmed grew annoyed. He put out his gloved hand to her.

"Come with me," he said bluntly.

The words, his own, born of impatience, echoed in his

mind. He had spoken very similar words centuries before, a
lifetime ago, on the other side of Time, in the air of a world
now gone, to another woman who was trying his patience.

*Come with us if you want to live.*

Theophila stared down at him; Achmed could see the instant when the decision was finalized in her eyes. She gathered her things, took his hand, and jumped down from the
wagon, ignoring the stares and bewildered mutterings of the
Panjeri, then followed him back to the horses and mounted
the one he had brought for her.

The mail caravan guards, seeing that the Firbolg king's
business was completed, passed the word up along the line,
preparing to resume their journey. The caravan leader waited
long enough for the two strange people to begin to ride,
then called to his own wagon drivers.

"Move on, lads. We have to catch up with the sun."

# 25

It took the better part of a day for the various factions
to sort through their own pecking orders enough to choose
a symbol to represent their interests.

Ashe spent that time cloistered with Rial and Tristan
Steward, comparing their observations and setting an agreed
standard for participation in the remainder of the colloquium.

"This nation is sorting out some of the most grievous
decisions ever to face a realm," he said quietly to the Lord
Roland over their sparse noonmeal served in the cavernous
dining hall of the palace; a good number of the cooks and
servants had fled after the funeral, fearing the unknown, but
trusting in their anonymity, assuming if a friendly regime
took Jierna Tal, they would be rehired, since no one would
recognize them anyway. "Whatever system replaces Leitha,
I mean to see that it maintains its status as a friend to the
Alliance. And while privately I agree with you in principle,

Tristan, that Sorbold is stronger and an easier nation to deal with as a whole, not as a conglomeration of independent states, it is not for us to decide, or deride, what they choose to become in this new incarnation of their realm. Not to mention that strong neighbors aren't always good things."

The Lord Roland fixed a demeaning stare on his sovereign and childhood friend.

"When we were lads, I remember you saying once that there were leaders, and there were politicians," he said in a surly tone, "distinguishable by whether they looked inward or outward to find the courage of their convictions. I am sorry to see which one you have turned out to be."

"I agree that a monolithic Sorbold is more stable," Rial inserted hastily, hoping to forestall the response he saw brewing. "But there are some legitimate points raised by the nobles. The needs of some of the larger city-states sometimes have gone unmet in the game of power the empress played with some of the smaller ones. The One-God knows that the outlying states with a shipping concern need more military might, more naval support; the pirate and slave trades have flourished in Sorbold for years, the gladiatorial arenas grown in scale and popularity as blood sport becomes more and more brutal. It's an atrocity that Leitha turned a blind eye to; I don't blame Damir, whose lands border Tyrian, for his concern."

"Though Kaav's protestations are disingenuous," Ashe said. "His central lands are the largest mining regions, anthracite and silver, sulfur and salt. Where do you think he gets his workers for those terrible places?"

"From the slave trade," Rial agreed.

"Perhaps we have coddled them too long," said Tristan Steward. "Ever since it broke away from the Cymrian Empire at the end of the war, Sorbold has been like a great, looming blight to the south, a nest of scorpions and Gray Assassins hiding in the rocks, biding its time. A more sensible tack to take would be to begin the process of reabsorbing them into the Alliance, rather than trying to make peace accords with them."

"And how would you enforce such a reabsorption, should they not wish it to happen?" Ashe asked disdainfully. "Their army is five, perhaps six times the size of the united forces of Roland—"

"But is dwarfed when you add Tyrian and Ylorc."

Ashe put out his hand quickly to stop Rial's acid reply.

"Let me not hear such talk again, especially while we are guests in this place," he said with a terrifying softness, his voice quavering with the multiple tones of the dragon in his blood. "You are putting ideas on the wind that have no support, but those words have power, and may bring about unintended consequences. What you are advocating is a return to days that are gone, and for good reason."

"Why do you fear that?" Tristan shot back. "Why do you not wish to annex what is unstable, to make it a part of the whole, where we would be safe from it?"

Ashe drained his glass and stood up from the table.

"Because, unlike you, I have no desire to rule the world. Sooner or later, the world comes to resent it."

𝒯he colloquium reconvened at sunset.

The various factions of Sorbold had gravitated toward each other, so that the inner table was divided into four distinct groups—the nobility of the nine large city-states Tryfalian had listed as worthy of independence; the counts of the remaining states, sitting silently and smoldering across the table from them; the Mercantile in the presence of Ihvarr and Talquist; and the army, whose sole representative was Fhremus.

Nielash Mousa had, by his appearance, gotten no sleep the night before. His face, which normally bore the puffy wrinkles under the eyes of a man of his years, sagged under the weight of the import of the proceedings, his dusky skin flushed and sweaty. He stepped into the center of the square, cleared his throat politely, and then spoke as the silence deepened.

"Before we set about the task of another Weighing, I ask if anyone present has a concern or objection that they wish to voice."

No one spoke.

The benison nodded. "Very well. Since I am to conduct this Weighing, with the aid of Lasarys in the keeping of the records, I feel that I should submit myself to the Scales for their judgment beforehand. The Scales detect more than the eye can ever see, more than the mind can rightly know. They know a man's heart, and a man's destiny; if they adjudge me to be false, I have no defense against it." He fingered the holy symbol around his neck, a representation of the Earth. "My office resides in this symbol. If I am not worthy of it, if I have violated any of my vows or compromised my holy oaths, I will be found wanting." He eyed the crowd as a smile took up residence at the corner of his mouth. "Bear this in mind for yourselves as well."

As the assemblage exchanged nervous glances, the benison removed the chain from his neck and handed it to Lasarys. The priest walked hurriedly to the top of the steps where the Scales loomed and reverently set the holy symbol down in the western plate. Then he stepped aside and nodded anxiously to Mousa.

The Blesser of Sorbold mounted the steps to the top of the platform, his back straighter than Ashe had seen it since arriving in Sorbold. He closed his eyes and stepped carefully onto the other plate.

For a moment the Scales did not move. Then, with a creak of the great wooden arms, the chains that held the plate rattled, and the benison was lifted aloft, then balanced perfectly with his holy symbol.

Ashe, watching from the outer circle, felt a swell of amazement. It never ceased to impress him, the sight of a man's weight balancing in the air against a tiny symbol like the ring, a sign of the power of the ancient Scales. He thought back to their history, how Gwylliam had valued them enough to bring them across the sea from Serendair, rescuing them from being obliterated in the cataclysm. It was one of the truly great accomplishments in his grandfather's sordid life.

Nielash Mousa remained still for a moment, his eyes closed, as if listening to voices no one else could hear. Then he opened his eyes, inhaled deeply, and stepped down from the Scales, sanctified by the Earth, and prepared to conduct the Weighings. He collected the holy symbol, which he kissed and returned to its place around his neck, then signaled for Lasarys to place the Ring of State in the western plate.

"Very well. Assuming no one wishes to dispute the findings of the Scales—" He paused for a moment, then, hearing no comment, plowed on. "I invite the factions to present their cases. Once we know which faction's vision for Sorbold the Scales determine to be the right one, we will weigh anyone within that group who wishes to present himself as emperor."

"What if our faction disputes that there should *be* an emperor?" Tryfalian called out.

Mousa considered for a moment. "Then the vision articulated by the person chosen from the faction by the Scales will be enacted—whatever it may be." He turned to Lasarys amid the murmuring that broke out at his words, then turned back to the assemblage.

"Who brings forth a symbol from the army?"

Fhremus pushed his chair away from the table and stood, taking a moment to stare at each of the other factions. Then he ascended the steps to the platform. He held aloft a shield that blazed with a golden sun; it glinted in the rays of sunset.

"This is the shield of the empress's regiment, the column which has protected and defended the throne of Sorbold for three hundred years," he said stiffly. "The army does not seek to rule, merely to guard and sustain whomever the Scales choose as the rightful voice of the realm." He coughed, then met the eyes of the assemblage. "If the Scales select our faction, the vision will be to remain a single nation, with a leader selected by the Scales from the military, and coronated as emperor."

Nielash Mousa motioned him to place the shield on the plate. The commander kissed the shield and set it down to be weighed.

The Scales did not move. The shield remained hovering at the place it had been, outweighed by the Ring of State.

"Your wisdom has been borne out," said Mousa to Fhremus, who nodded and retrieved his weapon. "It is not from the military that the visionary who will lead Sorbold will come. Who is next?"

"I—we are next," called Tryfalian, his voice booming over the square. He strode to the steps and mounted them without looking back, ignoring the whispering that had begun.

"What symbol do you present?" Mousa asked.

Tryfalian held up a large brass wax seal. "This seal was presented to my grandfather by the empress, for the purpose of stamping trade agreements on behalf of the Crown," he said. "It is a symbol of the autonomy which she granted to the city-states, an autonomy that will be furthered should the Scales weigh in favor of the Greater Nobility, the counts who steward the nine largest states. Should this be the choice of the Scales, the empire will be dissolved; autonomy and freedom will be granted to the nine large provinces which between them comprise more than three-fourths of the landmass and population of the current state. They will absorb the remaining eighteen, after meetings to discuss the specifics."

Mousa nodded and indicated the western plate. Slowly Tryfalian approached the Scales, and knelt, laying the heavy seal in the plate to be weighed against the small ring.

The Scales tipped immediately, dumping the heavy seal out of the plate onto the reviewing stand, where it rolled quickly to the edge. Tryfalian lunged to keep it from falling onto the bricks of the square, and landed on his stomach, the seal banging against his knuckles with a crunching sound that made the onlookers wince.

"Perhaps the empress favored you, but the Scales apparently do not, Tryfalian!" one of the lesser counts shouted derisively over the laughter that bubbled up from his faction.

"Silence!" thundered Nielash Mousa. The assemblage froze at the steel in the benison's voice; Mousa was generally a soft-spoken man with a famously long temper. "You dishonor the Scales." He laid a hand on the shoulder of the Count of Keltar as he rose, glaring at the lesser counts, then waited until Tryfalian had taken his seat again.

"Who will present next?"

The Mercantile and the lesser counts looked at one another blankly. Finally Ihvarr stood.

"All right," he said testily. "The Mercantile will go next."

Quiet whispering rose up from the lesser counts as Ihvarr walked to the stand. Nielash Mousa met him at the top of the steps, then glared the lesser nobility into silence.

Ihvarr held up a single gold sun, the coin of the realm of Sorbold, imprinted with the empress's face on one side and the sword-and-sun symbol on the other, larger and heavier than a gold crown of Roland.

"This simple coin is the symbol of commerce in Sorbold," he said, his glorious merchant's voice filling the square. "It represents the wealth and power of trade in Sorbold, shipping lanes, mining interests, and linen weavers that are known the world over. While the Mercantile does not seek to rule, it does seek to keep the nation together. The men who plough the earth and the sea, who ply the trades—these are the lifeblood of Sorbold. I speak for them." He tossed the coin flippantly into the plate.

Slowly the Scales moved, scuffing the platform.

The arm raised to the inky sky, lifting the coin aloft, then brought it to balance with the Ring of State.

Ihvarr stepped back as if slapped. He looked quickly over

at Talquist, who was similarly stunned, and then to the benison, who nodded gravely.

"Take the coin off the plate," Mousa instructed.

Quickly the merchant leader complied.

"There must be a mistake," Tristan Steward whispered to Ashe, echoing the thoughts and comments of countless others in the factions and among the guests. "Surely the next emperor is not to come from the Mercantile?"

Ashe waved at him to be silent. "Why not?" he whispered. "You know the work of a head of state. Half of the time is spent in mind-numbing figuring of tariffs and grain treaties. These people *live* for that." He inhaled deeply, thinking of Rial's words earlier regarding the slave trade. "And perhaps with the Scales watching their movements, they will address the illegal trade that deals in human blood, lest they risk the ire of the Dark Earth."

The benison raised his hand for the attention of the assemblage. "We shall weigh the symbol of the Mercantile again, so that there can be no doubt," he said. "Ihvarr, place the coin in the plate again."

The eastern Hierarch did as the benison instructed. Again the Scales lifted the coin high to the darkening sky, as if exalting it, then slowly settled down into an exact balance against the Ring of State.

"It is Weighed, and found to be in balance!" said the benison loudly, his excitement echoing in the stunned silence.

For a long moment no one spoke. Then a smattering of applause was heard, followed by a more rolling round of it. The eastern Hierarch looked out to his compatriot, who shrugged.

"Who will stand to be Weighed as a candidate for emperor?" Mousa inquired.

"Ihvaar!" Talquist shouted merrily. "If his illegitimate birth does not disqualify him, that is."

"Blackguard!" Ihvarr shouted back. "If it does, we will

surely be in difficulty, because you are a bastard, too, Talquist; a bigger one than I, by all accounts."

"Step into the plate," said Nielash Mousa impatiently. "Allow your amazement to render you speechless, rather than foolish, in the sight of the Scales."

Abashed, the Hierarch stepped onto the plate.

Immediately he was upended. With a rush of air and a swing of the wooden arm, Ihvarr was violently thrown to base of the reviewing stand; he landed with a sickening *crack* of his neck, then thudded heavily to the ground.

Talquist shot to his feet, rushing to Ihvarr's side, panic written all over his features.

"Help him!" he cried, shoving aside chairs to get to his comrade. "For the sake of the All-God—"

"Leave him," commanded Nielash Mousa sternly. "The Scales have spoken. Mount the stairs."

Talquist stopped in midstep. "What?" he asked incredulously.

"Present yourself for Weighing. It is the will of the Scales."

"Don't be a coward, Talquist," sneered one of the lesser counts. "The Mercantile is to lead us, to take the throne from the hands of the nobility, where is had rested for centuries, and place it for safekeeping in the dirt-stained paws of a merchant. It might as well be you! Throw yourself into the plate. Perhaps you will only break a leg instead of your neck."

Talquist, who had bent to close the glassy eyes of Ihvarr, stood again, his heavy features hardening into a frowning mask.

"Nobility, are you, now, Sitkar?" he said, staring into the ranks of the heads of the smaller city-states. "You only know one meaning of the word, apparently. There is far more nobility in the hand of a man who earns his bread, rather than stealing it from the mouths of those who do by a distant scrap of Right of Kings. Perhaps the Mercantile represent something that none in your faction ever could: an understanding that the Earth rewards the man who works it, honors it, respects it—not just feeds off it."

Without another word he walked to the stairs and ascended the platform.

And stepped into the Scale plate.

And was lifted high above the red bricks of the square, over the heads of the other contenders for the throne, aloft, as if a precious offering the Scales were making to the moon above.

Then balanced perfectly against the Ring.

Silence so profound that a man could hear nothing but the beating of his own heart filled the square.

Then the benison knelt reverently, followed by Lasarys, Fhremus, and the other citizens of Sorbold, some reluctantly, others in awe.

Finally the Blesser of Sorbold stood. He bowed to the Hierarch, then turned to the assemblage.

"Whosoever doubts the wisdom of the Scales, it is as if he is calling into question the integrity of the Earth itself," he proclaimed, his wrinkled features relaxed into a contented expression. "Let none be so blasphemous as to do so."

He turned to Talquist and offered him his hand to help him down from the plate.

"What are your directions now, m'lord?"

Talquist contemplated the question for a moment, then came to the edge of the platform and stood staring down at the assemblage before him. Finally he spoke.

"The first order of business will be to tend to the burial of Ihvarr, who was an honorable man, a loyal Sorbold, a defender of the nation, an advocate for the common man, and a good friend," he said simply. "After that we can set about sorting out the business of state.

"I am as shocked as anyone else, probably more so, at this turn of events. I would propose that, rather than move to a coronation, I be invested as regent for the period of a year, an office with which I am much more comfortable at this moment. The army will continue as it has, in its steadfast defense of the realm, the Mercantile will continue to ply their trades, the nobility may keep their offices—for the time being. If, after a year has passed, the Scales still say I am to reign as emperor, I will bow to their will and accept the Sun Scepter as well as the Ring of State, which I will wear beginning now. But until then, I wish only to hold the empire together, and get back to work."

The benison bowed deeply. "As you command, m'lord."

Talquist exhaled deeply. "Come, then," he said to assemblage. "Summon the chamberlain to tell the cooks to return and prepare all of us a well-deserved repast. We can sit together, at this table without hierarchy, as friends and allies, and drink to Ihvarr and the future of Sorbold. For this night holds great promise.

"For Sorbold, it is a new beginning."

Something in the words rang false against Ashe's ear. He turned to look more carefully at Talquist, but the new regent was obscured from view by Nielash Mousa, who hovered near him.

The benison turned to Lasarys.

"Command the bells to peal!"

Two days after the colloquium had concluded, Ashe was finally able to break away from the requests for his attention and depart for Haguefort. He bade the Blesser of Sorbold goodbye, wishing him well.

"Try and find an excuse to rest," he said, clapping Nielash Mousa on the shoulder. "This has been a difficult few weeks for you, but there is still much work to be done. Sorbold needs you well."

The weary benison smiled wanly and nodded his thanks. "We can but petition the All-God that the difficult times are behind us, not ahead," he said softly.

"Ryle hira," Ashe replied, using the ancient Liringlas expression. *Life is what it is.* "Whatever comes to pass, we will make the best of it."

The morning of their leavetaking was hot. The sun had

risen rapidly, energized as if with the renewed stamina of a new era, and burst forth into the heavens, eager to light the land. Ashe's men, sweating already at breakfast time, cursed mutely and wished for less solar enthusiasm, but nonetheless packed the caravan quickly and efficiently, departing the Sorbold capital speedily and without looking back.

As the Lord Cymrian's retinue descended the northern face of the Teeth, through the Rymshin Pass heading north to Sepulvarta, a cry went up from a single voice, which was picked up a moment later by the rest of the regiment.

"M'lord! M'lord!"

Ashe followed the fingers of the soldiers pointing west into the sun. Even before his eyes tracked, his stomach clenched in terror; his dragon sense discerned the approaching bird, noted the feathers it had shed, the strain in its wings, the rapid movement of its eyes as it searched from above for its perch on its trainer's glove.

"Sweet All-God," he whispered, reining his horse to a halt. "No."

It was a falcon.

# 26

## HAGUEFORT, NAVARNE

Rhapsody coiled the last of the sections of curly hair into a chignon and pinned it, more by feel than sight.

"Blue ribbons, or white, Melly?" she asked.

"Blue, I think," the girl replied, examining her young face seriously in the looking glass. "And can you entwine the crystals with them at the base as you did at the spring ball?"

"Of course." Rhapsody put out her hand for the ribbons, swallowing quickly as another dizzy spell signaled its approach. She blinked rapidly, trying to quell the unsteadiness, and improvised by running her hands along the sides of Melisande's hair to smooth it.

"There," she said when the unsteadiness had passed. "How is that?"

"Wonderful!" Melisande replied, turning to hug her. "Thank you. I wish the Lirin hairmistresses would teach me to plait pretty patterns as they taught you."

"I was a poor student, I fear," Rhapsody said, brushing a kiss on the side of the girl's head. "You should see some of the configurations they are able to weave. Once I attended a meeting with the sea-Lirin ambassador with an accurate depiction of the coastline of Tyrian embroidered in my hair." The young girl giggled. "Next time you come with me to the Lirin lands I will ask them to teach you, too. Now, come. Help me find your brother."

Melisande put out her hand, and slipped an arm around Rhapsody's waist to steady her. Together they strolled up the front entranceway of Haguefort, past the walls of rosy brown stone blooming with fragrant floral ivy, taking their time on the stairs.

The sounds in the distance told Rhapsody the carriage and its escort were close to being ready to leave; she could hear the drivers, little more than moving shapes in the distance, calling to each other, making final preparations; a squeak of doors indicated that the carriage was being stocked.

"Is Gwydion here?" she asked a little nervously, scanning the swimming green horizon for her adopted grandson.

"Behind you," came a voice that was deeper than it ought to be, with a slight crack in its tone. Rhapsody turned and smiled fondly at the blurry shape now in front of her.

"I was afraid you would be caught up in your archery, and not remember to come and bid me goodbye."

"Never," said Gwydion Navarne solemnly. She opened her arms, and awkwardly he came into them, embracing her carefully, as if she might break.

"I'm not made of glass, you know, Gwydion," she said as Melisande ran off to inspect the inside of the carriage. "Please don't worry so."

"I'm not."

"Balderdash. You're lying; I can hear it in the frequency of your tone." She reached up and laid a hand on his cheek, the smooth, boyish skin rough with an emerging beard. "Tell me what is troubling you."

Gwydion looked away. "Nothing. I never really like it when you leave. Particularly in a carriage, and even more so when you refuse to allow me to go along."

Rhapsody inhaled and held her breath, cursing herself for being thoughtless. Gwydion's mother had been mercilessly slaughtered after kissing her seven-year-old son goodbye and heading off to Navarne City with her sister to purchase a sturdy pair of shoes for one-year-old Melly. She had forgotten the circumstances until now, though she had noticed his reticence to say goodbye each time she left for Tyrian or some other place.

"I will be back to see you shoot those new arrows," she promised, running her hand up and down his arm as if to warm it. "Do you like them?"

The lad shrugged. "I've used but one, and it was true. I am saving them so that you and Ashe can both see me use them in an archery tournament."

"Wonderful!" she said brightly, her tone belying the nausea that was rising again. "Now, will you escort me down to the carriage? You know how much Anborn hates to be kept waiting. He'll be bellowing any moment."

"Let him wait," Gwydion said, his humor returning. "He's going to bellow anyway. You may as well give him something real to bellow about."

"They've put in a silver bucket with *ice* in it!" Melisande called up from the roadway in amazement. "And it's shaped like a knight's helm! And there are cherry and lemon tarts!"

Gwydion Navarne brushed some stray pebbles from her path with his toe. "Will you commend me to the dragon?"

"I will. I'm sure that will please her. She's really quite kind and has an interesting sense of humor."

"I have no doubt," Gwydion said, offering her his arm. "If she didn't, the population of western Roland would be hanging upside down, drying into bacon in the world's biggest smokehouse somewhere north of Gwynwood."

Rhapsody put her hand over her mouth. "Ooh," she mumbled, rushing to the side of the keep's wall.

The young duke-to-be turned away and scratched his head awkwardly.

"I can't wait to be able to talk to you the way that I used to," he said remorsefully. "I am so sorry."

"I can't wait either," she said after a moment, reaching for his arm. "Perhaps Elynsynos will know a way to bring me back to my old self again."

"Well, I know a way for you not to have to suffer like this too long."

"Oh? How?"

The boy's eye glinted merrily.

"Stay far away from Ashe the next time."

𝕿he road to Gwynwood wandered for a while through a mixture of sparse forests and open fields before it passed into the thicker white wood for which it was named.

The summer sun was high in the sky, but the forest was cool, the light flickering in through the carriage window in lacy patterns. Rhapsody drowsed against the cushions, enjoying the feel of the gentle breeze on her face.

The debilitating illness had lessened in the three days she had passed at Haguefort. Though she was sometimes sick, and often unsteady, more often than not the symptoms of her condition were confined to blurry vision and a sudden lack of balance that overwhelmed her, even when sitting or lying down. *Another few days, and I will be with Elynsynos, deep within the quiet of her lair, at the edge of her underground lagoon.* The thought made her smile.

The rumble of the carriage wheels, the muted clip-clop of the horses' hooves, the occasional twitter of birdsong that made it past the curtain at her window, the sounds of a journey happily undertaken blended in a soothing harmony. It was a peaceable feeling.

She heard her name being called from out the left window; it was Anborn's voice, and he sounded almost merry. For all that he protested an unwillingness to be tied to a single place, or kept in a task not of his own choosing, the General seemed quite pleased to be out with a small guard regiment, traveling some of the most verdant and beautiful forest on the continent.

"Hello in there," he bellowed. "You alive, m'lady?"

She moved to the window and stuck her head out.

"Define 'alive.' "

"Aha! She lives!" the General said cheerily to his troops, the eight soldiers and two drivers who had accompanied them. "You must make an effort to let us know you are still among the living from time to time, lady."

"Sorry," Rhapsody said pleasantly. She closed her eyes and enjoyed the feel of the strong breeze, cooled by the green leaves of the forest canopy, as it billowed over her face and buffeted her hair. It was a feeling similar to being at sea, the constant motion, the stiff wind. A sensation she enjoyed.

Anborn rode close to the carriage. "Do you wish to stop for noonmeal?"

Rhapsody opened her eyes and smiled involuntarily. Aside from the high-backed saddle that had been crafted to support him, there was no visible sign that this was a man without the use of his legs. His lameness was even less noticeable because, to a one, all the saddles of the guards riding with him had been similarly outfitted, so that the General could ride any mount he chose. He looked as hale and imposing on horseback as he had the first time she had ever beheld him, when he almost ran her down on this very forest road.

"If the troops would like a break, we can stop," she said. "I'm not hungry."

Anborn snorted. "They had breakfast," he said haughtily. "We'll go on; we're making good time."

"I'd like to stop at the Tree when we pass near the Cir-

cle," Rhapsody said, gripping the window to steady herself
as a new wave of unease rolled over her. "How much longer
until we are there?"

Anborn looked around at the forest and the position of
the sun. "Tomorrow afternoon."

"All right." She pulled the carriage blanket up to her
shoulders. "Then, by all means, let us stop and take noonmeal. Knowing you, Anborn, you won't give them the
chance to eat again until tomorrow."

The General smiled slightly. "As m'lady commands."

Shrike, as ever riding at Anborn's rear flank, his dual
stonebows in his lap, spoke up.

"Thank the gods. I was planning to rip the bark from the
next tree we passed and swallow it."

$\mathcal{T}$he deeper they traveled into the greenwood, the easier
the journey became.

Anborn called the carriage to halt every few hours when
he determined Rhapsody to be awake, giving her a chance
to stretch and feel solid ground beneath her feet for a while.
After a few moments, when she deemed herself ready, she
was packed carefully back into the coach, and the guard
regiment set off again.

As the afternoon sun fell below the tree line, flooding the
forest with shafts of dusty golden light, the General called
the carriage to halt for the night.

"I think you've had entirely enough jolting and jouncing
for one day," he said as the coach doors were opened. "Time
to rest. We'll build a fire and sleep for the night."

"Don't refrain from traveling on my account," Rhapsody
said, taking the arm of the guard who stood at attendance
to help her down the carriage steps. "I'm just sleeping in
here. I've done no work at all today."

"Welcome to the privileged life," Anborn laughed.

As the soldiers set about laying camp, Shrike assisted the
general off his mount and onto a bedroll near the pile of
sticks and branches in the clearing that would be the camp-

fire. Rhapsody settled down next to him, and was handed a mug of cider and a plate of biscuits.

She unbuckled Daystar Clarion from her belt and pulled the sword gently from its sheath; it came forth with a quiet hum, the same pitch as the clarion call that it could wind when drawn in anger or need, but almost inaudible, resonating quietly in the still air of the darkening forest.

The bond to elemental fire deep within her sang a harmonic in response; the music hummed in Rhapsody, quieting her stomach and her mind.

The soldiers watched, fascinated, as she extended the sword of billowing flames and touched the kit of sticks and branches; it ignited immediately, the fire leaping in the wind, showering the twilight with bright sparks that crackled and winked like fireflies.

She rested the sword across her knees, her elbows holding it in place, impervious to the flames, and listened to the gossip and banter of the four soldiers who were not standing watch as they relaxed around the fire and ate their simple meals.

There was something refreshing, invigorating, about being in the forest at night in summer, she thought, breathing deeply to take in the cool, moist air that stood in such contrast to the dry heat of Yarim. Perhaps being in this natural setting, with the full green of the season, the warm, rich scent of the earth, the sheltering canopy of tree branches above her, was improving her condition. She felt better, though she was still off balance and unclear in her sight.

Many leagues away in the distance she could hear the song of the Great White Tree, a deep, primeval melody that stretched throughout the forest, humming in all the things that grew there. She closed her eyes and listened, entranced, letting the music fill her mind and clear it.

Softly she began singing a song of home that her seafaring grandfather had sung to her when she was a child.

> I was born beneath this willow,
> Where my sire the earth did farm

Had the green grass as my pillow
The east wind as a blanket warm

But *away! away!* called the wind from the west
And in answer I did run
Seeking glory and adventure
Promised by the rising sun

I found love beneath this willow,
As true a love as life could hold,
Pledged my heart and swore my fealty
Sealed with a kiss and a band of gold

But *to arms! to arms!* called the wind from the west
In faithful answer I did run
Marching forth for king and country
In battles 'neath the midday sun.

Oft I dreamt of that fair willow
As the seven seas I plied
And the girl who I left waiting
Longing to be at her side

But *about! about!* called the wind from the west
As once again my ship did run
Down the coast, about the wide world
Flying sails in the setting sun

Now I lie beneath the willow
Now at last no more to roam,
My bride and earth so tightly hold me
In their arms I'm finally home.

While *away! away!* calls the wind from the west
Beyond the grave my spirit, free
Will chase the sun into the morning
Beyond the sky, beyond the sea

Anborn, Shrike, and the soldiers listened, their conversation dying away when the first notes sounded, rapt at the melancholy melody. When she was finished, the circle of men drew in a deep, collective breath, and let it out again in a synchronous sigh.

"Now for another, if you are up to it, lady," Anborn said, draining his tankard. "Can you favor us with 'The Sad, Strange Tale of Simeon Blowfellow and the Concubine's Slipper'? It's a favorite of mine, as you know."

Rhapsody laughed, feeling the tightness in her chest and abdomen abate a bit. "A Gwadd song? You want to hear a Gwadd song?"

Anborn adopted a comic air of injury. "Why not?" he demanded. "Just because the Gwadd are tiny folk—"

"Make good footstools," added Shrike rotely.

"—doesn't mean they aren't fine singers—"

"Tender when stewed with potatoes—"

"And crafters of wondrous ballads—"

"Can substitute as haybutts for crossbow practice—"

"All right!" Rhapsody choked, mirth making her ribs hurt. "Stop that at once." She sat up as straight as she could and cleared her throat. "I need my harp," she said, positioning herself more comfortably. "Would one of you fine gentleman be so kind as to retrieve it from the carriage?" The guards rose quickly to their feet, looking askance at the ancient Cymrians so willing to be crude in front of the lady, to no apparent displeasure on her part.

Anborn sighed comically as one of the men jogged to the carriage to get the instrument.

"Sounds better on a concertina," he said knowingly to Shrike.

"Or a fiddle strung with Gwadd-gut."

Rhapsody put her hand over her mouth to quell the mixture of nausea and laughter that rose up at the comment. "One more statement like that, Shrike, and I will move over near you so that when I retch, you can be the direct beneficiary of it."

"Tsk, tsk," intoned Shrike, shaking his head. "Never known her to be so mean and ornery before, have you, Anborn? Wonder what's got into her? Oh, wait—that's right. It was your nephew."

Anborn cuffed his oldest friend on the ear and glowered at him.

Quickly Rhapsody took the lap harp from the guard, tuned it and began to play the comically heartrending air from the old land, the song of the Gwadd hero Simeon Blowfellow and his lost love's shoe.

"Another! Sing another, lady," Shrike encouraged when she had finished the tragic tale.

"How's for a lullabye?" Rhapsody asked in return, shifting the harp to her other knee. "Not just because it's late, but because I need to practice." The men nodded their assent, and she began to sing an old, soothing night air, the origins of which she didn't remember.

> Sleep, little bird, beneath my wing—

Anborn turned suddenly pale in the reflected light of the campfire; his hand shot out and gripped her forearm.

"Sing something else," he said tersely.

Rhapsody blinked, taken aback. "I'm sorry," she said quickly, trying to discern the expression on his face, but could only make out the shadow of his eyes and mouth.

"Do not be sorry. Sing something else."

Unnerved, she thought back to the wind-song that was her own lullabye as an infant, knowing that none of those assembled would have heard it before, and so would not take a dislike to it as Anborn apparently had to the last one. Haltingly she began to sing it, her voice reflected in the gentle crackling of the campfire, the pulsing of the flames that licked the blade of Daystar Clarion.

> Sleep, my child, my little one, sleep
> Down in the glade where the river runs deep

The wind whistles through and it carries away
All of your troubles and cares of the day.

Rest, my dear, my lovely one, rest,
Where the white killdeer has built her fair nest,
Your pillow sweet clover, your blanket the grass
The moon shines on you as the wind whistles past.

Dream, my own, my pretty one, dream,
In tune with the song of the swift meadow stream,
Take wing with the wind as it lifts you above,
Tethered to Earth by the bonds of my love.

When she was finished, Anborn looked over at her for the first time since the air began.

"Lovely," he said quietly. "Where did you learn that one?"

"From my mother," Rhapsody said. "She had a song for everything. Liringlas ascribe a song to almost every event in life. It is tradition among the Lirin that when a woman discovers she is with child, she chooses a song to sing to the growing life within her. It is the first gift she gives to the baby, its own song." She looked off into the darkness beyond the campfire's blurry light. "Each of my brothers had his own, but this is the one she sang when she was carrying me. The Liringlas mother sings the song she has chosen through the course of each day, through mundane events, in quiet moments when she is alone, before each morning aubade, after each evening vesper. It's the song the child comes to know her by, the baby's first lullabye, unique to each child. Lirin live outside beneath the stars, and it is important that the infants remain as silent as possible in dangerous situations. The song is so familiar that it comforts them innately. Puts them to sleep."

Anborn exhaled. "A noble tradition. Have you chosen one yet for my great-nephew or niece?"

Rhapsody smiled. "No, not yet. When it is right, I will

know it. Or so they told me. Now, if you'll permit me, I think I will sleep. Rest well, gentlemen." She stretched out to sleep by the fire.

Anborn watched her affectionately through the better part of the night, his brow furrowing when she winced in pain in her sleep, his eyes shining as she slumbered peacefully.

After the watch had changed, Shrike came over to him and crouched down beside him.

"Withdraw for a moment," he ordered the four guards who had come off watch. They looked to Anborn for confirmation; the General nodded.

When the soldiers were out of the way, Shrike drew a thin, battered cutlass and held it out to his old friend.

"Take it," he said.

Anborn looked away. "Not tonight."

Shrike shook the weapon at him. *"Take it,"* he said, more firmly.

Anborn declined again. "I cannot bear it tonight, Shrike."

"If you are going to be lost to melancholy thoughts, at least go into that heavyheartedness with having experienced the sight, not just the memory."

Finally the general turned and looked at his man-at-arms, who, as always, stood just behind him, at his back. He sighed and took the cutlass, holding it up to the firelight so that it reflected in the blade.

Shrike stood very still, watching Anborn as he sat, lost in memory, reliving a moment in time gone forever, a sight that Shrike, alone in the wide world, by virtue of a Namer's word bestowed on him long ago, had the power to allow him to see again.

When the image faded, he returned the cutlass to the man-at-arms and took hold of his useless legs, stretching them.

"I suppose I should thank you," he said distantly.

"No need. You never do."

"For good reason," the General said as he settled down to sleep. "There are some things a man should abstain from

allowing himself to see, no matter how desperately he wants to. Now summon the guards back and let them rest."

𝔍n the morning, the journey to the dragon's lair resumed, through fair weather, three warm days and three cool nights, uneventful and easy.

Until the first bolt struck.

# 27

𝔈arly morning on the fourth day, they were half a day's journey from the narrowest crossing of the Tara'fel river when Shrike lurched forward in his saddle.

Shrike always rode rear guard, directly behind Anborn, covering the General's back literally as he had for centuries figuratively. So when the first bolt was released at the beginning of the ambush, it was aimed at Shrike, riding at the end of the guardian circle behind the carriage in which Rhapsody slept.

Despite his years, Shrike was blessed with uncommon speed, and so had time to catch a fleeting glance of the double volley of bolts that severed the spinal columns of the soldiers riding before and to the sides of him as the men reeled forward simultaneously, their legs suddenly as useless as Anborn's.

The bolt aimed at him had caught the high-backed saddle, shocking him with its impact, but giving him the opportunity to wheel in his seat and fire his crossbows into the eyes of two of the men who had appeared from the trees behind him. He noted the rustling of the branches, the rise of dirt and dead leaves into the air as they fell back, but did not hear them hit the ground.

Time slowed maddeningly; he could hear the pounding of his heart, the scream of the horse as it reared, the crashing of the forest branches all around them. In that one last, instantaneous moment of sight, before the second bolt struck him, before the blood welled into his throat, Shrike heard his own voice, from which he was quite dissociated, loose in a shout of alarm.

"We're under *attack!* Drive on! Drive on!"

The third bolt split his breastbone, ripping his breath away. Shrike fought the darkness dropping in from the corners of his eyes as the crossbow fell from his left hand, the bolt gouging the horse as it skittered down its side, and put all of his concentration, all of the torn spiderwebs of his conscious focus, into one last shot.

He fired again.

The bolt went wide, or so it seemed, and yet it appeared to him, in the haze that had settled now in his eyes and mind, that another body fell from the trees.

He noted an impressive absence of pain as he rolled off the twisting horse's flank, heard nothing now but the pounding in his ears, the emptying of his heart as the blood gushed out of his chest, pooling onto the forest floor beneath his face.

He heard Anborn shouting his name, the sound growing dimmer until in reverberated into nothingness.

Ride! Surround the carriage!" the General thundered, reining his horse back as Shrike fell to the forest floor, his life spilling out into the loam. He slapped the horse, using the hand signal it knew, directing it across the road, bisecting the pathway, and, stonebow in one arm, he drew his bastard sword with the other, murder in his eyes.

Rider and animal halted; then galloped forth at an inverse angle again, dodging another hailstorm of bolts. Anborn leaned forward over the neck of the horse, hearing the sickening tattoo of the careening carriage wheels as the drivers beat their team, the guardian soldiers thundering along beside it, then charged forward into the woods from whence the crossbow fire had come, slashing with fury unleashed.

The crunching of bone, the spewing of blood, of leather, of brain, the true, solid reflections of the accuracy in which his marks were met, did nothing to quell the fury that had boiled over, and was now scorching all in his path. Gone was the detached pragmatism with which the Lord Marshal had conducted himself through some of the bloodiest campaigns in the history of the continent. He could not contain the anger, laying on a slack-faced crossbowman so viciously that after six rapid blows the corpse was unrecognizable.

He heard in the distance the sound of hammers firing and stopped, reining the stallion in place, then turning in horror.

Ahead of the carriage the crossbows fired again. One of the drivers, shot through the forehead, fell heavily to the ground, taking the reins with him as he slipped under the wheels.

The coach wobbled crazily, tilting off its wheels, as the royal guards struggled to keep up with it, firing at any movement they saw in the woods at the edge of the roadway.

From either side of the carriage, two of Rhapsody's guards attempted to leap from their horses to gain control of the coach and drive it to escape. One succeeded, the other making a grab for the running board, only to be shot as well.

"Fly!" Anborn roared to the riders and the coachman, but they were out of range of his voice.

He sheared the reins and swept around, driving his mount back through the forest edge, bearing down on two men on foot who had turned and were fleeing toward the forest road. Man and animal, in single-minded concentration, rode the first one down; Anborn waited until he felt the horse's hooves crush the first man's head like a melon before firing into the back of the neck of the second, sweeping him out of the way with the bastard sword as he spun and fell.

Ahead in the tree line he could see shapes moving, a score or more, and knew that it was only the rear flank of the force that had laid the ambush. His gorge rose as he leaned close to the neck of the stallion in pursuit, knowing the carriage was probably surrounded by now, the guards outnumbered or dead.

He did not think about Shrike.

\* \* \*

Rhapsody woke as she was flung across the carriage.

In the haze that had settled into her mind since conceiving the child, she struggled to come to consciousness, her perspective thrown off kilter both by the wildly tilting carriage and her own internal lack of balance. At first she couldn't even remember where she was, fraught in the clutches of the strange and exaggerated dreams that had been plaguing her.

She heard voices outside the carriage window, the shouts of her own troops, and, more distantly, muffled calls in a language she didn't understand.

Shakily she felt for her sword.

*This can't be happening,* she thought, trying to clear her head and at the same time hold on to her stomach as the carriage swerved again, slamming her to the floor.

As her ear banged against the planks of the jolting carriage floor, she could hear a whooping cry go up, and her blood ran cold.

It was a call of impending victory.

The seneschal was waiting half a league up the road.

He could hear the sound of the carriage approaching on the breeze, followed by the keening cry. He looked over his shoulder and called to Fergus, at the head of the remaining troop mounted atop the horses they had acquired in the last week.

"There's the signal. She's coming. Take her off the road."

Fergus gave a quick nodded and gestured to the troops, then kicked his horse forward into a rolling canter.

The seneschal raised his hand over the metal drum half full of oil in front of him. He opened the door in his mind that would let the demon come through, invited.

*Kryv,* they whispered together in a single voice.

With a billowing roar the oil ignited, ripping into a sheet of flame. A rolling plume of black smoke and sparks ascended, torching the green leaves in the canopy above the road. The fire quickly settled into a hot, bright blaze, a contained inferno.

As the troops rode past, the archers, headed up by Caius, hung back, their long bows, nocked with tar-tipped arrows, at the ready.

As the carriage wove down the forest road, the remaining six guards covered the driver, spurring their horses desperately, trying to keep time with the panicked team that was struggling to break free from the burden it was towing.

Two more pockets of assailants, one on the left rear flank, the other ahead on the right, rode out of the woods, firing a cross-hail of bolts, some aimed at the guards, but more trained on the driver and the team.

Rhapsody's driver and guards were now so badly outnumbered that it was all they could do to keep the carriage on the road. The rear flank seemed bent on driving them right, while those approaching from the woods ahead were veering left. The driver's hands, bloody from gripping the reins, threatened to give out as he yanked the team left, away from the gullies at the side of the road.

As they crested a rise in the road, another phalanx of riders, three this time, charged out of the woods, directly perpendicular to the coach. They charged, firing first at the driver, who slumped on his perch, then at the carriage and the guards, hitting some of each, driving the team northward, off the road, and into a low-lying area just beyond.

Rhapsody's remaining guards, borne down on now by four times their number, stopped and drew, interposing themselves between the oncoming marauders and the carriage.

It was like trying to hold back the sea with a shield.

The attackers fell on the guards, slashing them to ribbons, driving their horses off into the forest with the bodies still hanging from the saddles.

Up ahead, the three riders propelled the driverless carriage closer and closer to the deep swale off the road. One rode alongside the team, slashing with a sword at the hitchings, hacking until the team separated from its burden and galloped off, still yoked together, into the deep green shadows of the forest.

The driverless carriage, with one last great jolt, teetered on the edge of the swale, then overturned, crashing down on its right side. It lay in the gully, vibrating, its wheels still spinning impotently.

From atop a slight rise in the forest road, the seneschal nodded with satisfaction.

"Set it afire," he called to Caius, who was turning pale where he stood. "Stand ready to take her when she comes out."

In response, the archers dipped their pitch-tipped arrows into the fire barrel, renocked, and, at a second signal from the seneschal, let fly.

The missiles sailed through the air and sank quickly into the wood of the carriage, echoing with the pleasant pattering sounds of rain on a wooden roof.

The seneschal gestured a third time; the breeze picked up, racing along the forest road, driving leaves and small branches ahead of it.

The carriage smoldered for a moment, then, as the wind blew through, tore into flames.

Farther back along the forest road, Anborn could see the black smoke from the fire that was engulfing the carriage. A curse more profane than any he had uttered in centuries tore forth from his throat; he swung his bastard sword all the more deeply across the chest of the last of the attackers near him, slicing the man open from nipple to nipple, then urged his horse forward again.

He charged up the forest road in the direction of the black smoke.

\*     \*     \*

ʄor a moment the fire burned, unabated, and seemingly unnoticed.

Then, in the middle of the smoke, the door that had at one time been the left side entrance to the carriage opened unsteadily, and Rhapsody's hands appeared. She was holding Daystar Clarion, drawn, in her hand; it resembled nothing more than some sort of firebrand, blending in with the flames that were surrounding her. She tossed it aside for a moment where it rested, unheld, as she pulled herself out of the carriage, holding a wet kerchief over her lower face, and crawled out onto what was now the top.

All around her the forest appeared to be burning, though she knew from her tie to the element of fire that, for the moment, it was just the coach and the dry grass of the swale directly under it. Just beyond the great sheets of flame she could see figures hovering, some on horseback, some on foot.

None of them were her guards.

Her mind, foggy and thickheaded a few moments before, honed down into clear, pragmatic thoughts. She had nothing to fear from the flames; she was the Iliachenva'ar, the bearer of the elemental sword of fire, and as such was impervious to it. So she determined she was better suited to waiting inside the circle of bright heat and light than the guards were.

She was wrong.

A door of sorts seemed to open in the firewall, parting as if in response to a command. The men on foot moved through the flames, approaching her cagily.

*Oh gods,* she thought, racking her brain for solutions. *They must be hosts of F'dor, or a demon's thralls at least. Oh gods.*

She looked over her shoulder.

Eight or nine more men were behind her, approaching her slowly, their blurry shapes crossing and blending into one another in her confused vision.

Struggling to quell the panic that was rising, she coughed

to clear her throat from the smoke, and grasped Daystar
Clarion again, concentrating on the deep connection that she
had to the blade, drawing its power through her hand to
steady herself. She thought back to her training under Oelendra, the previous Iliachenva'ar. The ancient Lirin woman
had bound her eyes, making her spar with her opponents
blind, requiring her to use the inner vibrational signatures
that the weapon allowed her to see.

She closed her eyes, focusing on the power of the sword.

In her mind she could see them more clearly, rainbow-
colored figures with cool blue weapons in their hands, their
red hearts and faces pounding with heat. There were fourteen of them altogether, surrounding her, slowly broaching
the spreading flames that were spreading from the burning
carriage. She dropped the kerchief and raised the sword
slightly to her side, holding her other hand out, palm up, as
if it were a shield.

"Stay back, or you will die," she said as loudly as she
could over the crackling roar in a voice that rang with a
Namer's authority.

To a one all fourteen froze, hovering in the smoke at the
fire's edge.

Rhapsody turned slowly, her sword at the ready, her eyes
still closed, so she could better watch the attackers. For a
moment no sound could be heard save that of the burning
carriage.

A hundred and a half yards up the road, a distant figure
in a calf-length cloak and hood standing near a barrel of
blazing fire shouted something in a tongue she didn't understand.

The men blinked and shook themselves, as if shaking off
the effects of her words, then swarmed forward in great
strangling circle.

"Come, then!" she screamed, her voice harsh with anger.
"Die, if you insist."

Her nausea and imbalance vanished as battle rage swept

through her. Cold calculations, instantaneous, appeared in her mind.

The first advantage she could perceive was their intentions toward her; she could tell by their postures and the way they held their weapons that they were not advancing to kill her, but rather to take her captive, seeking to spare her from the edge of their blades.

She had no similar compunctions where they were concerned.

Rhapsody raised the sword over her head, and quickly drew a circle of protection around herself, catching the note of the sword with her own voice. The thin circle of light hovered over her head, reflecting the light of the fire, diverting the currents of the wind around her, obscuring her now as much to them as they were to her hazy eyes.

Up the road, where the cloaked figure and a number of others stood, an angry shout went up in a voice that chilled her, though she had no idea why.

The four marauders on foot before her slowed, trying to maintain her attention so that she would not notice the two others approaching from the rear. She waited, keeping her back to the closer phalanx, until she knew they were close enough, and then spun and jumped, laying on the two closer ones.

The sword rang out with a note of vengeance, the flames leaping from the blade, as she struck, two-handed, first across the eyes of one, then returned a quick sweep back, slashing the throat of the other. With her eyes closed she could not see the flashes of astonishment on their faces before they began to drown in their own blood, but she had already turned to set against the charge from behind her.

She was laying about her capably, slashing at hands that tried to subdue her, lunging away from poles swung to knock her feet out from under her, following the patterns of her training and her deep elemental bond to the ancient weapon, when Anborn reached the carriage.

The heavy thudding of his crossbow firing, catching the

assailants' notice for a split second, gave her the opportunity to drive her blade deeply into the stomach of one who had rushed her from behind, impaling him as he reached for her. Anborn fired again, a double bolt shot that dropped another horseman, then turned to behead a foot soldier who was trying to knock Rhapsody to the ground with a polearm.

With the speed and synchronicity born of training from the same master, the two silently divided up the attackers, turning their attentions to the targets each had chosen. Anborn reloaded one-handed and fired again, taking down a horseman who was charging, then turned the hilt of his sword upward, clenching his teeth, and brought it down with all the strength he could muster on the head of the marauder who stood beneath him. Following his lead, Rhapsody dodged and ran, leading those on her into the path of his bolts.

Another shout went up from the road, a ringing voice shouting orders, as the figure in the cloak began striding toward the fray.

From behind him another group of seven men on horseback rode forth, barreling down the road, as the archers dipping their arrows into the flaming barrel again.

The last of the fourteen immediate attackers vanquished, Anborn urgently put out his arm to her, leaning forward in the saddle.

"Rhapsody! Come!"

She leapt over the writhing body in front of her and ran to Anborn, reaching for him, preparing to be hoisted onto the horse before him.

Archers, aim for the horse," the seneschal said. "Caius— take the rider."

She was within a half-dozen yards of Anborn when the beautiful black stallion lurched and stumbled, then crumpled to the ground, throwing the General, who had himself pitched to the side, tumbling headfirst off its back.

Her concentration shattered, Rhapsody gasped in horror and bolted for her friend. She covered the last few feet by sliding to her knees, covering him with her body, desperately checking him for signs of life. His clothes were burning; she snuffed the flames with a word, struggling to stanch the tears that had sprung into her eyes.

The General lay on his back, his eyes glassy but focused on her. He attempted to smile, his clammy hand trembling as it patted her, in a futile gesture of comforting reassurance.

"Get out of here, you pretty fool," he whispered hoarsely. "You are outnumbered, and they are coming."

In the distance the seneschal peered through the flames, and saw her bending over the body of the rider.

*Whore,* muttered the demon. *Miserable, rutting whore.*

Rage burned in his brain, a fury that was his own, not that of the F'dor.

He grasped the hilt of Tysterisk, not breaking his stride, and pulled it angrily from its scabbard.

As the elemental sword of wind came forth, it brought with it a gust as stiff as a gale. From the burning forest floor a wind-devil rose, funneling currents of air that caught the sparks from the burning carriage and swept them through the forest glade, igniting it. The green leaves, hithertofore resistant to the smoldering fire from the carriage, succumbed to the hot, burning wind and tore with flame, lighting the sky with an intensity vastly brighter than daylight.

The seneschal gestured to the horsemen.

"Dismount," he said sharply. "The horses will not know they are safe from the fire with me. Follow."

Rhapsody felt the fire rise, felt the heat around her increase to the point of scorching, watching the skin on Anborn's face begin to blister with it.

She looked over her shoulder to where the riders and the cloaked figure had been, and saw that they were still coming, moving quickly through the flames.

She turned back to the General, who was starting to go gray, even in the bright orange light of the burning forest.

"You must help me, Anborn," she said softly. "Live; I need you."

The General blinked but said nothing.

Rhapsody bent closer and whispered in his ear. "I cannot escape them," she said. "I cannot see well enough; there are too many of them. I cannot allow Daystar Clarion to fall into their hands; you understand the import of this."

The glassy eyes of the General cleared for an instant, then began to cloud over again.

Quickly Rhapsody traded swords with him, rolling him onto his side and slipping Daystar Clarion beneath his rigid body, then took his hand and concentrated on his true name, speaking it to heal him, to make him whole with it.

"Anborn ap Gwylliam, heal," she commanded in her Namer's voice. "Rest in curative slumber, appear lifeless until these men leave." She chanted his name over and over, keeping an eye on the shapes approaching rapidly through the billowing smoke of the fire.

The General's eyes cleared, and the color returned to his skin at her words. He tried to rise, but Rhapsody pushed him gently back to the ground and bent so that her lips were next to his ear.

"The sword will protect you from the flames," she whispered. "Keep it safe, Anborn. The foresters will come when they see the fire; if you wait here, and feign death, help will come. Can you hear me?"

Anborn nodded slightly and closed his eyes.

The marauders were now within twenty yards. Rhapsody leaned over Anborn, her chest against his shoulder, and kissed his cheek.

"Live, live for me, Anborn," she said. "Get word to Ashe about what happened here; tell him, the children, and my Bolg friends that I love them. Remember that I love you as well."

The General squeezed her hand. An understanding passed

between them, the instinctive shared comprehension of the duty, of harsh reality, and of what Kinsmen do when death looms.

℞hapsody stood, Anborn's sword in her hand, struggling to regain her concentration, and stared into the swimming conflagration before her.

The figure in the cloak gestured to the others.

Three of the men stopped and trained their crossbows on her.

The other four, armed with swords, knives, and poles, began circling, splitting up to surround her.

As the marauders closed ranks around her, a detail occurred to her, pathetic in its irrelevance. She concentrated on the fire within her, calling forth a sliver of flame that licked up the blade of Anborn's sword, a pale imitation of the rolling waves of Daystar Clarion, so that if her assailants had discerned the fiery blade they would not notice the difference. The irony and insignificance to her impending confrontation made her snort with wry amusement.

"Drop your weapon," said the figure in the cloak in the common tongue.

There was something chillingly familiar in his voice, an aspect that made the hairs at the back of her neck stand on end. She stood stock-still, refusing to dignify his command with a response.

The crossbowmen set the hammers.

The swordsmen closed ranks.

The Lady Cymrian did not blink.

The figure in the hooded cloak came to within five yards of her and stopped.

"Not even so much as a flinch," he said, admiration in his pleasant voice. "You are just as you were, a fighter to the end. And it's just as stimulating now as it was then. More so, in fact; you are even more beautiful than you were. Who could have imagined it?"

Her grip on the sword tightened.

"You would stand and fight, wouldn't you? Even surrounded as you are, outnumbered eight to one, you would
still not yield." The man in the hood inhaled deeply and let
out an encompassing, pleasurable sigh. "This is going to be
such fun."

Rhapsody said nothing, just checked her grip, her heart
pounding. She numbly thought of her unborn child, keeping
her heart out of the dialogue, and silently begged its forgiveness.

The cloaked man chuckled, signaled to his men to hold
the line, then sauntered casually forward.

"I told you I would return for you one day," he said, his
voice barely containing his excitement. "I am *so* sorry that
I am late."

Rhapsody's already tremulous stomach went cold. There
was something in the voice that horrified her soul, that
harked back to a time of darkness beyond comprehension,
but her rational mind assured her, in the midst of her rising
gorge, that it was not possible.

A stench of the old world, like the reek of an open grave,
permeated her nostrils, making her dizzy, nauseated.

When he was standing directly in front of her, the man
took down his hood. His face was wreathed in a cruel smile,
his light blue eyes glittering brightly in exhilarated anticipation.

"Hello, Rhapsody darling," he said.

The Lady Cymrian's face went slack, then white, even in
the light of the burning forest. Her grip on Anborn's sword
slackened as her hands became suddenly cold and sweaty.

The blurry face that had been shielded by the hood was
familiar and yet alien. She thought she recognized the shape
of it, but there was a skeletal aspect to it that she knew
she had never seen on a human face before, a kind of feral
angle to the lines in cheeks, a demonic fire in the familiar
blue eyes. A chill ran down her back and radiated through
her, and suddenly the death she thought she was facing a

moment ago paled by what stood before her now.

"It's not possible," she whispered.

"How cliché. Now, Rhapsody, surely I took you in enough exotic positions, put you through enough paces, to prove to you that anything—*anything*—is possible."

Horror crept over her like blood oozing from a mortal wound.

"No," she choked. "No. No. *No.*"

The seneschal laughed aloud. "Do you remember how aroused I used to become when you said that to me? Harder than a sword hilt. I used to make you say it before I knobbed you, and during sometimes, because it made the feel of your inner muscles all the more thrilling, knowing that you were resisting me, but could do nothing to stop it." He leaned forward slightly, casting a glance down, then laughed aloud.

"Look," he said. "It still has the same effect!"

Rhapsody shook her head violently, her thoughts jumbled, her breathing quickened, her eyes darting around, seeking escape.

"No," she said again. "It's not possible."

The seneschal sighed blissfully. "This is better than I had hoped. I feared you might have actually been happy to see me, and then it would not have been so enjoyable. You were such fun to vanquish, Rhapsody. I've never had the equal to it. I cannot wait to know that feeling again. But let me just state right now that you will not be able to resist me, in any sense of the word. Don't become resigned, however; that will make the conquest less enjoyable." He took a step toward her.

The sword in her hand was pointed at his throat in the next heartbeat.

"Stay away from me, Michael. I may die, but I will take you with me."

The three crossbows were lifted and pointed at her head.

The seneschal nodded to the other men as he untied his belt.

"You want to take me, Rhapsody?" he said teasingly, with an unmistakable undertone of menace. "It would be my pleasure to oblige you.

"Hold her," he said.

# 28

## OFF THE NORTHERN COAST

From the deck of the *Basquela*, Quinn could see the smoke begin to rise far away over a towering cliff face in the mammoth, unbroken rockwall that rose up from the shoreline and ran the length of the coast.

He watched the sky nervously for a long time, waiting for the signal, but it was not yet forthcoming.

Finally he turned to the crew, who were watching the sky as well.

"Let's take her in a bit more shallow," he said to the mate, who nodded. "We wanna keep drawin' deep as long as we can, to stay out of sight, but we don't wanna keep His Honor waiting when he's ready to embark."

"No, we certainly dunna," the mate agreed hastily as the sailors scattered to their posts.

"Did you pull any eels?" Quinn inquired of a motley deckhand who had been fishing since daybreak.

The sailor shook his head. "Just blackfish. They're pretty oily."

"The creature don't like blackfish," Quinn objected.

The deckhand shrugged. "That's all that were bitin'. If it's hungry enough, it'll eat 'em." He tossed the bucket he had hung on the deckrail to the captain.

Quinn scowled and caught the bucket, then hurried across the deck to the door that led down into the dark hold. He seized the battered lantern that hung on a hook next to the door, lighted it quickly, then carefully made his way down the creaking wood ladder to Faron's makeshift abode.

The creaking of the ship was louder down here in the dark, the stale reek of bilge vying with the unholy stench that lurked beyond in the shadows.

When the gleaming green pool was in sight, he rattled the bucket noisily.

"Faron?" he called, nerves in his voice. "Breakfast."

The green pool began to roil, and the creature broke the surface, water streaming from all of the openings in its hideous head. Quinn struggled to contain his revulsion; the green glow of the water was from the monster's waste, and to see it pouring from its misshapen mouth made his stomach turn violently.

The bulbous eyes fixed on him in the dark, the wrinkles in its face bunching around what would have been a forehead on a human, its distorted features set in a look of evident displeasure.

"No, he's not back yet," the captain muttered. "Soon."

The creature hissed, saliva spraying from the open sides of its fused mouth.

"I brought ya some nice blackfish, Faron," Quinn said in as soothing a voice as he could muster.

The creature spat, screeching in anger.

"I'm sorry—'twas all we could muster. This ain't your home by the docks, Faron; eels don't abound here."

Faron eyed him contemptuously.

"Well? Do ya want 'em or not?"

The creature stared at the captain for a moment longer, then nodded, a look of ominous purpose in its cloudy eyes.

As Quinn took a few steps forward, Faron reached into the depths of the shallow pool, fishing around for something. When he found it he held it up.

Quinn held up the light to better see what it was.

In the creature's gnarled hand was a ragged oval, glittering with color, though its surface was primarily gray. Quinn had never seen such a thing, but had heard the seneschal refer to the monster's ability to read *the scales,* and supposed this must be one of them.

"You showin' it to me?" he asked. "Is it for me?"

The creature nodded, beckoning the sailor nearer with its grotesquely twisted hand.

Hesitantly Quinn came forward and held the lantern closer. He bent forward, trying to stay far enough away to keep from inadvertently touching the freakish being in the pool that the seneschal seemed to love so dearly.

The light from the lantern flickered across the etching on the scale's surface. At first Quinn could not discern the pattern of the lines, but after a moment, the image became clear; he stepped back in horror.

It was the crude rendering of a gallows, a body hanging limp from the noose.

"Me?" Quinn squealed, recoiling. "Are you saying that is for *me?*"

Faron's eyes gleamed triumphantly, and a hideous grimace that might have been, on a human, a smile, spread across the wrinkled face.

The sight of the arrogant look in the monster's eyes made the panic in Quinn change to anger.

"Bugger you, Faron," he said nastily. "Sit in your shit and rot, you floating freak."

The creature's smile only grew brighter.

Quinn shoved the pail over to the edge of the pool and scurried back up the steps, trying to ignore the hideous popping and rending sounds behind him.

## NORTHERN GWYNWOOD, IN THE FOREST

"Shoot me now," Rhapsody said to the crossbowmen, without taking her eyes off the seneschal. "Until my last breath, I will kill whoever approaches me."

The seneschal crowed with laughter, his fingers working at the laces of his breeches.

"Oh, Rhapsody, how I've missed you these many centuries," he said, fondling himself as he struggled with the lacings in his excitement. "You always know how to make the event all the more thrilling."

For only the second time, the Lady Cymrian addressed the seneschal directly.

"So do you, Michael. I'm sure your men would appreciate the entertainment."

The light in the blue eyes grew more excited. "Indeed. You recall how I used to take you before the eyes of my men in the old land, don't you, Rhapsody? My favorite was having you on the breakfast table, or on horseback while giving morning orders. What fun it will be to do it again now, here, in the forest, surrounded by the dead bodies of your guards."

Rhapsody smirked. "Well, for *them*, at least," she said haughtily, nodding at the seven men. "I'm sure these ruffians are no different than your other lackeys, and would derive sincere enjoyment out of seeing their leader so compromised, so unable to sustain the act for more than a few seconds, so pathetic, so—so *small*. I have no doubt they would get as much amusement as the others did privately at your expense in the old world."

The seneschal stopped, his hand in his trousers, his skeletal face slack with shock.

"Amusement?" he demanded. "Lies. My men would never have dared to joke at my expense."

The Lady Cymrian laughed harshly. "Perhaps not to your face, Michael, 'the Wind of Death.' But it was your own soldiers who coined your nickname—Michael, the *Waste of Breath*. Not your adversaries, though of course they made copious use of it, and coined many of their own."

"You are a liar," he said coldly.

Rhapsody smiled with equal frost in her expression. "You don't remember me as well as you think, Michael," she said. "I don't lie. Not even when forced anymore."

The expression on his face blackened, and when he spoke, the harsh tone of the demon was in his voice.

"You lied to *me*," he said, the words resonating palpable

hatred. "You pledged your faith to me. And how did you live up to that oath?"

"I swore to love 'no other man until this world comes to an end,' " Rhapsody said quietly. "I never said that I loved you, only that I would love no other than the man who had my heart then, and still does. And in case you do not know, that world *did* come to an end, a rather horrifying one, in volcanic fire. I misled you, because you would have raped and murdered a tiny child if I didn't. But I did not lie to you. Your injured feelings will earn no remorse from me."

Like a storm building, the seneschal's body tensed, and his face hardened into a terrifying aspect.

"Hold her down," he said again to his guards. "We will see who is injured, and whether or not you feel remorse."

Fergus looked uncomfortably at the fire spreading to the outer canopy of the forest.

"M'lord, we must get back to the ship," he said quietly, casting a glance through the tree line as the flames leapt skyward, filling the air above with thick smoke. "Most of our guards are dead, and Quinn said this was a holy wood. There must be foresters or nature priests who will respond when they see the smoke."

*More flame*, the demon urged. *More flame. Take the girl on your own time.*

The seneschal rested a hand on his forehand, trying to press the voice into silence, but the F'dor spirit was too excited by the building inferno to be quelled.

*More burnings! More flame!*

"Disarm her, then," he said viciously to Fergus. "Bind her hands and I will drag her by the hair to the promontory."

Slowly Fergus and the other three swordsman began to circle Rhapsody.

"Lay the weapon down, lady," the reeve said soothingly. "It's far too big a sword for you, anyway. You will only succeed in hurting yourself. We mean you no harm."

In response, Rhapsody raised the sword a slight bit higher, her grip unwavering. In her mind she remembered

Achmed's advice long ago, deep within the Earth, as Grunthor trained her for the first time in the weapon's use.

*First, however you initially grasp the sword, change your grip a little, so that you focus on how you're holding it. Don't take your weapon for granted. Second, and far more important: tuck your chin. You're going to get hurt, so expect it and be ready. You may as well see it coming.*

She inhaled deeply, trying to keep her distorted vision from being apparent to her captors, as she turned the grip of the sword ever so slightly.

*You're spending too much time trying to avoid the pain instead of minimizing it and taking out the source of what will injure you further or kill you. If Grunthor weren't holding back you would have been dead in the first exchange of blows. You should accept that you will be injured and decide to pay him back in spades. Learn to hate; it will keep you alive.*

Rhapsody could hear her own voice, naïve, innocent, in the darkness of the tunnel that ran along the roots of the World Tree.

*I'd rather not live at all than live that way.*

*Well, if that's your attitude, you won't have to worry long.*

*No*, she thought, her will steeling like ore tempered in the forges of Ylorc. *No. I have too much to fight for. Too much to protect.* Her eyes narrowed as hatred rose up in her soul, the righteous loathing of a woman long abused, a mother whose unborn child was in danger, a queen whose friend and protector lay comatose on the burning forest floor.

*I am going to get hurt now,* she thought; the realization did not terrify her. *And I am about to lose here. I have to protect my abdomen, bide my time, and wait for the right moment.*

Slowly the swordsman stepped closer.

*But I will take as many of you with me as I can,* she thought, glancing from the swordsmen to Michael, who was watching her in a state of agitation clear even through her

hazy eyes. *And I will not let you have me again, you piece
of demonic filth. Not while I live.*

The voice of Oelendra, her Lirin mentor and the last one
to bear Daystar Clarion before her, echoed in her brain.

*You've got a good start, but now we're going to train you
to fight like our people do.*

*Do you think that the Lirin way of fighting is better than
that of the Firbolg?*

*Aye, at least for Lirin. The Bolg are big, strong, and
clumsy, the Lirin are small, fast, and weak. You rely too
much on your strength, not enough on agility and cunning;
you just don't have the body mass to fight like a brute.*

Slowly she lowered the blade.

As soon as the sword was pointed to the ground, the
swordsman behind her dashed forward, the flat of his sword
aimed horizontally at her neck as the others moved nearer.

She gave no sign she had heard him, no indication she
was aware of him, until the last second before his impact.

Then spun around, going low, and sliced his knees out
from under him with Anborn's bastard sword.

A geyser of blood shot forth, spraying her clothing and
face. The forest seemed to erupt with a blast of wind knocking her off her feet; she could feel the other six of Michael's
men fall on her, tearing her weapon from her hands, ripping
the cloth of her shirt; she curled like a ball to protect her
child as she fell, numbing her mind against the pain of the
bruising, the jerking of her legs, the slamming of her back
against the ground again and again.

*Spare my baby,* she prayed to the One-God over the howls
of pain from the man whose leg she had severed and the
blows her own body was sustaining. *If I live, spare my child.*

For all that it seemed an eternity of torment, it was over
in a few blinks of the eye.

Rhapsody lay on the burning ground, her face bruised and
blooded, breathing in the dirt of the forest floor, feeling the
heat all around her rising with Michael's madness.

He strode across to where she lay—she could hear his

footsteps approach, and struggled to keep her fear from consuming her—seized the ropes that bound her hands, and hauled her to her feet before him.

He stared down into her face, his eyes a swimmingly cruel blue light before her own; in that moment Rhapsody felt she was staring directly into the Vault of the Underworld where the race of demons had been imprisoned.

Then his lips were on hers, lips that stung with acidic fire, pressed heavily against her mouth hard enough to bruise it.

All the horror of the past roared back in an instant. Rhapsody began to tremble violently, as agonizing memories flooded her mind, hideous moments from the past locked away deep with her nightmares. Against her will, she gasped aloud.

Michael pulled back from the kiss and stared at her, misreading her expression. He took her face in his hands and pressed his body, with its steel-like skeleton covered by a musculature that felt more dead than alive, against hers.

"Bite, and it will be the last thing you ever use your teeth for," he said quietly as he ran his hands over her golden hair, loosing the ribbon and letting it fall to the ground. "They are only a hindrance for how I plan to make use of your mouth, anyway."

Then he thrust his tongue harshly between her lips, stealing her breath.

Rhapsody tried to separate her mind from her body, as once she was able to do, but the revulsion was so strong, the overwhelming stench of human flesh in fire reeking from his skin as his excitement grew, that she could not block out what was happening. Her stomach rushed into her mouth and she vomited, the force of it driving Michael back a few steps, reeling in disgust.

She was bent over in the throes of nausea when he recovered and strode angrily back to her, slapping her full across the face with a force so violent it threw her backward onto the ground.

"Whore!" he screamed, the sound of it harsh with the tone

of the demon. "Miserable, rutting whore! You endure the rancid juice of your husband's loins, no doubt, but you are repulsed by *me*?"

As he reached down to grasp her again, the reeve called out to him.

"M'lord! We risk notice! I strongly suggest we get to the promontory and back to the ship. There you can have her, undisturbed, in the privacy of your cabin, and she will be unable to escape. And Faron is waiting."

The seneschal stared down at Rhapsody, curled on the ground, blood coming out of her nose, then reached down and seized her hair, pulling her to her feet.

"Bring my horse," he ordered one of the remaining swordsmen who had been futilely attempting to bind the wounds of the man with the severed leg; he stood, looking helplessly at his writhing comrade, then ran up the road to retrieve the mounts.

From behind the seneschal Caius's voice spoke up nervously, weakly.

"M'lord, we must go back to the first ambush point and retrieve Clomyn. He is grievously injured, dying; I can feel it." He passed a sweating hand over his gray face.

The seneschal turned and stared at him angrily.

"Are you blind?" he snarled, gesturing into the conflagration that was spreading like a meadow wildfire through the green forest to where the coach had first come under attack. "He is ashes by now."

Caius was staring into the blistering wall of light and heat. "No, no, Your Honor, he's alive, though barely. He's my heart twin, sir; I can feel what he is feeling, hear what he hears, just as he hears me. Please, I know he is alive. We have to retrieve him before we go."

The demonic host that was once Michael glared at the crossbowman. When he spoke, his voice dripped venom.

"Very well, Caius. By all means. Go get him." He wrapped Rhapsody's hair around his hand several times and dragged her to where the lackey had brought his horse to a halt, lifted her by the collar of her shirt and her belt and threw her across the animal's back.

"But—m'lord—will you open a—a wall in the fire, as you did before?" Caius stammered.

Michael turned, his shoulders visibly tense beneath his cloak, and regarded the shaking crossbowman.

"Of course, Caius," he said solicitously. "Here." He gestured casually toward the wall of fire.

A slim passageway in the flames opened, leaving a blue slice of air.

Caius's face relaxed somewhat, his color returning with the light that flickered off it.

"Thank you, m'lord," he mumbled quickly as he dashed into the passageway.

As soon as the crossbowman had entered the flames, the seneschal gestured again, and the passageway disappeared.

Caius, swallowed in flame, screamed noiselessly, drowned in the sound of the inferno and the cracking of the burning trees.

He turned and bolted from the fire into the area where the others stood, still clear from flame but about to be engulfed. Two of the swordsmen seized him and rolled him in the loam of the forest floor, snuffing him amid the spreading sparks.

"The next time you question my decision, Caius, I will wait until you are deeper in to close the passage," the seneschal said smugly. "Then you and your heart twin can be forever mixed in the same ashes."

He mounted the horse behind Rhapsody's supine body and pulled her up so that her back was lying against his chest. Her eyes were glassy, her breathing shallow, but her heartbeat was strong, he noted, as he pulled her shirt the rest of the way from the waistband of her torn, bloody trousers and slid his hands up under her camisole, allowing himself to revel in the soft skin of the breasts he had dreamed about across endless time.

Rhapsody merely slumped forward, too spent to keep her head up and her back erect.

*I have to protect my abdomen, bide my time, and wait for the right moment.*

She battled to keep a tenuous hold on consciousness as the marauders rode off, westward, toward the sea.

And lost that battle.

# 29

Anborn came slowly to consciousness on the forest floor, where already the fire had charred the trees, reducing much of the wild bushes and scrub to hot ash, and had moved on.

All around him, before and behind, the world was burning.

The General groaned as he raised his head up to look around him, then laid it down again, too heavy to sustain. The heat on his back was searing, so hot that he could not imagine that he was not already burning alive.

For the smallest of moments, he thought of closing his eyes again, laying his head down to rest, and letting the fire sweep over him, through him, take him into its maw and swallow him, chew him into ashes and spit him out into the wind, where he could float across the sea, all around the wide world, ebbing and flowing in an endless current of air, like the Kinsman he had been.

The thought shook him from his dying reverie as the memory of Rhapsody's last words came back to him.

*Live, live for me, Anborn. Get word to Ashe about what happened here; tell him, the children, and my Bolg friends that I love them. Remember that I love you as well.*

Whether those words were the inescapable magic of a potent Namer, the command of his sovereign to whom he was sworn, the call of a fellow Kinsman, or the last request of the one woman in the world whose love and friendship

he valued, they held power, a power great enough to make
him lift his head and shake off the warm and peacefully
endless sleep that glowed just beyond the edge of his awareness.

As his eyes cleared, he saw the destruction around him
was far more widespread than he had even imagined. Every
tree in the forest for as far as he could see was aflame, the
fire growing in intensity as it spread north to the Tara'fel
River.

He had to get out of the forest and back to where he could
summon help.

Anborn braced his hands against the ground and lifted his
upper body to look.

It was there still, smoldering quietly beneath him, drawing
the destructive power of the flames into itself, sparing his
hide from immolation.

Daystar Clarion.

For a moment the General lay and stared at the blade.
Gone were the rippling waves of fire that rolled from hilt
to tip in Rhapsody's hand, a sign of the bond between element and Iliachenva'ar. A bright glow of starlight was still
imbued in it, but the fire was stilled, taken away by the man
that had borne the sword of air. Though he had never seen
it, he had heard tales of the weapon, a blade wielded in the
old world during the Seren War that preceded the Cymrian
exodus.

Tysterisk.

Its power was unmistakable. He could feel it, sense the
command that the figure at the end of the road held over
the element.

Kinsmen were brothers of the wind; this man could command the wind itself.

Anborn's mind raced, trapped in his unresponsive body.
He thought of Rhapsody, how terrified he knew she must
be, though she had put on a brave face for him. The thought
of what might be happening to her, or that she might in fact
already be dead, caused a surge of relentless rage to build

in his heart until it overflowed in a seething flood of anger.

He rolled with great effort onto his side, then reached with hands that trembled with the strain for the elemental sword. He sheathed it with some effort across his back, then extended his arm as far as he could, feeling around on the ground for a root, a living bush, anything with which to gain purchase.

The blackened husk of what had once been a bramble of some kind was just beyond his reach; Anborn pushed forward, his hands in the burning loam, stretching the muscles of his upper body until he seized the husk and, finding it holding firm in the ground, dragged himself a few paces forward, knowing that the fire moved far more quickly than he could.

All conscious thought submerged; he had but one single-minded task, to crawl in any way he could, out of the burning forest and back to the Filidic Circle at the Great White Tree where they had been a few days before. Surely there would be help to send after her.

Slowly, agonizingly slowly, the General stretched and reached, dragging himself by vegetation when he could grasp any, by the strength of his fingers and elbows when he could not, hauling himself with almost imperceptible success through the smoking leaf matter and other burning detritus of the forest floor.

Time passed with a cruel sluggishness. The inferno around him grew hotter, brighter, at the outskirts of his vision, but Anborn paid it no heed, focusing instead on the few handsbreadths of ground before him, pulling himself arduously along, to find himself doing it all over again, and again, moment by brutally painful moment.

After what seemed like forever, he came across the body of the archer who had shot Shrike, a crossbowman with his stonebow still beside him. He took the opportunity to rest and catch his breath for a moment; he rolled onto his side, wincing at the crushing pain in his ribs, and tore off a rag from his shirt to stanch the bleeding in his hands, wrapping them in the makeshift bandage, then looked around again.

Within arm's reach the burning skeleton of a horse lay, its high-backed saddle melting in the heat. A battered cutlass lay next to it, reflecting the fire. Anborn reached for it with a hand that shook violently, not feeling the pain in his back.

The bodies of all the other attackers must have already been consumed by the fire through which he was crawling; he had been breathing their ashes, inhaling their remains and their souls, on his crawl along the burning forest floor.

Even Shrike's.

For the first time since entering battle he thought of his friend and mentor, a humble sailor who had served on the crew of the *Serelinda,* the last ship to leave the Island before it sank beneath the waves, transformed by the journey across the Prime Meridian into a surly, immortal soldier. He had been a loyal if sometimes reluctant follower of Gwylliam, Anborn's father, then of Anborn himself, for almost fifteen centuries between them, and had always given a perspective that could only have come with the wisdom of someone who had lived through the death of two worlds.

As he lay on his side, Anborn felt grief creeping in, a grief the likes of which he had not known for centuries. He closed his mind to it, held it at bay; it would only serve to divert him from his overwhelming task.

Once rested, he crawled to the body of the archer and, after spitting in its lifeless face, he seized it by the jaw and dragged it along with him, knowing he would need it for his purposes.

Above his head, the massive limb of a towering tree crashed through the canopy, roaring with flame, then collapsed to the ground nearby. Anborn shielded his nose and mouth from the ash and burning leaves that rose in its wake.

His lungs, already stinging with the caustic cinders he was inhaling, began to burn.

\*       \*       \*

When finally he began to choke, gagging blood from the creosote and fire residue that had thickened the air to the point of being black, Anborn had to acknowledge that if he was alone in his effort, he was not going to succeed.

It was time to give in to the one last lifeline he had.

For a moment the world around him hummed with a destructive static, too loud and full of noise to hear anything. Impatiently he rubbed his ears, cursing his useless legs, and tried to block out all noise, all clamor save for the gentle song of the wind.

It took him a long time to hear it, but finally a tiny breeze picked up, perhaps generated by the fire itself. Anborn listened for the fluctuations in it, the subtle whine as it changed directions, whistling with power.

The General summoned all his strength, lifted his head, inclining it to the west, and spoke the call that he had answered but never put onto the wind himself until this moment.

*Leuk, the west wind, the wind of justice, hear me,* he rasped in the Ancient Lirin tongue, the only words in the language he knew, his voice thick with smoke and pain. *By the star, I will wait, I will watch, I will call and will be heard.*

As he spoke the call of the ancient brotherhood of soldiers, he thought back to the last time he had answered it, a clear, soft cry on the wind of a snowy forest in the black of a storm. He had followed the source to discover a woman, shivering in the cold, leading a freezing horse over which an unconscious gladiator was stretched.

A woman who had become the Lirin Queen, the Lady Cymrian.

A gladiator who she had taken into the realm beyond life and death and left there. He had returned to be chosen by the Scales as the Patriarch.

He winced at the irony of it all now.

He had thought then he was rescuing her, rescuing them both, though at the time he had wanted to put the brute to death. When he felt the pull, the intrinsic magic, wrap around him and transport him on the back of the wind to where he was needed, he believed he was going off to save a fellow Kinsman. He knew now that in doing so he had actually rescued himself, been absolved for his crimes in the Cymrian War that had haunted his dreams and his waking moments.

He had finally been able to sleep after that.

And now she was gone. He had failed her, had broken his oath to his nephew to protect her, to keep her, and their child, safe. The agony was too great to be borne.

From deep within his viscera another cry came forth. He called to north wind, the strongest of the four, in hopes that it would carry his cry farther, for Kinsmen, as he had noted to Gwydion Navarne, were few and far between.

"By the star!" he shouted, inhaling more of the smoke, "I will wait, I will watch, I will call and will be heard!" He coughed from the depths of his lungs.

The towering walls of fire roared in response.

No other sound could be heard.

Anborn struggled to fend off the despair that hovered near the edge of his consciousness, whispering to his doubts. Not all Kinsman calls were answered, he knew; he himself had thought he heard two only a few weeks before, had listened, stood ready to go, but the doorway in the wind never opened to him. He had not been able to find the one who was calling for help.

Just as now, perhaps, there was no one to answer him.

*Jahne, the south wind, most enduring,* he rasped, his voice beginning to give out from the smoke. *By the star, I will wait, I will watch.* He swallowed, trying to force the sound from his throat. *I will call and will be heard.*

Time seemed to expand around him, twisting on the heat of the fire like glass in a blower's hands.

The smoke was sinking now even to the forest floor, the ground on which Anborn's head now lay. The General buried his face in the crook of his arm, trying to breathe, but it had become laborious to do so.

No one was coming.

The General rolled onto his back and stared up at the blazing orange sky above him, punctuated by bands of smoke, black and gray, sparked with flashes of intensely bright light that fizzled and died.

*There is no one left to answer the call,* he mused, watching absently as the great trees of Gwynwood broke under the weight of the flame and fell, the forest, the ancestral lands of his grandmother, the dragon Elynsynos, reducing to ash before his eyes.

Anborn could feel the skin on his face, once healed by Rhapsody's power of Naming, start to crack with heat again. He took one last breath, turned as much to the east as he could, and whispered the name of the last wind.

*Thas,* he said softly. The wind of morning. He swallowed, remembering its other appellation. The wind of death. *Hear me*.

His voice, clogged with smoke, had lost all of its tone, leaving only the sandy fricatives of his dry tongue and rattling teeth.

*By the star, I will wait,* he whispered. *I—will watch.* He swallowed, once more trying to force the sound from his throat. *I—will—call*.

His lips no longer moved.

At the edge of the sea, a man the color of driftwood looked up from the patterns he was drawing in the sand, as if hearing distant voices on the wind. He stared into the gray-blue-green of the ever-changing horizon, listened again, but heard only the cry of the gulls.

He shook his head, and went back to his pictures in the sand.

## 30

When the Kinsman heard the call, he was on horseback, riding across verdant green fields on the way home.

He paused and reined his mount to a stop, sitting up high in the saddle, tilting his ear to the wind, endeavoring to catch the sound again, the plaintive words that he had heard once before, long ago, in a language long dead.

*By the star, I will wait, I will watch, I will call and will be heard.*

He didn't recognize the voice, a thick rasp that signaled its speaker was very near death, but he didn't expect to.

He looked around at the undulating highgrass, rolling placidly in the warm breeze; the sun was just beginning to wane, hanging in the sky high over the western horizon, casting afternoon shadows to the east, the direction in which he had been traveling a moment before.

He heard the voice again, weaker this time, but clear; it had caught the wind that was blowing in his direction.

*By the star, I will wait. I—will watch. I—will—call.*

Then nothing.

The Kinsman searched the pockets of breeze, looking between the gusts that bent the grass of the wide fields for a doorway, a path of some kind, that would lead him to the one who was calling, as had happened the only other time he had heard the call. But there was no swirling vortex in the air, no misty tunnel to ride through, as there had been before. Nervous now, he dismounted and shielded his eyes, staring beyond the waving ocean of grass to the edges of the horizon, but finding nothing.

He turned to the west, from whence he imagined the call had come.

And blinked.

The ground in front of him had begun to shift; the highgrass parted as the earth split, unraveling noiselessly, the darkness below the surface suddenly filled with bright light. Before his eyes the hole grew deeper, wider; the wind blew through, snapping the cloth of his tunic, beckoning to him.

He shook his head, having never imagined that the wind would call to him through the Earth, though it hardly surprised him. He seized the huge horse's reins and led the animal into the passageway en route to answer the Kinsman call.

The moment they had passed through, the tunnel closed up as noiselessly as it had opened, leaving nothing but an endless sea of verdant meadowgrass, waving in time to the breath of the wind, beneath the afternoon sun.

Anborn was still on his back, watching the forest canopy burn off above him, the black leaves floating on the smoky wind into the unseen sky above, when he felt a tremor within the Earth, a rumbling that went up his back to the base of his neck.

He blinked as the heavy wall of smoke above and around him began to shift near to the ground. Bright streaks of light flashed intermittently from the forest floor, piercing the gloom that hovered above it; the ground trembled as if in the midst of an earthquake.

Slowly, and with the last of his strength, he rolled onto his side, his ash-caked eyelids blinking more rapidly to clear his vision.

Even hovering near death as he was, Anborn could sense the presence of deep magic, of elemental power at work, an occurrence that never failed to leave him simultaneously awed and frightened. He had seen much of this ancient magic at work in the days of the war, watched his parents wield it for ill, and had seen the fallout from it. Even when it was used for good, as Rhapsody or his nephew sometimes made use of it, it still set his teeth on edge, and his mind humming with nervous anticipation.

He was too weak to rise further, to be in any position

other than all-but-prone, as the whirling smoke and light grew in intensity, but he knew that if this was a Kinsman coming in answer to his call, he could be no worse off than he had been a moment before.

In the fiery haze he thought he could see a figure appear, coming toward him, leading what appeared to be a horse, though its outline was hazy and impossible to define. The searing light from the ground disappeared, leaving the figures backlit only by the raging fire all around them.

When finally the Kinsman and his mount emerged from the smoke, Anborn squinted to see who it was, his eyelids still heavy with ash. The man was almost upon him before recognition set in.

The General stared in astonishment for a long moment, then rolled onto his back and sighed, breaking into weak, croaking laughter.

"Bloody *gods!*" he rasped, coughing shallowly. "You?"

His rescuer's brow furrowed as he squatted down beside the ancient Cymrian warrior, clicking to the enormous horse.

"Rather odd ta be laughin' now, Oi'd say," Grunthor said dryly, catching hold of Rockslide's reins. "But each to 'is own. Can Oi hoist ya without damagin' ya further?"

Anborn nodded with difficulty, clutching the cutlass. "Have to—get word—to—Haguefort," he whispered, his voice faltering. "They've—taken—Rhapsody."

The amber eyes of the Firbolg giant darkened with alarm. "Where? *'Oo?*"

The General shook his head, struggling to keep from succumbing to unconsciousness. "I don't—know. Had—Tysterisk." He gestured weakly.

"Where did they go?" the Sergeant demanded as he slid his arms under Anborn's back and lifeless legs.

"West," the General whispered. "Into the—fire."

Grunthor saw Anborn's face begin to go gray; he lifted him carefully and started to carry him to the horse.

Unable to speak, Anborn grasped hold of the body of the

bowman on the ground, refusing to let go, then lapsed into unconsciousness.

Grunthor pried Anborn's fingers loose of the corpse's wrist, then continued his trek, laying the General over Rockslide's back for a moment. Quickly he tore off his own tunic, threw it on the ground and kicked the body into it, then lashed it to the back of his saddle with a length of rope. He stared for a moment into the belly of the inferno, then mounted and, holding the dying Kinsman before him on the horse, rode off, hell-bent, for the Filidic Circle at the Tree.

When Anborn came to consciousness in the gray hours of the next morning he was looking into two of the most unpleasant faces he could imagine seeing, only slightly less surly than his own.

The first was that of his rescuer, the gray-green hide and amber eyes in the heavy features of Firbolg mixed with some other race—Bengard, he thought he recollected Rhapsody saying once. The Sergeant-Major, with whom he had once served in Rhapsody's honor guard, was silently staring down at him, consternation deeply etched in the lines and crevices of his face.

Beside him was Gavin the Invoker, the quiet, taciturn forester who had been the most trusted advisor of Llauron, Anborn's brother, succeeding him as head of the religious order when Llauron left to commune with the elements, abandoning his human form for a dragon one. The expression in the Invoker's eyes denoted a less personal anguish that Grunthor's, but a more widespread one. Anborn understood his torment; a forester's soul was tied to the forest, and until this fire there had been no more beautiful, deeply magical forest on the continent than Gwynwood.

And it was burning.

Anborn's head felt as if it would split open. His skin and eyes, though protected from the scorching flames by Daystar Clarion, were red from the heat and stung maddeningly. He struggled to sit up, but Gavin quickly laid a hand on his shoulder and pushed him down against the pillow of the bed in which he lay.

"Stay. You have had the attention of healers, but you are still weak. How do you feel?"

"Bugger how I feel. Did you find her? Has there been any word at all?"

"No," Gavin said quietly. "The fire has been contained. But there is no trace of Rhapsody."

"Oi'm about to send birds to 'Aguefort and Ylorc," Grunthor said brusquely. "What did ya want with the body Oi dragged out wi' you?"

"He's a witness," Anborn said, his voice returning slightly. "The bastard took down Shrike; if only for that and nothing else I would have left him to burn alive if I could have. But the Patriarch is said to be able to speak with the spirits of dead; this is the only clue to what happened to Rhapsody that isn't ashes now. I shall take this piece of filth to Sepulvarta and have the Patriarch wring the information from him."

Grunthor nodded. "Sounds like fun. When 'e's done with 'im, Oi want a turn. Oi'll torture 'im so brutally 'e will feel it in the Underworld." He stepped back and started for the door.

"Sergeant," Anborn said, his voice ragged from the forest smoke.

Grunthor stopped.

"Tell Haguefort to send out a falcon. A regular messenger won't be able to locate Gwydion if he's on the road."

The giant Bolg nodded and started for the door again.

"Sergeant," Anborn said again.

Once again Grunthor stopped.

"My life is yours," Anborn said heavily, in the custom of the ancient brotherhood of Kinsmen. "Thank you."

The Sergeant nodded, and a hint of a smile played on his bulbous lips. "Good. Oi'll find a way to put you ta good use. Always did want an Ancient Cymrian 'ero to serve as pissboy to the Firbolg army." He took hold of the cord of rope that served as a door handle and withdrew from the Filidic hospice, closing the door behind him.

Gavin gently squeezed the General's shoulder. "I sought the spirit of the forest through the Great White Tree once the fire was contained," he said, his words halting; the Invoker rarely spoke, so words were arduous for him. "Rhapsody, if she still lives, is not in Gwynwood, nor anywhere within the great western forest. That forest runs from the Hintervold to the Nonaligned States, Anborn. Either she has been taken away by sea, or—"

"Don't even whisper the word," Anborn said acidly. "They took her alive. If they had wanted her dead they would have filled her full of bolts before my eyes. Don't even whisper the word."

The Invoker stared down at him.

"I will leave it for others to pronounce. It is not a reality I want to be the one to invoke. But you must be prepared to accept what may have come to pass here."

*A*s Grunthor strode through the grounds that comprised the Circle around the Great White Tree, the Filidic priests and foresters scattered, hurrying to stay out of the way of the giant Firbolg who was their Invoker's guest, but nonetheless looked as if he was ready to bite the head off the shoulders of anyone who got in his way. With a jaw that size, and tusks that were visible in the corners of his mouth, jutting above his lips, there was no question that it would not have taken more than a single bite.

He made his way out of the forest through neatly maintained gardens, bursting with fragrant flowers and medicinal herbs, that surrounded the healers' area, to the edge of the wide, circular meadow where the Great White Tree stood, an ancient wonder older than any living thing in this part of the world.

Grunthor could see its branches even before he came into the clearing, great ivory limbs that spread like immense fingers to darkening sky. It had been a while since he had seen it, and the sight caused him to momentarily slow his steps, marveling at the white bark that gleamed in the sun, its breadth and height—it was easily fifty feet across at the base, and the first major limb was more than a hundred feet from the ground, leading up to more branches that formed a expansive canopy reaching over the forest that surrounded it.

Around its base, set back a hundred yards from where its great roots pierced the earth, was a ring of trees, one of each species known to the Filids, the religious priest of the western continent, who tended this holy place, said to be the last of the five birthplaces of Time, and the Tree that grew here. It was here the element of Earth had its beginning; Grunthor, tied as he was to the Earth, always felt a surge of power here, a strength he could draw on.

He stopped long enough to absorb it, knowing he would need that power to get through what was to come.

Then he made his way to the aviary, a central tower built where Llauron's strangely angled house had once stood.

The guard at the door at the bottom of the tower, a forester like Gavin, met him, bowing slightly.

"Get two birds, fast ones, trained ta fly to 'Aguefort and Ylorc," Grunthor ordered.

The guard spoke quietly with the woman who tended the birds, who eyed the giant Bolg for a moment, then hurried up the ladder to the aviary. She returned a moment later with two doves, one gray, one white, and said something to the guard in a language Grunthor didn't recognize, handing something to him.

"They will be spooked by a—a stranger, sir," the guard said nervously. "If you will put your messages in these, we will see to it that they are sent." He gave Grunthor two small brass leg cases for the birds.

The Sergeant took the casings, looking around at the dirty smoke wafting eastward over the Circle as he slid the messages he had written inside them. He scrawled something additional on Achmed's before wrapping it and sealing it in the leg holder.

The irony of the moment caused his throat to tighten, recalling how Rhapsody had taught him to read and write during their endless trek through the Earth along the Root.

He hoped she remembered the fighting lessons he had given her in exchange.

He watched as the birdkeeper ascended the tower again, into the branches of the high trees in which it was built. A moment later he saw her step out onto a balcony at the top of the tower and release the birds; they banked immediately to the east, flapping their wings in unison, then caught a warm updraft, flying off together into the sun.

He closed his eyes and willed them to hurry.

## HAGUEFORT, NAVARNE, AT THE ARCHERY RANGE

At noon the master of the range called for the close of flights.

Gwydion Navarne sighed dispiritedly. Three center shots out of twenty in the last quiver. It was probably just as well that the range was shutting down; his aim was getting progressively worse.

He unstrung the bow and was gathering the quiver up, preparing to see what arrows he could retrieve, when he caught sight of Gerald Owen, moving as quickly as the elderly man could across the wide, grassy range. The look on his face caused Gwydion to drop both the bow and the quiver and run to the chamberlain.

"What is it?" he asked the puffing man.

Owen stopped and bent over at the waist, his hands on his knees.

"Word—has come in by—avian messenger, for the Lord—Cymrian," he said, breathing heavily. "Rhapsody has been taken prisoner, or killed."

The young man who would soon be duke heard the

words, felt the electricity of the statement hum in his skin as his stomach went icy, but his mind refused to allow their meaning to penetrate. He had heard horrible news too often in his young life, the tidings of his mother's death, and had witnessed that of his father in battle. This was too much.

"No more," he said. He stared blankly at the chamberlain. "No more."

Gerald Owen laid his hand on the boy's thin shoulder. "Come with me, Master Gwydion," he said with a tone that was both gentle and authoritative. "I've summoned the falconer. There is no time to waste; the bird can't sight at night. It has to away by at least fifty leagues before nightfall, or it will come back without delivering its message."

Gwydion Navarne nodded numbly and followed Gerald Owen back over the darkening fields, the sun overhead not casting as much as a hint of a shadow.

# 31

## NEAR THE SEACOAST

Rhapsody was jostled from her waking nightmare into awareness as the seneschal reined his horse to a halt.

Throughout the course of the ride the creature she had known as Michael in the old world, now a living corpse, once despicably human, now truly demonic, had berated her relentlessly, punctuating his discourse with new gouts of wind and flame released for emphasis, burning everything in sight. As each new fire erupted she was overwhelmed with the reek of burning flesh, the unmistakable fetor of an excited F'dor.

Her hold on her stomach had already been tenuous; she now was roiling in the dry nausea of horror. The heat of the demon's breath on her neck, coupled with the skeletal hands groping her body, probing beneath her clothes, fondling her, revolted her to the core of her being and made her wish for death.

Her touchstones of comfort had been polluted, deviated, into thoughts that only served to make her despair. Any memory of Ashe caused her soul to bleed, knowing how terrified he would be for her. Far worse, any reminder of the child she was carrying made her quake with fear, praying that its presence would not be discovered.

As each hour passed, her belief that she would be able to escape from her captivity lessened. Michael never left her alone, never let her out of his sight for a moment, assuring her repeatedly that this was the way she would be passing her days from now on.

"Do you remember our last fortnight together in Serendair?" he had inquired as they rode, his lips tracing the line of her neck to the shoulder. Rhapsody had closed her eyes, trying to block the memories, but they came flooding back— the captivity, the depravity, the total breaking of her spirit which only served to feed his perverted enjoyment. "It is a time I hold dear in my heart, Rhapsody. A return to those glorious days is at hand. When we return to Argaut, you will be the courtesan of the seneschal, the minister of Justice, by day, the whore of the baron by night." She tried to close her mind and senses to the rise of the stench that indicated the demon was even more excited at the prospect.

Michael had inhaled deeply, breathing in the smoky air with vigor, then pulled her closer so that his lips were next to her ear.

"I will make you love me again, Rhapsody. You have never ceased to be mine, remember that. I owned you long before any other man did; I will drive the memory of him out of your heart, and from between your legs. You will be so full of me soon that there will be room for no other anywhere in you."

She thought of her child and fought back tears.

Finally, after time undetermined, the burning forest began to thin, the trees winnowing into outer forest growth, then

copses and glades, with wide expanses of open land between
them, finally disappearing altogether.

Rhapsody, her sense of smell heightened since the child
was conceived, caught a trace of the sea air the moment the
burning forest was behind them. As they rode on, the wind
grew heavy with salt as they traveled west, heading straight
for the seacoast.

The sound of the ocean came up with a gust of wind as
the sun began to descend. The greatest fear in Rhapsody's
mind, being alone with Michael when the group made camp
for the night, was cast aside as she realized that the voyage
he had been alluding to was imminent.

She had foolishly believed the nearest place they could
embark on a vessel would be Port Fallon or Traeg, the most
northerly of the major and minor ports along the seacoasts
of Avonderre and Gwynwood. She had already been planning her escape, hoping to find assistance in the crowds of
Port Fallon or among the stoic fisherman who plied the cold,
windswept waters off the tiny inlet of Traeg. Now it was
becoming clearer that Michael had other means, other plans.

She was in even greater danger than she had known.

The riders came to a halt at the opening of a rocky promontory, a great precipice overlooking the churning sea. The
sound of wind and waves crashing in concert against the
cliff walls below rang with a familiar tone, the discordant
wail she had heard within the well of the prophetess's temple in Yarim.

Manwyn's voice rose up in Rhapsody's mind, smug and
mysterious.

*Rhapsody will not die bearing your children. The preg-
nancy will not be easy, but it will not kill or harm her.*

*Was Manwyn predicting something else?* she wondered
dully as Michael seized her by the waist and hauled her off
the horse. *Mayhap this is what she saw.*

Her death at Michael's hands. Or at her own, faced with
an even worse fate.

*One should beware the Past, lady. The Past can be a*

*relentless hunter, a stalwart protector, a vengeful adversary. It seeks to have you; it seeks to aid you.*

*It seeks to destroy you.*

She struggled to remain upright as the strong sea wind roared over the promontory, buffeting her face, whipping the tatters of her shirt.

Michael took her wrist and dragged her forward on the promontory; it was a wide ledge, narrowing to a distinct point, where the wind was fierce. His dark hair streamed behind him like a triumphant banner, matched by the cloak, now blowing behind him as well; he seemed invigorated by the wind, Rhapsody noted. She struggled to keep from trembling in his grasp, but was finding it hard not to do so when faced with the reality of her captor's strength; aside from his obvious advantages of size and strength, he was evidently tied to two elements, air and fire, both of which he seemed able to command at will.

And he was the bodily manifestation of a F'dor.

The sun turned red as it sank toward the ocean, hovering only a few hands from the horizon.

Michael ran his cadaverous fingers through the hair at the nape of her neck, running the skeletal digits through the tresses, entwining them. He jerked her head up and turned her so that they were looking southward and pointed to the left of the setting sun, his arm bathed in bloody light.

"There it is, my love, our ship of dreams, come to sail us away from this place and back to Argaut, where I will make good on all my promises to you."

He waved his free hand high in the air; a shower of black fire shot forth, burning through the dusty afternoon light in a screaming arc.

As the searing light faded she could see the ship, anchored deep. In response to the flash of fire, the sails began to rise.

Rhapsody started to shake with the effort to hold back from sobbing. *I will not give this bastard the satisfaction of making me cry ever again,* she thought, though her resolve was fading in the face of the circumstance.

She peered over the end of the promontory. The volcanic rock of the cliff stretched down directly into the sea a hundred or more feet below; leaving a shoreline scored with jagged rocks. The waves crashed menacingly below, surging violently against the cliff face. Rhapsody closed her eyes and staggered slightly as her balance shifted, leaving her nauseous and faint.

"Please," she choked, "move back from here."

The seneschal laughed harshly and pulled her away from the edge of the promontory, back toward his seven men, who were reconnoitering, getting their bearings and making preparations to descend to the ship.

"You are afraid of heights? Now, that's odd, Rhapsody. I hadn't realized you were afraid of anything. Perhaps it explains why you never liked being on top."

Rhapsody swallowed her retort. Her head cleared as they moved away from the churning sea, making her realize that there was nothing to be gained by infuriating him.

"How did you survive, Michael?" she asked softly, no tone of contempt evident in her voice. "I have long believed you dead."

The seneschal turned and looked down at her, his blue eyes piercing, as if trying to gauge her intent. Rhapsody forced herself to return his gaze without any of the disdain she felt, and had always felt, for him, searching his face for changes.

The chiseled lines of his jaw and cheekbones were the same as they had been when she had known him in the old world, but they had gone much more hollow; it was as if the skin was stretched over the framework of his face a little too tightly. When he was excited, however, he seemed to thicken, his gaunt frame gaining flesh, probably from the presence of the demon rising in his blood. She had seem similar physiological changes in Ashe, when the dragon was getting the better of him.

But while the dragon in Ashe's blood was covetous and petty, avaricious and difficult to reason with on occasion, it was an innate part of him, a trait handed down from his grandmother and great-grandmother that had come into prominence because of a near-fatal blow, coincidentally from another F'dor, and the extreme measures that had been undertaken to save him in the land between life and death, the realm of the Lord and Lady Rowan. It was as much a part of him as the color of his eyes or his ability to ride a horse, and had as many endearing aspects as annoying ones.

Michael's physiological manifestations were a sign of an evil spirit that had moved into his flesh as if it were an inn or a brothel, making itself at home.

But the eyes were the same. They were the same blue, like a cloudless summer sky, with the same propensity to gleam with unholy excitement, the same unstable gaze that could break like a sudden thunderstorm without warning. His eyes had always haunted her.

Those cold blue eyes were now tinged with the flame of the Underworld itself.

"Did it matter to you when you thought I was?" he asked quietly. His face was guarded, but Rhapsody believed she saw a vulnerability there, beneath the rictus of the demon.

"Yes," she said directly and honestly. The belief that she had escaped him, would never again have to see his face, had been one of the few happy thoughts that comforted her when she came out of the Root and discovered the Island was gone.

"I found a way to live forever," he said simply. "It involved taking on a partner."

"You sold yourself to a demon?"

"In a manner of speaking, but in truth it made out far better in the deal. I am not a mindless host, Rhapsody; it is *I* who am in control."

*Liar,* the demon whispered in his mind. *Cast me off, then, and see if you can still make that claim.*

Rhapsody could not hear it, but saw his face suddenly

contort, and knew he was struggling with the monster. She stood as still as she could, fearing that the ire would turn on her if she moved.

"Your Honor! We've found the pathway down to the sand beach," Fergus called from the southern side of the promontory. "If we leave now, we can be at the shoreline before dusk. The longboats are already on their way."

Michael's grip on Rhapsody's arm tightened again, causing her to gasp against her will. He dragged her back over to the rim of the promontory, and stared out over the ocean, now bathed in rosy golden light.

Rhapsody looked out on the sea. Away from the base of the cliff walls below them, to the south, she could see a sandy shoreline past the rocks, where the incoming tide rolled in breakers, whispering up the beach and rolling away again, unlike the mad crashing of sea against stone wall that was the shoreline directly below.

Three longboats had been launched by the vessel that lurked in the depths, rowing smoothly to the sandy shore.

"Take an archer and start down," the seneschal ordered his reeve. "When you get to the switchback, light it and signal me; I want to know where it is if it has gone dark before we make it down." Fergus nodded, lit the lantern and signaled to one of the bowmen, disappearing into the rocky boulders that lead down the cliff face to the beach.

"Why are you tarrying, Michael?" Rhapsody asked, a nervous edge to her voice. She was exhausted and overwrought; her normal reserve was beginning to crumble.

And she feared she already knew the answer.

He turned slowly and looked down at her thoughtfully. A beam of red sunlight broke through the low-lying clouds at the horizon, illuminating his face, making it glow with a demonic sheen.

"Isn't this a romantic spot?" he asked, his grin widening to the point of being malefic. "We have at least an hour before the longboats land. That should be plenty of time." He tossed his head in the wind whipping up from the bellowing sea, his eyes sparking with its power, then fixing on her with a gaze that terrified her.

"I have been waiting for this for a very long time, Rhapsody. I've mourned the loss of you ever since the day you escaped from that ratty tavern, the Hat and Feathers, or some such thing, in Easton; do you remember? I sent my man to bring you to me, but you never came. They told me the Brother had taken you—was that true? What happened to him?"

"The Brother—is no more," she stammered, her teeth chattering from fear and the chill of the night wind coming off the cold sea.

"Good. So, before we make our way down to the beach, before we spend the next six weeks on board a cramped ship tossing its way across the world, I intend to have you here, in the wind, on solid ground. I'll be denied no longer. I want to make some boulders fall into the sea." He patted one of a pair of large rocks that formed a V near the promontory's edge.

Rhapsody wrapped her arms around her waist, her eyes darting all around her.

*One should beware the Past, lady. It seeks to have you; it seeks to aid you.*

*It seeks to destroy you.*

The seneschal saw her, and his face hardened into an angular, malevolent mask.

"There is no escape, Rhapsody. You have run out of excuses and diversions. This is going to happen now. Resign yourself to it; you know the way this works." He pulled off his cloak and tossed it on the rocky ground.

"Spread out and block the wide edge of the precipice," he said to the five remaining men. They moved into position in a straight line, blocking the area where the promontory connected to the land.

"Light, m'lord," called one of the bowmen. He was staring down the path where the reeve had descended.

The seneschal tossed Rhapsody to the ground, her back

to the promontory's edge, her face to the line of soldiers, then crossed to the south end of the promontory and looked over the edge to where a tiny flicker of lanternlight waved back in forth in the oncoming dark.

"Fergus has found the switchback," he said to the men. "Good. All right then." He turned to take a step back onto the promontory.

Just in time to see Rhapsody lunge for the cliff's edge.

For a split second he and the others stood in shock as she bolted for the end of the promontory. Then a harsh sound of fury tore forth from his throat.

"Stop! Stop her!"

Caius fired; Rhapsody lurched forward, a few paces from the edge, the bolt lodged in her sword belt.

Bent over at the waist, wincing in pain, she saw the guards running toward her. She met Michael's eye for the last time.

Then threw herself over the edge of the cliff and into the sea.

# 32

$\int$or a long moment, the only sound that was heard on the promontory was the howl of the gusting wind.

Then, a moment later, a scream of rage, dual in its origin, rocked the cliff, the harsh tones of the thwarted demon blending discordantly with the rage of a psychotically cruel, unstable man who had been denied the prize he had crossed the ocean to reclaim. It was a sound horrifying enough to make more than one of the hired mercenaries lose control of their water.

The wind rose in response to the scream of anger, blasting the promontory, shaking loose a hail of rock and causing it to rain in great dusty sheets down into the roiling sea.

The seneschal ran to the cliff edge, his muscles thick and corded as he moved, and peered down into the crashing waves that were battering the base of the volcanic rockwalls a hundred feet below. There was no sign of her; he had hoped against hope to see her clinging to the rocks, or washing out to sea on the violent tide, but there was nothing but the endless ebb and flow of blue-gray water, foaming with turgid froth, swirling in the dark light of dusk.

He threw back his head and screamed at the sky.

*Noooooooooooooooooooo!*

The malodor of the demon, the reek of burning flesh, rose into the wind, making the soldiers gag and tremble as sparks of black fire erupted into the air.

They peered over the edge of the precipice themselves, searching in the fading light for a sign of the woman below, but all they could see and hear was the relentless pounding of the angry surf against the rockwalls, the black tide swelling away from the volcanic cliffs, churning back to the sea in a wicked undertow.

The seneschal was clutching his head, writhing, as though locked in battle with an unseen spirit that was gouging at him. The soldiers, frightened now, hedged together, looking to each other for direction; in the absence of the reeve, there was no subleader to turn to.

Finally the seneschal jerked upright and glared at them.

"What are you waiting for?" he demanded, his voice crackling with rage. "Get down there, you fools! Comb the beach, search the rocks—find her!"

"M'lord—" one of the bowman began.

The wind shrieked in fury as the seneschal snapped his arm in the man's direction and made an angry, sweeping gesture toward the edge of the precipice; a gale-force gust swept the man up from behind and heaved him over the promontory's edge. His scream was lost in the cry of the wind as he fell. The others could not help but notice his body bounce off the jagged black rocks that lay about the bottom of the cliff below, the waves seething over them, to be sucked a moment later into the depths by the undertow.

The seneschal watched as well, studying the course the

body took. Then he turned and eyed the men again.

*"Find her."*

The men scattered, hurrying down the path to the switch-back that the reeve had lighted a few moments before.

Michael stood in the screaming wind, staring down into the roiling water. The waves undulated like the grass in the Wide Meadows had, the grass that for more than a millennium reminded him naggingly of her hair, prodding him with memories made all the more aggravating by futility.

*For this we traveled across the world. What a colossal waste.*

"Silence!" the seneschal screamed, clawing at his own face. "Do not torture me with your smug insights. You know *nothing.*"

*I see nothing as well, nothing but surf and rocks.*

The veins in Michael's neck corded thickly, his face hot with fury.

"Would you care to see them close up?" he snarled, stepping closer to the cliff's edge. "For I have lost the only thing I wanted. Life unending has suddenly become a burden. Perhaps we should follow her into the sea. Would that please you, you self-satisfied parasite?"

The demon went suddenly silent.

The seneschal's eyes opened wider, and he stared down into the watery frenzy below, contemplating it. He could feel a sudden sweet madness take hold, a desire to throw himself onto the arms of the wind, to drift down, then plummet, ending the torment from the demon and the loss of Rhapsody in one swift, tumultuous leap.

*No. Step back.*

He shook his head violently, spattering the sweat from his brow into the cleansing wind.

*She was not worthy of us. She despised you. Could you not tell that?*

"I don't believe you," the seneschal said lightly, but his undertone was menacing. "Did you see her face when she told me she thought I was dead?"

*I saw it. I saw disdain.*

"Nonesuch," the seneschal snapped. "You saw remorse, and longing."

*You are not only blind, you are pathetic.*

From below voices could be heard in snippets on the rising gusts of wind; the seneschal looked to the south, where lanterns were being lighted on the now-dark sand beach, their tiny flames spreading out wide, circling the edges of the sea, approaching the rocks but driven back by the force of the tide, sending ripples of light out over the black water.

The demon's voice in his mind changed; it took on a warm, sweet tone.

*Go down, then, if you must. Search the shoreline. You will not find anything—no one could have survived those rocks. But search, for you will not be able to rest until you do. Then, once you have made your peace with her being gone for certain this time, let us return to the ship, and back to Argaut. Much is waiting for us to revel in back home.*

Michael inhaled silently, watching the fallowing sea, until darkness had consumed the shore.

*Come,* the demon wheedled. *Let us go down to the sea again. See for yourself. Faron is waiting.*

The seneschal nodded reluctantly. "Yes," he said aloud. "It's time." He stared ruefully one last moment into Rhapsody's rocky grave of smoldering water, trying to blot from his mind the way she had met his eye before she jumped. The message had been unmistakable.

Death, even a violent and painful one, was preferable to being with him.

"Whore," he whispered into the wind coming up from the rocks below.

"Miserable, rutting whore."

# 33

## THE CAULDRON, YLORC

The long ride home from Sorbold had given Achmed an interesting window into the woman he had hired.

At first, her somewhat slight stature and angled face had reminded him of strongly of Rhapsody, as well as her unwillingness to be disturbed in her work or manhandled, even by her own family members. But the more he observed Theophila, the more intrigued he was by the differences between them.

Rhapsody had always been as transparent to him as clear glass. Her motives and intentions were obvious, and while she had subtleties and nuances to her character, for the most part she was as easy to read as the mile-high letters carved by river canyons into the cliff faces of the mountain passes in the High Reaches back in the old world.

Theophila, on the other hand, was more opaque than the stained glass she and her fellow Panjeri crafted.

For the vast part of the journey she had said nothing, preferring to ride in silence over the rocky steppes that edged the Manteid mountains from Sorbold northeast to Ylorc. She was even quieter once they entered the mountain passes, glancing above her every few minutes like a prey animal nervously watching for predators above.

While he found her silence to be preferable on balance to Rhapsody's prattle, there was something different about the vibration that emanated from her. While the natural music that surrounded Rhapsody was soothing to the sensitive network of nerves and veins that scored the surface of his skin, the Panjeri woman had more of a crackle to her, a sort of static that hung in the air that she passed through. It was fascinating, though it kept his natural defenses on a high state of alert.

On rare occasion he had even tried to engage her in conversation, or what to Achmed passed for conversation, terse and pointed questions about her training, her experience, her requirements. Theophila responded in short, clipped answers, preferring to keep her concentration focused on the unfamiliar terrain through which they were traveling.

When they camped at night, neither of them got much sleep. The level of understandable distrust had not subsided in the few days since they had met, and so each traveler tended to sleep upright, drawn, ostensibly to be ready to respond to any threat coming upon them from roving animals or brigands, but there was little doubt in either of their minds that the other was on the list of things of which to be wary.

On the few occasions that Theophila did speak, she had gone into great length about the type of tools and supplies she would need, despite not having seen the project site. She had brought a small bag with her, and in it he presumed there were a few hand tools: a saw, perhaps, tile nippers, and the badly balanced groziers and files he had seen her using on the glass windows of Sorbold. But the Panjeri owned the more significant tools and all of the supplies, she had said, and so he would need to be prepared to outfit her completely.

*She's a tool-slut,* he thought in amusement, watching as she scrawled the list. *Like Rhapsody and her weakness for clothes.* Every woman he had known, no matter how formidable, had a secret obsession for something.

She also knew how to handle a horse. When she thought he wasn't looking, Achmed had heard her speaking to the animal he had purchased in Yarim, checking its hooves, gentling it with words in another tongue. Her hands were small but strong, and she employed them rather than her feet to direct her mount. It was a soft side that she gave him no view into when she knew he was paying attention.

Six days after they left the Rymshin Pass, the towering peaks of Grivven and Xaith came into view. Achmed watched Theophila from behind his veils, noting how quickly her dark eyes took in the sight of the multicolored mountains, rising, fanglike, in a multiplicity of colors and hues, blends of black and purple, green and blue above rolling mist that made it appear as if they were in the clouds above. Those two peaks had been hollowed out in the Cymrian era, and now had been restored and expanded into outposts that never slept, housing thousands of soldiers in watchtowers that could see for fifteen leagues across the Krevensfield Plain.

"Ylorc," he said simply. Theophila nodded silently.

He brought her in through the main entrance to the Cauldron, giant arched gates hewn from the very stone fabric of the mountain, past giant ramparts and bulwarks fashioned on a scale as if for holding back gods. Achmed chuckled to himself at the look of undisguised wonder on her face, remembering how he, Grunthor, and Rhapsody had first entered Ylorc through a storm sewer drain, itself a massive architectural marvel, though obviously less grandiose. As ever, he had no need to examine his motives.

He had wanted to impress her, to overwhelm her. Even to frighten her a little.

Great brass bells rang at their approach, the martial sound echoing off the peaks of the Teeth and through the earthen walls, rattling the massive tapestries in the inner hallway. Two hundred Bolg soldiers, glowering in their dark leather armor, their greaves and vambraces forged of blue-black rysin-steel, lined the colossal corridor that led past gigantic statues left over from the Cymrian era, recently restored to glory, or at least cleanliness, by the Bolg artisans.

Theophila followed the Bolg king as he turned down the deep tunnel that led to the Great Hall, lined on both sides with uncounted pedestals, most of them mismatched, on which various items sat, gathering dust.

"What's all this?" she asked, her voice reverberating in the cavernous hallway.

"Gifts of state," Achmed replied, walking past necklaces

and pitchers, seals and other court treasures, all casually displayed. "Trinkets and frippery that various leaders of other nations sent as gifts when I took control of the Bolglands. Bribes. Appeasement. Dust collectors."

The Panjeri woman's dark eyes glittered in the shadows from the torches that lined the halls.

"Some of them look priceless."

"No doubt they are."

"Well, then why are they so carelessly displayed?"

Achmed snorted. "Because I don't care about them. I would have sold the lot of them in the fish market, but my— minister of protocol insisted that they needed to be kept in case any of the fools came calling."

Theophila smiled slightly. "Why don't the pedestals match, at least?"

Achmed shrugged. "You find a pedestal in an old closet somewhere, you haul it out, stick a bowl on it, and put it in the corridor. It becomes a diplomatic statement. They don't have to match."

"Ah. And yet you are willing to spend two hundred thousand gold suns on stained glass. You have an interesting sense of aesthetics." Theophila lapsed into silence and followed him up the corridor to the Great Hall.

Shaene was sifting a large pile of wood ash into a barrel amid the scattered shards of the many frit attempts that had failed when Achmed and the new stained-glass master entered the tower of Gurgus.

The Canderian artisan gaped for a moment, then closed his mouth quickly and made his way across the marble floor, his boot heels sounding in the high-domed chamber. He wiped his hands on his leather apron as he approached.

"Welcome home, Your Majesty," he said with exaggerated politeness to Achmed. "I trust you had a good trip." He smiled brightly at the woman, who met his gaze without registering a facial expression.

"Where is Rhur?" Achmed demanded brusquely.

"He and Sandy went to check the kilns." Shaene's smile grew brighter and more obsequious. Achmed ignored him and went to one of the worktables, where many generations of test shards lay next to seven glass plates wrapped in burlap. Theophila followed him, her eyes taking in the tall, slender room, its lofty, tapering tower that reached into the sky above. He pointed to the circular domed ceiling, temporarily sealed with wood, divided into seven equal sections in rays around the centerpiece support.

"This is the project: I need to have that ceiling inlaid with seven colored panes of glass, all equal in size. The circle is to be divided up in eighths, each section accounting for one eighth of the area, the last eighth accounting for the lead cames, the support sections that divide the colors one from another." The Panjeri artisan nodded.

"The forges that are available to you here rival—no, best—anything you have ever seen before. There are four furnaces the size of three oxcarts in length, a fritting furnace, a melting furnace for working the glass, an annealing furnace for cooling, and a furnace for spreading the glass sheets. If you have need of another, or any other tools, I will have them made for you.

"Here is the challenge," Achmed continued. "Each section must be precisely the right color—I have a gauge I will show you. Additionally, it must be strong enough to withstand the thin air and the battering winds at the top of this crag, but at the same time flawless, without bubbles or imperfections. And the glass must be translucent enough to cast a clear, colored shadow on the floor of this room; different colors will shine at different hours, depending on the position of the sun. If it's done correctly, a rainbow will arch across the floor at midday."

"Do you have a schematic to indicate where each specific color goes?" the stained-glass master asked.

"Yes. Rhur has it now, most likely."

Shaene shook his head. "Probably Sandy, actually."

Achmed exhaled, remembering the nervous look on

Rhapsody's face as she reluctantly copied the corresponding colors onto the diagram.

"I will make certain you have the plans," he said to Theophila. He picked up one of the burlap-wrapped plates and pulled off the cover. In his hand was a small plate of glowing green glass, as thick as the length of his thumb.

"This is supposed to be a gauge of the correct green—there is one for each color," he said, handing it to Theophila. "In addition, you can test the opacity by holding it up to sunlight. If the glass has the right translucency, supposedly some sort of rune appears, some kind of writing, that can only be seen if it's not too thin, not too thick."

"I take it you have never seen the rune," Theophila said, running her fingers absently through the multicolored shards on the table.

"No."

"Not surprising. You are using the wrong materials."

"Oh? And what should we be using?"

She picked up a shard, fingering it carefully, then held it up to the light.

"You are using the wrong type of wood for ash, for one thing. What concentration of ash to sand are you using?"

"One and one half parts ash to one part sand."

The sealed master shook her head. "No. Two to one. You also need a finer mesh to sift it; this is still too coarse. And you need to be using different wood. This has too high a concentration of potash in it."

Achmed swallowed, thinking. They had used the same wood that Gwylliam had used—the harvest of the deep forest glades to the east within the Hidden Realm of Canrif, past the dry canyon. "When the original tower was built, they used the same wood that we are using," he said, picking up a blotchy yellow piece.

The artisan arched an eyebrow. "Are you certain?" she asked, looking through the test piece again. "There is wood of all different sorts around here. You've used the soft woods of the eastern forests, have you not?"

"Yes."

She chuckled. "You should be looking *west,* not east. The foothills on the western side of your realm are full of cherry and, even better, beechwood, which has more sodium in it— much better in glass making. Additionally, you can find wormwood and nettles strewn all over the steppes—we passed enough of them to realize your brave boast about lining every mountain peak of the Teeth with stained glass. And finally, we can harvest the szeksos."

"Szeksos?"

The artisan nodded. "Salt crusts that you find on arid land, such as that between here and the Sorbold border. Very commonly seen on steppes. They are probably the remains of ancient saltwater ponds. Whenever the Panjeri come across them, we harvest them. They make a wonderful additive."

Achmed had been listening in an almost grateful admiration. Hearing the confidence in her voice, after so many months of failed trial and error, gave him renewed hope that his undertaking might have a chance after all.

"I've brought back barrels of minerals to use as colorants," he said quickly, stepping over the broken glass and nodding to Rhur as he came into the tower. "I'm assuming you'll want manganese for the purple, copper for the red, iron for the yellow, cobalt for the blue—"

"Perhaps," Theophila shrugged. "I may use the traditional metallic oxides, but I have my own recipes as well. Different types of ash make for different colors, different temperatures do as well."

"What are the ingredients?"

The Panjeri woman did not smile. "Your two hundred thousand gold suns purchases my time and labor," she said blandly. "It does not buy my secrets."

Rhur signaled for the Bolg king to excuse himself; when Achmed waved at him dismissively, the Firbolg artisan cleared his throat and spoke, something that occurred so rarely that both the king and Shaene were startled by the sound of his voice.

"Majesty." He beckoned with his head again.

Achmed tossed the shard into the pile and hurried across the room. He took the small scrap of oilcloth that Rhur held out to him; it was a message that came in from the aviary.

In Grunthor's hand.

He stared at it for a long moment, trying to make sense of the words, then suddenly looked up at all three artisans.

"I must go," he said quietly to Rhur. "I don't know when I will return. Make certain she gets anything she needs—*anything*. Have the tool casters begin work on whatever she designs. See to it that she is made comfortable in the ambassadorial guest quarters. But confine her to that section of hallways. I don't want her loose in the Cauldron while I'm gone." Rhur nodded. "Now, go to the quartermaster; tell him to reoutfit me right away. I have to leave immediately for Sepulvarta."

He turned back and met the stares of the men and the woman.

"I have to leave suddenly, Theophila." He looked around quickly. "Rhur will see to everything you need. I—I will check in with you as soon as I get back. You can work independently, without my oversight, from what you have seen, yes?"

"Once I have the plans, yes."

"Good. Shaene, make certain she gets them."

Without another word, the Bolg king fled the chamber.

Out along the corridors of the inner Cauldron he ran, past hallways and guards who blinked but said nothing as he rushed by. Firbolg workmen and citizens passing in the corridors moved quickly up against the walls to keep clear of him; from the look on his face, the last thing they wanted to do was get in his way.

Achmed slipped into a thin tunnel that served as a vent for the circulating system of heat that warmed the inner reaches of the mountains in winter, now dormant in sum-

mer's heat, and followed it out onto a rocky eastern ledge
that overlooked the Krevensfield Plain. He tried to calm his
frantically racing heart, inhaling deeply until he could feel
his internal center, focusing on his own heartbeat.

Then, tremulously, he closed his eyes and pulled back the
veil over his skin-web, letting the gusts of warm summer
air billow over it, searching for the familiar rhythm on the
wind.

Only the wind answered him.

He cast a wider net, opening his mind until his head
throbbed with the effort of it, combing each pocket, each
gust, desperately striving to catch even the tiniest flicker, the
smallest flavor of Rhapsody's heartbeat, a rhythm that was
as familiar to him as his own. He waited a long few moments, tasting the air, inhaling it deep to see if he could
capture an infinitesimal particle of it within himself.

Nothing.

*Rhapsody,* he called silently, casting her name like a net
into the wind, then pulling it back with his mind, hoping
for a fragment, a flicker, anything.

Nothing.

Cold waves of fear began to rise and fall, radiating from
his stomach out to his extremities.

He barely felt them.

Achmed shifted his focus and combed the wind, seeking
Grunthor's heartbeat. It thrummed in his skin-web immediately, pulsing in the familiar rhythm of his friend's life
signature. Distantly the buzz of the other thousand or so
survivors from the Island were there as well.

Only Rhapsody's was missing.

Breaking from his search, Achmed ran at breakneck speed
to the livery where the quartermaster had saddled his horse,
mounted, and rode off west toward Sepulvarta before almost
any of the Bolg had even realized he had returned.

Omet returned to the work site in the tower a few
minutes later, having completed his rounds of kiln-checks,

to find a stranger in the inner sanctum, the Bolg king's second-most-restricted area after his own chambers.

She was consulting with Shaene and Rhur, crouched over a pile of wood ash and glass shards when he came in. At first he didn't even realize that she was a woman, because her build was so slight, her hair so short, and her stance so aggressive that immediately he assumed she was a man.

All misconception of that was shattered a moment later, when Shaene noticed him standing there.

"Ah, Sandy!" the oafish artisan called, waving Omet into the room. "You're just in time to meet the king's new hire, a sealed Panjeri master. Theophila, this is our fellow suffering glassmaker, Sandy."

The woman crouching on the floor looked up and nodded, her face impassive, dark eyes lighting on Omet for a moment, then returning to her conversation with the two men.

"Say, Sandy, do you have the plans? The king wants Theophila to have them."

At those words, both Theophila and Rhur looked up at him again.

As their eyes met, Omet went suddenly white. His jaw clenched into a firm grip, so tight that the tiny hairs in his beard vibrated.

"Well?" Shaene demanded impatiently after a moment. "Do you have them plans or not?"

"Er, no, not with me," he lied, holding as still as possible and hoping the drawings would not be revealed in the canvas he carried. "I must have left them near the kilns. I'll have to go to the forge and get them."

"Well, for the gods' sake, don't lose them. The king will push you into the kilns himself if you do."

"Where—where is the king?" Omet asked, running a hand through his sweaty hair.

Shaene looked up from the ash pile on the floor. "He just left the mountain on somethin' urgent. Said he didn't know when he would be back." He took in the pale look on Omet's face, noted where the boy was staring, and laughed.

"Slacken your trousers, lad. She's too old for you."

The woman rolled her eyes and turned back to the table. "No hurry on the plans today. I'll want a tour of the forge and the ovens first, and an inventory of the materials and tools you have."

"Very good, mum," said Shaene.

"Excuse me," Omet said quickly, then slipped out the door again.

Once around the corner, he leaned up against a wall for support, suddenly light-headed and sick.

He knew this woman, though her hair had been cropped short, and she was wearing clothes the like of which she never would have been seen in normally.

He prayed she did not know him beneath the head of hair and the full beard he had grown since last she had seen him.

In the foundry of Yarim.

All the world began to spin, and fear worse than any he had known roared forth, threatening to consume him.

The guildmistress had come to Ylorc.

# 34

In the heartbeat before she bolted for the edge of the cliff, Rhapsody remembered something.

The last time she had run from Michael, in the company of Achmed and Grunthor, they were in the Wide Meadows of Serendair. They had come across a cadre of nomadic Lirin, wanderers known as Lirinved, the In-Between, who traveled betwixt forest and field, making homes in neither place. She and the two Bolg, though meaning no harm to the Lirinved, were nonetheless strangers in their lands, in bad days to be strangers. Achmed and Grunthor, hidden with her in the highgrass of the meadows, had drawn weapons silently in preparation for the confrontation that no one wanted, but was to come.

That was the first moment she had understood the true,

deep and inexorable power of a Namer, the rank of Singer she had just achieved through her self-study and constant practice.

Because she knew the true name of the highgrass, *Hymialacia,* in which they were hiding, she had been able to whisper it, over and over, weaving into her chant the names of other distractions—the clouds above, the warm wind, hummocks and pits. In that way, just for a moment, she had altered the vibrational signatures of each of the companions, camouflaging them, blending them into the highgrass until they actually *became* the Hymialacia while she sang. For the time they were hidden, transformed thus, the wind had blown through them, the sun had beat down upon them, but cast shadows that looked like those belonging to blades of grass, not a Firbolg man, a giant, and a Lirin woman. The Lirinved had walked past, close enough to touch them, never knowing they were there.

That power, that Naming ability, was the only thing that had even the slightest chance of saving her now.

Even if it would not, there was no other recourse than but to try, she reasoned. Preferable to die in a fall from the precipice than to live in the fetid clutches of a human-demon who would defile her body, torture her soul, and worst, eventually become aware of her child.

Her mind refused to imagine what he would do then.

There was no other option.

But what word, what name, could possibly spare her from a fall from that height? Her mind raced furiously as she lay on the ground where Michael had thrown her, the cloth of her torn shirt rippling in the wind raging up the cliff face, spilling over onto the promontory, tangling her flying hair, as he conferred with his men.

Droplets of salt spray borne on the wind slapped her face, stinging her eyes with salt. Her mind registered them first as rain, making unconscious note of them a moment later, then shifting suddenly back to her first impulse.

Rain.

*Typta,* she whispered in her Namer's voice, feeling the hum of the different vibration in her teeth.

The tone was true.

She concentrated on her own note, *ela,* and prepared to alter it with the roundelay.

Within the next beat of her heart Rhapsody was on her feet, running with all her strength for the cliff's edge, chanting with the last of her breath.

*Typta. Typta, Typta.*

She felt the wind waft over her, lift her slightly, like raindrops on an updraft, caught the exhilaration of speed, hearing the shouts behind her, but blocking them, focusing with all her concentration on the edge of the precipice looming before her.

*Typta. Ty—*

She felt the reverberation of the bolt in her back and side before the pain, a thudding lurch that threw her balance off, shattering her concentration. Then an instant later the waves of shock radiated through her, a sickening jolt of opposing vibration that tore the breath from her.

The impact strained the muscles of her abdomen; Rhapsody bent over, trying to catch her breath, and as she did she saw Michael at the place where the land began to split into the promontory. A look of shock was frozen on his face, a face with eyes that burned red at the edges, whose ancient skin was drawn like a mummy's over the sharp bones. It was a face far worse than the one that had haunted her dreams; seeing it made any other option unthinkable.

She closed her eyes before she leapt, fearing that if she saw the sight of the crashing waves, the jagged rocks at the shoreline again, she would lose her nerve. The wind that caught her was cold, coming off the northern sea; it clouted her awake, forced her eyes open as she fell, swirling toward the ocean in the careless embrace of the air.

*Typta,* she chanted as she plummeted, her hands still bound, her cheeks distended in the breeze and from the pull of the Earth. *Typta. Typta, Typta—*

A wave swelled suddenly over her face, filling her mouth with water, choking her. She did not feel the impact of her fall; not then. The breath was knocked out of her, so she could not inhale, which in the initial seconds probably kept her alive.

A roar of green and white, then an echoing silence as she was pulled below the surface, followed by a thick drumbeat, like an underwater wind. Rhapsody's eyes burned from the salt, her lungs from the lack of air. Above her, before all went green, she could see Michael's face and the faces of his cohorts staring down from the cliff top, or at least she imagined that she could. She could hear their voices, though her ears sank into the water quickly.

They were staring directly down at her.

They didn't see her, even though she was there beneath them.

Because, for a moment, she was rain.

The incoming tide caught her then. In the first moments she had been floating in the crest of the waves, the foam itself, light as a raindrop, skittering across the surface. As soon as the chant was broken, her mouth filled with water, her mass returned, and with it the whole force of the raging sea.

Like a heavy curtain falling, the world suddenly went from green to black.

*Don't breathe,* she thought, fighting to find the surface in the darkness, and failing. The thick noise of the waves, muted, pounded in her ears.

Then, with a great swell, she was caught up, spinning wildly, struggling for purchase where there was none, nothing to grasp or bear against, nothing but evanescent water slipping through her hands, out from beneath her. It was a sickening sensation, akin to being hurled through the air, only worse, roiling and tumbling with the madness of the waves.

Until she was slammed into a wall of solid rock.

Against her will, Rhapsody gasped, inhaling a rush of

caustic seawater. Before her lungs burst she broke the surface, gagging, choking, spitting, clawing desperately in the
dark at the vertical rocky surface before her, a wall that rose
as far up as she could reach.

Above her there was only enough air space for her nose
and the upper part of her face to bob out of the water; past
that, overhead, her tied hands scraped a similar rockwall,
this one horizontal. She was bleeding, she noted distantly,
as her face impacted the hard ceiling above her with a swell
of the waves, her side stinging as well from where the bowman had shot her.

The noise of the sea had diminished a bit; it echoed now
in the dark, roaring with the ebb and flow of the waves, but
not with the same broad, endless crashing she had heard
atop the cliff. That was only when her ears were above the
surface; with each new wave she was submerged again,
hearing only the muted swishing and the sound of bubbles
beneath the water.

How long she continued to bob in the dark, catching insignificant breaths of air, Rhapsody could not be certain, but
it seemed hours, days, years, a punishment of eternal pro-
portion. Her skin stung from the salt; her limbs grew tired,
so she gave up the struggle to move and instead concentrated on floating, trying to quell the panic that swept over
her with each wave, pounding on her lungs.

Finally it seemed as if the space above her where there
was air was growing larger; she could no longer touch the
ceiling with her hands when she crested the surface. After
some time light broke through the darkness behind her, a
small, white slice of visible sky that her stinging eyes could
barely make out. It grew ever larger with each rolling wave,
until finally there was a goodly space above her, and enough
light to make out where she was.

She had been swept on an incoming wave into a tidal
cave, a volcanic hollow in the endless cliff face that made
up the many miles of shoreline from the northern Hintervold
all the way down to her own lands in Tyrian, half a thousand

miles away. Rhapsody choked back the irony; it was in just
such a cave that she had postulated the water source that
fed Entudenin had its mouth.

In the back wall of the cave she could see a shallow ledge
of sorts, hewn from the rock over millennia by the slow,
insistent carving of the currents; she let the next incoming
wave carry her to it, clutching with all her might as she was
battered once more against the back wall of the cave. It took
her three tries to roll up onto the ledge and remain there
after the wave receded, but when finally she was able she
sat upright, her back against the smooth, irregular cave wall,
and struggled to clear her lungs of the brine she had inhaled.
Her stomach rose to her mouth and she retched, glad to be
clear of the saltwater.

Numbly she felt for the locket around her neck; it was
still there, hanging on its thin gold chain. Still coughing, she
opened the clasp; a tiny, thirteen-sided copper coin that
Ashe had given her in their mutual youth, and she had carried through two worlds, tumbled into her hand. She sighed
in relief; having it with her still was like having a part of
him there, too. Rhapsody quickly closed the coin back inside
the locket and set about clearing her lungs.

When she could breathe again she stared out the cave's
opening; the light that spilled into the cave over the swirling
waves was pink. *Dawn,* she thought weakly. *I have been
here all night.* Now the tide was going out, emptying the
cave slightly, though she could still not see the bottom in
the swirling water beneath the ledge.

*Risa hilue,* she whispered in the tongue of her mother's
people, Liringlas, the Skysingers, who greeted the sun in its
rising and setting with song. *Welcome, sunrise.*

The turbulent sea growled relentlessly in answer.

𝒜s the outgoing tide carried the longboats back to the
*Basquela,* Fergus, the seneschal's reeve, squinted in the red
light, struggling to keep his master at all times in his sight.

The seneschal had said nothing from the moment they

had launched, staring behind him at the rising sun cresting the towering coastline, silent as death. The sounds of morning on the sea—the cry of the gulls, the music of the wind—went unnoticed, the sky-blue eyes of the minister of justice glassy and unfocused. Fergus knew better than to annoy the seneschal with idle conversation or ameliorative attempts, so instead he merely called to the oarsmen, directing them back to the frigate in smooth, unhurried strokes.

When finally their longboat reached the ship, the reeve signaled the majority of the crew aboard, wanting to give the seneschal as much time as he needed before climbing the ladder that would be the final step in abandoning his quest. He stood silently behind his master, clutching the guy rope but saying nothing, staring at the misty cliffs in the distance, flat and stolid gray with the bright sun rising above them.

Fergus had learned long ago that the moods of the seneschal were like the wind, unpredictable, often fierce; he had weathered storms of temper that had raged for hours, like the howling of a hurricane. But if one watched carefully, occasionally one could gauge the signs of a lull.

He thought he saw one now, brought on by a combination of wretched disappointment and exhaustion.

"Your Honor?"

At first the seneschal said nothing, then finally inclined his head.

"Hmmm?"

Fergus swallowed and took the risk. "Are you ready to embark, sir?"

The seneschal sat quietly until the sun fully crested the forbidding cliffs, brightening the froth rolling at their base with bands of sparkling light, then nodded, his head slightly atilt, as if his neck had been broken.

He stood as the longboat was hauled aboard, then climbed free of it once it was on deck, and stumbled for the door of the hold, the rest of the crew hovering as far from his path as possible.

Down the ladder into the black underbelly of the ship he crawled, his chest heaving with pent-up despair.

He felt around in the darkness at the bottom of the ladder, lurching and floundering blindly until he came to the green pool.

"Faron?" he whispered. There were tears in his voice.

The meniscus on the top of the smoky water broke almost instantly as the twisted child came forth, a look of concern in its cloudy eyes at the sound of pain in its father's voice.

The seneschal sank to his knees on the wet planks of the floor, and bent over the edge of the pool; he threw his arms around the boneless child's misshapen torso, leaning his head against it, and began to sob in deep, racking spasms.

"Dead, Faron, she's dead," he moaned, venting his grief to the one entity in the entire world he could trust with it. "Flung herself from the cliff top, rather than come with me." He began to wail, his speech slurring into incomprehensibility, muttering nonsensical words over and over again.

Faron's occluded eyes widened in panic, then tempered. Its gnarled left hand came to rest on its father's head, the contorted fingers gently caressing his hair with the overgrown nails. The creature sat, emitting no sound, just listening to the outpouring of anguish that made the mist that hung over the glowing green pool swirl and twist as well.

Finally, something occurred to the creature. Without pausing in its comfort, it reached below the surface of the water, feeling around for a moment, then pulled forth a dark green scale and the lock of hair that the seneschal had given him long before to scry with.

Faron continued to pat the head of its father, who had settled into quiet hiccoughing, as it ran the scale and the hair through the pale green currents, finally pulling them up to stare into the rune inscribed on it.

The cloudy eyes blinked.

Then the creature began to squeak, tapping its father on the shoulder with its arthritic digit.

Michael looked up dispiritedly.

"What, Faron? What is it?"

The creature's strange, fused mouth was contorted in a hideous wave of muscle and lip tissue, the flaccid skin at the sides of its face flapping excitedly.

It held up the scale.

"What is it?" the seneschal asked again, beginning to sense the creature's message.

The creature let go of its father's head long enough to catch the lock of brittle hair; it turned it between its bent fingers, holding it over the dark green scale, then shook its head in rapture.

The seneschal took Faron's face gently in its hands.

"You are looking through the death scale?"

Faron nodded.

"And you do not see her?"

The creature nodded again, exhilaration evident in its contorted face.

The seneschal looked at Faron intently. "Are you saying that—she is—still alive?"

Faron wriggled happily, nodding vigorously.

"Are you certain, Faron?"

Faron nodded yet again.

*"Where?"*

The mutant child shook its head.

The senechal's eyes were on fire, but he endeavored to keep his voice steady, so as not to frighten Faron. He kissed the creature's head amid the wrinkles of loose skin and wisps of white hair.

"Can you continue to scry for me, Faron? See if you can find any clue, any direction at all."

The creature nodded and slipped back beneath the surface of the glowing water.

Invigorated, the seneschal leapt to his feet and started to cross the pitching hold.

*Stop. No more.*

The voice of the demon, respectfully silent in Michael's misery, spoke up harshly.

*You looked,* it said, black fire crackling in its voice. *You searched everywhere; your men combed the beach in the dark and the light. There was nothing there.*

"She's alive," the seneschal retorted, heading for the stairs. "We must turn back."

*Enough of this foolishness. We will return to Argaut.*

Michael chuckled as he began to climb the ladder back to the deck.

"What? And miss all the lovely burning?"

*Burning?*

"Yes," the seneschal said warmly as he opened the door to the world above. "It is about to begin in earnest now."

# 35

## NAVARNE

On the morning of the day Ashe returned to Haguefort, the smoke from the fires burning along the western coast had begun to drift over Navarne, hanging loosely in the summer sky, coloring it from clear blue to a hazy gray, lacing the wind with the rancid residue of trees that burned too soon, while they were still living.

The smell had been burning the inside of Gerald Owen's nostrils all day, irritating his eyes as well. He had to squint into the gray miasma of the air to see the riders galloping up the road, pushing their horses too hard, even when the shouts had gone up for half a league that they were coming.

Ashe had not slept for four days since receiving the tidings. That he was still able to maintain a seat on his horse caused Owen to marvel; the Lord Cymrian had undoubtedly stopped at each way station along the mail route, trading mounts, and no doubt was feeling the effort in his legs and hindquarters, but he had disregarded that, spurring the horse mercilessly for the last half-league.

He did not wait to dismount before looking for answers.

"What happened?" he demanded, his face haggard but his eyes burning with consternation. "Has she been found?"

Owen signaled subtlely to the stablemaster to lead the horse away after he helped the Lord Cymrian down.

"No, m'lord. Your uncle and the Sergeant-Major are awaiting your arrival in the Great Hall."

"Sergeant-Major? What S-ergeant-Major?" Ashe asked brusquely, ignoring the salutations of his guards as he hurried past them.

"Er—the Lady Cymrian's friend. From Ylorc, sire," Owen said, trying to keep pace.

"Grunthor? What's he doing here?"

"It was he who brought Anborn back to Haguefort, m'lord."

Ashe shook his head and made his way as rapidly as he could into the keep.

In the Great Hall he found them, the General and the Sergeant, poring over a map of the western continent. The sight of his uncle caused the anger that had been brewing behind his eyes to explode.

"Where is my wife?"

The soldiers looked up at him.

"If we knew that, Oi wouldn'ta sent for you, sonny," Grunthor said curtly. "Now, don't go gettin' all peevish. Won't help."

Ashe stopped in front of Anborn. "I entrusted her to you, Uncle. You swore you would guard her with your life. She's gone, but you still seem to be here, unless you are a very hale ghost. What happened?"

Anborn lowered his eyes. Grunthor's brow darkened; he interposed himself between the Lord Cymrian and the General.

"Oi know you're upset, Ashe," he said quietly, but in a deadly tone. "You ain't the only one, but you're the only one 'ere who didn't walk through fire ta try an' save 'er. Don't start be'aving like yer grandparents, or you'll be lookin' for 'er alone. Ask yerself—would the Duchess want you browbeatin' the General? 'E's doin' a right fine job of it to 'imself without yer 'elp, thank you very much."

Ashe inhaled, his eyes locked with Grunthor's. Then he let his breath out slowly to try and calm the rising ire of the dragon in his blood; the wyrm was panicking at the loss of its treasure, threatening to rampage.

"I apologize," he said to Anborn, noticing for the first time the fresh scars and bandages. "I know you must have done everything you could. Tell me what happened."

The General did not speak for a long moment. Finally, when he did, Ashe noted that his voice sounded older than he had ever heard it.

"We were barely more than a day out from the dragon's lair when we were attacked in Gwynwood north of the old forest outpost of Penn-yg-Naral," he said stiffly. "I counted at least thirty of them altogether—and some masters of the stonebow. One of them killed Shrike; he was the first casualty, riding rear guard."

Ashe exhaled. "I am sorry, Uncle."

Anborn waved his hand in the air sharply, as if to deflect the sympathy.

"She held her own. They overwhelmed the guards, set her carriage alight, cornered her—sick as she was, she fought back. I almost had her out of there, but they took down my horse. And then, because of these cursed useless legs, there was no escape for her. She knew it, so she traded swords with me, knowing that to allow Daystar Clarion to fall into their hands might be fatal to the continent." Ashe nodded, his eyes gleaming.

Anborn's voice became hoarser. "She healed me, told me to tell you—both of you, and the children—that she loved you. Then she said some blasted words over me that put me to sleep, caused me to appear dead, until they were gone." He coughed to clear his throat. "But we saved the body of one of the bowmen—all the rest, our men, their men, Shrike—all of them burned to cinders in the fire that ensued.

"The man who took her carried the elemental sword of

air, Tysterisk. Though I have never seen it, I am certain of it—he commanded the wind with the power of a god. He torched the entire northern forest, nephew. The Invoker is probably still working to extinguish it. Unfortunate that your father has gone off to play with himself amid the ether; he might have been able to summon rain or quiet the flames before it burned a good piece of the continent." At the mention of Llauron, Anborn's eyes darkened.

"Did you see where they took her?"

"No. But I am certain it was into the fire. They came from the west, even though we were hit first from behind, from the east. I am the world's biggest fool for allowing her to fall into such a simple trap."

"None o' that," Grunthor said gruffly. "We got a bad enough enemy to fight without you giving 'im any free shots at yer arse."

"So where were they from?"

"No idea. I did not recognize them, and their garb was foreign."

Ashe began to pace the stone floor of the Great Hall. "Then they were probably heading to the sea, perhaps to Traeg or Windswere, or even down to Port Fallon."

"If they was takin' 'er to sea," Grunthor said. " 'Oo knows?"

"The *bowman* knows," Anborn said acidly, "which is why we saved his misbegotten body. We have to take it to Sepulvarta, to the Patriarch. He can wring the truth from his corpse, chase his spirit into the Vault of the Underworld and wrestle the information out of him—or so it's rumored."

Ashe paused in his pacing, looking doubtful. "Those may be folktales, Uncle," he said uncertainly. "Having worn that ring myself, though not as Patriarch, I recall nothing of that in the Office. I fear that may just be wild tales and wishful thinking."

Anborn snorted. "Perhaps. But I am willing to make the journey on the chance that it is not."

"I know you are," the Lord Cymrian said, running his

hand over the backs of the chairs that stood beneath the tallest windows at the end of the Great Hall, where he and Rhapsody had heard petitions for aid and supplications for relief every month for the last three years during Days of Pleas. "But you will not. I need you here."

The General's face blanched, then turned a livid shade of purple.

"It will take more men than you have in your army, nephew, to confine me so when the lady to whom I am sworn is—"

"Anborn," Ashe interrupted, his voice ringing with quiet authority and the deeper, more menacing tone of the dragon, "I do not question your willingness to do so, or your fealty to Rhapsody. But we know very little still about the motivations behind this. For Rhapsody's sake, and for the security of the continent, it is imperative that we make no missteps here. Calm and order must be maintained, and we must do all that we can before word of her disappearance comes out. Once it is known that she has been taken, chaos will break out. The ensuing uproar may compromise her safe return, or even her life."

He turned to Gerald Owen, who had quietly withdrawn and now stood at respectful attention in the doorway.

"Aside from those in this room, who else in Haguefort knows?"

"Only young Master Gwydion, m'lord."

Ashe considered for a moment, then turned back to Anborn.

"One of us must seek Rhapsody's return, while the other stays in Haguefort, keeping a watchful eye on the Alliance, maintaining order and as much secrecy as possible. Can we stipulate that I must go, and you must stay?"

Anborn glared at him balefully. The dragonesque pupils in Ashe's eyes expanded infinitesimally, but otherwise he did not move. Finally the General nodded, then stared down at the floor, his face suddenly older.

Ashe turned to Grunthor. "Will you accompany me to Sepulvarta, Sergeant?"

"Aye," Grunthor said. "And 'Is Majesty will be meetin' us there; Oi directed him so in the message Oi sent by bird."

Ashe's breathing loosened. "Good," he said in relief. "Achmed can track her by her heartbeat. Though it pains me to say it, he is our best chance to find her now." His attention returned to Anborn. "Grunthor, will you excuse us, please? Owen, please have another horse restocked and ready to go in ten minutes, with provisions for Sergeant-Major Grunthor as well."

"Yes, m'lord." The chamberlain waited respectfully for Grunthor to leave the hall, then quickly followed, closing the heavy door behind him.

Ashe walked slowly over to where his uncle sat, staring out the window. He stood in silence for a moment, studying the ancient Cymrian's face, watching the shadows flicker across it.

"I know what a sacrifice you are making, staying in this place yet again at my request," he said finally. "I know, too, that Roland and the rest of the Alliance will be safe in your hands."

Anborn said nothing, just continued to stare out the tall window.

"I also know that she has no better friend in this world than you, Uncle," Ashe said quietly. "And that if it were possible for anyone to have saved her, she would have been saved."

"Get out of here," Anborn said flatly.

Ashe waited a moment longer, then turned and left the Great Hall.

As he passed the Grand Staircase in the foyer, he saw Gwydion Navarne waiting on the steps, his shoulders square, but his face pale as death. He gestured to the boy to follow him.

When they reached the doors to the keep, Ashe strode past the guards and stopped at the top of the stairs that overlooked the roadway, where only a few short weeks before Rhapsody had eschewed the carriage he had provided for their journey to Yarim. He closed his eyes, remembering the look of comic horror on her face, trying to freeze the moment in his memory.

"I *will* bring her back, Gwydion."

The boy inhaled deeply but said nothing.

Ashe turned and regarded him thoughtfully.

"You've heard those words before, haven't you?"

Gwydion nodded. "It's what my father said when he rode out to the place where my mother's carriage—"

"I know."

"Do you?" the boy asked sarcastically, his voice rising with barely contained hysteria. "Do you know, Ashe? Did you know she was attacked by Lirin? Our friends, our neighbors, a race my father loved and trusted, who he counted as his friends. Did you know that they cut her head off? That they kept on sawing at her neck, even when my father's soldiers were shooting them point-blank? That she was still clutching Melly's baby shoes, even while—"

He stopped and broke down as Ashe pulled him into his arms.

"No one lies on purpose," Gwydion Navarne choked, his face buried in his guardian's shoulder. "My mother didn't know she would never come home when she told me she would. My father didn't know that he couldn't bring her back, except in—pieces. Rhapsody didn't know that she would not return to watch me shoot the albatross arrows she brought me from Yarim in an archery tournament. And you can't make any promises, either. Everyone leaves. And no one ever comes back. So don't tell me you *know*. You know *nothing*."

Ashe squeezed his shoulders, then pulled back and looked down into the youth's tearstained face.

"I know your grandmother," he said, smiling slightly. "I know that she will fight with everything she has to come back to us. I know she has an even better reason now, a child to protect, to live for. But I understand why you don't want to hear the words again. So instead of making you a promise you won't believe, I will ask you to make one for me, that I will."

Gwydion Navarne nodded slightly.

"Stand to serve Anborn," Ashe said, noting that the quartermaster was almost done outfitting the horses. "Stay with him, and keep his spirits up. Aid him in whatever he needs to keep order while I am gone. His task is critical; help him in it."

"I will."

For the first time since returning home, Ashe mustered a melancholy smile.

"He likes you a great deal, Gwydion, and I know you have a fondness for him too."

"Yes," the boy said. "I do."

"Cherish that bond," the Lord Cymrian said. "It is a precious thing, one that I always longed for in my heart, but that never came to pass. I am at least happy to see that he has found the ability to share it with you. He is a great man." He dropped his voice into a conspiratorial whisper. "A colossal pain in the privates, but a great man."

Gwydion Navarne did not smile in return.

"What I am asking of you is a man's task," Ashe said, signaling his readiness to Grunthor, who was standing beside the quartermaster, ready to mount up. "But you are up to it. You have been a man for a long time, even if you haven't the beard yet to prove it." He patted Gwydion's arm, then turned and jogged down the stairs.

Gwydion watched until the two men had ridden out of sight, east into the ascending sun, before breaking into sour, hidden tears that burned like acid.

# 36

## SEPULVARTA

The journey to Sepulvarta, under most conditions, took six days from Haguefort on horseback, assuming a minimal encampment and watch. Ashe and Grunthor, determining that to be too long, forwent any troop accompaniment, preferring to rely on their natural or ingrained abilities to go without sleep for extended periods and the well-supplied mail route along the trans-Orlandan thoroughfare, where fresh horses could be had every eighty leagues.

Grunthor had been unwilling to part with Rockslide. The flexibility of the horse trade meant individual mounts were lost, rotated out as need be, so he settled for the heaviest war horse in Haguefort's stable, a battle mare with dray bloodlines, apologizing to the animal as the quartermaster packed it.

"Poor ol' girl," he said, eyeing the heavy hocks and strong gaskins. "Gonna be putting you an' all the rest like you through your paces. You'll be glad Oi'm offa ya by day's end." He patted the animal's shoulder and neck. "Hmmm. Used ta say the same thing to ol' Brenda back at the Pleasure Palace."

The holy city, sometimes called the Citadel of the Star, lay to the southeast, a tiny, landlocked independent nation-state bordering Roland, Sorbold, and Tyrian. The religion of the Patriarch, known generally as the Patrician faith of Sepulvarta, had adherents in all three of its neighbors, but, while Roland was overwhelmingly Patrician, and most of Sorbold could be counted among the faithful, the vast majority of the Lirin citizens of Tyrian were followers of the Invoker and the practice of the Filids, the nature priests of Gwynwood.

Two days out from Sepulvarta, Grunthor and Ashe caught

sight of the towering minaret known as the Spire, a slender campanile that was one of the greatest architectural achievements in the Cymrian era, designed and built by an ancestor of Stephen Navarne. Broad as an entire city street at the base, it tapered up into a needle-like point a thousand feet in the air, crowned at the top with a silver star, the symbol of the Patriarchy. It was said that the pinnacle contained a piece of pure elemental ether, part of a fallen star that now glowed at the top of the Spire, sanctifying the basilica beneath it with the most powerful of the five elements, and lighting the way to the city.

It glowed in the clear air of the summer night, like a star that was tethered to the Earth.

Midmorning on the fifth day of travel, the two men arrived at the outskirts of the holy city. They had gone overland for much of the journey, but now caught up with the north-south roadway that led to the only entrance into the walled city. Grunthor dismounted reluctantly as they prepared to join the thoroughfare, shaking his head at the sight of the mass of humanity that was traveling the roadway, pilgrims and merchants, beggars and clergy, all wending their way to and from Sepulvarta.

"All the time we saved is gonna be lost if we don't get around this," he grumbled to Ashe, who was feeding the two pack horses they had brought with them, one of which carried the bowman's body.

The Lord Cymrian's appearance and demeanor had deteriorated in the intervening days. Worry was etched in the lines around his eyes, and his hair and face, unkempt and unshaven, were now hidden beneath the cloak of mist he had worn for so many years when he was a hunted man.

"What do you suggest?" he asked bitterly, his voice terse with shared frustration.

The Sergeant contemplated the question for a moment. Then he nodded to the horses.

"Hitch 'em to the next post we come to," the giant said.

Another half a league up the road they came to the barracks of the mail caravan, where the convoy quartered, picked up messages and supplies, and changed guard. Ashe nodded at the heavy metal posts outside of the barracks.

"Will those do?"

"Yep."

The two men secured the animals. Ashe nodded toward the well.

"I'll get water."

"All right," Grunthor said, shading his eyes while watching the thickening crowds of travelers clog the road to the holy city.

Once the horses and the men were refreshed, Ashe went to untie the pack animals.

"Wait," Grunthor instructed.

"Why?" Ashe asked.

"Ya wanted to get there faster?"

"Yes."

"Then cover yer ears, sonny."

Ashe opened his mouth to ask what Grunthor had planned, but before he could the giant Bolg threw his head back and screamed. It was an earsplitting, gut-tingling sound that struck panic in the hearts of men and horse alike; Ashe had forgotten Rhapsody's description of it, and Grunthor's tendency to employ it when need be.

The swirling crowd of travelers panicked, the horses among them rearing in fright, clearing the roadway or dashing off into the surrounding fields.

"Now we can go," Grunthor said, untying the reins.

They made their way quickly to the city gates, past the staring throng of unsettled pilgrims, into the teeming streets of Sepulvarta.

The Patriarch's manse was not difficult to find; they had both been to the basilica, the enormous cathedral that was the center of the Patrician faith. The manse where the head of the church resided was attached to the basilica, high on a hill near the city wall. It was a beautiful marble building, its engraved brass doors guarded by soldiers in bright uniforms.

The two men approached the guards, and were instantly rebuffed at spearpoint.

"What is your business?"

Ashe considered for a moment. Word that the Lord Cymrian was in Sepulvarta might compromise them, and ultimately Rhapsody, should the information come out. He knew how easily secrets carried on the wind.

"Please tell the Patriarch that he who supped with him on the way to the Cymrian Council three years past seeks an audience now."

The guards exchanged an amused glance, then laughed.

The travelers exchanged a glance as well. Grunthor rolled his shoulders as if working loose a cramp; Ashe saw that he was removing something from the massive bandolier that he wore on his back which held many of his prized collection of weapons. The guards were still in the throes of their merriment when the long bullwhip lashed, wrapping around their throats and the tips of their spears, pulling the two of them together, entwined in its leather cord.

With a great recoil of Bolg musculature, the Sergeant hauled the two encumbered guards into his proximity and glared down at them.

"P'raps you didn't 'ear my friend. 'E said please.' "

"As usual, you are the very pinnacle of subtlety, Sergeant," Ashe said. He addressed the fettered guards quietly. "Is Gregory still the Patriarch's sexton?"

The soldiers glared at him from within the coils of the bullwhip around their throats.

"Yes," one of them spat.

Ashe took the end of the bullwhip and disentangled one of the soldiers. When the guard reached for his knife, Ashe's hand locked on his wrist and dragged the soldier close enough to meet his direct gaze. His tone was polite.

"Kindly ask the sexton if he will meet with two weary travelers, one of whom is going to kill and eat your fellow guard here in the street if you don't return with him immediately." He shoved the soldier toward the door of the manse.

"Oh, now, *that* was subtle," Grunthor remarked as the soldier hurried off. "Glad for the lesson; thank you, Ashe. Though Oi must admit Oi don't partic'lary appreciate you makin' promises regarding who Oi will and will not eat." He eyed the guard like a side of beef. "Oi'm partial to Lirin myself."

"Who said anything about you?" Ashe said sourly, watching the doorway for the guard's return. "I am not only impatient, I'm hungry."

A moment later the ornate brass doors swung open, and a tall, thin, middle-aged man emerged.

"Lord Gwydion?"

Ashe and Grunthor looked at each other in surprise.

"Yes?"

"Please come with me, both of you."

Grunthor went to the pack horse and untied the bowman's body.

"Oi'm sure 'e woulda invited you, too, if 'e knew you were 'ere," he said comfortingly to the bagged corpse, slinging it over his shoulder.

The sexton led them into the rectory. The heat of the sun disappeared the moment they entered the building, a place of few windows and marble walls that blotted out the light completely, leaving a dark and dismal feel to the interior of the beautiful building. Heavy tapestries hung on the walls and ornate brass candlesticks held large wax cylinders that provided the only light. The pungent scent of incense did little to mask the sharp odor of mildew and stale air, made even more vile by the reek from the corpse they bore.

The sexton led them down long hallways, past sallow-faced men in clerical robes, finally stopping before a large carved door of black walnut, and opened it, gesturing for them to enter.

In the sparsely decorated meeting room beyond the door,

which had a large gilt star embossed on the floor and a pair
of enormous braziers, now cold, two men were standing
near a heavy walnut table at the top of a small rise of stairs.
The taller of the two was the Patriarch of Sepulvarta, his
muscular shoulders seeming somewhat bent with worry beneath his silver robes.

The other was the Bolg king.

"Sorry; I just arrived myself," Achmed said to Grunthor
as the two men came into the room. The sexton closed the
door behind them. "Didn't have a chance to get word back
to the guards that you were coming."

"No 'arm done," Grunthor said as he came to greet the
king and the Patriarch. "Ashe 'ere picked out someone 'e
wants ta kill and eat in the street for supper while we were
waiting. Should be entertainin'."

Ashe's face had lost its composure. He stared at Achmed,
terror lying deep in the recesses of his eyes, almost too
afraid to speak.

"Have you heard her heartbeat?" he asked nervously.

The Dhracian shook his head.

"Oh gods," Ashe whispered, his voice breaking.

The Patriarch sighed, then gestured to the table.

"Sit," he said to the three men. "You have traveled far,
and are weary in body and heart. Tell me what I can do for
you." He eyed the body on Grunthor's back. "Lay that on
the table."

"My wife is gone from the reach of my senses, Constantin," Ashe said as he sank into a heavy walnut chair. "She
was taken in an assault on her carriage in the wilds of
Gwynwood eleven days ago. There is no trace of her, and
before I send the combined armies of the Alliance out to
comb the countryside, I wanted to consult you and seek the
guidance of the Ring of Wisdom. I fear that calling attention
to her disappearance may jeopardize her safety, but as the
days pass, and there continues to be no sign, I fear inaction
more."

The Patriarch nodded his head, his broad brow knitted

with consternation. "Who is this?" he asked, pointing at the body on his council table.

"A witness that Grunthor carried from the burning forest. A bowman, apparently, who killed Shrike, Anborn's man-at-arms. He was in the company of the bastard who laid the trap for her. Anborn suspects whoever he is, he is in possession of an ancient sword known as Tysterisk, a blade imbued with the pure element of air. Like Kirsdarke, the blade I bear, the sword of elemental water, and Daystar Clarion, Rhapsody's weapon, the sword of starlight and pure fire, Tysterisk is legendary from the old world, but has no history on this continent. If this man really is in possession of Tysterisk, he must have come by it somewhere else in the world. And he isn't a Cymrian; if he were, I would know him."

"One can be from the Island and not a Cymrian, can one not?" the Patriarch asked, looking at the shroud-wrapped body.

Achmed and Ashe exchanged a glance. "I suppose," Ashe said after a moment. "But those on Serendair who did not refugee with Gwylliam did not enjoy the immortality that the Cymrians did. They fled to nearer places, not crossing the Prime Meridian as the Cymrian Fleets did, and lived out the remainder of normal life spans, or so the history texts say. The sword might have left the Island with a refugee, then been handed down, or lost, as Daystar Clarion was for a time before Rhapsody found it."

The Patriarch rose. "Let's have a look."

The other three men stood as well while the holy man carefully unwound the cords that bond the shroud around the corpse.

The stench of decompostion was strong as the linen was peeled back, but not as overpowering as it might have been; the body had been cured, like ham or fish, in the smoke of the burning forest, and so the flesh had dried to the bone, much of the bodily fluids evaporating in the ferocious heat.

"He died with his eyes open," the Patriarch said, more to

himself than aloud. "Good. He will have seen more."

Suddenly, as if catching a scent of fire on the wind, he looked up, then leaned over the decaying corpse and inhaled deeply, closing his eyes. He did it again, as the other men looked to each other. When he opened his eyes again, they narrowed.

"Can you smell it?" he asked softly.

"What?" Achmed asked.

The Patriarch passed a hand over the body, as if brushing away unseen currents of wind. "It's there, though faint, unmistakable. The malodor. F'dor."

For a moment, silence reigned in the council room of the manse. Ashe, who had begun to tremble immediately at the word, spoke first.

"No, Your Grace," he said haltingly.

The Patriarch turned away from him and looked to Achmed, whose body had tensed almost imperceptibly.

"For nineteen years of my life I carried such a taint within my own blood," he said, his voice deep and certain. "I would know that stench in any form. It is undeniable. Somewhere in this man's life he was touched by a demon spirit; most likely not a host, but perhaps a thrall to one."

"So somewhere there is another F'dor alive, walking the continent," Achmed said, trying to absorb the words, struggling to contain his blood rage, the racial hatred of F'dor that screamed like needles in the veins of every Dhracian. "Of this you are certain?"

"Yes. Or there was; where it currently resides is unknowable until we speak with this man."

Achmed turned to Grunthor. "Get back to Ylorc," he said tersely. "Guard the Child." The Sergeant nodded and turned toward the door, only to be stopped by the Patriarch's large, rough hand on his arm.

"Tarry but a moment, Sergeant," Constantin said gently. "I may have need of you until we have heard all that we can. Then you can go."

"Is it true," Ashe said desperately, trying to blot the image of Rhapsody in such a demon's clutches from his mind, "that you can see into the realm between life and death?"

The Patriarch said nothing, just passed his hand over the moldering flesh, thinking.

"Can you speak with the spirits of the dead, Your Grace?" Ashe asked again, more forcefully this time.

"No," Constantin said flatly. "It is not to the spirit of a dead man that I can speak, but rather to his blood." He looked askance at Achmed as he spoke.

"I assume you know that a few years ago, in the time of this world, I was a gladiator in the arena of Sorbold," he said, his thunderous voice now soft. "It was Rhapsody that dragged me from that life, brought me beyond the Veil of Hoen, to that place between life and death that you mentioned, Lord Gwydion, the realm of the Lord and Lady Rowan. I know you visited that place, too, in your hour of need, but you left upon being healed.

"I chose to stay. Had my mother not been of Cymrian descent, I would doubtless be dead now; I remained within that drowsy place of healing and wisdom for centuries, aging, growing old, though on this side of the Veil, only a few short months passed. Much of what I learned of blood, and of healing, I learned in that place.

"But not all of it. Some of it I learned in the arena. I was born with a tie to blood; in my youth, that bond made me a skilled and relentless killer. Now, in my old age, I try and use it for healing, to be a blood saver, not a blood letter." He ran a finger carefully down the gashes in the bowman's body.

"In the arena, I used to hear blood sing the death of my opponents. Sometimes it rang a story, sometimes not. Perhaps it was this cheering, rather than that of the crowd, which motivated me. It was too long ago to say adequately."

He caressed the body again. "This man is quite dead. He has little life left in his blood, if any, perhaps no more than a whisper or a hum left for me to trace. But I will endeavor to trace it, if that's what you wish, for Rhapsody. And to find out whatever clues we can to the origins and intents of this man's master. The dead know more than the living, but it is not easy to hear them when they tell what they know."

The three men nodded silently.

The Patriarch excused himself and returned a few moments later, clad in a white robe, rather than the silver one he had been wearing, and carrying a tear-shaped religious vessel known as a lachrymatory, a canopic urn, a cinerary bowl used to store burial ashes, and a censer of burning incense. He was followed by two acolytes bearing white linen cloths, which they spread on the table beneath the body.

"Whatever this man did in life, he is entitled to the same rituals in death as any who sought succor under my roof would be offered," he said, his deep tone denoting the refusal to hear dispute. He waited until the acolytes had lit the ceremonial braziers, then gestured for them to leave, closing the door behind them.

As silence took hold in the room, the Patriarch set the burning censer on the table, then uncorked the crystal ampulla that hung on a chain around his neck, a tiny phial with many facets that contained a blood-red liquid. He anointed his own eyes and ears with the contents of the phial, then the chest of the corpse above the heart. Then he made a countersign on his own lips.

"You will tell me who has taken the woman," he said, his deep voice ringing in the tones of a Namer, or a king.

Next, he opened the lachrymatory, and with great care poured a drop of the liquid into the rotting eye sockets of the body, quietly chanting a prayer. The liquid in the lachrymatory emitted a sound that hummed familiarly in Achmed's skin; after a moment he recognized it as Ocean's Tears, living water from the sea. He had one such drop in a protective case, hidden deep within the Loritorium where the Earthchild slept.

The body on the sheeted table seemed to swell slightly,

rehydrating, its shrunken flesh and stretched skin reinvigorating a bit.

The Patriarch then moved his robes aside about his waist. From a belt sheath he took forth two implements, a tool that looked like a burnishing roller and a curved ceremonial knife with a platinum blade.

As the three men watched, Constantin firmly sliced into the chest of the cadaver, not wincing at the black ooze that slid out, coating his hands. He sawed down the length of the dead man's chest, cutting through bone and all-but-dry viscera, then carefully wiped the bloody blade and his hands on the edge of the canopic urn, meticulously collecting every drop.

He set the knife down across the corpse's legs, then took the roller and pressed down on the chest, wringing the blood drop by drop from the rigid flesh.

More than an hour passed, then two, as the Patriarch continued to work, squeezing the blood from the body into the canopic urn. When he had collected enough to barely cover the bottom of the container, he held it up to his ear, closing his eyes.

No sound could be heard in the cavernous room; each man held his breath, lest the release of it disturb the Patriarch's ear.

Finally, Constantin looked up.

"There is very little of this man's soul left behind," he said quietly, reverently, his blue eyes gleaming sharply. "There is but one tie he had in life, to another heart that beat in time with his own. This man was a twin, and not just any twin, but a heart twin, someone whose physiology is so similar to his brother's that their pulses matched. It is that one fragile tie, thinner than the silk of a spider's web, that binds even the slightest bit of his soul to this realm; elsewise, if not for that connection, he would be beyond our reach in the Afterlife, or the Vault of the Underworld, more likely."

Achmed and Grunthor nodded, while Ashe, who had

grown gray with the effort to remain calm, merely listened.

"I can hear but one word in the clotted remains of this man's blood."

"What is that word?" Ashe asked nervously.

" 'Seneschal,' " the Patriarch replied.

"Seneschal?" the Lord Cymrian repeated. "Like a regent, or a castle protector?"

The Patriarch shrugged. "Sometimes it is a judge, someone who is appointed by a sovereign to oversee justice," he said. "Do you know of any in the Alliance?"

"No," Ashe said. "For a short time, Tristan Steward was a seneschal of the House of Remembrance, but of course that is gone now, burnt to ashes and being rebuilt."

The Patriarch held up his hand "Shh," he said suddenly. "There is another whisper, even fainter, perhaps something that he did not hear himself, but that was heard by his twin."

The three men held their breath again.

From the depths of the rotting corpse's sundered chest, a tiny puff rose, like a wisp of smoke. The words were so slight as to be almost inaudible, but they were spoken in a woman's voice, a voice they all recognized.

*Stay away from me, Michael. I may die, but I will take you with me.*

"Michael?" Ashe demanded. "I know of no one named Michael." He turned to the Bolg, whose eyes were locked, a look of disbelief passing between them.

The Patriarch raised his hand for silence. He took the roller in hand and laid on again, wringing the blood from the body. Like a sigh, the words came forth, infinitesimal, fragile.

*Perhaps not to your face, Michael, the Wind of Death.*

"*Hrekin,*" Grunthor sword softly.

"The Wind of *Death?*" Ashe demanded, terror rising in his voice. "Is that not the evil soldier she was trying to escape from in the old land when you two—"

"Yes," Achmed said shortly.

"And he has her?"

"Apparently," spat the Dhracian, his voice frosty. He turned to the Patriarch, whose white robes were now spattered with dark blood. "Where? Ask him where?"

The men waited in anxious silence as the Patriarch posed the question. He held the canopic urn up to his ear, but whatever story was in the blood was so faint that he could not hear it. Finally, the holy man met their gaze and, seeing the horror boiling beneath the surface, he lifted the bowl to his lips and drank. The Ring of Wisdom on his hand glowed brightly as he swallowed.

He clutched the table then, steadying himself against the nausea and the shock that took him into its clutches, his face going as white as the upturned edges of his beard. Constantin put his hands over his ears, trying to keep the faint sound from escaping.

"On the seacoast," he stammered, clutching the table again. "North of Port Fallon."

Ashe and Achmed turned simultaneously and started for the door, only to be stopped in their tracks by the ragged voice of the Patriarch.

"Wait." He steadied himself against the table, breathing shallowly. "Do not leave this place before you hear me, and before you have a chance to answer my question. You owe me this."

The two sovereigns waited in silence, along with the Sergeant-Major, for the Patriarch to recover. It took but a moment. After a few deep breaths the color returned to Constanin's face. *He has doubtless inhaled or ingested more than his share of blood over the years in the arena,* Achmed thought, watching the elderly man straighten his wide shoulders, then cross to the summoning bell and pull the cord.

The two acolytes returned a heartbeat later.

"Ritually burn the body," the Patriarch instructed. "Place the ashes in the cinerary bowl, and scald the table with holy water." He turned back to Ashe and the Bolg. "Come with

me to the basilica. If there is even a breath of life remaining
in this man, I don't want to speak in front of him, for just
as he was able to hear what his brother heard, even in death,
so it might work the other way."

# 37

𝕿he Great Basilica in Sepulvarta was the centerpiece of
the city, with towering walls of polished marble and an
overarching dome that was taller than any in the known
world. The myriad colors and patterns of the mosaics that
graced the floor and ceiling, along with the exquisite gilt-
work on the frescoed walls and the windows fashioned in
colored glass, all contributed to its grandeur, but it was the
sheer height and breadth of it that made it the masterpiece
of all the elemental temples, great architectural marvels left
over from the Cymrian era, still standing long after that
empire had fallen and crumbled to dust.

The Patriarch led the three men up a cylindrical rise in
the center of the sanctuary to a plain, stone table edged in
platinum that formed the altar of the basilica. On this altar,
the body of his predecessor had been ritually burned amid
the flowers and feathers that were the burial tradition for
clerics of the faith of Sepulvarta.

When the Patriarch was in the center of the sanctuary,
standing directly beneath the aperture in the towering ceiling
through which the Spire could be seen, he spoke. His words
did not echo in the vast hollowness of the mighty cathedral,
but rather remained close to the ears of those who heard
them.

"Tell me of this man, this Wind of Death," he said, his
deep voice resonating but not carrying. "Who is he to you
that you know of him?"

The three men looked at one another. Ashe spoke first.

"No one," he said, his eyes red with worry and lack of

sleep. "I know little of him; Rhapsody does not speak of him much. He was someone who tortured her in the old world; I know this because I have held her through the nightmares of him, dreams that were horrific to observe, and so I am certain they were reflective of one of the worst times in her life. But I do not know him."

The Patriarch absorbed the Lord Cymrian's words, then turned to the Bolg.

"Yet you did know him, or of him," he said, watching them with the bird-of-prey eyes that had served him well in the arena.

Achmed exhaled. "He and I served the same master," he said, weighing his words carefully. "In his case, his servitude was voluntary. Mine was not."

"You were allies, then?"

"Never," Achmed spat. "Neither allies nor enemies. He was filth, chaotic in his nature, impulsive and cruel. I knew of his actions, but I was in no position to stop them, nor of a bent to do so even if I had been able. At that time all I sought was the return of my name, which our master owned, and with it my freedom. It is true, however, that Rhapsody was on the run from him when we came across her. By taking her with us, away from the old land, we thought we had spared her from him. Since he had not crossed the sea with the fleets, we had every reason to believe him dead, until that corpse spoke his name a moment ago."

"You as well?" the Patriarch asked Grunthor.

"Yep. Oi only knew 'im by reputation. 'E was ruthless and talented at destruction. O' course, that made 'im a bit of an 'ero to the Bolg and the Bengards, my people."

"I had other reasons to believe him dead," Achmed said, staring at the distant ceiling above him. "There was a hero, the real kind, in the old land, a half-Lirin, half-human soldier called MacQuieth, now long dead himself."

"I have seen his name," the Patriarch said. "It is inscribed on an altar in the water basilica of Abbat Mythlinis in Avonderre, on the coast where the first Cymrian fleet landed. I attended a service in my honor there upon my investiture."

"My mother was descended of his line," Ashe said quietly.

"History says that it was MacQuieth who killed Tsoltan, the F'dor that was the Waste of Breath's master as well as my own," Achmed continued, his voice tight with the strain of containing his anger. "I could only assume that in order to get to Tsoltan, MacQuieth would have had to have gone through Michael, would have killed him first. They were known to be bitter enemies."

"If he was as unstable and cowardly as you say, perhaps he deserted," Ashe said tensely. "There is no reason to believe that a man who tortures women and kills children for the sheer enjoyment of it would hold to his post when the tide of the war began to turn."

Achmed waved his hand impatiently. "Perhaps. But how he survived is unimportant. What is important is that there is another F'dor loose, one that inhabits a host with a propensity for chaos, rape, and murder, without the long worldview of the last one we dealt with. If he really does carry Tysterisk, the situation is even more dire, because that would give him the power of both wind and fire. What before was fear for Rhapsody has now become a fight for the survival of the whole continent. I cannot even begin to put words around how bad this is."

The eyes of the Patriarch maintained a calm and steady gaze. "You are incorrect that it does not matter how he survived. It may be critical for several reasons. If he is the host of a demon, under normal circumstances, he would have been subsumed to its will long ago; that is how F'dor function. Each of them is a distinct entity, an individual in an unholy pantheon that was born at the beginning of time. Thus they are limited in number, unless they discover another way to propagate."

The holy man fell silent for a moment; the others looked awkwardly away, knowing that he himself had been the product of such a breeding. He looked up again quickly.

"If a demon has taken him over, what had been his personality should have been completely subjugated to its will," he continued. "Since he came after Rhapsody, this does not seem to be the case. This is cause for some concern. There must be something untoward, something different about this symbiotic relationship. That worries me.

"Moreover, it causes me to wonder what sort of ties he has in this land. Clearly your ties to him are but weft thread, not the warp."

"What do you mean?" Ashe asked.

The Patriarch studied the Lord Cymrian. "Did you see the Weaver when you were in the realm of the Rowans?" he asked finally.

"No," Ashe said. "Or if I did, I don't remember. I recall very little from that time; I was too badly injured. My only memories are of fragments of faces, and hazy, pain-filled dreams."

"The Weaver is one of the manifestations of the element of Time," the Patriarch said seriously. "Those who know the lore of the Gifts of the Creator generally only count five, the worldly elements, but there are others that exist outside the world. One of them is the element of Time, and Time in pure form manifests itself in many ways. The World Trees, Sagia, the Great White Tree, and the three others that grow at the birthplaces of the elements, are manifestations of Time. As is the Weaver. She appears as a woman, or so it seems, though you can never recall what her face looks like after you see her, no matter how much you study it at the time. She sits before a vast loom, on which the story of Time is woven in colored threads, in patterns, the warp, the weft, the lee.

"The Weaver is the manifestation of Time in history," he continued. "She does not intervene in the course of events, merely records them for posterity. It is a fascinating tapestry that she plaits, intricate in its connectivity. All things, all beings, are threads in the fabric; it is their interconnectivity that weaves what we know as life. Without those ties that the threads have to one another, there is merely void; absence of life. And in those ties, there is power.

"Those ties bind soul to soul, on Earth and in the Afterlife. It is the connection that is made in this life that allows one soul to find another in the next. This is the means by which love lasts throughout Time. But other things last throughout Time as well.

"Sometimes the ties that are forged in enmity are as strong as those woven in love. Souls that have the need to finish business that is steeped in hatred can transcend many things, many realities, if the tie is strong enough. From what you have told me, none of you have the connection that would give you any power over this man, if he is still man, though more likely he is man-in-demon. The tie is not strong enough, the weft thread of the fabric, where lives cross, but don't intertwine.

"But the tie between him and Rhapsody, that is different. There is a direct connection there. This makes her both more powerful, and more vulnerable where he is concerned. It is the warp thread, the most basic of connections. And so she will therefore be more equipped to fight him than either of you. If she has been unable to prevail—as it seems is the case—there is little you will be able to do against him."

"Nonetheless, I will give my life, and afterlife, if need be, in the effort," Ashe said. "Thank you for your help, Your Grace. Excuse me now; I have to find my wife." He walked to the stairs that led up to the sanctuary, only to be stopped by the deep voice of the Patriarch.

"Wait. You have not answered *my* question."

"What is it?" Ashe asked, struggling to maintain his patience.

"What was decided by the Scales?" the holy man asked. "I have had no word from Sorbold on the outcome of your discussions."

"I would be interested to know that as well," Achmed said.

"They weighed in favor of the Mercantile," Ashe replied.

"The Mercantile?" the Patriarch demanded. "Who?"

"The Hierarch of the western guilds, a man named Talquist," the Lord Cymrian said. "He seemed levelheaded and considerate; he will rule as regent for now, by his own choice, until the period of a year passes, at which time, if he is still confirmed by the Scales, he will assume the throne as emperor." He stopped when he saw the Patriarch's face go pale. "Your Grace? What's wrong?"

"Talquist?" the holy man said softly. "Are you certain?"

"What disturbs you about him?" Achmed asked.

The Patriarch sat down unsteadily on the chair at the top of the sanctuary. "You could not have brought me worse news," he said to Ashe, his deep voice absent of the power it usually had.

"Why?" Achmed demanded. "Tell us why."

The Patriarch stared out the aperture in the basilica's ceiling at the Spire rising into the endless blue above him.

"Talquist is a merchant in only the kindest usage of the word," he said finally, watching the wisps of cloud pass overhead. "He is a slave trader of the most brutal order, the secret scion of a fleet of pirate ships, which trade in human booty, selling the able-bodied into the mines, or worse, the arenas, using the rest as raw materials for other goods, like candles rendered from the flesh of the old, bone meal from the very young. Thousands have met their deaths in the arenas of Sorbold; I cannot even fathom how many more have found it in the mines, or the salt beds, or at the bottom of the sea. He is a monster with a gentleman's smile and a common touch, but a monster all the same."

"And yet the Scales confirmed him," Ashe said. "I witnessed it myself."

"Why did you not say something before you left?" Achmed asked the Patriarch incredulously. "If you knew this was a potential outcome of the selection process, why did you not intervene?"

"Because it is not for me to decry the Scales," Constantin answered. "They are what confirmed me to my position in the first place. How could I decree their wisdom to be faulty without invoking a paradox?" He sighed heavily. "Besides, to acknowledge my past in the arena would be to open the realm of the Rowans to scrutiny that would not be welcome there. And finally, he was not the only man with blood on his hands who was in the running. If I were to decry everyone I thought unfit to be emperor, Sorbold would be a leaderless state. Truth be told, I was hoping they would decide to disband into city-states, but the Scales decided otherwise."

He rose and put his hand on Ashe's shoulder.

"I shall intercede with the All-God for your wife, and your child, each day," he said. "As well as for your efforts to find this Wind of Death, which now is the Wind of Fire. I pray that, as I have undergone a change of heart in my time behind the Veil of Hoen, Talquist too will experience such a transformation. Perhaps the fact that he did not immediately demand coronation as emperor is a sign of that."

"I doubt it," Achmed said. "In my experience, men who had a thirst for blood and power only grow thirstier the more they are fed it. You may be the only exception I have ever met."

The three men thanked the Patriarch and descended the stairs together, leaving him beneath the aperture of the Spire, staring into the sky.

At the door of the basilica, Grunthor grasped Ashe by the shoulder.

"Child?" he demanded. "Ya didn't mention this; why?"

"Leave for Ylorc at once," Achmed ordered. "There is another Child who is our responsibility, a far more grave one than finding Rhapsody. Or Michael." He turned to Ashe.

"If we hunt for them together, we have a better chance of finding her," he said, "though I still do not hear even a hint of her heartbeat. No matter how far she has been from me, ill or injured, even within the earth, I have never lost the sound of it until now. I suspect that he has killed her;

that would be like him. So though I know you will be seeking her, blind to everything else, understand that I am seeking *him* now. If we find him, we might at least be able to discover what he did with her. Are we clear on the distinction?"

"Yes," Ashe said shortly.

"All right then." He pulled Grunthor aside to confer with him.

"Back in Ylorc is a woman named Theophila, from a tribe of nomadic artisans known as the Panjeri. She has access to the forge and is to be given anything she needs for her work on the Lightcatcher. She also has a temper. Don't anger her—I've searched for the last year and a half to find her."

Grunthor eyed him doubtfully. "Yes, sir."

"Travel well," Achmed said. "I'll bring Rockslide back when I return."

The Bolg Sergeant shook his head. "Bring back the Duchess, sir. Don't get lost in the blood rage or the fact that it's Michael, and forget who we're *really* missin' 'ere."

Achmed and Ashe were already gone.

## JIERNA TAL

𝕴f there is nothing else, m'lord, I will be going back to the Chancery now," Nielash Mousa said to the new regent, bowing slightly with deference.

Talquist looked up from the heavy mahogany table and smiled from among the depths of the sheaves of papers. His swarthy face glowed in the dusky light of afternoon, which was darkening outside the window in the advent of a coming rainstorm.

"No, nothing in the world, Your Grace," he said warmly. "I think all is well on its way to normalcy again. Thank you for everything you have done to facilitate this transition."

The exhausted benison smiled as well. "It has been my pleasure. Please send for me if you have any need, m'lord."

"I shall. Now go home and get some rest. What I need is

you hale and healthy, and you won't be if you don't look after yourself."

"Very well. Good evening," said the Blesser of Sorbold, bowing slightly again. He turned and followed his retinue from the enormous library.

Talquist watched him go, then returned to his papers.

After a few moments, a man slipped in through the open double doors, closing them quietly behind him.

The regent looked up, amusement in his eyes. He reached for the Canderian brandy that was breathing in the open crystal decanter on the table next to his paperwork and pointed to an empty glass. The man shook his head, declining the drink.

"I suppose I should actually have said those words to you," Talquist said, refilling his own glass. "Thank you for everything you have done to facilitate this transition."

Lasarys blinked nervously, his eyes unused to the light.

"You are welcome, sire," he stammered.

"You seem fretful, Lasarys. Why?"

The sexton tried to meet the dark eyes of the regent, but found it too draining. "I—am merely tired, m'lord. It has been a difficult few weeks."

"Ah. I see." Talquist sat back and crossed his hands over her stomach. "No doubt you have had to follow the benison about, tending to the guests of state—are they all gone now?"

"Yes, m'lord. The Diviner left this morning."

Talquist glanced out the window to the courtyard below, where the column of the late empress was running drills.

"Indeed. He and I were up quite late in discussions with Beliac. So you are now relieved of your duties as host, Lasarys. You may return to your dark hole within Night Mountain and tend to your beloved cathedral. The Living Stone you harvested from it for me was invaluable in achieving my ends; thank you."

The sexton looked ill. Talquist did not look at him.

"What is the matter, Lasarys? Are you having second thoughts? It's a bit late, wouldn't you say?"

"N—no, m'lord, no second thoughts," the sexton said quickly, wringing his hands.

Talquist rose and came to him then, laying his heavy hands on the trembling priest's shoulders.

"I know you love that dark cathedral as if it were your own mother," the regent said softly, his voice caressing every syllable. "And that whittling off even the smallest of pieces of animate clay was like cutting off your own mother's breast. You don't have to make excuses, Lasarys; I know your heart. I learned much about you when I was your acolyte. And I wish that I could promise you that it was the last time you should ever have to endure such a thing, but there is no need to lie now. I am emperor; or will be in a year's time." He patted the priest's cheek. "Now go back to Terreanfor, and tend to it as lovingly as you always do. While you are skulking about in the dark, begin looking for other places from which to harvest. It's better to begin secreting it away now, rather than have to kill one of the Living Stone trees, or the elephants! Ah, how I love those elephants, those dark, glowering monsters. Let us spare them until the very end, shall we?"

The sexton nodded, unable to speak coherently.

Talquist smiled. "Good. Summer is high, but it will end in time. The earth will go dormant, life settling underground to hide, hibernate, as we hide and hibernate. But in spring, Lasarys! Ah, spring."

He strolled onto the balcony, whistling merrily.

# 38

## THE CAULDRON, YLORC

Omet was up all night, working feverishly.

Shadows leapt madly across the rough stone walls of his chamber within the second wing of the guard barracks; Omet had always preferred living among the soldiers to sharing a guest quarter with Shaene, mostly because, in addition to snoring and having a penchant for the petty, Shaene was a hired artisan, temporarily housed in Ylorc for the duration of the stained-glass project. Omet had every intention of staying here.

*Somewhere in those mountains greatness is taking hold,* Rhapsody had said to him three years ago when they parted at the border of Yarim and Ylorc, following his rescue from the guildmistress's foundry. *You can be a part of it. Go carve your name into the ageless rock for history to see.* From that moment he had been inspired to, in fact, do just that, rather remarkable given that a few days before he could not imagine his future past the next turn of the day, the next in an never-ending cycle of watching the ovens and kilns.

And it was coming to pass. The Bolg had made him at home, as much as they were able, had taken him in as one of them, not as a distrusted stranger; he knew the rarity of his good fortune, and understood what made a half-Lirin woman like Rhapsody, so utterly out of place in the rough land of cannibalistic demi-humans, love the place and the people as much as she did her own race in Tyrian.

He had the same unquenchable desire to spare the place, and its king, from whatever destruction Esten was planning. That desire fought with another strong urge.

The urge to run as fast and as far as he could away from the Cauldron and never look back.

But even as the rushes of panic swept through his blood, he knew there was no wisdom in flight.

After all, sooner or later, everything made its way to Esten.

He had taken one risk, however. In between stretches of drawing, to rest his hand, he had jotted careful notes, written in a bad combination of phonetically spelled Bolgish and the common tongue when necessary, detailing what he had seen the guildmistress do in the king's absence, as well as recording his own actions, and the place in which he had hidden the original drawings.

More of Rhapsody's words came back to him now as he sweated in the light of the lantern, copying and blotting, copying and blotting.

*Don't limit the uses of your skill and imagination. I believe that you could become one of the great artisans of the Rebuilding.*

Omet held the parchment he had been working on since leaving Gurgus up to the lanternlight. He chuckled at the irony of what she had said.

The plans he had redrawn were an impressive copy of the original, even in his own modest estimation. He had rendered them on pieces of ancient parchment that had been discovered, in a casket full of rice, on one of the lower levels of the vaults in Gwylliam's library, sealed with an ancient wax mark; undoubtedly they had once been documents, but the intervening centuries had caused the ink to dry up and disappear as if it had never been quilled into the paper.

Having found a convincing canvas on which to scribe his deception, he devoted the remainder of his waking hours to the careful copying of just enough of the elements of the original plans to, with any luck, be convincing. With a careful hand he drew lines of scale where the piping schematic had been, deleting all references to the wheel, leaving only the very basic diagrams of where the colored glass was supposed to go.

He prayed it would be enough.

Once he put the falsified plans in Esten's hands, it would be an endless game of cat and mouse, trying to stay out of her sight as much as possible without attracting her notice of his absence. Thinking about it made Omet's skin erupt in cold beads of sweat.

She had unconsciously given him until the morning to produce the plans, which would afford him the opportunity to stop by the forges and dry the ink on them. He pushed back his chair nervously, blotting the parchment one last time, then slipped quietly out of his room and down the corridor to the tunnels that led to the great forges.

Fearing that Esten and some of the others might be touring the kilns and glass ovens, he climbed farther down the stone tunnels and passageways to the great searing inferno at the base of the mountain, where the steelworks lay.

The heat was searing in this place of melting ore and glowing hot metal. Two separate forges blasted day and night, a commercial smithy that produced the standard weapons sold via trade agreement to Roland and Sorbold, and a specialty forge that produced Achmed's original designs: *svardas*, the heavy but well-balanced circular throwing knives with three blades; short, compact crossbows with extra recoil for use in the tunnels of Ylorc; split arrowheads and heavy darts for blowguns, balanced and designed for deeper penetration; midnight-blue steel drawknives that were really razor-edged hooks that replaced the makeshift close combat weapon of many Bolg; and, of course, the disks of the king's own cwellan.

It was this forge alone that was allowed to run hot enough to shape the blue-black alloy of rysin and steel.

And since Esten had been promised tools of her own design to be manufactured in his forges, no doubt she would be given access to this heavily guarded metalworks, whose source of flame was a vent to the fire that burned at the heart of the Earth itself.

The prickles of cold panic rose from his feet again. He looked past the half-dozen tiered galleries of anvils and fires, worked by three thousand Bolg at each shift, stoking the flames, smithing the ore, forging the steel, running the damper system that vented the heat and soot out of the mountain in summer, or recirculated it, filtered, through the tunnels of Ylorc in winter for heat. Satisfied that no one was watching him, he unfurled the scroll and allowed it a moment's exposure to the searing wind from the forges, then quickly wrapped it in leather again before it could ignite.

He was under siege, though he did not believe at the moment the enemy that threatened him was aware of it.

What had brought Esten to the mountain was not in doubt for him. She was here to extract revenge. How she planned to do it was unclear, but her means of getting inside Achmed's impenetrable mountain had been, like all her machinations, flawlessly plotted, brilliantly planned. The wolf was in the henhouse, and the farmer had unwittingly invited her in and held the door for her.

It would not end well.

It was only a matter of time.

*Here's for it, then,* he thought as he made his way up the dark corridors to the towering crag of Gurgus that would one day be made into a Lightcatcher.

But not while Esten was still within the mountain.

He only hoped he could live long enough to explain to the Firbolg king what he had done.

Esten waited in the wind at the top of a bluff, watching for the mail caravan to arrive. The sun was setting over the Krevensfield Plain, reflecting on the clouds and the waving fields of grass, blanketing them with gold that turned red at the edges, a warmth that hinted ominously of things to come.

The sweet sensations of summer hung heavy in the air around her. Esten allowed herself the momentary pleasure of closing her eyes and breathing them in: the smell of the wind on which rain would come soon; the odor of verdant grass, bursting with life, arching toward the descending sun in a kind of joyful agony; the relentless whine of insects, the ever-cooling gusts of air, the pinpricks of distant light in farms and outposts as lanterns were lit to battle the coming darkness.

A moment was all she allowed herself. Esten opened her eyes again quickly, watching for the mail caravan that was arriving from Yarim. She pulled her knees up to her chest, thinking, allowing her mind to wander down metaphysical alleyways where death, ever-present, lurked, waiting.

It had been six days since the Bolg king had brought her to this place, and six days that he had been gone.

After almost an hour, the caravan pulled into sight on the steppes beyond the rocky hills where she lurked. In the lead were the first third of the two score and ten soldiers that accompanied it, followed by four wagons and a coach, with the balance of the forces deployed around them.

Following the official caravan was the informal convoy, the travelers who sought the protection of the soldiers and each other, believing that safety did lie in numbers as well as in arms. There was a ragtag group with this particular caravan; a few farmers traveling to or returning from market, some pilgrims on their way back from holy sites.

And one familiar business associate.

While the caravan was putting in to the outpost at Grivven Tower, the guildmistress slipped quietly down from the foothills, clad in her simple black trousers, shirt, and summer cloak, a dark blue shawl over her close-cropped hair, blending in with the growing darkness. She hung back in the shadows, waiting patiently until the convoy dispersed for the night, the soldiers retiring to the guest barracks, the stragglers making camp. Then she stepped silently out into the moonlight long enough for Dranth to find her.

He saw her right away, came to her quickly, following her into the shadows of the cliffs, carrying a small chest wrapped in burlap and a large sack. When she had determined their meeting place to be safe, she inclined her head; the guild scion nodded in return.

"You are looking very well, Guildmistress," he said quietly. "Is everything unfolding as you planned?"

"Everything," Esten said confidently. "It was easier than I could have imagined to infiltrate the Panjeri; they took me in without question. I would have never guessed my father's upbringing would prove so useful to me one day. And the Bolg king is every bit as obsessed with his project as we had heard from the Hierarch in Yarim. A good thing that is; without the distractions he would be more formidable than I ever could have imagined. But between the deaths of the Sorbold royal family, the colored ceiling he wanted blown into the pinnacle of a mountain crag, and whatever took him away unexpectedly, he is not concentrating. He will be caught completely unaware."

"Good." Dranth handed her the burlap-wrapped chest. "Here is the picric acid you asked for—do be cautious, Guildmistress. Remember to keep it wet, so it is merely flammable; when it dries—"

"I am well aware. Thank you, Dranth. Did you perform the tests on it that I asked of you?"

"Yes. Glass, being a liquid, holds it in a liquid state, if it is applied after the annealing. Until it is dried by intense heat again. The remaining acid is housed in green barrels and will be delivered by the caravan at sunrise."

"Very good." Esten set the chest down, then reached into the folds of her garments.

"In exchange, here are the maps I've drawn, the stockpiles I've noted, and my analysis of the Bolglands' infrastructure, as well as their obvious treasury, manpower, armed capabilities, and the like," she said, handing the papers to Dranth. "Disseminate them. For the right price, of course."

"Yes, Guildmistress."

"They are still keeping a tight rein on me, but I have managed to charm one of them, an idiot artisan from Canderre, into bringing me what I need or describing some of the areas that I have not been cleared to go into yet. Though he has yet to tell me where the Bolg king sleeps."

The guild scion's face twisted with a hint of concern, ironic as it was.

"Do you want us to infiltrate the mountain, mistress? So that you are not alone?"

Esten smiled wickedly.

"Do not fret about me, Dranth. When the Bolg king finally returns, I will be the only one left alive in all of the godforsaken mountain."

She waited until his shadow had been swallowed by the night before climbing the misty hilltop, being buffeted by an insistent wind as she pulled herself over the ridges, and making her laden way across the dark mountain fields of rock and scrub to the warmth and light of the Cauldron once more.

# 39

## THE NORTHERN SEACOAST

The tide was rising again, Rhapsody knew.

The first time it had happened she had panicked, had believed for more than a few moments that she would drown as the tidal cave filled to the top with caustic brine, churning relentlessly in circular torrents, spinning violently out with the current as it flooded.

She had been asleep that first time, drowsing in exhausted half-slumber on the one solid spot in the cave, the ledge onto which she had crawled. Her hands were free; it had taken but a moment and the true name of corn silk—*tesela*—to soften the rope that had been wrapped cruelly tight around her wrists to the point where she could break it.

The crossbow bolt that the archer had fired had lodged in the leather sword belt at her waist; by sheer luck it had hit the joint between the belt and the scabbard, missing her kidney, but nonetheless leaving a wicked bruise and a deep scratch in its passing, both of which stung to the point of agony in the swirling salt water. She had taken the belt off and was working the bolt loose; without her sword, the tip was the only sharp metal implement that was on her when she fell.

Despite her chanting, she had hit the water harder than she realized at the time. The only mercy in her plummet was that she missed the rocks; between the fall, the impact, the seawater, and the lack of balance she had already been experiencing, she had been all but unconscious when swept into the tidal cave by the incoming tide.

After the first time the tide fell with the ebbing current, leaving the cave half full of water breaking against the back wall, she had taken the opportunity to feel around, still virtually blind in the half-light. There were cracks in the back wall of the cave through which gusts of air could be felt while the tide was low, but little else. In addition, she could see the ocean current that swirled in the cave, that had caught her and pulled her inside, sparing her from being battered against the rocks; it was a spiral current with a cross-undertow. She knew that it would be almost impossible to bear up against it if she tried to swim out, being compromised in both strength and mass. *I have to find fresh water,* she thought, her mind fuzzy from exhaustion, *and food. If I grow any weaker, I will die in here.*

*But first I must sleep, and in sleeping, heal.*

The slumber into which she had fallen was so deep, so dreamless, that when the first wave broke over her she didn't feel it.

It was not until a rolling breaker doused her, drenched her again, that she woke with a start, fear permeating her to the depths of her being.

The tide turned quickly, rushing into the cave with a force that frightened her even more. Rhapsody was submerged almost instantly, again being battered about the cave but never swept out of it, held in place by a relentless current. She braced her now-free hands against the rocky ceiling as the waves bobbed her up to it, tilting her head back to keep her eyes and nose out of the brine.

As she hovered in the water, feeling the slimy rush of seaweed pass her, she slapped it aside, trying to remember her father's words, spoken to her as he taught her to swim as child in a deep pond a lifetime before.

She called on the memory now, trying to make use of the lore to calm her racing heart.

*Too deep,* she thought. *It's too deep.*

*Stop flailing.*

Her father's voice rang in her memory, as clear and authoritative as it had all those years before.

She stopped flailing, remaining motionless, letting the current lift her.

The water of the pond had been cold, as the sea was cold; green scum floated on the surface as the seaweed floated past her now. She could not see the bottom of the pond, just as she could not fathom the depth of the cave.

*Father?* she whispered, her lips tasting of salt.

*I'm here, child. Move your arms slowly. That's better.*

*It's so cold, Father. I can't stay above it. It's too deep. Help me.*

*Be at ease,* her father had said. *I'll hold you up.*

Rhapsody took a quick breath, and felt the tightness in her lungs slacken a little. The memory of her father's smiling face, his beard and eyebrows dripping, rivulets of water rolling down his cheeks, rose up before her mind's eye as it had from the surface of the pond so long ago. It was an image she had concentrated on before, in the belly of the Earth, making her way along the Root of Sagia, the World Tree, in a place as foreign to her soul as this one.

*The water won't hurt you, it's the panic that will. Stay calm.*

*It's so deep, Father.*

A spray of water as he spat it out. *Depth doesn't matter, as long as your head is above it. Can you breathe?*

*Ye-e-ss.*

*Then never mind how deep it is. Concentrate on breathing; you'll be fine. And don't panic. Panic will kill you, even when nothing else wants to.*

Rhapsody closed her eyes as another wave crested over her face.

*Panic will kill you, even when nothing else wants to.*

*No,* she thought, *I will not panic. I didn't throw myself off a cliff only to be vanquished by something that means me no harm.*

She tried to float on her back, and managed it for a while, bracing herself against the cave walls with one hand, holding her other elbow close against her side to minimize the exposure of the grazed skin to the salt. She cleared her mind, listening to the rhythm of the flooding current, the rising tide, and heard a music in the water, a cadence and tone she could concentrate on to maintain her calm.

After time uncounted, the current ebbed, and the tide fell again.

As the ledge became visible Rhapsody contemplated her options. She thought to call to Elynsynos, the dragon whose lair had not been far off when she was taken by Michael's men; but discarded the notion, knowing that the beast could not sense her through water. Her eyes stung with salt, knowing that Merithyn, Elynsynos's lover, had perished for that reason.

She had also considered shouting the Kinsman call for aid as once she had done, summoning Anborn to her side in her hour of need. But Michael was master of the element of air; if the wind betrayed her, he would find her.

There was nothing to be done but to use her own wits, her own survival skills.

No one could come to her aid but herself alone.

Rhapsody made her way to the ledge once more and stared down into the green swirling water.

Below the surface she could see movement, a slithering motion that made her skin go cold.

*Snakes?* she thought hazily. *No, eels.* The cave was full

of them, black, oily ones, swept in on the last tide, not yet pulled out again with the ebbing current. A source of food, and of water. Choking back her disgust, she untied the closures of her torn shirt, pulled it off, then retied it into a snare of a sort.

*I will live through this,* she thought, running her hand over her abdomen. *We will live through this together, you and I. And we will get out of here.*

The wind whistled through the cave, then fell silent.

 $\mathcal{T}$ he seneschal did not wait for the last longboat to land before he began kindling the black fire.

Each of the oared vessels sported a lantern at the prow, hanging over the edge of the ship to light the shoals and reefs over which the longboats skimmed on their way to shore and ship and back. Now the demon in man's flesh seized hold of the first, wresting the handle free with a savage twist.

An exposed rim of sharp wire gleamed in the sun. The seneschal ran the edge of his finger along it, drawing blood that hissed with fire from another world.

He unhooded the lantern and held up his finger, allowing the blood to drip into the well of the lantern.

From the drops tiny tendrils of caustic smoke rose, kindling a moment later into sparks that caught a breath of life in the air. A sliver of flame, black and liquid, twisting and transforming in a gloriously malevolent pattern of color, heavier than that which burned in the air of the upworld, caught the wick of the lantern and glowed.

The flame suddenly darkened, snapping evilly, then sprang to a more intense, more rampant light.

Michael turned to the fresh coterie of soldiers and sailors who had come ashore with him. He handed the lantern to the leader of the first group of four men, reaching for the next lantern to light in the same fashion.

"Comb the coast," he ordered as his reeve divided the men up into smaller raiding parties. "Check every privy in every hut in every fishing village. If you find her, drag her out, then burn the house of whomever has been sheltering her."

His blue eyes shone wildly in the dark.

"If you don't find her, burn everything in sight."

As the troops and raiding parties were saddling up and dispersing, both on horseback and on foot, the seneschal drew Caius, his trusted bowman, aside.

"I have a special assignment for you," he said, his voice betraying excitement tinged with anxiety. "Quinn says she made her home a few days' ride inland from here, in the first stronghold along the transcontinental roadway, in a keep known as 'Haguefort' in the province of Navarne. See if she has crawled home. And be sure to leave it in ashes, whether she has or not.

"If you come across her husband in the confusion of the evacuation, make sure you dispense with him first," he continued, his bony face hardening, its sharp angles delineating the aspect of the demon that dwelt within him. "But cut off something as a souvenir; make sure it's something she will recognize."

"How will I know him?"

Michael shrugged. "If he is old or young enough to walk without assistance, assume any man you find in her house is her husband. Be thorough. Kill everyone you can, children too, Caius. *Everyone*."

Caius nodded and pulled himself up on his mount.

"Remember, even though you are shooting in your brother's memory," Michael said with a sudden jolt of jollity, "try and limit your kills to one bolt. Any more than that, even to honor poor, sausage-handed Clomyn, and you will find yourself outnumbered and out of ammunition."

Caius's eyes narrowed at the offhand mention of his heart twin, but he said nothing, just nudged the horse east toward the thoroughfare that would lead him to Navarne.

# 40

𝓤nder the best of circumstances, the Bolg king and the Lord Cymrian would not have made easy traveling companions.

Under the worst of circumstances, in which they now found themselves, they discovered a surprisingly fluid pattern of companionship that was born of necessity.

Neither man had any need of or tolerance for camaraderie or conversation. Achmed spent his waking moments fending off the myriad vibrations in the wind, combing each pocket of air for a flicker of Rhapsody's heartbeat, a trace of the stench of whatever F'dor spirit was now feeding off of Michael, a man he had loathed in the old world, but had never tracked before. Ashe, with the minutiae of awareness of the dragon in his blood, was unconsciously sorting through the infinite pieces of information that assaulted his senses, most of it banal and inconsequential, none of it indicating that his wife was still present in the world of the living.

As a result, they traveled in a mutual silence that suited them both.

They rode the borderlands between Roland and Tyrian, staying far enough off the road to avoid notice and the interference of the human and animal traffic that traveled the thoroughfare there, stopping at the first Lirin outpost in Tyrian long enough to send a coded message to Rial in Tomingorllo, the hilltop palace in the forested capital city.

More than the endless days and nights of silence, another unspoken synchronicity seemed to develop between them. Achmed's blood rage, the propensity of hatred for F'dor present in the makeup of all of the Dhracian race, was simmering beneath the surface of his conscious control, a volatile anger that drove him to the hunt to the exclusion of everything else. No diversion, not the need for rest, or hunger, or even the desire to rescue a treasured friend, the woman who was the opposite side of his own coin, could break the concentration fomented by the primal need to seek and destroy that was driving his every waking breath.

Ashe, too, had fallen into a primal state that was just barely on the inside edge of containment. The dragon in his blood, awakened from dormancy and invigorated by the ministrations of the Lord and Lady Rowan in the effort to save his life, was lurking at the edge of his reason, whispering constantly in his mind, but it was not singular in its purpose as Achmed's blood rage. It was easily led off the path by other things it desired, difficult to rein in, seeking and coveting endless items that led away from the path Ashe was pursuing.

So both men were fighting inner battles in preparation for an outward one, Achmed trying to keep from falling into the bottomless chasm of single-minded concentration that blood rage demanded, his entire essence locked on his prey; Ashe from being driven insane by the multiplicity of the dragon's rapidly shifting focus.

Both men had relegated the hunt for the Lady Cymrian to the back of their minds. While there could be no question that each considered her to be the primary object of his search, the looming threat of a F'dor loose on the continent, lurking somewhere in the Wyrmlands, subjugated the need to save a single human life to secondary focus, even a life that was as precious to them both as hers.

They both knew, without discussing it, that she would agree.

Northwest, following the setting sun, they rode, leaving the open lands of way stations, farming villages, and tiny towns along the thoroughfare, to the sea cliffs, two weeks' ride encumbered, ten days by their estimates, not knowing where they were to look, just hoping to start with the coastline north of Port Fallon and continuing up the beach until they found one of the things they were looking for, knowing the other would not be far away.

If she was still alive, or hadn't been taken away by sea.

It was this thought that had both of them in the clutches of unspoken fear. The sea, like the wind, was a great source of masking vibration; if Michael had taken her aboard a ship and sailed away with her, Rhapsody's heartbeat would be lost in the endless churning turbulence of the waves.

"How useless to have such powers, such gifts as we have, when they cannot be employed in the sparing of Rhapsody's life, the saving of the continent from the scourge of another demon," Achmed had mumbled in a rare moment of speech at the campfire's edge one night.

Ashe sat silently for a long time, watching the twisting patterns of the flames.

"We shall just have to employ the tools of ordinary men, our wits, our endurance, and our luck, should we be fortunate enough to have any fall from the sky into our laps," he said, his voice dull with exhaustion. "For in the end, our titles, powers, and lands asides, that is all we are—ordinary men."

"Speak for yourself," Achmed retorted, draining his battered tankard and settling down to sleep that was less than restful.

By the eighth day of their journey from Sepulvarta, those tools, both ordinary and extraordinary, were put into use: Achmed's skin-web sensitivity to vibration feeling the change in the air, a sort of dusty heaviness on the already-thick summer wind, Ashe's dragon sense picking up the newly caustic feel of the world around them.

And both of their noses inhaling the scent of fire, rancid, odious fire that reeked of the Underworld.

## HAGUEFORT, NAVARNE

Gerald Owen burst through the doors of the Great Hall, startling the Lord Marshal from his paperwork, with Gwydion and Melisande close behind.

"Lord Anborn! There is smoke hanging in the air over Tref-y-Gwartheg! Word has come from the coast in north

Avonderre that two of the fishing villages are in flames, and that the fire is moving this way. Word also has it that armed men have been seen up and down the coast, just before each of the blazes has broken out. They are burning wantonly, starting at the shoreline and moving inward toward the forest."

The General turned his upper body toward the tall windows behind the chair.

In the distance he could see it as well, the gray haze that hung over the treetops at the horizon, a bellwether of encroaching fire. He had seen it before.

But never with the dark tint it left in the sky.

There was something more ominous than the obvious warning signs of a moving brushfire that was spreading to a forest. Something about the fire.

He turned back as quickly as he could.

"Owen, evacuate the keep," he said, reaching his strong hand out to Melisande; the trembling girl ran to him and buried her face in his shoulder. "I will deploy our forces to assist the Invoker in containing the fires, and hunting down whoever it is that is setting them. Send word to Gavin by avian messenger."

The elderly chamberlain nodded and turned to leave.

"Wait," Anborn instructed. "Summon the captain of the guard for me, and have him send the message. You take Gwydion and Melisande and leave immediately with the civilians for Bethany. I will send part of the force to clear the local villages as well. But get the children out of here."

"I am not a child, and I am going nowhere," declared Gwydion Navarne. "I am duke of this province, thank you, and will stay here with you to defend it."

The look on the General's face was an odd mix of fury at being defied and affectionate admiration.

"You're not duke yet, lad," he said sternly, though his eyes twinkled in the deep lines of his face. "My nephew, your guardian, is still regent of your lands, as well as both of our sovereign. It was he who told me to defend the Alliance in his absence, so your authority is null. Your responsibility—your *duty*—is to your sister; now take her and get out of here."

"But—"

"Do not argue with me, cur!" the General roared. "Take your sister, and go with Owen to Bethany, or I'll set fire to you myself!"

Silence fell heavily over the Great Hall. Then, after shaking off his shock, the young duke-to-be nodded distantly and put his hand out to his sister.

"Come, Melly," he said.

Anborn gently separated the sobbing girl from his shoulder, patting her back encouragingly. Gwydion Navarne stepped forward and put his arm around her, leading her from their late father's keep without so much as a backward glance.

## ABBAT MYTHLINIS, THE BASILICA OF WATER, NORTH OF AVONDERRE

𝒯he seneschal stood between the gusts of sea wind in the shadow of the great stone edifice at the shoreline of the sea, watching as darkness crept in from the horizon. He felt the warmth of the lanterns on the rectory and other buildings behind him come to light, the people inside them doubtless eager to combat the windy dusk that loomed at the edge of the sea, gray beneath low-hanging clouds heavy with rain to come.

The dark beauty of the coming storm hovering over the architectural marvel before him gave him pause, silencing the demon that had been cackling in glee at the destruction they had left in their wake.

The temple reached up out of the darkness of the crashing wind and surf, its oddly angled spire pointing away from the fallowing sea. The base of the mammoth structure was built from enormous blocks of quarried stone, gleaming gray and black in the light of the setting sun, irregular and pur-

posefully shaped, mortared together around tall beams of
ancient wood. Carefully tended walkways, formed by great
slabs of polished rock embedded in the sand, led up to the
front doors, which were fashioned from planks of varying
lengths.

The entire cathedral had been designed to resemble the
wreck of a ship, jutting from the craggy rocks and sand of
the beach at an ominous angle. The immense entrance doors,
with a jagged notched pattern at the top, appeared to depict
a vast hole torn in what would have been the keel. The
crazily angled spire was the representation of a mast.

The colossal ship had been rendered accurately, down to
the last nautical apparatus. The moorings and riggings, detailed in exquisitely carved marble, were a half-dozen times
their normal size.

The seneschal whistled in admiration, wondering what
had inspired such a strange and magnificent undertaking.

Farther offshore behind the main section of the basilica
was another part of the cathedral, an annex connected to
the main building by a plank walkway. It was evident to the
seneschal that the annex and the walkway were only visible
at low tide, as now, submerging into the sea when the current flooded back in. This additional part of the temple
evoked the wreckage of the stern. A gigantic anchor, lying
aslant on the sandbar between the two buildings, served as
its threshold.

The seneschal shuddered involuntarily. With Faron out on
the sea in a ship, he did not enjoy viewing the celebration
of a major traumatic shipwreck, if that's what this building
was constructed to represent.

Despite the care that had been taken by whatever architect
designed it to elicit the feeling of an off-balance wreck unevenly resting on the sand, it was obvious that the enormous
edifice was sound and solidly built. It stood, undisturbed,
amid the churning waves of the raging sea, giving no quarter, no inch to the sand.

The seneschal turned to the quartet of soldiers on horseback behind him, awaiting his orders.

"Search the rectory and the other buildings," he said, his eyes darting around at the lights flickering off the rolling waves. "Perhaps they are giving her shelter. Then, if you don't find her, burn the priests alive. There are bound to be more of them than you, so when you are ready to go in, let me know, and I will assist you."

The soldiers nodded and set about preparing for their maneuver.

The seneschal opened the great doors of the basilica and looked inside.

His eyes took in the cavernous basilica, its ceiling towering above him, the distant walls arching up to meet it. Great fractured timbers of myriad lengths and breadths were set within the dark stone. It looked a little like the fragmented skeleton of a giant beast, lying on its back, its spine the long aisle that led up forward, ancient ribs reaching brokenly, helplessly upward into the darkness above.

Round windows in the design of portholes were set high in the walls, undoubtedly affording the temple light by day. A single line of translucent glass blocks of great heft and thickness had been inlaid in the walls not far up from the floor. The churning sea was diffusely visible through them, bathing the interior of the basilica in a greenish glow.

The seneschal shuddered again. He was now outside of one of his elements, away from the wind, inside the holy place of an opposing and stronger element, water.

Besides, the ground beneath his feet was stinging him through his boots, hissing with smoke.

Blessed ground.

The demon within him screamed in anger and pain.

F'dor could not broach blessed ground.

"Rhapsody?" he called, his voice echoing in the cavernous cathedral. To his ears it sounded harsh, like the voice of the demon in his head. He winced; in the never-ending struggle for dominance in their shared body, it appeared that at the moment, the F'dor had the upper hand. He swallowed hard.

With a great swing of annoyance, he slammed the cathedral doors shut.

He strode across the walkway and down to the water's edge, wading into the low sea. He made his way to the sandbar on which the temple annex stood, the great rusting anchor on its doorstep, and put a foot onto the sandbar.

No smoke rose from his boot.

The annex, unlike the basilica itself, was not blessed ground.

Cautiously he stepped the rest of the way onto the sandbar and stepped inside the open doorway. He turned around and looked at the back door of the cathedral.

Two copper doors, blue-green with salt spray, inscribed with runes, bore raised reliefs of swords which had been wrought into the metal, one pointing up, the other down. Scrolled designs ran down the blades, similar to ocean waves, and the points were flared in a similar pattern.

In the background of the relief was a coat of arms, an engraving of a winged lion.

The seneschal caught his breath, then laughed harshly.

It was the family crest of his most hated enemy in the old land, MacQuieth Monodiere Nagall.

Inside the annex's archway was a simple, hollow chamber open to the ravages of the sea and the air. When the tide returned, much of the annex would submerge again.

Unlike the temple, which was an edifice built to look like a ship, the annex was a piece of a real one, wedged upright, bow skyward and aslant, in the sand. Whatever ship had been broken apart and now formed the annex had been a sizable one, judging by its wreckage, which appeared to be the better part of the stern and midship. Its deck had been stripped away, leaving nothing but the hull, which now formed the walls of the annex. It was evident that the ship had been built of something other than ordinary timber, something that had not decayed or corroded with time.

Also wedged into the sand in the center of the annex was a block of solid obsidian, gleaming smooth beneath the pools of water that danced across it with each gust of the wind. Two brace restraints of metal were embedded in the stone, their clasps open and empty. There was not a trace of rust on either one.

The surface of the stone had at one time been inscribed with deep runes that had been worn away over time by the insistent hand of the ocean. Now it was smooth, with only a bleached shadow marring the obsidian where the inscription once had been.

Attached to the front of the stone was a plaque, with raised runes similar to the ones they had seen in the copper doors. Like the braces on its horizontal surface, the marker was unaffected by the scouring waves.

The seneschal crouched down and examined the plaque. Its inscription was in an old language, one he barely remembered, and contained a good many characters he could not make out. But the largest of the words caught his eye immediately. A smile began at the corners of his mouth as he read the word once, then again, then a third time, after which he threw back his head and laughed uncontrollably.

*MacQuieth,* it said.

The horrific sound of the laughter blended with the scream of the sea wind, the harsh cry of the gulls. The seneschal could barely contain his mirth, but more so, another emotion.

Relief.

MacQuieth had been his bane in the old world, the one man whom he knew, deep in his heart, that he feared.

There was something freeing about staring down at his hated enemy's tombstone, something so vindicating that he could not help but give in to his basest instinct.

Quickly he unlaced his trousers and urinated on the stone, still laughing aloud.

"I have lived long enough to actually see it, your grave," he said as he put himself back together. "Please accept my humble gift of *holy water* to bless it; I hope you can feel it as your bones rot in the sand beneath it. But most likely you are nothing but sand yourself by now anyway."

He glanced quickly around the annex again and, seeing nothing, went back across the sandbar and waded to the shoreline again, where his soldiers were waiting. He drew Tysterisk, the handle coming forth glowing with excitement, the blade intermittently visible on the gusts of wind.

"Aim your fiery arrows for the cracks between the tiles of the roofs," he instructed the soldiers. "All you need is a spark to catch. I will take over from there."

The men nodded. A volley of arrows and bolts shot forth from bows, traditional and cross, raining like hail on the rooftops of rectory and the other outbuildings.

The seneschal raised the sword hilt above his head, where the wind danced around it in visible swirls.

The tiny sparks on the roofs roared to life.

The seneschal swept the sword through the air again. Once more, the sparks burst open, igniting the rest of the stone buildings into orange-red stone boxes of fire hot enough to melt the walls.

As the screaming rose in chorus, the seneschal and his men started up the beach, north, looking for more places that Rhapsody could be hiding.

It had almost become an excuse for the burning, instead of the other way around.

# 41

GLASS WORKSHOP, THE CAULDRON, YLORC

"How does the melt look, Shaene?"

The journeyman ceramicist peered in through the window of the enormous kiln.

"Red hot," he said smugly.

The sealed master did not smile. "Dull, or bright?"

Shaene looked in through the window again, then shrugged. "Hard to say, Theophila. Fairly bright, I suppose."

The woman pushed him impatiently out of the way and looked in herself. She exhaled in annoyance.

"One might think *you* would recognize *dull*, Shaene," she said. "Sandy, increase the heat. I need it to glow like blood spurting from a pumping heart."

"Lady!" Shaene groaned in pretend shock. "What a gruesome reference! And I can't say as it's a color I've ever had the opportunity to have seen. Honestly."

Omet cranked the damper of the furnace open a little wider, allowing for more direct contact with the natural flamewell, averting his eyes, saying nothing. He had no doubt that the woman knew exactly the color of which she spoke.

The test frits had been fired, all save the last, the purple, and now lay on their racks, cooling, awaiting the comparison to the old plates. Omet went about his work, the dizzy sensation of fear that had been clutching his viscera mounting.

He knew that the colors were true by eye; whatever else she was, Esten was a skilled glass artisan, ceramicist, and tile artist. It was rumored her Yarimese father, who had traveled with the Panjeri in his youth, had taught her the nomadic glassworkers' secrets from childhood, before she killed him for the family's money to start off on her own. By the time she had become mistress of the Raven's Guild she had gained entry into the best schools and guild workbenches in the world, and she had made a life's work of it, employing the tile foundry as a creative outlet as well as an effective cover for the less savory workings of her business.

His hands trembled slightly as he turned the racks of the cooling frits. If the colors were true, whatever rune was inscribed in the test plates would be visible. Omet had no idea what information that might reveal, but its mere presence would signal that the color formulas were correct. Once that was achieved, Esten was poised to fire the enormous rolls that would be cut into sheets of glass to be embedded in the tower's ceiling.

And what that would lead to, he had no idea.

Though the Firbolg king had said little about the purpose of the project, Omet had had enough exposure to the original plans to know that the tower was more than a mere work of art. The stained glass was the final piece that would make it into an instrumentality of some sort, some kind of funnel of power that must be very great for Achmed to be so insistent on it. Omet had no use for magic, especially when he didn't know what it would bring about, but that had mattered little while the king was in the mountain. Whatever ends Achmed was building his Lightcatcher for, Omet trusted they were not threatening to him.

Now, with the king gone, and a vengeful killer in control, that was no longer the case.

Black eyes were suddenly staring directly into his.

Omet jumped.

The eyes focused even more intently on him.

"Where did you learn to turn racks like that, Sandy?"

Omet struggled to keep from shaking visibly.

"Shaene," he said simply. It was a lie, but safer than revealing that his technique had come from endless instruction by her own journeymen when he was indentured to her in the foundry of Yarim.

Esten watched him complete the rotation, then nodded, satisfied; she touched the rack and, determining it to be cool, took the red frit out and returned to the worktable.

"It's true to my eye. Let's have a look, then, and see if the test plate agrees."

She held the ancient plate of glass up to the light of the open ceiling above, then carefully slid the newly cooled frit in front of it. She waited for the clouds overhead to pass, then eyed it, the other artisans hovering behind her.

Delight broke over her face as a beam of sun shone into the tower, glowing through the double layer of red glass.

"I see it," she said quietly. "But I can't make out what it

says. Can any of you? Come here and look while I hold it."

Rhur and Shaene each looked over her shoulder at the pieces she was holding aloft, then shook their heads. "Don't even recognize the symbols," Shaene said, returning to his work. "Those aren't any letters I've ever seen. Looks like scratchings or numbers of some sort. Sorry, Theophila."

"Come here, Sandy," Esten said, her eyes still on the test glass. "Do you recognize this writing?"

Omet set his tools down and came over quickly, not wishing to draw her notice further by dawdling. He peered over her shoulder as well, inhaling and holding it so as not to breathe on her.

In the translucency of the glowing red glass he could make out some old symbols in a language he could not read, but had in fact seen many times on the original documents. Until the Bolg king had gone to Yarim, no one had any idea what the symbols meant. Rhapsody had translated them, had scratched their meanings onto the diagrams next to the places the runes appeared.

This one was merely the symbol for red.

He shook his head, then walked quickly back to his workbench where the Bolg apprentices and journeymen where preparing the colorants to be added to the ash and sand in the huge vats near the furnaces.

Esten continued to stare at the symbols for a moment longer, then shrugged. She took each of the remaining test plates and held them up to the colored frits, seeing symbols in all but the last.

"Oh well. No time to be lost worrying about it. All right, Rhur, tell the furnace minders to set up the large sheets of frit in each of the colors except violet; we haven't got the formula right on that one yet. We'll get the fritting started on the other six. Once they're fired, grind them down and get them ready for the melt."

"Grind them down?" Shaene asked incredulously. "You going to add something to the mix, lady, and remelt them? An enamel?"

Esten's eyes glinted sharply. "Yes, just a protective glaze, so that when they're annealed they will be stronger. I had it sent from Yarim—it's in those green barrels. No one is to touch them save for me. The glaze is expensive. Now, set about it. I want to have the ceiling installed before the king returns."

Omet smoothed the surface of the wooden board on which the panes were to be cut, dusting it lightly with chalk. When the board was as white as his hands now were, he took the can of water and sprinkled it, then rubbed it down vigorously to make the surface reflective and easy to see.

Once the board was prepared, he looked at Esten, who was busy giving directions to the journeymen, and exhaled quietly.

He reached for the tin-tipped compass, the instrument with which she would draw the window sections, which he was expected to go over with red pigment, noting where the support cames, the leading that bordered each section, would go.

His hand was shaking. No matter how much he tried to control his terror, despite being blessed with a nonchalant aspect and a deadpan expression, there were subtle signs of the fear—the gleam he could see on occasion in his eyes reflecting in the undulating glass, his mouth, dry as the sand and ash from which that glass was formed, the way his voice would occasionally refuse to come forth from his constricted throat.

His quaking hands.

*Has she noticed?* he wondered, watching the masquerading guildmistress cutting pieces of other glass sheets with a red-hot iron cutter, trimming it with her shoddy groziers. *How long will it be before she realizes I belonged to her once, lived under her lash, languished in the inferno of her foundry, witnessed her send the bodies of the dead slave boys to the kilns, and hundreds of other crimes?*

Amid all those wonderings, the one he had no question

about was what would happen to him when she discovered him.

*Please let the king return soon,* he prayed to whatever god might hear him.

He could feel the gaze from her black eyes on his neck.

"Sandy, get the stonemasons in here," she said curtly. "It's time to measure for the tracery supports."

Omet nodded without turning around, grateful as always to Shaene for his stupid nickname, and to Rhur, for his unwillingness to speak much. His true name was still guarded because of both of their idiosyncrasies. He rose from his workbench and left the room quickly, heading for the quarry where the masons worked.

He had considered telling Rhur, or Shaene, to be wary of the new artisan, not to use his name in her presence, to try and stall the work until the return of the king. But he could not do that. He had seen her in action, had watched her overtly tossing unfortunate boys who tried to escape into ovens, covertly assigning them to tasks that would inevitably drown or asphyxiate them, knew in the depths of his soul that to speak any of his terror out loud would only hasten his end.

He knew what everyone who knew her name knew.

No secret could be kept from Esten for long, let alone forever.

# 42

## IN THE TIDAL CAVE

After the first few days, Rhapsody managed to settle into a routine, trapped within the tidal cave.

She had made one valiant attempt to swim out with the ebbing current, only to confirm what she already knew—that the spiraling rip tide was too strong for her to bear up against. She was caught almost immediately in the undertow and found herself fighting to keep from drowning.

So she had to look around for another means of exit.

The first thing that she knew she had to find, after warmth, was water. Drying herself during the times when the tide was low was easy enough; the elemental bond to fire in her soul allowed heat to come forth upon her command, and she took every opportunity to summon it, using the warmth to dry her hair and clothes, reveling in the comfort of not being wet until the next time the current flooded, keeping her body from losing too much heat.

Water had been more difficult to come by. A small amount of freshwater condensation could sometimes be gathered from the ceiling of the cave when the tide was high, but it was never enough to slake her thirst. She had to content herself with the blood of the eels that swarmed abundantly in the tidal cave, trapped when the current ebbed, then eating their flesh raw to preserve as much of the liquid as possible. Occasionally she caught a few oysters, fish, or sea urchins that got swept into the cave, but after a few nightmarish days the source of her nourishment hardly mattered.

*We will live through this together, you and I,* she had promised her unborn child.

She would do whatever she had to in order to keep that promise.

*I am a Singer, a Namer,* she thought, caressing her abdomen while watching the gray sky turn pink from her perch on the natural ledge in the back of the tidal cave. *And also because I am your mother, I must tell you the truth.*

She closed her eyes, remembering Ashe's tender words to her on the night their child was conceived.

*And what do you plan to give me for my birthday?*

*Someone to teach your morning aubade, your evening vespers to.*

A tiny shaft of sunlight broke through the gloom at the horizon. Rhapsody cleared her throat, ragged from the salt, and quietly sang one of the ancient aubades, the love songs to the sky that Liringlas had been marking time with for as long as she knew.

Welcome sunrise
Touch the mountains with
Tentative light
Blend the clouds with gold
And gently disturb the dreams of the night

Welcome daybreak
Fill the silence with
Songs of the birds
Lift the sky-lantern to the sound of
Music that swells without singers or words

Welcome morning
Fire of dawn, light of the day
Warming the world with your glow
Awaken again we, your children
Who, chanting the aubade, know
That we have welcomed sunrise.

"Not my favorite," she said to the unborn baby when she was finished, "but the first one your grandmother taught me. We must learn them in order; they have a pattern, as you will see."

More and more she had begun to talk aloud to the child, her only regular companion in the prison of her tidal cave. The baby had become her touchstone, her reason for enduring the hours underwater, the thirst, the hunger.

During the times when the tide was high, she had stopped struggling, and instead viewed the hours as instruction in the music of the sea. While floating on her back, she could make out songs on the waves; at first they were wordless, mere melodies of swirling currents, rushing and ebbing along with the seawater. She tried to concentrate on floating, knowing her child was floating within her as well.

*If you are not frightened in your small, dark cave full of water, I must not be, either.*

Once she had banished the fear from her mind, she could hear it then, the lore of the sea, songs from all the shores that the ocean waves touched, some fragmented, some clear and long. She spent most of her quiet hours listening to the chanties of sailors, the call of the merfolk, scraps of lore from the ancient city of the Mythlin, now silent beneath the waves, the weeping of the families of those lost on the sea; it was an indescribably beautiful symphony of life, of history, sad, heroic, glorious, mystical.

And it was being sung to her, and to her baby.

*How lucky you are in a way, my child, to have this time,* she thought one night as the moonlight was reflected on the low water of the cave, swirling in great silver ripples. *You are being steeped in elemental magic—the baptism of the sea, the fire that warms and dries us when the tide is low, the sheltering cave of earth that was formed in fire and cooled in water, the wind that blows through, singing its ageless song. One day you will make a fine Namer, if you choose to be one.* The thoughts were enough to help her keep despair at bay.

Most of the time.

One afternoon, when she was not feeling so strong, and misery had taken a greater toll that it was usually allowed, Rhapsody looked up from her ledge to see bright eyes in a small brown furry face staring back at her.

She started, reeling back against the wall.

The animal started as well, disappearing beneath the surface of the water.

As she skittered back, her boots scraped for purchase on the ledge, sending a small hail of black rocks that had broken off from the wall into the swirling water.

Rhapsody watched, fascinated, as the black igneous formations floated in the surface, spinning in spirals. A moment later, the otter she had seen appeared, bobbing the volcanic rock in front of its nose, guiding it out of the tidal cave.

She pondered what she had seen that night as she floated with the rising tide, trying to think of a way she might make use of what she had seen.

By the time the tide had fallen, she had an idea.

Every few hours she would use the bolt tip that had lodged in her belt to scrape free pieces of the back wall of the cave, tying them within her shirt. *If I can bind them together with something, seaweed, strands of my hair, it would make for a tiny raft of sorts,* she reasoned, trying to keep from shredding her fingers too badly. *If I can use it to aid my floating when the tide is high, perhaps I can use it to obtain purchase, to work my away around to the front of the cave, so that when the tide falls, it will take me with it.* She patted her abdomen and silently corrected herself.

*Take* us *with it.*

Each evening that the tide was low, when the weather was clear, she would watch for the pink light that filled the cave, signaling that the sun was about to set.

Even more than the sunrise devotions, Rhapsody had always loved the vespers, the evensong that bade the sun farewell with a promise to be standing vigil until it rose again the next morning. It was a dual devotion, a requiem for the sun, marking the completion of another day as a requiem sung at a funeral pyre marked the completion of a life; it was a greeting to the stars, the sky guardians of the Lirin, as well.

*I will not forget you,* she whispered as the light in the sky dimmed, disappearing beyond the horizon into night. *Please do not forget me.*

The phrase rang in her memory, familiar; she pondered while floating where she had heard it before, then remembered as the water swirled around her ears, singing its ageless song.

They were the words, simple in their formation, spoken by her dear friend, the dragon Elynsynos, to her lover, Merithyn the Explorer, before he left her lands and returned to his king, Gwylliam, with the joyous news that there was a land, a verdant, beautiful land, that would take the refugees of Serendair in, would make them at home.

He had promised, and then died at sea on the way back.

As she watched the first star rising at the horizon, twinkling in the deep cobalt blue of the late summer night, Rhapsody wondered what might have come to pass if the sea had not taken him, had he made it back to her, to their children whom he would not live to see. *How different would things be now,* she thought, her hand, as ever, resting lightly on her belly.

She thought of their descendants, Manwyn and her two mad sisters, the Seers of the Past and Present, the first now dead, the second living a frail and harmless life, moment by moment, in an abbey in Sepulvarta. Edwyn Griffyth, Anwyn and Gwylliam's eldest son, a self-imposed exile in Gaematria, the mystical island of the Sea Mages. Llauron, Ashe's father, now lost in time somewhere, communing with the elements in a vaporous dragon form, one with them. And Anborn. Tears welled up in her eyes as her mind came to rest on him, remembering the sight of his body lying in the burning forest, his legs, lost in the effort to spare her three years ago, useless to save him.

A litany of sadness, all born of that one failed promise.

Merithyn's promise.

Still thinking of Anborn, she remembered their time together around the fire, singing the song her mother had sung to her for him.

*A noble tradition. Have you chosen one yet for my great-nephew or niece.*

*No, not yet. When it is right, I will know it.*

*It's the song of the sea,* she thought, the music of the endless waves, ever-present but ever-changing, eternal, endless.

Like love.

Touching all the kingdoms of the earth, but free to rove the wide world, home anywhere it went.

*As I hope for you,* she thought.

She wondered if some of the melodies she heard in the sea were endless vibrations put on the wind by Merithyn; there was lore in the waves that told of his love for Elynsynos, songs she resolved to learn and sing for the dragon one day.

And as the thought brought her warmth in the last light of the setting sun, the child's name rang in her mind, a paean to the hapless explorer that was its great-great-grandfather, and to the man who would be its father.

"If he agrees, boy or girl, I will call you Meridion," she said aloud to the child, wanting it to be the first to hear the name spoken. "Merithyn was the past; Gwydion is the present, but you, Meridion, you will be the future, with ties to all three."

The ocean roared its approval; all else was silent.

# 43

## TRAEG, NORTHERN SEACOAST

From the southern tip of the cove where the Water Basilica stood, the fire spread northward, burning villages and small towns, open farmland and forest, leaving smoldering wreckage that continued to burn with the acrid taint of the Underworld.

The Filids of Gwynwood deployed their foresters all along the coast, the men and women who normally traveled the woods, serving as guides to pilgrims who were making their ways along the Cymrian trail, a historic path of sites the First Fleet of refugees had established upon coming to this new land. That duty, and their countless other tasks of forest stewardship, were abandoned in the effort to contain the burnings, but the firestarters were elusive; occasionally one or two men, sometimes up to four at a time had been seen, traveling the winding roads or untrodden paths that led up the sea coast. They were looking for a woman, a yellow-haired woman, they said on the rare occasions they stopped; not long afterward, a crop of black fires, hissing and resistant to normal methods of extinction, would break out nearby.

Villagers began taking up arms, posting guards, in the effort to protect themselves from the purveyors of the dark fire; blacksmiths could often be seen, hammers in hand, lurking on the roads outside of town, or patrolling the outer edge of villages by day and night.

The demon that clung to the seneschal reveled in the intense heat and the heavy smoke at first, but as the days passed and the woman was not found, there was only so much joy to be had in the ashes.

*We need to move inland,* the incessant voice insisted, nagging at the base of Michael's mind. *Or south to Port Fallon, where there is more wood, more ships, more buildings, more people. There is nothing here along the desolate coast except for a few thatched hut villages, a tiny town here and there. There is not enough death. What good is fire without destruction, without murder?*

The seneschal clawed at his skull in frustration.

"Have you failed to notice how very few of us there are?" he asked the demon angrily, feeling it bristle at the affront. "I have a handful of men. The coast is hundreds of miles long, which is the only reason we have not been captured yet. This is not Argaut; we are not in power here."

*Yet.*

Michael glanced around, looking for signs of the longboats. In the distance over the waves he could see dim lights glowing diffusely in the semi-darkness, undulating on the waves.

He inhaled deeply, reveling in the scent of the fire that had consumed the dock here in Traeg, the tiny, windswept fishing village, the northernmost on the seacoast.

"I am going back to the ship," he stated flatly, looking around to make certain that none of his men were near enough to hear him arguing with himself. "I must consult Faron one more time; perhaps the scales have scried something in my absence."

The demon screamed in fury.

*You execrable, accursed fool! Enough of this idiotic search! The woman is gone; she is not to be found. It is time to move to the next step; either set sail for Argaut, or turn and move inland. But we will wander no more in this vain exercise in futility!*

"As ever, it is not your decision, m'lord," the seneschal replied in a deadly tone. "You may come along, or you may exit now, but you may not direct. If there is a blacksmith or a dock whore you would like to inhabit, by all means go. But if you wish to remain with a more powerful host than the human rats available to you, you will cease your prattle and go back to seething sleep whilst we row out to the ship."

Faron winced at the sound of the door to the hold opening, at the approach of the lantern that stung his eyes with unwelcome light.

Out of the darkness the seneschal stepped, carrying a burlap sack that twisted and writhed in the air.

"You're in luck today, Faron," he said, his voice barely hiding the raw edge that had been there since his conversation with the demon. "The deckhands have pulled in some lovely eels, the kind you favor; big ones with the heads still on."

The hermaphroditic creature's milky eyes lit up with excitement. The seneschal tossed Faron the bag; it fell short of the pool and landed with only its bottom in the glowing green water.

Faron stared at the bag in dismay, then at its own diminished hands, curled under and soft of bone. The creature looked back at the seneschal and mewed pathetically.

Michael stared at Faron coldly.

"You can't do it alone? You need my help?"

Faron nodded slightly, a look of confusion turning to one of guarded alarm.

Without another word the seneschal swept the bag from the floor, tore open the drawstring, pulled forth the twitching sea creatures and ripped their heads off, slicing the flesh thinly, then fed it off the knife to his child.

When the creature was sated, and the eels were gone, the seneschal patted Faron, then plunged his fingers deep into the soft tissue of the creature's head.

"Where is she?" he screamed, digging his knuckles down to the bone, lubricating them with the blood that spurted out of the holes.

Faron gasped deeply, then shrieked in agony.

Michael twisted his fingers more deeply in.

"Tell me, Faron, or by the gods, I will pull your head from your shoulders and eat your eyes."

The creature collapsed, moaning and twitching desperately.

The seneschal loosed the metaphysical ties and allowed his essence to flood in through the holes in which his fingers remained.

"Show me, Faron, look in the scrying scale and *show* me where she is!"

Faron's body went rigid, then swelled with the influx of life. Michael's corporeal form shrank away into its mummified state, its bony fingers still clinging stubbornly to the holes in Faron's skull.

The seneschal stared down into the blue scale, the side with the clouds clearing from in front of the eye.

At first all he could see in the green water was the waves of the sea crashing against a rocky seacoast with no beach-line. Then a moment later he recognized what he saw from the triangular shadow that was being cast on the sea.

It was the same promontory from which she had fallen.

With a savage twist the seneschal disengaged himself, leaving Faron bleeding and whimpering in pain. Once his body had rehydrated, he stared down at the sobbing child without the pity he had once had in his eyes.

"You had best be right this time, Faron," he said contemptuously. "For if you have sent me off again for nothing, I will toss you into the sea; instead of feeding off eels, you will be feeding them with your own flesh. My child or no, you are of no use to me if you cannot at the very least read that scale."

He wiped the blood on his hands onto his trousers, then climbed the ladder up onto the deck again.

Rhapsody was listening to the sea tell her the story of a pair of lovers who had communicated by seagull and messages in glass bottles when the mangled body was swept into the cave on the tide.

In fright she backed up on the ledge, trying to keep away from the waterlogged corpse, its eyes missing in a face that had been battered into shreds against the rocks just outside her tidal cave. The body was mostly nude, clad only in a shirt that looked as if it had belonged to one of Michael's regiment.

*He's here,* she thought, panic flooding through her as the current was flooding the cave. *He has found me; Michael has found me.*

After a few moments her calm returned.

This might have been one of Michael's men, but he had been in the water for weeks, probably as long as she had been in the cave. The waves had given up the dead body grudgingly, and not before having their fun with it; the corpse had absorbed at least twice its weight in water, and was swollen and bruised, distended almost beyond recognition as human.

Worst of all, the body caught on a snag near the front of the cave, then slowly swirled throughout the tidal hideaway, scraping the edge of the rock on which Rhapsody now sat.

She put her head down to ward off the stench that was rising from the body; it had baked in the summer sun, absorbed the water from the sea, and now, with its penis and testicles cleanly broken off against a gouging rock formation, it was dissolving by pieces in the tidal cave, sheaves of skin and hair floating loosely, ready to separate.

Horror crept over Rhapsody as she realized the import of this event.

The body was now her companion. It would be bobbing with her when the cave flooded, bumping up against her in the wild current, trapped with her in the endless cycle of floating and resting, floating and resting.

*I have to get out of here now,* she thought desperately.

She looked to the tiny suspended mat of igneous stones she had bound together, plaiting strands of her long hair to serve as a rope to hold them. *It's not ready,* she thought frantically. *It's still too small.*

She glanced at the body again, knowing that in a few hours it would be dancing with her in her endless vigil. The thought made her shudder violently.

"I have to get out of here," she said again aloud.

Perhaps it was her own mind filling in the space; she heard an internal voice, perhaps her own, but young-sounding.

*We have to get out of here.*

*Right,* Rhapsody agreed silently. *Give me one more night to plait and bind; in the morning, when the tide flattens, we will try to make our escape.*

She didn't even have the strength to wonder whether Michael was gone yet or not.

# 44

## TRAEG

By the time the two sovereigns had reached the seacoast, neither of them could expect to be warmly welcomed into an inn.

The journey overland had been a brutal one, with little

rest and less success. In each place they stopped, they arrived too late; village after village had been burned,
scorched by half or more, some reduced to ashes that smoldered in the wind. In Traeg, the northernmost of the tiny
villages, the whipping wind that battered the coast had long
been seen as both a friend and adversary, but with the elemental sword of air in the hand of one who was spreading
dark fire, it had served only to broaden the destruction,
carrying the deadly sparks throughout the boatyards, burning
the docks to cinders.

It was at those docks Achmed and Ashe came to a halt
one afternoon, staring at the devastation in silence.

Neither man had taken the time to shave or bathe, their
outward appearances deteriorating from both the grime and
soot of the road and the added toll that worry was taking
on both of them. Under normal circumstances, an unkempt,
hooded traveler would have gone unnoticed in a rough place
like Traeg, but because of the rumors carried like sparks on
the wind of pairs and trios of men who came through coastal
towns, seeking a blond woman, leaving behind buildings in
flames, they had dismounted at the waterfront to find themselves the objects of steely-eyed scrutiny.

"It will be harder to convince anyone to trade horses
now," Ashe remarked as they stopped in what was left of
the tiny village square.

"If there are any to be had," Achmed said.

They looked around for signs of life and found them; a
tiny salt shop stood open, its walls glazed in black soot but
still sound; the smithy was undamaged as well, and a large
tavern with an ash-covered sign in front was apparently
open for business by the look of things, men wandering in
and out, calling to one another.

The two travelers walked up the cobbled path that led to
the establishment, lined at one time recently with neatly
tended flowers that now sat twisted and burnt. As they
passed the inn's signboard Ashe stopped suddenly. He
crossed over a row of black shrubbery to stand before it for

a moment, its name and symbol obscured by a layer of soot. He wiped the center of the signboard clear with his sleeve.

In the center of the board was a gaily painted rendering of a fancy headpiece surrounded with gilt words. Ashe wiped his sleeve across it again, then stood back in silence.

THE HAT AND FEATHERS, the sign decreed.

He signaled excitedly to Achmed. "This may be a portent," he said.

"How so?"

"In Yarim we went to Manwyn's temple, Rhapsody and I. Amid her rantings, the Seer mentioned something about a hat and feathers."

Achmed looked over his shoulder at the three men who had gathered on the inn's stoop and were watching them closely. "What else did she say?" he asked quietly.

Ashe glanced at the men, then turned slightly to shield his words from the wind.

"She said that Rhapsody would not die giving birth to my child," he said haltingly. "That was why we sought her counsel."

Achmed's face was impassive. "Anything else?"

"Yes. She told Rhapsody to beware the Past—'it seeks to have you, it seeks to aid you, it seeks to destroy you.' She also characterized the Past as 'a relentless hunter, a stalwart protector, a vengeful adversary.' "

Achmed snorted in annoyance. "And you are only thinking to tell me this now?"

"They were rantings. She also told us the what was good on the menu of the local tavern and made recommendations on mementos to bring home to Stephen's children."

Achmed started for the door. "She sounds like a keeper. I may go and see if she wants to leave that godforsaken temple and come live in Ylorc."

Ashe caught his elbow.

"Wait," he said quickly. "There is one prophecy more." He waited until the Bolg king had drawn close enough to hear without being overheard. " 'Long ago a promise made, long ago a name conveyed, Long ago a voice was stayed—three debts to be paid.' "

"And did this mean anything to Rhapsody?" Achmed asked.

"No, but I have been pondering the words as we traveled. The only one I can make any possible sense of is the 'promise made'; Rhapsody told me long ago she had been forced to lie against her will, had given her word to a cruel, evil bastard about something he might misinterpret in return for the safety of a child. I believe that man is the seneschal we seek, the one you called the Waste of Breath."

Achmed said nothing, merely nodded.

"Let us make our inquiries here," Ashe said, his eyes red from exhaustion. "This is the last of the coastal towns; if no one here has seen her, I don't know where else to look."

"I doubt they have, but one might surmise that they could have seen Michael," Achmed retorted, gesturing angrily at the ruins around them.

Together they shouldered their way through the gathering of townsmen who were still observing them and went into the tavern.

A lanky man with a sailor's manner and a beard interposed himself in the doorway. "Can I help you, mates?"

"We are seeking victuals," Achmed replied, casting his eyes around the tavern.

"And ale," Ashe added. "And fresh horses."

"Canna help you with the latter," the man said, "there are none to be had. Those few that survived belong to the barkeep here, and he keeps them for the needs of Gavin's foresters who are fighting the fires and seeking the firestarters." Without breaking his gaze away from them, he called to the barkeep over his shoulder.

"Hie, Barney! Customers."

The young man on the other side of the bar looked up and motioned them nearer, signaling subtlely to the men at the door as well.

"What'll it be, gents?"

"Food and drink," Achmed replied. "We're not particular, unless it's mutton. If all you have is mutton, just give me ale and bread."

"Bread and ale and thin cabbage soup is all I have," the barkeep replied, setting two tankards on the board in front of them. "We have been a little—busy, as you might have noticed."

The travelers nodded. "Did anyone come through here before the fire, asking after a woman?"

The barkeep exchanged a glance with the men at the door.

"Aye," he said. "Three of 'em, one dressed much like you, sir."

"Do you know where they went?"

The barkeep shook his head. "You might ask Old Barney; he may know. He'll be here soon."

"Old Barney? Is that your sire?"

The thin young man laughed. "I see you gentlemen don't frequent taverns much."

"I've drunk in my share," replied Ashe, exhaustion making him testy. "Why do you say that?"

"Had you not noticed that all barkeeps are called Barney?"

Achmed shrugged. "As long as he keeps pouring my ale I've never thought to ask his name. Unless knowing him personally makes it cost less, I don't care."

The young man's forced smile dimmed a notch. "It's an ancient tradition, an old story. One that predates this land."

"Oh?" Ashe asked, loosing his tentative hold on the dragon slightly to assess the man more thoroughly. His awareness noted the barkeep was not Cymrian, nor were any of the others huddled at the door, watching them intently, blades not drawn but at the ready. "Would you favor us with the telling of it?"

The barkeep exhaled. "Not much to tell. In an old land, far across the sea, long ago a barkeep named Barney overheard something that he shouldn't have heard; 'tis an occupational hazard amongst us, for good ale makes lips loose, and there are many in the taverns to whom a friendly face behind a bar seems the best friend in the world after a few pints. But this particular Barney, now, he was unfortunate enough to be the only man in the pub when something was witnessed or said that a fellow of large influence and small conscience did not want known, or repeated, or discovered.

"So the fellow hired the best assassin of the day, told him the name of the town thirty leagues away, and the name of the victim—a barkeep named Barney—paid him a handsome sum to send him on to the Afterlife. Not being from the area, he did not know the name of the tavern, but they both reasoned it would be fairly easy to discover.

"The assassin arrived in town, and made discreet inquires—much the way you folks are doing." The barkeep raised an eyebrow, then continued as he wiped off the tavern board. "He asked the first few men he came across where he could find a tavern with a barkeep named Barney. And he got three different answers.

"He went a little further into town, and tried again, learning not only the names of four different taverns, but the fact that barkeeps are a nomadic lot; we tend to move around quite a bit, unless we own the tavern. The nature of the business, so to speak, and a precaution for our safety. Word had apparently spread of the original Barney's plight, and so all the barkeeps in the town decided quickly that it was better for them all to share a single identity and the name that went with it, rather than allow their friend to pay for another man's mistake.

"So the tradition continued. It spread all across the old land, a place that now is lost to the sea, and when those who came here from that place began building alehouses—which of course is often the *first* order of business—they all became 'Barney' as well." He smiled slightly and went back to drying his tankards.

"That's a fine tale, and this is fine ale," Ashe said, putting his battered tankard back on the bar. "So does Old Barney own this establishment?"

"Aye," said the barkeep. "This one, and this one alone, though I know he had one of the same name long ago and far away. He's a right old man, sir—mayhap not the original Barney, but he might have known him." He laughed at his own joke.

A slight commotion rose from the door; the group of men parted as an old man with a thick head of white hair passed through, whistling merrily.

"Speaking of which—here he is," said the barkeep.

The man pulled the hat from his head and ran his hand through his hair, spattering off the spray of the sea, then hung his hat and jacket on a peg by the door and came to the bar, a gleam in his blue eyes. He ceased his whistle in midnote.

"Just tellin' these gents the story of our name, Barney," the young barkeep said, putting the clean tankards under the bar. "They've been asking after those men who came through here three days ago."

Old Barney nodded as he came around behind the bar; he reached for an apron beneath it and as he stood his eye caught the faces of the two travelers. He stood suddenly straighter, then leaned forward and quietly addressed them both.

"Pray come with me, sirs. I'm sure we have a better, more private table for gentlemen of your stature." He turned and beckoned for them to follow him to the rear of the tavern.

Achmed and Ashe looked at each other in surprise. Neither was wearing any insignia or markings indicating their position; in fact, the journey had been arduous enough that their appearance had caused them to be denied entrance to a few establishments along the way. They rose from their stools and followed Old Barney to the back table he had indicated.

"You know us, Grandfather?" Ashe asked as they slipped into the rickety chairs.

"Aye, m'lord," the tavernkeeper replied, nodding his head deferentially to each of them.

"How?" Achmed demanded.

The old man's eyes took on a gleam.

"I am of the Island, too," he said in Old Cymrian. "I was there at your investiture, Lord Gwydion; I fought that day in the battle against the Fallen, though I am not as spry a man as I once was. And I saw you there, standing as host of the Moot, Majesty," he said to Achmed.

"Please speak Orlandan, Grandfather," Ashe said quietly. "Though I understand you, my grasp of Old Cymrian is academic; my father insisted I study the language, but it was long dead ere my birth. It is important that I grasp fully everything you have to say."

"Once again your inadequacy compromises us, Ashe," Achmed said.

"Why do I not know you?" the Lord Cymrian asked the elderly man, studying the shining blue eyes, the wrinkled face, the thick head of hair whiter than salt. "I wore the Patriarch's Ring of Wisdom for a time, and believed that it revealed to me the names of all those from the Island who were still alive. And yet I know you not—why?"

The tavernkeeper smiled. "Because my name is not my own, m'lord," he said pleasantly. "It belongs to a brotherhood that predates the exodus. My fealty to that brotherhood is more elder, and more powerful, than any pledge I, like the others who fled the destruction of Serendair, made to your grandfather Gwylliam. So, with respect, you have no claim on me." He leaned forward slightly. "But your wife does."

"Rhapsody?" Ashe demanded, his voice rising involuntarily; Achmed stepped on his foot to bring him into a low modulation again. "You have seen her?"

The old man shook his head. "Not since the Council, m'lord." His eyes widened as realization set in. "She—she is not the woman for whom they are searching?"

The travelers' eyes met; after a moment Achmed nodded.

"Yes," Ashe said, trying to keep his voice from betraying him.

Alarm flooded the old man's features. "No, gods, no. Not again, gods, not again. What happened?"

"Again?" Achmed demanded. "Tell us how you know her."

Old Barney looked over his shoulder for a moment and, noting that the tavern had returned to its normal business, tuned back and spoke.

"I knew her in the old world," he said sadly. "She was a favorite patron of my wife, Dee, and mine. She used to study her music in my tavern, taking a back table, writing away on sheets of parchment, never causing a problem. We both loved her. I would not be here speaking with you now if it hadn't been for her."

"Why?" asked Ashe.

The barkeep's eyes blinked in the dark tavern.

"An accident, I'm sure, m'lord. On the last day I saw her in the old world, she handed me a bit o' music she had graphed, telling me it was my name, and that if I should ever come upon a troubadour, I should get him to play it for me. She was in a hurry at the time, on the run from a dangerous man, so I slipped the paper into my apron pocket and forgot about it. I never saw her in that world again.

"A fortnight or so later, a traveling minstrel did come into the old Hat and Feathers—I kept the establishment name when I built the new one—and, in barter for a pint, I asked him to play the tune Rhapsody had graphed for me. It was a catchy melody, one that fit my mind well, as it should, bein' my name and all. I had no understanding of Lirin Namers and their powers—she was just a sweet girl in a bad situation, and the tune was pleasing to my ear, so I whistled it every day; got to be an unconscious thing. Drove poor Dee to distraction, may she be restin' peacefully in the Afterlife.

"The Seren War came and went; my beloved Dee grew old and passed from this world to the next, life went on, day into day, year into year, century into century, and yet I didn't seem to age past the point I had been on the day she gave the scrap of music to me.

"I didn't figure that out 'til much later, though. I just thought perhaps I had a Lirin ancestor, or some other long-lived type. Until the day I met up with a Lirin Namer aboard the ship I was leaving Serendair on; he was a pleasant fellow, and addressed me by my name, though I was certain he had never seen me before, and could not have known my profession. 'How do you come to know my name?' I asked. He laughed and said, 'You told me yourself, good man. It is the tune you are whistling.'

"I came to know him on the voyage—we both had refugeed with the First Fleet, and traveled in Merithyn's convoy of ships—and it was in the course of that time I learned what had accounted for my longevity. In the whistling of my name, over and over, each day, I was in a sense *remaking* myself, returning myself to the 'vibrational state,' whatever that be, I had been the day before."

His eyes gleamed brighter in the smoky air of the tavern. "Then, arriving here, we all had it, that immortality; some cherished it, others grew to hate it, but they, unlike me, had not already had the stroke of luck to live well past my time before I even left the Island. Had it not been for that last gift of your wife, Lord Gwydion, I would never have come to this place. And while I have seen a great many terrible things, and lived through times when I wished I were in the Afterlife with my Dee, I have to say that on the whole, it has been a gift unparalleled."

Ashe put his hand over the old man's; it was trembling, the distended knuckles of the arthritic fingers shaking violently.

"The man who was pursuing my wife that day," he said quietly, trying to contain the emotion in his own voice, "did you know him?"

Old Barney's eyes opened even wider, their pale blue irises and white scleras standing out in stark contrast to the dim light of the tavern.

502 *Elizabeth Haydon*

"Michael, the Wind of Death," he whispered, as if afraid
to say the name aloud. "Yes, I knew of him, saw him once
or twice in fact. Why?"

"It is he that may have her now, or is at least pursuing
her," Achmed said bluntly. "Most likely he is also the one
who is laying waste to the seacoast. He is no longer the
Wind of Death, but the Wind of Fire, being the whore of a
F'dor spirit."

"Gods," Old Barney choked, making a countersign upon
his forehead. "No."

Ashe's grip tightened on his hand.

"Help us," he said tersely. "I believe you can. Rhapsody
and I saw the Prophetess of Yarim, the Seer of the Future,
at the beginning of summer; she uttered a prophecy that may
have partially been about you."

The old man trembled more violently. "Manwyn? Manwyn—named me in a prophecy?"

"I don't know for certain, but it seems so," said Ashe.
"She told her to beware the Past, that it sought to have her,
to harm her, and to aid her. And then she said: 'Long ago
a promise made, long ago a name conveyed, long ago a
voice was stayed—three debts to be paid.' "

"I—I don't know that I have ever been spoken of in a
prophecy before," the elderly barkeep said nervously.
"Your—great-aunt frightens me; I witnessed her madness at
the Councils long ago. To know that she may have seen me
through her sextant is a terrifying thought, m'lord. I am only
a simple barkeep, and a very old man."

"But do you seek to aid my wife?" Ashe asked desperately. "I believe that you might be the 'past' that seeks to
do so."

"Yes, of course," Barney whispered. "For though she is
mad, the Seer's words are true; a name was conveyed, my
name, as I have told you, and I am alive as a result. It is a
very great debt I owe her, and I am eager to repay it. I just
do not know—"

His voice trailed off suddenly as a thought occurred. His

face became serious, the fear dissipating in his eyes.

"Perhaps I do at that," he said softly.

"Tell us," Achmed demanded.

"Please, Grandfather," Ashe added, trying to quell the dragon that was rising, impatient, in his blood.

"You said that it was Michael, the Wind of Death, that pursues her now?"

"Yes."

Old Barney nodded.

"I know a secret, one that I have shared with no one, not in this life or in the Afterlife," he said quietly. "I have guarded it all these years. But perhaps in telling you now, I can repay the debt I owe Rhapsody, and aid her as once she aided me. It may be a secret of power in these times."

"What is it?" Achmed asked, clutching the table board, he had not touched his ale, and was focused on the man as if he wished to feel rather than simply hear his answer.

The old man drew closer as the noise of the dim tavern grew louder in the distance. His words were spoken so softly that both the sovereigns had to strain to hear him.

"MacQuieth lives," he said.

# 45

*S*ilence reigned for a moment in the back of the tavern.

When Achmed and Ashe had recovered their voices, they spoke at the same time, their words tumbling over one another.

"Where? How do you know? MacQuieth Monodiere Nagall? Impossible—he has been dead for fourteen centuries. What—"

"Shhh!" Old Barney hissed, his eyes darting furtively around the tavern; satisfied after a moment that they had not been overheard, he turned back to the two sovereigns.

"King Achmed, Lord Gwydion, you must listen to what I tell you without argument, for I am telling you the truth," he said clearly. "Though history records his death, history is sometimes wrong."

"He was a Cymrian and a Kinsman," Ashe said softly, taking care with his words. "If he was alive, he would have felt the call of the Council horn, if not for this last Council, then certainly for all those that were held before it. Every Cymrian, no matter where he or she was, felt the compulsion; it only grew more difficult to ignore when resisted, leading to death if held at bay long enough. He never came; he can't be alive, Barney."

The old barkeep sighed in annoyance.

"I can tell you why that is not true, m'lord," he said evenly. "The reason for your misconception is because you don't understand *why* the horn worked as it did. I was there, however, so what I bear witness to is what I have seen with my own eyes, and heard with my own ears." His face took on the same faraway expression it had held when talking the moment before about the old world.

"As each man, woman, and child of Serendair boarded the ships that would sail to this new land, they were presented with two things: a dipper of water from the Well of the Before-Time, and the silver horn of the king. Gwylliam had decreed that each refugee would drink from the Well, believing that it would guard their lives and health in the course of the passage, and for the most part he was correct. It is still not known decidedly what gave the Cymrians their agelessness, the ability to cheat Time, though many theories abound. Personally, I would guess that the living water from this ancient well might have been largely, if not solely, responsible.

"As for the horn," the old man continued, "Gwylliam, your grandfather, had decreed that any Seren citizen wishing to sail to the new continent must pledge his or her fealty on the horn, and swear that they would come, in times of need or council, in answer to the horn's cry. Because of the import of the moment, and the presence of such primordial elemental power, it was a promise that could not be broken."

"Yes," Ashe agreed. "And we know that MacQuieth sailed with the Second Fleet—"

Old Barney's voice crackled with controlled anger. "Lord Gwydion, if you would listen, you would cease to sound so much like your grandfather. If you are to seek MacQuieth's help, you will want to separate yourself as much as you can from that lineage." Ashe lapsed into silence.

"MacQuieth did not pledge fealty to Gwylliam on the horn. It is a long story as to why, a tale you have no time for now, but suffice to say that MacQuieth hated your grandfather, his king. He was old at the time of the Island's peril, and volunteered to stay and watch over the last hours of Serendair, but the king wanted to assure the Second Fleet, and commanded that he lead it. MacQuieth blamed your grandfather for the death of his son, Hector, who, in his place, stayed behind when the fleets sailed to protect the Island in its last days. When the Sleeping Child erupted, and the Island was lost, Hector was lost with it.

"And all who were part of the story knew that was how it would end—Hector, MacQuieth, and Gwylliam. So while MacQuieth accepted what was to come to pass, his loathing of Gwylliam never abated. When he was presented with the horn, on which he was to place his hand and swear fealty to your grandfather, MacQuieth instead spat into the sea. 'I'll not pledge,' he said to the soldiers lining the gangplank. 'I have given all I have to give. If you require more of me, I will stay behind with my son.' Faced with this choice, the soldiers looked at one another and, knowing MacQuieth was the commander of the entire Second Fleet and captain of the ship they were boarding, they let him pass. So he made no promise, as the rest of us did. And when the horn of the Council sounded, while we were all impelled to come in response, he heard no summons, felt no compulsion. He remained hidden away, out of the sight of Time."

"He walked into the sea," Ashe murmured, thinking back to the endless history lessons his father had imparted to him. "He stood on the shores of Manosse, where the Second Fleet ultimately landed, knee-deep in the surf, and stood vigil for the Island. The only person he would tolerate the company of was his daughter-in-law, Talthea, the Favored One; I remember witnessing her death when I was a small child. When he felt the Island's death in the waves, he walked into the sea and disappeared. Everyone assumed he drowned, for he was never seen again."

Old Barney smiled. "Ah, yes, Everyone. He is surely the wisest of men, since he always knows so much; as a barkeep I've heard his false assumptions and half-truths for a millennium. How do you think that Gaematria, the Island of the Sea Mages, has remained unmolested all these centuries there, alone, in the middle of the Wide Central Sea? MacQuieth guards it from the depths. There is a whole world beneath the waves of the ocean, Majesties, a world of high mountains and deep chasms, of unimaginable wonders, of beings that rarely, if ever, are seen on the drylands. Do not assume because something is not within your senses that it is dead; there are many places in the world for a man to hide if he does not wish to be found."

"Will he aid us in our search for Michael?" Ashe asked, suddenly invigorated. "My mother was descended of Talthea; I am of his line, and carry Kirsdarke, the sword of which he was in his time the bearer."

"Aye," Barney said seriously, "but you are also descended of Gwylliam, whom he may never forgive."

"Perhaps, then, he will do it for Rhapsody?" Ashe persisted, desperation creeping into his voice. "She met him once in the old world—she was looking for me."

Barney shook his head. "If MacQuieth does anything, it will be because of Michael," he said. "He needs no reason other than that. There are ties there that are far older and far stronger even than the fact that you are of his blood. But I cannot speak for him—bartenders never make promises for ancient heroes. It's bad form."

Achmed and Ashe looked at each other, then chuckled.

"Thank you, Barney. We will guard his secret as well," Ashe promised.

"Where is he?" Achmed asked.

The elderly Cymrian barkeep stood and pushed his chair in.

"Come, and I will show you."

## ATOP GURGUS, YLORC

In the cool of the evening, the glassworkers, exhausted from twelve days of work without cease, sleeping in five-hour shifts, stumbled out into the fresher air of the corridors that led out into the mountain passes, finished except for one giant panel.

The woman known to the glassworkers as Theophila was standing at the top of the grade, directing the finishing touches on the sealing of the circular dome of glass. After three major and two minor adjustments she still was not satisfied, and so was perched on the top rigging of the dome itself, dangling over the massive drop below it, soldering the edges of the tracery that bordered the green and yellow sections.

A number of the Bolg stonemasons who had participated in the building of the tracery supports, the framing of the glass, stood silently and somewhat helplessly to the side, watching the woman, who was harnessed to a nearby support. The thin air at the mountain's summit was causing her to struggle for breath; the Bolg were waiting to see if she would finish, expire from lack of air, or plunge to her death first.

When she finally was satisfied, she signaled to Shaene, ever-present, hovering obsequiously.

"All right, Shaene, have them pull me in."

The Bolg masons grasped the ropes that ran through three pulleys, maneuvering her away from the glass dome below and back to the rocky ledges. She unhooked herself from the support wires, pulled off her heavy goatskin gloves and threw them to the ground, then began walking down the mountain pass back to the Cauldron, then stopped.

"Put the cover on," she called back over her shoulder.

A great circular dome of wood was hoisted into place and laid gently over the newly positioned glass. Satisfied, the woman turned and started off again.

"You are a brave woman, Theophila," Shaene puffed, struggling himself to catch his breath in the mountain air and keep up with her. "Let's go back inside now, so you might rest."

The woman eyed him scornfully. "Rest? I have a last panel to fire, Shaene, and the color formula isn't right yet. I've tried everything I know—different types of ash in the melt, stirring with iron posts to shade the purple, baking it longer. It's still not true. I may have to send you or Sandy off to Yarim for some different metal ores to experiment with."

Shaene laughed in a sudden bark of amusement.

"You had best send me, then, Theophila. Sandy won't have no part of going to Yarim, but you should tell him you're sendin' him anyway; it will be fun to watch."

The woman showed no particular interest, trying to avoid being trapped in conversation with the Canderian artisan. "Sandy will go where I direct him."

"Yes, lady," Shaene said hastily. "But he'll turn white when you tell him he has to go. I'd like to watch, if I may," he added lamely.

The woman stopped and leveled her gaze at him for the first time. "Why would he turn white?"

Shaene leaned forward conspiratorially. "He came from there a few years back," he imparted importantly. "He's terrified of what he left behind."

"And what was that?" Her tone became suddenly warm, sweet and thick, like malt.

Shaene looked into her endlessly deep eyes, saw the corners of her mouth turn up in a sensuous smile, and blinked rapidly, trying to quell the swelling that was coming in response. *She is so beautiful,* he thought, *beautiful and alone. If it has been as long for her as it has for me—*

"A witch," he said, his voice rumbling with a huskiness it had not had a moment before. "A hideous woman, or so he says, the mistress of his old guild. Evil incarnate, he said. But then, what can you expect from so young a lad? He knows nothing of the world." He forced a laugh, trying to sound debonair. "And how truly evil women can be."

The woman's forehead furrowed, her brows drawing together darkly.

"Sandy?" she said aloud, half to herself.

"Oh, well, his name is actually Omet," Shaene said, wiping the sweat of exertion off his brow with a stained handkerchief. "I call him Sandy because of the desert he comes from."

"Yarim isn't sandy," the woman said distantly, as if her mouth were still engaged in a conversation her mind had long abandoned. "It's clay. Red clay."

Shaene shrugged, then gestured to the guards at the entrance to the Cauldron as they approached.

"Just a nickname," he said. "So shall I meet you back at the kilns, or in the tower workroom?"

The woman turned to him and smiled broadly, then drew close to him in agonizingly slow steps.

"Neither," she said sweetly. "You have been working far too hard, Shaene; I don't want to compromise you." She chuckled, giving him a meaningful look. "Not that way, at least."

"I'll—urgh," Shaene fumbled. "What—what do you want me to do, then?"

"Wait for me in your quarters. I have some cleanup to attend to, and then I will join you for supper."

Shaene nodded dumbly as the Panjeri woman winked at him, then turned and walked into the tunnel that led back into the Bolg seat of power.

Something in his head did not add up.

But he was much too far past the point of the clarity of reason to do the figuring.

# 46

## TRAEG

Old Barney led Ashe and Achmed out the back door of the Hat and Feathers. As soon as they stepped outside, the smoke of hickory wood was cleared from their heads by the fresh sea wind, itself still heavy with ash, but clearing.

Barney gestured as they passed the remains of a livery, the iron hitching posts out front the only survivors of the fire that had claimed it.

"I'll procure four horses for you, three riders and a pack-horse," he said, not slowing his gait. "They'll be here when you are ready to leave. If you need but three, leave whichever you judge to be least hale."

"Thank you," Ashe said; Achmed nodded.

All around them the wharf was growing busy with pas-sersby, workman clearing away the rubble of the burnings, urchin children begging alms, fishermen bringing in the day's catch, hauling nets that had seen better days' bounty.

The closer they came to the waterfront, the stiffer the wind became. At high gusts it was almost a struggle to stand upright; after one particularly violent squall Barney turned to them and, seeing their hair and veils plastered against their faces by the wind and spray, laughed aloud.

"Welcome to Traeg, by the way," he said, holding up a crooked arm to shield himself from the gale. " 'Tis our claim in history, the home of the wind in this part of the world, or at least a place it feels comfortable enough in to stay for long stretches without abating."

*How appropriate,* Ashe thought as they followed the bar-keep off the loosely cobbled road and across a sandy bluff. *The great Kinsman, a Brother of the Wind, makes his home near Traeg. It's fitting.*

Barney stopped a dozen yards from the edge of the bluff, pointing down a rocky train to the beach.

"If you're to find him, you'll find him down there most likely, m'lords," he said, pulling his hat down farther over his eyes. "He's sometimes out near the breakwater, or walking near the seawall, though some days he remains in his keep, attending to whatever business an ancient hero attends to. But do have a care; there are sometimes wastrels and floaters around these parts, beggars, sailors that were tossed off their ships when their captains put into port here and refused to be allowed back aboard. They are a ragged lot, with desperation in their eyes; hunger'll do that. I used to bring food to them occasionally, the day's leavings, until they fell upon me and beat me bloody one day. Since then I've stayed clear of the beach. Watch your backs."

"Thank you," Ashe said, giving his hand to the old man, resting the other on his arm. "For this, and for what you did those many years ago to spare Rhapsody. When I find her, I will bring her by so that you two might visit and reminisce."

The old man smiled sadly, but said nothing.

He stood and watched as the sovereigns made their way down the rocky path to the beach below the bluff, then walked to the bluff's edge and looked down from below.

He could see them in the distance, making their way across the sand to the water's edge, looking up and down the shoreline, buffeted by the fierce wind.

Barney then looked out at the beach at the foot of the bluff. The tide was rising, the waves creeping ever closer, rolling in amid a swirl of windy froth.

In the wet sand at the water's edge was a strange drawing, a vast picture of simple lines, depicting a skull, Barney thought, or perhaps, upon second reflection, it was a head, its eyes set wide apart in a shallow, soft face, the line of the mouth missing below the flat nose.

As if the lips were fused.

## ON THE *BASQUELA,* OFF THE
## NORTHERN COAST

𝕿he seneschal put the spyglass to his eye, scanning the black lava coastline, watching the breakers batter the jagged rocks below the promontory.

It was a sight that had come to haunt him not only in his waking hours, but in his dreams as well. As a demonic host, Michael had little need for sleep, passing a few hours in a sort of dreamlike meditation, the voice of the F'dor droning in his mind like an endlessly crackling fire.

It was during those times that the promontory appeared in his inner vision, as if it were mocking him. That jagged cliff, coming to a point over the rocky water, seemed to laugh as the brutal tide smashed over it.

*She is here, hiding from you,* it jeered at him. The words had played in his mind, burning like acid, until the seneschal no longer knew whether they were portents of some sort of prophecy, the taunting of his infuriating guest, or his own self-doubts, which had always been vociferous, clanging at him, chewing on his confidence.

He watched the rocks for a long time, looking for a sign of life of any kind, and saw nothing but the endless crash of the waves, the boiling froth of salt water and foam.

Then, as if put into his mind by a less malevolent spirit than the one that actually lived there, a thought occurred to him.

*Perhaps there is a cave behind all those rocks, behind that swelling tide,* he thought, though his mind rejected the notion that she could have survived in such a thing. He and his men had certainly seen many such crevices in the towering rockwalls all along the coast, but they had been shallow enough that even at low tide they were submerged. Still, the cliffs here were taller than most, the wind more violent, so it seemed worth examining that such a thing could be so.

"Quinn!" he shouted to his appointed captain.

"Aye, sir?" Quinn answered, exhaustion in his voice. He

had not had a decent night's sleep since assuming the captaincy, and was now praying daily that the seneschal would give up and let them go home to Argaut.

"Take us back. I want to drop anchor tomorrow, and put in to shore the next morning."

"Yes, m'lord," said the sailor wearily.

The seneschal turned to his reeve. "Fergus, select two of the remaining crew and get a strong cordon of rope. I want them to rappel down those cliffs and see if she is hidden in back of the rocks."

The reeve's face remained placid. "As you command, m'lord."

"You and they will accompany me in day after tomorrow. If we do not find her, there will be fiery repercussions for all involved."

"Yes, m'lord."

The seneschal moved closer and spoke softly into the reeve's face.

"Even you, Fergus."

The reeve sighed. "Yes, m'lord." He had expected nothing less.

# 47

## TRAEG

For two hours the men waited in the biting wind, wandering up and down the beach along the shoreline.

After an hour the sun had begun its descent; it was still high, given the length of the summer days, and the afternoon still bright, but the light had shifted into the hazy gold of later day, and with that shift came the human pigeons.

Where the ragtag wanderers and beachcombers had been hiding during the brighter hours was a mystery. Ashe thought his dragon sense had discerned them in and among the rockwalls, in flat depressions and tidal caves where they could sleep away the day's heat at low tide. Now that the current was flooding and the tide rising again, they came out of the rocky edifices, some making their way to the docks, others shambling out onto the sandbar, searching the edges of the seawall for the remains of the day's catch caught and tossed back.

Achmed was growing more surly with each passing moment. Water was an element he loathed in any form; it masked the vibrations of the world to which he was sensitive. Beside the sea, at its windiest, his irritation was at its high; the conundrum of the crashing surf not only made it impossible to concentrate on any signal he might normally have felt on the air, but in fact added to the cacophony that already was assaulting his sensitive skin.

"I used to come down to the seacoast to practice adjusting for air currents with my cwellan shots," he remarked to Ashe near the fire they had laid after a batch of raggedy women had assailed them, begging alms. "I am a little rusty. Perhaps I should take some target practice."

Ashe said nothing, tossing a handful of coins to the women, who scurried after them in the sand, then ran off, gibbering, up the path to the remains of the village.

"Stop that," Achmed said angrily. "They'll only come back with their friends and whatever leprotic spawn they have waiting up there."

"They're sea widows," Ashe replied mildly, his eyes beginning to burn from staring so long down the shoreline. "Women whose husbands plied the seas, sailors, fisherman, who never returned. My whole family's sorry history began when Merithyn never made it back to Elynsynos. Alms for starving widows is the least I can do."

Achmed rolled his eyes. "When are you ever going to understand that penance and penitence for the deeds of others who died long before you were born, but happened to share the same blood, is ridiculous? You can't make up for the sins of the past that your family committed; in truth, if you go back far enough, you would be responsible for the misdeeds of everyone in the world. Get a hold of yourself."

Ashe made an ugly masturbatory gesture in response. "*You* get a hold of yourself," he said contemptuously. "Spare me your bile and worldweariness; my wife would not agree with you." Then he returned to his vigil.

"Well, you are correct at least in that," Achmed retorted, shielding his eyes. "Rhapsody thinks the world's pain is her personal responsibility to heal. Fortunately, if she lives, she will have enough time to waste in the ultimate discovery that even if it is, she is not up to the task."

"If she lives?" Ashe demanded, turning on the Bolg king in anger. "Did you *really* just say that to me?"

"Yes, that was not the cry of the wind echoing between your ears," Achmed replied. "Have you not noticed that her presence is missing from the wind? I find no semblance of her heartbeat. I hope I am wrong, but you must prepare yourself to face the possibility that she is dead, that he killed her, certainly violated her, threw her in the sea, or took her away with him. Give in to the hatred that the possibility spawns in you; it will make you even more focused on what needs to be done—finding the F'dor."

"Stop," Ashe said, his face growing florid with effort to keep the dragon from rampaging. "Do not speak of such things to me—not yet. I do not need more reason than I already have to hate this man, to hunt this demon, to rend him when I come upon him until there is nothing but a shadow where he once occupied space in the wind. You are prodding powers within me that it is already a daily struggle to contain; don't enflame my ire for your own purposes. Whether you think you are assuring my concentration on the task at hand, or merely tormenting me for taking her away from you, all you are doing is treading on the thin ice of disaster."

Achmed opened his mouth to respond, then shut it quickly. He exhaled angrily.

Near their fire a ragged old man was wandering aimlessly, flicking a long stick of driftwood, drawing shapeless pat-

terns in the wet beach. The pursuit of his artwork was tossing sand onto the fire, making it hiss and threaten to die.

"Move back from there," he called out in annoyance, but
the ragged man ignored him, continuing his lazy patterns
amid the dunes and sand drumlins.

Achmed strode over to the fire and interposed himself
between it and the elderly sand artist.

"Shoo," he said. "Warm yourself if you wish, otherwise
back away."

The man turned in the general direction of his voice; Achmed could see that his eyes were cloudy with the cataracts
of age, possibly of exposure to the sun; they seemed almost
burned on the surface. The irises of those eyes, like his skin
and long, unkempt hair, were the color of driftwood; in fact,
the Bolg king noted, the old man had been sleeping in a
sand drumlin near the water's edge since they had been
there, and he had mistaken him for a long pile of jetsam
washed up on the shore.

After a moment, it seemed as if he had finally heard Achmed's instruction. The man turned away and walked off
purposefully into the sea.

"What—what did you say to him?" Ashe said in disbelief,
watching the frail legs disappear in the waves. The breakers
were growing in intensity; it seemed unlikely that so little
body mass as this elderly man had could stand up to even
the gentlest of them.

"Stop—come out of there," Achmed shouted. He grunted
in exasperation and then, seeing the old man had not heard
him, followed him reticently out into the shallow surf.

"Come out of the water, you old fool," he growled. "I'll
not fish you out if you get sucked away by the undertow."

The old man spoke, his voice carried to them by an incoming gust of wind.

"I don't know you," he said. "Go away."

"Come out of the water."

In response, the elderly fellow squatted down in the surf.
He turned slowly, facing them. It was not clear if the squint

on his face was a grimace or a smile. Then he stood, turned toward the depth of the sea, and walked away from them again.

He was in surf up to his calves before Achmed broke into a run to catch him. The Dhracian grabbed the old man by the arm.

"What are you doing? Are you deaf?"

The ancient face turned to look at Achmed's hand on his arm, but the man took another step, knee-deep now. Achmed grasped the other shoulder and turned the old man's whole body toward him, away from the depths.

"Don't hurt him," called Ashe, looking down at the scratching the old man had made in the sand.

Achmed wasn't even certain that the face in front of him could see. The clarity was mostly gone from the eyes. In the breath while he was pondering, trying to think of something calming and harmless to say, he thought he caught a flash of recognition in the hazy eyes.

Suddenly his feet were out from under him. Whether it was a wave or a leg that had upended him, he had barely time to inhale before his whole body was submerged.

His hatred of water overwhelmed his senses, and he tried to push with his elbows against the gravelly bottom of the sea to get up, but he felt the old man's knees come down on both of his forearms, and he suddenly realized that it had been no chance wave that swept his feet out from under him.

He was being intentionally drowned.

He struggled to stay calm in the face of the panic that was threatening to consume him. He made another attempt to overpower the man holding him beneath the waves, to slip or shift the old man off, but it was like trying to move the weight of the whole ocean.

*A*t the sound of the splash, Ashe looked up; Achmed was gone.

The old man was stooped, almost on his knees in the

water, expressionless and calm. Ashe strode out into the surf
a step or two before he could see Achmed's legs flailing
underwater. He ran the remaining steps, drawing Kirsdarke,
and leveling it at the old man's ear.

"Get off of him," he commanded.

Never before, with dragonesque eyes staring down the
shining blue coral filigree of the sword, had a man not lost
his breath, dropped a beat, been given pause at least. But
the old man, like a rising tarpon, flung one hand from the
water to Ashe's wrist and twisted the hilt away from him
with the other hand, simultaneously, with hardly a splash.
A surge swept through his arm and hand, like a cross-wave;
Ashe blinked. Kirsdarke was gone from his grip, now
clutched in the bony grasp of the old man.

He had no need to turn around to know that the sword
was now stretched at his own neck. He cursed silently and
grabbed Achmed's robe, dragging him out of the water.

𝒰nderwater, with his eyes closed, Achmed felt the flutter of what he thought were Ashe's footsteps. As he realized
he couldn't break free on his own, he willed himself to calm,
to wait for the opportunity that Ashe's attack would present.
As his struggles ceased amid the rushing rhythm of the
waves around him he heard a great sounding, almost a bell
of a heartbeat, which he hadn't heard since he left Serendair.

It was MacQuieth's heartbeat.

And it was thudding directly above him, practically pulsing through his own forearms where the ancient hero was
kneeling on him.

He nearly gasped, and listened harder, knowing that if the
ancient hero had recognized him as the Brother, the master
assassin from the old world, it would explain why he was
drowning right now.

Distantly, in echoes and waves, impossibly far and faint,
he heard another familiar tone. Before he could really catch
hold of it, he was being dragged upward, as abruptly as he
had been submerged, Ashe's face before his eyes.

For a few moments there was nothing but the attenuated silence of the beach, the surf cuffing the rocks, their soaked clothing dripping, Achmed choking, while Ashe witnessed a transformation with his dragon sense. The already tall figure who now held the water sword was growing, not in the sense of size, but like a sponge or a dried plant or fruit, revivifying.

As the life, the vigor returned to the driftwood-gray skin and eyes, it returned to the voice as well. It was still somewhat salty, but resonated as much as it had whispered before. There was flesh in it, where before it had been merely skeletal.

"Where did you get my son's sword?" The unwavering blade dripped slightly and glowed a fierce blue. "If you speak more than five words, you will die."

Ashe's mind raced in shock, pondering what to say.

"We're hunting Michael," Achmed spat, slavering seawater. "He's alive."

# 48

Shades of expression blew over MacQuieth's features in rapid succession as if huge gusts of wind threw great masses of cloud across his face. Possession of the sword, recognition of an old foe, Ashe's affront, and that name, all had to be chewed into a mass for comprehension, by a mind whose reason spent most of its time adrift.

"He can't be" was all the ancient hero could muster.

Ashe found words this time.

"Yes, lord. He carries Tysterisk. He's taken my wife, put the forest and the shore to flame. He's become the host of a F'dor."

The old man drew the sword toward him and took it in both hands. For the first time, he seemed to feel weight in it. He slowly crouched until he was almost sitting in the surf again, with the tip of Kirsdarke dangling in the waves, his eyes resting on the sword, but wide, as if he couldn't really tell whether he actually held it before him.

"Who are you?" he said again softly. "I don't know you. Go away." He ran his hand down the shimmering blade, which was glowing more intensely blue than either man had ever seen it in Ashe's hand. "If the tyrant sent you, return to him and tell him I'll see him in the Afterlife. Tell him to bring his sword."

"Tyrant?" Achmed queried.

"Gwylliam is dead," Ashe said.

"Good," the old soldier said, ignoring the spray that was pelting his face. "I thought he'd never die. With his elixirs and machines and engines. A thousand years from now, nothing left but his ego. No telling what there'd be left of me to fight it. Not even enough left to spit on. Here!"

He heaved sword at Ashe.

"You came to use it," he said contemptuously. "Give it your best." He stood stiffly, ankle-deep in water that alternately pushed and pulled the sand beneath his feet.

With him standing now, his eyes clear, his body no longer looking so frail, or his mind so brittle, Ashe and Achmed finally had a good look at him. Though not nearly as tall as Grunthor, or as his legends had proclaimed him to be, MacQuieth was exceptionally large for a half-Lirin. What they originally thought were layers of ragged clothing was really his body underneath, both taller and broader than Ashe, with what once must have been black hair and eyes, both gray now, only slightly cramped hands, and either sufficient command of the sea or strength in his legs to be unmoved by the running waves.

Achmed stood and stepped back, shaking his head.

"No," he said. It did not escape him that the old soldier had subtly, sagaciously manipulated both of them into the deeper water, that the beach was fairly close behind him, and that now that he had the sword, there was no way they were escaping without coming to whatever agreement suited

MacQuieth, whose heart, he noted, still rang like a great bell.

Ashe caught part of the hilt of the sword, and was so spared the indignity and vulnerability of fishing for it in the knee-deep water. He also stood and said, "No, m'lord." Then he carefully wiped the blade on the upper part of his cloak and sheathed it.

"We have come for nothing like that. We have come because we need to find Michael. We need to stop him and rescue someone he's taken. We know only that he landed near here, but we cannot track him—"

"And you can't kill him if you happen to find him. You don't know how to kill him as he deserves to be killed, as he needs to be killed, if he's going to stay dead." MacQuieth finished Ashe's statement, and at last looked at him without the lens of combat in his eyes. "Are you Merithyn's heir as well as Gwylliam's?"

"Yes, sir. And yours."

The ancient warrior scowled. "Nonesuch. None of my line would ever blend their blood with the spawn of that cur."

"Cynron ap Talthea did. She was my mother. Many generations removed from you, but undeniably of your line."

"How disappointing for both of us. And on whose authority have you come to hunt this creature, and disturb me?"

"Our own," Achmed said. "Few others know he is here."

As he stood in the receding current, Achmed thought that it looked as if the tide were taking out MacQuieth. He looked more drawn with every breath, more reduced or distant from the rush of battle and grip of the sword.

MacQuieth fixed his gaze directly at the Firbolg king, but addressed the Lord Cymrian.

"You know you travel with the Brother, the great assassin who, in his time and way, was more terrible than the one you seek?"

"Yes," Ashe said, "but a world away from his former self."

MacQuieth turned back up to the shore, apparently tired of the tide, tired of questions.

"A world away? No. The world follows us in our travels. We're there, no matter how far we've run; trust me." He trudged slowly toward the shore, with the two younger men sloshing out of the waves behind him, then turned and glared at them again.

"What do you want?"

With no time to confer, neither of the sovereigns said anything for a minute. Then Achmed motioned to Ashe to speak.

"Michael landed near this beach. He has been up and down the coast, burning villages mostly. We wish to get ahead of him, trap him somewhere."

"Stop. *Who are you?*"

"Didn't you just tell me who my ancestors were?" Ashe asked, growing desperate, not knowing what to say to answer the man's questions without angering him, then giving up, realizing it would be impossible to know.

"I can smell your blood," MacQuieth said with a glower. "The sword has tasted it. Him, the sea knows, and I can tell by the way he moves who trained him. I have no idea what the world looks like now; most often I don't care. Once a man passes his millionth day, they mercifully run together. But to find the bone in the soup, the oasis in the desert, the island, the killer, I have to know what the wind looks like, how many years have passed, whether this is a new road or an old wall. When my senses were young and on fire I could track a porpoise, a hawk." He gestured at Achmed. "I was ready to track *him* before he was said to have died. Tell me what I really need to know."

Ashe straightened his shoulders, feeling the wisdom in his blood course through him.

"I am Gwydion ap Llauron ap Gwylliam, tuatha d'Anwynan o Manosse," he said simply. "Lord Cymrian by election. And long ago, before the exodus, before the real onset of the Seren War in which you fought for the life of the Island, before all that, a young girl came to you in the streets of Easton and asked if you had seen me. You had not, and you told her so, kindly, she says. Now, if she is still among the living, she may be in the clutches of the Wind of Death, the anti-Kinsman, he who would use the element of air to destroy armies, murder soldiers, rather than to aid them in their time of need. He is the host of a demon-spirit, though a strange permutation of the normal parasite relationship; apparently his loathsome personality was so strong, so evil, that it did not succumb to the monster's will, was not subsumed by it, but rather coexists with it in the same body. So whatever murderous tendencies, whatever depravity lived within his mind when you fought him, still remain, only more powerful now."

"I did not fight him," the elderly soldier said, turning away and walking up the beach toward the rockwalls of the cliffs. "I fought Tsoltan, his master. Michael ran. Had he been man enough to stay and fight, you would not be seeking him now."

The wind howled as the two sovereigns followed him around rocky outcroppings and hummocks of driftwood.

"What were you drawing in the sand?" Ashe asked, hurrying to keep up with the old man.

MacQuieth shrugged. "Whatever the sea tells me," he said, and nothing more.

On the north side of a large formation of boulders at the cliff face they saw what they realized after a moment was a small hut that never saw visitors. In front there was a battered shield that had been converted into a distiller for water and little else.

The ancient hero disappeared into the rocky enclosure, reappearing a moment later with a wedding ring encrusted with diamonds in his hand, which he slipped onto his smallest finger.

"Do you have horses?" he asked, examining the ring on his hand.

"Yes," Achmed said. "On the bluff."

Without a word MacQuieth walked away, heading to the path that led up to the top of the pass.

Ashe glanced westward over his shoulder at the red sun hovering just at the edge of the horizon, ready to plunge into the rolling gray sea.

"Did you wish to sing your vespers, Grandfather, the requiem for the sun?" he asked respectfully in the Lirin tongue.

MacQuieth stopped abruptly.

"No," he said, then started up the path to town again. "I no longer remember how."

# 49

At the top of the hill, at the outskirts of the village, four horses were waiting, three saddled, one packed with provisions.

The healthy tinge MacQuieth's skin gained when he held the sword in the sea had begun to recede. The farther he moved from both water and weapon, the grayer he grew, first in hair, then in face, and finally in eye. By the time they had reached the horses he had begun to look somewhat frail again.

His will, however, seemed not to have diminished at all. He studied the horses for a moment, speaking in a strange tongue to each of them, then summarily chose the one onto which Ashe had already begun to bind his gear, dumping it unceremoniously onto the ground.

"Barney's packed the wrong animal for dray," he said, the wind whipping through his hair and the horse's mane in time. "That horse is smarter than the one in the lead. The leader's a stupid animal. He would lead better with his arse than his head." He mounted the horse he had chosen with the fluidity and grace of a young man. "Must be a Cymrian horse. Think I'll call him 'Gwylliam.' "

The two sovereigns smiled wearily.

"Just the back end of him," Achmed said.

Those were the last words the ancient hero uttered that day. He turned his head to the wind, listening as if for the Kinsman call, then clicked to the horse and rode off to the north along the coastal road, seemingly unconcerned as to whether the others were following him or not.

Achmed watched the process of the hunt with interest. Unlike his method of tracking heartbeats, the singular concentration on one specific trail, MacQuieth seemed instead to be looking for what was not there, searching in between the pockets of air to find a man-spirit that was using the element to wrap around himself, shielding him from normal sight and even his own extraordinary abilities and Ashe's.

They all but flew over the ground, Ashe and Achmed frequently looking at each other in surprise—surprise at their companion's age, surprise at the toll the years had taken, surprise that he could still ride as well as his legends said he did. The greatest source of their surprise, without question, was that they had even found him at all.

They rode through much of the night, stopping finally in a sheltered spot to sleep and sit watch.

"The wind in which he hides is on the sea, but it is moving," the ancient warrior had said before settling into a dark shadow cast by the light of their campfire for the night.

The two sovereigns sat watch through the early hours, watching the coast and listening to the crashing of the dark waves against the shore below them; there was a shriek in the wind as it howled over the bluffs on which they were making camp, as if it were warning of something dire coming.

Finally, after the midpoint of the night had passed into the next day, Ashe rose and stretched.

"I'm going to sleep," he said, reaching skyward with his arms to loosen his sore muscles. "Another long day of riding tomorrow."

Achmed continued to stare at the fire.

"Sit down for a moment," he said quietly. "I am about to repay you for rescuing me today."

The Lord Cymrian inhaled, then sat down again.

"Rhapsody is alive," the Bolg king said. "I heard her heartbeat in the sea."

Ashe sat up straighter. "You are certain of it? She's alive?"

Achmed scowled. "I was certain of it at the time. I don't want to be held to what may have happened since. But when I was beneath the waves while you took your time to get to me, I heard it—impossible to gauge distance in all that god-forsaken water. I never could have imagined that I would be able to hear it through the damnable element; it has always been a barrier to me before. Perhaps I should have MacQuieth stand on my head whenever I need to scry hereafter."

The Lord Cymrian lapsed into a grateful silence, contemplating his world.

"Thank you," he said finally.

"We had best make plans as to how we are going to deal with Michael if MacQuieth is able to track and ultimately find him," Ached said quietly. "In the old world Dhracians generally hunted F'dor alone, but the one we killed a few years ago was stronger, fiercer somehow; I don't know if I am merely not as potent in the ritual as a full-blooded Dhracian would be, or if crossing Time has anything to do with it, but I do know if Grunthor and Rhapsody had not been there, I would have been lost to it."

"What do you propose?"

"Once we get within striking distance, I will begin chanting the Thrall ritual," Achmed said. "It ties a net of power around the demon, keeping it from escaping the host's body, so that both die together. You will be able to tell if it has taken when I move my hand as if winding yarn about it; if the tether has hit its mark in the demon's soul, the host's body will lurch, as if being dragged." Ashe nodded. "That is the moment when you want to strike.

"As a Dhracian, I can hold the demon's spirit in its body, keep it from escaping, while the host is being killed. Done properly, a Dhracian can do it alone; the vibration of the Thrall will eventually cause the host's head to cave in. But we had best take no chances. I will get him into Thrall, and you drive the water sword through him. If you do it right you can gouge his heart out of his chest and throw it, still beating, onto the ground, so that we can watch to be sure he dies in body and soul."

"Poor technique," MacQuieth muttered from the shadows where he lay. "You never fully extend until the blade is inside your target. Push it out his back instead."

$\mathcal{A}$she was sleeping on his back by the remains of the fire when the dragon in his blood felt the dawn break gently over the sea.

He sat up, stiff and sore, and looked over to the place where MacQuieth had been.

Nothing was there.

Ashe sat forward quickly, looking with his eyes, but allowing his dragon sense loose to find the old man.

It only took a moment. The sensitive vibrations in his blood told him that MacQuieth was near the edge of the cliff wall that towered over the beach below.

The Lord Cymrian rose, stepping quietly over Achmed, who slept fitfully next to the remains of the fire. He followed the path back to the overlook, his dragonesque eyes scanning for the ancient warrior.

What he found was the feeble old man he had met the day before, the progenitor of his family back so many generations that it was impossible to count, a hero who had slipped with Time into a state bordering on dementia.

The driftwood-gray had returned to his wrinkled skin, the color of extreme age mixed with a life led almost exclusively outdoors. He was wandering close to the edge, seemingly blind to the bluff that ran above the seacoast, on which he was walking.

Ashe caught the urge to call out to him in his throat; he could tell, with the inner sight that allowed him to observe many hidden things, that MacQuieth was not playfully risking death by walking so close to the end of the land.

He could not see anything.

Ashe willed himself to be calm, to move with great deliberateness so as to not startle the blind old man. As his senses wandered over the hero, he thought he had ascertained the reason why he was suddenly sightless.

The dragon had made note of the blood that had pooled in the back of MacQuieth's eyes during the night; it had coated the back of the inner lens, leaving the man without sight. An hour, perhaps more, of being upright, and the blood would drain away from the back of his eyes, allowing him to see again.

For the man who had carried Kirsdarke, carried the essence of the sword of water still, each awakening was a reminder of the drowned. When first he came to awareness he was paralyzed, frozen even beyond shivering.

Blind.

As if trapped beneath ice, the old man had to struggle to come to awareness, to awaken, a much more difficult battle to wage against exhaustion than any man of regular years faced. He deliberately, patiently melted the burden of time that he carried with each liquid-heavy breath, pushing his chest to make more breaths, tiny lapping waves to erode the years.

Even so, it appeared as if he were losing his battle to awaken.

Ashe felt his throat constrict. He waited until the old soldier had gotten his legs under him, then quietly drew Kirsdarke, the blade the old man had borne gloriously throughout so many centuries of life, and held it in outstretched hands, hoping that its ancient bond to MacQuieth would give him strength to draw on again now.

"The All-God give thee good day, Grandfather," he said deferentially, using the polite form of address that the young used to speak with their elders.

As at the waterside the day before, the hero seemed to

strengthen before his eyes, taking on the same patient, enduring power of the waves of the sea below them. The fragile old man shook the tangled mess that was his head.

"If He were to do so, I would be gone from this life now," he said soberly, without melancholy or self-pity. "All of the years I have ahead of me, and all those behind, would I trade for but one day in which to see what has been lost to Time once more."

"I understand," Ashe said.

The soldier cocked his head in the Lord Cymrian's direction. "Do you? Hmmm. I think not." An amused smile crossed his lips. "But I suspect one day, a thousand years or more from now, you will."

He turned to face the sea, letting the rising sun bathe his face with its light.

"The sun—I can feel it," he murmured, his eyes open in the intense glare, reflecting the burning light. "I know it's there. Like the Island, sleeping now beneath the waves, its towers crumbled into great mounds of sand, the great seawalls that proved to be futile broken, strewn about the bottom of the ocean floor like the playthings of a child. I feel its warmth; but I see it not.

"When the Second Fleet landed in Manosse, when my— duty was discharged, I stood in the sea and waited for the Island's end." MacQuieth closed his eyes to the golden light, lifting his face to the sky, following the path of the sun. "I felt it; it was many days, how many risings and setting of the sun I do not remember, but all that water, all that sun, all that salt burned the surface of my eyes. I did not care; I had no need of them. Anything that I had wanted to see was no longer visible.

"But finally, one day, it was over; I felt the sea shudder with pain as the Sleeping Child rose, consuming Serendair and the islands north of it in volcanic fire, felt its depths burning." The soldier ran the back of his hand across his eyes in memory.

"You know the order of the birth of the elements? How

the older they are, the more powerful they can be? Ether was first; it is the only one not born of this world, but came rather from the stars. That is why the F'dor fear certain types of diamonds, by the by—they are crystal formations not of this earth, but that fell from the heavens in a blaze of light, cooling and hardening into a prison of fire."

He held up his hand, not looking at it; on the index finger the ring he had taken from the hut blazed, brilliant, in the morning light.

"Ether is the only element that came before fire, so it is the one that holds more power. Water came after it, then wind, then earth; over those three elements fire holds sway."

"But water quenches fire," Ashe said.

MacQuieth turned on him like a badger on its prey, his cloudy eyes leveled at him.

"Tell that to the people of Traeg, or any of the other villages that burned to ashes along the coast of the sea," he said scornfully. "Tell that to the islands of Balatron, Briela, and Querel, that *melted* in the heat of the fire that burned, unquenched, in the boiling waves. I may have burned my eyes, staring at the sun on the sea, fire on the water, to the point of being sightless, but it is you, Gwydion ap Llauron ap Gwylliam, who are being blind."

"Ashe," the Lord Cymrian said quietly. "Call me Ashe. Then you don't have to utter the name you loathe. I am not my grandfather; I would hate to have my kinsman think of him when talking to me."

The ancient warrior smiled then, his eyes seeming to clear a bit.

" 'Ashe,' " he said, rolling the word around in his mouth. "Sounds like a version of the story of the cinder girl who becomes a princess. I am old; you will learn it in my tongue. 'Aesch.' " The harshness of the sound scraped against Ashe's eardrum like teeth on bone.

"And what am I to call you, Grandfather?"

MacQuieth shrugged.

"I could not care less what you call me," he said. "I am

not here to do your bidding. I will not answer unless I am moved to. I am only here to find the one you seek as well. But one thing—do not use my name. If he hears it on the wind, he will flee. Even as you see me now, old and wasted as I am, he would run rather than fight me."

Ashe nodded. "You were telling me of long ago. What did you do?" he asked gently. "After you felt the death of the Island?"

The ancient hero stared off, still sightless, into the horizon at the waves rolling up the gleaming sand, over the fragments of shells and pebbles, rushing white to the end of the froth, slipping away, with the top layer of sand, back into the maw of the sea.

"I went to bury my son," he said.

Above the crashing waves a seagull screamed; the shrill sound broke the thundering silence that rolled in, like the waves, on the warrior's words.

"It is a strange thing, walking the world through the sea," MacQuieth said, almost as if talking to himself. "There are wonders untold, great mountains that dwarf anything in the upworld, trenches and chasms that surely must reach to the center of the world itself; treasures of man, buried in the sand beneath wrecks of ships; treasures of the ocean, coral in colors never imagined, towering threads of spider-lace rock and creatures that defy description. More of the world exists down there, far from the minds of the ignorant masses, than ever will be known in the realm of land. There is magic unfathomable to be seen if a man's eyes are open to it."

He looked overhead as a flock of seabirds passed on the warm wind, following the shadow. *His sight returns,* Ashe thought. *Thank the gods.*

"But of course my eyes were not open to the sea's wonder, but to its terror. I knew that I would find devastation there, but could not have begun to imagine how hellish, how truly terrible the sight of it would be. The towers of Tarte-chor, the great city of the Mythlin, once the jewel of the sea, gone, along with the rest, swept away by the roiling current. The hundreds of thousands souls that lived there gone as well, atomized, turned into vapor, foam on the waves. In breathing the water around the place where the city had been, I knew I was breathing the dead.

"It was a kindness that Tartechor went the way it did, however. For all that it was horrific to view the place where there had once been such opulence beneath the waves, and now was nothing but ever-shifting sand, it could not begin to compare to the horror of the sight that was once Serendair. Where there had been highlands, there was nothing beneath the waves but rubble and ruin, melted statues and stone gates jutting from great mountains of broken earth, the towers of Elysian castle now pebbles in the swirling current. They had built seawalls, levies, in the last days, in the vain attempt to hold back the inevitable." MacQuieth shook his head, smiling sadly. "That must have been Hector. My son would have been filling bags of sand to the last." The ancient soldier fell silent. Ashe stood alongside him as the sun crested the horizon and set sail for the pinnacle of the sky.

MacQuieth bent down and gathered a handful of sand, contemplating it for a moment, then allowed it to run through his fingers onto the ground again.

"If you know the ways of the Liringlas, you know that we bury our dead by committing their bodies to fire on the wind beneath the stars. We sing of the life of the dead, of their dreams, their accomplishments, their good works. There was much to elegize for Hector. He was a man of surpassing greatness; he was my hero." The soldier exhaled deeply. "But there was nothing to bury, nothing to put on a pyre, just loose mountains of ruin that towered almost to the very surface of the sea. And ash; even in all the time it had taken me to walk through the sea to the other side of the world, when I came there were still clouds of ash swirling in the current, clouding the water, fouling it, despoiling it, with transient earth. How was I to find my son in all that rubble, all that thick, gray haze? I could not sing the requiem for my own son; how could I ever sing it for another?"

For a long time the two men stood, one lost in thought, the other in memory, listening to the whine of the wind. Suddenly MacQuieth looked up sharply to the north.

"He comes," he said simply.

## OFF THE NORTHERN COAST

The *Basquela* dropped anchor as the sun was at the pinnacle of the sky.

The seneschal's face, even more drawn and thin than usual, hardened as the ship came to rest on a fallowing sea that was beginning to pitch with the winds heralding that a storm was coming.

He pulled the spyglass from his robes and fixed it on the pointed promontory, scanning once again the rocky crags, the jagged coastline.

"Where are you, Rhapsody?" he muttered, searching through the mist from the crashing surf, the haze of the misty sunlight darkening as clouds began to pass overhead.

*Dead,* the demon answered bitterly, or hidden far beyond your reach. *One last time; abandon this madness and turn for home.*

Defiantly, Michael clutched the rail and leaned into the wind, shouting her name at the top of his lungs.

In the depths of her tidal cave, working feverishly as she sat on the ledge to expanded the floating net of lava rocks, Rhapsody thought she heard her name in the whistle of the wind in the cave.

*The salt is getting to me,* she thought, desperately plaiting the strands of her hair she had shorn from her head with the broken crossbow bolt, eyeing the body that was swirling in the circular current, dissolving before her eyes. *Tomorrow. We will get out of here tomorrow.* It was a promise she had avoided committing to until this day.

The she heard it again, shouted in a voice filled with anger and obsession.

*Rhapsody! I am coming for you! I know where you are; I see you! I will be with you today or on the morrow! Rhapsody!*

She clutched the floating mat closer to her chest; then, after a moment, her fear turned to steely resolve.

*Not in my lifetime.*

# 50

## THE CAULDRON

Shaene was snoring prodigiously in his bed within the ambassador's chambers of Ylorc, having long given up on supping with Theophila, when he felt an odd sensation, as if his big toe had been licked.

In his sleep he pulled his foot away rapidly, only to feel his leg held down by pressure.

The Canderian glassmaker struggled to open his eyes. As he did, a thrill shot through him, originating at his crotch, where a warm hand other than his own had made itself at home.

He sat up slightly, only to feel the body that was hunched over his, head between his legs, press him firmly to the mattress again.

The coverlet was pulled back by a woman's hand, revealing a small dark head. Similarly dark eyes in a grinning face looked up at him.

"Shhhhh," the woman said, running her hands briskly up and down his thighs. "I am sorry I am late."

The sounds that came forth from Shaene's throat were unintelligible as words.

Theophila returned to her task.

He let his head fall heavily back against the thin pillow of his bed, surrendering without any resistance whatsoever to the delicious sensations that were being visited upon him below the coverlet, watching the ceiling turn strange colors as the blood rushed away from his brain and streaked rapidly to other parts of his body. Arousal, long arrested, long denied, roared forth from deep within him; he went from soundly asleep to fully primed in a few beats of his rapidly pulsing heart.

"Theophila—"

As if to silence him, her ministrations became all the more eager, all the more intense. Fire of a sort broke out between Shaene's ears; his head hummed with static, as though it had been completely cut off from the rest of his body.

He moaned foolishly as she pulled back suddenly, stopping before he lost control completely. The erotic sensations that had been flooding through him a moment before were now replaced by prickling guilt, an embarrassment that she had been able to tell how close to the edge he had come with almost no stimulation. He started to speak, to apologize, only to find his mouth covered with her own, her lips as hot as the forges under the mountain.

Shaene abandoned any conscious thought, any ability to move. He did not have the energy to marvel at his good luck, or pinch himself to ascertain the reality of his situation, or wonder at her motives. He merely lay back, rigid in all parts of his body, and tried not to laugh or wheeze or cough as the beautiful woman who had appeared in the dark beneath his blankets rode him vigorously, sending lightning strikes of pleasure through his lonely flesh.

She was a master at building him to the point of release, then backing him quickly down, only to soar to a dizzying, frightening height again a moment later. Her scent, a spicy blend that made his nostrils tingle and his head swim, wrapped around his conscious thought as she whispered erotic words to him in his ear, teased him, coaxed him to fantasize about making love in strange places—on a windswept mountain pass, near the heat of the forges, in the Bolg king's own bed.

He found himself straining to answer, muttering replies and directions to each of the imaginary venues, only to find his mouth covered again with hers. After the last of the fantasies, when he had murmured how they would have to wait for the changing of the shift of guards at the ninth corridor in order to sneak down the left-hand hallway to the private chambers of Achmed the Snake, to copulate as she had wished on the silken sheets of his bed, she had stopped for a moment, causing waves of prickling shock to roll through him.

"Where?" she demanded, bearing down on him, causing him to gasp with pleasure. "Tell me. Where is the ninth corridor?"

"I—I don't know," Shaene answered breathlessly. "I've never been allowed near there."

The Panjeri woman's eyes grew steely; if he had been looking into them, Shaene would have been terrified, but he was spared from the sight because his own head was tilted back, gasping for air.

He was thereby also spared the sight of those angry eyes resolving into annoyance as she plunged deeper, knobbing him so relentlessly that he could no longer hold on to any semblance of restraint. Indeed, she ceased holding back altogether; if anything, Shaene had a fleeting impression that she went from being amorous to being impatient in the wink of an eye, wishing the act to culminate quickly.

Involuntarily he obliged.

Spent and brainless, he groaned as she rolled off of him, missing the fiery heat that had surrounded him a moment before. Shaene reached for the warm body beside him and missed; he raised his head and looked around.

Theophila was gone.

Omet was deep in the throes of a nightmare, a dream about his mother.

He had had many such dreams in his life, though they had been fewer and farther between since he had come to the mountain with the other slave boys rescued from Yarim. One by one those children had left Ylorc; orphans, they had no family to return to or that they remembered, so they had been placed by the Lady Cymrian with childless couples that she knew in Tyrian and Navarne, far away from the burning clay and horrific memories of the foundry of Yarim and the dark, clammy tunnels they had been forced to dig beneath it.

But Omet had stayed. He was no orphan, or at least he didn't think he was; his mother had apprenticed him out of need and the desire to no longer pay for his upkeep. She had known the life to which she was sentencing him, had been fully aware of the guildmistress's reputation, and had not come to visit him once in the five years of his apprenticeship. He blamed her for all but the last.

But now she was with him at his bedside, weeping quietly, begging his forgiveness as she often did in these dreams, telling him of her sorrow at his loss, and how she had mourned him each of the days of his apprenticeship, praying for him, making offerings on the Patriarch's altar so that the prayers would be melded with those of other mothers of slave children, channeled through the benison to the Patriarch up to the Creator, the All-God himself.

*I am so sorry, Omet,* she said in the reverberating voice of the dream world. She brushed a heavy lock of hair away from his forehead.

Omet sighed in his sleep.

His mother's fingers were callused from years of manual labor, but gentle as they caressed his forehead.

*I've missed you,* his mother whispered in his dream.

"Have you?" he murmured. "Have you missed me?"

"Oh, very much, Omet. Very much."

The words were clearer, closer. Omet opened his eyes to find Esten sitting beside him on the bed, where his mother had been a moment before in his dream.

She was caressing his hair.

Her knife pressing against his throat.

Omet inhaled raggedly through his nostrils, letting his breath out cautiously, the knife blade sharp.

"You didn't think I recognized you, did you, Omet?" she said sweetly, the light from the lantern on the bedside table making her eyes glow wickedly. "But I've known you from the beginning." She ran her free hand through his thick, straight hair and cupped the beard on his chin, letting her fingers linger there. "Once I own someone they are mine forever. Surely you knew that, didn't you, Omet?"

He stared at her in silence.

Esten moved closer, her back arched like a cat hunting. There was cruelty in her eyes that was mirrored in her muscles, an intense, deliberate movement that carried as much threat as his mind could imagine. She sat on his chest, pinning his arms down with her legs.

"Tell me what happened that night in the foundry," she said softly, pressing the blade infinitesimally closer; the tension making his mouth taste iron. "How did the Bolg king get past all of you? How many men did it take to overcome my journeymen? Tell me, Omet, how did he do it?"

The artisan said nothing.

With an artless flick of the blade, Esten shaved off a tiny section of beard and the top few layers of skin, drawing but one drop of blood.

"Tell me," she said menacingly, her voice dropping. "The vein that my knife leans against would be most difficult to close once opened."

Thoughts of that night flashed before his eyes. He had been awakened, quickly tied and gagged by Rhapsody while Achmed scouted the area.

"Alone," Omet whispered. "He was alone."

Esten lifted her head at a different angle, studying his face. "Liar. There were thirteen men and two dozen half-grown boys missing as a result of that night. He could not have been alone."

"He was alone," Omet insisted, struggling to breathe with

the knife at his neck. "He—killed most of them with—his cwellan."

"Cwellan?" The knife did not move as her other hand produced a blue-black rysin-steel disk. "The curved weapon he carries on his back, that fires these?"

"Yes," Omet whispered. "He bound me, and the other apprentices. Vincane—fought him. The—Bolg king locked him—in the kiln."

The cruel eyes glittered. "That explains the stench. Did he kill the slave children? Bury them beneath all that slip?"

Omet thought of the long ride to Ylorc with the rescued boys, Rhapsody and Achmed maintaining order until they could be turned over to the Bolg guards in the northern Teeth.

"Yes. All dead. Buried in the slip. Along with the journeymen."

"Why? Why would he do that?" The lines of her brow knitted together, drawing her face into a terrifying mask of concentration. "If he is some sort of do-gooder king, off solving the problems of the world, why would he seal my slave boys under a fired mountain of clay?"

"It was—Vincane who upended the first vat," Omet said quickly; it was the first truth he had told. "He was—trying to get away."

Esten's eyes narrowed, and her mouth drew into an even tighter line.

"How did he fire it? How did it become solid?"

Omet struggled to breathe, trying not to encourage the blade point any closer. "I don't know. He had bound me and taken me out by then."

"Hmmm. I still don't know why he chose to risk my wrath by interfering with my work, though it may have had something to do with wanting his mudfilth artisans to be the ones to dig out Entudenin. He is a curious fellow, isn't he? Well, no matter. He will get what is coming to him."

Omet said nothing.

"Just as you will, Omet." Her free hand reached behind

her over her shoulder as her knife pressed deeper against the vein in his neck; the world went black for a moment. Omet fought to stay conscious.

When his vision cleared she was holding up a shiny metal flask before his eyes. She uncapped it with her thumb and held the vial to his lips.

"Drink," she said simply.

"No," Omet replied. Death as the outcome had been something he had accepted from the moment he recognized that she had come to the mountain; a sense of finality and peace came over him, leaving him fearless for once.

Esten blinked. "You defy me? You are braver than I thought." She bounced sharply on his chest, knocking the wind out of him; Omet gasped for breath, and as he did, she poured the scorching liquid down his throat.

The heel of her hand was up against his chin in a flash, snapping his neck back and forcing him to swallow.

Omet gasped again, her hand still sealing his mouth shut, as the caustic liquid tore down his gullet. In a matter of seconds he felt the heat spread to his limbs, leaving them weak, useless.

Esten climbed off him quickly.

"If you move it will bring on the coma more rapidly," she said flatly, straightening her clothes and flicking her wrist; the knife disappeared. "I need you to linger in fever for a while to distract your friends, until the Bolg king returns to the mountain." She cocked her head and watched him with interest as the heat rose up in his face. "Your mother would be proud of how you met your death, Omet, and I'm sure you are appreciative that I gave you this gentle way out, unlike the rest. At least you do not have to live with the effects of picric exposure, as the others will."

Her face brightened and she leaned closer. "It really is a quite lovely substance. Those who get it on their skin or breathe it in, as your Bolg and glass artisan friends have done, will find their eyes, hair, and skin turning a glorious yellow, almost the color of goldenrod glass. They will succumb to a variety of lovely agonies—bloody urine, twisted and melting internal organs, convulsions, stupor, eventually leading to a blessed, if painful, death."

Esten picked up Omet's right hand, now flaccid and unresponsive, and dropped it heavily to the bed. She stretched out beside him, sliding her arm under his neck, as his breathing grew shallow and his face turned gray. With one last tender gesture, she laid her head on Omet's shoulder, turning her lips so he could hear the words she whispered to him.

"But for the Bolg king—he has the best in store for him! The glaze we annealed into the ceiling glass—that was picric acid, Omet, a delightful substance when wet, as it is now beneath the wooden cover of the dome. I'm sure you recall it from your lessons in my foundry. When it dries, do you remember what it does?"

Omet, who was breathing shallowly, slipping into unconsciousness, did not respond, but he knew the answer in his last moments of awareness.

Picric, dry, exploded.

He was too far gone to feel the warm kiss she placed on his temple, too deep in the grip of the poison to hear her leave.

## 51

### ON THE NORTHERN SEACOAST

That night they camped when the path along the seacoast grew too treacherous to be forded in the dark.

They passed the night without a fire, keeping low to the ground, until the edge rains of the storm began in earnest.

Lightning rippled through the sky in waves of heat, becoming more focused as the storm grew in intensity. Crackling flashes shot the heavens through with pulsating light, followed seconds later by the deep rumbles of thunder, echoing off the sea cliffs, frightening the horses.

The travelers broke camp and hurried northward along the seacoast, watching the thrashing waves pound the shore, ignoring the sting of salt spray mixed with the fresh water of rain.

Finally they took shelter in the ruins of a small village on a cold inlet, where the lava cliffs that lined the whole of the western coast rose even more dramatically into rocky ledges and promontories above them. One small brick building with a tiled roof half crumbled away remained standing near a tall seawall; all else was ashes.

They quartered the horses next to the seawall as the sky opened above them, drenching men and animals to the skin, then climbed one after another into the broken building, leaning up against the wall that still had a bit of roof to it, gaining only partial shelter.

A nest of rats that had been the only tenants prior to their arrival scurried out of the half-hut as the three men shifted uncomfortably, seeking whatever dry place they could find. The old man chuckled as the rodents disappeared into the rain.

"I slew the last Seren rat years ago," he said. "Poor old Nick. I did him the favor of helping him pass through to the Rat Afterlife, if there is one. He must have come on one of the ships of the First Fleet."

"The rats gained immortality in the passage from the old world as well?" Ashe asked incredulously.

"Aye," MacQuieth said. "Cymrian rats. And you thought only the people wouldn't die." He shook his head at the memory. "Too grizzled for even his own kind to eat. I didn't have the heart to eat him either."

"Tell me something, if you will," Achmed said, taking off the veil that shielded his face and wringing the water from it. "Something that has long puzzled me. It is said in legend that it was you that slew Tsoltan, the F'dor-priest who was once my hated master. How did you do it? You are not Dhracian, and yet you killed him, both man and spirit. I need to know, especially if it will help us in the battle that is to come."

MacQuieth leaned back, oblivious to the rain.

"I hunted him," he said, his voice heavy with the memory. "I was young then, in what I thought was my prime. I was the shadow of the king, the queen's champion, the black lion. In those days, those times, there were those who said I had wings. And on days when the wind was at my back, I almost believed them. If you remember but one thing about me, remember this: I have never failed to complete a quest that I undertook alone.

"And I work best alone. I am no minister, no advisor, no ambassador. I had no wish to be a general, just in the vanguard." He broke his gaze away from the endless sheets of rain long enough to meet Achmed's eye. "In the days after you left, I *was* the vanguard.

"But I was also a fool. When the Seren War began I had no idea such a thing as F'dor existed; they had been long bound, imprisoned in the Vault of the Underworld for ages before. The lore of them had been lost, or I ignored it. I carried the courage of the fool, or it carried me. I had met children of the four other Firstborn races, Seren and Mythlin, the children of the stars and the sea. I had struggled with wyrmkin like you, Aesche, the spawn of earth, and knew the Kith well; many of them were Kinsmen, brothers of the wind, born as they were of the element of air. The missing element should have been obvious, but I forgot about the children of fire.

"Tsoltan had been the nemesis of my king, and therefore my nemesis, from the beginning of the war; it was just a matter of time before my comrades and I uncovered his identity. When we did, I went after him alone.

"I caught him outside the Spire, his lair in the old world, on an errand he could not leave undone." MacQuieth's voice warmed in the telling; his eyes looked out into the sheets of blinding rain, as if seeing past them into history. "His men, his retainers were nothing. I fell on them with such fury that the water sword smoked, atomizing lives, wrenching souls and organs from their houses like an avalanche, or a tidal wave." He chuckled softly. "I love the sound of the blade, the feel of steel on bone. It was glorious.

"The demon itself, now, that was another matter. At first, of course, it fought. It had no idea who I was, or that I carried its doom in my teeth. It had every strength—strength of time, strength of element. And I had one advantage—it could not afford to kill me."

"Why?" Achmed asked.

"Because," MacQuieth said matter-of-factly, "I was carrying it within me. I was its host."

Achmed choked on a stream of rainwater pouring from the broken roof, coughing violently.

"What did you say?"

"I took it into myself, into my body; like you said Michael has done; I invited it in, swallowed it." His face grew darker. "And then I wrestled with it.

"I had to unravel my own darkness from the demon's so I could kill the spirit from vision rather than anger. My race, my sword, my solitude; I was the shadow of the king. That gave me a pool of strength. I drowned it. Held its fire under the waters of my life. Eventually it came to begging, wheedling, before it finally surrendered, whispered itself away. I had killed the body long before, so when it gave up and dissipated on the wind, it was well and truly gone. Not even enough of a spark of black fire to light a candle to guide me home from the depths of the Spire, a place of consuming blackness.

"You did not think it was merely time that has made me into the frail human refuse that I am? Gods, no. My frailty, my dissipation, comes from life, not time; from the things I visited upon myself, such as the battle I have just related to you, and the spirit-breaking demands that others have visited upon me." He glared at Ashe for a moment. "None so much as Gwylliam.

"But I have no regrets about having spent myself as I

have," he said, his voice softer now. "Immortality is foolishness. Everything dies, goes. Mountains age and fall, islands slip into the sea. And if not these F'dor, with their endless appetite for destruction that brings the curtain down, then it will be someone else, some fanatic who will snare the sun and pull it into the earth. Sooner or later, life ends. Those who seek to cheat that concept are worse than the F'dor in their ceaseless hunger for oblivion."

Achmed looked over to see Ashe trembling.

"What is it?" he asked sharply.

"I cannot do that," the Lord Cymrian whispered. "I have lived with the touch of the F'dor, have felt the demon's fingers reach into my chest and tear out a piece of my soul; I know the torments of sharing being with it. I cannot fight the beast like that."

"Nor can I," Achmed said.

MacQuieth looked at them both intently. "Not even to save your wife? Your friend?"

Neither man answered.

A flash of lightning crackled through the sky in the distance, lighting the sea.

The ancient warrior shook his head. "I am sorry. I have told you but one method to kill the demon; it will not work for you, though others might. You may be good men, good kings. Even a worthy husband and a worthy friend. But you are not Kinsmen. Neither of you are made for it; your senses of self are too strong. You were put on the Earth to rule; Kinsmen are not rulers. We are a brotherhood that sees through darkness and time, but one thing we are blind to is that we have a purpose other than to serve."

"I will do it if I must," Ashe said, looking up into the darkness of the half-roof. "If the demon slips away from Achmed during the Thrall, I will do whatever I must to keep it from escaping."

MacQuieth smiled and tapped the scabbard that held Kirsdarke.

"I doubt you will need to," he said, his voice clearer and

stronger than they had heard it. "You bear the right weapon.

"We all live on the blade of balance, a slurry of water, air, fire, and earth. The great swords allow one to alter the balance. There were five elemental swords made. A million were forged, but only five made, consecrated—not all together, but each in its time by loving hands. Daystar Clarion by the Seren, born in the twilight of the gods. Fired and finished by starlight. It's an old power, but it's distant, far away from us. There was a fire sword, now gone, combined with the sword of the stars. The blade Michael bears is born of wind, but wind is fleeting. It is water that will vanquish dark fire when wielded by the right hand. The sea is the one thing that still touches us all. Earth is broken, wind is lost, fire is quenched. The waters touch us all. Kirsdarke is our sword."

Achmed, loather of water, inhaled deeply.

"Look at me if you do not believe in the enduring power of water," MacQuieth said jokingly. "Salt is a wonder as a preservative. There are fish in the depths of the sea hundreds of years old, did you know that? Trust in the sword, and in yourselves. And, if it appears you are about to fail, remember that living forever is not always a blessing."

A rumble of thunder punctuated his words.

# 52

*A*nd then it was morning.

The rain remained, gray and foreboding, coming and going on the wind, leaving behind an ever-present mist that shrouded Achmed's senses in a maddening fog.

They followed MacQuieth, trusting in his tie to his nemesis from the old world, though each step into the mist coming off the turbulent sea made their confidence, if not their resolve, wane slightly.

The ancient hero had stopped at one point along the rough land overlooking the sea and quietly lashed his horse to a

tree in the last copse he saw. The others followed his example, noting that the forest of Gwynwood to the east still
hung in heavy smoke from the fires that had so recently
burned there.

"He is here," MacQuieth said quietly. "Close to the sea."

At the edge of the promontory, Michael glared impatiently down the cliff face at the two soldiers Fergus had
chosen, hovering on ropes over the rocks below.

"What do you see?" he shouted into the rain-heavy wind.

One of the men looked up to the precipice and shook his
head.

"Keep going!" he screamed. "She's down there! I know
she's down there!"

*You know nothing. You only hope she is down there.*

The voice of the demon-spirit seethed with disgust.

Michael clawed at his face. "Silence!" he screeched.
"Stop taunting me!"

*Very well. I will leave that to the woman if you find her.*

Down at the sand beach to the south the seneschal's eye
caught a flicker of movement; he turned to see Fergus, who
was posted below, waving triumphantly.

He looked down the edifice below, where the two soldiers
hung suspended over the thundering waves and black, jagged rocks. He made a beckoning gesture. The wind, in response, carried their voices up the cliff face to him.

"Cave down here, m'lord!"

"I knew it!" the seneschal shouted, clutching his hands
tightly in excitement. "Rappel deeper, keep going."

He was staring down into the updrafts from the sea, the
salt spray buffeting his face, when he noticed that an odd
sound, a vibration of a sort, had been scratching at his eardrum. He waved it away, like a bothersome fly, but the noise
only grew louder, more intense; a moment later it grew almost painful.

He turned in the breeze and stared off to the east at the
wide edge where the promontory began.

Three figures stood there in the mist, or two and a partial figure, he noted an instant later. To his left, farthest north, was a vague figure swathed in mist, blending into the heavy vapor as naturally as the rain itself. He wouldn't have even noticed the figure if not for the sword it wielded, a sword that glowed intensely blue.

A sword he recognized from the old land.

*Kirsdarke,* he mused, his mind running slow. *I thought it had been lost with the Island.*

The demonic voice in his brain fell suddenly silent, giving him the sensation, for the first time since he had agreed to take it on, that he was alone in his own skin.

To his right, southward, stood another figure, this one draped in black. Its hand was raised in the air in a gesture of halting.

Between his ears he felt an explosion as the demon panicked, cursing in the profane language of its race.

*A Dhracian,* it spat.

Michael's head turned quickly to the figure between them. At one time the man might have been tall, but now was bent, bowed with age; he stood, frail, looking as if the wind itself could blow through him, hanging back, out of the fray.

"I don't have *time* for this!" the seneschal bellowed. "Begone!"

Achmed was in the throes of the Thrall ritual when the figure that MacQuieth had led them to gestured at them.

"I don't have *time* for this—Begone!"

The irony caught him off guard, almost made him break the ritual, swallowing the wry laughter that welled up within him.

*So appropriately named,* he thought, clearing his mind again. *The Waste of Breath.*

He raised his left hand, calling to each of the four winds, the entities that gave the Thrall ritual its power.

*Bien,* Achmed thought. The north wind, the strongest. He opened his first throat and hummed the name; the sound echoed through his chest and the first chamber of his heart. He held up his index finger; the sensitive skin of its tip tingled as a draft of air wrapped around it.

*Jahne,* he whispered in his mind. The south wind, the most enduring. With his second throat he called to the next wind, committing the second heart chamber. Around his tallest finger he could sense the anchoring of another thread of air. When both vibrations were clear and strong he went on, opening the other two throats, the other two heart chambers. *Leuk.* The west wind, the wind of justice. *Thas.* The east wind. The wind of morning; the wind of death. Like strands of spider-silk, the currents hung on his fingertips, waiting. Four notes held in a monotone.

The man on the edge of the promontory stared at him in shock, then reached to his side and drew his blade.

Tysterisk came forth from its scabbard in a blast of keening air. It hissed and howled like a gale blowing around a mountaintop.

Achmed's hand contracted, and with a graceful swing of his arm he tossed the ball of wind that had formed in his palm, feeling the four winds knot together, anchored to his palm, around the demon-spirit that dwelt with Michael.

He tied the net, then wrapped the metaphysical threads around his palm.

Ashe, seeing the signal, stepped forward out of the mist that came both from his cloak and the rain-heavy air.

"Where is my wife?" he demanded, his voice ringing with the multiple tones of the dragon, soprano, alto, tenor, and bass; it vibrated through the earth of the precipice on which they stood.

Michael smiled, then turned and pointed off to the southwest at the shadow of a ship hovering in the sea.

"Servicing my crew," he said, his grin broadening. "They are taking turns with her. By now she's doubtless on her third or fourth round. I have ravaged her seven times myself. Like old times, it was. And will be again. And again."

Fury roared through Ashe; he found himself stepping forward, then stopped, waiting for the sign that the Thrall had taken.

Achmed jerked his arm, drawing the threads of the wind taught with a snap.

Michael's eyes widened; even from the distance they could see the white gleam suddenly in the gray haze.

His body lurched slightly in Achmed's direction.

The Dhracian's excruciating song grew louder.

As Achmed slowly approached the edge of the precipice, balancing the invisible web of wind, he noticed Ashe shifting his grip on Kirsdarke's hilt.

Michael stood as if thunderstruck, watching them approach, his sword hilt in hand, not moving.

When they were within a few paces of the seneschal, Achmed wrapped the net of wind tighter, and gave it another pull.

Michael's arm wrenched back.

Ashe began his approach, lifting Kirsdarke, its blade running in frothing rapids of blue and white, aiming for the seneschal's throat.

With a vicious sweep, Michael sliced through the air in the direction of the Dhracian, severing the ropes of wind.

*Hrekin! I should have known,* Achmed thought as he desperately tried to gather the tattered threads of the Thrall.

Michael gestured savagely and Achmed felt his breath ripped from his body, choking off his strange song in midnote.

A gust of wind exploded over him, blasting him into the air, hurtling him off the promontory and far into the sea.

# 53

Ashe reared back in shock as the Bolg king's body flew over the edge of the cliff. He raced the few steps to the point of the precipice and pointed the sword at the pounding surf, reaching into his own elemental bond to the sea, commanding it to bring forth a wave to catch the Dhracian and speed him away from the rocks, knowing that while it would spare him death from the impact, it would not save him from drowning.

Michael threw back his head and laughed into the wind; the breeze caught the dual tones of his voice, the joyous chortle of the man, the harsh, cackling screech of the demon.

"You did this in jest, did you not?" he said to Ashe, who was staring desperately between the waves, searching for signs of Achmed's black robes. "You thought you could contain me with a Thrall ritual? I command the *wind,* you fool. I *am* the wind, the Wind of Fire, the Wind of Death." His voice grew harsher as the demon came forth, causing the clear blue eyes to redden at the edges.

"I will eat your soul," he said as he moved closer to Ashe, the blade of his weapon finally visible, the outline burning with black fire. "I will keep you alive for a while, however; tonight you can come with me to the ship. Before I let the crew bugger and keelhaul you, I'll grant you a boon; I'll let you watch me violate your lovely wife, who is mine to play with now."

Ashe gripped Kirsdarke's hilt, breathing shallowly.

MacQuieth's voice rang out, as if in his palm.

*Go. Save him.*

He turned and looked behind him. The ancient hero was standing erect, his body rehydrating as if with the elemental power of the water sword.

*Leave this to me,* Ashe heard in his mind; it was as though the words were vibrating through Kirsdarke's hilt into his hand, through his heart and to his brain. They were not spoken lightly, but with grave depth, the command of a Kinsman, his kinsman, his ancestor.

The Kirsdarkenvar.

*If you remember but one thing about me, remember this: I have never failed to complete a quest that I undertook alone.*

Ashe turned to MacQuieth began to offer him the sword, holding its hilt to him.

The old man shook his head. Ashe heard the voice one last time.

*He may command the wind, but I am the sword.*

In his mind he recalled the words the soldier had spoken in the dark of the crumbling shack the night before.

*The sea is the one thing that still touches us all. Earth is broken, wind is lost, fire is quenched, The waters touch us all.*

*Kirsdarke is our sword.*

Ashe grasped the sword tightly, the frenetic currents of power running through his arm, changing his mass, the water within him, so that it was vaporous, sea spray. With the last of his corporeal strength he bowed slightly to his forefather, and then, with a great leap, followed Achmed into the sea.

Rhapsody was floating at the edge the tidal cave, her back braced against the wall, clinging to the mat of igneous rocks, when she heard the voices, the shouts of the men above.

"Cave down here, m'lord!"

*No, gods, no,* she thought. *He has found me.*

She grasped tighter hold of the mat and slowly, agonizingly inched closer to the edge of the cave, staring out in her muddy vision at the swirling water beyond. The tide was low; if she went now, they would see her, but if she stayed—

There was no alternative.

*Come, my child,* she thought, taking a great breath and reaching, her hand slippery, around the outside edge of the cave. *Now for it.*

With all her strength she pushed the mat out ahead of her, diving beneath the waves and kicking off the wall with as much force as her legs could summon.

The current caught her and dragged her down immediately, swirling in a vortex of spray and rock. Immediately the breath was torn from her lungs and she struggled not to breathe, her body battered by the crags beneath the surface.

Tumbling, whirling end over end, she clung to the mat, its buoyancy useless in the overwhelming flood of the tide.

Rhapsody was suddenly lifted by the swell that dragged her, powerless and choking, whisking her rapidly out to sea. She was vaguely aware of bodies falling or hanging from the cliff wall above her, but all other thought, other reason, was lost in the mad roar of the waves.

The seneschal watched in amazement as the second man who had threatened him leapt from the cliff.

He turned to the last, the half-figure, expecting to see some third champion, some last show of this land's muster against him, noting in surprise that it seemed healthier, somewhat taller and broader now, but was still nothing more than an old man in ragged clothes, approaching with a half-smile on his wrinkled face. With a deep bow Michael stepped aside and presented the cliff's edge.

"Pray, don't let me stop you," he grinned. "By all means, throw yourself off as well."

"Come to me," the old man said.

Michael's brow furrowed. "I beg your pardon?" he said, more puzzled than angry, at least for the moment. "You must be addled, old man; clearly you do not see where you are, or have any idea to whom you are speaking."

"No, I do know," the aged man answered. "But I was not speaking to you."

The seneschal rolled his eyes, irritated now, then stopped when the realization came over him.

The old man was speaking in the harsh guttural tones of the language of the F'dor.

"Who are you?" he demanded, raising Tysterisk menacingly.

"I am one is who far more hospitable than you, Michael," the man said, walking closer. "A much better host. I have lived longer than you have, without even a sword for a crutch, nor any help from a demonic guest; my elemental power precedes yours in the order of birth of the Creator's gifts. I am stronger, and truer, and a better choice than you in every way. I would have killed you long ago if you had not been the coward that you are, would have torn your life from your useless body and buried you in a midden or a pile of manure, so that as you rotted at least some good would come of you one day." He stopped within reach of the seneschal. "I am the black lion. He who stands in the shadow of the king. The queen's champion. And after escaping me all these years, I am finally come for you. But it is not you I want."

The seneschal began to tremble with a mixture of rage and terror, his hand gripping the sword.

"MacQuieth," he whispered, "you should have died with the Island."

"And you should have died long before. It matters not what should have happened, only what happens now." MacQuieth put out his hand in a gesture of welcome and spoke in the dark and ancient tongue again. "Come. Abandon him. He will only disappoint you ultimately, if he has not already."

The seneschal lifted his free hand and pointed it, palm front, at the ancient warrior. Instantly a swirl of black fire appeared and billowed forth, fed by the wind, blasting over the old man in front of him.

It burned for a second in the hot air, then fizzled, snuffed as if by a wet cloth.

MacQuieth merely stared at him.

Fury blackened Michael's brow. With a vicious swing, he sliced at MacQuieth's throat, only to hear the voice in his head speak commandingly, bringing him up short.

*Stop.*

MacQuieth did not move.

Within his mind, the seneschal could feel the demon considering its options.

Michael clenched his teeth to quell his panic and rage. "Surely you are not fool enough to consider *him?* You have the master of Wind; you yourself are the servant of Fire! What good would *water* do you? If you want another sword I'll dredge the bay where the last fool dropped it. You can't accomplish your burnings with water. This man is a husk!" He stepped forcefully through the demon's command and resumed his swing.

MacQuieth's left arm came up sharply against the flat of the sword. Michael's blow went high, and he stepped back, the edge of the precipice now at his heels.

All of the Seren history, the reports of his scouts, all he had forced from his memory about this nemesis came rushing back to mind. He tried to suppress it, tried to clear his mind of the fear, the jealousy, the *awe* in which he had held the ancient warrior, the king's shadow, the queen's champion, hated himself for his grudging admiration, his loathsome inadequacy in the face of the warrior's reputation, his unparalleled might. Michael tried to forget the day he had taken the demon's offer, had escaped this ancient hunter, the craven relief he had felt being spared from MacQuieth, he believed, for all time.

But he could not force any of it from his mind.

Because the F'dor remembered it, too.

The demon was leafing through him. It was preparing to choose.

He stood, almost slack, on the edge, his eyes frantically scanning MacQuieth, noting with vague, detached interest that he could see a dangling hand. He appeared to have broken the old man's arm; slashed it; one of the forearm bones jutted sharply through the skin, blood spurting quietly around it.

*What kind of man seeks out a duel and brings neither armor nor sword?* he wondered.

The F'dor was at that moment asking the same question.

With a slight smile that had no joy in it, the ancient hero spoke.

"Does this mean you yourself are not already master of fire alone, Michael? A pity. Without acting as a host, on my own I have been to the soft places beneath the sea."

The hush of this whisper quenched the wind. It took Michael a moment to realize the import of this terrible utterance.

MacQuieth knew the entrance to the Vault of the Underworld.

For the first time in years, the demon in his mind was silent, contemplating the possibilities.

In the depths of his brain, Michael felt its loyalty shift like a scale plate that had fallen to the earth with a thudding certainty.

The seneschal's face contorted with rage.

"You want him?" he screamed. "Go to him! I will kill you both!"

He leapt on the ancient warrior, blood in his eyes.

MacQuieth opened his arms and threw them around Michael's waist, catching him low, slamming him to the rocky ground of the promontory. As they grappled, MacQuieth stretched his mouth up so that it was just outside of Michael's ear.

"Waste of Breath," he said with a derisive snort. He reared back, staring down at the man beneath him on the ground.

Then he drove the jagged, exposed bone of his forearm into the seneschal's abdomen.

Michael gasped.

With a burst of strength, a wave of energy that caught the demonic thrall off balance like a sudden swell of the sea, MacQuieth pushed as hard as he could against the rocky ground of the promontory, raising the impaled seneschal and himself to a stand at its edge.

Michael struggled for purchase, too close to bring even the ephemeral blade to bear, he smashed the Kinsman against the face with the air sword, striping his eyes with blood, gashing him open with cruel, gaping wounds from the weapon's edge, but he could not get a grip on the ground.

Suddenly it seemed as if he were floating at the crest of surf, buoyant, without limitations, in the wake of a great rolling wave.

He saw the ground and sky flash intermittently as the cliff edge rolled closer. Michael made a final grab for the edge of the promontory and missed, swept up in the flood that was the man clinging to his body, piercing his flesh with the warrior's own bone, violating him, swallowing his demonic soul.

Knocking Tysterisk from his hand.

Michael felt darkness swallow his mind as the power of the wind sucked from his body and soul in one horrific rending sound.

He could feel in the recesses of his mind the demon searching madly for a different host, anything to flee to, but MacQuieth had made certain that escape was impossible; even the horses had been left too far away to refugee into.

Through the pain Michael tried to call to the wind to hold him aloft, but it barely slowed their descent. It was as if the ocean itself already weighed him down.

His scream blended with the howl of the wind and was lost in the fall to the rocks below.

Achmed pitched at the crest of the wave that caught him, flailing helplessly in the wide expanse of the sea.

*Don't panic*, he willed himself. *Don't panic*.

The overwhelming immensity of the waves caught him, cloaking his senses, stinging his skin like acid. He struggled not to breathe, not to succumb, trying to resist the torrent that held him, knowing if he could just relax long enough to get out to sea the waves would calm and he would be able to float.

But he didn't have it in him.

The endless green water closed over his head; the myriad vibrations that assailed his senses every waking moment suddenly went silent, replaced by the muted noise, the deep, murky thudding of the sea that now enclosed him like the sky.

The last hazy thought in Achmed's head before the breath was squeezed out of him was a memory from the old world. It was the recollection of a day when, on horseback and girded in full chain mail, a bridge had given way beneath him, tossing him and his mount into the great river that bisected the Island, swollen and roaring with the rains of spring. It was the closest he had ever come to death that was not of his own choosing, and the panic, the helplessness as his body was flung about in a flood of confusion came rushing back to him now, closing the darkness in around him.

He was losing consciousness when a firm, strong grip that seemed to grow ever more solid caught him by the neck and dragged him up out of the quiet green depths and into the cold, bright realm of the air again.

"Peace," Ashe said, "I have you. Float now."

The two men hovered for what seemed like forever, watching the cliff in the distance anxiously, bobbing in the rolling waves.

Ashe stretched out his draconic senses, trying to find a likely place to make landfall. In dismay he watched, holding Achmed's head above the surface of the water, as an indelible image flashed into his mind's eye.

Two falling men were locked in mortal and immortal combat, a demonic shadow in the breech between them. Wedged together in body, bone impaling flesh, and locked in spirit, a bridge of black fire and evil from before the dawn of Time, the entity that had once been Michael was flailing desperately, struggling to separate himself from the grimly determined Kirsdarkenvar, whose ancient mien was set in an aspect of concentrated calm. As the bodies pitched off the cliff, just before they impacted the rocks below, Ashe was knocked momentarily senseless by the wave of elemental power that had entered the sea, merging wind and water and dark fire in a miasma too overwhelming for his dragon senses to bear. He struggled to hang on to consciousness and braced for the impact of the tidal wave that was rising from where the two had fallen.

A plume of steam and black fire shot into the sky; the sea at the foot of the cliff boiled to its depths, lighting the cliff face and covering the surface of the ocean with a rapidly approaching wave of froth.

"Hang on," Ashe said to the Bolg king as the swell approached; it was half as high as the cliff, churning madly as it came.

Ahead of the wave a body tumbled, rolling along the crest of a foreswell, curled around something buoyant that kept dragging it up again.

"Gods," Ashe whispered, treading water, clinging to Achmed as the wave approached. "Oh, gods. Take a breath."

He dove, with Achmed in tow, swimming parallel to the current, knifing through the water as the first shock of waves swelled underneath them, then passed.

The dragon in his blood, primed by the blast of power, had caught a flash of golden hair in the wreckage that was being dragged out to sea.

Faced with a lack of free hands, and the need to hold up a drowning man, catch his wife, or lose the weapon to which his soul was tied, without hesitation Ashe let go of the sword he had carried as Kirsdarkenvar, allowing it slip into the spinning green depths. He reached out and snagged the ratty mass floating in the wake of the wave and turned it over quickly.

"Oh gods," he gasped, shaking the stunned Dhracian's arm. "Rhapsody."

A larger foreswell to the oncoming wall of water broke over them, death's harbinger. Awash in a buoyant green world that spun around him, Ashe dragged his wife's limp body against his chest, holding her in the crook of his arm, struggling to hang on to the Firbolg king, who was only semiconscious and trying not to flounder.

The sky above him roiled in green and black, as caustic steam blasted the air from the battle of the elements raging between MacQuieth and Michael, the ancient Kirsdarkenvar and the Wind of Fire. The cliff faces in the distance disappeared, swallowed by the churning seas and the smoke.

And in that moment Ashe knew he would not be able to hold on to either of the two people he was clutching when the wave reached them.

Their bodies rose on the last foreswell as the wave neared, blotting out the sun.

In the final seconds before the wave hit, Ashe recalled the look of certainty in MacQuieth's eyes, the eyes that in the morning were blind to the world of the sun.

*He may command the wind, but I am the sword.*

*The waters touch us all.*

*Kirsdarke is our sword.*

From the salt in his blood the answer came.

*The waters touch us all.*

*Kirsdarke is our sword.*

*I am the sword as well,* he thought.

He opened his fingers of the hand that gripped the water-stunned Firbolg king and called on his bond to Kirsdarke.

He could feel its hilt, the only solid manifestation of the weapon when it was in the sea, brushing the tips of his fingers, at the edge of his grasp.

He clutched it, willing it to take a vaporous form, and, loosing the Bolg king for the space of a heartbeat, drove the sword into Achmed's chest, wrapping his arm around him once more.

"Hold on to the sword!" he shouted over the thunder of the roiling sea. "Breathe!"

Ashe turned to the unconscious Rhapsody in his other arm and snapped her head back, trying to find her face in the tangle of hair and seaweed. He pressed his mouth against her blue lips, then gripped the hilt of Kirsdarke, sending all of the water in his body, all the power of the element he could summon from the raging sea around him, into the watery blade, hoping his air would transmute into Achmed as well. Drawing the water from Rhapsody's lungs, blasting the exhalations of air through the weapon into those of the Firbolg king.

And, still clutching his wife and the impaled Firbolg king, kicked down to the depths of the sea.

The scream of the waves muted instantly into a deep rumbling thudding as he sank like the heaviest of stones, dragging the other two down with him.

Rhythmically he breathed into Rhapsody's lungs, feeling his breath spill out of her mouth as it rose in a swirl of bubbles that were instantly lost in the dark churning water above them. His hand still grasped the sword that pierced the Bolg king, but whether Achmed was alive or not he could not determine.

Around his ears the sea bellowed in rage at the affront, the violation of the elemental battle, screaming angrily as the black fire of the demon churned on its surface, spun into its depths. He could hear the ocean's anger, and its fear, felt in his mind its tale of the events as they unfolded, of the struggle between the two beings of flesh and element, the raging maelstrom of water against wind and an even more ancient and dark fire.

From the corner of his eye he could see the wave pass above them, felt the swells beneath it pass through his body, one with the water now, concentrating on keeping the breath in his wife's mouth, the sword hilt one with his hand.

From the deck of the *Basquela,* Quinn saw the wall of water towering off the shoreline, felt the backswell, then watched in horror as, in direct controversy to nature, it began to rush toward them, into the open sea.

*"About!"* he screamed to the thunderstruck crew, who broke out of their rigid stares and scrambled aloft and to their posts, endeavoring to take the ship into the wind.

Quinn himself could only stand at the rail, frozen, his keen sailor's eyes wide with horror, his mind calculating the impact and the inevitability of it.

There was no escape.

"Turn her into it!" he shouted into the wind to the mate who was frantically trying to gain control of the wheel. "If it hits us amidship we're done for!"

The blast of wind that tore around the approaching monolith of water swallowed the mate's reply.

Quinn turned back one final time, riveted by the sight of lightning and blazing fire rolling within the tidal wave, swirling in dark colors of brimstone and blood.

In the moment before it hit the ship, Quinn could swear he saw the wave's yawning maw, a towering face in the vertical sea of sightless black eyes and a titanic mouth screaming in demonic madness, turning the very ocean against itself.

He whispered a prayer to the god of the Deep, a sailor's entreaty he had learned as a cabin boy, wondering dully as the deck rose into the air amid the sharp cracking and snapping of the ship being rent into pieces how the sky and the sea had become one.

When the wave passed, Ashe could feel it, sweeping out to sea, contrary to nature, flattening as it went, dissipating into nothingness. The current steadied, then resumed rolling toward the shore, eternal.

As if nothing had happened.

Slowly he kicked up to the air, dragging the Bolg king, his wife still locked against his chest in a mad embrace of breath. They broke the surface, the sun stinging their eyes, the salt excoriating their nostrils.

Ashe tilted Rhapsody back so that her head pointed to the sky and pressed her against his chest, drawing the seawater from her lungs, willing her to breathe, then turned to Achmed, still impaled on the vaporous sword. He pulled the elemental weapon from the Bolg king's chest and slid it through his belt. He looked out to sea where the ship had been, and saw the rapidly sinking mains'l disappearing beneath the surface of the waves.

Suddenly exhausted, he lay back in the tide, holding tight to Rhapsody and Achmed, and let the eternal pull of the sea carry them to shore.

# 54

## HAGUEFORT, NAVARNE

When Caius entered Haguefort, there was no guard at the gate, no one in the foyer, no one in the corridors or on the stairs. It was as if the keep had been abandoned in the advent of a coming hurricane.

Which, in a way, it had been.

He crept quietly through the entranceway, taking pains to not allow his footsteps to echo on the polished stone floor.

The crossbowman was making his way through the enormous dining hall when a middle-aged woman in an apron appeared in the buttery doorway; Caius shot her through the forehead one-handed without breaking his stride, and without looking back.

Berthe crumpled to the floor without a sound, the blood that pooled beneath her forehead and into her open eyes whispering quietly as it bled.

Caius walked silently through the corridors, past the beautiful displays of armor and antiquities, looking for anyone who might have been the husband of his master's quarry, but finding nothing but empty silence.

Until he entered the Great Hall.

At the far end, beneath the tall windows, a man was sitting in a heavy wooden chair at a similarly heavy wooden table, sorting through parchment scrolls. When he looked up, their eyes met, and Caius froze.

It was the soldier he had seen in his dreams, the crippled

man who rode in a high-backed saddle through the burning
leaves swirling on the forest wind to rescue the woman his
master sought.

The man who had killed his twin.

Caius could read the man's thoughts as he raised his
crossbow and sighted it at the soldier's heart. The soldier's
first glance had gone to the windows behind him, trying to
determine if escape through them was possible, the thought
immediately discarded because of the height. Next the soldier glanced around for another exit, but there was none
between Caius and him. He could see the futility register as
the last thought came into his head.

There was no escape.

Generally Caius never spoke to his victims, determining
conversations with the imminent dead to be a waste of energy. But in this case, the look on the face of the man who
sat behind the desk was so insolent, his expression so hard,
that he made an exception.

"You killed my brother," Caius said accusingly.

The soldier's expression did not change as he spoke a
single word, likely to be his last.

"Good," he said.

The anger of insult coupled with the grief of loss flooded
through Caius. He raised the bow a fraction of an inch
higher, taking the time to be deliberate, to enjoy this moment.

He cocked the crossbow.

There was a flash seemingly behind his eyes as his bolt
whizzed harmlessly over the head of his brother's killer.

*Impossible,* he thought.

It was his final musing as he fell sideways, a white-
feathered arrow skewering his brain through the temples.

Anborn, who had been gritting his teeth and tensing his
abdominal muscles in the hope of twitching as little as possible when the arrow pierced him, blinked and pushed himself up with his hands on the table. He stared down at the

body on the floor, then looked to his left where the arrow had originated.

Gwydion Navarne stood, still in his archer's stance, his hand holding the bow trembling slightly. His other hand was still frozen at the anchor point behind his ear.

After a long moment, he turned to meet the gaze of the Lord Marshal, who still remained behind the table, rigid in body and face. Gwydion regarded his mentor seriously.

"I believe you owe me, or rather, my bow, an acknowledgment of your misjudgment," he said blandly. "I told you, as an archer I merely needed to be sufficiently proficient to penetrate a haybutt." He walked over to the corpse and turned its head over with his toe, admiring the clean breach of the man's skull between the temples. "And as you can see, I can."

Anborn only continued to stare at the crossbowman on the floor. Finally he shook his head and turned to the future Duke of Navarne.

"Are those the albatross arrows Rhapsody brought you from Yarim?"

"Yes."

A reluctant smile broke over the General's face.

"I suppose we have to acknowledge a center shot for both you and my mad Auntie Manwyn. Two miracles have occurred today; you managed to pull off a fine shot, even with a silly longbow, when you weren't even supposed to be here, and she actually got a prediction correct. I do believe the world is coming to an end."

Gwydion Navarne smiled. "Or perhaps it is just beginning."

# 55

## THE CAULDRON

Esten waited in the shadows impatiently, watching with grudging admiration the precision with which the semi-human beasts that were the Bolg held a watch. There was no perfunctory movement, no yawning or evidence that the ritual was rote. The king's guards took their duty seriously.

All the better.

She would have preferred to slip in and slit their throats but she had taken so long and spent to much time setting the trap that she didn't dare tip her hand now.

So she waited.

It had required painstaking hours to covertly search the general vicinity of the corridor whose general location she had knobbed out of Shaene. But in the end, it was the Bolg king's meticulous security that gave her the clue she needed. His inner sanctum must lie beyond this most guarded of intersections.

Somewhere in the distance she could hear an uproar, a sound of muster, or something like it, rumbling through the mountain, but the guards did not deviate in their watch. Upon consideration of it, she realized that the noise had been building for the better part of the day, like preparations in the face of a coming storm. This deep inside the mountain, however, little impact could be felt.

*In truth,* she mused, hearing the three-quarter-hour bells sound, *it probably* is *overkill to trap the king's bedchamber.* The tower had been brilliantly constructed, the subterfuge of the snare was so subtle, so unexpected, that she fully expected to blow the top off of Gurgus, crumbling the rest of the peak in upon itself, burying the king and all the Bolg he allowed to be present at the inauguration of the tower with it.

But it never hurt to have a backup plan. And she wanted to be certain that the Bolg king paid for his incursion into her guild, for the loss of her tunnel into the artery below Entudenin.

She wanted him to suffer horribly before he died. If her timing was good, he would be enjoying the full effects of the exposure before he was crushed to death.

The last communiqué she had sent to Dranth had included the general directions she had knobbed out of Shaene. The memory of riding his shapeless body, his pathetic wheezing beneath her, gave her a chill of disgust that she shook off, wanting to be ready when the watch changed. As long as the idiot's information was good, the Raven's Guild would have detailed maps and schematics to the most sensitive areas of the inner Teeth, she knew, along with the intelligence she had gathered and passed along previously.

Her opportunity presented itself just as the soldiers crossed in front of the triple pass, a juncture where three major tunnels met in the dark basalt walls of the inner sanctum. Esten had been timing the dead space, the moments in between when one shift of soldiers had left and the next arrived; it was never more than a matter of seconds. When she saw it, she slipped around the corner of the corridor and down the left-hand hallway, blending into the shades of dim light and fuzzy darkness, running her hands along the veined walls, until she was standing before what could only be the doorway to the king's own bedchamber.

Like everything else about the king, the doorway was concealed, hidden amid the striations that marbled the stone of the walls. Esten marveled at the masterly hiding of such a large aperture; had she not known that this was the right corridor, in a labyrinth that contained hundreds of corridors, even she, with her extensive training and experience in ferreting out the hidden, never would have found it.

*That disgusting tumble was worth it after all,* she thought.

The catch that served as a handhold to the door was locked.

With the speed born of years of practice, she took her thin picks from her mouth where she carried them and set about opening the lock; it was a puzzle lock of ancient design, with an undoubtedly obscure code, but she did not need to know what it was to pick it. Instead, she reached into her pocket and pulled out a small vial of quicksilver mixed with filings of lead; a drop applied to the shaft of the pick formed an impression of the inner works of the lock. With the lightest of touches, she turned the makeshift key.

The door opened silently.

Esten slipped inside and closed the door quietly behind her.

Her bright, dark eyes, raven's eyes, scanned the room.

The king's bedchamber was a surprising mix of austere décor and lush linens. The walls, the sheets, the wooden canopy over the bed draped in satin, were all in black; the marble desk, the wooden chairs, the enormous chest at the foot of the bed, everything formed of dark materials. It was a place of deep quiet; there was a sense of thick, solid softness evoked in the room, a place where someone with much on his mind could sleep restfully.

Esten smiled.

Quickly she set about searching the chamber, opening each small chest, each drawer, examining the nooks in the wardrobes and finding very little. The Bolg king might be lord of the ruins of one of the richest empires in history, but he had taken little material wealth for himself.

Methodically she continued her search, finding nothing of note, until she pulled back an area of the silk tapestry on the floor and discovered a tiny irregularity that would have been unnoticeable to any but the sensitive fingers of the mistress of a guild of professional thieves.

She ran her finger around the outline, checking for traps and finding none, then carefully sprang the locking mechanism.

A small reliquary in the slate of the floor opened, in which a rectangular box the length of two of her hands rested, swathed in a velvet covering.

Esten stared into the hole for a moment, then reached in and took the box; when she opened it, her brows drew together.

In the box was a key of a sort, a strange, curving key that looked like it was made of bone, like a large rib.

She slipped the key into an inner pocket of her shirt, closed the box, put it back in its velvet pouch, and resealed it in the reliquary. Then she went back to her search.

The chest at the foot of the king's bed gave her the greatest effort. The traps were so devious she could not wait to put some variations of them to use back home in Yarim. When she finally was able to spring the lock, she opened the lid, only to have a dank wind slap her across the face. Esten blinked in surprise; she was staring down a long passageway of rough-hewn steps. Where it led to, she had no way of fathoming.

$\mathcal{S}$andy! Get up, you lazy sinner!"

Shaene pounded on the door again; the noise of the barracks was so ever-present that Omet had no doubt grown used to it. Why the boy insisted on bunking with the soldiers in the ascetic quarters was beyond Shaene's understanding; the ambassadorial suite to which he had been assigned was far more comfortable, though certainly not opulent. If one was to be forced to live, as a result of an ill-thought-out contract, in the land of the Firbolg, one might at least opt for the most comfortable accommodations available.

Hearing no reply again, Shaene turned to Rhur.

"Maybe he's ill," he said the to the Bolg artisan.

Rhur grasped the door handle, expecting to find it locked; Omet was fanatical about locking his door of late, ever since Theophila came to the mountain. To his surprise, and that of Shaene, it opened easily.

The stench of illness hung in the tiny windowless room.

"Gods!" Shaene cried. "Omet?" He and Rhur hurried into

the room; in two steps they were at the young man's bed-side.

Omet's eyes were open, staring sightlessly at the ceiling. His skin was the color of the stone walls around them, except for his cheeks, in the center of which two bright spots of fever burned, hot as the fires of the forge.

"Get a healer!" Shaene screeched, the sweat of fear springing from his skin, leaving his hands trembling. Rhur disappeared; Shaene stumbled to the bedside table and, with shaking hands, poured water from the face-washing basin atop it onto the towel that was folding neatly next to it. He hurried back to Omet's bedside and laid the wet cloth gently over the boy's forehead; the towel turned quickly warm.

Shaene clutched the hot, limp hand atop the covers and began to rotely chant the prayers he could recall from youth, from the last time he had sat vigil by a young man's beside. In the earliest days of his apprenticeship his old brother Siyeth had contracted scarlet fever, had wasted and died in his bed before Shaene's eyes; the sights and smells never left his memory.

From what he could remember of Siyeth's death, Omet looked worse.

He had no comprehension of how much time was passing now. Rhur returned with Krinsel, the midwife, who was the chief of the Bolg healers, and several of her assistants; they had ministered frantically to Omet, only to see him edge closer to death.

"Come on, lad, come on," Shaene muttered, patting the young man's forearm impotently. He turned to Krinsel, who shook her head, then to Rhur, who watched, as always, stone-faced, but with eyes that held deep worry.

Suddenly Shaene sat up straighter, as if struck.

"Rhur—the tower! We can take him to the tower!"

The Firbolg artisan's brow furrowed. "Why?"

"Do you recall the wheel? Sandy said that the tower and the wheel worked together for healing, I think."

Rhur shook his head. "We know not how it be used,

Shaene," he said quietly in the common tongue tinged with the harsh accent of the Bolg.

"It can't come to harm, though, can it? We'll put him below the glass ceiling and set up the wheel." Desperation rose in Shaene's voice. "We can't just stand here while he burns to death from fever!" He gestured toward the healers. "Send them to the journeymen, the apprentices, and tell them to get take the wooden cover off the dome. You and I can make a litter out of his cot, and carry him."

Krinsel and Rhur exchanged a silent glance, then a few words in their native tongue, and finally a nod.

Shaene exhaled deeply. "All right, then." He patted Omet's arm again. "Hold on, boy. Perhaps all your efforts are about to be repaid."

# 56

Esten stared down into the dark passageway, struggling to decide what to do.

*Something of grave import must lie at the bottom of this tunnel,* she thought, patting the pocket of her shirt where the key was concealed. *There is nothing in the king's bed-chamber itself that requires the level of guard he has posted, or the concealment of the door, or the traps. Any thief stealing his way into this place would be bitterly disappointed.*

And yet there was a passageway hidden at the foot of the king's own bed, a sign that when he was in the mountain, he himself was the last line of its defense.

It was tempting, difficult to resist.

And yet Esten's time in the mountain had taught her that such passageways could go on for days, could misdirect, lead into other twisting hallways, designed to confuse, to cause the traveler to lose his way. It was possibly a journey for which she was not prepared. She just did not have the time to risk it.

A prickle ran over her skin, a shiver that she cursed, because it denoted a weakness in her she could not abide. The tunnel recalled the one she had been digging in Yarim beneath Entudenin, or, more accurately, her slave boys had been. While she was not averse to going to check their work, to correct their direction, there was a limit to the length of time she was comfortable remaining underground.

Living within the mountains of Ylorc had been difficult, but it was a difficulty she could abide. Esten was accustomed to back alleys, to dark buildings, to sewers beneath city streets, to the shadows in which all of her people lurked, hidden, waiting for the time to emerge, then blend quickly back into the darkness again. The tunnels, passageways, and rooms of Ylorc reminded her more of those alleys, those sewers; they had been built for men, after all, in the Cymrian era.

But this tunnel was different. If she was going to traverse it, she would need supplies and light.

She shut the chest and carefully reset the traps, meticulously following the order in which they had been originally laid.

Esten slipped out of the secret door and closed the entrance, when a great shadow appeared at the end of the hallway.

She glanced up, started, to see a giant there, a brutish man seven and a half feet tall, a cache of hilts and weapon handles jutting from a bandolier across his back. His skin was the color of old bruises; his horsehide-brown hair and beard dripped with rivulets of rainwater.

And his broad, tusked face was wreathed in a horrific scowl.

" 'Oo are you?" he demanded, his thunderous voice echoing off the basalt hallway. "And what are you doing 'ere?"

Esten's mind, finely honed from years of nefarious trade and knife's-edge situations, focused quickly. She folded her arms across her chest and scowled back.

"My name is Theophila, Grunthor," she said, taking a calculated risk that there could only be one fitting the description the Bolg king had given her. "And I am here because I *sleep* here now."

The ferocious anger melted into a look of shock that resolved into mere surprise, dimming finally into embarrassment.

"Oi do beg yer pardon, miss," the giant Sergeant said sheepishly, running an enormous paw through his dripping hair. " 'Is Majesty did mention you to me, o' course. Oi just didn't realize you were, er—"

"Knobbing him?" she said playfully, relaxing her stance visibly so as to mask the motion of drawing her blade. "Good. He promised to be discreet."

Grunthor cleared his throat awkwardly.

"My apologies again," he mumbled, then, seeing no anger or retribution in her eyes, broke into a wide grin. " 'Is Majesty asked me ta make certain you got everythin' you need. What say you we go to the mess hall and have some grub? We can get ta know each other better." He gestured down the feeder tunnel toward the soldiers' dining hall.

In return he received a glittering smile.

"That would be nice," she said simply, walking to meet him as he turned away from the hall toward the feeder tunnel. She manipulated the blade into her palm.

*Kidney,* she decided. *Such a large target, and he's giving me a clean shot at it.*

She increased her speed infinitesimally, holding her blade point-down, raising it just as she moved within range to strike, watching the movement of his soft leather jerkin over the vulnerable area of his back.

Her eyes narrowed slightly as she concentrated, aiming her blow between the moving muscles of his back.

Which continued to shift more than she expected as Grunthor swung fully around with the hand-and-a-half sword she had never seen him draw, separating her head cleanly from her shoulders with one beautiful, fluid motion.

Faster than anyone of that bulk should ever have been able to move.

Esten's dark, bright eyes had just enough time to blink open in shock before her head fell away from her shoulders; her body pitched forward on the ground, shuddering, while the head tumbled end over end, dousing the black walls with spurting blood, to land, spinning, on the floor just past the Bolg king's door.

The Sergeant-Major crouched down beside the body. He rolled it over onto its back; as he did, the blade fell from her lifeless fingers. Grunthor picked it up and shook his head, clucking in mock disapproval.

"Lesson One," he intoned in his drill instructor voice, "when you're in 'and-to-'and combat, always go for *distance*." He held up the slender knife beside his sword. "No matter what they tell ya, size *does* matter."

He searched the headless body quickly, uncovering several phials and odd coins, and, hidden in the inner pocket of her shirt, the key that had been the rib of an Earthchild. The amusement on his face drained away as he rose and strode down the hall to where the head lay.

He picked it up by the hair and stared into the wide eyes.

"Sorry, miss, but I knew you just weren't 'is type," he said solemnly. " 'Is Majesty tends ta favor a woman that can keep 'er 'ead about her in a crisis." *And only one alive at the moment,* he thought. *The king would never 'ave compromised the Sleeping Child for you, darlin'.*

As the head tilted to the side, a pair of thin silver picks fell from the flaccid mouth.

Grunthor winced in mock dismay.

"My, you would have been a real pleasure in sack, wouldn't ya? Makes my privates shudder ta think about it."

He jogged back up the hall and dropped the woman's head onto her belly, then summoned the guards on duty down the hall.

"Wrap this thing up in a cloak and take it to the armory," he ordered. "Be careful; she's a real treasure trove of all sorts of 'idden things, some of which might kill ya. Carry 'er by the cloak. And get a new quartet of guards on duty."

He waited until the soldiers had removed the body before opening the door to the king's chambers.

As he did, the floor and walls around him rocked with the reverberations of a violent explosion.

Instinctively Grunthor threw his arms up to shield his head, as debris and sand rained down on him. His head jerked in the direction of the sound, then turned back to the doorway.

Faced with the horrific choice of intervening at the Loritorium or the Cauldron, he pulled open the secret entrance and made his way in haste down into the cavern of the Sleeping Child.

# 57

$\mathfrak{I}$t had taken Rhur and Shaene only a few moments, after placing Omet on the floor of the tower chamber, to find the wheel they had tested in the closet where they had stored it. It stood, untouched, wrapped in oilcloth, propped up against the back wall.

It took a bit longer to get it into place. The last time the wheel had been installed Omet had helped carry it, had assisted in its hanging—had, in fact, headed the effort up. Two pairs of hands bearing the large steel-and-crystal artifact were decidedly less well suited for the task than three; still, the two glassmakers persevered, and after a few agonizing moments and several close calls, they finally managed to get the thing into place as it had been when they tested it as a threesome.

Shaene knelt over Omet while Rhur continually watched the wooden dome overhead.

"Omet," he said gently, his voice filled with uncharacteristic certainty and wisdom, "hold on just a few moments longer. Soon the dome will be removed, and the sun will break out from behind the clouds; the colored glass you helped make will be reflected on the floor. Imagine how proud you will be then."

Omet was still gray in the face and breathing shallowly, staring at the ceiling.

The two men, both artisans, one Bolg, one human, both friends of the young man dying on the floor, waited anxiously, watching the life slip from him breath by breath.

Finally, amid a great scraping and a thunderous jolt, the men looked up to see the wooden cover being slowly shifted away by a team of artisans outside the tower on the crag above.

The base of the tower, still awash in a messy array of pots, tools, beams of wood, and makeshift workbenches, took on the diffuse glow of early morning; the day had broken, the storm had passed, but it was still a few moments until full sun, when the rising orb cleared the horizon completely.

Shaene continued to whisper words of encouragement, his voice growing tenser and Omet grew paler.

A glimmer, warming to a rosy glow; the two artisans looked up to see the sky above beyond the seven-eighths-complete circle of exquisitely colored glass brighten to a clear, cloudless blue.

As Shaene watched, transfixed, Rhur went to the cooling rack in which one final experimental frit of violet glass rested, waiting to be tested. He searched through the piles on the workbench until he located the violet test plate, while Shaene futilely patted Omet's face.

As Rhur was heading back to where the young man lay, he heard a deep, ragged intake of breath from Shaene, and looked down.

Stretching across the stolid gray stone floor of the tower was a slice of glorious color, multihued and shimmering; the rich shades of light looked for all the world like pools of melted gems, precious jewels in liquid form, evanescent, gracing the dull gray of Ylorc with a momentary splendor of surpassing beauty.

Shaene stared overhead, gawking; Rhur held the test frit up to the light in front of the plate.

In the depth of the violet proto-glass he could see the runes, symbols he did not recognize.

*Grei-ti,* violet. The New Beginning.

Shaene lumbered to his feet, gesturing toward the wheel. "Come on, Rhur! Help me loose it!"

Together the men gave the wheel a push; at first, nothing happened. Then, with another shove, it starting gliding slowly across the metal tracks. As it traveled it slowed; a tonal vibration sounded, a clear, sweet note that caused the wheel to hover slowly in time with it. The vibrant light from the multihued ceiling above them caught in the crystal prismatic refractors, sending spinning flashes of color dancing wildly around the room, resolving as it slowed into a gleaming, pulsing arc of red light which came to rest on the floor where Omet lay.

*Lisele-ut,* red.

Blood Saver.

Neither man recognized the tone, of course; it was Namer magic, ancient, deep lore from another time, another land. If they had thought about it, they might have realized that the precise notes Gwylliam had left directing the construction of all the pieces of the Lightcatcher, from the exact shades of colored glass to the varying thickness of the metal on the support rails which produced the differing tonal vibrations as it rolled, worked in harmony of light and color to tap the ancient power of vibration, a magic left over from the creation of the world, still extant in every living thing.

But they did not grasp the nuances of what they were witnessing. They only knew that Omet, who a moment before had appeared more dead than alive, now lay in the rosy light that had been caught from the sky above, attuned to a precise color and pitch; he was breathing in time with the music of the tone, as if it had filled him, adjusted his heartbeat, his tides of breath, all the vibration that was his living essence, to itself.

And in doing so it was healing him.

Shaene lost his composure. He bent over the young man, still in the clutches of fear that was now abating to relief, and wept. He felt Rhur squeeze his shoulder from behind and looked up to find the dour-faced Bolg smiling. It was the first time Shaene remembered seeing it happen.

They watched, transfixed, as the slowly moving wheel continued to hum, the tone deepening as it lost speed, the red light waning, warming to a brighter, darker orange.

As the shadow of the healing red light passed from his face, they could see that Omet's skin was hale again, filled with a natural, healthy color. His eyelids flickered, and his head moved from side to side, as if shaking off sleep.

The men listened, rapt, as the tone changed in time with the movement across the rails. The light on the floor shifted completely then, from the red of the first section of domed ceiling to a full shaft of the next color, orange.

*Frith-re.*

Firestarter.

Shaene exhaled deeply as the room took on a sudden warmth. He looked up into the glass rainbow arching above him, minus its violet end piece, to the clear sky beyond.

"What a magnificent day this looks to be," he said to Rhur.

Which were the last words anyone in the room heard before the world exploded.

Once he had found the Earthchild to be sleeping still, resting undisturbed, Grunthor sealed the tunnel and hurried back to the Cauldron, making his way to Gurgus.

He could not get to within three corridors of it.

All around the section of the Cauldron beneath that peak the tunnels had collapsed, turning passageways into impenetrable walls of shale and rubble. Bolg soldiers were scurrying through the surrounding tunnels, evacuating the rooms that had not fallen in upon themselves, carrying out the injured and the dead, coughing violently in the encompassing cloud of dust.

"Criton!" Grunthor whispered, staring at the devastation. "What 'appened?"

No one around him answered.

Desperate now, Grunthor ran to the thick wall of detritus that filled the corridor to the top. He concentrated, reaching deep within himself to touch the elemental bond he had to earth, channeling it out through his hands and into the crumbled rock around him.

Summoning his earth lore, he tunneled into the wall of debris, feeling the shale and rock slip away from him as if it were melting at his touch. He dug in deeper, pushing his body through, making a passageway.

In the rubble he could see the wreckage of bodies, though at the outer edges at least there were none. He found two buried in the deeper in, recognizing them as he passed as Rhur and Shaene, both of whom had been crushed beneath tons of broken shale and enormous pieces of basalt, the remains of a large piece of the peak of Gurgus.

"Aw, *no*," he muttered upon finding Shaene, who was compressed upright. "Dammit."

He continued to press forward through the broken fragments of the mountain peak until he broke through, his eyes stinging from the dust, which was also collecting in his throat and nose, to an opening beyond the wall of rubble.

There, on the floor of the tower, in a sparkling rainbow of colored glass shards, Omet lay, his eyes closed, flecked with blood from the rain of glass, but otherwise spared. Grunthor was dumbfounded, judging by the pile of broken bits of glass, that the young man had not been sliced to ribbons.

He crawled carefully over the confetti that was all that remained of the beautiful domed ceiling, past the shattered workman's tables, and lifted Omet out of the pile of shards, hoisting him over his shoulder.

Omet moaned as his upper body hung down Grunthor's back.

"Grunthor?" he whispered, his long, straight hair inverted over the floor.

The Sergeant turned and headed back out through the wall of debris.

"What?"

Omet struggled to speak clearly, even though he was being jostled madly, and hanging upside down.

"Theophila—is really—the guildmistress of the—assassins and thieves' guilds of—Yarim."

"Oi'm a head of ya on that one," Grunthor replied, ducking to keep from scraping Omet's back on the ceiling above him.

The young artisan gestured with his arm.

"Rhur and Shaene; they're around here somewhere, I think. I heard them talking just before—"

Grunthor patted the small of Omet's back, his face impassive but his eyes raging.

" 'Ush now," he said firmly. "There will be plenty o' time for talking after Oi've gotten ya out of 'ere and you've 'ad a chance to rest."

€ight days later, the scion of the Raven's Guild received a package by way of the mail caravan from Ylorc.

Dranth broke the seals and tore off the parchment in which it was wrapped carefully; Esten had thus far only sent nonfragile articles and papers, but he wanted to take no risk of damaging the contents. By the odor issuing forth from it, the package might have already suffered some damage and spoilage from the heat of the mail carriages.

Upon pulling off the last piece of the carton, Dranth, the guild scion of the most soulless, deadly coterie of thieves and assassins in Roland, took a step back from the table, slapped his hand over his mouth, and then vomited all over the floor of the guildhall.

Grunthor had not even bothered to shut her festering eyes before shipping her head back to them.

# Epilogue:

## Tying the Threads

The rolling backswell from the wave from the explosion beneath the surface of the sea unceremoniously disgorged the Kirsdarkenvar and the two who clung to him onto the black, unforgiving sand of the rocky beach.

The purchase of ground, even sandy ground that slipped and whispered into the sea as the breakers rolled over it, felt like a lifeline to Ashe. He let go of the sword and rolled quickly over onto his belly, checking to see that Rhapsody was breathing and, finding that she was, turned to the Bolg king, who was coughing his lungs up onto the sand.

The next wave that foamed up the beach was shallower, tracing echoes in the outline of the last, but not reaching where it had left them. As the water rolled back, it littered the shore with splinters of wood and rope, the detritus of the ruined ship. None of the pieces were more than the size of driftwood.

Ashe drew his wife into his arms and pressed her body up against his to impart to her what warmth he could. The dragon in his blood assessed her frantically, finding some of her body weight to be missing; her skin was sunken and pale from the salt and the endless exposure to the water during her time in the cave, her hair matted and dark, ragged in varying lengths from where she had sawed it off. He choked back tears at the thinness of her hands, her neck.

But she was home, returned to him from the sea.

And within her their child still grew, strong; he could feel its presence, vibrant.

He pulled her closer, speechless with relief, matching his breathing to her own, reveling in the ragged sound of life coming from her, and let his head fall back on the sand, his eyes blind in the sun above.

Beside him he felt the Bolg king rise, still clearing the sea from within himself, and wander down to the shoreline.

*        *        *

Achmed stared down the windswept beach to the black,
jagged bed of boulders over which the sea crashed, where
MacQuieth had taken the beast into the sea. Where once
there had been boiling steam and turgid froth was now
peace; the sea had returned to its ever-violent pounding
against the shore, the waves rushing in a great swell of white
water, to hurry back out again, dragging the undertow with
them.

Gingerly he put his foot in the water.

"Do you see him?" Ashe asked, rising from the sand and
pulling Rhapsody up with him. "Do you see anything?"

Achmed squinted, then shook his head.

"Michael?" Rhapsody whispered, her voice harsh from
the salt.

Ashe put his arm around her.

"MacQuieth," he said. "It was he who found Michael,
who took him into the sea, wrestled him off the precipice,
perhaps even taking the demon into himself." He fell silent,
a sense of loss overwhelming him.

"Could he have survived?" Rhapsody asked, leaning
closer to the water's edge and staring up the beach into the
crashing surf. "There are thousands of places to be caught,
to hide; believe me."

Achmed exhaled sharply, then waded into the sea past the
crest where the waves were breaking. Slowly he bent down
until his skin-web was submerged, listening. After a moment
he stood rapidly, shook his head, and strode back out of the
sea.

"No," he said. "His heartbeat is gone, as is the stench of
the demon. I heard it once; it rang like a great bell. There
is nothing here now but the sound of the waves."

"Such an incalculable loss," Ashe said softly. "Imagine
what he has seen, what he could have told us. In just the
few days we spent with him, I learned more of the Island,
and of my line, than I have ever known in all the time before
that. Now I can finally see the stock of soldier from which

Anborn comes; both Kinsmen." He shielded his eyes from the red glow of the sun at the horizon's edge, a bright slice of diminishing fire. "Anborn studied him endlessly, worshipped him; it was MacQuieth on whom his whole life's plan was modeled. Such an incalculable loss to us. And yet—"

His mind went back to the sight of the old man walking, blind, in the light of the morning sun, unable to see it, feeling its warmth, its glory just beyond his sight.

*The All-God give thee good day, Grandfather.*

*If He were to do so, I would be gone from this life now. All of the years I have ahead of me, and all those behind, would I trade for but one day in which to see what has been lost to Time once more.*

*I understand.*

*Do you? Hmmm. I think not. But I suspect one day, a thousand years or more from now, you will.*

"And yet what?" Rhapsody asked.

"And yet there is nothing to mourn," Ashe said simply. "He is at peace."

Rhapsody nodded, brushing the heavy snarls of her hair out of her eyes, remembering words she had spoken once to Elynsynos long ago, consoling her over the loss of her lost sailor.

*Sailors find peace in the sea, just as Lirin find it on the wind beneath the stars. We commit our bodies to the wind through fire, not to the Earth, just as sailors commit them to the sea. The key to finding peace is not where your body rests, but where your heart remains.*

"I will sing a requiem for him," she said.

"And for his son," Ashe said. "Hector; the one who stayed behind in the Island's last days. MacQuieth could never bring himself to sing it; perhaps you could do it for them both."

Rhapsody nodded, brushing the salt from below her eyes. She gathered what strength she had left and walked to the water's edge, Ashe's hand still in hers, and touched Achmed's shoulder.

The men stood silent on either side of her as she lifted her voice, harsh and brittle like a crone's, chanting the ancient vesper to the sun, the song of the funeral pyre, for the father and the son, both now resting in the sea.

She sang in the lore she had learned in her time in the cave, the ancient melodies the sea had taught her, blending the keening call of the wind with the rhythm of the waves, endless and enduring, in all the colors and subtle tones that had filled her ears while floating in its embrace. It was a song that resonated within her now, in her blood, from her grandfather who had left the lowlands to ply the sea, in her heart, from the lore she had learned, in the child she carried, steeped now and forever in the lore of the water world, the hidden mountains, the unseen splendors, the treasures that lay beneath the rolling waves.

She sang of the lives of two soldiers, one cut short, one lingering far beyond reason, both stalwart guardians, both now part of the never-ending rhythm of the sea, part of its lore.

Part of its song.

The ocean roared in time, the salt-flecked air above the churning waves buffeting her face, all the colors of light wrapped within its swirling, eternal dance. It was a symphony of time, an endless dirge, an elegy, a lullabye, a song of creation, of desolation, of quiet, relentless guardianship, of inevitability. *Time carries on,* the sea seemed to sing. *Live your human lives, however long; they are but a flicker in the eye of eternity.*

She sang the sun down, then fell silent, her voice, like her strength, all but gone. She turned to her husband and spoke while she still had voice.

"Did Anborn live?" she asked tentatively. Achmed nodded. Rhapsody sighed deeply.

"Thank the One-God," she whispered to Ashe. "Sam, please take me home. I need to see Anborn, to let him know that he did not fail me; and Gwydion. I need to make good on my promises to him. Then, if you will come with me, I still need to go to the dragon's lair." She smiled slightly, remembering the music of the Explorer she had learned. "I have some songs I have to sing for her. The silence of her cave will do me wonders. After all that constant noise, what I crave most is peace."

Ashe drew her closer, his eyes sad.

"If I have learned one thing from this, Rhapsody, it is that men like Achmed and Anborn are right; there is no such thing as lasting peace, just lulls between episodes of strife," he said softly. "But I mean to see that those lulls last as long as they can for you, and for us all." He ran a hand over her ragged hair. "Now, come; I will take you home. On the promontory above there is a sword hilt glinting in the sunlight; I suspect we should gather it before we go. Tysterisk was once the weapon of Kinsmen; my namesake may have use of it one day."

Rhapsody smiled weakly. "Thank you for helping me make good on my promise to return to him and Melisande," she said, her voice a harsh whisper. "Let us get there with all due haste; I don't want them to suffer a moment longer."

Ashe nodded, raising the back of her hand to his lips.

"There is a stop we should make first, a place we can eat and get some rest that I know you will like. There's someone there, an old friend of yours, who has been waiting a lifetime to see you again." He put his arm around her waist to support her and led her up the beach to where the horses waited.

Achmed stared at the sea for one last moment, his eyes scanning the waves, which were still slowly washing up the broken debris from the ship, then turned and watched the bedraggled couple moving slowly along, arm in arm, allowing himself a wistful moment.

Then he shook his head and followed them up the coast.

"Why do I have a sickening feeling Barney will be serving mutton?" he muttered to himself.

An Excerpt from

# Elegy for a Lost Star

Book Five of
## THE SYMPHONY OF AGES

## YLORC

When the mountain peak of Gurgus exploded, the vibrations coursed through the foundations of the earth.

Above ground, the debris field from the blast stretched for miles, ranging from boulder-sized rubble at the base of the peak to fragments of sand that littered the steppes more than a league away. In between, shards of colored glass from windows that had once been inlaid in the mountain's hollow summit lay like a broken rainbow, glittering in the sun beneath an intermittent layer of sparkling dust.

Below ground, a small band of Firbolg soldiers felt the concussion rumble beneath their feet, though they were some miles east of Gurgus. A few moments of stillness passed, as dust settled to the floor of the tunnel. When Krarn finally released the breath he was holding, the rest of his patrol shook off their torpor and resumed their duties. The Sergeant-Major would flay them alive if they let something as small as a tremor keep them from their appointed rounds.

A few days later, the soldiers reluctantly emerged under a cloudless sky, having reached the furthest extent of this section of their tunnel system, and the end of their patrol route.

Krarn stood on the rim of the crater-like ruins of the Moot, a meeting place from ancient times, now dark with coal ash and considered haunted. Nothing but the howl of the wind greeted him; no one lived in the rocky foothills that stretched into steppes, then out to the vast Krevensfield Plain beyond.

Having finished their sweep of the area, his men had quietly assembled behind him. Krarn was about to order them back into the tunnels when the hairs on his back—from his neck to his belt—stood on end.

It began as the faintest of rumblings in the ground. The tremors were not enough to be noticed on their own, but Krarn noted the trembling of vegetation, the slightest of changes in the incessantly dry landscape, little more than the disturbance that a strong breeze might make. He knew that it was no wind that caused this disturbance; it had come from the earth.

Silently ordering his men into a skirmish line, Krarn's eyes scanned the area, looking for any more signs. After a few minutes, the feeling passed, and the earth settled into stillness again. Nothing but wind sighed through the tall grass.

"Aftershocks," he muttered to himself.

With a shake of his head, Krarn led his men back into the tunnels.

And in so doing, missed the chance to sound a warning of what was to come.

*A*s the days passed, the tremors grew stronger.

The surface of the Moot, baked to a waterless shell by the summer sun, began to split slightly, thin cracks spreading over the landscape like the spidery pattern on a mirror that had broken but not shattered.

Then came steam, the slightest of puffs of rancid smoke rising up ominously from the ground beneath the tiny cracks.

By day it was almost impossible to see, had eyes been in the locality to see it. By night it mixed with the hot haze coming off the ground and, caught by the wind, wafted aloft, blending with the low-hanging clouds.

Finally came the eruption.

Waves of shock rolled through the earth as if it were the sea, waves that intensified, growing stronger. The earth began to move, to rise in some places, shifting in its underground strata.

Then, with a terrifying lunge, it ripped apart.

The rumbling beneath the surface suddenly took on movement. It started outside of Ylorc but traveled quickly. It was heading north.

Unerringly, determinedly north, toward the icy land of the Hintervold.

All along the eastern rim of the mountains, then westward across the plains, a movement within the ground could be felt, a shifting so violent that it sent aftershocks through the countryside, uprooting trees and splitting crevasses into the sides of rolling hills, causing children miles away to wake in the night, shaking with fear.

Their mothers held them close, soothing them. "It's nothing, little one," they said, or uttered some similar words in whatever language they were accustomed to speaking. "The ground trembles from time to time, but it will settle and go quiet again. See? It is gone already. There is nothing to fear."

And then it *was* gone.

The children nestled their heads against their mother's shoulders, their eyes bright in the darkness, knowing on some level that the shivering was more than the ripples of movement in the crust of the world. Someone listening closely enough might sense, beyond the trembling passage, a deeper answer from below the ground.

Much deeper below.

As if the earth itself was listening.

Deep within her tomb of charred earth, the dragon had felt the aftershocks of the explosion of the mountain peak.

Her awareness, dormant for years, hummed with slight static, just enough to tickle the edges of her unconscious mind that had hibernated since her internment in the grave of melted stone and fire ash in the ancient Moot.

At first the sensation nauseated her and she fought it off numbly, struggling to sink back into the peaceful oblivion of deathlike sleep. Then, when oblivion refused to return, she began to grow fearful, disoriented in a body she didn't remember.

After a few moments the fear turned to dread, then deepened into terror.

As the whispers of alarm rippled over her skin it unsettled the ground around her grave, causing slight waves of shock to reverberate through the earth around and above her. She distantly sensed the presence of the coterie of Firbolg guards from Ylorc, the mountainous realm that bordered the grave, who had come to investigate the tremors, but was too disoriented to know what they were.

And then they were gone, leaving her mind even more confused.

The dragon roiled in her sepulcher of scorched earth, shifting from side to side, infinitesimally. She did not have enough control of her conscious thought to move more than she could inhale, and her breath, long stilled into the tiniest of waves, was too shallow to mark.

The earth, the element from which her kind had sprung, pressed down on her, squeezing the air from her, sending horrific scenes of suffocation through her foggy mind.

And then, after what seemed to her endless time in the clutches of horror, into this chaos of thought and confused sensation a beacon shone, the clear, pure light of her innate dragonsense. Hidden deep in the rivers of her ancient blood, old as she was old, the inner awareness that had been her weapon and her bane all of her forgotten life began to rise, clearing away the conundrum, settling the panic, cell by cell, nerve by nerve, bringing clarity in tiny moments, like pieces of an enormous puzzle coming together, or a picture that was slowly gaining focus.

And with the approaching clarity came a guarded calm.